Dragon Dale Beta

Book 1 Initialization

Nathan J. McDougal

Last Legend Publishing

COPYRIGHT

For more information, address: nathan.mcdougal@gmail.com

First Edition June 2022

Book cover design by Charlie Utting

ISBN 978-1-7337999-3-5 (paperback)
ISBN 978-1-7337999-2-8 (ebook)
LCCN [0000000000]

www.nathanjmcdougal.com

Contents

Part I

Chapter 1: The End

It was times like this, lying in a state of complete and utter darkness, that Dante imagined himself to be nothing more than a thought, floating in the ever-stretching infinity of the universe. No more than an idea, no, the mere spark of an idea, hovering in the vacuum of space. His entire existence persistent upon nothing other than the fact that it was by his own choosing that he even existed at all, and if he so desired, he could choose to exist no longer, and like a thought slipping from memory, the idea of Dante would dissipate into the darkness, and he would truly become nothing.

The darkness broke. The words "Now Loading..." blinked across the otherwise blank television screen and shafts of white light cut through the darkness of Dante Battle's bedroom. The light from the loading screen woke him from his pseudo-meditative state and illuminated the modest yet cozy room, revealing, in a soft silver glow, what the darkness had previously concealed: A full-sized bed, a dresser, a nightstand and a small desk. The walls were speckled at random with an assortment of old posters, all of them featuring either dark-skinned movie stars, professional athletes, or melanated comic book characters. Among the posters hung 8 picture frames. Each one a certificate awarded to Dante Battle. Some were still white and crisp, some yellowed with age, all neatly hung and set with great pride.

Dante stretched out in front of the glow of the television set. He lay leisurely across an overstuffed beanbag chair at least a size and a half too small for his long and limber frame. His body was wrapped tightly in dense well-constructed muscle, which itself was wrapped in the deepest shade of coconut brown skin that seemed to give off an iridescent glow of silver and blue when reflecting the white light of the television screen against the background of a pitch-dark room. With his fierce brown eyes, broad nose and full lips, he was a striking figure to behold, though there was no one around to see him.

He sat up and leaned forward. The influx of light from the television screen made him wince and lift one hand to shield his face from the brightness. In the other hand he gripped, with loose familiarity, a video game console controller.

Dante's eyes flashed toward the alarm clock. It was 2:46 AM. He was admittedly a little sleepy, his eyes even burned a little, but exhaustion didn't matter. In a few short moments, the late night would be well worth the effort.

He put his controller down briefly in order to put on a headset, a pair of large, well cushioned over-the-ear headphones with an adjustable microphone and a noise cancellation feature. The noise cancellation feature wasn't really necessary, considering there were no other sounds to cancel, but he turned the feature on anyway. With the headset in place and his controller in hand, he was ready, and just in time too, because as he adjusted himself in the beanbag chair a series of bold words flashed across his TV screen.

"Adventurer, prepare yourself. Once your companions have gathered, the battle will commence!"

Trumpets blasted from the TV's speakers. Dante knew the message well, it meant that he was in a battle queue waiting to be paired with other players looking to undertake the same in-game mission as him, in this case, a boss fight. MMORPGs, or Massive Multiplayer Online Role-Playing Games, often had these types of mechanisms in place to group players together, allowing them to take on more difficult content by working in small teams. Being grouped with random strangers was not without risk. You never knew what kind of personalities you might run into. Over time, however, he had grown used to it and prided himself on being able to work well with most other gamers he encountered.

Dante could see there were already three people in their party, which meant they only needed three more to begin battle. As the system slid him into the pre-fight waiting area a number of voices began to chatter into his headphones.

"Who's ready to do this?" one of the voices chimed in. It was a male voice; one Dante had played with a number of times before.

"Maverick, I see they let you back online again?" Dante said into the mic of his headset.

"Wait a minute, is that Dante? Thank the Gaming Gods my brothers and sisters we have been sent a savior!" Maverick responded in the accent of a southern preacher, a Baptist, by Dante's account.

"Yo, Dante, welcome back my man, glad to have another able body on this run," said another voice. This one was also a guy, and also familiar.

"Thanks Goose. You know me, always glad to be of service!"

"Ha! Don't believe those lies, Goose," shouted Maverick. "Our little power gamer friend here wants to defeat Nebuchadnezzar just as bad as we do. Once he completes the main campaign of Dragon Dale 7, he'll have finished off the entire franchise."

"Wait a minute," said Goose, "You've completed every Dragon Dale game?"

"All except one," Dante responded, attempting to sound nonchalant, but both Maverick and Goose could tell he was grinning from ear to ear on the other side of his headset.

"And he has the completion certificates to prove it!" Maverick's bragging on Dante's behalf made his grin even wider.

"But how?" Goose seemed genuinely mystified, "You're only what, 19? The Dragon Dale Series is older than you."

It was true, mostly true. Dante had recently turned 20-years-old, and the Dragon Dale Series was about to celebrate its 25th anniversary. To Goose's point, the first Dragon Dale game was released before Dante had even been born and when Dragon Dale 2 was released, Dante was still in diapers, yet to master the fine motor skills necessary to operate a joystick. Yet each of the frames hanging on the wall of Dante's room held a certificate in which Last Legend Games offered its congratulations to Dante Battle for his completion of yet another chapter in the Dragon Dale Saga.

"Thank God for older brothers," Dante responded, and left it at that.

"Thank God indeed," Maverick's Baptist preacher accent had apparently returned to share a word. "I say thank God indeed, as they have passed on their infinite wis-dom to our gaming messiah and as it was prophesied, so it has become, for he has returned. Can I get an Amen?"

"Amen!" Shouted Goose.

"And in his pres-ence, there shall be no boss battle that we shall not overcome!"

"Mmmm-Hmmm" co-signed Goose only serving to encourage Maverick's sermon further.

"I-I-I-I say, no wea-pon formed against us shall prosper."

"Preach preacher!"

"I-I say, no magic spell thrown at us shall succeed."

"Whoo!"

"Hi, is this the queue for the King Nebuchadnezzar final boss fight?" The new voice was soft, feminine, and not nearly as moved by the spirit.

"I say, no area-of-effect spell shall have an effect on our area!"

"Maverick," Dante cut in. "We've got more players joining the party."

"Sorry to interrupt," replied the newest gamer.

"Don't mind him," Dante said to the feminine voice. "He's just committing blasphemy, and yes, this is the queue for Nebuchadnezzar."

"Oh great, uh... Hi. I'm Amabilis and um, just as a heads up, this is my first time running this fight and I don't really know all the mechanics."

"Ah, no worries," said Maverick, back once again in his regular voice. "Goose and I have run this a few times and haven't won it once, not that it matters, seeing as how we have Dante here. He'll know exactly what we need to do to win." He said, as if victory was already assured.

"Oh wow, well that's great," Amabilis said with a nervous giggle in her voice.

"Don't go telling people that," protested Dante. "This is *my* first-time fighting Nebuchadnezzar, too."

"Well, it's true," said Maverick. "And it's only his first time because he's been on a hiatus from the game for the past few months, otherwise he'd have already beaten the boss, and the rest of us would be out of luck. Trust me Amabilis, this guy is tough."

"You guys in an Adventuring Company together?" Amabilis asked.

"No, we're not in an AC." Dante answered.

"But we've played together tons of times, so I can attest to Dante's skills, if that's what you're wondering about," added Maverick.

"Oh no, I wasn't doubting-"

"Yeah, I've run a bunch of quests with Dante as well, and he is the real deal," said Goose.

"No, no, you've got me all wrong," said Amabilis.

"Don't mind them," said Dante. "They're just teasing the both of us."

"Level 85 Ninja, Omath here." The new voice was male, and unlike either Maverick or Goose, his tone was short, dry, and direct.

"Welcome." Maverick responded, almost matching Omath's tone.

"Welcome," said Goose.

"Welcome," added Dante,

"Welcome..." muttered Amabilis.

"We've got 5 so far?" asked Omath.

"Yep," said Goose.

"Who's healer?" Omath asked.

"Um, I'm a healer, well I guess I'm *the* healer," said Amabilis.

"Have you run this before?" Omath's questions were coming sharply and in quick succession.

"Well, no. I was just telling them this is my first-"

"Aw man, this is the healer's first run of Neb." Omath interrupted.

"I'm running tank." Dante interrupted Omath before he could continue. "I'll be holding the hate and watching the healers back. She'll be ok." He hoped he sounded reassuring.

"Your funeral," said Omath, in a tone that led Dante to believe that a shoulder shrug followed the phrase even though he could not see it. "I'm not trying to go through a bunch of wipes tonight though."

He's one of those, Dante thought. For some players, getting wiped out, which was when an entire party died in the midst of a mission and had to start over, made them angry. Dante didn't think it was that big of a deal. Wipes happened all the time. They were a regular part of games like Dragon Dale 7, which was known to be one of the more difficult MMOs.

"We're not going to wipe." Maverick responded, without elaborating.

Dante wondered if he needed to talk Amabilis through the basics, but figured she knew the deal. In any MMO, players were usually either tanks, healers or damage dealers. The tank's job was to stand at the front lines and divert enemy attention away from the rest of the party, this usually results in that player taking lots of damage, that's where the healer came in, their role was to cast healing magic on party members to keep them healthy and in fighting shape. Lastly were the damage dealers, whose sole purposes was to inflict as much damage on to the enemy as possible.

Aside from the players, there was also an unseen force at work as well. Hate, or sometimes called aggro, it could best be described as the enemy's attention span. In an MMO, an enemy will attack whichever player whose actions garner the most attention, or, in other words, generate the most hate. Dante's thorough understanding of those roles and rules, among other things, was what made him such a reliable player, but on an enemy, he had never faced, with players he had never played with, he knew nothing was guaranteed and a wipe was always possible.

"Hello all," The voice was feminine, definitely a girl but lower than Amabilis', maybe more mature, or just maybe more confident. "Level 90 Black Mage, Morrigan," the voice said as she spoke the ceremonial greeting of the veteran gamer.

"Welcome," the others spoke in chorus.

"Party's full. Let's get this show on the road," said Omath.

"Oh Noble Warrior, the fate of Deos now rests in your hands, go forth and may the gods be with you!"

The television flashed and Dante saw his avatar appear on screen. It was a miniaturized digital representation of himself, clad in heavy metal armor and holding a large sword and shield. Standing among him were five other characters, each a different size and shape. He recognized Maverick and Goose, he then spotted the two female characters who were both playing mages, one a cleric wearing white robes and the other a black mage wearing dark robes, and then, by process of elimination, he identified Omath.

The six characters stood on a small plot of barren land. The ground beneath their feet was dark and cracked, like scorched earth. The area they could move within was small. The rest of the screen was filled with parts of the stage that could be seen but not acted upon. At the top of the screen were a massive pair of free-standing wooden doors at least twenty feet in height. The entrance gate to the boss' area loomed over the players, extolling a sense of impending doom. On the other side of the door waited the creature. At 3 am in a dimly lit room where the only source of light came from a glowing television screen, those large double doors sent a shiver of apprehension through Dante. He couldn't help but smile. This was why he loved the Dragon Dale games. They really knew how to pull you in.

Colossal stone gargoyles flanked the doors. From the mouth of each, vast amounts of water poured, dropping into jagged trenches carved into the rocky ground on either side of the players. The water formed a makeshift moat which flowed under a small land bridge that led up to the boss area entrance gate. It was all intricately detailed and the sight of it gave Dante an idea.

"Alright, we're here. It's the final stage. Let's do it," barked Omath.

"One second," Dante interrupted. "One thing we need to do really quick."

Dante walked his character over to the water's edge, pressed a button on his controller, opened a menu, and scrolled down to an option called emote. He then selected an action labeled 'Highender's Prayer'. A small notification bubble popped up on his screen asking, "Would you like to include Hassan the Merciful as well?" Dante clicked 'yes' and his screen avatar pulled a coin pouch from its belt, reached into the pouch and extracted a coin, bowed his digital head and tossed the coin into the water.

"What are you doing?" asked Omath.

"I need everyone to do it." Dante said. "It's in the menu as Highender's Prayer."

"I know what it is," said Omath, "but why are we wasting our time? It doesn't actually do anything, and it costs one gold coin and one HP."

"Just entertain me," Dante said with little enthusiasm.

Maverick, who played as a large lizard man, followed suit, and Dante watched as his avatar went through the motions, as did Goose and Amabilis. After the three of them complied the black mage gave in. Seeing as he was now the odd man out, Omath caved as well. The moment Omath's character dropped his gold coin into the water, the television blared out a trumpet call and a message scrolled across the screen.

"Your party has been given the War God's blessing, 5% increase to attack and defense."

"Wow, what was that?" Omath asked.

"Highender's blessing," Dante answered. "He's the god of mercenaries, assassins and sell swords. The people of Deos pray to him by dropping a blood-covered coin into a body of water before a big mission. I knew once I saw that option in game it had to unlock something, it just has to be performed under the right conditions."

"How would you know something like that?" Omath asked.

"He is an expert in all things Dragon Dale. He has completed every single game in the franchise," answered Maverick.

"All except one," Dante said. "Come on, let's go knock this guy down."

As the party approached the large wooden doors, the gate swung open and the digital adventurers poured through, weapons drawn. The gate led to a vast and open area roughly the size of a football field. In the center of the field was a tree nearly as tall as a skyscraper. Dante recognized it immediately as Yggdrasil, The World Tree. Sitting directly in front of the tree was a large black throne made from gigantic slabs of stone, and in it a man at least three times as tall as Dante's. He had red skin, a long dark grey beard the color of smoke, and bright orange eyes that glowed like hot coals. On his head, he wore a crown made from volcanic roc covered sparkling red jewels.

"That's Nebuchadnezzar?" Amabilis asked nervously.

"*King* Nebuchadnezzar." Maverick responded. "Flame giant and destroyer of worlds."

Nebuchadnezzar slumped on his throne. His left hand propped up his chin and his right hand rested on the handle of an enormous club. His eyes drooped; he looked bored.

"Come challengers. Come forth so that I may break you, as I have done all the adventurers that have come before you." His voice boomed through both Dante's headset earphones and the speakers of his television.

"For Deos!" Dante yelled into his headset before dashing toward the giant guarding the world tree. Nebuchadnezzar stood from his throne with his club in hand and began to swinging it over his head.

The players clashed in battle with the evil king. Dante was out of his bean bag chair and onto his feet, mashing buttons frantically on his controller and yelling instructions and directions into his headset.

"Maverick, get the adds. Amabilis don't worry about healing me for now, just focus on the damage dealers!"

"But you'll die," she protested.

"No, I won't," Dante responded. "Nobody is gonna die today."

After fifteen full minutes of button mashing, barking orders, dodging attacks, and dealing damage, Nebuchadnezzar fell. He dropped his club, fell to his knees, and then collapsed face down in the dirt. Trumpets blared.

The party let out a cheer and cries of congratulations flooded in over the voice chat.

On Dante's screen, a notification popped into view. "Congratulations! You have attained level 100!"

"Dante just reached max level! Congrats my man!" Maverick called out over the headset.

"Thanks!" Dante responded.

"Man, you earned that." said Goose.

"Yeah man, you did good..." Omath's words were cut short.

"Hello?" Dante said, tapping the side of the headset with his hands. Silence. "Anyone there?"

Suddenly, the television went blank, but before Dante could call out in protest, words began to flash across the screen.

"You have defeated a great evil threating this world and have saved the land of Deos. You now stand in the center of the lost city of Dragon Dale in front of the fabled Yggdrasil, the tree of life. From its branches hangs the God Fruit, which, when eaten, will grant a single wish. One such fruit hangs low and appears to be well within your reach. Do you dare take the fruit?"

An option of 'Yes' and 'No' appeared on screen.

"Oh wow, this must be the end game cutscene. Guess it's private." Dante said to himself, attempting to justify why he had suddenly been cut off from the other players.

He moved his cursor over "Yes" and hit the select button. The television dinged in confirmation. The screen flashed again, and Dante could see his avatar standing before the Yggdrasil Tree, the God Fruit in his hands. More words populated on screen.

"Champion of Deos, Great Hero of Dragon Dale, you hold in your hand the God Fruit, the deepest desires of your heart are now within your grasp. What is your wish?"

Beneath the question appeared a series of options, a list of possible wishes. Dante read them silently, one by one.

1. **'Immortality,'**
2. **'Infinite Power,'**
3. **'Unimaginable Wealth,'**

and the last option listed was,

1. **'To Play Again,'**

Dante couldn't help but laugh. "Wow, this has never happened in any of the other Dragon Dale games before." Dante felt trapped between amazement and disbelief. He was astounded at how unbelievably cool the ending sequence was but confused by the fact that he had already beaten both Dragon Dale 8 and Dragon Dale 9 and their end game sequences were not nearly as intricate.

Before his mind could drift any further, he looked back to the screen, focusing on the list of possible wishes. "The deepest desires of my heart..." he mumbled to himself, and once again his mind drifted but this time it was to thoughts of his mother and his brothers, he looked around his room, his old childhood room, a room that he once shared with both Bryan and Malcolm, shared it until the three of them had gotten too big for one room and they then began spreading out, first all *over* the house, and then *out* of the house. First Bryan moved out, then Malcolm. After that, it was just mom and Dante, and he had the room all to himself. Then a couple of years ago, *he* left for college. Now his mom was gone. There was no one left but Dante. He had the whole house to himself, just Dante and his wishes. His eyes began to well up with tears, but he fought them back.

"One wish." He said aloud. An idea formed in his head.

The Sword Saint was a powerful class of warrior that every true Dragon Dale enthusiast had longed to play, however, one that had yet to be made available in any previous incarnations of the game.

"I would choose to play again, but only if I could play as a Sword Saint this time. Now that would be dope."

At the conclusions of Dante's words, the television dinged in confirmation and the 'To Play Again' option blinked repeatedly.

"Hey!" Dante yelled, looking down at his hands to make sure he didn't accidentally graze the controller and pressed a button unintentionally. "I didn't even choose anything yet!"

The television seemed unaffected by his words. The screen flashed again, and a new message displayed.

"Congratulations Adventurer, you have completed The Main Story of Dragon Dale Seven."

Then, in smaller, less grandiose lettering, an additional message appeared.

"Last Legend Games tracks player progress. With your permission we would like to send the data of your game's completion to headquarters for our records. This will assist us in improving Dragon Dale games in the future. Would you like to submit your gameplay data?"

An option of yes and no appeared on screen.

This is what he was waiting for. In the early days of his childhood gaming every time he completed a Dragon Dale game, he had to wait for an alpha numeric code to flash across the screen, copy it down and then send it into Last Legend Games via mail and in return they would send him back a certificate of completion. Once the video game console systems began connecting to the internet, the game completion data would be submitted automatically after a question such as the one he had just received. Now, with this final 'yes' his collection would be whole. He had now completed every Dragon Dale game to date.

He sat back and smiled to himself. Maybe now he'd go back and start again with the original Dragon Dale 1. He was sure it was still in the house somewhere. He removed the still silent headset and then stood up to go find the old game cartridge and the system to play it on, when his screen blinked one more time and he looked up to see his avatar standing outside the gate of the boss area once again. All of the other PCs were gone with the exception of a lizard man warrior who still meandered on screen as if waiting for something.

"Aw snap," Dante scrambled to put his headset back on. "Maverick!"

"Dante? What happened to you man? I thought you got disconnected. Right after we beat the final boss you vanished."

"Oh no, I went into the final cutscene, where you get to eat the God Fruit and make the wish and stuff. I figured they were private cutscenes, and that's why they cut the voice chat."

"God Fruit? You mean from the World Tree? Nah brother, we didn't get that cutscene. Must have been a Level 100 exclusive or something. You just went silent and then your avatar disappeared. After a few minutes of celebrating everyone else left too, I figured I'd wait to see if you came back on."

"Oh wow, that's strange. Thanks for waiting on me though."

"Aye, no worries bro, seems like you unlocked some cool secret alternate ending or something. Don't spoil it for me. I'm gonna get to Level 100 and come back and see it for myself." Maverick laughed.

"I like the sound of that." Dante responded with a smile.

"Oh and Dante," Maverick spoke with a bit of hesitation in his voice, "I know you're only playing because you're on a bit of a break from college and of course now that you've hit max level and finished the main story line, you can check this one off as done, but as I'm sure you know this game is like never-ending with all the side quest and the bonus content and stuff, so, if you do decide to like... stick around and keep playing, maybe consider starting that AC with me and Goose. I think a lot of gamers could benefit from your knowledge and skills." Maverick let out a breath, as if he had been holding it the entire time. "Well, haha, that was my sales pitch. Anyway bro, think about it, and either way, send me a message next time you're online."

"Thanks Maverick, I'll give it some thought. I really enjoy playing with you guys."

"Yeah, same here, we work well together. I think our company would have a real kind of family vibe, you know?"

"Yeah, um, aye Maverick, it's getting late man. I'm gonna log off and grab a little sleep. I'll catch up with you next time I'm online."

"Alright bro, catch you later."

"Later." said Dante, shutting down the entire console without bothering to log off or even close out the game. He pulled off his headset and tossed it on the bed, then went back to pondering the possible location of his old copy of Dragon Dale 1 when his laptop beeped. "What is it now?"

Dante's computer sat on a desk in the corner of the room adjacent to the TV. The now illuminated screen flashed an alert. New email. He walked over to the laptop to disable the notifications. The last thing he wanted was to be bothered every time he received a spam email message, but as he neared the computer, he read the subject line:

"You're invited to play Dragon Dale Beta,"

"What is this?" he said to himself. Dante looked at the email's 'From' address and saw the name Last Legend Games. His heart rate increased. He pulled up a chair and sat down at the desk, then clicked open the message. As he read, his hands began to shake.

"Greetings Adventurer,

Our records indicate that you are a faithful Dragon Dale Player and that you have met the criteria necessary to be part of a unique opportunity. Dytorus Corp and Last Legend Games would like to invite you, DANTE BATTLE, to the closed beta test for the newest installment in the Dragon Dale series. This is a PRIVATE event and will be taking place exclusively at the Last Legend Games Corporate Headquarters in Oxnard, California. If you would like to attend, please be aware that all airfare and hotel expenses have been arranged and will be provided at no cost to you. As stated, this is an invitation only, closed beta test for the currently in development Dragon Dale 10. As a loyal and dedicated champion of Deos, your feedback is of the utmost importance in helping us continue to make the Dragon Dale Saga bigger and better. Please follow the instructions in the link below to confirm your flight and hotel reservations.

We look forward to seeing you in Deos!"

"Unbelievable." muttered Dante, a smile creeping across his exhausted face. He was going to California to become a Dragon Dale Beta test player.

Chapter 2: Brother Malcolm

Dante didn't really remember falling to sleep. He didn't recall getting into bed *or* crawling underneath his blankets. He didn't even remember dreaming. He was, in fact, missing a very large chunk of time where he went from sitting at his computer, to now having the shrill sound of a ringing phone wake him from slumber.

He reached out from underneath a mass of blankets and felt blindly on the nightstand, found the phone and pulled it back into the void of sheets and pillows that were piled on his bed.

"Hello" answered Dante, in a gruff and scratchy morning voice.

The voice on the other end of the phone spoke in a crisp and clear articulation, an obvious recording, but one that Dante recognized as if it were a member of his own family. "This is Global-Tech Securities, you have received a call from..." there was a brief moment of silence, as if someone was supposed to say something, as if a voice was supposed to be inserted but nothing, no sound came. "An inmate at San Marcos State Correctional Institution. As a precaution, this call may be recorded or monitored. To accept the charges for this call, please press '5' or say, 'I accept'. To deny the charges for this call, please press '2' or hang up."

"I accept!" Dante yelled into the phone, flinging the covers from his back and jumping out of the bed.

"Thank you," said the recording. "your call is now being connected."

"Malcolm?" said Dante, cupping the phone with both hands.

"Hey D, what cha doing baby bro?" His big brother's voice was rough on its edge but still gentle in tone and smooth in delivery, a voice like the blade of an old knife that you trusted not to cut you... so long as you handled it with respect.

"Mal! Ah man, it's good to hear from you. Umm.. I'm not doing too much of anything, actually. I'm just here at the house, still getting things in order and what not. But how are you? How are you doing?"

"Aw D, don't worry about me. I'm good kid. You know your big brother always gon be good. Right?"

"Ha-ha, yeah, yeah I know."

"I called to check on you," the voice on the phone became low and solemn. "I didn't really get a chance to talk with you at Mom's funeral."

"Yeah," said Dante, his tone also dropping to match that of his older brother. "But at least they let you come to the service."

"Yeah, in chains, shackles and with armed guards." The knife's edge flared up when he spoke this time, but then quickly subsided. "But yeah, you're right. At least the let me say goodbye."

Dante could feel tears welling in his eyes and wanted desperately to fight them back, but even more desperately, he did not want to sniffle on the phone with his older brother. So, he just remained silent.

"Have you talked to Bryan since the funeral?" Malcolm asked.

"No," said Dante, "We talked about school for a little while afterwards, then he got to complaining about you, then he asked if I wanted to go grab a bite to eat, but I suspected that would consist of more Malcolm-bashing, so I told him I'd take a rain check. He said he had to get back to D.C. for work and we haven't talked since."

"That was 3 months ago." Malcolm sounded more than a little annoyed. "That's your big brother my man."

"*Our* big brother," corrected Dante.

"I'm pretty sure he's disowned me by now. Can't have a convicted criminal as a brother putting a blemish on his flawless military service record."

"I'd never disown you." Dante said this with a finality to suggest this portion of the conversation had come to its end.

There was less of a word and more of a sound made on the other end of the receiver as Malcolm either grunted his approval or sniffled and coughed. "Speaking of school," said Malcolm, "How is it going college boy? How is the team looking this year? What the grades looking like? Tell me about the girlies. Come on, give me the whole run down."

"Oh yeah, well, there is nothing to report at the moment because I haven't been back yet."

"I'm-sorry-you-said-what-now?" Malcom spoke in a single breath as if it were one word.

"I haven't been back to school since the funeral." Dante replied.

Silence.

Dante could feel the knife's edge flare up again and the hairs on the back of his neck stood on end.

"Dante, it's been 3 months."

"Yeah... about." Dante replied.

Dante heard a distinct thud on the other end of the phone. Someone yelled "Battle" and then he could hear his brother exchanging words at an elevated volume with someone off phone. He came back to the line, even more composed than he had been when they first began talking.

"Dante, you are in college on a combination athletic and academic scholarship. How will you maintain said scholarship if you are not at school to neither participate in your athletic events nor excel at your academic pursuits?"

Dante knew that when his brother was truly angry, he would begin to speak slowly as well as uncharacteristically proper. This was done in an attempt, on his behalf, to eliminate any miscommunication before he fully lost his temper.

"Yeah, I know," his voice quavered a bit, "It's just, since Mom died, and right before that, you and your trial..." Dante's voice quivered. He swallowed. "They gave you 15 years, and-and Bryan is saying that's what killed Ma, that it broke her heart to see you go through that..."

"D..." Malcolm tried to cut in, but Dante wouldn't give him an opening.

"*I* don't believe that. I know that's not true. But now you're in there and Bryan is back off serving in whatever secret branch of the military he's in and the two of you hate each other and, man it's just a lot right now man... So, yeah, I just needed some time. I just needed some time to myself. Some time at home." Dante sniffled.

"D, look bro, I get it. I do. There is a lot on you, and in all honesty, it's not fair. And for that I am sorry, because a lot of it, nearly all of it, is my fault. But look here baby boy, you cannot run from it.

"It's hard and it's gon' be hard, right up until it gets easy. I know that right now you are feeling like you're by yourself out there, but you have to know that even if they keep me in this cage for the rest of my life, you are not alone." Malcolm was silent for a brief moment. "Man, you remember we used to play all of those video games when we were young?"

"Of course." said Dante, who had now made his way to the bathroom and was wiping snot from his nose and tears from his eyes.

"You remember we always played on what difficulty?"

"Hard mode," Dante laughed.

"You right, because if you can win on hard mode, you know you won because you were the best. The game didn't *let* you win, it didn't *give* you the win. It means you won because you are the fastest, the smartest, and the toughest person in the room. Now am I right or am I wrong?"

"You're right." replied Dante.

"So, you remember that D, we play on HARD MODE."

Dante sniffled, breaking the silence on the call.

"But then again, what do I know? I'm facing 15 years." Malcolm said.

Dante laughed out loud. His brother laughed. And though it was a sad fact, they both were happy to hear each other happy, if only for a moment.

"Aw man," said Dante "Speaking of video games. Last night I beat Dragon Dale 7!"

"Dragon Dale 7? Which one is that?"

"That's the one that you play online. It's an MMO. It's like four years old at this point, but a lot of people still play it. I had been playing it off and on over the past year, but since I've been at the house, I've been catching up on a lot of old games. I beat Dragon Dale 9 again last month and then last night I finally beat Dragon Dale 7."

"So that's what you've been doing for the past three months, playing old video games?"

"The old ones, the new ones, everything we used to play back when we were kids. But check this out. Last night after I finished 7, I got an email from Last Legend Games."

"Last Legend Games? That's them people who make the Dragon Dale games?"

"Malcolm, will you let me finish!?"

"Go ahead!"

"Last night I got an email from Last Legend Games inviting me to their headquarters to play the beta test version of the new Dragon Dale 10!" Dante announced with obvious excitement.

"Dooooope," responded Malcolm, "What's a 'beta test'?"

"Oh my God bro, you are old as dirt!"

"I'm 28, you nerd. That's not old. I'm sorry if I don't keep up with all the new tech lingo while I'm in *prison*, college boy."

"A beta test is when tech developers let people test out a product that is still under development so they can find any errors, and then fix it before release. The cool part is I get to play Dragon Dale 10 before it comes out."

"Haha, nah bro that definitely is very cool my man. I'm happy for you, and a little jealous as well, I gotta admit."

"Mal, the beta is in California. It's in a week. The company is paying for airfare and hotel and all of that stuff. I was wondering, since I'm going to be out that way, would it be cool if... if I came to visit you? I could tell you all about the new game and everything."

There was a brief moment of silence. And then it sounded like Malcolm took a breath, as if he was about to speak, but at that moment, the audio recording cut in.

"You have two minutes remaining on this call." said the recording.

"D," said Malcolm coming back to the line, "I think that's a great idea. I'd love for you to come visit me man, but you gotta promise me one thing."

"What's that?" Dante asked.

"After you come to Cali and play your game and check on your big brother, promise me you'll go back to school and talk to your coach and make sure your scholarship is still intact."

There was another brief silence.

"You have one minute remaining on this call."

"Dante? What? You don't wanna come no more?"

"No, I still want to come," Dante responded quickly this time.

"Well... do you promise?"

"Yeah Mal, I promise."

"Good... I'll see you soon then, knuckle head."

"Alright." Dante laughed.

"Dante," said Malcolm, "I love you, bro."

"I love you too Mal, I'll see you soon."
The phone call ended with a distinct click.

Chapter 3: Orientation

Dante stood in the lobby of the Last Legend Games HQ surrounded by floor to ceiling glass. Natural sunlight flooded the first-floor lobby, bouncing off the many reflective surfaces. It was like standing in a Crystal Palace. Blinding. On a 15-foot wall, scroll posters featured the most prominent characters from the Dragon Dale franchise, and Dante felt as though he were standing before a shrine.

He stared in silent reverence, not noticing the security guard standing behind the front desk staring daggers into him. Nor did he notice when she called out to him.

"Excuse me, sir!" she said a third time and finally, Dante snapped to attention.

"Oh yes, um hello..." Dante approached the desk, embarrassed by his sheepishness. "My name is Dante Battle. I'm here for the Beta test."

"Of course, you are," said the security guard, rolling her eyes, annoyed with Dante. She was a fair-skinned middle-aged woman with dark hair pull back into a tight neat bun. "Sign in here, take a name tag. You all have been advised to use your gamer handles on the name tags as opposed to your real names," she said. "Once you're signed in, go over to the Theater Hall and wait with the others." She pointed to a far corner of the lobby where a group of people gathered before a large, open door.

Dante signed in, scrawled his name onto a "Hello My Name is..." adhesive tag and then attached it to his jacket before making his way to the constantly growing group gathering in the room across the lobby floor. He had seen the group when he first entered the building and had simply taken them for Last Legend Game Studio Employees, but as he got closer, it became clear that the ever-growing throng of bodies was made up purely of Beta testers, like himself.

There were a lot of them. Upon entering the Theater Hall, Dante found himself surprised that so many people had received the invitation to play the beta, although when he thought about it, it made sense that they would need a lot of players for it to be a true test. The room itself was huge, in the style of an amphitheater or a college lecture hall, positioned so the person on the back row was sitting at a higher elevation than the person on the front row. Although when Dante entered the Theater Hall, no one was sitting, instead everyone was standing around talking and chatting amongst themselves. So Dante stood as well.

"You're here for the Beta too?" a voice cut in on Dante's private thoughts. Dante nodded, looking into a pair of bright blue eyes belonging to a young man, probably around Dante's age, wearing a head of messy brown hair, the smatterings of a wiry goatee, and a big broad grin. The tag on his shirt said his name was Alexaldrin. He must have taken the whole 'Write your gamer handle' thing seriously. Dante had only written his name. Coincidentally, it was also his handle.

"My whole life stopped when I found out about this. I told myself I wouldn't miss it for anything in the world."

Alexaldrin was a few inches shorter than Dante, not abnormal considering Dante himself was roughly 6'2. By comparison, Alexaldrin was squat and stout. He reminded Dante of someone built to play fullback, or maybe hind catcher.

"Are you from here? California, I mean." Dante asked.

"Las Vegas actually. Before you ask, I'm not a gambler. Whenever I say I'm from Vegas, people always assume I have a thing for gambling."

"Makes sense," Dante responded, "it's kind of like working in fast food. Once you spend so much time around the stuff, really see how it's made, they say you lose your taste for it."

"Exactly. You think that's how these guys feel too?" he asked, motioning to the Last Legend employees walking by, going to and from their respective departments within the building.

"No, not even close," said Dante. "These guys are a part of making the best video games that the world has ever seen, even if the world doesn't know it yet. No way that ever gets old."

Alexaldrin grinned. "I couldn't agree more. I'm Alex Peerson. It's nice to meet you." Alex extended his hand toward Dante with the intentions on shaking.

"Dante Battle," said Dante, returning the gesture by shaking Alex's hand in return.

"I'm so glad that I'm not the only Dragon Dale nerd here." Alex had a look of unbridled glee on his face, "I hope you don't mind me calling you that, a nerd I mean. I don't mean any offense by it. It's just that I noticed how you were looking around earlier, and then just now how you answered the fast-food question. Listen, I'm just happy to run into a kindred spirit. I was overhearing some conversations earlier and a lot of these guys are what you might call 'too cool for school' and others are just plain toxic."

At that moment Alex fell face first into Dante, knocking him back a step, and if Dante had been any slower in bracing himself, the two of them would have fallen over right in the middle of the theater hall floor. Dante looked behind him to see what had caused him to go careening forward and saw a big meaty back moving away from the two of them.

"Yo man, watch it!" Dante called out. "You almost knocked us over!"

The meaty back turned around to reveal that it was attached to an entire meaty man who looked more like a professional wrestler than a gamer.

"Oh, sorry, home boy, didn't see you there. I'll try and be more careful next time."

Dante grimaced.

"Speak of the devil," said Alex. "That's Arnold Fangloski, one of the guys I was talking about. He's here for the Beta too. He's a complete and total jerk. He's been complaining about everything from his hotel room to the plane ride all morning. He's not a fan of any of the past Dragon Dale games and all he keeps saying is how much he knows this one is going to blow. I don't know why he was invited; he definitely doesn't deserve to be here."

"It takes all kinds I guess." Said Dante, trying to hold back his own rage at Fangloski. He imagined that fighting in the Last Legend Games headquarters building would probably get him kicked out of the beta test. But still, he considered it.

"Hello everyone, everyone, may I have your attention please? Can everyone please take a seat?" A young man, no older than 27, was at the front of the room, with his hands in the air. He was Asian American. Handsome in the traditional sense. He had high cheekbones and a prominent chin, and he accented his face with large square framed glasses that made him look both studious and somewhat authoritative. He wore jeans and a white button-down long sleeve, although it was covered by a dull red cardigan sweater that looked as if it had been washed a few times too many. He wore no name tag, but instead a Dytorus Corp Employee Badge, which hung from a lanyard around his neck. Alex sat right next to Dante. "Hello everyone, I'd like to thank you all for coming and take this time to officially welcome you to the Beta Test for Dragon Dale 10!"

The crowd of gamers, which now easily numbered more than a two hundred, erupted in applause. Dante refrained from joining the celebration and choose instead to politely observe.

"My name is Stephen Choi, and I will be one of your many game guides for the duration of the Beta. I know you all are eager to get started. We have a very large group here and a lot of ground to cover, so what do you all say we get things under way, shall we?"

At this, the group of gamers hooted and cheered, they clapped and whistled until Stephen raised his hands to calm them so he could continue speaking.

"So, we begin with a tour of the facility, followed by character creation, and then we will log on to Dragon Dale 10!" he said with a flourish.

Again, the crowd went wild.

"In an effort to be more expedient, efficient and to offer a better overall experience, we will be breaking you all into small groups, our some of you might even call them parties." Stephen smiled.

The gamers let out a collective chuckle and Dante yearned to be out of this large group that seemed to be laughing, cheering, and thinking as one organism. At that same time, a number of other lanyard wearing employees filed into the Theater Hall. The "game guides" as they were so called, began taking out beta testers in spontaneously generated groups of four. The employees approached the gamers in much the same way kids in junior high approached one another at a school dance. A game guide would walk up to a gamer or group of gamers, exchange a few polite words, share a fake and forced laugh at some mildly amusing comment and then the game guide would invite the Beta tester to dance, or rather to begin their tour of the facility. The room was beginning to empty almost as quickly as it filled.

Dante felt silly for not realizing that there would be so much social interaction at an event like this and kicked himself for not mentally preparing to be more outgoing and sociable. Now he felt caught off guard, and as a result, any attempts to seem charming or likeable would come off as awkward and clumsy. On top of which, he wasn't really interested in meeting new people, he just wanted to play the game.

Dante stood, and as he stood Alex moved over, attempting to make room for him, but in the process bumped into a blond-haired young woman sat on the other side of him.

"Personal space buddy." She spoke in a way that was hard to tell if she was joking or truly upset.

"Sorry." Said Alex.

"That was my fault." Said Dante, speaking around Alex in an attempt to apologize as well.

"What are you doing, bro?" asked Alex, confused by Dante's sudden movement.

"I'm trying to get up and go-" Dante began, but before he could explain any further, Stephen Choi was standing in front of them rubbing his hands together and smiling his charming and likeable smile.

"Alright, what do you guys say? Are you ready to take the tour?" asked Stephen. He seemed genuinely excited.

"Heck yeah, we're ready," said Alex. "Are you going to be our guide?"

"Ya darn tootin!" Stephen replied, doing his best impression of a southwestern cowboy accent.

"Nice! We got the number one guy as our guy!" said Alex, jabbing Dante in the ribs with his elbow in a poor attempt at a celebratory nudge.

"Well, I wouldn't say I was the number one guy." Said Stephen bashfully. "It's more like I just ended up as the guy with the announcer's job."

Alex chuckled too. Dante watched awkwardly, willing the moment to pass quickly. He noticed the blond-haired girl that Alex had bumped into was observing the situation as well, and she was not chuckling either.

Stephen turned to the young woman. "And shall you be joining us as well?" he asked with an air of false chivalry.

"Only if you vow to never use phrases like 'ya darn tootin' ever again," she said dryly.

"Oh, you drive a hard bargain but... consider it done! Welcome to the team. And now we need one more to round out the group." Stephen's eyes scanned the room. Most all the other gamers seemed to be either talking with a guide or already engaged with a group of gamers. But then apparently, he spotted someone because he said, "Oh give me one moment please" and then dashed off to the far corner of the room, before coming back a few seconds later with another young woman. "Friends and gamers, I present to you the fifth member of our merry band."

Their new group member, a black girl, had a chin that never dropped below a heading of 98 degrees, and as a result when she looked at either Dante or Alex she had to look down the length of her pierced nose to make eye contact. She wore her hair in the natural way, pulled back slightly in the front, but from her ears and back, her springy black curls stretched out in every direction. Her dark brown skin showed little to no signs of either make up or flaw and the expression on her sharp and angular face reminded Dante of the expression 'if looks could kill'.

Her expression screamed "I'm only interacting with you because it seems to be a mandatory requirement at the moment," and Dante realized that perhaps he was not the only one who was less than excited about the high amount of social interaction required of the Beta participants.

Stephen led 'Team Stephen', through a number of floors in the Last Legend Headquarters building, describing how company founders Arthur Hirsch, Michael Edwards and Benjamin Sandberg started out by developing a turn-based tabletop, pencil-and-paper role-playing game in their garage. After experiencing enormous success in the tabletop gaming community, the three friends and business partners decided to develop a computer game, and that's how the original Dragon Dale console game came to be.

Dante knew all of this information already, but still, he told himself, it was fun to hear it firsthand on an official Last Legend Games Corporate Headquarters Tour, and he imagined that there had been worst things that he could have been forced to suffer through as he waited for a once in a lifetime opportunity.

"So, when exactly did the old guys decide to sell out to the corporate over lords and where do they stand on all of this?" asked Robyn. She asked this question out of nowhere, interrupting Stephen as he explained the inspiration behind Dragon Dale 4.

"Well," he said looking caught off guard, "It is true that Last Legend Games was purchased by the Dytorus Corporation about five years ago, and this collaboration..."

"Hostile takeover," Alex fake coughed, then nudged Dante and winked.

"We think of it as a strategic partnership," said Stephen. "Dytorus Corp brings us newer technology, and more manpower. Even this building that we're in is a Dytorus Corp addition to the Last Legend Legacy. New body, same soul. That was the idea behind the acquisition, and as you've seen, the quality of the Dragon Dale games has not dropped since Last Legend Games joined the Dytorus Corp family of companies."

He was right, Dante thought. Last Legend Games had always had a cult following, so when it was announced they were being sold to the oversized and often vilified multimedia and tech company the Dytorus Corporation, a large section of the gaming community was concerned, Dante one of them. People feared that the games they once loved would be turned to cheap imitations of their former selves, just blind money grabs churned out by a mindless machine. But as Stephen had said, everyone's concerns were unfounded, after Dytorus acquired Last Legend Games the Dragon Dale Franchise didn't drop in quality, on the contrary, subsequent games got better, yet, a large number of gamers were still apprehensive in regard to Dytorus Corp.

"Anyway, that's enough corporate politics for one tour, get enough of that by the water cooler am I right?" said Stephen, attempting to change the subject, "Let's prepare to move on to Character Creation, for that we will head down to Sub Floor 1 fill out a few forms and get this show on the road."

Alex let out a "Whoo!" which was followed by a very sarcastic "Ya-hoo"" from the blond-haired girl, while Dante and the other girl in the group, who he had identified as Morrigan by way of her name tag, remained silent. Dante felt a bit of sympathy for Stephen, as he knew out of all the groups of Beta testers any game guide could have ended up with, Stephen had perhaps gotten the most difficult bunch. With the exception of whichever game guide ended up with Fangloski.

Sub Floor 1 was very different from the rest of Last Legend HQ. It was below ground level, so no more of the big bright natural light Dante had seen in the lobby. The upper floors were all individual cubicles or employee desks sitting on modern and open floor planning, traditional corporate decorative affair. On Sub-floor 1, the environment was more reminiscent of a hospital or science lab, the walls were thicker, the doors were all heavy and metal and they all had to be opened by scanning a badge. The only thing that remained the same from the upper floors to the Sub Floor was Stephen's upbeat attitude.

"So, before we actually start Character Creation, I'll have you guys fill out a little paperwork. An NDA, for one, Dragon Dale 10 is still unfinished and the guys in legal are just dead set on having something in writing saying that you guys won't spill all the beans before the specified time. You met them earlier, you know how they are. We'll also have you guys fill out a couple of other forms. The team will record your vitals. You know the standard weight, height, blood pressure. Hmm what else?"

"Wait a second, what do you mean record our vitals, why would you need to record our weight, height or blood pressure?" asked Morrigan.

Stephen looked puzzled by the question, "Well, that basic biometric information will help us out tremendously in the Character Creation Phase and also, we do have to ensure that everyone meets some basic health parameters to actually log into the game. We need baseline statistics to compare against once you get in game. You know, reference points. The game can be... intense."

"I'm sorry," said Dante."I don't follow."

"Yeah, because none of that made any sense," said Robyn.

Stephen slapped his hand against his forehead. "Of course! It keeps slipping my mind that you guys don't know yet." He put the back of his hand to the side of his mouth like he was saying something he didn't want anyone outside of 'Team Stephen' to hear, but he was wearing his same high energy grin as he said it. "I'm not supposed to tell you until after you sign the NDA," he whispered. "But you guys are cool, so what they hey!" He leaned forward. "Dragon Dale 10 is a fully immersive VR MMO." He spoke with the same bravado as in the Theater Hall.

"Virtual Reality?" asked Alex.

"Of course, Virtual Reality." answered Robyn before Stephen even had a chance to respond.

Dante grimaced. He had played a number of Virtual Reality games before and in all honesty, he always found them lacking in the areas of substance, style, and execution. They often came off more as gimmicks than serious games. It was odd, he thought, that a franchise as large as Dragon Dale was doing something as risky as releasing their flagship title as a VR game.

"Okay," said Morrigan, "I still don't see why you need our health information."

"Well, this isn't your run-of-the-mill VR experience. Dragon Dale 10 is so convincing we've found that the mind often cannot distinguish the difference between real danger and the simulated kind, so as a precaution we need a base line of all of your biometric information so that we can monitor your heart rate and blood pressure while you are logged into the game and if either gets too high, we'll pull you out," he paused. "Look," he continued. "You can always pull out of the beta test. By the time it hits market, all of this will be ironed out, anyway." Suddenly Stephen looked serious, or maybe it was genuine.

Dante got a queasy feeling. A VR experience so advanced that your mind couldn't tell the difference between what was real and fake? That sounded like perfectly executed Virtual Reality, groundbreaking technology compared to what was currently on the market. If what Stephen was saying was true, that made the play test an even more historic event than Dante had originally anticipated. But then why was their game guide trying to talk them out of the beta? Was he implying the unfinished game was somehow dangerous?

They were in Last Legend Games HQ, which was owned by Dytorus Corp, a multi-billion-dollar company. There was no way there were going to invite a couple hundred people into their building to test out something that was not absolutely safe.

"I'm in." said Dante aloud. The rest of 'Team Stephen' looked up at him.

"Me too." Alex announced.

"Yeah, I mean, obviously," said Robyn half-heartedly.

Morrigan rolled her eyes, but otherwise remained silent.

"Great, now that we've got that settled, let's move on," Stephen said, ushering the group down the hall. "You know," Stephen clapped Alex on the back as they walked. "You all are a pretty good group; I think I lucked out when I got you guys!"

Chapter 4: Character Creation

When the tour ended, so did 'Team Stephen'. Dante and Alex sat in slightly uncomfortable chairs in a narrow room with heavy metal doors on either end. The same uncomfortable chairs that they occupied lined the walls of both sides of the room and at capacity could hold about twenty people at a time. Currently there were only ten occupants, all guys, including Dante and Alex.

Each of the occupants held a clipboard, upon which, were a thick stack of papers. Dante thumbed through the paperwork reading, signing and initialing as he went. There was a strict non-disclosure agreement, as he expected. He signed it. No protest. But then he flipped to a Liability Waiver that absolved Dytorus Corp of all wrongdoing in case of participant personal injury or death. Dante paused, tapping his pen against his chin. This was odd. Death? He looked around the room, everyone else was busy signing and flipping papers. There's no way this waiver would ever hold up in court, he thought to himself, so he signed.

The next few pages were lists of more personal questions like, "Do you enjoy working in groups or do you prefer to be alone?", "Do you consider yourself a leader or a follower?", "Are you a good listener?" "Do you feel you perform well in high pressure situations?", and so on and so on. Many of the questions were really just the same question asked in three to four different ways. Dante counted at least 6 times that they asked him about working in groups, on a team, well with others, or cooperatively.

"Is this a personality test?" He asked looking up and over at Alex for some sort of confirmation. But Alex merely shrugged and then grunted a series of syllables that Dante interpreted as "I don't know," then dropped his head and went back to filling out his paperwork.

Dante was halfway through the questionnaire when one of the doors at the end of the room opened and in walked Arnold Fangloski. He was hefty and muscular and moved with the unmistakable confidence of an athlete. He held himself like he was fully aware of both his size and his power. He wore cargo shorts and a t-shirt a size too small, and on his chest his name tag simply read

Fang. He was almost as wide as the room itself and as he walked between the rows of chairs, he kicked the extended foot of one of the other gamers. "Oh, sorry!" said Fangloski, on his face a smile that showed he didn't mean it. He looked down the length of the room, spotted Dante and winked at him, and then with his clipboard in hand, plopped down into the first open chair that he came across and began to complain.

"Jesus how much paperwork is this? Are there tax forms in here too? Good God man, I thought I came here to play a video game, not retake the SAT."

Dante gritted his teeth. The 'home boy' comment from earlier was fresh in his mind. This guy thought he was all strength, but Dante knew better. He'd noticed a ring around Fangloski's left knee, an indention from wearing a knee brace, which hinted at an injury, a weak point. Dante made a mental note.

"You done already?" Alex asked Dante.

"Oh yeah," Dante said, not realizing that he had been sitting there for the past minute and a half just blankly staring down at his completed paperwork. He stood and took his clipboard to a reception window.

"Thank you, they'll call your name shortly," said the receptionist.

With a smile and a nod, he went and sat next to Alex, who was still filling out the questionnaire and having a tough time with a true or false question that read simply:

"I feel that my life lacks direction."

Alex had filled in and erased both the 'true' and 'false' bubble multiple times from the looks of it.

"You need some help?" Dante asked, partly teasing.

"Oh thanks," replied Alex, "but I think I'm about done. Just a couple more to go now."

Dante shrugged. Not every joke got a laugh. Absent-mindedly he looked at Fang who was filling in bubbles much too fast to actually be reading the questions. Dante's name was called.

The Dytorus employee waved him into the next room, which was large and filled with advanced and expensive looking machinery. The employee that had called Dante was a small woman with short dark hair and a petite face. Her features were soft and when she smiled, she gave the impression that her natural disposition was both gentle and kind.

"My name is Sara," she said with her kindergarten teacher's grin. "And today I'm going help you design your character." She led Dante to a large padded chair, one of eight in the room. They looked like dentist or the eye doctor chairs, large metal and leather contraptions that take your feet off the floor and lean you back to look up at the ceiling.

Sara pulled up a stool and sat down at the station that corresponded to Dante's chair. She fed the bubbled in questionnaire into a slot on one of the machines and immediately it began to whir and buzz. "Oh wow," she said sounding more than a little surprised. "It says here that you've completed all of the currently available Dragon Dale titles."

"Umm yep," said Dante sheepishly.

"Okay that's quite the accomplishment, let me be sure to update that to your character profile that will unlock additional selection options." She typed and talked at the same time most of which she did without ever turning and looking at Dante.

"Really?" Dante said trying not to sound too excited. "You mean like bonus content?"

"In a manner of speaking, yes."

"Aw man that's awesome."

"Do you have any other talents?" she asked.

"Talents?" said Dante.

"Yes?" she said, still facing her screen. "Do you speak another language, can you play an instrument, anything like that?"

"Uhhhh no." said Dante, feeling a flush of shame.

Sara turned around. "Well," she said, looking him up and down, "you look fit enough, do you play any sports?"

"I went, I mean I go to Milgrad University, and I have an athletic scholarship to play..."

At that moment Fang burst through the door of the character creation room with a Dytrous employee following closely behind him.

"Alright let's get this character created so I can get into this game!" he shouted.

"Right this way Mr. Fang, sir." Fangloski was led to the chair directly across from Dante. Fang plopped own into the chair rattling the entire station and its surrounding machines.

"Well," said Sara, turning back to Dante but obviously startled by the commotion, "Yes as you were saying, you are a college level athlete, that is worth noting, one moment." She turned back to her keyboard and begin typing once again.

"I'm sorry, Sara." Dante said, "But what does this have to do with creating my character?" he asked.

She turned to face him. "Dragon Dale 10 allows users to unlock and access special in-game talents and skills based off of their real life talents and skills, so if you spoke more than one language in real life, you would have a knack for learning languages in Deos, if you knew how to play an instrument in our world you would be able to pick up an instrument in that world."

"Oh wow," said Dante, "That's a pretty amazing idea."

"Yeah, I thought so too," she giggled and turned back toward her keyboard and monitor. "So, any other talents?"

"Um well my only other talent is that I know way too much information about the Dragon Dale Franchise." said Dante jokingly.

She turned to him and didn't respond, but Dante thought he saw an expression of concern crease her forehead.

A few minutes later Dante held another clipboard. This time the questionnaire featured nothing but questions pertaining to Dragon Dale lore, ranging from what form of government rules the city-state of Dalgonia, to which Dante knew the answer was a Monarchy, to who is the principal deity in the Deosian Patheon, a question to which Dante felt there was no correct answer seeing as the principal deity is actually Desus the God-King of Creation, however not many Deosians pray to Desus and their aren't many temples built in his honor, on the other hand the most commonly known and most worshiped deity in the pantheon is Desus's eldest daughter Hathor the sun goddess. Dante simply wrote Deus, and then pointed the issue out to Sara when he handed in his completed questionnaire.

She nodded and said, "I think that tells us just about everything that we need to know right there." She fed the completed questionnaire into the same machine as she had the personality test question and then typed in a few new keystrokes into her system. "Okay," she said, "Now for the fun part."

A thin red light appeared above Dante's head as he reclined in the chair, and then ran down the length of his whole body.

"What was that?"

"A body scan." She replied with a smug smile. "And now I can remake you in whatever image you choose." She rolled to the side to show Dante her screen. On it he saw a free-standing silhouette of himself positioned like he was leaned back in the chair, which then slowly unfolded itself to a standing position with his arms slightly out spread about three quarters of the way up.

Sara hit a button and the figure on the screen changed from Dante's form to that of a large hulking figure, she hit the same button and it changed again to a lithe, thin figure with distinguishably pointy ears, she hit a differ button and the figure took on distinctly feminine curves around the hips and breasts.

"We can set your race, your gender, your complexion, your body type, all to your preference, and then we'll go in and select your job class. After that you'll be good to go. So, what will it be? Do you want to be a half-orc, a half-elf? A dwarf? Male... female?"

"I'm going to be male." Dante said. "And human."

Sara hit a series of buttons and Dante's silhouette returned to its original shape. "Human? That's a surprise. How about your complexion? I can fully manipulate your skin color."

"No, I would like to keep my complexion as is," said Dante.

"Alright. Well should I bulk you up a bit?"

"No, I'm fine there too, I like it just like that." Dante said, looking at the screen where a full color rendering of his character had come into focus.

"That is pretty much you exactly as you are now," Sara said.

"Pretty much," said Dante.

"I'm sure I don't have to tell you this but, you do know that half-orcs get a stat boost to strength, elves a boost to magic and agility, half-elves magic and charisma. Every race has their area of expertise, humans are just..."

"Jack of all trades, master of none," Dante said before she could go any further. "Humans are also known for their high adaptability, so I was hoping that they would still get their stat boost that can be placed in the three individual stats of the player's choosing? It's not as good as some of the other races, I know, but it allows for greater customization," said Dante, his eyes glued to the screen.

"Yes, yes of course, okay. Any idea where you want your stat boost to go?" Sara asked.

"Strength, agility and intelligence." Dante replied without hesitation.

"Ok got it, let me get this finalized. I'll be right back, and we'll finish up."

Sara hopped up from her stool and left out of the character creation room, at the same time Fang's technician left. Arnold Fangloski smiled at him from across the room.

"Hey there superstar," Fang said, hunched over in his chair looking, in Dante's mind like a great big hairless ape.

"What are you talking about?" Dante replied.

"You're obviously somebody's quarterback, or point guard. I can tell you're an athlete so don't try to deny it. I can smell it on you." Said Fang with a look in his eye that made Dante question his sanity.

"Are you ok?" Dante asked.

"To be decided," said Fangloski with a shrug, "The way I see it, you're my only competition in this whole thing, the rest of these losers are couch potatoes living in their momma's basements, but you, you're a competitor, and that just means I have to get you out of the way early."

"It's a Beta Test not a competition, there's nothing to win."

"You think they flew in 200 gamers from around the country just to test out a game? They could have gotten a bunch of locals to do that. No, there is more at stake here then just checking some game for bugs, and whatever it is, it belongs to me." Fangloski stood up and stepped in front of his chair. "And if anybody tries to get in the way of what's mine," he said attempting to loom over Dante who remained unfazed, "He's going to end up getting himself hurt."

Slowly and deliberately, Dante stood. "I don't know if you are stupid or just plain dumb but if you don't sit back in that chair, I'm going to put you in a chair... permanently." Dante spoke his last sentence slowly, enunciating every word and syllable. He felt the toes curl on his right foot, he'd give Fangloski three more seconds and if he didn't step back, he was going to grab him by the collar of that too small t-shirt and kick hard as he could into his bad knee.

"What are you two doing?" said a man's voice from the far end of the room that lead deeper into sub Floor 1. They both turned and saw a man approach. He looked in his mid to late 30's, clean shaven with his hair greased back. His face was chiseled and stern and looked like it was carved of stone. He was wearing black boots with military style roll-out pants and a white t-shirt tucked neatly into his waist. He was as tall as Fang and twice as fit. When he walked, he leaned forward and moved like he wanted to get to where he was going before he needed to be there. Around his neck hung a pair of military-issued dog tags, that bounced off his chest as he walked, jingling in rhythm with his steps. He moved with purpose. His sudden appearance caught both Dante and Fangloski off guard.

"We were just..." Dante began, but was caught off.

"I don't want excuses," the man said, his voice stern, but not harsh. "I want results. I told everyone to have this done by yesterday, and here the two of you are lollygagging. The briefing is at 1400 hours." The man was now in arms reach of both Dante and Fang, and now that he was closer Dante noticed that he also wore a thin gold chain around his neck, the end of which was tucked decidedly into his t-shirt, a small heart shaped pendant pressing through the white cotton of the man's shirt.

Behind him were two more men, one a tall, thin, serious looking Caucasian man in glasses and the other a young Hispanic man with a crooked nose and a buzzcut. They all wore the same style of clothing, only the men in the back wore black collared polo shirts instead of simple white t-shirts.

"Yesterday?" Said Fang looking confused, "we just got here today."

"What?" said the man. "What do you mean you just got here today? We go live today." The man reached down and pulled a folder from the front of Fang's chair, opened it, and then smiled. He reached over and grabbed a similar folder from the front of Dante's chair and did the same. A look of realization spread across his face. He let out a short single syllable laugh that sounded more like a grunt then an expression of mirth.

"Good Afternoon Captain Pope," said Sara, walking back into the room from the waiting room door, along with Fang's technician. "I see you are getting acquainted with two of our volunteer beta test players."

"Apparently they don't build these video game players like they used too. For a moment I thought these were a couple of my guys," Pope said, handing the folders to the tall thin man who then put them back in their rightful places without a word. "I am Captain Marcus Pope formerly of the United States Army, currently head of the Dytorus Corp Mobile Security Team." The men behind him straightened up even more, which to Dante seemed impossible considering they were already standing pretty straight. "This is David Lansing," he motioned to the tall man, "and this is Rodney Hernandez," he motioned to the man with the crooked nose. Each man merely nodded.

"Captain, I'll finish up here and then join you and your men at station 4 for your character creation," said Sara.

"*You're* creating a character?" Dante blurted.

The Captain locked his bright blue eyes onto Dante, and he felt as if the thin red light was shining on him again. Up close, the Captain really looked like an action hero. He smiled. No, not a smile, it was more of a smirk really, a smug, arrogant, self-satisfied, smirk. Like the expression you'd expect to see from a fox before devouring a rabbit.

"Why indeed I am." The captain said.

"The Captain and his team will be joining the Beta Test as Combat Consultants," said Sara. "They'll help us ensure the combat is... properly balanced."

"Now that's pretty cool," exclaimed Fang. "That's how you build a great game, around the combat system, and you create a great combat system by consulting people who have actually been on a battlefield."

At that Captain Pope turned his attention from Dante to Fangloski and Dante felt himself breathe again. The Captain's smirk turned to a wide mouth smile.

"My thoughts exactly," said Pope. "Have you ever served in the military?"

"Unfortunately not, Sir. I wanted to enlist but my father insisted I take a wrestling scholarship to Alcoa State instead."

"I used to wrestle myself a bit back in school, that was before I joined the service of course." The captain did a playful jab toward Fang who immediately rolled into a defensive position, elbows up high near his chin and his forearms by his ears. He bobbed back and forth to give the Captain no opening to attack. "Ah, excellent technique, your father's a smart man, and you were a smart son to listen to his advice."

"Thank you, sir," said Fang.

Dante frowned. Fang was being so respectful, when all morning he had behaved like a complete Neanderthal. Why the sudden change of heart for the head of security, was he that afraid of being kicked out of the beta? Or did he really believe that there was some secret prize to be won?

"Please no need to be so formal, call me Marcus, or Pope, that's what all my men call me. Well, to my face anyway." Captain Pope laughed at his own joke, and on que Fang joined in. "We'll get out of the way and let you all finish, you boys enjoy your game, maybe we'll see you on the other side."

"It would be an honor, sir." Fang looked ready to salute. Dante rolled his eyes.

Pope and his men left.

"It would be an honor sir?" Dante said looking sideways at Fang.

"Oh, shut up superstar, what would you know about being a patriot."

"Nothing apparently, other than when you do it, it looks a lot like kissing a-"

"Alright Dante are you ready to finish up your character build?" asked Sara, waiting for Dante to return to the station chair.

He and Fang cut eyes at each other and went back to their respective stations. Dante took his seat.

"Okay, so we have everything in order the only thing left is to choose your job class, which of course as you know is selecting what style of fighter your character will be. Let's see you have the option of battle guard, monk, mage, cleric, rogue and oh, oh wow that's interesting, never seen that before."

"Seen what before?" Dante asked, his interest thoroughly piqued.

"Well it looks like due to your gaming history; you have unlocked an additional job class. It says here that you can also play as the Sword Disciple class if you'd like."

Dante's heart thudded. "But Sword disciples become Sword Saints," he said.

Sara pursed her lips, reached into a cabinet under her keyboard and pulled out a large binder. She began flipping through its pages. "Okay yes, it says here that *'A Sword Disciple can graduate to the status of Sword Master and then to the status of Sword Saint'*. Also, there is an asterisk here that says that Sword

Saints are very rare and that the job class of Sword Disciple has an abnormally high difficulty and learning curve especially in the early stages and should be approached with caution. Which I would imagine is why it's not made available to all players; this is actually the first time I've seen it in the options. Let's read through the rest of the options..."

"I choose Sword Disciple." Dante interrupted.

"Are you sure? I mean at least for the Beta wouldn't you like to try something with an easier entry point?"

"No," Dante said. "Absolutely not. I've been waiting my whole life for this. It's definitely Sword Disciple."

"Alrighty," Sara said, typing in a few commands on her keyboard. "I'll get your starter equipment loaded in and that will be that." She hit one last button and the entire station whirred to life, then with a final beep, a thick plastic card popped out of a slot in the front of the chair. Sara gently pulled the card free and handed it to Dante. "This is it, all of your character data has been loaded onto that keycard, you'll use that to login. If you head back out to the waiting room someone will come and grab you in a second and take you to the login area."

"Thanks." Dante said. He flipped the card over in his hands, it was six inches long by three inches wide and completely blank, with the exception of an embossed symbol like a number eight turned on its side. Dante recognized it as the infinity symbol, it also served as the Dytorus logo.

The deeper he'd gone into Sub Floor one, the more he'd seen of the Dytorus Corp branding and the less he'd seen of Last Legend Games. He assumed Dytorus owned all of the technology, or maybe bank rolled the research. Regardless, he didn't really care that much, he had more important things on his mind. He was on his way to becoming a Sword Saint. He gripped his key card and stood to leave, looking forward to finding Alex who he knew would truly appreciate the gravity of this moment.

"Dante," Sara called out to him once more. He turned, his face still beaming with excitement. She, on the other hand, looked worried, her eyes dark and glistening. She opened her mouth to speak when a large figure walked up behind her. She didn't bother looking back but Dante noticed her expression changed. "Have fun, okay."

"Yeah, I will. Thank you. Thanks for everything. And uh, catch ya later Captain." Dante gave Pope a half-hearted salute and left the room.

Chapter 5: Now Loading...

"Alright Ladies and Gentlemen, right this way. Follow me," said Stephen in his upbeat tone, leading the Dante, Alex and a random assortment of new gamers deeper into Sub Floor 1. The Sub Floor of the building seemed larger than the upper floors. Everything looked identical. Dante knew that if they hadn't had Stephen there to guide them, they would have gotten lost in that labyrinth of underground hallways and metal doors.

After a number of twists and turns they came upon a set of hospital style double doors. Stephen waved his lanyard in front of the scanner and the doors swung open. Inside, 10 large tube-like machines that looked like MRI machines filled the room.

"Welcome to the VR login room." Stephen announced.

Alex had been walking beside Dante and now turned to him. "They're so... big." If all the gamers from the theater were to be hosted in machines like these, they were going to need a lot more login rooms.

That's because they're powerful," Stephen said. "Fully immersive. These things will transport you to another world. When it's time to go to market we'll have a scaled down version of course. That one is still being calibrated."

"Is it safe?" Asked one of the gamers.

"Oh yes, yes very." Stephen nodded his head and leaned on of the machines. "We have logged on with these particular pods numerous times."

"We, as in you?" quipped one of the gamers.

"We as in me." Stephen quipped back, pulling out a key card bearing the Dytorus logo. One just like the card Dante had received from Sara when he created his character.

"So, you've played?" "What was it like?" "How real does it look?"

The excitement from the gamers was palpable.

"Alright, alright hold on a second," Stephen said attempting to regain some order. "You will all be logging on momentarily and at that time, all of your questions will be answered. But first a few announcements. Before character creation you all answered a series of questions, the way you choose to answer these questions were loaded to your character profile, we used that information to match gamers into compatible parties. Each party will have four beta players, one game guide, which will be someone such as myself and three combat consultants. Now the game is still being calibrated for battle difficulty, so the combat consultants are there to assist with battling monsters and taking on tough quest and things of that nature. Please do your best to follow their directions as they are only there to enhance the game experience. Now if you please, can I have everyone step up to a VR pod, no need to push, there is one here for everyone. Hand the technician your key card, place the helmet on your head like so and then lay back on the platform." Stephen was placing a large white helmet over his head; it came down over his ears and had a fold down visor. It reminded Dante of a motorcycle helmet, only with large sections of it missing. Stephen's visor was currently in an upright position, so he was still able to see the gamers as they made their way to their VR pods.

Dante stepped up to an unoccupied pod near the center of the room. He watched as Alex claimed the pod next to his. He handed the waiting technician his Dytorus Key Card and was handed a white helmet in return. Dante slid the helmet on and the technician helped him with the straps. It fit snugly over his head and ears, the inside was cushioned and soft, turning out to be a lot more comfortable than he expected. The helmet covered his forehead, the back of his head and the direct top of his head, but there were still spots of his exposed hair that he could reach up and touch if he felt so inclined, it was like expensive boxing headgear.

"I'm going to load in your key card now sir," said the technician as Dante sat down on the platform.

"Okay, thanks." He replied with a bit of a weak smile. Suddenly, he felt nervous.

A crack of mild static and an electronic voice began speaking into his ear. It was Stephen, speaking through the helmet's built-in headphones.

"Alright party people, everyone is on a pod and it looks like all key cards are loaded, now what you have on your heads is the prototype technology for the new Dytorus in-home Virtual Reality Home Entertainment System. Each helmet is equipped with over five thousand neurotransmitters, which both send and receive small electric signals to your brain, allowing you to act as the video game controller for your character in the game world without moving a muscle. As I stated earlier, we have used these devices a number of times, and they are one thousand percent safe. Now if I could have everyone pull down the visors on their helmets."

Dante reached up and flicked down the white visor, which came down to the bridge of his nose and blocked everything in the room from view. The only thing stopping him from sitting in total darkness was the small amount of light that streamed in from the bottom of the visor, like light that squeezed in through the bottom of a closed door.

"Alright, now everyone can go ahead and lay back on the platform, slowly now. The technicians will assist you."

Dante felt hands guide him backwards as he leaned back and stretched out on the makeshift cot.

"There you go," said Dante's technician, barely audible through the helmet.

"Alright, now," said Stephen over the headphones. "The visors are screens that project super high-resolution images at very close range, but the human mind is difficult to fool. That's why we have the pods. The platform will now slide into the pods and the pod will create a host of high-resolution images and sounds all around you, a full 360 degrees."

Dante's breathing quickened and his heart thumped in his chest. The platform began to move, and as it crept further into the tube, the light that had forced itself up through the bottom of Dante's visor grew to less and less and until it vanished completely, and he was in complete darkness.

"See you all in Deos," Stephen said, and the headphones went silent. Dante felt like he was in a sensory deprivation tank, a breeding ground for bizarre hallucinations and anxiety attacks, especially for an emotionally distressed mind.

"Well, shit." Dante muttered to himself, just to keep the silence at bay. He feared being trapped alone in the dark with nothing but his thoughts to keep him company. Resorting to an age-old technique he had perfected while waiting on other video games to load, he closed his eyes under the visor and imagined that the darkness around him extended further than just the interior of the VR pod. He imagined, instead that it extended for all time in every direction. He imagined that the whole world, that the whole universe was covered in darkness, and that he was merely another shapeless being floating in that great void.

A bright line shone from somewhere beyond his closed eyes. He blinked his eyes open, expecting to stare at a blank screen, but instead found himself in a white room, no longer laying in the VR pod platform at all but rather sitting upright in a chair. He was alone. Alex, Stephen, the other gamers and the other pods were gone and all that remained was this bright white, borderless room. He tried to stand but found he couldn't move. He looked down at himself, he wasn't tied down or strapped to the chair but when he tried to move, his body wouldn't budge. He started to panic. Was he paralyzed? Did something go wrong with the VR Pod, did it fry his brain, put him in a coma, was he... dead? His initial panic graduated to irrational fear and he began a desperate struggle to stand up from the chair move a finger, move a toe anything to prove that he had some type of control over his body and his mind.

"Don't bother, you can't move," said a voice. Clear and distinct, it was a man's voice but one that he had never heard before. Dante looked up and in front of him was the back of a man who a few moments ago had not even been standing there. Was he mixing a drink? Dante heard a metal stirrer, the clinking of ice and a glass being filled full of amber liquid. At the same time, or perhaps it had been there the entire time, music played. It was an instrumental version of 'Copacabana'.

"You are bound, as they say." The man said with a chuckle. He turned around with the drink in his hand and a dancing shuffle in his step.

"What's happening? Where am I?" Dante asked. He swallowed hard imagined he'd clear his throat and try again with a bit more authority in his tone. But when he next opened his mouth to speak his lips were now reacting in much the same way as his body. They would not move.

"Nuh-unh-un, I need you to listen, not speak." Said the man. He took another sip of his drink and then sat the glass down, on what Dante thought was about to be mid-air but once the glass landed safely on the surface Dante realized it was a white table. Everything in the room was the exact same shade of white so much that it was impossible to distinguish one thing from another. With the exception of the man that is. He was the solitary figure in stark contrast to everything else in the room. He was of middling weight and average height, probably 5⊠11 maybe right at 6 feet if Dante had to guess it. He wore a suit, but more in the style of a military officer as opposed to a businessman or a politician. He had jet black hair combed toward the back of his head, a thick and full beard and most distinguishable of all an eye patch that covered his left eye. The man shuffled ever closer to Dante and as he did Dante smelled blood and metal. Dante clenched his teeth and braced himself, as expecting a punch to the gut.

"You are about to enter into the world of Deos. However, what you need to know is that Deos is a dangerous and treacherous place."

If this was Dragon Dale 10's cutscene he would be sure to complain about it. It was terrifying and not exactly instilling confidence that he was going into a great gaming experience.

"Pay attention now!" said the man, and his voice seemed to boom throughout the entire room when he spoke. "I'm about to give you a very important history lesson."

"In the beginning, Deos was a land of Gods. But the immortal Gods soon grew bored, so to entertain themselves they began to pit mortals against monsters, and mazes, and eventually each other. And because Gods like to argue and cheat, in their infinite wisdom, they did one more thing to legitimize their little game. They put a system in place to help them keep score. It's called Universal Quantification, and it means everything in the land of Deos has been assigned a value, or better yet, a level, and the more you live, grow, learn and experience things in Deos, the higher your level will grow.

After a time the Gods grew bored of the mortals and the game and left the land of Deos, but since they all agreed on something for once in a millennia, Universal Quantification and a number of other things from the God's Era remained in place and are staples of the Deosian culture and way of life." Over the course of his explanation the man had gotten incredibly close to Dante. "Now," he said, looming over him. "I imagine you're wondering why I'm telling you all of this?"

The man leaned face to face with Dante now. The smell of blood and metal was overpowering. Dante's head wobbled and for a moment he feared he would pass out from the stench. The sound of music had been replaced by the clanging of swords, and if Dante was not mistaken the distant boom of cannon fire. He heard the echo of men screaming, blood curdling howls and cries for help, all of which intensified as the man inched closer and closer. The white room seemed to vibrate and fall out of focus as the man's good eye stared into Dante's. He was not fully sure how or why, but Dante knew that if he could see what was beneath the eyepatch, he would go insane from sheer terror. And as if aware that Dante had made this realization, the man answered his own question.

"Because in order to play the game, you have to know the rules." And with those words Dante's chair pitched forward, sending him tumbling through a floor that was no longer there, through white space until he hit solid ground with a hard thud, and everything went black.

When he opened his eyes again, he was lying face down on a bed of dark green grass with blood in his mouth, in the land of Deos.

Chapter 6: Welcome to Deos

Dante spat out the blood filling his mouth. He had busted his lip in the fall. He tried to lift himself up to his hands and knees and took a hard breath in through his nose before pushing off.

"Whoa now, slow down partner," said a familiar voice, just outside of Dante's vision.

He raised himself to his knees, sat back on his heels and saw Stephen, squatting in the grass next to him.

"That was quite a spill you took." Stephen said with a smile. At least it looked like Stephen. His face seemed more angular than before, and the tops of his ears were sharply pointed at the end. His clothes were different, too. He wore loose dark brown crudely made clothing that looked crafted by hand. His pants were tucked into shin-high brown leather boots and over it all he wore a large dusty white robe.

"You ok?" he asked.

"Um, yeah. I just busted my lip. Must have been from the fall." Dante replied.

"Well I'll say," said Alex. "You materialized at 10 feet off the ground and landed face first in the dirt, lucky you didn't break your neck!" Alex was standing on the other side of Dante, and he could tell it was him primarily by his tone of voice, but also because of how he looked out from behind bright blue eyes and messy brown hair, only now, his once wiry goatee had grown into a full beard. It wasn't very long, but it was thick and shiny.

"Alex?" Dante said in astonishment.

"Alexaldrin Oreheart, at your service." Alex took a deep and dramatic bow. He was draped in the same type of rudimentary fabric clothing as Stephen, only he had a few pieces of leather armor clad around his shoulders, chest and forearms and then layered in between the fabric and the leather Dante could see he was wearing a chainmail shirt.

"You're a dwarf!" Dante said in surprise.

"He's a dwarf. You're late. Are there any other very obvious things you'd like to point out while you hold up our gameplay, Mr. Observant." Robyn stood a few feet in front of Dante and beside Morrigan.

"Robyn, you're here? Morrigan? But you weren't in the group that logged on with us?" Dante said, still disoriented from the fall.

"And you are still pointing out the obvious," replied Robyn.

"Well, hello to you too," said Morrigan, glumly.

"Dante, parties are predetermined based off of the personality test you all took. So the system determined the four of you would complement each other the best." Stephen was still beside Dante down on one knee.

"Well I think your system might be busted," Dante said, using his thumb to wipe more blood from his lip.

"Yeah, well, speaking of busted, let's see what we can do about that bleeding," said Stephen. With his thumb, fore and middle finger extended and his ring and little finger slightly curled inward, he waved his right hand near Dante's face. There was a sudden sensation of warmth and when he removed his hand Dante noticed that the pain in his mouth had gone. He wiped away what little blood that remained on his lip and was surprised to find that it was no longer cut.

"Healing magic?" Dante said looking up at Stephen in bewilderment.

"Healing magic." Stephen replied, who's face seemed to be locked in the position of an unwavering smile.

"Are you guys just going to sit here all day and repeat after each other and smile or can we explore the game?" Robyn drummed her foot impatiently.

Dante surveyed his surroundings for the first time. The sky was a startling and bright crystal blue, speckled with pearlescent white clouds that looked like something from a dream. Thick blades of ankle-high grass spread like an endless green ocean as far as the eye could see. Dante's first impression was that the virtual world was more valid than the real world had been. He could hear the distant song of chirping birds and swore he could smell the sweet scent of jasmine. How could a video game recreate that?

"Glad we ended up in the same party," said Alex to Dante.

"Yeah me too." Dante replied, coming back to himself. "Nice to have at least one friendly face around here." Alex smiled. "You know, you're pretty tall for a Dwarf," Dante commented. "Well at least taller than I expected."

"Low center of gravity." Alex said in response, "hard to knock down, even harder to knock out, the ultimate tank. Dwarf Battle Guard!"

"Haha right on." Said Dante, extending a fist toward Alex. Alex pounded the top of Dante's fist with his own, Dante returned the gesture in kind.

"And a bromance is born, now will you guys come on?" Robyn said.

"Do you ever quit?" Alex sounding genuinely concerned.

"Actually, I'll be here all week." Robyn gave a shrug. She was dressed similar to the others, rough fabrics and leather, only, all of her clothing was dyed in a combination of deep dark browns, reds and greens. She also had a hood covering her head although her bright blond hair still streamed down both sides of her face and poured out over her front collar. Morrigan stood next to her, not looking nearly as impatient but somehow still just as annoyed. She was wearing a full-length robe nearly as dark as Robyn's leathers layered with a pelerine cloak that cut off at her ribs. Her face was exactly the same as it had been outside of the game, all the way down to the nose ring, except for her ears. Like Stephen's, they were slightly pointed at the top and her hair was in a series of braids that hung down her back and lay draped over her shoulder as well.

"Man, you guys look great." Dante said as they approached the girls. Morrigan's head darted towards Dante's direction as if she hadn't heard him correctly. "No, I didn't - I don't, mean it like that, I mean in the game. In the context of the game everyone looks really great, really life like."

"The advances of modern technology." Stephen said bashfully. "Anyway, you were the last piece to the puzzle and now that you're here we'll charge forward, off to adventure and all of that, but first how do you feel?"

Dante was dressed in much the same way as everyone else, rough handspun fabrics, fitted with pieces of snug fitting leather armor. The fabric felt just as uncomfortable and itchy against his skin as it looked on everyone else and the leather armor pieces were thick and hard but otherwise lightweight, easy to move in.

At his waist Dante noticed that hanging from his belt was a sword almost as long as his leg. Its handle was made from dark ebony wood, wrapped in leather and capped with a simple brass pommel. It invited him to reach down and pull it from its sheath. He stared at it for a moment and thought of the man in the white room. He thought about his temporary paralysis and the chair and the gut wrenching feeling that he had felt in his stomach as the man moved closer to him and where he expected to find fear, he found instead excitement, and now he yearned to grab the sword handle. The palm of his hand began to sweat and itch, the world began to vibrate as it did in the white room and out of near desperation, he grabbed the sword handle, and it all stopped. Slowly he pulled the sword from its sheath and it sang, the hauntingly beautiful sound of metal on metal, almost as if it were thanking him for bringing its glistening blade out into the sun. He stared at the sword in admiration, holding the handle with one hand and then two. It was hefty, it had weight, but it was not heavy. He imagined he could wield it with one hand easy enough, or he could use both hands if he was trying to cleave something in two. He switched back to one hand, flicked his wrist and spun the sword around before placing it back into its sheath.

"Boys and their toys." Robyn said to Morrigan but cutting her eyes at Dante.

Dante looked up at Stephen and saw something he hadn't noticed before. He quickly looked over to Alex, then Robyn and then Morrigan. Each of them had a small transparent box floating to the right of each of their heads, in it was each of their respective names, adjacent to their names were the words 'Level' and the number '1' followed by a series of different words that varied for each of them. Beneath each row of words was the letters 'H' and 'P' above a long white bar, and beneath that was another bar headed by the letters 'MP'. "You guys have status boxes by your heads." Dante said with a smile.

"The brilliant observer strikes again," said Robyn. Dante looked at her with an expression that said he was growing annoyed with her commentary, but she only smiled and winked back at him without speaking.

"Well that brings me to my next point, a few quick announcements if you will," said Stephen.

"More announcements?" Morrigan rolled her eyes.

"These you will definitely want to hear. It's a few things on game mechanics."

"Well please, don't start the party without us." The voice came from behind Dante. He turned to find a large figure approaching. The voice and the steely, determined walk were familiar.

"Captain Pope," Stephen said. "Welcome back, any luck on your survey?"

"We didn't find much, but I see you all did. Glad to see our last warrior has arrived. Welcome to Deos, soldier. What happened, you get held up at the border?" Pope said, speaking to Dante.

Behind Pope was a tall man with long angular features and very sharp pointed ears and the other was the man Dante recognized with the crooked nose, Lansing and Hernandez. Lansing had a long bow slung across his back and Hernandez had a sword and shield. Pope had, attached to his back, a very large and menacing looking crossbow that looked as if it had to be held with two hands to be fired. Similar to Dante, Robyn and Hernandez, Pope had also chosen Human as the race for his character avatar. Although, in the light of the Deosian day he seemed both taller and bulkier than Dante remembered, his strong Greco-roman features and overall rugged good looks seemed to transfer all but perfectly from the real world to the virtual one.

"Yeah," replied Dante, "I got caught up in that cutscene in the white room with the guy with the eye patch," Dante explained.

Pope looked confused.

"You know the cutscene, when the guy gives the history of Deos and talks about the Gods and Universal Quantification?"

Stephen and Pope exchanged a curious glance.

"I had no cutscene," said Alex, "There was a *countdown* and then we came straight here."

"Yes, must have been a glitch of some sort, or perhaps you fell asleep momentarily, the pods have been known to induce odd dreams, besides it has been a long and exciting day, either way, we'll get it all sorted out once we get back," said Stephen. "For now, let's get a move on."

"Finally." said Robyn.

Dante was prepared to protest but decided not to waste his breath considering the luck he was having with secret cutscenes.

"Alright, so game mechanics," began Stephen. "As Dante has pointed out, you each have a status box to the right of your heads. This little box will give you basic information about anyone that you meet, including their name, level, class as well as their HP and MP. HP stands for Health Pool, or Health Points and MP stands for Mana Pool or Mana Points or..." Stephen rolled his eyes and shook his head from side to side like he was tired of saying the word 'or' "Magic points," he said reluctantly. "Fun fact. You can make these status boxes appear and reappear as you like just by concentrating on them, and also the status box will only show you a character's name, class and level if they've told it to you. Otherwise, you'll just see question marks. If you drop down to zero hit points your character falls unconscious. If you keep taking damage while you're knocked out, or if you somehow sustain a substantial amount of damage when you are near zero, then you are facing character death, but hopefully that's not something we'll have to worry about." Stephen said with his characteristic game show smile.

"Alright last big-ticket item of the day. Do you all remember these?" Stephen was holding up his key card, at least it looked like his key card, only now it was larger and it was no longer a card at all but a small, leather-bound notebook. "This is your spirit tome, and in game it is the single most important item that you own. This book is the physical manifestation of your character's soul. It contains within it your every stat, exploit, achievement, and success. Everything you do and everything you are is recorded in this book. It is your passport in the Land of Deos."

They were standing on a ridge, surrounded by mostly open, grassy fields and a few patches of dense trees, but to one side was the open blue sky and a steep drop off. Stephen turned and threw his small notebook over the edge. The little book went flying into the air and out of sight in an instant. Both Robyn and Alex gasped in surprised, Morrigan let out a high-pitched squeak of excitement and Dante's eyes grew wide.

"Why would you do that?" Dante asked.

"To show you this." Stephen held up his right hand and a shimmering blue mist appeared, within it, small blue lights twinkled like tiny distant fireflies in his hand before, materializing from the smoke, another notebook appeared in Stephen's hand. "The spirit tome is bound to you, as a matter of fact its soul is bound to you. You can't lose it, no one can steal it, heck no one can even read it unless you allow them to. Now I'd like everyone to go ahead and summon their spirit tomes before we head out."

"How?" Asked Alex.

"We don't have menus here, everything is done by force of will. Now this is more than just thinking about what you want. You have to think about it, imagine it, visualize it, and then force that image from your head to your hand. You have to drag it out of your imagination and into physical being. Go ahead and give it a try, sometimes it helps to use the words, try closing your eyes and saying, 'Spirit Tome' to make it easier."

Dante did as he was instructed. He closed his eyes and imagined his keycard in the form now of a small black book, he then imagined the image of his notebook traveling out of his head down to his shoulder through his arm into his hand and... there was a sudden feeling of tightness, as his entire arm clenched up and when he opened his eyes, he was holding a small notebook.

"Well done," said Stephen, as almost instantly notebooks begin to appear in the hands of the other players as well as that of Pope and his combat consultants. "This is the basis of conjuring all magic in Deos. Summoning your spirit tome is a low-level spell that everyone has access to, but even the skills and abilities of the warrior classes work in much the same way. Take a moment to look at your spirit tomes, you'll undoubtedly find some useful information inside, and once you're done, we'll proceed to the nearby city of Illdershire."

Dante looked down at his tome. The first page was blank but as he turned to the second page, he found what looked like the traditional character sheet that he would have found in any RPG, his name, class, and level were all there. Dante, Sword Disciple, Level 1. There was also some additional information such as his title, and current experience. He had no title as of yet and his current experience was zero. On the following page he saw a breakdown of his detailed stats his strength, agility, and constitution scores among others.

- Strength – 13
- Agility – 13
- Constitution – 10
- Intelligence – 12
- Wisdom – 10
- Mind – 10
- Charisma – 10

Each of these base scores, Dante knew, influenced his other stats. He knew, for example, that his constitution score effected the size of his health pool and that his strength and agility score combined in some way to influence his attack score, even if he didn't know the exact formula. At the moment his attack was at thirteen, but if he was able to increase either his strength or agility that attack score would also increase, making him that much more deadly in combat. In Dragon Dale, players could increase their stats by increasing their level or by upgrading their equipment. The general rule of thumb was higher stats meant a more capable character, but for now, at least for Dante, these stats were just numbers.

He thumbed through the remaining pages and saw that there was a section for Skills and Abilities, Magic Spells, and even Currently Active Quest. It was just as Stephen had said, apparently everything that there was to be known about his character could be found within the pages of his book, which at the moment was almost completely blank.

"I know this was going to be amazing, but I never imagined it would be like this. It's like we're actually in Deos," said Alex.

"Yeah, this is like nothing I've ever even heard of before," Dante said.

"Say, so what's your setup anyway? Human Battle Guard?" Alex asked.

"Oh no," Dante smiled just realizing he had yet to share the news "I'm a sword disciple."

Alex dropped his spirit tome, which disappeared in a flash of blue light.

"Did you say you're a Sword Disciple? But, that's not possible, Sword disciples become..."

"Sword Saints," Dante said with a grin. He turned his open Spirit Tome toward Alex who bent forward to read it, then used one of his meaty hands up to keep his head from spinning away.

"I completed all nine Dragon Dale games and I have the completion certificates, so they have it on record, they said that unlocked the job class for me."

"I knew I shouldn't have listened to my dad when he said to stop wasting my time playing those stupid games. Thanks a lot dad, I could have been a Sword Disciple!" Alex said to the sky.

The party began walking away from the cliffside, toward the direction Stephen said was east. Dante had no real way to know that it was east seeing as no one else in the group had a compass, with the exception of the combat consultants. Stephen moved in front of the group, with Pope and his men closely behind and behind them, Dante and the group of gamers. A small part of Dante was convinced that they weren't even in a video game. Every detail was accounted for, every blade of grass, every flying bug, even every smell seemed legitimate. Nothing revealed they were in virtual reality except for the status boxes that he could see to the right of the other players' heads, and even those felt like something he'd experience with a pair of augmented reality glasses on, or through an AR app on his phone. Dante was simply astounded that he had to keep reminding himself that everything he was seeing, he was not seeing at all, but instead he was lying in a VR Pod in the Sub Floor of the Last Legend Games Headquarters building. He refrained from saying this aloud so as not to spoil the experience for the other gamers, but he felt it was important to remind himself.

Suddenly, Pope stepped in front of Stephen and stopped him from moving forward. In an act of streamlined military style coordination, Hernandez shushed the gamers as Lansing drew his bow and nocked an arrow, aiming it at the empty open clearing in front of them.

"What's wrong?" asked Alex in a whisper.

Hernandez simply held out and extended an open hand palm to say stand still and be quiet.

Dante could find nothing out of place. Then he heard twigs breaking and small branches snapping and bounding out of the trees came a deer. Or something that looked like a deer. its fur was a burnt orange, like the color of autumn leaves, while on its back were thin white stripes that streaked down its sides. Its graceful neck led up to a small almost triangular shaped head offset by a pair of large ears at full attention.

"It's an Illder Doe," said Dante in a hushed voice.

"A what?" asked Pope.

"An Illder Doe, its harmless, it doesn't even have horns, it's not even a stag."

"Lansing." Said Pope. To which Lansing raised his bow and pulled back the bow string, aiming his arrow at the illder doe while it merely stared at the group not really sure what to make of what it was seeing. One of its ears twitched.

"You're going to shoot it?" Morrigan whispered.

"You eat meat don't you?" replied Pope without so much as turning his head in her direction. "Lansing, take it down."

On Pope's command, Lansing released his arrow and it zipped in the direction of the illder doe, but before it struck, the biggest wolf Dante had ever seen leapt from the tree line, clamped onto the doe's neck and wrestled it to the ground. The arrow sailed gracefully over the heads of the wolf and the deer as it struggled and lay still on the ground.

The entire party let out a collective gasp of surprise by the wolf's vicious and violent entrance. Dante was sure that he heard Hernandez swear in Spanish and he was definitely sure he heard both Robyn and Alex swear in English.

The wolf slowly released its grip from the neck of the dead doe, its maw dripping blood, teeth bare and growling, its eyes focused on the nearby adventurers.

"I think it just wants the deer," said Stephen, sounding nervous. "So if we just back away, I think we'll be ok." Stephen took a step back, and Robyn, Morrigan, Alex and Hernandez took a step back as well. Pope pulled his oversized crossbow from his back and pulled a lever on the side, loading it with a crossbow bolt the size of an arrow.

"It's only one wolf. Hernandez on me," ordered Pope.

"Wait, a second," warned Dante.

"What is it!" shouted Pope angrily.

"It's never just one wolf." In one fluid motion Dante pulled his sword from its sheath.

On cue, a number of throaty growls came from the tree line and two more wolves appeared behind the party, darted out of the trees and took positions at a distance of about 100 feet. Ahead of the group, a wolf joined the one that had just killed the doe. The group were now surrounded.

"Is there a pause button?" shouted Morrigan.

"No, no pause button," said Stephen.

"What's the policy on dying?" asked Robyn.

"It should be avoided. If you die the system logs you out and you log back in tomorrow."

"Looks like I'll see you guys tomorrow." Robyn replied.

"Hernandez, you hold off the two in the back, Lansing and I will kill the two in front and then we'll sweep around and clear out the back two," Pope commanded.

"Captain Pope!" Dante interrupted.

"What is it kid?"

"We can take the two in the back, no use in wasting Hernandez as a babysitter."

"No no," said Robyn. "Let Hernandez babysit."

"I think you're in over your head kid."

"Sir, Alex and I will tank the two in the back."

"We can what?" Alex called out.

"We'll make an opening for Robyn and Morrigan to get a clean kill shot. Stephen will stay in the middle between both our groups and heal whoever gets hurt sir, trust us. We can handle the two in the back."

For the first time since the wolf appeared Pope looked back over his shoulder at Dante. He was smiling.

"Alright kid you got it. Hernandez on me."

"Yes Captain." Hernandez called out moving forward with his sword and shield in hand.

Dante gripped tightly to the handle of his sword. Hunched over, knees bent, his eye darted between the two growling, snarling wolves.

"Aw man what have you gotten us into?" Alex asked.

Dante concentrated on the wolves in front of him and watched as their status boxes shimmered and glowed. Their HP bars flipped from solid white to multicolored bars that flowed from dark red to yellow to green, Dante remembered a great deal more detail about not just wolves but these wolves in particular.

"Listen," he said to Alex "You and I are going to get back to back and we are going to move closer and closer to the wolves."

"What?" said Alex in disbelief. "We're just level 1 these things have to be level 10 at least!"

"These are Illdershire Black Wolves and they are level 3. As long as we stay back to back, we stop the wolves from getting behind us. These wolves are known for being extraordinary pack hunters that attack their prey from multiple angles, we can take that option away and use it against them." Dante turned to Robyn. "When Alex distracts the wolf sneak up and stab it in the back!" Dante yelled back.

Robyn nodded grimly.

"Morrigan, I'm going to try and hold the other one, I'm not built to tank like Alex is but if you see an opening to blast it with a spell, do it, don't worry about me I'll get out of the way."

"Al-alright" Morrigan said hesitantly.

Dante and Alex put their backs together and begin to move in slowly on the wolves. They counted their steps aloud so as to stay in lock step with one another and not get tripped out or lose pace.

"1-2, 1-2, 1-2,"

Under ordinary circumstances it would have looked and felt silly, but precaution was better than coolness. Dante kept his sword blade in front of his body and Alex kept his shield raised and as that got even closer to the wolves Dante had another idea.

"Alex, do you have a taunt or a provoke ability, something meant to grab the enemy's attention."

"Yeah, in my spirit tome there was an ability called 'War Cry'. Why?"

"Okay at the count of five do your war cry, the wolves aren't going to have a choice but to come barreling at you, I'm going to catch this one on my side, you catch the one on your side and then Robyn will come up and help you kill that one."

"Are you sure this is going to work?" Alex asked.

"This is MMORPG 101, of course it's going to work."

"MMORPG 101 is done from your living room couch, not in an actual field with wolves the size of cows."

"Five, four, three, two,..."

On the count of one Alex's shield and axe begin to glow red hot as if they had just been pulled from a blacksmith's furnace. He banged the axe and shield together and then threw them open letting out a roar that echoed and shook the ground and the teeth in Dante's head.

"FOR THE HONOR OF ONINGRAD!" he yelled and for a moment the wolves shuddered as if the volume of the banging and yelling hurt their sensitive hearing, but the moment the sound passed, just as Dante suspected, they bolted forward, launching themselves at Alex.

The wolf closest to Alex hit his shield with a crash. It landed headfirst into the wood. Alex leaned back into the blow and then used his new dwarven weight to push back on to the wolf, springing it off the shield and back a few feet. It landed on it paws and was right back on the attack coming at Alex with teeth and claws.

Enraged by Alex's War Cry, the second wolf attempted to blow past Dante and attack Alex from behind, but since the two fighters were back to back it collided instead with Dante and his raised sword. For a moment, they stood locked together, the wolf's jaws bearing down, the only thing keeping him from going into the wolf's mouth the relatively thin metal blade that was currently strewn across the thing's teeth like a makeshift prop rod. Fearing the stress from the wolf's jaws might snap his sword, Dante twisted his body and pushed, forcing the wolf to pull back and let go of its grip but not without first losing a fang in the process. The wolf let out a low growl and looked at Dante with rage flickering in his eyes.

Alex's wolf was still on the attack, it snapped and clawed, and its every attack was met with a reply from Alex's shield, all of which only seemed to frustrate it more. It was so preoccupied with trying to chew through Alex's shield, that it hadn't noticed Robyn creep silently from behind like a serial killer from a horror movie. She stepped closer. The wolf made a hard headbutt into Alex's shield, bounced off and landed in her lap. Both shocked and surprised Robyn plunged her daggers into the wolf's back haunches. The wolf let out a surprised yelp, Robyn screamed, and the wolf with all fangs bared, twisted its body turning to bite down on Robyn's throat in retaliation to her surprise attack. But before it could get too far, a dwarven axe cleaved its skull, nearly splitting it in two and stopping it dead.

Meanwhile Dante's wolf was still whole and still very angry. Its large jaws snapped viciously, narrowly missing the opportunity to take off an arm or a leg. He managed to block the ferocious bites by swinging his sword at just the right moment, hitting the interlocked teeth, an impact which the wolf withstood repeatedly though Dante wasn't exactly sure how, but he also didn't feel now was the best time to question it. He knew only that the attacks seemed to be coming faster and if he was going to survive this encounter, he was going to have to swing his blade with even more speed.

Dante swung again, a cross slash, his right arm coming down and forward across his body. The sword glanced off the wolf's fangs, this time however, the recoil from the blow forced the wolf's head down toward the ground and in that instant Dante saw an opening. If he could get his sword arm back up and bring it down on the wolf's exposed neck before the beast could regroup, he might be able to wound it bad enough to turn the tides of the fight.

Time slowed. The sword was heavy, his arm; tired, and with every passing moment Dante could see the already small window of opportunity closing. Then he remembered what Stephen said, imagine it, visualize it, will it into being. He imagined the sword being over his head again, he imagined himself having enough time, imagined his sword coming down on the wolf's neck like a guillotine. And suddenly he felt something in his arm, suddenly the heavy iron sword didn't feel so heavy, it didn't even feel like a sword, it didn't even look like a sword. The handle of his weapon came up with ease, the blade became a grey blur, the weight moved behind the action, and just as Dante felt the sword's heft returning, he brought it down on his target.

The blade arched like something so real and solid it could not be denied. It sliced the wolf through the neck with speed, rendering flesh and cutting through bone and collapsing the wolf to the ground without even a yelp.

Dante didn't catch his whole neck. He must have hit it right between the neck and shoulder because the wolf was still alive. It moaned, and whimpered and tried to crawl, but the wound made it nearly impossible for the wolf to move. Its status box only had a few hit points left; it was in the red section of its now multi-colored health bar. And though he knew it was not a real wolf, that it was only a series of ones and zeroes, he felt bad for it, so he took his sword, put it over the beast's heart, and pushed. The whimpering stopped. The HP blinked away, and the wolf and its status bar died.

Chapter 7: Wolves, Raptors and Adventurers...

"We won!" Robyn jumped up and down while hugging Alex. "I thought we were all dead for sure."

"That was quick-thinking Dante, good work," said Stephen.

"Thanks," said Dante still standing over the wolf he had slain. Everyone else seemed to be celebrating, but something about it all felt... off. He knelt down near the body and placed a hand on the still animal's dark black fur. He wanted to see how real it felt, but when he came in contact with the wolf's coat, he felt an intense cooling sensation gather in the palm of his hand. Swirling blue light coalesced between his fingers and the unmoving wolf. Then almost as quickly as the light appeared, it vanished. In its place, Dante felt something cold and rough in his palm.

He pulled away shaking his hand and saw something fly from him and the thud of an object hitting the ground. Nobody had seen. They were all still busy celebrating their first victory. Dante stood and took a step back away from the wolf corpse, rubbing the palm of his one hand with the other and frowning.

"He's right," said Pope. "That was impressive. You should be proud."

Hernandez walked over to Dante and nudged him. "You actually surprised the captain, that's not easy to do. These wolves are pretty monstrous, let me skin this thing for you this hide might come in handy later."

"Oh no, you- you don't have to do that," said Dante.

"No man I do, you stepped up when it mattered, practically saved my ass. Stopped me from having to fend off two of those things at once."

Dante assumed he wouldn't be taking no for an answer, so he stepped back, and Hernandez went to work removing the wolf's jet-black fur covered hide from its body in one large clean piece.

"Are anyone else's ears ringing?" Dante asked.

"I thought it was just me." said Alex.

"Oh yes!" said Stephen. "In all the excitement I forgot to mention it, that ringing you're hearing, that's the notification system. It's meant to inform you that new information has been added to your spirit tomes."

Dante called up his spirit tome and the ringing stopped. He opened the notebook.

- You have unlocked a new ability.
- 'Scan' has been added to the abilities and skills list
- You have unlocked a ranked skill 'Sword Technique'.
- Your Sword Technique has risen to a rank of 'F'
- Four Illdershire Wolves have been defeated.
- You have gained 800 Experience points!
- You have a total of 800 Experience Points.
- You have obtained Level 2, Congratulations!

What was Scan? Dante flipped to the Skills and Ability page to see he had a new listing.

"Scan – Due to your quick wit and keen eye you are able to make split second observations and then pull from a vast body of knowledge in order to recall intricate details about your enemies, allowing you, at times to pinpoint weaknesses and determine the ideal angle of attack. Your knowledge of the Deosian landscape, its flora, fauna, people and its culture are said to be so all encompassing that some suspect your skills border upon that of the telepathic."

Wow, so he was now a Sword Disciple Level 2. On the next page he found all of his stats had slightly increased and his Sword Technique stated Rank 'F'. Here he frowned. He imagined he had done a little bit better than an 'F' in that last fight. At least maybe a 'D'. Dante flipped back to the Skills and Abilities section and looked specifically at the Skills portion of the page. He thought it was odd that he didn't have any Job Class based Attack Skills, every class usually started with at least one. He expected to find something like a 'Spinning Sword Slice' or a 'Divine Heaven Blade', those were the types of skills the Sword Saints from all of the previous Dragon Dale games used. So, what was the big deal, where was his 'Devil's Heart Lighting Stab'?

"I leveled up!" shouted Robyn.

"Yeah, so did I." said Alex.

Dante closed his tome and let it disintegrate in an arc of blue light, he looked up to see everyone smiling down into their books looking satisfied, everyone except Morrigan. He approached her.

"Hey, didn't you level you up too?"

"Yes, I did." She said.

"Why the long face? I thought for a second you didn't get any experience point based off the way you were frowning at your book." said Dante.

"That's because I shouldn't have." said Morrigan. "I didn't fire off a single spell, I didn't help you at all." She said shaking her head. "You killed that wolf by yourself. I didn't earn any of these points."

"Hey, it no big deal. I doubt I even gave you an opening to fire at the thing anyway. We were all kind of just fumbling our way through it trying not to become dog chow," said Dante with a smile and a laugh.

"Well to me it is a big deal. I carry my own weight and I earn my keep, and I'm not some downtrodden damsel in need of a pep talk either, so save it for someone else. The truth is I messed up, I froze, and I didn't contribute a single thing to the group, but it won't happen again, I can promise you that." she said as she stormed off toward the front of the group where Pope and Lansing were waiting to begin the march again.

"Man, you sure did something to piss her off." Hernandez said, handing Dante the wolf fur rolled tight like a blood and fur-covered sleeping bag, and making his way to the front of the group.

Dante stuffed the tightly the fur into a small satchel that he wore on his waist opposite his sword. It would now fit little else. Spotting something on the ground, he reached down and picked up a small blue gem. It was the size and shape of one of the wolf's fangs, only it was made of rough blue crystal. Was this what he had pulled from the slain wolf? He shrugged, he could find out what it was and how it worked later, for now he had two souvenirs from his first battle.

Pope, Lansing, Hernandez, Alex and Dante all kept their weapons unsheathed and at the ready, and before long Dante's sword became cumbersome in his hands. After about a mile the trees thinned down to nothing more than a mass of tall grass and the group relaxed. Dante sheathed his sword. Alex, Hernandez and Lansing put their weapons away as well. Pope kept his crossbow in hands, propped casually and carefree against his large broad shoulders. Dante imagined it had to weigh a ton, though Pope showed no signs of exhaustion or strain from carrying the burden of its weight.

The sun was behind them now and as it neared the horizon the sky turned a bright shade of purple and orange.

"How much further to town?" asked Robyn.

"Not far," replied Stephen.

They'd walked for nearly an hour and had probably covered about two and a half miles from the starting point of the game. He thought it was odd that they didn't spawn inside a city or town to begin with but figured he would add that feedback to his list of notes for the 'post beta discussion'.

Now that they were free from the shadow of the tree line and seemingly away from any lurking dangers Alex was back to his talkative self. He started recapping the battle with the wolves, complimenting Dante's on the spot strategy, their back-to-back combat tactics and Robyn two-fisted sneak attack. Then Robyn, who had up to that point been pretty much nothing, but constant sarcasm and snarky comments began reenacting the battle along with Alex, this time playing the part of Dante and going back-to-back with the dwarf, then pretending to slash her make believe sword at an imaginary wolf.

"How did you manage to kill that thing by yourself?" she asked, a little out of breath after slaying her invisible wolf.

Dante cringed and looked up the path at Morrigan who seemed to be purposely ignoring the three of them. "I think I just got lucky really."

"No way," replied Alex, "I caught sight of that final blow, you moved like a blur, was that a Sword Disciple Class skill?"

"I don't have any Sword Disciple skills yet."

Alex laughed, "What do you mean, every job class starts with at least one skill, I have War Cry."

"I have Backstab!" said Robyn.

"Morrigan, don't you have some starter spells...." Alex was beginning to ask when Dante interrupted him.

"I unlocked a character skill in the last fight, but I don't have any offensive class skills. Not yet anyway."

"Quiet!" Pope spoke in a low stern voice. He had pulled the cross bow from his shoulder, had dropped down to one knee and seemed to be focusing all his attention on a group of boulders that lay about 60 yards ahead. When Dante looked out toward the boulders to see what had put Pope so on edge, he saw a tail flutter by and dash behind one of the rocks.

"What was that?" asked Morrigan. The entire team stopped in their tracks.

Amidst the wide-open green field there was a gathering of large round boulders stacked atop and among each other. They looked like colossal stone marbles left there by some giant child who had abandoned them long ago. Something among them moved.

Lansing, Pope and Hernandez stood side by side in the middle of the clearing staring out at the rocks. The three of them formed a makeshift wall with the rest of the party peeking out and around them.

"More wolves captain?" Dante asked, moving up to join them.

"No, not this time," replied Pope. "Not sure what these things are."

Dante watched the boulders intently and after few seconds the thing lurking between the rocks remerged. It was definitely not a wolf. It was feathered like a bird, but looked and almost moved like a lizard. It had long thin legs, with feet tipped with large black talons. It was streamlined and aggressive in its design, as if made for speed, for hunting and chasing. It had a long tail almost twice the length of its body, and though it had no visible scales, or so much as a forked tongue, it had the cold-blooded eyes of a reptile.

"Whatever they are, there's three of them," said Pope.

Dante took a second to focus on the status box of the original creature, what had started as a box containing nothing more than a solid white health bar topped by a series of question marks, changed under Dante's focused gaze, to a multicolored bar once again, flowing from red to yellow to green from one end to the other end. The question marks changed themselves also, revealing to Dante the creature's name and level and bringing to mind a slew of other facts. This, he realized, was his 'Scan' ability at work.

"That's a Cockatrice Raptor," Dante said aloud, "Level 5, very aggressive pack hunters, usually found in the Onin Highlands." Dante looked back to Stephen, "I thought you said we were outside of Illdershire."

"We are," whispered Stephen. "That rock formation is called The Devil's Marbles, it sits just a few miles outside of Illdershire."

"Well, these things shouldn't be here." Dante responded

"How do you know all of this?" Pope asked in a low voice.

"I played these games a lot growing up. When I created my character, they let me take a quiz to test my knowledge on the game's lore. I guess I did pretty good on the quiz and as a prize they gave me an ability that reveals enemy information. It's called 'Scan', it's been in a number of the past games. It's a really simple ability but it comes in handy."

"So, you're like, a really good scout?" said Hernandez attempting to simplify Dante's long answer.

"Yeah, I guess you could say that." Dante replied.

"What else can you see?" Pope asked.

Dante looked back to the raptors. "They're all level 5," he said, "but one of them is injured."

One of the raptors was missing nearly a quarter of its health bar, a fact that hadn't revealed itself until Dante performed his scan.

"I'd say that puts us at a distinct advantage!" said Robyn, excited.

"Yeah," agreed Alex. "There were four wolves but there are only three of these things and one of them is already hurt. I say we hit'em fast and hard."

"Best idea I've heard all day. Let go and collect our E-X-P!" said Robyn eagerly. "Morrigan, what do you say?"

"I say what are we waiting for?"

"It looks like our little sharks have gotten quite the taste for blood." said Pope with a smile. He was still down on one knee when he took a moment to pull back a lever on his large crossbow. Dante noticed an arrow move smoothly into place when he did so. He then pulled another lever, positioning another arrow above the loaded one, and then he pulled another lever yet again, loading a third arrow into the crossbow's open inner chamber.

"I've never seen a crossbow like that in Dragon Dale before?" Dante whispered.

Pope looked up at him and smiled. "You spent your time studying video games, I spent my time studying firearms. It appears both of our time was well spent."

"Should we reconsider this? We defeated the wolves unscathed but it was close," Stephen said.

"And that's exactly why we shouldn't have any trouble with these things," interrupted Robyn. "They're *level 5,* think of the E-x-p." Her green eyes glistened in the sunlight.

"I say we attack," agreed Morrigan. "I mean, this is part of the game isn't it, why so much debate on if we are going to fight monsters or not."

"Yes of course," said Stephen, "But in Dragon Dale 10, players must be both cautious and strategic about the battles they undertake. We don't have to fight everything we encounter."

"We out number them, and one of them is injured. Let's go for it!" said Alex.

"Dante, what do you want to do?" asked Alex.

"Does it matter?" Dante asked pulling his sword from his sheath.

"Not really," said both Robyn and Morrigan.

"Captain?" said Lansing nocking an arrow and raising his bow.

"Give the gamers what they want I say, that is what we're for here after all." Pope replied.

He began to give orders, and when everyone was in place Dante could see it was a strong setup. Pope and Lansing would fire their ranged weapons at the Raptors from a distance, the aggressive predators would come charging in toward the group meeting the shielded warriors first. This would slow their assault enough for Dante, Robyn, Morrigan, Pope and Lansing to launch a counterattack, and finish the raptors off in one fell swoop.

"Which one is the injured one?" Pope asked.

"The one there in the middle," Dante pointed out, "with the damaged wing."

"Lansing," said Pope.

"Yes sir." Lansing raised his bow and pulling back slowly on the string. Dante watched as the head of his arrow glowed red hot. Lansing released and a stream of red light streaked across the green field striking the unsuspecting Raptor square in its already injured wing. It let out a shriek of pain, and Dante watched as its health bar immediately dropped down to one half.

"You hit it!" Alex yelled out from behind his shield.

"Of course, I hit it," said Lansing, nocking another arrow.

All three raptors turned their heads toward the group of adventurers and let out a distinctive and high-pitched screech. The raptors attacked, wing held out to their sides, heads tucked low toward the ground, long feathered tails streaming up toward the sky. They were a terrifying sight and lightning fast.

As the birds rushed, Pope and Lansing concentrated their firepower on the already injured raptor. Lansing released more arrows and Pope fired with his oversized crossbow, all three of his preloaded arrows in quick succession. His aim was extraordinary. Each hit took the monster's health bar lower, though did little to slow it down. It continued its advance.

Pope reloaded his crossbow. Meanwhile, Lansing fired new arrows from his quiver with impressive speed that almost matched the captain's rapid fire. The injured Raptor let out a shrill squawk and all three raptors begin to move side to side as well as forward in a serpentine pattern, as if there were attempting to dodge the flying projectiles. It worked. Lansing's shots all grazed off the side of its slender body. Its health continued to drop but now did so much more slowly, than it had before.

"It's too fast captain, I can't get a clean shot."

Pope didn't respond. He shouldered his weapon, fired off three more shots, hitting the injured raptor in the shoulder, the leg and then 'thwack!' an arrow landed right between its lizard-like eyes. It hit the ground in a slump about 30 paces out from Pope and Lansing, dead, but it had soaked up way more damage and attention than the party had intended and now its packmates were poised to strike.

The remaining two raptors split up, one going for Alex and the other for Hernandez. A cockatrice with shiny grey and blue plumage dashed in front of Alex and while still at a distance of some ten feet away the creature leapt into the air, coming down on top of Alex with its razor-sharp talons. Alex, surprised by the raptors sudden jump, raised his shield just in time to avoid being skewered by the force of the blow and the full weight of a creature twice his size.

The other raptor was covered in black and orange feathers like a large and deadly oriole. It leapt to attack Hernandez from above, but at the last-minute, Hernandez rolled out of the way and swiped at the creature with his sword. He grazed it drawing blood and a screech of anger. The raptor turned on him kicking and biting when *thunk, thunk, thunk*, three arrows struck from behind, hitting the raptor in the back. Confused, it turned to find Pope walking toward it at his determined pace, pulling back the levers on his crossbow. The raptor abandoned Hernandez and attacked the easier, more wide-open target when another arrow hit it in the chest. Lansing was behind Pope firing over his shoulder. The arrow to the chest had stopped the raptor in its tracks, it was down to half of its health bar and the flurry of attacks were leaving it disoriented and jolted. Pope brought the butt of his heavy crossbow down on the creature's head, turned it around and fired three more shots into it at point blank range.

All this time, Alex was on his back, the only thing between him and the grey and blue raptor his thin wooden shield. The bird creature was squawking in Alex's face, its snout-like beak open to wide reveal hundreds of thin, needle-like teeth. Dante swung his sword, but as if sensing the incoming attack, the raptor leapt, dodging Dante's blade. In the moment of reprieve Dante helped Alex scramble to his feet and then the two of then faced the raptor. Its eyes registered that it was outnumbered, but what it didn't see was Robyn, creeping around behind it in the confusion, daggers drawn.

She didn't notice Dante waving his head no, trying to ward her off, and she was just as surprised when the raptor swung its large and powerful tail in a sweeping motion, taking her feet from underneath her and putting her on her back in much the same way it had done Alex. It turned around with a roar and seemed as if it was about to pounce on Robyn, but in an act of desperation, Alex lunged, slamming into the creature with his shoulder. Dante helped Robyn to her feet while Alex rolled away from the raptor. Suddenly he let out a scream of agony. The cockatrice had bitten him, hard, on his leg.

Morrigan got there first. She raised her hands high above her head and then jutted them forward toward the raptor as if she was pushing a person that could not be seen. At the same time, she yelled out "Ignis!" and huge orange flames shot from her hands, covering the raptor in fire. It screeched loudly, releasing Alex, but now aflame and running in circles. Morrigan stumbled and fell. The raptor, running blind, was coming straight at her and without thinking Dante put himself between her and the cockatrice, thrusting his sword, impaling the monster on his blade, it flailed wildly, screeching and squawking, attempting to claw Dante's eyes out with the small talons that tipped the end of its wings, there was another distinctive 'thunk' and a thick crossbow bolt arrow went through the raptor's head and its body went limp on Dante's sword.

The first cockatrice was dead, the raptor in front of him was charred black, had an arrow sticking out of either side of its head and now its sharp pointed tongued lolled out of its open mouth. Dante dropped his sword in disgust and let the bird monster drop to the ground. He turned his head away and saw Morrigan still sitting in the grass from when she had fallen.

"I don't need your help." She coldly pushed his hand away. "I didn't need your help then either, I had it under control."

"What is your deal?" said Dante angrily, "You came to help Alex, I came to help you, that's how a party works, trust me."

"I *don't* trust you; I don't know you and I don't trust you. So do us both a favor and get over yourself."

Dante would have said more but saw that Alex was still laying on the ground. "What's wrong?" Dante asked, running over.

"It's the Cockatrice bite," Stephen said, pulling up Alex's pant leg revealing a series of puncture wounds where the teeth had broken the skin. They weren't bleeding, instead they looked like cleanly pierced holes in his flesh.

"Can't you heal it?" Robyn asked.

"I already cast a healing spell on it." replied Stephen, "that stopped the bleeding, but it didn't seal the wound. That's because of this." He pointed to an area around the holes in Alex's leg that was turning a pale chalky grey.

"Cockatrice venom," said Dante. "It turns portions of their victims to stone, so they can eat the rest of you when they're ready."

"We need a de-petrification antidote to stop the process from spreading and taking his entire leg," said Stephen.

"Where can we get one of those?" asked Robyn.

"Probably Illdershire," answered Dante.

"We can't, he's not going to make it with his leg like this," said Stephen.

A shout from up ahead broke the silence. Hernandez, Pope and Lansing had gone ahead to explore the large rocky area where the raptors had been first spotted. Apparently, they had found something, and he was motioning for rest of the group to come join them. Dante hooked Alex's arm around his shoulder and he and Stephen helped to get him up to the boulder site.

They arrived to a grizzly scene. Corpses were laid out between the boulders, whole parts of each fully turned to stone, a leg, an arm, the entire head of a particularly frightened looking man, completely petrified, the parts of the bodies that had not been turned to stone had been chewed and mangled down to the bones.

They propped Alex against one of the large round boulders. He was sweating buckets and looked like he might throw up at any moment.

"You alright?" Dante asked Alex.

"Yeah," replied Alex. "It really hurt when it first bit me, like someone had put a hot poker into my leg, and even afterwards it was pretty bad, but now that Stephens's healed it, it just feels kind of numb."

"Looks like we found out who injured the one raptor." said Pope.

Of the dead bodies, all were wearing armor and holding weapons.

"I think they were adventurers," said Dante. "I mean, not gamers like us, but NPCs, as in they were already part of the game." Dante spotted a human who looked like he had been chewed on, but in his hand, he held an empty glass vial. "We can check them for supplies!" Dante said, "If they were adventurers, they may have a de-petrification antidote in one of their bags."

The party begin tossing the dead people's things and Dante noticed Robyn collecting each of their coin pouches, emptying out the contents into her own.

"I found something," Stephen said, holding up a small glass vial filled with a bright red liquid. "This has to be it." He had pulled a belt pouch off of one of the dead NPC adventurers, the top flap was still open and Dante could see that the inner lining of the pouch was cushioned with some type of soft fur and inside there were a number of small glass bottles each one holding a different color liquid.

"Red are health potions, blue are mana potions and green is...?" said Robyn, thinking out loud.

"Green is an antidote for poison," said Morrigan. "Yellow is for curing petrification and paralysis."

Everyone looked at her. "Dante isn't the only one that plays Dragon Dale," she said. "The color coding of potions is action-adventure gaming 101."

"She's right," winced Alex. "It's yellow for petrification, can someone pass it here, I can't feel my toes anymore." Alex pulled up his pant leg. The chalky pale color had spread across his skin, looking dry and cracked in some places.

Stephen removed the vial filled with yellow liquid from the pouch, pulled out the stopper and handed it to Alex who took it in a shaky hand, threw his head back and emptied out the contents in one gulp. He began to choke and gag, but somehow managed to keep the yellow liquid down.

"What's it tastes like?" asked Robyn.

"Like rock," he coughed.

"Hey, take a look at what I found." Hernandez was holding a small ruddy burlap sack with a drawstring opening at the top to help keep it closed. It looked, Dante thought, like an old potato sack, three feet in length, until Hernandez sat it on the ground letting most of the sack crumple to the floor. Now it was nearly flat with only the top open. Hernandez stuck his hand in, then up to his wrist, then his forearm, then his whole arm all the way up to his shoulder. Even though the bag was nearly flat against the ground Hernandez was still able to fit his whole arm inside as if the bag had no bottom. "It's like there is more space inside the bag then there should be." he said pulling his arm out, whole and unscathed.

"It's a Plunderer's Pouch!" said Robyn.

"A what?" asked Hernandez.

"A Plunderer's Pouch is an enchanted item. The inside of the bag is really a pocket of extra dimensional space. You can fit almost anything inside there, within reason, and the bag won't ever get much heavier or much bigger than it is now."

"I think I'll hold on to this," Hernandez said, placing the sack with his other belongings.

"Hernandez, Lansing and I will clear out these bodies," interjected Pope. "Stephen, you tend to Alex, the rest of you, prepare to set up camp, we may as well bunker down here for the night."

"Bunker down for the night?" said Morrigan, "Here?"

"I thought you said we were just outside of Illdershire?"

"Well, we are," said Stephen, jumping up from Alex's side.

"Then why aren't we going on to the city?" asked Morrigan.

Pope didn't bother explaining himself in the slightest, instead he and his men began lifting the corpses of the NPC adventurers and carrying them away from the rounded boulders. That left the gamers staring coldly at Stephen for answers.

"Alex is not really in any shape to travel at the moment, it looks like he'll need a little time for the antidote to actually take effect and on top of that, the sun is setting. Illdershire is still at least an hour away on foot and believe me, we don't want to walk around outside of a city in the dark."

"So, we're going to just sit out here all night, meaning our bodies are going to just sit in the VR pods all night."

"Oh no," Stephen let out a forced laugh, "No, no, not at all. I'm sorry I should have explained. Time passes differently here in Deos then it does in the real world. It seems that we've been here what an hour, an hour and a half?" Stephen asked.

"I'd guess more like two hours," said Robyn.

"Well, we've actually only been playing for 30 minutes," Stephen replied. "You see, because we communicate directly with the brain via the neuro transmission helmets, we can send and receive information at four times normal speed. In the game world, time is compressed. We're not on the same clock as your body on the outside."

Morrigan still looked apprehensive. Robyn looked worried, and Dante didn't know how to look. The idea of time compression made sense, and in MMO the passage of time was important, but he definitely didn't feel like only thirty minutes had passed since he had arrived in Deos.

"In addition," Stephen continued, apparently trying to top off his sales pitch. "Nights in Deos don't last long, they are intentionally made to be much shorter than the days, so in effect, to 'bunker down for the night' really means nothing more than setting up a camp fire and stretching out on your bedroll, and once you close your eyes we fast forward to the morning and continue our journey to Illdershire. I'm sorry if I did not properly explain this portion of the game experience earlier, I thought we'd be in the city by now."

"Why didn't we start in the city in the first place?" Robyn asked.

"Exactly, what game starts you off in the wilderness, with no supplies and no preparation," added Morrigan.

"This is the Beta test. Each group was started in a random location across Deos, so this is just where we happened to spawn." Stephen was starting to sound defeated, and, in a way, Dante felt bad for him, he was after all just doing his job.

"If you don't want to stay, then I could log you out," said Pope returning from his dirty work flanked by Lansing and Hernandez, "but your Beta experience would end there. You would not be able to log back on again."

"Why not?" asked Morrigan.

"Because the purpose of the Beta test is to *test* all of the game's features, the combat, the magic system, the interaction with the NPCs," said Pope. "With time compression and night and day cycles and with the camping systems, if players pick and choose to log in and out on their favorite and least favorite parts, well we wouldn't be able to gather the proper data needed to improve the game."

Morrigan was silent and didn't reply.

"The choice is yours. I can log you out if you would like." Pope's smile was disingenuous, but not threatening, it was a smile of arrogance. And Dante realized that it was that air of superiority that he recognized Pope had in common with his eldest brother Bryan.

"Since the nights are short, I think we'll be fine," said Robyn, walking up and grabbing Morrigan's hand, "Come on Morrie, use that magic of yours and help me build a fire." She led her to a clear spot near where Alex was sitting.

"We'll do one more patrol before we settle in. We pulled a few bedrolls from the supplies of the NPCs so everyone doesn't have to sleep in the dirt. Dante can you grab some wood and sticks to keep the fire burning?" asked Pope.

"Yeah, sure." Said Dante. He looked over at Alex who was massaging his own leg but stopped to enthusiastically give Dante a thumbs up.

"Make sure you don't wander to far from camp." Pope said in a stern voice. "It's getting dark soon."

Its dark now. Dante thought as he walked away from the large boulders. The sun met the horizon and most of the sky was a deep dark purple and only a thin strip of orange and pink light gave off any indication that there had previously been daylight.

There was a ringing in his ear. It had actually been there since the defeat of the raptors, but in the chaos and confusion of trying to find a cure for Alex's bitten leg, Dante had been ignoring it. Now in the silence and solitude it was hard to ignore. He summoned his spirit tome and opened it to the notification page.

- Three Cockatrice Raptors have been defeated.
- You have gained 1200 Experience points!
- You have a total of 2000 Experience Points
- You have obtained Level 3, Congratulations!

Another level. The had been in the game a couple of hours and had already quickly climbed to level 3. He smiled to himself as he walked, this was the part of the game that he loved, growing and getting stronger. At this rate he figured the whole party would be killing level 3 wolves in one shot within the span of a few battles. Then he heard a growl.

It came from behind him. He turned around and saw standing between him and the stack of boulders that was his makeshift camp, a large angry wolf. He wasn't sure where it had come from or how it had gotten behind him, he wasn't that far from the camp, but apparently somewhere along the line he must have let his guard down. He pulled his sword from its sheath and when he did the wolf's growl grew. He thought of calling out to the others for help but when he tried to look past the wolf to see who was in ear shot, the wolf moved. Not towards him, but into his line of sight, as if... as if it was purposely trying to block his view. Dante stared at the wolf for a moment, it looked similar to the one they had encountered earlier, his eyes drifted up to its status box.

'Illder Shire Black Wolf, Level ???'

He focused on the status box for a moment, wolf's solid white health bar became multicolored. But the information above it remained unchanged. Its level was still a series of question marks.

"What's going on?" Dante said aloud.

In response the wolf let out a low bark. When he did, two more wolves emerged from behind Dante, also growling.

"I guess I won't be coming back with that firewood." Dante said to himself.

"Put away your sword human, you'll be *coming* with us," said the wolf standing between Dante and the camp.

Dante paused. Squinted. "I'm sorry, did you just speak?"

"Put away your sword and come with us. Willingly or by force," said the wolf. "I prefer force, but I have been directed to give you a choice." Its voice angry and throaty, was just the way Dante expected a wolf to speak, if he suspected wolves spoke.

"Directed by who?" he asked.

"PUT AWAY YOUR SWORD!" the wolf shouted.

"Okay," said Dante sheathing his sword, "okay, putting the sword away. Just... just stay calm and let talk this through."

"Be silent, meat. You will follow us, if you fall behind, you will be killed. If you attempt to escape, you will be killed. If you breathe in a way that I do not like..." the wolf paused for a second and simply stared at Dante.

"I... will... be killed?" said Dante.

"I'm glad to see we have reached a mutual understanding of one another."

Without another word the wolf bolted, dashing south into the darkened grasslands. The wolves behind Dante lunged forward forcing him to follow. They bound through the grassy plains with incredible speed, the dark, now sunless sky concealing their movement. Dante had to run at a full sprint to keep up. And based off the wolf's threats he was afraid of the consequences if he could not keep up for long. The wolves maintained their feverish pace much longer than Dante thought possible. He ran along with them until his legs ached and his lungs burned and the stitch in his side commanded that he stop and rest and just when he was convinced, he could not maintain his speed a second longer, the lead wolf suddenly dropped from view. Before Dante could react, or even stop running, the ground beneath his feet gave way and he found himself tumbling down a steep hill.

He rolled and tumbled for what felt like forever and finally landed at the foot of the hill with a hard thud. Dante lay there for a moment, flat on his stomach his heart thumping in his chest, and he wondered how this all could come from a video game. He pulled himself to his hands and knees.

"Is this to be taken as a sign of tribute or insult?" said a voice so deep and strong that Dante could feel it reverberate in his chest.

He raised his head and saw, laying stretched out in the moonlight, a gigantic wolf, roughly the size of a truck. It was completely black with hungry yellow eyes. Behind the giant were upwards of fifty, smaller wolves all sitting and staring, like well trained dogs awaiting a master's command. He began to scramble backwards but found that the steep hill kept him from moving too far. He was pinned in.

"There is no doubt that the gesture is meant as an insult, father," said a wolf smaller and less intimidating by comparison, and whose voice Dante recognized as the one that had led him there. "I say you bite off his head and be done with it."

"I only jest my son; I know the boy means no insult," said the gigantic wolf, "Do you boy?"

"No, of course not... sir." said Dante, not really sure how to address a giant wolf.

"Do you know why I have summoned you here boy?"

"No, I do not... sir."

"It is because earlier this day you and your kind encountered four of my wolves, a battle ensued, all four of my wolves were slain and none of your comrades were slain."

"Oh, yes."

"My wolves were young and inexperienced, but they were still knowledgeable enough in the ways of the hunt to wipe out a small pack of level 1 know nothing adventurers," said the wolf leaning its large black snout close to Dante. Hot breath shot from its nostrils. "So, imagine my surprise when I find out that among the rabble of men that killed my wolves, there was a boy that not only used the tactics of the hunt against *my* wolves, but that this boy also killed one of my wolves singlehandedly."

Dante did not like where this conversation was going, but also, did not see any way out of it.

"And then" continued the great wolf, "you and your companions happened across a group of raptors." At the mention of the raptors the other wolves in the area begin to growl and let out low yelps and barks. "and once again, you were successful."

"Is this revenge?" Dante asked with a dry throated gulp, "for killing the wolves?"

"Revenge?" said the great wolf. "No boy this is a request."

"A request?" said Dante.

"There is a change taking place in Deos, the raptors have come down from the north and have invaded our lands, and as a result war has erupted. Now normally the affairs of beast have no bearing on the affairs of men, but this time I think we will both find it beneficial to see an end to the raptor menace."

"You want me to... kill raptors?"

"No, I ask that you go to the heart of their nest and kill the *Alpha* Raptor, once you do this, the rest of their pack will become disorganized and chaotic and my wolves will do the rest. Complete this task, help us retake the Illdershire Plains, and you and I will enter into an alliance. You shall find the plains a safe haven for yourself and your friends, at all times."

"But father," said the young wolf.

"SILENCE!" said the great wolf in a tone so loud and terrifying that for a moment Dante thought his heart had stopped. "What say ye boy? Do we have a deal?"

"Umm... I would be glad to help sir, but, you see, I am a part of a group, so I would have to discuss it with them first. Now I'm sure they would like to help as well, it's just. I don't want to say yes to you right now and then if I can't deliver on that promise, I'd hate to have you come hunt me down in my nightmares. So, if it's okay I need to discuss with my friends."

"Yes, discuss it with your pack if you must but for now return to them. Janis, take him back to his friends."

"Yes father," said the young wolf.

"Um sir how will I find you to tell you our answer."

The great wolf's ears perked up, "I am Canis Romulus, there is nothing done on the Illdershire Plains that I do not hear. There will be no need to find me, once you have made your decision, I will know."

"Talking wolves? You've been out there for over an hour, by yourself *in the dark* and you come back and expect us to believe a story about talking wolves?" Morrigan was in an especially foul mood by the time Dante returned and told everyone what happened.

"I mean, we're in a virtual world based off a fantasy role playing game, it's not that far-fetched of a concept. We just literally fought giant lizard-bird hybrids that tried to turn one of our friends into stone, but it's the talking wolves that you have a problem with?" said Dante.

"No, it's you I have the problem with," said Morrigan.

"Me?"

"Yes, you! You're smug, you're arrogant, you're selfish, you're self-absorbed."

"You just met me today, these are blind assumptions based on what exactly?" Said Dante.

"How about the fact that you just ran off into the dark for an hour and left everyone here worried sick."

"I was taken hostage by wolves!" Dante screamed.

"People!" yelled Pope attempting to bring order to the situation. "The important thing is that Dante is back, unharmed. There is no point in arguing."

"Well," said Alex, who Dante noted was looking a whole lot better and appeared to be back to himself again. "Wouldn't it be in your book, I mean, it sounds like he gave you a quest, something like that should be in your Spirit Tome."

"Alex you're a genius, Look, I'll show you right now..."

"Don't bother." Said Morrigan, "I don't need to see your spirit tome to know you're a jerk." She walked to the other side of the camp and sat next to Robyn, who had been quietly watching the fight with wide-eyed glee.

Dante sat next to Alex.

"Man, what is Morrigan's problem?' he asked in a hushed whisper. "She has been giving me nothing but attitude since we got here. I tried to be nice to her, she told me to get lost. I tried to help her up when she fell, she told me to get bent. Then I got lost and almost did get bent and then when I came back, she tried to bite my head off."

"Well, earlier today *may* have been ego driven," said Alex.

"What do you mean?"

"You don't know who she is, do you? She's Morrigan Le Bey, she's like semi-famous online gamer. She was a really big deal up to about a year and a half ago, then she kind of started to fade away."

"Why?" Dante asked.

"Not sure," Alex said "There were rumors floating around the internet that she was a bit of a diva and hard to get along with, but then I also heard that she wasn't really a gamer, that it was all an act and it was actually her older brother who was the one behind all the game play videos and she was just the face of the brand to attract an audience or something. I don't know, you know how people can be online. I'm sure her frustration with your 'help' has something to do with that."

"Those sound like a bunch of insecurities that have absolutely nothing to do with me," Dante said coldly.

"But I'll also say this, when you were missing a little while ago, I think she was just genuinely worried."

"Worried why? It's just a game." Dante looked at his hands, "Worst case scenario, one of us dies, we logout, wakeup in the VR pod and log back in tomorrow."

"Yeah, but it's not really that simple. After being bitten by that Raptor and feeling that pain in my leg... I'm telling you, they have to recalibrate the system because as it is currently, you do not want to die right now. I just think Morrigan tapped into that, and for better or for worse, her yelling at you really just means she cares, at least on some basic level of friendship."

"Well she's got a funny way of showing it." Dante said. "If that's how she treats her friends, I'd hate to see how she treats her enemies."

Chapter 8: Urthlanders in Illdershire

"Ladies and Gentlemen delivered to you as promised, the lovely little town of Illdershire!" Stephen said. He was facing toward the party but was walking backward as he spoke, in that of the spirit and manner of a true tour guide. His arms were spread wide and lifted high as if everything around him were being offered as a gift. Dante hadn't seen him this cheerful since they had been on the tour of the HQ building. Finally, Stephen seemed to be back in his element. Perhaps he helped design the town, Dante thought, and now he was anxious to show off to them the results of all his hard work.

Illdershire was impressive. The entire city was surrounded on all four sides by a fifteen-foot-high stone wall with armed guards on each side of a gate that let travelers flow in and out of the town. The gate itself was an intricate stone archway with a heavy wooden door that was raised and lowered by a system of pulleys and chains overseen and operated by a number of guardsmen. They entered in through the western gate and were met by a young guardsman in a metal plated chest piece underset by a chain mail shirt. He had carried a long spear and spoke in a loud clear voice.

"Welcome to Illdershire, I hope you journey here was without incident." said the gate guard warmly.

"Yes, well we ran into a bit of trouble along the way, but we are definitely glad to be here now," Stephen replied.

"And we are glad to have ye!" said the guard.

"Why thank you. You see my friends and I are here..." Stephen began, but the guard cut him off.

"Ah no need to explain, It's obvious why you are here. Come on in." He ushered them through the gate. "Now, what you want to do is take the main road straight toward the center of town. After a ways or so you'll see a tavern and inn called the Thirsty Dragon, it'll be on your left. That's where you want to go."

"Well thank you good sir!" said Stephen gratefully. "I appreciate your help."

"No, thank you Adventurer, Illdershire appreciates your service." The guard bowed his head and moved on to the next traveler.

Dante mentioned to Stephen that the gate guard spoke to them so casually that it almost seemed as if they had been expected. And he wondered for a moment, if they were being somehow mistaken for someone else. Stephen, however, quickly dismissed the idea and explained to the party that Illdershire sat in the geographical center of Deos and regularly received a large number of travelers and what they were experiencing was nothing more than the infamous 'Illdershire Hospitality' in action.

Once they had made it past the gate and into the city the party found themselves walking on wide cobble stone streets lined on both sides with timber framed houses and shops. Two and three story-high buildings with balconies overlooked the street below.

Wood-framed windows underset by crisscrossing wooden beams could be seen across the side of almost every building. People, horses and carts all hobbled up and down the busy streets. There were humans and halflings, half-elves, high elves, dwarves and half-orcs. There was so many people of so many races and of so many colors he imagined that there was no limit to the types of people you could run into.

"Alright everyone," Stephen said in his tour guide voice. "We are in the western district at the moment, I suggest we head to the nearest tavern, recollect our thoughts and plan out next course of action." Said Stephen.

Morrigan looked as if she was about to say something but then Pope spoke up.

"I think that's a good idea Stephen," said Pope. "Let's go to the Tavern together and once we've got our bearings you can all go out and explore the town on your own or in pairs, however you like. We can all meet back at the Tavern in an hour. Then we can logout, take a short break and pick back up from inside the city when you log in."

"I like the sound of that," said Robyn.

They walked further into town collecting, Dante noticed, the occasional stare or turned head as they went. Odd for a town keen on travelers, but Dante put it out of his mind as it seemed no one else in the party really seemed to notice or care. They were all much too busy to notice, much too preoccupied with the sights and sounds of a bustling Illdershire to notice anything as subtle as a lingering glance.

Previous Dragon Dale games had failed to do the towns and cities of Deos true justice. In its current incarnation Illdershire was alive in a way that Dante had never experienced. The yelling of merchants attempting to lure potential customers near their shops or carts, the banging of metal on metal as some unseen black smith worked his craft, the smell of live animals being ushered or led down the road. It was a hive of sensory activity that was difficult not to get lost within and in some ways almost overwhelming.

After a short time they could see ahead of them just a few buildings away a sign for their destination, The Thirsty Dragon.

"Wonder if they serve food in there. I'm starving... I think." Alex said, rubbing his stomach.

"We can eat food here?" Dante asked.

"Oh yes," answered Stephen. "We encourage it. The consumption of food offers a number of in game benefits."

"Master Dwarf! Mas-Master Dwarf!" yelled a creaky old voice from the side cart. "Did I hear you say you were hungry? Come, you must come to Madam Humphrey's Fruit Cart I have just the thing for you." The voice and the cart belonged to an old woman. She wore a drab blue dress, a red vest and her stark white hair was pinned back inside of a white cap. "I have just the thing for a hungry adventurer. Peregrine Fruit, come, come here milord, have some." The woman waved Alex over with one hand and the other hand held steady a large prickly green fruit the size of a small watermelon.

"What's Peregrine Fruit?" Alex asked.

"Ah milord, it is a Deosian Delicacy grown here in the central region and served in a variety of ways. It revitalizes the body and restores the mind, replenishing strength and vigor to the weary and healing the ills of the sick." Said the lady who was apparently Madam Humphrey.

"It does all of that?" Robyn said with wide eyes.

"Oh yes mi lady, its often called the miracle fruit. Come you must try some." From a shelf in the back of the cart the old woman pulled out a large knife and with one decisive chop, cleaved the large spiky fruit clean in two. It split open revealing a sectioned interior like an orange or a grapefruit. With the agility that comes only with age and experience the woman grabbed one of the halves, and brought the knife down again, then took the quartered piece of fruit in one hand and with the same knife, quickly separated the meaty interior from the hard and spiky rind that covered it. She moved quickly and with purpose, performing this task so fast that no one standing by watching could protest or even attempt to deny her offer to taste the fruit. By the time they knew what was happening she was already holding a wet and slimy de-rind quarter of the Peregrine Fruit in her hand.

"Oh geez," Robyn held her nose. "that smells."

Dante could smell it to, but he didn't want to say anything for fear that it might be taken as rude.

"Yes," said the Madam Humphrey, "This is how ye know it's good and ripe."

"Ripe or rotten?" Robyn mumbled under her breath.

"Yes, it takes some getting used to, but once you do, it'll be yer favorite, this I promise." She dropped the deskinned quarter on to her table and took the knife to it, cutting it into long chunks. She then reached back into her cart and pulled out a handful of wooden skewers then jabbed them through the length of the cut fruit. They looked like slime covered pineapple chunks on a stick, Dante thought. She picked up one of them and held it out towards Alex. "For you milord, free of charge."

"Free?" Alex said, looking a bit guilty now that he had been reminded a price was normally associated with interactions such as these.

"Yes of course, I can tell this is your first visit to Illdershire. It is my duty to make sure you first visit is a pleasant one. Please take it, you will enjoy."

Alex reached out and took the Peregrine Fruit. Madam Humphrey smiled. A small tight-lipped smile that Dante assumed could only be interpreted as, "Won't you give it a taste?"

Alex must have interpreted the expression in the same way because he then began to slowly bring the fruit toward his face. Reluctantly he opened his mouth, closed his eyes and took a large bite of fleshy yellow fruit. As he pulled it away from his face strings of slime clung to his lips and beard. Eyes still closed, he chewed. And chewed. And chewed some more. Then he opened his eyes. Rolled around the fruit in his mouth and then swallowed. Then without saying another word he took another slimy bite. This time he chewed with his eyes open, looking as if he was lost in deep thought.

"It's amazing!" he looked at the fruit as if it had somehow transformed from what the old woman had given him. "It's savory and sweet, but the slime, the slime is kind of salty."

"Oh god I think I'm going to throw up." Robyn put a hand over her mouth.

"You guys have got to try this."

"I think I'll just take you word for it." Dante said.

"I'm telling you, it's your loss." He turned back to Madam Humphrey, "Can I buy some of this?"

"Well of course my dear! I sell it raw, roasted, chilled, salted and pickled. Which way would you like?"

Alex purchased a jar of raw Peregrine Fruit and another jar of pickled Peregrine Fruit for which he paid a total of 5 copper coins. Dante found that they had each started the game with a coin pouch containing 5 silver coins. It was 10 copper coins to a silver and 10 silver coins to a gold. They could get a few of the basic necessities with the coins they started with, but Dante knew they would quickly need to find a way to earn more.

"Now if we could proceed to the Thirsty Dragon." said Stephen, looking a little disgusted as Alex stuffed his jars of fruit into his waist satchel.

The party walked past the next few buildings unhampered, arriving underneath the large wooden sign of The Thirsty Dragon Tavern and Inn. They walked inside to find a large open room with walls of wood and stone. About the room were scattered sturdy wooden tables of varying sizes. The tavern was filled with people. In a corner of the room a half-elf stood playing a string instrument that looked like a small guitar while a female elf drummed away merrily on a tambourine. The air was thick with the pungent smell of tobacco smoke and the distinctively sticky-sweet smell of spilled beer.

Pope moved past Stephen and waded through the sea of patrons and tables settling at an empty booth near the back of the tavern. The rest of the group followed, all taking a seat at the large table. Moments after they were seated a young woman in an apron approached the booth with a weary smile.

"Fine mornin' to all, is there anythin' I can get ye?" she asked in a heavy accent. "Will ye be having a bit o' breakfast, or will ye be startin' ye day drinkin' like the rest of these here degenerates?"

"Hey!" called out a large and obviously drunk man sitting a table over. "Who you calling a de-gen-a-rite?"

"You, ye bloody lush, now go back to yer mug and mind yer own business before I give you a good wallop!" said the barmaid shaking a fist at the man. Then with the same weary smile she looked back to the table. "So, what'll it be me loves?"

"I think we'll have the breakfast." said a wide-eyed Stephen.

"Coming right up!" she said vanishing from the side of the table just as quickly as she had appeared.

"This all seems like very advanced technology for a video game." said Morrigan.

"I'm not sure if that's a compliment or... not," said Stephen leaning forward to speak so he could be heard over the chatter and noise of the room.

"I mean to say, this is all just leaps and bounds beyond anything else I have ever seen or heard of. I just- I just don't know how you do it."

"Well," said Stephen bashfully, "It's something that has been in the works for quite some time and there a number of very talented people putting in a lot of long hours to make this project a success."

"Perhaps some early morning ale wouldn't be such a bad idea after all," said Pope abruptly, and he raised a hand for the barmaid.

Every head in the room turned at a loud bang at the tavern door. A row of heavily armored soldiers marched through the doorway of the Thirsty Dragon. There were six, they stepped through the door in pairs, once in, the turned, faced each other then each took a single step backward creating between them an open lane big enough for someone to walk through.

A thin man with a handlebar mustache and spectacles, wearing a peculiar blue suit and matching pillbox cap strode into the Thirsty Dragon between the rows of soldiers. His eyes jumped from table to table until he spotted Dante and the others.

When he was close enough to see his ears, Dante realized that he was a half-elf. "Greetings fair adventurers, I am Caspin, the mayor's aide, I hope your journey from..." he paused, "Ah yes where *did* you all journey from?"

Every patron in the tavern seemed to be waiting on the answer to this question. Stephen had handled the NPC interaction up until now, but his lack of response left an awkwardness nearly unbearable. Finally, Alex said, "Earth?"

"Urth," said Caspin, "A far off and exotic land I imagine, as it is not one with which I am familiar. Be that as it may, we are grateful you for coming and the Adventurer's Guild for sending you. Now, the mayor would have you wait no longer, as he knows you are anxious to hear the details of our town's request and we are anxious to the task done. So, please come with me." And with that he turned on his heels.

The gamers, consultants and game guide looked at each other in befuddlement, all except Dante who had a good idea exactly what was going on.

"Illdershire Hospitality my foot!" Dante said in a hushed whisper, "They think we're adventurers sent here to do quest."

"How did you miss that?" Robyn asked Stephen.

"I'm not privy to every available storyline. They vary greatly based off of player actions," Stephen said, sounding more than a little annoyed.

"Are you coming?" asked Caspin standing in the doorway, armed guards on either side of him.

The adventurers had little choice, they filed out of the tavern behind the mayor's aid. Behind them, the barmaid approached the table with an arm full of food, but before she could protest, a large cloaked figure arrived at the table in their place, mumbled to her a few words and then withdrew a large pale green hand from his cloak and dropped two gold coins before following the group from the tavern.

Caspin led the party to the center of town. They walked in tow with the train of soldiers, humans, half-elves, elves and dwarves, all dressed similar to the gate guard. The townspeople of Illdershire, who Dante noticed had only stolen glances of them before, now stopped what they were doing to watch them pass. They traveled over a small bridge through an expertly manicured garden filled with exotic flowers and then into the shadow of a large brick and stone behemoth that looked like a cross between a large gothic mansion and a small castle. It loomed out and over every other building in the city.

The mayor's building had glossy wooden floors and high ceilings, the smooth stone and wood paneled walls were covered with either intricate woven tapestries, decorative wallpaper, hand painted works of art as well as the stuffed and mounted heads of a variety of animals that Dante assumed had been hunted and killed either by the mayor himself, or an extraordinarily ambitious interior designer.

A host of official looking dignitaries seemed to be awaiting their arrival, among them a well-dressed, middle-aged human who paced back and forth between the others looking unusually anxious. At the sight of Caspin, his look of anxiety turning to one of beleaguered relief.

"Ah Caspin, you have returned, and am I correct in assuming that these are our courageous heroes from the Adventurer's Guild?"

"Yes milord." replied Caspin with a deep bow. "Noble Adventurers it is my honor to introduce you all to his lordship the venerable Cedrick Lesmiester the Third, Mayor of the Great City of Illdershire."

"Oh, Caspin no need for such formality." said the mayor. The party members straightened from their half-hearted bows. "He is stickler for decorum you see. Well here now let us see what we have. Yes excellent, excellent." he stepped forward shaking the hand of each party member one by one. When he got to Robyn and Morrigan he bowed slightly and gave each of their hands a gentle peck in the chivalrous tradition and then let out a boyish chuckle. When he reached Dante, the mayor grabbed his hand with a firm grip. "Oh hoho, with such fine and strong adventurers as these I dare say our concerns shall soon be over. That reminds me, I must make another introduction. Um Captain Dunbar, Captain Dunbar please come here, come meet the adventurers."

At his call one of the dignitaries broke off from a conversation that he was having from one of the other Illdershire officials and made his way to the mayor's side. "You have summoned me lord mayor." He had heavily lidded eyes and wore a formal military officer's uniform, decorated with a number of sparkling and shining metals.

"Yes, yes Dunbar. I wanted to introduce you to the... Well, where are my manners. I mustn't keep simply calling you Adventurers. Your names please, tell us your names."

They gave their names to the Mayor and his host of accompanying officials, at the conclusion of which the bearded man nodded, and Dante noticed a slight grimace flash across his face, his mouth upturned into a disapproving sneer right before responding with, "It is a pleasure to make your acquaintance, I am Alphonso Dunbar, Captain of the Guard for the Great Town of Illdershire. I'd like to thank you personally for your help with this... minor problem of ours. We shall all be glad to have these vermin properly exterminated."

As the guard captain spoke Dante couldn't help but overhear the Mayor whispering to Caspin nearby. "Did you walk them through the town from the tavern, yes and well what was the reception like, the people seemed to take notice did they? They seemed encouraged? Inspired? Good, good, we want to communicate the message they the Mayor's office is taking bold and decisive action to remedy this concern as quickly as possible. The last thing I need is to give my political opponents another a reason to drag my name through the mud like a cheap Dalgonian wh-"

"My Lord," interrupted Captain Dunbar. Mayor Lesmiester looked up from his conversation with Caspin, and Dante quickly turned his head to avoid any awkward eye contact with the mayor only to find everyone else in the atrium doing the same thing. "We have a meeting with the Merchant's Guild shortly, as well as the talks with the representatives from El Arden Ka that we must prepare for." said Captain Dunbar.

"Oh yes, yes you are quite right Captain." The mayor turned to the gamers with a large unabashed smile. "While it has been a pleasure to meet you all, I do regret to inform you that I must take my leave as the ceaseless demands of office call me elsewhere, but as I do, I leave you all in the very capable hands of my aid and assistant, Master Caspin."

"Um... thank you... your lordship." said Stephen with another slight bow.

"Do not mention it." said Mayor Lesmiester with another laugh, "Fare thee well, and may the gods guide you until we meet again."

Caspin turned on his heels, faced the adventurers flashed a weak smile and the said simply, "Follow me."

They were led through the large atrium, passed a number of armed guards and into a spacious, book-filled room on the first floor.

It was explained to the party that Illdlershire had an issue with wolves and raptors. The two predators were competing with one another for hunting territory and the competition was spilling over to the nearby farmland, roads and villages so travelers on the Illdershire Plains were suffering from frequent and excessive animal attacks. Both the wolves and the raptors were reported to be ambushing merchants traveling to and from the city as well as guard patrols that were traveling the area attempting to keep the merchants safe. The mayor felt that either one or both of the animal groups need to be culled in order to bring about peace to the area. And to that end the Adventurer's Guild was contacted to assist Illdershire in dealing with its overactive predator problem.

"So, you need us to go kill wolves and raptors?" asked Robyn.

"Shaving the population will only serve as a temporary solution. Ideally the mayor would prefer something more permanent, killing the pack leader of either the wolves or the raptors, or both. The loss of leadership would drive them from the area, restoring safety to Illdershire and peace of mind to the townspeople and the merchants that we so deeply count on for commerce and trade." said Caspin.

Morrigan looked at Dante but did not speak.

"So, marching us through the town streets, I'm assuming that has to do with the peace of mind portion of the plan?" asked Dante with a smirk.

"The mayor felt a public display of the brave adventurers would boost the morale of the townsfolk during these trying times." Caspin replied.

"Yeah, well that's politics. Anyway, let's talk compensation," said Robyn.

"Oh, why yes of course," replied Caspin, a little taken aback but the sudden change in course. "we'd be glad to offer twenty gold per adventurer for the completion of the task, with solid proof of course."

"Fifty gold, plus a ten-gold deposit per adventurer up front. So that we can properly prepare for the expedition. And the rest upon our return with proof that we have killed one of the pack leaders." said Robyn.

"Thirty-five gold, with your ten gold deposit, and the rest when you return with proof." said Caspin, apparently back on solid ground.

"Agreed." said Robyn, extending her hands to shake with Capsin, who took and shook her hand graciously and with a smile.

"I'll have the agreement drawn up right away. Please wait here." He said and he turned and walked into another room.

"What are you doing?" asked Stephen.

"I negotiated us a better reward?" said Robyn, confused by the question.

"Yes, after you accepted a quest that wasn't meant for us, without discussing it with any of us!"

"What," Robyn said with a laugh, "Of course it was *meant* for us. They think we're the NPC adventurers that the Raptors killed. They think that because they are supposed to think that, we were meant to find those adventurers, we were meant to come in through the western gate, and we were meant to be offered this quest in their place. It's the run of the mill 'mistaken identity trope' it's a common RPG storyline."

"Oh... yes, well of course, well... I didn't know you had figured it out so quickly." said Stephen.

Robyn rolled her eyes. "Dante's not the only gamer here you know." she said sarcastically.

Dante shrugged, he too had recognized what was happening some time ago, but Stephen hadn't, and that worried him, considering that Stephen should have been the first person to know what was going on.

A moment later Caspin reentered the room with a rolled-up scroll of parchment in his hand followed by a single soldier carrying a small open chest which was filled with money pouches.

"Our official request and promise of payment." Said Caspin handing the scroll to Robyn, "and your deposit." He motioned to the open chest. "I look forward to seeing you all again when the task is done." said Caspin and without another word he left the room.

Placing the gold coins into his own money pouch Dante and the other left the Mayor's building with their first official quest and, thanks to Robyn, a bit of gold to finance it.

"So, do we still want to logoff for a while or..." asked Alex.

"Logoff?" said Robyn loudly. "Why? Things are just getting good, we've got gold, we can go shopping and then we can do a major quest, probably will even have a boss battle at the end of it."

"That's what I was thinking," said Alex in agreement.

They looked at Dante. "Do you want to log off?" asked Alex.

"Of course not." said Dante, who feared that if he logged off, he may not get the opportunity to log back on. The three of them looked at Morrigan, who in return cut her eyes at them all.

"I don't know why you all are looking at me, Captain Pope is the only person who has ever mentioned logging out." said Morrigan.

Now all four gamers looked slowly toward Pope. "I'm glad to continue if you all are up for it." he said.

"Yes!" said Robyn, "Then its settled, we shop for supplies then we go Raptor hunting!"

"Wait," said Alex, "So we're going after the Raptors and not the wolves?"

"Oh well," she said now a little less enthusiastically, "I figured since Dante had already gotten that mission from the wolves yesterday, we could kill two birds with one stone... no pun intended."

"And yeah," added Dante, "I don't think you want to go after the leader of the wolves, they get a lot bigger and a lot meaner."

"Yeah, well I don't think the Raptors are going to get any nicer." said Morrigan.

"Well the wolves were here first..." Dante began.

"So, we're choosing which monster we like best now?" replied Morrigan.

"No, I was saying they may be more deeply entrenched, there are probably more of them."

"Adventurers don't usually discuss their plans openly in the streets like this." said an unfamiliar voice.

A large figure in a dark cloak stood a few feet away. He was large and blocky, as big as Pope, his face concealed in the shadow of his large hood, his body enveloped by a cape.

"Do we know you?" asked Stephen.

The figure pulled the hood from his head, revealing a face covered in pale green skin, offset by green eyes and topped with a head of emerald green hair. He had a stubbly beard growing across his face and from his mouth grew two oversized canines that protruded upwards from his bottom lip, so large that they remained exposed, even when his mouth was closed, like the tusks of a boar.

"An orc," mumbled Dante.

"Half-orc actually," said the stranger. "You know you all left the tavern without paying for the food you ordered."

"Are you here to make us pay." asked Robyn defiantly.

"No," replied the half-orc, "There's no cause for concern. I took care of it for you."

"So, you want repayment then?" said Robyn.

"I seek no repayment, just a word to the wise to be more careful in the future, few other places are as forgiving as Illdershire."

"Duly noted, thanks for the advice friend." Waving a hand Robyn turned her back to the stranger, but the stranger didn't move.

"The young swordsman is right," said the half orc, "the wolves have been in the Illdershire Plains for a long time, the raptors are an invasive species. If either one is going to be driven out of the area it would have to be them, they don't belong here, they are throwing off the natural order."

"I'm sorry sir, but *you* don't belong *here*, and you are throwing off *my* natural order, so could you please just go!" said Robyn loudly. But still the stranger did not move. Instead his stony faced drew up into a smirk, invoking the ire of Pope.

"I think it's time you move along friend," Pope said taking a step toward the stranger. They were still some ten feet apart, but still the stranger seemed unfazed by Pope's threatening gesture.

"I am what some might call a naturalist and I have come to Illdershire to investigate this disturbance between the wolves and the raptors. Now I have identified the Raptor nest north of here and intend to travel there, seeing as our goals align, I came to inquire if you all would like to travel together."

"I said move..."

"Wait, wait, wait," said Dante, "You know where the Raptor nest is?"

"That I do." said the half-orc.

"And you're willing to lead us there?" asked Dante warily.

"That is what I propose," said the stranger.

"And why is that?" asked Robyn suspiciously, "Are you trying to get in on the reward? You looking to make some type of a name for yourself? You some aspiring Adventurer or something?"

The half-orc let out an open mouth laugh that surprised everyone in the group. "No, I have no desire for any reward. I do not seek to make a name, and as for adventuring," he let out another giggle, "I know that you all are not who the town of Illdershire assumes you to be. Oh you are adventurers, but you have not been sent by the Adventurers guild. A detail that makes little difference to me, but to the guild and to the town this is a detail of great import. However, I have a history with the guild, so if we were to travel together to complete a task both you and I were prepared to do individually anyway, I think we would both find mutual benefit, me from the company and you from the circumnavigation of a considerable amount of explanation and confusion."

"Ah. Blackmail," said Morrigan.

If you choose not to accept my offer, I will say nothing of the fact that you are not from the guild. The choice is yours to make freely. I was simply pointing out another benefit."

"We accept!" said Dante.

"What?" said the remainder of the party in unison.

"Great" said the half-orc, "I am Shinto Mongore Merciful and I look forward to our journey together."

Chapter 9: Into the Raptor's Nest

"I don't know why you would agree to work with some random stranger we've only just met." said Robyn, still annoyed by Dante's decision to accept Shinto's offer.

"For the same reason you agreed to take a quest meant for a group of dead NPCs," Dante replied without looking at her, instead looking at the variety of cloaks draped over the wooden frames shaped like men. The cloaks were hooded, were trimmed with animal fur. He thought about the wolf hide stuffed in his satchel and wondered how much gold it would cost him to have it cleaned, treated and made into the shoulder mantle of a cloak for himself. He smiled at the idea of donning a shadowy black cloak the same color as the wolf's fur, lined with the fur of the wolf from his first kill. He scratched his chin. Perhaps new leather armor was more practical. He touched the cloak hanging from the nearest dummy, the dark brown cloth was rough and hand spun. Dante concentrated on the item and after a moment a small box popped into his view.

Wool CloakQuality: Fair

Condition: New

An item status box, or rather an information box. So, items had levels and apparently conditions. Dante's mind drifted back to the white room.

"Universal Quantification..." he muttered.

"Dante!" screamed Robyn, "are you listening to me?"

"Did you know items and equipment have status boxes too."

"I've been telling you off for the past ten minutes and all you have to say for yourself is that items and equipment have status boxes?"

"I think it would be more fitting to call them information boxes, but yes." Dante looked up to find Robyn glaring at him. "Are you still talking about the Shinto thing?"

"Yes 'I'm still talking about the Shinto thing!'" she said. "I made an executive decision to take that quest because it was a decision that was going to bring us gold and experience points. You made a decision that will most likely cost us gold by bringing some shady half-orc on to our mission."

"Are you all done?" asked Stephen.

The gamers along with their game guide were all wandering curiously around an items shop, the RPG equivalent to a general store. They were supposed to be stocking up on supplies for the journey ahead.

Alex had made it a priority to purchase more yellow de-petrification potions. He felt much more comfortable knowing that he had plenty of the anti-stone potions on hand, despite the purchase clearing him out of gold coins. He preferred to be out of money then face a nest full of creatures that might turn him to stone with a single bite.

Morrigan, who had started the game with a quarterstaff that she was not particularly fond of, spent five silver on a dagger, which came with a leather belt and sheath that allowed her to position it right at the small of her back. Not the ideal setup for a magic user in Dante's opinion, but he didn't dare tell her how to play her character.

Robyn, aside from her constant scolding of Dante, had conducted quite the shopping trip. In addition to the two daggers that she started with she had purchased six throwing knives, a one-handed crossbow, twenty cross bow bolts, a set of lock picks, a second set of lock picks in case anything happened to the first set, a crowbar, a hammer and a backpack with 50 feet of rope strapped to the side.

"Never know when you might need fifty feet of rope," she explained.

All in all, she spent 85 gold. She had pulled quite a few coins off the NPC adventurers when they were looking for the petrification solution for Alex, and she felt it best to go ahead and put the coin to good use.

Dante hadn't bought anything yet. He couldn't think of anything he really needed, at least not for the amount of gold that he had on hand. He couldn't afford new armor yet, and he was happy with his current weapon, at least for now. He was equipped with an iron long sword, it was the starter sword, yes, but it had served him well thus far and it wasn't like he could exactly afford a new one any way. The Item Shop had a small selection of bladed weapons in addition to their potions and armors and other assorted items. They carried daggers of both iron and steel, as well as short swords and long swords of the same metal types. Dante had taken a look at a steel longsword, which would have been the next step up from his current sword, but the going price on a blade like that was fifty gold pieces. He only had ten. After everyone else had made their purchases, they all stepped back out into the open Illdershire streets.

Most of the Illdershire townsfolk passed by Dante and his friends with a smile and a nod, or at most, a simple tip of the hat, but as he stepped out onto the cobble stone streets six pairs of eyes stared at Dante with unwavering determination. He looked up to see three young boys ogling him with looks of wide-eyed amazement. When he was sure that he was the actual subject of their fascination he approached.

"Something wrong?" he asked curiously. The boys looked at each other at first, each one nudging the other to go forward with the next step in their previously agreed upon plan. Finally, one of them stepped forward.

"Is it true you're an adventurer?" asked a boy with a head full of shiny black curls and a skin tone nearly as dark as Dante's.

"I am." Dante replied.

"See, I told you!" said one of the other boys from behind, a half-elf with pointy ears and sharp features.

"Are you Fer de Lance?" asked the third, a thick-limbed half-orc.

"Um, Fer de Lance?" said Dante confused.

"You know, Fer de Lance, the Adventurer, leader of the Myrmidons!" said the curly headed boy.

"Oh," Said Dante with sudden realization, "No, I'm not Fer de Lance. Sorry," he said apologizing when the boys looked crest fallen.

"I told you it wouldn't be Fer de Lance," said the elf to the orc.

"Well what is your name?" asked the curly headed boy.

Dante dropped down to one knee so he could be on eye level with the young boy. His small brown eyes gleamed in the Deosian sunlight and he stared back at Dante with a such a brilliant sense of admiration and wonder that Dante begin to suspect that this was the beginning of some new quest.

"My name is Dante."

"Dante?" repeated the boy, "Are you one of the adventurers from Urth Land?"

"Urth Land?" repeated Dante.

"Yes, my father said that the Mayor's aide came to the tavern to fetch some adventurers who were meant to go kill the wolves and the raptors and he said that they were from the land of Urth."

"Oh!" Dante said surprised, "Earth, yes."

The curly-headed boy smiled, happy to have been right about something. "I'm Edmond," he continued, "this is Mondego," he motioned to the elf, "and this is Jacopo." he motioned to the half-orc.

"Hi, Edmond, it's nice to meet you." replied Dante with a smile.

"I like your hair." said Edmond in the characteristic way that children say things without warning or filter.

"Thanks," said Dante. The texture of their hair was nearly the same, curly, black and full, but the styling of their hair was different. While the boy's hair grew freely in every direction, Dante's hair was cut low in the back and on the sides, and was thicker on the top, while in the front of his head, on the right side of his face starting at the edge of his hair line and going back about a third of the way towards the back of his head, he had a part, a thin line etched deep into his hair. A line cut so deep that his dark brown scalp could be seen through the knotty black curls. "I like your hair too." Dante replied.

Edmond beamed. "We wanted to come see the adventurers. I bet Mondego a whole copper that Fer de Lance would be here."

"Well," Dante said reaching into his coin pouch, "sorry to disappoint you guys, but I'll tell you what. What do you say I reimburse you for what you lost on your bet, plus interest?" Dante pulled three coins out of his bag and flicked one to each of them. They caught the coins in their hands, each of their eyes growing wide.

"This is a gold piece!" said Edmond, "It takes my father a week to earn this much coin."

Now Dante's eyes went wide, he had not intended to pass out a week's pay to a child.

"Yes, well... it is the duty of the Adventurer to serve the people of Deos, so... don't mention it."

"Dante," Alex called out from behind him, "You ready? We have to go meet Shinto at the East Gate."

Dante stood, the boys looked up at him with their mouths still open the gold coins still gleaming in their hands. "Well looks like I have to go... you boys be good now, it was nice to meet you." Dante turned to leave, and he felt someone tug at his arm. It was Edmond.

"Master Dante, do you think I could be an adventurer one day too?" he asked.

"Um sure, if you work really hard, train every day, listen to your parents and um always try your best to do what's right, then I think you'll make a fine adventurer." He turned and walked away but he knew the three of them were still standing there, still watching him. He didn't look back, but instead joined a waiting Alex.

"This has to be the greatest video game I've ever played in my life." Dante said.

It took a few minutes for the party to walk over to the east gate and once they got there, they saw the half-orc Shinto waiting for them to arrive. Dante's head was still reeling from his interaction with the young boys. They'd seemed so authentic, so honest, it had truly been like interacting with real children, the way they talked to him, the way they looked at him. So much of Edmond reminded him of himself; so much of the three of them reminded him of his brothers.

He had been making notes in his head, saving all of his feedback for after the demo was done, but after the interaction with the boys he could no longer contain it.

"Hey Steve," said Dante slightly out of breath, "I um... I want to talk to you about something."

"Oh, hey Dante, what's wrong?"

"Oh, nothing's wrong, it's the opposite. I wanted to take a second to tell you how impressed I am with the game so far. The sense of immersion, the details, the interaction with the NPCs, this is all really been unbelievable. I'm really glad that you guys invited me out to take part in this Beta test. It feels like a once in a lifetime opportunity."

Stephen looked over at Dante and flashed him a half-hearted smile. Dante noticed his face looked weary and exhausted. "I'm glad you are enjoying it Dante." Stephen said solemnly. "You are taking to it very well, you seem to be a natural here. One of the main goals when selecting players for the Beta was finding people that could survive *and* thrive in Deos. Not only people who reacted well to total immersion into this new world, but people who garner a certain type of reaction from the world itself. A certain amount of acceptance. I think it goes without saying that you *are* that type of person."

"Wow thanks," Said Dante, "That's a pretty big compliment from a game developer."

Stephen looked at Dante with the same weary and exhausted expression once again, except this time there was no smile. "Look, Dante, there's something I need to talk to you about as well."

"Sure, what about?" replied Dante, when suddenly he slammed into Lansing's back.

"Sorry about that Lansing. I didn't see you there," Dante apologized.

"It's my own fault." Lansing looked flatly. "Doc," he said now looking to Stephen, "Captain Pope would like to have a word with you."

"Doc?" Dante said aloud, confused to hear Stephen referred to in this way. Silently and without looking at Dante, Stephen moved ahead and positioned himself next to Pope, where almost immediately Hernandez stepped between them blocking the two of them from Dante's view. He looked back to Lansing who was now walking beside him as they moved through the open grassy fields of the Illdershire plains. "Doc?" Dante said again.

"It's just an expression... chief." said David Lansing, looking at Dante with a slight grin.

"Oh," said Dante, deciding that there was no point in pushing the issue.

The group walked on in relative silence, Lansing was not the most talkative member of the party and any attempts on Dante's part to start a conversation were stonewalled with short often one-word answers.

"What line of work were you in before you started working for the Dytorus Corp?" Dante had asked.

"Military." Lansing responded.

"Oh cool, my brother is in the military, what did you do, you know, in the military?"

"Sniper."

"Oh wow, that's... intense. What brought you to Dytorus Security Forces?"

"Captain Pope."

"Oh... ok. Um, how are you liking the game so far?"

"It's fine."

"Right... fine. I... I can't argue with you there. Um, so what made you choose to go with elf as your race of choice." Dante had asked, finally finding a question that demanded a multi-word explanation.

This time Lansing looked at him with a cold and emotionless gaze. "Compared to the other races Elves have superior hearing, superior vision, enhanced reflexes and agility, but of course *you* knew that already."

"Oh yeah... I suppose I did."

After that Dante no longer attempted to make conversation with Lansing.

After a couple more miles they stopped. The group had come to the base of a steep hill. The landmass obstructed their vision from seeing anything further ahead, which was in vast contrast to the majority of the trip where the group was always able to easily see out in front of them for up to a mile. This abrupt loss of foresight made Dante anxious.

The hillside was dotted with a scattering of flowers not present in the plains. Large flowers with petals that started out as a dark red at the tips, but then flowed to bright and yellow at the center. Thin green vines connected the plants to one another creating a makeshift net across the side of the hill. Dante leaned in to examine the flowers more closely and observed a waxy dew coating the petals, on one of the flowers a small winged insect beat its wings desperately in an attempt to fly off the blood red petal, but it was trapped within the sticky dew of the flower, which flowed toward the center of the plant. Dante looked back at the hill and suddenly felt his stomach turn, he was staring at a hillside of carnivorous plants.

"The Blood Petal Flower," said Shinto coming up behind him, "the Raptors unintentionally brought the seedlings with them when they migrated to the area and, like their host, they are spreading aggressively. This is only the early stage of their development, if left unchecked they turn into something truly horrible. Once we clear out the nest, I can put something into the soil to kill the blood petal plants at the roots." Shinto bent and plucked a flower and Dante heard something that sounded like a distant screech. Shinto sniffed the flower, pulled a vial or bright green liquid from a pouch on his belt, poured a drop on the plant and immediately it shriveled into a dried-out husk. The half-orc dropped the remains of the flower, then turned and faced the group.

"This is the border between the Bleekmore Hills and the Illdershire Plains," he said standing before the hill. "It goes on for quite a few miles in either direction, east or west, but beyond this hill, nestled in the gap between this one and those surrounding it, the Cockatrice Raptors have made their den. That is where we will find the Alpha Raptor."

"You say 'we'," said Pope, "do you plan to enter the nest with us?"

"That I do," answered Shinto.

"I would have never expected such dedication from a guide who has decided to work for free." said Pope.

"I am no guide," replied Shinto. "As I stated before, our goals are one in the same, you all have come to slay the Raptor for the sake of Illdershire, and I have come to see the task done, but for the sake of others."

"A covert mission," said Pope with a smile, "Heard, understood and acknowledged. What do you know about this Alpha Raptor and its nest, what information can you share with us?" Pope asked.

Shinto squatted down in the dirt and began to explain the layout of the Raptor nest, but then suddenly Pope stopped him.

"Dante," said Pope, jarring Dante's attention from the flowers. "Come closer, I want your input on this."

Dante looked around surprised but then quickly joined the huddle around Shinto. The half-orc had drawn a rough circle in the dirt.

"The nest sits nestled in a gap between three large hills. From the southern hillside, which is where we are, there are two pathways leading into the nest. The eastern path on the right side of the hill and the western path on the left side of the hill. Now on the other side of the nest there are two paths leading north, that's not really relevant to our plans so it's of no concern to us. The idea is to storm the nest from the western side, The Alpha Raptor will be waiting inside, and it will fight ferociously to protect its nest, it will not retreat or run away. Once inside, we will become locked in a life or death battle." Shinto looked up at the faces of all of those surrounding him. "If anyone wants to back out, now would be the time."

There was a moment of silence.

"It's a boss battle." Mumbled Dante,

"What are you thinking?" asked Pope.

"Well," said Dante. "Based off the layout, we should send Alex and Hernandez in first, then I will follow closely behind supported by Pope and Lansing and Robyn, then lastly Morrigan and Stephen should fill in the back but stick close to the exit in case things get hairy, that way they can retreat."

"What about him, you left him out," said Hernandez, motioning toward Shinto.

"I'm not sure of your abilities Shinto so I wouldn't know where to place you, I'd say go where you're most comfortable."

"I'll go in first, ahead of your battle guard," said Shinto.

"The tanks should go in first. What I mean is, the guys with shields have the best chance of surviving head on attacks."

Shinto stood from his drawing in the dirt, reached his left hand behind his back and then pulled his arm back out with a small metal buckler now attached to his forearm. It was a circular disc slightly smaller than the shields carried by both Alex and Hernandez, but fastened to Shinto's large muscular arm, it looked more like a children's toy than a real piece of armor.

"I have a shield as well." said Shinto, pulling out a menacing mace with his right hand. "Among other things."

"Then its settled," said Pope, "We'll enter from the west. Alex and Hernandez, you keep the thing's attention and we'll make sure to keep your back clear of any other raptors that may be in the nest along with it. Stephen and Morrigan stay near the exit, do not let them trap us inside. Shinto, I imagine you will do whatever it is you do best."

"That I will." said Shinto.

"Let's move out!" said Pope with a tone of finality and on his command the group began to move, but as Dante made his way to his place in the marching order Pope stopped him. "Dante, before we go any further, I wanted to give you this." Pope reached out and handed Dante a sheathed dagger. Dante took it and pulled the blade from its holster. It was heavy but balanced, well made.

"What's this for?" Dante asked.

"Well, I noticed you only carry a sword and we're about to go into a nest, might get tight in there. I figured this might help you out in a pinch."

"Don't you need it?" Dante asked looking up at Pope a little concerned.

Pope pulled out another blade from behind his back, "I've got myself one as well." he said smiling.

"Attach it to your belt and keep it within reach of your off hand," Pope instructed. "Can't tell you how many times a knife was the only thing that stood between me and the grim reaper. Saved my life more times than I care to mention," Pope said with a wink.

"Thanks again," Dante said and put the knife on the small of his back like he had seen a number of the others do, then practiced reaching around and grabbing it with his left hand. It was quick and easy to reach, and he wondered why he had never thought of doing it before now.

"I guess that's what combat consultants are for," he said to himself taking his place behind Alex as they began their trek towards the Raptor nest.

As the party moved deeper into the path, the peak of the neighboring hill blocked the sunlight, casting a deep shadow. The blood petal flowers seemed to grow thicker and in larger number the further they went. Dante noticed their flower petals showing less and less of the bright yellow and now seemed to be overtaken by the rich blood-colored red. Their vines too now were thicker and heavier and the team had to trod and kick to drag their feet through the plants, the flowers' sweet sticky dew covering their boots and the hem of their pants and Morrigan's dress. Dante swore a bit of the dew got onto his skin and he felt a momentary burning, but Shinto was moving so fast between the hills he had no time to stop and pay attention.

After a short trek the group came to a large clearing. In the space before them there were no blood petal flowers, there was not even grass. Only bare ground littered with bones and the petrified remains of an unknown number of people and animals.

"We're in the nest." said Shinto in a whisper. He was crouched down low, moving forward slowly with his arms out to his side, the heavy metal mace in one hand and the metal buckler attached to the forearm of the other. Dante drew his sword. The other members of the party did the same. There was a small bend where the hill to the north and the south obstructed the view of the eastern and northern paths of the nest. They approached the bend stealthily, hugging the northern wall as they moved. As they turned the corner, a massive bird-like creature came into view.

The Alpha Raptor stood in the middle of the clearing. It was 12 feet tall, crowned with a tangle of twisted black horns. Its beak was jagged and sharp making the Alpha look much more dangerous and prehistoric then it's smaller counterparts. Dante focused on the large monster for a moment and its status box appeared, its health bar went from solid white to multi-colored but just as Dante suspected a series of question marks remained where the creature's level should have been.

There were five other raptors in the nest and Dante scanned each of them quickly, level fives, all. Dante and the party watched as each cockatrice laid down an offering before their leader and with a screech stepped slowly away. When the fifth raptor stepped forward it laid down a collection of meager scraps, the half-chewed carcass of an Illder doe from the looks of it. It let out a feeble screech and attempted to back away but before it could get far, the great raptor grabbed it within its beak, shook vigorously and threw the fifth raptor's lifeless body to the ground with a thud. At this sudden act of violence Robyn let out a small eek and immediately the Alpha Raptors horned head pointed in the direction of the western pathway. It's small lizard eyes locked in on the party then, with a shrill screech, the Alpha and the remaining four raptors advanced at speed across the clearing.

"Dante, split the team!" shouted Pope.

They were too bunched up. The Alpha Raptor hurtled towards them like a bowling ball while they stood like pins, waiting to be knocked down. Dante grabbed Alex's shoulder and pulled him toward the northern pathway.

"Robyn, Morrigan! Come with us!" Dante screamed.

"What about staying near the exit?!" Morrigan screamed in reply.

"Just move!" Dante yelled.

Meanwhile, Shinto rushed headlong into the charging raptors and met one of the regular sized monsters head on, the creature leading with teeth and claws and Shinto leading with his small metal buckler. The two of them collided and were soon wrapped up in a tangle of green skin and feathers.

The remaining three raptors split their attention. Two broke for Dante's group and one headed toward Pope and his men.

The isolated raptor fell directly into Pope's trap, it launched itself at Hernandez, only to find its attack deflected by his shield and then itself pelted by arrows and crossbow bolts so fast that it could not react. And within seconds Pope was upon the raptor, brandishing his dagger before burying it into the monster's skull.

"Crap, why did we get two?" shouted Robyn from behind Dante.

"Don't forget that they're jumpers," shouted Dante "Alex you meet the first one, I'll distract the second one, we'll go back-to-back like with the wolves!"

"Got it!" said Alex who readied his shield and axe as the raptors closed in.

"What do you want me to do?" shouted Robyn.

"I want you to watch out for that tail!" shouted Dante, and just as he did the first raptor leapt into the air. Alex held his shield high to block the oncoming attack and the second raptor, sensing an opening, dropped its head down low and opened its jaws wide, determined to take a large bite from Alex's exposed torso. In that moment, Dante dashed past Alex, dragging his sword along with him and with a vicious swing swiped at the raptors open mouth slashing into its jaws. Feeling the cold sting of the sword the raptor slammed its mouth shut immediately its sharp needle like teeth scraping across parts of the metal blade.

The leaping raptor landed onto Alex's shield, but Alex bent his knees and shifted his body, rolling the raptor from on top of him and sending the monster careening into the dirt.

The two raptors stood. The bird-like lizards attempted to circle them, but Alex and Dante moved as one, rotating with their backs to each other, both of them careful to keep his respective raptor directly in front of himself. And that's when Robyn struck. With her daggers out she ran towards the raptor in front of Alex jumped over its tail, rolled over in the dirt and came up on the other side of the beast before slamming both blades into its left flank. Taken completely by surprise, the creature's HP bar dropped dramatically.

"Critical Hit!" Robyn screamed, but as she did the raptor turned towards her direction, its angry lizard eyes focused in on her.

"For the glory of Oningrad!" bellowed Alex, banging his axe against his shield and instantly the raptor turned its attention back to him. Even Dante's raptor tried to shoot past him at the call of Alex's war cry, but Dante's sword came whipping across the monster's neck when it did, and it retreated.

Across the clearing the Alpha Raptor grabbed both Shinto and the raptor with whom he was locked in battle within its large beak, in an attempt to crush them both. As the alpha tossed its head back trying to swallow its prey the half-orc Shinto kicked the regular sized raptor further down the Alpha's gullet and at the same time pushed himself out of harm's way. Then, in a feat of acrobatics surprising for someone of his size, Dante watched Shinto jump from the Alpha Raptor's open beak, grab hold to the feathers on its neck, and then quickly scramble out of reach as the Alpha Raptor begin to snap wildly. Preoccupied with Shinto, the Alpha Raptor begin to buck and spin in circle, attempting to dislodge him. They were at a stalemate.

"Any ideas?" asked Alex from behind Dante.

"Nothing comes to mind at the moment." Dante replied. And it was then that the raptor in front of Alex burst into flames.

Alex reeled back and shielded his face. The Raptor let out a blood curdling screech where it stood, its entire body consumed by flames, its health bar plummeted down to nothing and when the flames stopped it dropped to the grown in a blackened heap. Behind the charred husk, Morrigan stood with her hands still alight.

"Jesus, Mary and Joseph..." said Alex.

Dante's attention was pulled and that was the opening his raptor needed, launching itself. Dante attempted to raise his sword with his right hand to guard his body but the raptor's large feathered head was already past his right arm. Dante leaned back in an attempt to escape and felt himself tripping over his own feet. Instinctively, he reached back with his left hand. The raptor was bearing down, and he was falling. His left hand reemerged with the dagger in its grip. He thrust upward, jamming the blade into the soft underside of the raptor's snout like beak. Hot red blood gushed from the wound, poured down Dante's arm and even then the raptor struggled, its winged and clawed feathered arms trying desperately to scratch Dante's eyes out. It wasn't until Dante's back hit the ground and he heard a distinctive "thunk, thunk, thunk" that the raptor stopped moving altogether, and its large body slumped upon him. The Raptor had three crossbow arrows sticking out of its head, one directly through its eye.

A large hand reached down and pulled Dante to his feet. It was Pope.

"Dagger came in handy I see," he said with a smile, pulling back the levers on his large crossbow, "Get that sword of yours ready, time to finish the job." Pope motioned over to the alpha Raptor who was still spinning in circles trying to get Shinto off its back, but the large green half-orc was locked on.

"Your friend bought us some time to get rid of the underlings," Pope said to Dante, "Good call having him come along."

Morrigan was sweating and looked exhausted. Her HP bar was full, but her MP bar was nearly empty. At that moment Stephen ran over to her with one of the blue vials from the potions pouch already out and uncorked. He handed it to her, and she drank the whole bottle in one gulp.

"Lansing, lay down some cover fire," shouted Pope. "Alex, Hernandez, north, south. Keep this thing distracted and confused. Robyn, give me that rope. Dante on me, we're going Raptor hunting." Pope, looped the coil of rope over his shoulder and took off in a sprint toward the Alpha Raptor, and almost instinctively Dante took off after him. The two of them were running at full speed toward a monster the size of a small building. Lansing arrows were shooting overhead, hitting the Raptor in its large broad chest. Dante saw Alex flanked on his left, running along with them struggling to keep up, he knew on the other side would be Hernandez. The Alpha Raptor, fully aware that it was being swarmed, abandoned trying to dislodge Shinto and let out an ear-splitting screech. Hernandez released a deep guttural roar as primal and prehistoric as the Raptor's, the sound of which must have surprised the raptor too because when the monster heard his cry, it turned all of its attention toward Hernandez. Immediately Pope unloaded his crossbow, firing three shots into the raptor and then throwing the strapped cross bow across his back, without a second thought he pulled out the dagger from the small of his back and placed it in between his teeth and then launched himself into the air and latched on the side of the Alpha in much the same manner that Shinto had.

Dante stood in awe of the savagery of both the giant monster before him as well as its attackers. The Alpha Raptor attempted to twist its long neck and contort its body to grab hold of Pope before he, like Shinto got out of its reach. In a fit of panic, Dante thrust his sword in the air, lodging his blade between the raptor's beak and using it as a makeshift prybar, keeping the jagged beak from closing on Pope back. He struggled to hold his position as Pope climbed further out of reach and after a few moments, he ripped the sword from the Raptors grip and the metal slid across the monster beak drawing sparks, as if he had glanced the blade across stone. Before he had time to think he thrust his sword upward again this time penetrating the body of the great bird. It let out another loud screech and one of its large feet came up and kicked Dante in the chest. It felt like being hit by a truck. He flew through the air, landing on the ground with a hard thud. The world spun and for a moment he thought he might pass out, but when he looked up, he saw a twelve-foot-tall prehistoric horned bird charging him and quickly, his vision cleared. He reached instinctively for his sword, but his heart sank when he looked and saw that the hilt still protruding from the body of the charging raptor. He stood to his feet and pulled the dagger. This was it; he was going to be trampled, skewered and eaten and if that kick was any indication of what was to come, it was going to hurt, a whole lot more than any video game should. For the first time he could see his own status box within his field of vision, his health bar had been cut in half by the raptors one attack. The Alpha Raptor bounded forward and right as Dante braced himself, Morrigan stepped in front of him.

"What are you doing?" he yelled out to her.

"Killing the boss." That's when Dante saw Alex, who let out another loud war cry and unable to help itself the Alpha was distracted and veered off of its path. On its back, Pope had taken the rope from around his shoulder and tossed one end of it to Shinto and now together the two of them were leaping from the raptors back and with the rope pressed against the back of its neck. They pitched forward and their combined weight in addition to the raptors misguided balance caused it to heave forward and fall in the dirt. It hit the ground with momentum and slid forward another five feet stopping a yard in front of Morrigan.

She set her feet, cocked back both arms and then in one flush movement thrust them forward only this time there were no flames, instead, Dante felt a sudden drop in temperature and smoky white mist poured from the palms of Morrigan's hands, covering the pinned down alpha as it lay struggling in the dirt. Frost and ice crystalized on the raptor's head and neck. Dante watched as the Alpha's HP bar dwindled down to nothing. But then the smoky white mist stopped. Morrigan's magic faded and almost immediately the ice crystals began to melt. Dante looked to Morrigan and saw that her MP bar was fully depleted.

The Alpha shook its head, shaking free the remaining frost and ice, but before it could stand Shinto came from nowhere and slammed his mace into the thing's head, cracking and crushing horns and splitting open the raptors skull. The alpha Raptor's HP bar fell to zero and its body dropped in a lifeless heap.

"Is it dead?" asked Robyn.

"Yes," said Shinto, "It's definitely dead." Shinto took a seat in the dirt obviously exhausted and possibly a bit frazzled.

For a moment they all stood around the giant bird in silence, as if not really sure of what to do next. Dante walked to the other side of the now dead alpha raptor and pulled out his sword, wiped it clean on the raptors feathers and placed it back into its sheath. This is usually where you get a "Congratulations you defeated Gur'lock the Raptor King" message to scroll across the screen, Dante thought. And then he realized that there was a ringing in his ears. Dante took a moment to summon his spirit tome then read the notification page which had, as he had expected, changed once again.

- You have been issued a new quest, "A Favor for Wolves"
- You have been issued a new quest, "Exterminators for Hire in Illdershire"
- Four Cockatrice Raptors have been defeated.
- You have gained 1600 Experience points!
- The Alpha Cockatrice Raptor has been defeated.
- You have gained 2100 Experience points!
- You have fulfilled the primary objective for the quest "A Favor for Wolves"
- You have fulfilled 1 of 3 primary objectives for the quest "Exterminators for Hire in Illdershire"
- You have a total of 5700 Experience Points
- You have obtained Level 4, Congratulations!

"We've gained another level." Dante said aloud. And as if by reflex, the other gamers pulled out their spirit tomes.

"Wow, we are leveling up really fast," said Robyn.

"Well, we have been taking on some tough monsters. Stuff that has been much stronger than any of us could have taken on alone, and we've been beating groups of them." said Alex.

"Yeah, and the first few levels do normally go by pretty quickly," added Morrigan.

Dante's eyes scanned over his notifications page once again. He noticed that the messages really seemed to stack up if you didn't stop and check the tome at regular intervals. He saw that the quest given to them by the Mayor's aid was marked with a message and now that they had killed the Alpha Raptor they were one third of the way done. He imagined collecting proof and then taking it back to Illdershire were the other two primary objectives of the quest. Dante also noticed the quest he received from Canis was listed in his messages and it appeared to have now been fully completed, which was good though he expected its conclusion to come with a bit more fanfare.

"Hey guys look what I found!" said Hernandez. He was standing on the far end of the clearing, in the spot where they had seen the regular raptors giving their offerings to the Alpha, only Hernandez was holding up a large oblong spheroid the size of a man's head, Dante recognized it immediately as an egg. Before long most of the party was examining the cluster of eggs. There were over thirty of them.

"So that's why they were bringing it food." Alex said.

"We should take some." said Hernandez looking up at Pope, who himself seemed to be considering the suggestion thoughtfully.

"Take a few, put them in the plunder's pouch." Said Pope. "Destroy the rest." Without hesitation Lansing and Hernandez began grabbing the large eggs and carefully placed a number of them into the bottomless bag Hernandez carried, the remaining they begin to simply pick up and throw, splattering the ground in a mess of yolk and shells.

"Dante, you need healing, you're down to half," said Stephen.

"Oh yeah, thanks," said Dante almost so distracted by the crushing of the eggs that he had forgotten about the pain coursing throughout his entire body. Almost. "What do you need me to do?" asked Dante.

"You just stand there." Stephen said with a smile before placing a hand onto Dante's shoulder. As he did golden light radiated from his hand and wrapped itself around Dante's upper body, immediately the pain he was feeling subsided and he could see at the top of his vision, his HP bar slowly increase back to full and then fade from view. As the health bar increased and the golden light swirled all around Dante, Stephen leaned into him and spoke in a low and mumbled voice. "Once we get back to Illdershire I need to speak with you in private," said Stephen. Dante looked up to see an expression of deathly seriousness on his face, and then suddenly he broke into his characteristic gameshow host smile again. "I think that oughta do you for now," he said loudly.

"Got him all fixed up Doc?" said Pope from behind Dante.

"For now, at least." said Stephen with a smile.

"Great, mind if I borrow him for a minute."

"He's all yours."

Pope motioned Dante over to space that was slightly away from the rest of the party.

"Dante, I just wanted to say, you did good out here today. You've got a real knack for this stuff."

Dante was confused by the exchange that had just taken place with Stephen and it took a moment to register what Pope was saying.

"Oh, no, I didn't really do anything. I mean you... you climbed up on the things back and helped Shinto bring it down. I... I just got kicked in the chest."

"Well you watched my back, stopped it from picking me out of its feathers like a little bug. What I'm trying to say here is that, you're dependable, reliable. You're a leader. Quite frankly, Dytrous Corp could use someone like you. Last Legend Games could as well."

Dante couldn't believe what he was hearing. "Really?" he asked. "You mean like a job?" Is this what Fang had been talking about. Was the Beta really a large-scale recruitment exercise?

"I'm just saying, if you keep going the way you are, I see a big future for you here." Pope said.

"Wow, Captain, thanks. That... that means a lot coming from you. I-I don't know what to say."

"Call me Pope, and you don't have to say anything. Just keep up the good work, soldier."

"I will," said Dante. "Oh, and Pope, sir. Your dagger." Dante held out the sheathed blade, but Pope didn't take it.

"You keep it." Pope said with a smile. "It's already saved you once, no doubt it will come in handy again."

Chapter 10: Disconnect

With a last stroke from Alex's axe and a mashing of bones, the Alpha Raptor's head was severed from its body. Lansing wrapped it in large brown cloth and with Dante's help they forced the large and battered head into the plunder's pouch, the mouth of which opened and stretched to fit the skull through before swallowing it and returning to normal size.

"I love this bag!" said Hernandez throwing it easily over his shoulder.

Shinto placed a hand on the alpha raptor's decapitated chest, and in a spark of blue light, the half-orc held a cloudy blue jewel in the same hand, one much larger than the blue gem Dante had found after the wolf battle.

"What's that?" Dante asked.

"This is a mana crystal," said Shinto, as though answering a question a child should know.

"Of course," said Dante realization dawning, "A mana crystal." In the Dragon Dale games, mana crystals were often dropped by monsters. Adventurers could exchange them for gold and prestige. The blue wolf fang must have been a mana crystal as well, and touching a recently slain monster was how they were obtained. The jewel from the raptor was huge by comparison. Seeing his apparent interest the half-orc handed the large mana-crystal over to Dante, initially without saying a word.

"Oh no I couldn't; it's yours." Dante replied to the gesture.

"I have no need for it. You will undoubtedly find more use for it than I."

Reluctantly Dante took the large blue crystal and placed it in his pack. "Thank you," said Dante. But the cleric seemed unconcerned with his gratitude.

"We should leave," said Shinto, "it's only a matter of time before more Raptors arrive."

"No need to tell me twice," said Robyn. "Let's go collect our reward."

The party moved with speed through the narrow passageway, trampling the blood petal flowers in their rush to avoid more raptors.

At the entrance of the nest, where the blood petal flowers and the bare ground met, Shinto removed a small hatchet from his belt, dug a shallow hole in the dirt with a trowel and poured from his vial of bright green liquid. The plants reacted violently, shriveling and dying, their dark red petals turning black.

"Let's go," he said and soon they had re-joined the rest of the group, who were trudging ankle deep through living flowers, while the disease slowly spread toward their direction. Far-off screeching came from the dying plants.

When Shinto and Dante caught up with the rest of the group, they found the gamers already deep in the midst of conversation.

"I am about ready for a break," said Robyn, "I'm starving."

"I'm hungry too, now that you mention it." said Morrigan.

"Oh, I still have some pickled peregrine fruit if you guys want some?" said Alex digging into his satchel for the jar he purchased from the fruit seller.

"Thanks, but I think I'd prefer real food. Not virtual slime melon," replied Morrigan.

"Oh, I cannot wait to take a hot shower and stretch out on that big soft hotel room bed." said Robyn stretching her arms out toward the sky as she walked.

"I can't wait to get to the mini bar," said Morrigan.

"We should all go out for drinks later tonight," said Alex, "You know, to celebrate."

"What was that stuff you poured into the ground?" Dante asked as he struggled to keep pace with Shinto.

"Something to kill the Blood Petal Flowers." Said Shinto moving at such a brisk walk that he was nearly running.

"It looks... deadly."

"Things are meant to kill often are," Shinto said without looking at Dante.

"Will it kill us?"

Shinto had now made his way to the front of the group but at this last question looked back over his shoulder and scowled at Dante confused. "Unless you plan to drink it in large amounts, then no, it will not kill you."

"Then why are you going so fast, like... like you're trying to get away from something. Like you're afraid."

"And you seem as if you are not afraid, which to me is not a sign of bravery, but one of ignorance, considering that you have proven to know little about your location and even less of your circumstances."

"What's that supposed to mean?"

"It means that it was only by good fortune that all of you made it out of that Raptor's nest alive and intact and if we would like to keep it that way, we should get back to Illdershire quickly."

Stephen suddenly stopped walking.

"Stephen? What's wrong?" asked Morrigan.

"I can't do this any longer." he said a look of exasperation across his face. "There is something that I have to tell all of you, and I have to say it now."

Everyone in the group stopped and looked toward Stephen, many of the squinting not really sure at what they were seeing

"Stephen..." said Pope.

"No Pope! Enough is enough. I can't keep this up for another second. I'm telling them now and there is nothing you can do to stop me."

Pope pulled the crossbow from his back and pointed it in Stephen's direction.

"Stephen." said Pope once again.

"Are you going to shoot me Pope? Is that it? Are you really willing to go that far to keep me quiet?"

There was a collective gasp from the group of adventurers as each of them took a step backward away from Stephen. Dante opened his mouth to say something, but Pope raised a hand to silence him.

"Stephen, I want you to shut up and then slowly and carefully walk to me." Pope said while staring down the site of his crossbow.

"No!" Replied Stephen, "I will not shut up. I will not be silenced, so if you're going to shoot me then damnit just shoot me!"

Pope pulled the trigger on his crossbow and the loaded bolt arrow flew through the air, zipped passed Stephen's ear and with a loud crack hit a large thick green vine, snapping it in two before it could inch its way any closer to Stephen's head.

There was, this time, an unmistakable noise, a screeching squeamish squelch as the vine writhed and wriggled in the air, a translucent green liquid squirting from its severed end like blood.

Stephen turned to see what was happening behind him, completely unaware of the other tentacle like vines that had already encircled his legs and waist. The vines snatched tight, binding him in thick green coils and pulling his body into the air like a rabbit caught in a snare trap. Before anyone could even shout, Stephen hung suspended some six feet in the air with a look of shock and bewilderment on his face. Shinto pushed his way from the front of the group to the back examining the scene with wide eyes.

"Oh no," said Shinto, "It's worse than I feared." New vines lashed themselves around Stephen's suspended body further binding him and making it impossible to move, he looked as if he was in the early stages of being mummified.

"What's going on?" screamed Dante.

"It's a fully developed, blood petal flower, the Man Eater Plant!"

From beneath the suspended and bound Stephen the ground rumbled and then split open throwing clumps of dirt and broken shards of rock as a large green pod erupted from the soil. Seven feet tall and nearly four feet wide the massive green bulb proved to be the source and control of the thick green vines that held Stephen, who was now dangling even higher in the air. Without thinking Dante dashed forward, unsheathing his sword and slashing at the long living vines that held Stephen aloft.

"No wait," shouted Shinto, reaching out a hand to stop Dante but it was too late, he was already hacking wildly away at the monstrous plant. He severed one vine, then another, then another and then Stephen came tumbling out of the sky, hitting the ground with a hard thud, still wrapped tightly in the plant's cords. Dante pulled at the vines wound tightly around Stephen's body, but they wouldn't budge, even severed they seem to be constricting tighter and tighter around Stephen's torso, slowly squeezing the air and life out of him. Dante's hands burned with pain, the vines were covered in thick, black tipped thorns that cut into his skin which ached and bled. He could only imagine the pain that Stephen was feeling.

The pod's severed vines writhed and shuttered, spewing more and more of the translucent green liquid, which upon landing, acted like acid, eating through clothing and burning skin. For a brief moment Dante imagined that *this* is what hell must feel like, the burning pain from the plants splattering liquid and the agonizing pain from his sliced open hands, pain in a variety. But before he could retreat any deeper into his own mind a flailing vine lashed toward them and he was forced to use his body as a shield to cover the incapacitated and exposed Stephen, who still lay bound in front of him. The thorned vine slammed into Dante's back, and he felt a chunk of his HP dissolve as searing pain shot through him.

"Dante." Stephen choked between labored breaths.

"Dante, get out of there!" yelled Alex as a barrage of arrows slammed into the pod, spraying the ground and both Dante and Stephen with more of the burning liquid.

"Stephen, I'm going to get you out of here!" Dante said, grabbing hold to the vines that restrained him and struggling to drag his body out of the shadow of the giant pod.

But as he pulled, the gigantic bulb let out another wet squelching shriek and then like a living nightmare, the pod burst open, unfolding itself like a giant blooming flower. The pod unfurled into four massive petals that flapped and rolled like giant tongues, each one laden down the middle with long spiked barbs. Their interiors were a deep bloody red, similar to the flowers from which it had evolved, but towards it center where the four petals met it slowly turned a bright yellow and instead of a stamen or stigma, there was a large gaping hole, a maw, encircled by more sharp and jagged thorns that looked more like the teeth of a predator then the protective parts of a plant, each one at least a foot in length. Dante eyes grew wide as the gigantic plant lumbered forward, looking as if it may tip over on top of them. But then it pitched backward, and then to the left and then the right, like an invisible hand was wriggling it out of the soil. Dante looked down, and unable to control himself, let out a low moan as he saw that the plant was in effect yanking *itself* from the soil, pulling its roots from the ground and folding them over into makeshift feet. Something from inside the center of the plant sloshed and splashed and a bit of the green liquid spilled from its center hole hitting the ground with a loud smoking hiss. The Man Eater's digestives juices meant to dissolve anything it could manage to stuff into its maw.

"Who designed this?" Dante moaned in a halfhearted whimper not even aware that he was speaking. *The dagger*, his mind flashed as he struggled to pull Stephen further and further away with his bleeding hands. *Use the dagger.* He pulled the small blade from its sheath and cut the vines that were coiled around Stephen's chest. The game guide took a deep breath, as if he had just come up from being held underwater. Dante leaned forward to cut the vines binding his waist and legs, but Stephen stopped him.

"Dante," he said rasping, "I must tell you..."

"Stephen, we have to move-"

"Dante, listen," Stephen said, his eyes bulging as if he still was unable to breathe, smatters of blood and the welts of chemical burns splattered across his face. Time seemed to slow. The noise and chaos that surrounded them melted away and for a brief moment which somehow felt as if it would last an eternity, all that could be heard was Stephen's ragged and tattered voice.

"We are not in a game," Stephen whispered.

"What?" mumbled Dante, now his own voice echoed in his ears, he must not have heard correctly, he must have been mistaken.

"This is not a simulation, it's not virtual reality, this is real. We are in an alternate world." He coughed harshly and blood bubbled at the corners of his mouth.

"That... that doesn't make sense, that's not possible. We're in the pods, we're at HQ."

"The pods are the transporters that sent us here. This is Deos, and if you die here..."

Just then Hernandez and Alex ran past both Stephen and Dante, using their shields for cover and swinging wildly at the plant with their sword and axes. New tentacles were sprouting from the plant's maw. Arrows rained from overhead. For Dante, the world came slamming back into view, all of its noise and color and chaos crashing back down onto his senses.

"If you die here," Stephen choked, desperation darkening his eyes, "You die."

"What are you waiting for? GO!" shouted Hernandez, looking over his shoulder to see why Stephen and Dante had yet to escape, but his brief lapse of vigilance left him unguarded and in that moment a particularly thick vine swung in hard and knocked him off his feet, sending him slamming into the side of the hill.

Stephen took the dagger out of Dante's hand. "Pope can still communicate with Headquarters; he can get you all home, but he..." Stephen let out another cough, "You have to convince him." Stephen said, then using the dagger he bent down and cut the cords binding his legs.

Dante scrambled to his feet, large tentacle vines lashed out from the Man Eater Plant, swinging wildly, slamming into the ground and Alex's shield in quick succession like green bolts of lightning. Alex had given up swinging his axe and was merely hiding behind his shield now that Hernandez had been incapacitated.

"Alex we're retreating!" Dante screamed attempting to guard his eyes from the rubble and dust stirred up by the gigantic lumbering plant.

"Go I'll cover you," he called out, slowly moving backward as his shield was pelted by the thorny vines. Stephen had also crawled to his feet, Dante stopped to put a shoulder underneath his arm and help him scramble off to safety but as he did, he felt Stephen's body lighten. He looked down to see a new set of vines had found their way around his torso and in an instant, the game guide was snatched into the air his hands slipping from Dante's, their fingertips barley having times to grasp hold to one another. This time there was no mid-air suspension, The Man Eater Plant yanked Stephen violently upward, Dante could see his face clearly although the rest of his body had become a blur. Stephen mouthed the word "Run" before the tentacle vine brought him careening back down to the ground slamming him into the dirt before lifting him up again. A strong hand gripped the collar of Dante's leather armor and Shinto snatched him off his feet and threw him backwards. In seconds, the half-orc rescued Alex in the same manner. Then Dante hit the ground, hard.

Robyn was screaming. Screaming telling him to get up and run. He stood, dazed and confused and looked up to see the party all running in one direction. Morrigan was out in front, Lansing was helping Hernandez hobble behind her and Robyn and Alex were pulling Dante to his feet while Pope carried the limp and unconscious body of Stephen. Together, they hobbled toward the open Illdershire Plains in the distance. The horrible and wet shriek of the Man Eater Plant followed, but Dante didn't dare look back.

After what felt like an eternity, the red flowers disappeared from beneath their feet and the sounds of the Man Eater Plant faded, yet still they ran. They didn't stop until Pope fell to the ground on one knee, chest heaving and breathing heavily as he lay Stephen face up in the grass.

Stephen's eyes were closed, his body covered in burns, large purple bruises, a countless number of cuts, scrapes and thorn-sized puncture wounds. Pope kneeled over him and put a finger to his neck. When Pope put an ear to Stephen's chest, Dante noted that his perfectly sculpted face was, for the first time since they had arrived, shaken. His breathing was wild and uncontrolled, and his eyes darted from side to side as he listened intently for a heartbeat or sign of life, and then slowly, Dante saw all emotion drain from his face and he dropped back from a kneel to a seated position in the grass.

"He's gone." Pope said letting out a breath as if he had just ripped off a particularly nasty bandage.

"Gone?!" said Robyn, "what do you mean 'Gone', I thought, I thought we just logout?"

Pope didn't reply.

In Stephen's Status box, his HP bar was completely empty, and his name was greyed out.

Just then Shinto came bounding out of the path. He was sweating and breathing hard.

"How is he?" he asked pushing his was toward Stephen.

"He's dead." Pope said coldly.

Shinto fell down to both knees and put an ear to Stephen's chest. Pope stood and stepped backward giving the half-orc more room.

"I've already done that, he's gone."

"Silence." snapped Shinto, waving a hand in the air to signal to Pope to stop talking. He listened intently at Stephen's chest for another moment, then leaned back and placed a single hand on his forehead and closed his eyes.

"His injuries are too extensive," Shinto muttered.

"As I just said," said Pope.

Shinto ignored Pope's comment. "His injuries are too extensive for me to heal his body, but his spirit is intact and the energy is strong, so I can still save him."

"How?" asked Morrigan.

"I can perform a spell that separates the spirit from the body and puts the consciousness into a form of suspended animation. This will protect him from death until you can find a healer strong enough to restore him fully, or someone skilled enough to craft him a new body." Shinto stared at them for a brief moment when he said this.

Pope took a step forward. He narrowed his eyes focusing hard on Shinto as if he were trying to see something that had been previously hidden. "Restore him? Craft a new body? But he's... he's dead." Pope seemed somewhat confused and flustered. "His heart has stopped; his body has been destroyed. What could you possibly do for him at this point?" Pope asked.

The thin golden chain that Pope had been wearing when they first met had, in the chaos and confusion of the fighting, come free and now lay across his chest. At the end of the chain hung a small heart shaped charm, tiny and petite, like children's jewelry and hardly noticeable on Pope's hulking frame. Dante probably would have missed it, if it had not been for the way that it glittered in sparkled in the light. As if he could sense that he was being watched, Pope glanced at Dante and silently tucked the necklace back into his clothing once again. His eyes then shot back to Shinto, transfixed on his every movement. Pope took another step forward as if not wanting to miss a single detail of what was about to transpire.

"With the proper knowledge and intention, magic can achieve anything," Shinto said. "Not that one always should. But I have no time to explain, we must act quickly."

Shinto placed both of his large green hands over Stephen's chest, took a deep breath and when he exhaled Dante saw sparkling golden light emanate from hands and forearms and snake its way into Stephen's mouth, nose and eyes. Stephen's chest heaved as if he had taken a breath. His torso lifted upward pulling him up slightly from the ground and then with a jerk he slammed back into the dirt. The golden light that had seeped into him, now reversed its course and oozed out of him, only it was no longer light. Now it was in the form of a shimmering pink liquid, and it poured from his every cut and wound gathering into a mass above Stephen. The half-orc still had his eyes closed when his outstretched hands went from palm down to palm up incasing the floating mass of matter between his two large hands. After a few moments, the pink liquid emptied itself from inside Stephen's body, the body itself lifted from the ground and was absorbed into the amorphous blob, which then condensed, compressing itself into a large roughly shaped gemstone in the shade of an opaque rose-colored pink. Shinto opened his eyes and plucked the jewel from the air.

"This," Shinto said looking up at the adventurers, "is a spirit crystal, it contains within it the mind and the soul of your friend. It will allow you to keep his consciousness safe while you find the means to restore him. Guard and protect it, as long as it remains whole, your friend can yet be saved."

CHAPTER 11: INITIALIZATION

Dante had the rose crystal, Stephen's soul, in his pouch because Shinto had given it to him, but he wasn't sure why. Pope had been expecting it, he had all but asked for it. But once Shinto stood with the fully formed Spirit Crystal in hand, he walked right pass Pope and handed it to Dante instead. Perhaps, Dante thought, it was based off of how he had rushed in to try and save Stephen from the Man Eater Plant. Maybe Shinto assumed that he and Stephen were better friends then they actually were.

Truth be told, Dante himself wasn't even sure why he had rushed in after him the way he did. Something inside Dante had pulled him forward, had forced him to act. Maybe it was the fact that he was so accustomed to playing these types of games as a tank, and as a tank rushing head long into danger was simply part of the job description.

Playing these types of games.

He allowed those words to reverberate through the echo chamber of his inner mind as the party walked back to the town of Illdershire.

"So, are we still logging off after we collect our reward?" Robyn asked, breaking the silence and the awkwardly ominous mood that had overtaken the players since the loss of Stephen, though it was unclear why, seeing how, as far as they understood it, he was now simply waiting for them outside of his pod at Last Legend Games Headquarters

That was the understanding, at least, for everyone except Dante. He had heard something different right before Stephen had died. Something that he was forcing him to rethink his understanding of the world around him.

"That was our original plan," said Morrigan, "don't see why anything would be different now. Especially since we've went and lost our game guide."

"Yeah, about that," Robyn was walking backwards as she spoke. She also absent-mindedly twirled a dagger between the fingers of her right hand, all of which seemed unusually irresponsible but for Robyn completely casual. "The Spirit Crystal seems like a mobile respawn point, which, I must admit, is actually pretty cool, but what happens when he logs back on? Does he automatically respawn, or do we still have to like... have him restored?"

She was walking next to Hernandez who seemed to be only half listening to the conversation between the gamers. He was back up on his feet now, both he and Dante had been pretty banged up after their encounter with the Man Eater Plant, but Shinto had healed them using the same golden light that he had used on Stephen.

"I imagine that he respawns wherever the crystal is." said Alex, "In most MMORPGs when you die you respawn in the nearest town, but with a spell like that one, once its cast your party can simply pick you up and carry you with them, so the next time you log in, you respawn with the rest of the group and you don't have to run clear across the map to get back with your party."

"But that doesn't exactly make sense," said Morrigan. "Earlier, Stephen said dropping down to zero hit points renders one unconscious, while dropping extensively below zero actually kills your character, but in past Dragon Dale games, there was never really a distinction between falling unconscious and dying. That would mean in past games, characters weren't dying in combat, they were fainting. That's why whenever you dropped to zero hit points, someone could just cast restoration and bring you back."

"Restoration?" said a voice that had not previously been a part of the conversation. "Is this the spell needed to *resurrect* Stephen?" it was Pope, who had been walking in general silence up to that point and the sudden emergence of his voice caught most members of the group by surprise, even Hernandez, who jumped when he heard the captain speak.

"Well, yes... at least in most versions of the game," answered Robyn. "Restoration brings you back after you die."

"Technically," interrupted Morrigan, "Restoration isn't a resurrection spell. It doesn't bring you back after you die, it just brings you back to consciousness. Characters usually only die in the context of the storyline and in cases like that, there is no way to bring them back."

"I mean, if we're being technical then yes, I guess all of that's true, but I would assume with this being a fully immersive VR MMORPG things will be a bit different in this version of Dragon Dale," argued Alex. "Restoration may be used when characters are knocked unconscious, and maybe stronger spells are unlocked later in game to avoid having to logoff or be turned into a crystal. Maybe a spell like Restore Life or something."

"That's a lot of 'maybes'" Morrigan said.

"Is there magic that can reverse the effects of death? Yes or no?" asked Pope, sounding annoyed by the gamer's debate.

"Well we've just seen someone drop down below zero hit points and die," explained Alex, "And then we had an NPC tell us that *someone* could restore them to full health. I think that tells us everything we need to know." Alex looked at Morrigan as if expecting her to disagree, but she merely shrugged her shoulders as if she had no further argument. "So, to answer your question. Yes, in this version of the game Restore Life must exist and it reverses the effects of death."

Pope's eyes gleamed at the mention of this information, but he said nothing else.

"Dante what do you think?" Alex asked.

What did he think? Well, that was the problem now wasn't it? He was doing a lot of thinking and the more that he thought the more of a problem it became.

He thought about what Stephen had said, that they were not in a video game but instead, in an alternate world. Not a game but a real world. But they couldn't be, that just didn't make sense. And why did Stephen wait until they were being attacked by a monster to share with him such an extraordinarily vital bit of information? But no, no that wasn't true. Stephen *had* been trying to tell him something before, but he kept getting interrupted. Interrupted by...

Wait, wait, wait. This didn't make sense. This couldn't be a real world. He was seeing tiny floating boxes filled with names and information for God's sake? Now that was just like a video game, you do not see those types of things in a real world.

Then he thought about the White Room, the man with the eyepatch and Universal Quantification.

Suddenly his mind was filled with a memory of himself, his brothers Malcolm and Brian, and his parents. It was an old memory, for it featured his father. They were sitting in a park, on a blanket, and they were looking up at a rainbow that arced across the sky.

He had asked how. How was there a rainbow in the sky?

"Light reflects through particles of water in the atmosphere and it creates the optical illusion of the rainbow," his brother Bryan said.

"What?" Said Dante confused by this thorough and overly logical explanation.

Malcolm gave it a try "It's like a giant projection in the sky Dee. It's there, but it's not really there," he said.

Dante had nodded, but he was still confused.

His mother smiled. "That's just the way God made it," she said.

"Oh," Dante said finding this as the most acceptable answer.

"Yeah Dee," said his father in a deep baritone voice that rang in Dante's inner ear. "Some things are too magical to understand... at least for now," he smiled down at his son with a handsome bearded face, "But with a mind like yours, I'm sure you'll have it all worked out soon enough!" His father lifted him up high into the sky, sitting him on big broad shoulders as wide as the world, and Dante remembered being so high up that he could practically reach out and touch that rainbow.

He came back to himself and felt tears welling in his eyes.

He thought about everything that had taken place since he had arrived in Deos. He thought about how he had landed face first in the Illdershire Plains splitting open his lip. He thought about the sights, the smells, the sounds, the textures. He thought about the town, the busy streets, the smoky tavern, the shops and the food vendors. He thought about the people, the gate guard, the fruit seller, the bar maid and the interaction he had with those boys. The boys that looked up at him with admiration and awe too authentic to have had been programmed. It had all been executed perfectly, all of it. From beginning to end.

Since he stepped foot into Deos there had not been one technological glitch, hiccup or bug, not even a single drop in frame rate. This "beta" program had run seamlessly, often times, looking and feeling more real than the real world had.

Now how could that be? Dante thought.

When he thought about it, Stephen rarely ever seemed in control of anything once they had gotten "in game". Yes, he'd had an answer for every question, but in retrospect, it was almost always reactionary. As if he had read and memorized those answers from a script, as if he'd studied predetermined responses.

Then Dante thought about the pain, about the wolves and the raptors and the bumps and the bruises. The cuts, the scratches, the bites and the burns. It had all hurt. All of it. Real pain not simulated pain, not haptic feedback. Stephen had promised to turn it down, had mentioned that it was in the process of being recalibrated, but that could have been a lie.

Then Stephen wanted to tell him something, he wanted to talk to him about something that had wiped that disingenuous smile from his face but every time he had tried, he had been interrupted. By Pope.

Then, when he finally did get the chance to tell him what he had been wanting to tell him, conveniently with the threat of death literally looming over their heads, he had said that Pope was their key to returning home. No, actually he had said that *convincing* Pope was their key to returning home.

But why did he need convincing? Why would anyone want to be in a place where death lurked around every corner? And *did* he need convincing? The plan was to logout after they had killed the raptor and returned to Illdershire. The raptor was dead, they were on their way back to town. That was it, they were about to go back home. Even if this place *was* real, they were about to leave it, they were about to put it all behind them and in a few minutes it wouldn't even matter.

"DANTE!" shouted Alex.

"What is it?" said Dante, annoyed to have his thought pattern derailed.

"I asked 'what do you think?' about Restore Life being a high-level white magic spell that's unlocked later in game, maybe to make dying seem more consequential? But then they offer the spirit crystal spell as a low-level alternative so as not to be too unforgiving?" asked Alex.

To Dante, Alex's words were a mishmash of sounds and syllables that Dante's brain just could not make sense of at the moment.

"Um...I don't... I'm not sure, man I don't know." Dante rubbed his eyes and then his forehead.

"Are you ok?" asked Alex sounding a little concerned.

"Yeah, yeah I'm fine. Um, just... Why not ask Shinto? He's the one who cast the spell." Dante said almost more to the ground then to any particular person.

"Yeah, but Shinto is so standoffish," said Robyn with a shudder.

Shinto walked at the head of the group, leading the way back to town and showed absolutely no interest in the conversation that was taking place behind him.

"I don't think he likes us very much," said Morrigan with a heartless sort of chuckle in her throat.

Dante was still walking in the back of the group. Still racking his brain to reconcile what he had seen and experienced against what he had been told. He felt a pressure inside his head build and bubble until it came spewing out like a volcano erupting in anxious emotional frustration. "Are we logging out in Illdershire?" Dante blurted out, loudly taking most of the group by surprise.

"Um, yeah I think we said that still the plan," answered Alex cautiously.

"I'm not asking you," Dante said. "I'm asking *him.*" He pointed to Pope. "Are we logging out in Illdershire?"

"Well that was the plan, unless you all have changed your minds. I mean, I know I could go for a little break myself right about now." Pope's smile turned to a large toothy grin. "How about you?"

"I think Dante obviously needs a break," said Robyn. "Someone's getting grumpy." She used a high-pitched voice that trailed as it extended the syllables of the wordy 'grumpy'.

Alex slowed down so that he could walk alongside Dante. "Man, are you ok bro? You don't seem like yourself."

"Yeah, I'm fine I – I just need to talk to Stephen that's all."

"I'm sure he'll be waiting for us in the pod room. I mean, with the whole 'time compression' thing, he'll actually have only logged out a few minutes before us, right?"

"Oh yeah, that's right." Dante said bleakly.

"Hey, I'm gonna go ask Shinto about that Restore Life spell. I'll let you know what he says."

But before Alex could begin to move towards the front of the group the walls of the town of Illdershire came into view. They had returned.

When they arrived at the town gate, they were greeted by the same guard that had seen them out of the city a few hours earlier. Dante noticed that he seemed to avoid bringing up the fact that they were one party member short, but the momentary look of realization that crossed the guard's face let Dante know that he took count of their group number and noticed a single adventurer missing. With a solemn nod, he ushered them back into the city.

They passed through the town's cobbled streets and made their way back to the center of town. In front of the Mayor's building, Shinto stopped and told them he would wait for them outside.

"But why? You may as well come in. You've done so much I'm sure I can negotiate an additional share on your behalf," said Robyn.

"No, that will not be necessary." said Shinto, "Please go, see to your business. I will be waiting here when you return."

The group of adventurers, minus one, spilled inside the Mayor's building where they found a slightly surprised Caspian waiting for them.

"You have returned?"

"You didn't expect us to?" said Robyn.

"Oh, there was no doubt in my mind. However, little did I know that you all would be so... efficient." He looked around the group. "One of you is missing?" he said.

"Yes," replied Robyn, "He was gravely injured, we are having a friend see to his wounds while we finish up here."

Caspin stepped out of the room, returning a few moments later with a cart upon which sat eight more money pouches, each one fairly larger than the ones he had given them that morning. "Twenty-five gold each, and a pouch for your injured friend as well. Um, did you bring any proof of victory, as stated in the agreement?"

Alex and Hernandez both reached into the plunder's pouch and together pulled out the severed Raptor's head. The large head's tongue lolled from its mouth and its eyes rolled up into the back of its head, blood and some other as of yet unidentified liquid, dripped from its neck. They dropped it with a loud clunk onto Caspain's desk. The mayor's aide covered his nose and mouth with a handkerchief as his eyes begin to water from the head's stench.

"Why, I think that will more than suffice, I'll take the agreement as well." he said. At which point Robyn handed over the rolled-up scroll of parchment that Caspain had given them earlier that same day. "And we can mark this task as complete. The city of Illdershire thanks you for your service. My compliments to the Adventurers Guild, you are true professionals." Quickly Caspin waved in a number of guards to come and carry the raptor head away, before he himself ran out of the room, desperate for fresh air.

The party was led out of the Mayor's building and as promised, Shinto was still waiting for them exactly where he said he would be.

"Let us go somewhere where we can speak a bit more privately." Shinto said as the party approached. He led them away from the town center, and the crowds and towards northern Illdershire, where the streets were quieter, serene. The came to a clearing facing the interior of the city wall, west of another gate used to enter and exit the city. It was well within visual range, yet still far enough away to offer them the relative space and privacy to talk amongst themselves without turning heads of every passerby anxious to see the adventurers that slay the Alpha Raptor and saved the town of Illdershire.

"It is time for us to part ways." Shinto began before anyone else could speak. "I have business in the north ." The half-orc's eyes scanned over the group. "I know that you all are not of Deos." He paused for a moment as if he wanted the fullness of what he was saying to settle in. "It is my understanding that you all have come here for some sort of recreation. For sport, for some type of 'game'. I regret to inform you that whatever preconceived notions that you may have had about this land have been misplaced. Deos is dangerous, as you all have seen. And as you all have experienced with the near loss of your friend. He has been given a second chance, and in that same vein you all have been forewarned. Leave Deos. Return to Urth. Whatever powers brought you here should be able to take you back and restore your companion as well. Fare thee well. And I pray to the gods that we never see each other again." and without another word Shinto turned and walked away.

"Wow," said Robyn "You think you know a guy."

"Never had an NPC try and talk me *out* of playing a game before." laughed Alex.

"Is that the games way of saying it's time for us to take a break maybe?" suggested Morrigan.

"Oh, that's genius!" shouted Alex.

But Dante just stood there, stunned. If there had been any question, any lingering doubt, it had just turned and marched out like the half-orc. Dante pulled the spirit crystal from his coin pouch. Its rose-pink surface shimmered in the waning sunlight. They had to go home. They had to log off. And only one person could make that happen. Dante looked up to see Pope staring at him, a smirk across his face.

Chapter 12: A New Understanding of Things

Dante turned to Pope. He felt filled with a cold fear that slowly spread, warmed, became a molten magma of rage that filled his throat and erupted from his mouth in a growl. "Take us home now." He said, the seething rage that had started in his stomach now pouring out of his eyes as well as his mouth.

His fist clenched the spirit crystal, and not even fully aware of his movements, he shoved it back into his coin pouch and then marched across the landing toward Pope, stopping roughly some ten feet away from him. "Go ahead, log us out."

"Well," commented Robyn, "this is awkward."

"It doesn't work quite like that." Pope said calmly.

"What do you mean? How does it work?" asked Morrigan apprehensively.

"I have to send a message to the Control Team at Headquarters and tell them that we are ready to log off and then they'll begin to slowly pull us out, one by one."

"Oh, that makes sense I guess." said Alex.

"No, that doesn't make sense," interrupted Morrigan. "That is an absolutely terrible logoff procedure. You're saying we have to wait in queue to *stop* playing the game."

"Well that's the essence of a Beta Test Miss Le Bey, we're still working out the kinks. In the final version of the game the logoff procedure will be much smoother."

"You all keep saying that. But it's not true, is it?" asked Dante in a tone that made it evident that he was not really asking at all. "Ever since we've gotten here, the 'game' itself has run perfectly, but anytime we question about how it all works; you use the catch all excuse that 'we're in a beta test.'" Dante's words came out of his mouth like venom.

Pope merely looked on with his same carefree smile.

"I'm sick of the excuses, log us out and take us home now!" Dante demanded.

Pope only shrugged. "I told you, I have to message HQ first. They have to pull us out, or at least open a portal."

"Portal?" muttered Alex, more to himself then to the group.

"Do it." demanded Dante. "Go ahead and message them right now. We haven't seen any of you contact anybody, not even one time, since we've been in game."

Hernandez begin to shift restlessly on the balls of his feet, while Lansing stared blankly at Dante with cold calculating eyes, blinking every few seconds as if waiting for something. Dante could feel tension in the air begin to thicken with each passing moment. But he didn't care.

Pope continued smiling. "I can't message them here," he said looking around. "And we cannot log out from here either. We'd need to go outside the city, I'd need to start a small fire and then we would have to wait, maybe a couple of hours."

"A couple of hours? To log out?" now Robyn was chiming in.

"Let me guess, another 'Beta Bug' you guys are working on fixing eh?" said Dante.

Pope shrugged dismissively.

"Well I don't believe it. You can take us out of here and you can do it now. So, do it!"

"I'm not really concerned with what you believe." Pope replied. "I've explained to you the situation which is more than I do for most and quite honestly I'm starting not to like your tone."

"Take us out of here now!" Dante yelled.

"No." Pope responded.

The head of every gamer turned towards Pope.

"What do you mean 'no'." said Morrigan.

"Look guys, let's just head out of the city, he can send the message, we'll wait the two hours and we'll log out. It'll be fine. Remember it's not really two hours, there's the whole 'time compression' thing." Robyn was attempting to diffuse the situation, but Dante cut her off.

"There is no time compression." he shouted.

"What do you mean? Stephen explained it. Everything is sped up. Four times normal speed, brain processes faster then something or something." she said.

"That was a lie. They've been telling us nothing but lies. Time Compression, VR Pods, and that story about dying in Deos and waking up at Last Legend Headquarters. None of its true." Dante looked down his nose at Pope as he spoke.

"Dante what are you talking about? Where else would you wake up?" asked Robyn, attempting to laugh off Dante's comments, hoping that he was telling some type of odd joke.

"You don't wake up at all." He said coldly, " Because when you die in Deos you're really dead. Isn't that right, Captain Pope?"

Dante looked at the rest of the gamers. "Stephen told me everything. He told me that we're not in a video game. That we've been sent to an alternate world. That this is not a simulation of a Dragon Dale game. This is the world from which all of the Dragon Dale games are based." Dante looked at Alex, Robyn and Morrigan with pleading eyes, as if he wanted nothing more than for them to believe him. Meanwhile they looked back at him with expressions of horror, and he couldn't tell if it was because they believed what he was saying or if they thought that he had lost his mind. "Don't you see?" Dante took an aggressive step toward the other gamers, the look in his eyes manic. He held his hands out in front of him with his fingers flexed and crooked as if he were strangling an invisible victim. "Haven't you guys noticed, every time someone brings up the issue of logging out, they've conveniently cooked up a new obstacle as to why it can't be done. They need to collect data on the night and day cycles and the camping systems, or now we've gotten a quest so we may as well complete that first, and now it's a message has to be sent and we have to wait for extraction. Next they'll say the system is down and we can't be pulled out right now, we'll have to wait a few more hours. Don't you see. There's always going to be something to keep us from going home."

Seconds passed without anyone speaking and then Alex stepped forward with an outstretched hand, he looked as if he wanted to say something but wasn't quite sure what. No one seemed sure what to make of the things Dante was saying.

Then before anyone could say anything else there was an eruption of laughter. It started as a muffled chuckle but quickly grew to a full-blown outburst before long. Dante looked to find that Pope was letting out a head back, open mouth, stomach clutching laugh that seemed to shake in the chest of everyone around him. For a moment the gamers looked relieved at his reaction. Then he began to speak.

"You know what Dante?" He wiped a tear from his eye. "If anyone figured out what was going on. I suspected it would be Morrigan. But I guess I should have known it would be you." His expression turned dark, and his tone became low and cold. "In a way I'm rather relieved you've finally figured it out. The constant deception and idiotic excuses were becoming bothersome, and now that Stephen is indisposed, it would have been left to me to keep up the charade. I don't suppose it would have lasted much longer if that was to be the case. I don't really care to propagate fairy tales to keep people feeling comfortable about their situation. Face the dark reality of life. Soldier through. That's my motto."

The faces of the gamers sunk into themselves. They stared at Pope in silent disbelief.

"So... you're saying it's true, that this is all... real?" asked Robyn in nearly inaudible words. She looked as if she may cry.

"I knew it." said Morrigan, her hands covering her mouth.

"Yes of course you did," said Pope mockingly. "After Dante has exposed it and I have confirmed it. Turns out you knew it all along." His arrogant smile returning to his face, he looked as if he would burst out in laughter again at any moment.

"But... why *us*?" asked Alex.

"You're a means to an end." said Pope, his eyes cold.

"I don't know what you people are up to, and at this point I really don't care, but Stephen said that you know how to take us back. So, do whatever it is you're supposed to do because it's time for us to go home."

"I think I've already made it quite clear that no one will be going anywhere right now."

Dante pulled his sword from his sheath. The metal blade sung as it rubbed against the lining in the scabbard.

"Take us back, or I'll force you to take us back." Dante said with a look of cold death in his eyes.

Pope looked at Dante as if he were looking at a child. "If you think it will make you feel better, you are more than welcome to try."

Dante rushed Pope, sword high. He brought the blade down recklessly, not sure if he wanted to cleave the captain in two or scare him into submission. Neither plan worked. With unnatural ease, Pope side-stepped the swinging sword and brought a large knee fast and hard into Dante's stomach, lifting him off his feet. One of the girls let out a small scream as the air left his body. He hung there, draped like a rag doll over Pope's knee. For a moment he thought he would vomit, but before he even had a chance to cough, let alone regain his balance from being knocked airborne, a sharp elbow slammed into the center of his back, sending him plummeting face first to the ground. His head hit the hard dirt with a smack and everything in his vision went white. The side of his face buzzed and tingled with a severe sensation of pins and needles. Slightly dazed he scrambled to his hands and knees, but before he could pull himself together a large fist came crashing down into the side of his face hitting him with the impact of a sledgehammer. The blow to the head made the world around him spin, and he feared for a moment that he might fall unconscious.

Panic rose up within him, followed quickly by an overwhelming sense of confusion and disorientation. He wanted to stand, but the risk of losing his balance and falling face first back into the dirt was too great, in addition he didn't want to prompt another attack knowing full well he had no way to defend himself. Instead, he stayed on the ground, frozen on his hands and knees. He dry-heaved and hacked, choking on the same air that he was struggling to breathe. His back, head and abdomen throbbed with pain, and he couldn't help but wonder if he had broken something. He reached up and touched the side of his face, he felt like he was bleeding, but when he pulled his hand away, he found it to be covered in only sweat and the wet grime of the ground. Yet and still, he checked and checked it again, choking out breaths and searching for signs of an open wounds across his aching face

Pope gave only a slight tug to the pant leg of his trousers, pulling up the hem of his pants before squatting down so that he was close to eye level with Dante.

"You know, I had this puppy once, a small little brown mutt that I found in an alley. I brought it home and begged my father to let me keep it, and to my surprise, he agreed, but only under one condition; it was my dog, so it was my responsibility. It's funny, you remind me of that puppy. He was smart, brave and loyal." As Pope spoke Dante could feel his face begin to swell and tighten. "I fed him," Pope continued, "kept him warm, kept him safe, he'd follow me around all day and sleep at the foot of my bed at night. I loved that dog. But as time passed, he got bigger, got meaner, then one day he turned around and bit me. My best friend in the world, who I had plucked from the gutter, had turned on me. The damage was done, I had been betrayed and I was heartbroken." Pope paused, his penetrating blue eyes seeming to concentrate upon Dante with renewed focus.

"That's when my father came to me and told me something. He said that it was all my own fault. That I had brought this on myself because from the moment I brought the dog home, I had been treating him as an equal, and not as a dog. My father explained to me that dogs are pack animals and every dog in the pack falls within a hierarchy of leadership. That these animals, instinctually crave structure and discipline and when you deprive them of that you do a disservice to both the dog and to yourself." Dante's spinning vision had begun to settle, but now his head pulsed with the throbbing pain of an oncoming migraine and he felt a wave of nausea. However, his apparent distress did nothing to interrupt Pope's story.

"Now the lesson in all of this was clear. Keep a dog in a dog's place and you will never have to worry about being bitten." Pope smiled, "An easy enough lesson for the next dog, but what about my dear old puppy who wasn't quite a puppy anymore? Well, kinda like me, my father saw that relationship was ruined, but for different reasons. 'The dog has bitten you,' he said, 'and you may not want to admit it, but now you're afraid of him, even if it's just a little bit, he'll sense that, and once he does, he'll never respect you again, he'll never acknowledge you as pack leader. The hierarchy has been disrupted and it has to be set right,' then he asked me 'You remember what I told you when you first brought that dog home don't cha?' My dog, my responsibility." Pope pulled the dagger from the sheath that was attached to Dante's belt. It was the same dagger he had given him. He pressed the flat of the cold metal blade against the side of Dante's bruised face. Dante winced but didn't move for fear of the blade slicing into his cheek. Pope pulled the blade away slightly and Dante still remained unmoved.

"The dog had been tied up in our back yard since the biting incident, it looked pitiful, all droop eared and tucked tail, looked a lot like when I first found it as a puppy. Looked like it knew what it had done and what was coming. It's odd because me and my old man didn't have much of a relationship but somehow, we sure as hell seemed to have bonded over this. He came out with me, he had a beer in his hand, and right there in front of him, I bashed in my own dog's skull. I killed my best friend and restored the hierarchy. I was 10 years old.

"When the deed was done my father ruffled my hair and called me a "Good Boy" then he told me, 'Remember what you learned here today,' he said, 'Always keep a dog in a dog's place.'" Pope flipped the dagger over and then slammed the blade into the ground inches away from Dante's hand.

"I learned a lot from that day, but as I got older, I learned something else, people aren't really all that different from dogs. Tribes, races, cliques, clubs, gangs, countries, nations, they're all just glorified packs. We like to say humans are social creatures but all that really means is that by our very own nature we're nothing more than pack animals, even if we don't know it, we crave discipline and structure and we all fall into a hierarchy, and just like with dogs, if there is any confusion about who falls where on the hierarchy, it's up to the pack leader to put everyone back in their rightful place and do whatever is necessary to restore the hierarchy." Pope leaned in closer to Dante's bruised and battered face.

"Normally, when a man draws a weapon on me, I kill him." Pope's face was inches away from Dante's. "But, you know something, I like you and in a way, I can understand your frustration. So, I say we just forget this whole misunderstanding ever took place, we let bygones be bygones and we move forward from here with... a new understanding of things. We are in Deos on a mission. You will assist me in that mission, and once that mission has been completed to satisfaction, then and only then will we go home. Do I make myself clear?" Pope's smile was gone. His face was a blank expressionless mask.

Dante had stopped choking but was still trying to catch his breath. He didn't say anything in response to Pope question.

"Here we go with this 'new understanding of things' again." Pope said rolling his eyes. "From now on when I say, 'Do I make myself clear?' You say 'Crystal'. Got it?" Pope grabbed Dante by the scruff of his neck. Alex attempted to step toward the two of the them, but Hernandez stepped in his path and shook his head. "Now, *did* I make myself clear?" Pope asked again.

"Crystal." said Dante through clench teeth.

"That's a good soldier." Pope released Dante's neck with a slight shove.

Pope stood up to his full height and from the corner of his eye Dante could see the captain looming over him and knew, without a doubt, from their current positions he could crush him with a single stomp if he was so inclined, and in that moment he felt as significant as an insect. Dante spat a bit of blood onto the ground, still on his hands and knees. At the top of his vision, he could see his HP bar again, down to half. Three strikes had sent him down to half his Hit Points, and then there was another word within his status box that had not been there before. Right next to his name the word "stunned" was shown in parenthesis. His hands turned to clenched fist, digging into the dirt beneath them. All of his rage and fury had amounted to nothing when it mattered. He hadn't landed a single attack, but instead had ended up half dead and stunned after three unarmed strikes. He hadn't really known what to expect when he confronted Pope, but he hadn't expected it to go like this. And even more terrifying was he had no idea of what to do next.

"Now that we all know the full gravity of the current situation," Pope said to the other gamers again, "We can move forward amicably and efficiently and without all the needless pretenses. This world may be real, but as you all have seen, it operates off the same rules and logic as the video games you all love so much. The nature of my mission requires three things, the gathering of intel, thorough exploration, and the setting up of a forward base. What I need to know is, what are the next step that *you* all would take, to achieve those objectives in game?"

"Wha-what?" Alex asked, confused.

Pope looked annoyed. "Information, exploration and a base of operation, where can I go to begin to get all three? Not to mention the fact that we now must find a way to restore Stephen. That is now a *top* priority."

No one said anything. The gamers were all stunned. Robyn's eyes quivered with unshed tears. With a frustrated sigh Pope pulled his oversized crossbow from his back and pulled back one of its heavy levers. A series of mechanical clicking sounds broke the prevailing silence. The tip of the crossbow pointed at the cluster of silent gamers.

"Abilene Bay," Dante muttered from his position on the ground.

"What was that?" asked Pope. The crossbow now casually drifting over to point at Dante.

"You want to go to Abilene Bay." Dante said through labored breaths. He leaned back to sit up on his knees and wipe spittle from his mouth. Half of his face was still covered in dirt and grime and now the bruising and swelling, from where he had hit the ground and then been struck, were becoming visible.

Morrigan's eyes grew big as if the crossbow and the violence and the news had all registered at once. As if she was just waking from a dream. "Yes!" she said, snapping to life, "Yes he's right. Abilene Bay is one of the largest cities in Deos, you won't be noticed as easily there as we would be here, *and* you can set up an Adventuring Company," she started listing her reasons on her fingers. "They have libraries, taverns and guild offices. You can find information on nearly anything. You can resupply between missions, buy the best equipment, buy mounts and gain access to the airships, which will allow you to travel around Deos much faster. Abilene Bay is the center of the world for adventurers in Deos."

Dante said nothing else but sat back on his heels and let out a breath of defeat and submission.

This all seemed to thoroughly satisfy Pope, who's face returned to its signature smile. He squatted back down in order to come face to face with Dante. "You wouldn't be lying to me now would you soldier? Sending me on a wild goose chase because of those little loves taps I gave you?"

Dante kept his expression cold and emotionless. His eyes and words now dead and devoid of feeling he said, "No sir, it's as you said. We have come to a new understanding of things."

Pope reached down between the two of them and snatched up the dagger still standing upright in the dirt and tossed it back on the ground for Dante to reclaim. He looked at Dante with an expression of both satisfaction and fulfillment, winked at him before muttering in a clear voice, "That's a good boy."

Chapter 13: The Long March Home

Abilene Bay was 300 miles from Illdershire. A five-day journey on foot. And for that reason alone, Pope decided the party would leave first thing the following morning.

By Earth standards of time it would have been a Friday, but in Deos, Dante knew it was actually Skysday.

Sunsday, Moonsday, Starsday, Windsday, Rainsday, Skysday and Godsday. The Desoian days of the week. In Dragon Dale 7, certain magics did slightly more damage during certain days of the week, offering gamers a slight advantage if they waited to take on certain enemies on a certain day, but then again in Dragon Dale 7, a Deosian week was only eight hours long. Dante knew the time compression had not carried over and he sorely doubted that in the world of Dragon Dale Beta certain days of the week carried with them temporary magic skill boost. But then again, he didn't know. He had come to the realization there was much he didn't know.

Internally he decided to refer to his surroundings as Dragon Dale Beta, as opposed to the 'real Deos'. Primarily because the term 'real Deos', the idea of it, the thought of it and everything that it represented, brought to Dante's mind and stomach a feeling of deep despair and unease. He couldn't bear to accept this new reality.

Since the altercation with Pope on the previous day, Dante had not spoken a single word aside from his suggestion that they travel to Abilene Bay. None of the gamers had really spoken. The party had been overtaken by a deafening silence that had seemingly become the new rule of order within the group.

The night of, they had taken rooms in the Thirsty Dragon Inn. Robyn and Morrigan had taken a room to themselves, while Alex and Dante split a room with Hernandez and Lansing. Pope slept alone. Dante had assumed that Lansing and Hernandez were there to keep an eye on him and Alex, to make sure they didn't get any bright ideas, but it wasn't necessary in Dante's opinion. What were they going to do? Where were they going to go? Pope was their ride home. They were at his mercy. He didn't need anyone to stand guard. Reality itself was their prison.

That morning, Dante had woken from a dreamless sleep to find that nearly half of his face, the half that had slammed into the ground on the day before, while no longer swollen, was now severely discolored to a deep shade of purple and black. Large purple bruises had appeared on his stomach and back as well. Without the aid of potions or spells, the healing process on Deos was just as slow and painful as it was on Earth. He made his way down to the tavern on the first floor of the Inn where the others were having breakfast. Pope and his men sat at a table eating toasted bread covered in butter and some type of fruit jam, drinking coffee and having casual conversation as if it were just another day at the office. Morrigan and Robyn however, were sitting at a table alone, separate from Pope and the others, and they were not eating. Robyn's eyes were puffy and red. It looked to Dante as if she had been up all night crying. Morrigan's face was stony and cold, and as Dante entered the nearly empty tavern, she looked up at him without moving her head. Her dark eyes followed his movement from the stairs to the nearby table where Alex sat. He felt her eyes roll over his mangled face. She watched him as if she half expected another outburst, as if he'd once again go into a fit of rage and attack Pope one more time for good measure. But once he took his seat at the table with Alex, nearly half the tavern's distance away from the captain, she returned her attention to Robyn, rubbing her back and stroking her arm in an apparent attempt to comfort her. Alex had been the first to break their unspoken vow of silence.

"I ordered you something to eat." He said to Dante quietly, motioning to a plate of cooked sausages and poached eggs. Dante grabbed a fork and skewered his sausage mercilessly, chewing his food with a quiet and violent ferocity that put in the mind of anyone that may have been watch him the image of a dark and hungry wolf, ravenous and out for blood.

Across the tavern, Pope locked eyes with Dante, held up his morning mug and gave the gamer a casual nod and a smile as if greeting an old friend from across a crowded room. Dante skewered another sausage and began chewing it even harder.

After breakfast the party went back to the item shop to resupply before the 300-mile trek. The gamers roved around the shop in gloomy silence. They now had more coin, but also seemingly less desire to spend it. None of them really seemed to be in much of a mood for shopping, let alone discussing what they might need for their journey. In the end none of the gamers made a single purchase. The combat consultants on the other hand, Hernandez and Lansing, spent their gold liberally. They bought four tents and a set of camping equipment. They stuffed their new purchases in the plunder's pouch and the group made its way to the East Gate.

The town of Illdershire as seen in the light of the early morning sun, as well as in the light of a new dawning realizations of life and death, looked, for lack of a better term... different. The city streets and buildings that had just yesterday seemed wondrous and fantastical were now ominous. The looks from the Illdershire townspeople which had just seemed liked curious glances or even courteous smiles and nods, now looked to Dante like distrustful glares and the malicious bearing of teeth. He found himself walking through town with his hand gripped tightly to the hilt of his sword, prepared at any moment to pull it from his sheath, never knowing when he would be audaciously shoved into some frenzied and desperate fight for his life. Unsure when he would be forced to kill... or be killed.

"Are the saviors of our fair city leaving us already?" said a battered and weathered voice.

He turned on his heels, hand still on the hilt of his longsword, the polished metal gleamed as the first few inches of the blade came sliding out of its guard. Then Dante saw who it was that had spoken, and froze.

Guard Captain Dunbar stood stock and rigid, staring at him, his bearded chin thrust into the air, but his heavily lidded eyes drifted down to the nearly unsheathed sword. Dunbar looked back up to Dante and raised a questioning eyebrow, his gaze lingering on his bruised face.

Dante pushed his sword back into its sheath and relaxed his grip.

Captain Dunbar was not wearing his formal military attire, instead he wore armor. His plate metal chest piece was covered by a cloth tunic that bore the symbol of Illdershire. The fabric billowed in the wind, making him look more knightly and admirable then the guardsmen. From the Captain's waist hung a sword, just as long as Dante's own and looked to be nearly five times as wide, even within its sheath it looked as if Dunbar was walking around with a giant meat cleaver attached to his leg. Dante's eyes drifted back upward to meet the Captain's own.

"Am I correct to assume you all are leaving our fair city?" asked the Guard Captain. His words were calm but his back rigid, his tone adversarial. Dante's hand drifted back toward the hilt of his sword.

Pope pushed his way past the other gamers and stood before Captain Dunbar. With a heavy elbow he pushed Dante backward clumping him in with the rest of the group.

"Good Morning, Guard Captain," Pope said in a robotic voice of a well-trained military grunt. He stood as straight as a steel rod. "Now that our job is done, we figured we would get out of the way and let you get back to running your city sir." At this sudden acquiescence Guard Captain Dunbar seemed to relax. The feelings of tension seemed to dissipate.

"That was good work you all did exterminating those pests. It's a crying shame that they'd given my own men so much trouble." Dunbar looked back at the guards standing behind him who faces flushed red with embarrassment at his admonishment. "I thought I was going to have to leave the city and hunt the things down myself before long, good thing you all came along."

"We're glad to be of service sir."

Dunbar smiled at Pope. "You're different from most sell swords I've encountered."

"Marcus Pope, sir."

"Adventurer Pope. And is this your company?" Dunbar motioned toward the party.

"It is sir." said Pope without looking back.

Dunbar looked over the group with a quick glance, his eyes stopped and narrowed on Dante for a moment then darted quickly to the left of his head. Dante was struck with the sudden feeling that he had just been scanned.

"Impressive," said Guard Captain Dunbar "I suspect you have been formally trained in the art of war, you were a soldier by trade before you became a soldier of fortune?"

"Yes sir, in my homeland."

"The Land of Urth?" asked Dunbar.

"Yes sir."

"What was your rank?"

"Captain, sir."

"A Captain?" A large grin spread across the Guard Captain's weathered face. "Ha, so you know how it feels then? You know what it means to lead men, to be entrusted with duty and honor and the lives of your subordinates as well as the success of the mission?"

Pope seemed to swell up with pride. "I do, sir."

"Yes, yes I can tell. A warrior through and through."

"In the land of Urth, war is taught to all from a young age. We are born from conflict; none can escape it."

"So tell me Captain Pope, what brings you here, why did you leave the army of your homeland on Urth to make yourself a mercenary in this land of strangers?"

"I had a wife and a small child on, or rather in, Urth. I left my nation's army to care for them, turns out sir that I make a much better soldier than a citizen. Civilian life did not suit me well, sir."

"No, I wouldn't imagine that it would."

"When I went back to my old army, well they didn't have space for soldiers like me anymore, there were no more wars for me to fight, all of Urth was at peace. But then someone I know told me about the Land of Deos, told me there was a place where a man with skills like mine could still be of service, so I came."

"You left your wife and child to seek fame and fortune in a faraway land?" asked Dunbar an inquisitive eyebrow raised as if the question were more so a test of character then of curiosity.

"No sir, unfortunately, they had already left me." said Pope with a straight face.

Dante looked at the glittering gold chain partly concealed around Pope's neck and wondered how much of this story that he was telling the Guard Captain was true.

"Quite the interesting journey you have have had Captain Pope," said Dunbar, and with a smile he clapped Pope on the side of the arm. "I have no doubt that one day you will be united with your wife and child, and you shall find the peace that only we true warriors have earned from a lifetime of conflict. In the name of Highender and Hassan may this be so."

"Thank you guard captain," responded Pope with a slight bow.

"Yes of course, speaking of journeys what is your next destination?" asked Dunbar.

"We travel to Abilene Bay sir."

"Abilene Bay. That's five days' travel on foot, but only a day and a half to Black Water."

"Black Water sir?"

"Yes, Black Water, a small lumber town that sits between Illdershire and Abilene Bay, it will be your last place to rest and resupply before leaving the Illdershire Plains and heading into the Black Woods. A word of advice, when traveling through the Black Wood, stay on the Merchant Road. Even for capable adventurers such as yourselves the Black Wood is a dangerous place. Those who stray from the road often do not make it through, only the gods know what horrors lurk in that dark place."

"Thank you for the warning, sir."

"I wish I had more assistance to offer you, but unfortunately advice is all that I can spare at this time. Fare thee well." Guard Captain Dunbar extended a hand toward Pope, who for a moment simply started down at it, as if the offer of a handshake was an obscene and foreign gesture to him, and then before Dunbar could become offended, Pope clasped hold to his wrist. "If ever you return to Illdershire we must have a drink and exchange stories of battles past."

"I would like that very much sir," replied Pope with a slight bow of his head.

The party left Illdershire through the East Gate and began their trek towards Black Water. Dante was sure the name Black Water had appeared in a few past Dragon Dale games, he knew it was a small town, poor from what he could recall, but never significant. What he could remember more clearly were the Black Woods, a large untamed forest spread over hundreds of miles and filled with a high number of wild animals and feral monsters. In Dante's gaming experience it was one of the most hostile and inhospitable places on Deos.

They had been walking for roughly an hour when Morrigan fell into step beside Dante.

"I just wanted to say," Morrigan spoke in a low and gentle voice, different than what Dante was used to hearing from her. "I think it was admirable of you to stand up to Pope the way you did." Dante looked at her out of the corner of his eye, cautious to avoid direct eye contact. "Stupid, but admirable."

Dante wanted to say thank you but managed only a slight smirk. Smiling, even in the slightest, made Dante's sore face ache, and he winced in pain. Instinctively he rubbed a hand across his bruised temple and cheek and his eyes drifted up toward the front of their marching train. Pope led the way as they all walked silently along the Merchant Road.

The Merchant Road was a set of intersecting highways running across the land of Deos, connecting the four major city-states to one another by land. They were the most commonly traveled roadways in Deos, and how a majority of travelers got from place to place. At the end of the Eastern Road sat the Port City of Abilene Bay, on the opposite side of the continent at the end of the western road sat the human city of Dalgonia. To the north in the heart of the

Onin Mountains at the end of the Northernmost road sat the Dwarven Kingdom of Oningrad, and opposite it, at the end of the southern road was El Arden Ka the Elven Kingdom. Illdershire sat in the geographical center of Deos and from their position Dante and his group could use the Merchant's Road to travel to any of the four major city-states in roughly the same amount of time. The Merchant Road cut through hills, mountains, forest, deserts and over rivers, it offered safe and accessible travel across Deos for anyone willing to make the journey, all they had to do was follow the road to their destination.

The bricks of the Merchant Road fit so perfectly close together that only a thin seam indicated where one brick stopped, and the other began. The road stretched for miles and was twenty yards wide, large enough for three large horse drawn carts abreast, and those perfectly laid bricks, looked as if they had been put into place yesterday, even though the Merchant Road was one of the most ancient structures in Deos.

Dante looked down as he walked, but he was not counting the bricks of the Merchant Road, he was contemplating the conversation Pope had with Guard Captain Dunbar. He had told him that he'd had a family, that they'd left him, and that he'd lost his position in the US Army and that's how he ended up here. Dante wondered how much of it was true. Pope was a liar, but the best liars, Dante knew, instilled a bit of truth into their lies. Was there any truth to the backstory that Pope had told Dunbar? And if so, was there anything there that Dante could use against him to get himself and the others back home as soon as possible. He had to be smart. He had to think. He had to find a way home, otherwise he was going to die in Deos.

There was a sound of breaking of twigs or small branches and Dante snapped to attention, his hand shot to the hilt of his sword. No one moved. It was so deathly quiet Dante wondered if the others could hear his heart audibly thumping inside his chest.

A four-legged figure emerged and clopped onto the path. In a wave of déjà vu' it came back to him. It was a deer. This had all happened before. But this time it was slightly different.

It was an Illderstag, a deer the size of a large horse. From its head protruded great antlers, two singular horns that spiraled perfectly, pointing in opposite directions, appearing crafted by the hand of an artisan with great skill. The stag was beautiful yet intimidating. It snorted and hot white breath shot from its nostrils. Its front hooves pawed the ground, and with its vast size and sharp horns, it looked ready to either trample or skewer anyone in its path.

Looks like a deer, is the size of a horse and has the temperament of a bull.

The thoughts popped into Dante's head of their own accord, along with a bevy of other information including the creature's name, level and a full color health bar. Dante had scanned it.

Illderstag, level six. Unlike its female counterpart, this deer did not look skittish or frightened. It stood ten to fifteen feet away from Pope, Hernandez and Lansing, and it eyed them cautiously as their hands moved toward their weapons. It shook its head from side to side, its large horns moving through the air as if to showcase their lethality. At this Pope and his men stopped moving. If it decided to charge, they were too close to it to ready their weapons and attack it before it impaled at least one of them in the process, and from the way it behaved, any sudden movement would set it off.

From the back of the line, thick beads of sweat had begun to form on Dante's face and his bruised cheek and temple ached. He imagined the stag driving its horns through Pope's heart, then felt immediate remorse for the fantasy. Even if it was someone that he hated, and he definitely hated Pope, wishing death on someone, especially when the prospect of that death seemed so visceral and real, simply felt wrong. Guilt and rage twisted inside of him like a cyclone, and in a fit of impulse, Dante pulled his sword from his sheath.

As if beckoned, the Illderstag charged. One by one the adventurers dived out of the stag's path, narrowly dodging the wildly flailing horns and parading hooves. Pope, Hernandez and Robyn jumped to the left. Lansing, Morrigan and Alex jumped right, and Dante the last standing with sword in hand flung himself towards Alex and the others at nearly the last moment. He hit the ground and rolled, stopping flat on his stomach then popping back up to his feet so fast that it was hard to tell that he'd been any position but upright. Which was good because the charging stag cantered, turned and prepared to charge again. This time, Dante was first in line and the focus of the Illderstag's ire.

The stag stared at him with large wild eyes. Eyes that somehow felt familiar to his own, eyes filled with anger, desperation and fear. The stag let out another snort, pawed at the ground and charged.

"Dante," yelled Pope from behind him. "we've got a shot lined up, get out of the way!"

But Dante didn't move. Instead, he let his sword fall from in front of him and allowed it to drop down to his side, still gripped loosely in both hands.

"Dante, move!"

The stag hurtled forward. Dante's right foot slid back and for an instant it looked as if he would break out into a run but then but as quickly as his movement had started it had stopped. Now his feet were spread, as wide as his shoulders, and staggered with his left foot still pointed toward the charging beast and his right foot braced behind him and pointed off into the distance. His blade had been dragged from his side to now sit behind him lolling like a half-forgotten thing, yet still present still dangerous still lethal, like a dragon's tail. The stag increased its speed, dropping its head to lead with deadly twisted horns.

Dante took a deep breath, ignored the screaming from Pope, Alex, Robyn and Morrigan. They were telling him to 'move', to 'get out of the way', and a garbled mish-mash of other things, but in truth he could hardly make out one voice from another, let alone the words they bellowed. The sound of blood rushing and heart thumping was drowning out all other sounds, that is with the exception of the Illderstag's stamping hooves which seemed to be in rhythm with Dante's beating heart. As the stag charged, its four-legged form seemed to momentarily melt away and, in its place, Dante saw himself rushing forward, sword in hand being propelled by nothing more than anger, desperation and fear. The stag was upon him now, he would not be able to run, or leap or dive out of the way, even if he wanted to. And he did not want to. He did not know or understand why, but he could not run. If he was stuck there, if he was going to be trapped in Deos, he could not spend every waking moment also trapped in the emotions of anger, desperation, and fear.

The galloping hoofs faded. Dante took another deep breath and felt volcanic-like energy building within him once again, only this time there was no eruption of empty threats and reckless action. Instead, the magma shot through his veins sending energy through his entire body and extending as far as to his sword, whose hilt grew hot in his hands. The stag charged, and in the moment that it bucked its head forward in an attempt to gore him with one of its beautiful horns Dante swiveled on his left foot, gracefully stepping out of the Illderstag's path, and as the beast blew past him, he squatted into his stance and brought the sword forward in an upward slash so fast and with so much force that the blade became an orange-metal blur as it passed through the section of space where the stag's neck and shoulder should have been.

The stag stopped running, trotted a few more steps forward then turned to face him. Everyone froze. The yelling and screaming had stopped and just as when the Illderstag had first appeared it seemed as if no one dare move. The stag took another step before a red line appeared along its neck and shoulder where Dante's blade had struck. Thin droplets of blood became a spray of red as blood gushed form the wound and the stag fell to the ground in a heap.

"Bro are you freaking kidding me? Critical Hit, One Strike Kill! How did you do that?" screamed Alex in a voice much too loud, even for the outside.

"I-I don't kn-"

"Oh my God Dante, you're a maniac. I thought you were dead for sure!" said Robyn throwing herself into him and wrapping her arms around his neck before burying her face into his chest. He stumbled backwards partly from her weight slamming into him and partly from the surprise of her invading his personal space. He looked down to say something, to find that she was staring into his eyes. Her green eyes sparkled in the sun, and it seemed as if all of the crying from that morning and the previous night had run its course and her face looked to glow, if only slightly, with light and mischievous energy once again. For a moment he thought she might lean in and kiss him. Then a hand popped out from nowhere and smacked him playfully across the unbruised side of his face. "Don't scare me like that!" she said, before walking away from him with her face turned up and her nose in the air.

Morrigan simply eyed him, raised an eyebrow, pursed her lips and then looked away without saying a word. Dante oddly felt approval, followed quickly by judgement followed immediately by dismissal. He felt his face become flush and hot as blood rushed to his cheeks.

"What skill was that? That had to be a class skill! Was that a class skill?" asked Alex excitedly, he looked as if he was prepared to jump into Dante's arms as well.

"No, I don't know. I don't think so." said Dante in a hoarse voice, his throat froggy and dry from lack of use. Those few words were the most he had spoken since his incident with Pope the day before. His silent protest had gone on long enough he imagined, and he couldn't think of what purpose it served other than to remind everyone of the humiliation he had suffered on the previous day and his bruised face was already doing that well enough on its own. "Honestly," said Dante clearing his throat, "I think it was just blind luck."

"Blind luck?" said Hernandez, slapping Dante on the shoulder, "You killed that wolf by yourself and then you killed this thing in one hit. I'd say that makes you the luckiest sword fighter to ever live."

At the sound of Hernandez's voice and the feel of his hand upon his shoulder Dante shrunk back and instinctively reached for the hilt of his sword which had at this point been placed back into its sheath. Alex too took a step backward and let a hand drift eagerly toward his waiting axe. Hernandez, sensing the sudden shift in tension, locked eyes with Dante and kept his hand gripped casually upon his shoulder. Dante felt two quick pumps from Hernandez's hand and then saw his eyes flicker, motioning behind himself. Pope stood a few yards away, staring at Dante and the others, that ever-present smirk on his face. Dante's eyes drifted back to Hernandez, whose own expression appeared to be one of pleading, his eyes were wide, his mouth was narrow.

"Just go with it," he seemed to say. "Play along for now, the Captain is watching."

And Pope was watching, to see if Dante had truly come to heel, or if he still had fight in him. And Hernandez, without words, with a shoulder squeeze and a facial expression was urging him to play along, and really what other choice did he have. Dante's hand moved away from his sword.

"Yeah, I guess so." Dante muttered. His eyes darted back toward Pope, whose smile had now turned to a wide grin.

Pope approached the three of them, Lansing close at his heels as always. Pope squatted down over the carcass of the dead stag and examined the wound, a clean cut, sheared straight through the bone and even the edges of the wound around the fur seemed singed. "Is this edible?" Pope asked without looking up.

Dante looked down at him and knew immediately what he had in mind. "Yes, it is." He answered.

"Good. Hernandez, you help Dante skin and butcher this... horse-deer thing and Alex get the girls and I want the three of you to help Lansing set up day camp and get a fire going. We'll stop here and break for lunch, rest up before continuing until nightfall. No point in letting a good kill like this go to waste." He stood and wiped his hands on a spare piece of cloth he pulled from his back pocket. "Well done Dante, that was some pretty impressive sword work." Pope walked away without so much as a look back over his shoulder.

"Come on," Hernandez said to Dante, giving him a slight tap to the arm, then motioning toward the Illderstag carcass and pulling out a hand axe from his belt, "help me with this. Damn thing is nearly the size of a moose. You have a knife I can borrow?"

Dante pulled the blade he had received from Pope from the small of his back and handed it, hilt first, to Hernandez. In exchange Hernandez handed him his own axe to hold, and with no lack of fervor and enthusiasm Hernandez begin making small cuts in key places on the stags hide.

"Hold that steady." he said to Dante, who as requested began to push down on one of the stag's heavy legs with considerable force, and without warning Hernandez begin yanking at the animal's fur, pulling back its hide and exposing its raw muscle as if he was removing a particularly snug and stubborn article of clothing from a wearer two sizes too big. He continued in this fashion, repositioning Dante, having him hold the stag steady, or repositioning the stag, turning and flipping it with Dante's help, until the carcass was stripped. And once that was done, he took the legs in quarters, cut out the ribs, the flank, the shoulder, which he was sure to tell Dante had been perfectly cut.

"How do you know how to do all of this?" Dante asked.

"My dad used to take me hunting, taught me how to track animals, how to skin'em, process'em. After he died, I kept taking the hunting trips, I guess as a kind of a way to try and stay close to him, you know." Hernandez placed his axe back on his belt and used his forearm to wipe sweat from his brow. He couldn't use his hands; they were covered in blood. "Kind of fell in love with the outdoors somewhere in the process, my old man always said I had a talent for it, never knew the things he taught me would come in handy like this though."

Like neatly arranged blood stained packages, he wrapped the butchered meat in swaths of cloth and pieces of twine then he and Dante begin to place them gently into the plunder's pouch. Hernandez reached down and picked up the remaining butchered leg quarter, the only cut of meat that they had not wrapped in cloth and tossed it over his shoulders. Dante picked up the plunder's pouch, which itself had begun to grow quite heavy and tossed it over his own shoulder. With the heavy leg of venison strapped over his shoulder, encumbered, exhausted and covered in blood, Dante saw an advantage.

"Your father," Dante muttered, as they began to trek toward the waiting day camp only a short distance away, Hernandez didn't seem to hear him, or at least didn't react as if he did. They were barely out of earshot of the others and if Dante was going to act, he would have to act now. "Your father," he said a bit more loudly.

"Yeah, what about him?" said Hernandez, looking over his shoulder but still moving forward. It had taken them nearly two hours to process the stag, and Hernandez had done most of the work. Dante knew he was tired, anxious to get to camp and sit down and rest if only for a few minutes, which is what made now the perfect time to act.

"What would your dad say if he knew you had helped bring people here against their will, and now were helping keep them here, even though you know it's wrong?"

Hernandez stopped walking. He turned on Dante the venison still over his shoulder.

"What did you say?"

"I said, what would your father think about you kidnapping people and bringing them here against their will. About you holding them hostage."

"No one kidnapped you, you volunteered to come here. You got into that pod of you own free will, you created your own avatar for God's sake."

"I got into the pod to play a video game, I created a character to play a game, not to be transported to another world."

"Look, Dante. You're looking at this thing all wrong, you've been given the opportunity of a lifetime, you guys have been playing in a digital version of this world for years and now you're here, you get to be here and explore it and live it, just like the you've always wanted. This is supposed to be a dream come true for people like you." Hernandez spoke as if he simply wanted Dante to understand.

"Is that what they told you?" said Dante coldly, "Is that how they convinced you to go along with this, by telling you that we would be happy to be here, to die here."

"Dante," said Hernandez, exasperated. "I understand you're upset, but honestly its really just a matter of perspective. Captain Pope is tough but he's fair, and like I said before, he likes you. You've just gotta cool it, keep your head down, don't make trouble. Follow orders." Hernandez dropped the stag leg from his shoulder and took a step closer to Dante, his voice lowering in both tone and volume. "Soon enough," he said, in something slightly above a whisper, "We'll be meeting up with the other gamer groups, and when we do, there'll be a lot more combat consultants, I mean, more Dytrous Mobile Security Personnel, more trained fighters, like me and Lansing. There will be more gamers and game guides too. There is strength in numbers, and once we have those numbers the danger for you and your friends goes down dramatically. It'll be the trained soldiers that came here voluntarily that'll be taking all the risk and all you guys have to do is tell us how to navigate this place just like you've been doing. And in the end, everybody goes home, nobody is going to die Dante. Trust me."

"Tell that to Stephen." Dante said and brushed pass Hernandez to camp, where the others waited. Hernandez hefted the stag leg over his shoulder and followed.

Chapter 14: Twilight Council on the Shadow Covered Plains

The smell of grilling Deosian venison filled the small clearing where the group had cut camp. The meat was tender, with a taste like beef. It dripped fat and left a greasy residue on Dante's fingers and lips. They sat in silence, drinking from waterskins and eating their fill. Once the stag leg was nearly shaved to the bone and everyone, including Morrigan and Robyn who had skipped breakfast, had enough to eat, Pope instructed them to break camp.

As afternoon faded to dusk, the party marched east. The Merchant Road snaked endlessly before them and gave no hint of a town or much less the forest that bordered it, anywhere in sight. While they walked, Dante flipped casually through his spirit tome, which he hadn't checked since they were in the raptor's nest. The faint ringing sound in his inner ear had been continuous for nearly a day since the party had returned to Illdershire.

- You have been issued a new quest, "How to Resurrect Friends and Influence People"
- You have been issued a new quest, "The Long March Home"
- You have fulfilled all primary objectives for the quest, "Exterminators for Hire in Illdershire"
- You have gained 2000 Experience points!
- The Illderstag has been defeated.
- You have gained 300 Experience points!
- Sword Technique Rank Up!
- Your Sword Technique has risen to a rank of 'D'
- You have unlocked a ranked skill 'Skin and Butcher'
- Your Skin and Butcher has risen to the rank of 'F'
- You have a total of 8000 Experience Points
- You have obtained Level 5, Congratulations!

The increased level and rank in sword technique as well as the new ranked skill, which stemmed from him helping Hernandez skin and butcher the deer, were to be expected. The mystery, however, were the two new quests. Who had given them to him?

He turned to the Quest, Task and Missions section of the book, and found the entry for the first quest, "How to Resurrect Friends and Influence People"

A member of your party has fallen, as is usually the fate of most who call themselves adventurers, but by some mysterious stroke of destiny, your brother-in-arms has been given a second chance at life and has been turned into a spirit crystal. If you can find a spellcaster or otherworldly being not only powerful enough, but willing to help, you may be able to restore your friend to life.

"That's odd." Dante thought. The quest was about Stephen. It was about resurrecting Stephen. Even though Stephen wasn't a character in the game, or rather a character in the world. When something was a quest in the Dragon Dale games, the events leading up the quest were pre-ordained. Did that mean that Stephen was meant to die from the moment they arrived in Deos? Dante ran a hand across his head in frustration, then searched the same section of the spirit tome for the other quest that he had seen listed in the notification page, "The Long March Home" he read the entry.

You've been had! You've been brought to Deos under false pretenses. And now in a world not your own, you find yourself trapped in a hostile, mysterious and dangerous environment. Allies have become enemies; fantasy has become reality and your solitary hope, to get back to your own world in one piece, is in jeopardy. Your greatest adventure in Deos is at hand and the long march home begins now. You have chosen Abilene Bay as the first destination on your journey, and you have been tasked with looking for information, opportunities for exploration and a place to setup a base of operations. Supposedly attaining these three things will earn your safe passage back to the Land of Urth, but in truth, only time will tell.

Dante's eyes narrowed. Getting back home had become a quest, the main quest. There were even references to their conversations written in the quest description. He wanted to read the entry again. He wanted to analyze it backwards and forwards, dissect it, pick it apart, use it, reverse engineer it and figure out exactly what was going on and how to control it, which he was convinced he could do with information he deciphered from that spirit tome. But he could barely think straight let alone decode a magical book. He was mentally, physically, and emotionally exhausted. His concentration was shot, and he felt like his sanity was holding on by a thread. He simply didn't have the mental capacity to begin obsessing over the inner working of the spirit tome, no matter how enticing the thought might be. Instead, he closed the booklet and allowed it to dissipate in a flash of blue light.

The party continued walking until sun began to sink towards the western horizon and the sky faded from a sparkling blue to dazzling shades of pink, orange and purple. The party, led by Pope, veered from the Merchant Road and wandered some one hundred yards into the vast and open fields of the

Illdershire Plains. They searched briefly for a suitable clearing, one that still gave them clear view of the main road, that was free of too much debris or high grass, and preferably that was close to a stream or source of water, as their waterskins were beginning to feel light after a full day's travel. Fortunately, it did not take long before they found a location that met all their needs. A fallen tree lay strewn about the vast green sea that was the plain and about it lay three or four large stones roughly the size of tree stumps. From it, another two hundred yards further into the plains and away from the Merchant Road there was a small freshwater stream from which they could drink and fill their skins.

"Let's make camp here," said Pope and almost as if in anticipation of his words, Hernandez dropped the Plunder's pouch and he and Lansing begin removing the tents. They gave one to Dante and Alex, another to Morrigan and Robyn. Then they set one aside and immediately begin to pitch the other. The tents weren't much more then canvas tarps and wooden poles, which were apparently more than adequate for Hernandez and Lansing as they rather quickly constructed the first tent on behalf of Captain Pope, they then moved speedily to the last remaining tent. The gamers fumbled through the pitching of their own tents, and by the time the combat consultants had pitched the two, Alex and Dante, and then Morrigan and Robyn had pitched their own.

Their timing couldn't have been more perfect, almost as soon as they had setup their tents and built a campfire, the sun had disappeared behind the western horizon. The illumination cast by the crackling orange flames along with the dying rays of the setting sun offered just enough light for them to pull out and roast another large chunk of the stag meat. There was a long, drawn-out howl in the distance, as in the dimming sky, not one, but two moons begin to emerge, both in the form of large quarter crescents, one a bright green and the other a pale yellow.

"We need water," said Lansing dully.

"Can it wait till morning?" asked Hernandez looking at the darkening sky.

"It could, but it shouldn't, it would be better to have water now. We'll set out again in the morning and we'll be traveling all day, in order to avoid dehydration, exhaustion, fatigue, we need to hydrate tonight, trying to guzzle down water tomorrow when you're tired and thirsty will already be too late."

Hernandez frowned and as if on cue, another howl could be heard in the distance, though this one seemed closer than the last.

"I'll go." said Dante standing up from the rock that he had taken as his seat.

"Go where?" asked Alex who was also sitting on a rock.

"To get water." answered Dante.

"Why?" asked Robyn.

"Because we need it, Lansing just explained that."

"Yeah, but why are you going to get it?" asked both Robyn and Alex almost in unison.

Dante stood there for a moment, contemplating their question before answering. "Because someone has to go."

Pope let out a sound that was somewhere between a grunt and a chuckle but did not look up. He was sitting in the ground near the fire, disassembling and cleaning his large, oversized crossbow. Dante looked over in his direction at the sound of his laugh, but was sure not to let his eyes linger. When he looked back, he saw Alex standing up from his own stone seat.

"What are you doing?" Dante asked.

"I'm going with you; I'm not going to let you go alone."

"No, it's not far away, I'll be right back."

"I don't think any of us should wander off alone, especially as it gets dark, plus it'll be easier for two of us to carry the waterskins."

"No Alex, you stay here. I'll grab the water and come right back."

Alex stared at Dante in confusion. Robyn looked between the two of them as an awkward silence rose up like smoke from the fire. "Wh-what are you talking about?"

"You stay here, I'll go alone, I'll get the water, I'll come back." Dante spoke as if there was a language barrier interfering with the message that he was trying to relay to Alex, which in a sense may have been true because Alex still looked dumbfounded. Morrigan who sat on the log watching the conversation take place, merely closed her eyes and shook her head.

"For Christ's sake, just let him go. He wants to be alone," said Pope from his same position in front of the fire.

Alex looked to Pope then looked back to Dante, whose face didn't show the slightest sense of protest to this suggestion and simply said "Oh," then silently handed Dante his waterskin and took his place back upon his stone seat. Dante collected the empty waterskins from everyone else in the group.

Dante left the camp and headed to the narrow creek they had spotted in the broad light of day. He could hear the streaming water up ahead, and as he walked, he cursed Pope's understanding of his desire to be alone. He hated Pope, yet somehow of all the people he was surrounded by, no one seemed to understand him better. And Dante knew as long as Pope could anticipate his every mood and emotion, he would always be two steps ahead of him. The mere thought of this made Dante sick to his stomach, and once again he was glad that he had come out alone. He needed space and time to plan.

But before he could think, Dante heard a rustling. Instinctively he reached for his sword, but the thin ropes of 9 waterskin bottles strewn across his neck and shoulder impeded his movement and he ended up merely fumbling in the dark and entangling himself in the cords as he fought to get his hand to the sword's hilt. He saw nothing but tall blades of grass lit by the double moonlight. He was still within view of the bright orange glow of the fire from camp. He could run for it if he needed to, or he could shout for help, they could get to him in a matter of seconds. But was there a need. He had only heard a rustle after all. He couldn't go running back to camp or screaming for help based off a sound he had heard, especially after insisting that he go alone.

Dante turned his head away from the far-off flames and back towards the sound of the burbling stream, only to find himself staring face to face with a large snarling wolf whose glowing yellow eyes were the color of the moon and whose black fur was as dark as the night itself.

"Hello again, meat."

Dante froze. All thoughts or running or screaming were immediately quelled and dying as quickly and as painlessly as possible seemed the only logical course of action. Then Dante realized, as odd as it sounded, even in his own head, that he recognized that voice, and upon closer inspection, he also recognized the wolf.

"Well, don't just stand there like frightened prey, my father awaits. Come, he is just on the other side of the stream." The wolf turned and bound off toward the direction of the creek.

They ran through the shadowed covered plains until they came to the water's edge. Janis was so large that his gait was as long as that of a horse and he moved across the plains with startling speed. Dante trudged through the creek which was only came up to his knee at its deepest and was only about six feet across. As he stepped up onto the opposite bank Dante found Janis waiting for him, and along with the disgruntled looking wolf, was an even larger even more intimidating wolf that made Janis look like a cuddly puppy. Canis Romulus.

"The boy returns a conquering hero." said the gigantic wolf in a tone of voice that led Dante to believe that the expression on its face was supposed to be a smile.

"Canis Romulus" Dante said dropping to one knee and bowing his head, not fully sure of how he was supposed to greet the gigantic wolf.

"That is 'Lord' Canis Romulus to *you*, meat." snarled Janis.

"Janis, you will remain silent, or you will remove yourself. I will have no more insults or interruptions." At this the young wolf merely turned his head away from Dante and his father. He did not speak, and he did not move.

"Pardon my son, he is skilled in the ways of the warrior, but is yet unlearned in the ways of diplomacy," said Canis, his large yellow eyes blinking as they focused in on a now once again standing Dante. "As I understand it you are quite the warrior as well. The alpha raptor has been slain."

"Yes, my lord," said Dante.

"You have kept your word, Dante of Urth Land, and I Canis Romulus of the Illdershire Plains, will keep mine. You are a stranger in this land correct?"

"Umm, yes my lord." said Dante finding it odd that the wolf had not only called him by his name, but also knew he was from Earth.

"Then I shall offer a reward greater than a mere alliance. I offer you a place among us as a member of the Illdershire Black Wolf Clan," said Canis

Out of his peripheral vision Dante saw Janis jump to his feet, but the junior wolf kept his silence.

"From this point on, I bestow upon you the title of Black Wolf Dante, and know that if ever should you need it you have the might of the Illdershire wolves at your disposal."

Apparently unable to take anymore, Janis turned and disappeared into the darkness of the night, leaving without a word. Dante turned his head to watch the wolf bound away.

"Pay him no heed, Janis is young, stubborn, he does not understand that our world is changing and that if we wish to survive that we must change with it. You my son represent that change."

"Lord Canis, I am honored," said Dante, still unsure what any of this meant. Perhaps the look of uncertainty showed itself across his face, or perhaps it was the bruises, but one of the two had seemed to pique Canis's interest.

"You claim to be honored, yet your spirit seems troubled, young one. You carry wounds and bruises that I doubt were inflicted by the raptors. You come to me tonight smelling of grief, guilt and shame. Are you already in need of our assistance?"

"Assistance, from the wolves?" the idea finally hit Dante, what he had been offered. The wolves will assist him in his time of need, well, he only needed one thing. "You can help me? If-if I'm in trouble?"

"You have become an extension of my pack, I have chosen to adopt you as a son, it is my duty and obligation to help you and to guide you whenever you find yourself in trouble. This is my reward to you. As long as you are on the Illdershire Plains, you have the strength of the entire pack to aid you."

"I do need help. I am trapped here in Deos. I need to go home, back to Er-back to Urth, but the only person that can send me back refuses. Maybe with your help we could overpower him. Force him to see reason." Dante spat the words out uncontrollably.

"Infighting, among the humanoid pack," said the great wolf appearing to be in deep consideration of Dante's predicament. "You have become engaged in a battle for pack leadership with the current Alpha?" asked Canis thoughtfully.

"No, nothing like that, I mean yes, he is the leader, I guess technically. But I'm not challenging him to become the leader, I'm challenging him so that we can get home."

"You have challenged the leader, so that you may choose which direction the group will be led?" asked the wolf gently.

Dante let out a sigh, "When you put it that way, then yes. Yes, I did." He saw no point in arguing semantics with a wolf on pack leadership.

"Then if I may offer counsel young one, it has been my considerable experience that battles for pack leadership must be won of one's own strength and means. Otherwise we risk bringing disorder and instability to the pack when such victories are brought about by unscrupulous means."

"I have no desire to be pack leader, I just want to go home," said Dante and he felt as if he were about to break down there in the dark, in front of the great wolf, the two moons and every unseen thing in the plains.

"Yes, my son, but often it is not what is wanted, but what is needed that matters."

What is needed? Dante thought. What could possibly be needed that would force Dante to fight Pope for pack leadership. Pack Leadership. Dear God, he was even thinking like a wolf now. But what could he do? If the wolves wouldn't help him then he was right back in the same position he was in before. He dropped down to his knees, sure that he had never been more lost than he was in that moment.

"Dante," said Canis, his deep voice rumbling through Dante. "If it is your request, the Illdershire Wolves will wipe out your enemies. As I said, you are an extension of my own clan now and it is my duty to aid you, but as I also stated, it is my duty to offer you guidance and counsel as I would my own son. On a hard and difficult journey, there are no quick and easy detours, that's because the life of a wolf is meant to be hard, and the longer and harder your life has been, the more successful you have been as a wolf. Only dogs have an easy life. I will aid you along either path. But *you* must choose the path: Black Wolf Dante, or Dante the Dog."

Dante arrived back at the campsite a short time later, dragging along with him the cumbersome refilled waterskins. He dropped them down into a slump into the middle of the camp.

"How did it go?" asked Robyn. "Did you have any trouble?"

"No trouble." Dante replied.

"Did you get the alone time that you needed?" asked Morrigan, her voice dripping with false sincerity.

"I got exactly what I needed," replied Dante who then took a slice of the freshly cooked stag meat from near the fire, found a seat outside of his tent, and said nothing else for the remainder of the night.

Chapter 15: Black Water, Black Wood

Dante woke the following morning with the sensation that everything he had experienced over the past few days had been a fever dream. When he opened his eyes to the interior of a hastily pitched, drab green tent, he felt the cold dark sting of reality. A gentle blue glow, and the sound of morning birds filtered into the tent from the partially open entry flap that lay at one end. Dante turned his head to find a modestly bearded dwarf sleeping a few feet away, tucked snugly into his bed roll and hugging his axe and shield. Alex let out a loud snore that almost masked the sound of rustling outside the entrance of the tent. He turned back toward the tent's entrance and crawled slowly and quietly toward the opening, careful to not make a sound, though he wasn't really sure why.

If someone was outside his tent rustling around, it was most likely someone from the party who had gotten up early and had already begun to clean up the campsite, either that, or some animal had wandered into the camp in the early hours of the morning scavenging for food. Probably attracted by the smell of the roasted stag meat, probably some type of carnivore. In that case, Dante decided that a quiet crawl was indeed the most appropriate course of action, and then he even went so far as to begrudgingly pull out the dagger given to him by Pope, just to be safe.

Dante aligned his eye with the tent opening, careful not to move it. He half expected to see the Deosian equivalent to a skunk or racoon or some other type of large rodent roaming about the camp, instead he found Pope. He was sitting in front of the fire, which was alive with small flames that flickered hungrily in the light of the dawn. Amidst the tumbling of the fire, something sparkled in the sunlight. It appeared to be a large brass ring. Pope sat in front of the flames, huddled over himself with what Dante noticed was a piece of parchment, a quill and a small well of ink. It was early but the light was ample, and the morning air was warm, so Dante knew that Pope could not have needed the fire to see or for warmth, so why was he crouched over himself writing a by a campfire in a brass ring during the wee hours of the morning?

Pope hastily scribbled something onto the scrap of paper, put down his quill and then placed the message into the fire of the brass ring and sat quietly as it burned into ash. In a matter of seconds, the paper was gone and in nearly the moment after that, Pope used his waterskin to douse the flames, extinguishing them before reaching into the fire pit and removing the metal ring.

"What are you looking at?" asked a thick gravelly voice from behind Dante. The words seemed to emerge from nowhere, and in doing so nearly sent Dante flying out of his skin and the tent. He turned around with the dagger in hand raising the blade in a wide defensive arc, moving it with reckless and lethal speed. At the other end of the weapon, he found a wide-eyed Alex, awake and staring at him, just as surprised as he was. "and what are you doing with that knife?"

"You scared the crap out of me." Dante exclaimed lowering the blade and at the same time attempting to slow his racing heart.

"I could say the same to you," said Alex, "I don't think I've ever had a knife pulled on me before breakfast before."

"Sorry about that," Dante replied, "I guess I'm still a bit on edge."

"No, I get it. I think we all are. This... these past few days have been... unreal. It's been a lot to process, and I think we all have just been dealing with it in our own way." Alex swallowed hard. "I'm sorry, you know... if you feel like I've been crowding your space, I know we hardly know each other, and we've all been kind of thrown into this situation together, and I have this tendency to kind of latch on to people and just-"

"Alex, there is no need to apologize. If anything, I should be apologizing to you. I'm sorry about last night. I just needed a minute to clear my head, it wasn't anything against you personally. Honestly, I think you have the right idea, if we stand any chance of getting out of this mess, we're going to have to stick together. And I for one, think you and I work fairly well together, and If I were a betting man, I'd say I like our chances." Dante extended an open hand towards Alex, who for a moment simply stared at it, as if he was unsure of what to do. But then after a moment a smile dawned across his face, and he reached out and began shaking Dante's hand vigorously.

Just then Hernandez stuck his head through the tent flap. His eyes darted around the interior of the small tent at the center of which Dante and Alex sat curiously shaking hands. He started at the two of them for a moment, then blinked. "We're breaking camp and heading out in five. Get a move on."

Within the hour, the party was once again back on the Merchant Road and en route to their destination. They marched through the morning with little to no incident and only minimal conversation.

"When you were out getting water yesterday, we were looking at our spirit tomes and comparing notes." Robyn said to Dante as they walked. "We're level five now, and we've unlocked new abilities!"

"You what?" Dante said surprised at this second piece of information.

"When you killed that stag yesterday, it gave us all enough experience points to get to the next level and it just so happens that level five comes with new job abilities. I guess technically we all should be thanking you. You did all the work, but since we're all in the same party, we all gained a share of the experience."

Dante looked up and over at Morrigan. She was not looking back at him and she was not smiling. He knew from their first in-game battle that she did not like receiving unearned experience points and apparently learning that they were in fact not inside a game but in a world where survival depended on growing stronger didn't seem to change her opinion in the slightest. Dante felt Robyn nudge him gently with her elbow. He looked back down at her brightly smiling face, she was standing inappropriately close to him as they walked. He smiled back at her but took a few extra steps to put a small amount of distance between the two of them. Her smile grew even larger.

"So, what new abilities did you guys unlock?" Dante asked, attempting to steer the conversation away from awkward smiles.

"Thought you'd never ask," Robyn replied, pulling from behind her back a familiar looking dagger and coin purse. Dante stared at the two items for a moment, and then looked down at his own waist. He felt the small of his back and ran his hands across the place where his coin pouch used to be.

"Hey! Is that my stuff!?" he said, trying to figure out at what point in time could she have taken both his knife and his coin pouch without him knowing, and then he realized it. The nudge. "Did you just pick-pocket me?" Dante asked, partially shocked but mostly impressed.

"I unlocked the 'Nimble Fingers' ability and the 'Sleight of Hand' skill, I can use it to appropriate items from their owners, pick locks and a number of other very useful things. Not to mention, 'Sleight of Hand' is a ranked skill so the more I use it the better I get." Robyn looked as if she was about to burst with excitement. Dante had never seen her so happy; and in an odd way he found this comforting.

Dante was familiar with the 'Nimble Fingers' ability, it was a job ability usually unique to the Rogue class. When used in past Dragon Dale games it granted the player a temporary yet dramatic boost to their sleight of hand skill allowing them to pull off task that required agile and precise hand movement. Need to steal a key from a guard's belt, disarm a trap or open a particularly stubborn treasure chest? Then suddenly the 'Nimble Fingers' ability and anyone able to use it, quickly became indispensable.

Robyn tossed Dante his coin pouch and knife. He caught the pouch and then yelled out a swear word as he tried to catch the knife without grabbing hold to the blade. Robyn, Alex, Morrigan, Hernandez and even Dante himself laughed and cheered when he did manage to catch the knife with cutting himself. He took a small bow at the applause he received and then placed the knife back in its holster on his back.

"Alex, tell him what you got." Robyn said to the dwarf.

"I unlocked the 'Shield Bash' and the 'Helm Splitter' ability."

"Wait," said Dante, "You unlocked two abilities."

"And," Alex continued, "I now have shield technique as a ranked skill and axe technique as a ranked skill."

"You unlocked two job abilities and you unlocked two ranked skills?" Dante asked.

"So did I," chimed in Hernandez. "Only I didn't get 'Helm Splitter' I got a thing called 'Sword Dance,' but I did get 'Shield Bash'." Hernandez who normally walked at a speed that allowed him to keep pace with Pope and Lansing had slowed down just enough to fill in the gap of space that usually hung between the combat consultants and the gamers, and by doing so he was now able to inject himself into their conversation with relative ease. For a moment the gamers simply looked at him without speaking. Then they looked at Dante.

"Well," Dante said, not really sure why he had to be the one tasked with breaking up both the silence and the awkwardness currently taking place. "'Helm Splitter' is an ability unique to axe wielders, like Alex. You fight with a sword, so that's why you unlocked the 'Sword Dance' ability."

"Oh ok, that makes sense. And I'm guessing since we both carry shields, that's why we both got 'Shield Bash'?" said Hernandez.

"Well, that and because both of you guys are the Battle Guard class." Dante said. "You are versatile frontline fighters who can use a variety of weapons. Swords, axes, hammers, spears, but the shield is always essential to your class. At least in the early levels."

"So, since we're the same class, we get some of the same abilities, like 'War Cry' and 'Shield Bash' but since we choose different weapons, we also gain some unique abilities," said Hernandez, catching on fast.

The Battle Guard Job class concept was simple, you're a warrior, with a shield in one hand and a weapon of your choosing in the other. With your weapon arm you hack away at your enemies and with your shield arm you defend yourself from their attacks. Complexity occurs as key decisions made by the player effect the outcome of the character.

"Now the 'Shield Bash' ability is pretty easy to wrap my head around, I assume it simply allows me to whack things with my shield, but for the life of me, I can't figure out what a 'Sword Dance' is supposed to be," said Hernandez looking a little defeated at the admission.

"Oh that," said Dante, "well, 'Sword Dance' boost your mobility and attack power, or basically your speed and strength, but only for a short time. It's a really good ability, it carries over well to the higher levels."

"Oh ok, well that's pretty cool too then." said Hernandez, now looking quite pleased with himself.

"What about you Morrigan?" said Dante, "what did you unlock?"

"You first," Morrigan replied, her tone light, almost playful, but her eyes as cold and as penetrating as ever.

"What do you mean?" asked Dante, still smiling.

"I mean, everyone is telling you what abilities they've unlocked, but I'm anxious to hear what abilities you've unlocked. You did reach level five like the rest of us, didn't you?"

"I did, I mean, of course I did," Dante hesitated. "I didn't unlock any abilities when I hit level five."

"What do you mean you didn't unlock any abilities, what about that glowing sword thing you hit the stag with?"

Dante looked puzzled. His sword attack on the illderstag *had* felt odd, the sword handle had felt hot in his grip and then the blade did that thing where it became nearly as light as air, the same as it had done when he was fighting the wolf. But that couldn't have been an ability skill, could it?

"I don't- I don't know anything about a glowing sword. Honestly, I'm not really even sure how I did that whole 'one-shot-kill' thing with the stag, in truth it all kind of just happened. What I do know is that my spirit tome did not mention any new unlocked abilities for me at level five. The only ability I've unlocked is 'Scan' and then the 'Sword Technique' ranked skill but both of those were at level two."

"You didn't get anything for hitting level five?" asked Robyn astounded.

"My sword technique rank went up from 'F' to 'D'." said Dante, more so as if he were asking for approval than stating a fact.

"I think your character is broken." replied Robyn sarcastically.

"So, you expect us to believe that *you*, the Dragon Dale Gaming Golden Boy, performed an attack that killed an Illderstag in one hit and you have no idea how you did it? And even more than that, you're telling us we've been in Deos for the past few days and the only ability you've had access to is 'Scan'?" asked Morrigan, sounding mildly annoyed.

"Yes," said Dante, who too was beginning to sound annoyed.

"You're a Sword Disciple, which is a class that has never been playable in any of the past Dragon Dale games," said Alex. "Maybe this job class doesn't progress like the others."

Suddenly, Dante remembered something. "Sara, the woman that helped me at character creation, she mentioned that the Sword Disciple class was difficult to play in the early stages. She actually suggested that I play something different, but I refused." Dante thought back to that moment in the character creation room, when he was walking away with his completed keycard and Sara called out to him. He had been too excited about the beta, to blinded by his desire to play a stupid video game that he hadn't realized she was trying to tell him something. But now looking back he knew. He knew because he could recall clearly the look that had been on her face when he turned around was the same look that had been on Stephen's face. And when he thought back, the only thing that stopped her from saying anything was the same thing that stopped anybody from doing anything in regard to this world. It had been Pope.

"Earth to Dante!" said Morrigan abruptly.

"Wha?" said Dante confused, he had begun staring at the back of Pope's head as they walked and somehow forgot all about the conversation, they were in the middle of having.

"I was saying," said Alex, "you probably unlock your sword disciple abilities by some means other than level, like maybe it depends on your sword technique rank?"

"Oh, yeah... maybe." Dante replied. He hadn't given much thought as to why he wasn't unlocking abilities at the same rate as the other adventurers and perhaps if he were still under the impression that this was all an extremely elaborate video game, perhaps he may have been somewhat concerned. But currently as it stood, his priorities simply were not centered around unlocking abilities. His one and only priority was getting home, and in his mind, the sooner he was able to do that, the less it would matter what abilities he did or didn't have.

The sun was high overhead and the group had been walking for hours. In the distance, towards the direction in which they traveled, a large dark tree line appeared. And even though it was still some ways away, this rapidly emerging forest wall stood out in stark contrast to the open blue sky and wide rolling fields of the Illdershire Plains that bordered it. The dark trees that made up the wood seemed less like gentle plants that grew up from the soil silently and slowly over time, and seemed more like giant black spears covered in green leaves, spears that had both suddenly and violently jutted up from the ground in an attempt to impale the sky. The sight of the far-off tree line made him think of the man-eater plant and he wondered what types of horrific monsters lurked underneath the boughs of those black trees. His stomach lurched. Rarely had a place been so adequately named, he didn't need a map or a guide to tell him what he was looking at in that moment, it was undeniable.

"The Black Woods! We're almost there." said Robyn, not sounding nearly as concerned as Dante felt.

"Which means we're almost to the town of Black Water as well," said Alex.

"Thank the Goddess," said Morrigan, "I'm tired of walking and I'm tired of deer meat. I need a bowl of vegetable soup, a hot bath and a warm bed."

"I'll have what she's having," said Robyn.

"Glad you all are back to having a good time." said Pope his voice cutting through the air like a blade. Dante was convinced he felt the temperature of the plains drop by a few degrees.

"When we arrive in the town of Black Water, we will rendezvous with a number of other parties. That means more combat consultants, more game guides and more gamers."

Dante's eyes darted over in the direction of Hernandez, who he was sure was purposely not looking back at him. "It goes without saying," Pope continued, "but your fellow gamers will not be aware of the alternate world theory or the reality of it. I intend to keep it that way." Pope's smile faded. "I'm only going to say this once, you all are expressly forbidden from discussing the nature of this world with other gamers. As far as they are concerned this is still a video game and there is no reason for them to think otherwise."

"No reason for them to-" Morrigan seemed too surprised, almost too angry to speak clearly, "So you've been lying to us and now you want us to lie to other gamers as well? Why would we agree to that?"

"If you want to go home you then you'll lie, cheat or steal, if necessary," Pope replied calmly. "Do not tell anyone the truth about Deos." Pope's eyes scanned the group of gamers before him and then rested upon Dante. "Insubordination will not be tolerated." He said with an air of finality before he turned around and continued walking toward the far-off tree line.

Unlike Illdershire, Black Water had no outer wall to separate civilization from the wilds of the surrounding environment. Instead, there was a large wooden edifice that stood constructed over the Merchant Road. The wooden arch and entryway, served as makeshift gate into the town of Black Water. Extending from either side of the archway was a hastily constructed and poorly maintained wooden post fence. It ran along what Dante imagined were the boundaries of the town, but considering their poor state of repair, he doubted they were meant for either defense or protection of any sort, instead they seemed to be there only as a reminder of where the town itself stopped and the Deosian wilderness started. Not that much of a reminder was needed. Inside the fence, which meant inside the town, everything in the realm of plant life, was either dead or dying. No grass grew within the confines of the Black Water fence, but outside it, the vegetation grew lush and viscously. The town itself looked as if it were fighting attempts to be swallowed by the large ominous forest that loomed over its eastern half. The tall dark trees from the Black Wood cast a shadow that covered the town in its entirety, giving the impression that the town was perpetually overcast by clouds.

Black Water was small compared to Illdershire. As the players entered through the unmanned and unguarded western gate, Dante was sure they would have been able to see clear to the other side of town to the eastern gate if the town itself had not obscured it from view. It could not have been more than 300 yards from end to end. In addition to being covered in a thin layer of dirt and grime, everything in the village seemed to be crooked, leaning or lopsided. The buildings, mostly one-story hovels and cottages were built of brown stone and a wood so rich and dark, that even from up to a few feet away it appeared black. Black Water was depressing. The people waded through the streets sluggishly, looking just as crooked and lopsided, just as grimy and dust covered as their buildings. No one noticed the adventurers, and those who did pass a glance looked entirely disinterested.

"So much for a hot bath and a warm bed." said Robyn.

"More like a mud bath and an order of bed bugs." replied Morrigan looking around at the dank and desolate town.

"Maybe you can still get that bowl of soup at least," said Dante with a fragile smile. Morrigan looked up at him and allowed the smallest hint of a grin to cross her face.

The party followed Pope through town to the doorway of a large ramshackle building. It was, from what Dante could tell, the largest building in Black Water, and appeared to be the town's one and only tavern and inn.

"Welcome to The Sipper and The Sapling." said a short balding human with a thick bristly mustache and a large round pot belly. The man was smiling as he spoke, but looked far from happy. He seemed frazzled and worried and the sight of seven new patrons at his tavern door seemed only to make him all the more anxious. "Please have a seat, someone should be by to help you in just a minute." He said, falling over himself as he scurried across the bar, picking up empty mugs and righting overturned chairs as he went.

The inside of the tavern like the rest of the town was a mess. The Sipper and The Sapling looked as if it had just recovered from rather large and raucous party the night before. The barmaid, who didn't seem the least bit interested in hiding her sour disposition, was sweeping a pile of broken dishes into a small heap in a corner of the room. Dante noticed that there were other heaps of broken things in other corners of the room.

"Grab a seat, rest up, get something to eat, the others should be here before long." said Pope. The captain pulled out a chair from a nearby table and took a seat. However, when Alex reached for a chair at the same table, Pope's thick arm shot out like a rocket, pinning the chair in place and causing each one of the gamers to jump in reaction. "We'll sit here... you all can find a table somewhere else," said Pope.

"Sure," Alex said fretfully, "no problem."

Lansing and Hernandez took their seats at the table with Pope while Dante, Alex, Morrigan and Robyn made their way cautiously across the tavern to find a table of their own. The Sipper and the Sapling was for the most part bare of any other patrons. There were three men sitting at the bar, who would occasionally steal glances over their shoulders to shoot dirty looks at the four strangers making their way across the center of the tavern. There was also a couple of locals sitting at a table in the far northwestern corner of the tavern, distinguished by their brown dirt colored clothing and by the thin layer of dust and grime that covered the outer layer of their pale skin. Dante and the others grabbed a large open table in the far northeastern side of the tavern, near the bar, which sat behind them, but about as far away from Pope as they could get. They were also parallel with the tavern front entrance allowing them to see who came in and out of the building with relative ease.

"Geez, what do you think that was about?" Robyn asked, looking back over at Pope's table.

"Just more pointless alpha male posturing I'd say," said Morrigan.

"More so like a firm separation of roles in my opinion," said Dante. He looked over at Pope's table. "The prison guards." He muttered before looking back at his own table and into the faces of his fellow gamers, "and the prisoners."

For a moment they were all quiet and in that time Dante worried that he had said too much, if he had made everyone feel worse than they already must have been feeling with his doom and gloom observations. And then when it looked like Alex was going to say something there was a loud bang from behind them, from behind the bar. Their heads snapped to attention in unison only to see coming from a hastily opened door in the back of the tavern a fair skinned, dark haired woman carrying a large tray balanced with both food and drink.

Unlike everyone else they had seen in the town she was not covered in a thin layer of dirt and as a result her skin seemed to give off light by comparison. She looked strikingly similar to the other barmaid they had seen, if not only younger, more vibrant and if Dante was being honest radiantly gorgeous.

"It's rude to stare," said Morrigan flatly, and though Dante wasn't completely sure if she was talking to him or Alex, who he noticed was also looking a bit bashful, he still quickly looked away from the young woman and placed his eyes ruefully on the weathered wooden table in front of him. Behind them, the men at the bar had also seemed to come alive since the arrival of the beautiful young bar maid, and since Dante was purposefully not looking, he could not see them, but he could hear them.

"E'llo Liza!" said one of the men in a gnarled and gruff voice, doing his best to try and sound upbeat and cheerful.

"Hey there Liza!" went another. The man in the middle.

"How's it Liza!" said the third and last man, rushing not to be left out.

"Afternoon Mr. Arnum, Mr. Bailey, Sir Gus. Another round for the three of you?" replied the young woman.

"Whenever you get a chance me luv, and this round'll be on me, you know these two get grumpy when they don't get enough grog in their bellies." replied the scruffy voiced man with a forced chuckle.

"Sure thing Mr. Arnum, I'll grab that for you in just a moment."

"Liza, you know better than that. Call me Phineas."

"Hello there, you all look like new faces," said Liza. She was even prettier up close and Dante suddenly found himself at a loss for words. "Welcome to The Sipper and the Sapling, my name is Eliza, can I get you all something to eat or drink?"

Dante's mouth was dry, making it much harder than normal for him to speak, while Alex had turned a bright shade of red and was smiling goofily, an odd thing to see from a dwarf.

"Ahem," said Robyn, clearing her throat loudly bringing both boys back to reality. "I think we're interested in food and drink," she said, "but do you have a menu we could look at?"

There was a rude grunt from the direction of the bar and Dante was sure that it was from Mr. Arnum. Eliza ignored the grunt and instead replied to Robyn with a smile.

"Well, I don't have a menu, but I can tell you what we have available. As far as supper goes, today we've got roast hen with lentils and succotash it also comes with nut bread and mince pie all for two silver each, but it's all really good, and I don't mean nothing by it, but if you think you might want some of them vittles you gotta let me know quick because we only got so much and lately we been getting mighty busy in the evening and we always seem to run out before long. Now as for drink we have a number of options, we've got grog, we've got mead, and we've got ale, lagers and stouts. They're all four copper a mug so as far as their concerned you can just pick your poison." said Liza, her smile still as warm and welcoming as ever.

"We'll all do supper," Robyn replied. "And honestly, I'd really just prefer water over grog, mead, or ale. Especially considering I'm not really sure what the difference between any of them is."

Eliza giggled. "Oh well that's no problem at all," she said, "I'll bring out a pitcher of fresh water with your food. Nothing else to drink for anyone else?"

"Do you have anything with peregrine fruit juice in it?" said Alex, who seemed to have had managed to regain his ability to speak once again.

For a moment Eliza looked shocked and then her large warm smile came back bigger and even brighter than before and for a moment Dante thought that even she looked flushed. "Well actually," she began, "our grog is made with rum, which is made from Peregrine Fruit. It's the local favorite." She said pointing her smile casually towards the direction of the men sitting at the bar. Dante looked over his shoulder to find Mr. Arnum, Mr. Bailey and Sir Gus looking back in his direction, but instead of the angry glares that they had worn earlier they were instead now sporting slightly confused looks of suspicious bewilderment. Apparently, whether he knew it or not, Alex was on to something.

"I'll have the grog," said Dante abruptly.

"As a matter of fact, a mug of grog for each of us," he corrected himself.

"I don't want that-" Morrigan began, but before she could finish the statement Dante placed his hand over her hand and looked her squarely in the eye.

"Morrigan trust me," he said attempting to keep his voice flat and still "you're going to love the grog." Dante spoke words that he knew were liable to send Morrigan into tailspin, but he hoped that what his words didn't communicate, his eyes did. There was some odd hostility in Black Water being aimed towards outsiders and for whatever reason, Alex's obsession with Peregrine Fruit and the townsfolk's obsession with grog seemed to be instrumental in diffusing it.

At Dante's words and the touch of his hand Morrigan froze, she stared back at Dante and for a second, he thought she might explode in a fireball of fury and magic but then her eyes narrowed, then she pursed her lips and shrugged her shoulders and simply said,

"Okay."

"Well alright," said Liza, "four suppers and four grogs, I'll get right on it." Liza left the gamer's table and began making her way across the tavern towards Pope's table. The men at the bar were looking back at the gamers, when Dante made eye contact Mr. Bailey and Sir Gus turned back around in their stools facing the bar and the short fat mustached man who had now made his way back behind the counter. Mr. Arnum however held eye contact with Dante a bit longer than the others and then held up his mug and gave an approving nod before turning back around to rejoin his friends.

"Don't say I've never done you any favors." Morrigan said with a sly smile that made Dante uncomfortable.

"What?" said Dante, taken aback by this comment.

"You obviously needed a wing man, or rather a wing woman, so I did you the favor and played the part and agreed to let you order me that grag or crog or whatever it's called."

"It's 'grog' and allowing me to order you a drink is not fulfilling the role of wing man."

"Wing woman." Robyn corrected.

"Besides, I didn't need a wing man or a wing woman becau-;"

"Oh, you needed something because you were crashing and burning my friend." Morrigan interrupted.

"Dude why didn't you ask me to be your wing man?" said Alex from across the table.

"Because he was to busy stealing your grog idea." said Morrigan.

Dante let out an exasperated sigh, "I didn't need a wing man, or a wing woman because I was not making a pass at anyone. I did not order the grog to impress our waitress."

"Bar maid," corrected Robyn.

"I did it," Dante muttered through clenched teeth, "to diffuse the tension between us and the locals. They've been very hostile towards us ever since we've entered into town."

"Hostile, hardly anyone in this town has said more than two words to us." said Morrigan.

"Exactly," responded Dante, "but they haven't been as stingy with their dirty looks. Listen I'm telling you this town has some type of issue with either adventurers or outsiders or something, but the moment Alex mentioned peregrine fruit the entire vibe of the room changed. That's why I ordered the grog."

"So, you're saying that it had nothing to do with the pretty girl?" Morrigan asked.

"No, the waitress being pretty had nothing to do with me ordering the grog." Dante said clearly and deliberately, even to his own ears it sounded insincere and forced

"That's good to know, but the drinks are still four copper a piece all the same." Liza said. She had returned to the table with a large smile on her face. Dante's eyes grew wide, and his face felt so flush with blood he was sure that his brown skin had turned just as red as Alex's had been earlier. Eliza's tray held four pewter mugs overflowing with a steaming amber liquid. With a flick of her wrist and a tip of the tray the mugs slid nimbly onto and across the table stopping just short of each of their respective patrons. Had Dante not been so overwhelmingly embarrassed he would have undoubtedly taken a moment to be impressed, but as things were, he was still a bit busy loathing Morrigan.

"Can I ask you all something?" asked Liza who was now holding the tray with both hands. "I hope you don't take offense or consider it rude, but I just have to ask, are you all from Urth Land?"

"Um, yes." Morrigan answered.

"Well by Hathor, I just have to say, you all have really been like a breath of fresh air. We've been getting a lot of Urthlander Adventurers in here lately and I'll just say, they have been rubbing a few people the wrong way but you all, you all really seem like good folk."

"Thank you," said Robyn softly. Then with a smile and a nod Liza walked away.

"Well," said Morrigan, looking at Dante "to think I just thought you were being paranoid."

Dante grabbed his mug and took a large sip of the warm golden liquid inside it. As it entered his system he felt like a small bit of his worries and concerns melt away with every swallow. He looked at the mug and then looked back over his shoulder at the three men sitting up at the bar. They were all turned to look at him, each of them with a mug in hand. Dante took another sip of his grog, felt another problem melt away and then lifted up his mug and nodded his head in the direction of the three men at the bar. Mr. Arnum, Mr. Bailey and Sir Gus lifted their mugs and returned the gesture with a nod of their own, then without a word they turned back around in their stools to face the bar.

It was about then when a rather large group of loud and unruly adventurers entered into the tavern.

Chapter 16: The Other Urthlanders

Dante heard them before he saw them. The Sipper and the Sapling was now nearly a third of the way filled with what looked like the local townsfolk of Black Water, but the townsfolk are not what prompted Dante to turn around for a clear view of the tavern entrance. 15 to 20 adventurers entered the door in a large hulking mass and then quickly spread about the place like a festering wound distributing infection through an unsuspecting the body. They barreled through the tavern door, screaming obscenities at one another, while bumping clumsily and rudely into both people and furniture with neither acknowledgement nor apology to either.

At the forefront of the unruly band of new customers was a woman. She stood in stark contrast to the others around her with pale white skin and raven black hair. Hair which she had stylishly cut so that bangs covered her forehead and long swooping sides perfectly framed her model like face. She looked like, someone Dante imagined, he'd see in a café in Paris or Rome rather than a dirty tavern in the video game themed world of Deos. Of all the adventurers she seemed the most levelheaded. She gazed across the open floor and allowed her eyes to stop on to Dante's table for a brief moment then continued her search until she spotted Pope sitting quietly in his corner of the room. The woman approached Pope's table as the other adventurers continued to roar raucously around her. They brandished weapons, threw things at one another and above all laughed. Amongst all their antics however Dante noticed an almost impossible bubble of calm that remained persistent around the woman, whenever she moved the group seemed to move with her but never so close as to let their horseplay affect her poise, but never not enough for her to seem as if she was not a part of them. Dante watched as she exchanged words with Pope, who himself seemed neither impressed or bothered by the appearance and presence of the woman or the motley crew of adventurers that accompanied her. He simply sat contentedly nursing a mug of his own and mouthing responses to the dark-haired woman's inquiries without even bothering to look up at her.

The woman than pulled up a chair and took a seat at the table alongside the captain and his men. Once seated she motioned indiscriminately with her hand and Dante watched as nearly half of the adventuring party began to move toward her It was then that Dante made, what to him felt like, quite a startling distinction. It was not the entire adventuring party at large that behaved, on the whole, like a pack of wild animals. In fact it was probably less than half, however the ones that were rather unruly, were so loud and so rambunctious, and the group itself was so large and so intimidating that the very childish and immature actions of but a few members of the party made the entire band of adventurers seem more like a swirling mass of chaos than a civilized group of individuals.. In reality, the half of the group that bade the dark-haired woman's call were quiet and composed adventurers that moved with the discipline of soldiers: A half-orc, an elf, a half-elf, a dwarf and two humans.

They seemed to be presented to Pope, more so than introduced and by way of military decorum they had done everything but salute their new captain.

"More combat consultants," said Dante as he watched silently from his table across the tavern.

As the newest additions to the table begin to pull up chairs and find seats another member of the party shuffled over to Pope's table, an elf, lanky and tall, he wore robes that seemed a size and a half too big and looked to be uncomfortable enough in his own skin let alone his clothes. He stood hunched over and stooped as he spoke to the table. The dark-haired woman waved her arm and pointed a long manicured finger directly at Dante's table.

As she did every head in Pope's corner of the room turned toward Dante and his fellow group of gamers, who upon finding themselves suddenly at the center of attention, grew uncomfortable and turned back around in their chairs.

"What just happened?" Robyn said nervously as the four of them plopped back down in their seats.

"I think Pope just picked up six new combat consultants." Dante replied gloomily. He felt the color drain from his face.

"That's good right," said Alex, attempting to sound happy about the situation but not coming off as very convincing. "I mean, there's strength in numbers... right?"

"Strength for who?" said Morrigan. "The combat consultants are really just Dytorus Mobile Security, and Hernandez has already said they're all ex-military. Pope is tyrannical enough with only two goons under his command imagine how scary he's going to be with eight."

"Hernandez isn't a goon." protested Robyn. "I think at heart he's kind of a good guy."

"Well, he sure seemed like a goon when Dante was trying to stand up to Pope and get us all home," said Morrigan.

Robyn grew quiet and Dante felt his face go hot and flush with fresh humiliation all over again. A somber silence fell over the entire table.

"Excuse me," The gamers turned their heads to find the lanky elf with bad posture stooped over them in much the same way that he had been stooped over Pope's table. "I'm sorry to impose but are you all the gamers from... Team 25?"

Dante was caught off guard by the way the elf spoke, like he couldn't catch his breath and had to speak while breathing through his mouth.

"Forgive me," the elf breathed. "are you are the group," another breath "that logged into Deos with Game Guide" one more breath, "Stephen Choi?"

"Yes, Stephen was our Game Guide," replied Dante.

"And if I understand correctly... Stephen's character was... defeated by a monster... logging him out of the game... but not before leaving behind some type of... special resurrection gem?"

"Again, yes." said Dante.

"May I see it?" the elf asked. Dante noticed perspiration beginning to collect above the elf's brow and at the same time his breathing had seem to become heavier and a bit ragged. He loomed and leered over the table in a way that made Dante want to grind his teeth.

"Who are you exactly?" Dante asked.

"Oh yes of course where are my manners... My name is Dwight... I am the Game Guide for Team seventeen... I am a colleague of Stephen's... Captain Pope told me about the unfortunate incident with the plant monster... but also about the gem that was left behind afterwards."

"You mean the spirit crystal?" said Dante staring up at Dwight.

"Yes... the Spirit Crystal." The game guide repeated, sounding as if he would begin salivating on the table if he were made to wait any longer. Dante eyes darted to the right of the elf's head to find his status box hovering there with nothing, but the name Dwight listed within. The fields that should have detailed his class and level were nothing more than a series of greyed out question marks. Dante thought back to their last interaction with Guard Captain Dunbar and decided to give something a try. His eyes narrowed on Dwight's status box for the briefest of moments and immediately the questions marks changed themselves to a litany of pertinent information.

Dwight of the GreymangeLv3 High-Elf Cleric

Subclass Game Guide

Dante froze. He hadn't expected his scan of Dwight to work so well. It gave him information that he had never seen in a status box before. It listed not only his level and his job class, but he could also see his race and his subrace and there was even a subclass which was listed as game guide. Game Guide. That had to be a self-appointed subclass Dante thought. Dwight, thought of himself as a Game Guide so Deos gave him the subclass of Game Guide.

"So... may I see it?" asked Dwight again cutting in on Dante thoughts and snapping him out of the stupor that he had fallen into.

"Oh um yeah I guess so but, be careful with it." He placed the spirit crystal gently into Dwight's open and waiting palm, who upon receiving the jewel let out a sound that fell somewhere between a purr and a coo. His eyes glistened and gleamed as he stared down at the magic shard and Dante could hear his ragged breaths growing louder with each passing second.

"And you say... this was created... by an NPC... A cleric?" asked Dwight finally looking up from the crystal.

"Yes," said Dante, taking the spirit crystal out of the elf's still open hand and placing it back into his pouch. "An NPC," he said with a purposeful grimace, "a half-orc named Shin-"

"Wait... you said a half-orc... but I thought you said he was a cleric."

"He is a cleric,"

"A half-orc cleric... well that, that's just illogical, perhaps he was a druid or shaman... maybe even a monk but... a cleric, as a half-orc."

"No," chimed in Alex, I'm pretty sure Shinto was a cleric, he was casting healing spells left and right, he had a pretty clear mastery over restorative magic."

"It's just that... Healing magic takes a certain aptitude... and traditionally half-orcs are not thought to possess the skill necessary to... well they're more of what you might call... blunt force instrument." said Dwight. Dante stared at him for a moment and in that time decided that he did not like Dwight very much.

"Well, I guess it's odd that someone from your company designed an NPC that was both a half-orc and a cleric, huh?" said Dante staring Dwight squarely in the face.

The elf began to sweat again. "Why yes I suppose that is odd... I should perhaps talk to someone in design about that... I wouldn't want us to go about... creating inconsistencies in the lore and what have you."

"Yeah, wouldn't want that." said Morrigan dryly.

"Yes... well since we are to be traveling together... for the foreseeable future... if you were to bump into this half-orc cleric once again... please introduce me... I'd like to interact with the NPC's AI interface... maybe collect some data on that spell he used... it's of a particularly high level you see... and your average NPC shouldn't have access to it... It's not a big deal, just still working out some of the kinks... this is a Beta test after all."

"Yeah Dwight, sure no problem." Dante was annoyed to once again be fed the company line when he already knew what now seemed like such an obvious untruth.

Oh ho boys Dwight's been holding out on us! Hey, Dwight, go ahead introduce us to your lady friends? And I guess since they're here you can introduce us to your guy friends too." Blutrted out some random voice Dante had never heard before. On the heels of this rather loud and obnoxious comment came an eruption of loud and uproarious laughter the source of which was a smattering of rough looking adventurers who had suddenly come to all but surround their table. But when Dante looked around to find the wise guy who actually made the joke he found himself staring at a short, thin man who, for a moment, he almost mistook for a child. It did not take long for Dante to realize that the person that he was staring at was indeed an adult, for one thing the mug in his hand was a dead giveaway and if that wasn't enough the large and menacing axe that he had strapped to his back appeared to be anything but kid friendly. The little comedian carried himself with quite a bit of confidence as well. He had a long reedy face with thin wisp of hair where a mustache and goatee should have been. He was no taller than 4 and a half feet but even in his short height his slender limbs still looked long and lithe, giving Dante the impression that he was more agile and fast than to be expected at first sight.

"Why don't you take a picture bub, it'll last longer." The small man said to Dante and on cue the group of adventurers around him burst out in laughter once again. The rambunctious group stood at Dante's table en masse, laughing their heads off at one-liners that sounded like they came out of a 1980's comic book.

"Dwight who are your friends?" the small man asked in a tone slightly more aggressive than the last time he asked.

"Hello Duke... these are the gamers from... Team 25... They just arrived here today... from Illdershire."

"Oh, you guys are Team 25, you're the players we've been waiting for. 'Bout time you people showed up. I was getting sick of waiting around in this do-nothing town all day and night. I was going to have them log me off if you all didn't get here any sooner," said the small man, who then looked back at the other adventurers who all took the opportunity to nod and agree.

"Well... I'll let you all talk... you know... compare notes... discuss tactics... reflect on your experiences within the Beta... that sort of thing... I, I need to go speak with Corrine."

"Of course, you do Dwight," said the small man, "Go. Go running after your mistress Corrine like always." But before the mini comedian could finish berating him, Dwight was already making his way back over towards Pope's table. "Geez the guy is supposed to be our game guide but half the time we've been here he's been more like her errand boy," said the little man, obviously annoyed.

"Who is Corrine?" asked Dante looking at the little person, also mildly annoyed.

"She's the dark-haired woman at the table across the tavern, over there talking with the combat consultants. Hey, is it true that your Game Guide was K.O.'d by a monster?" the adventurers behind the tiny man begin to giggle.

"And who did you say *you* were... exactly?" asked Morrigan.

"Oh, me? Yeah well sorry about that ole Dwight there didn't actually introduce us did he. I'm Danger Duke, Halfling Barbarian and international man of mystery."

The Halfling part Dante had already surmised, but the Barbarian part explained the axe, and it also explained the clothes, the Halfling was clad in a patchwork of animal skins and furs that appeared to have been sewn together by some rather primitive needle work.

"I know what you're thinking," said the Halfling, "why would anyone roll a halfling as a barbarian, and the answer is-"

"You thought it would be cute," said Morrigan flatly, cutting him off mid-speech, "You thought it would be funny to have a frontline melee damage dealer in an uncharacteristically small package. It's not nearly as clever as you imagined." Dante bit his lip to stifle a smile.

"Did you say your name was *Danger Duke*? asked Robyn, not hiding her laugh in the least.

"It's my gamer handle." Said Danger Duke surprised by the fact that he was suddenly getting more questions than laughs. "What are your character's names?"

"Robyn Greenhood" Robyn replied.

"Morrigan Le Bey"

"Alexaldrin Oreheart"

"Dante... Battle." Dante said taking another sip of his grog. It had begun to cool and was not as nearly as good as it had been to start with. He would have to order another.

"Oh, I see," said Danger Duke, "You guys are *those* type of players." He said giving his group the side eye. "The super serious RPG players."

"Well, Dragon Dale is an RPG," said Robyn matter of factly.

"I just mean you guys should lighten up, it is just a game. Look let me introduce you to the guys." Danger Duke turned to the adventurers that stood around him and for the first time acknowledged them as something other than his own personal laugh factory.

"This is Saber Lord," Danger Duke said, pointing to a large green-scaled lizard man with two curved scimitars attached to his back. "He's a Saurian Battle Guard." Sabre Lord nodded and then, what looked like a force of habit, whipped out a long thin tongue, black and forked, which darted flapped up and down rapidly tasting the air before disappearing back into his snout like mouth once again. "Next to him is Torrent, he's an Elf Mage." Duke pointed to an inconspicuous elf in stark blue robes and a cup of ale in one hand. "Aside from Orion that's most of Team 17, which is my group. Over here starts team 12 that's Thorn he's a Half-Elf Druid." A spacey looking half-elf with a quarter staff waved when his name was called. "The Half-Elf next to Thorn is everyone's favorite female rogue, Cyanide." Danger Duke said the Rogue's name as if he was introducing a professional wrestler, to which Cyanide smiled smugly and then winked one eye at the table. "And last but not least, the beast from the east, the monster slaying master and our very own fanged phenom, The Kalgari Ranger, Mr. Wuddlekins!" Danger Duke formed both of his small hands into the shape of tiny L's and with a grand gesture that took his arm over his head and back down again he pointed both finger guns to a hooded adventurer standing near the back of the group. The hooded figure stepped forward and removed his hood revealing the head and face of a large feline, his fiery orange fur speckled with black spots like a jaguar, his cat-like ears twitching and alert. The Kalgari took a deep bow and when he rose, he allowed his large yellow eyes to fall upon the table moving slowly from Robyn, Alex, Morrigan and then to Dante before opening his mouth and in a deep penetrating voice he said:

"Meow."

The adventurers burst out laughing, slapping tables and rattling chairs overtaken by their giddiness. Their merrymaking caused such an uproar that the other patrons in The Sipper and The Sapling focused their attention to Dante's table. Mr. Barnum, Mr. Bailey and Sir Gus turned on their stools once again wearing glares and glowers as opposed to approving nods.

"Mr. Wuddlekins?" repeated Alex looking at the feline Ranger whose large pointed teeth were showing as he laughed heartily along with the others. "You named your character Mr. Wuddlekins?"

"Sure did." said the Mr. Wuddlekins plopping down in a chair and propping his feet up on a nearby table. "Had to damn near fight my game tech during character creation to get it done, but in the end, I told them if I couldn't play the character I wanted to play then I just wouldn't play the Beta at all. And so... Mr. Wuddlekins was born."

"The Kalgari are a race of cat people, but Mr. Wuddlekins sounds like an old lady's house cat!" said Thorn, still laughing quite uncontrollably.

"They get the joke Thorn; you don't have to explain it," said Cyanide punching the druid in the arm.

"Dude watch it, you made me spill my beer." Thorn looked down at his now wet tunic.

"It's mead not beer you dummy," said Torrent "and you wouldn't have spilled it if you'd been drinking it instead of baby-sitting it!" and without warning the elven mage lashed out and smacked the druid's mug from his hand spilling mead all over the table and floor in the process. The Adventurers burst into another fit of laughter.

Dante Morrigan Alex and Robyn simply looked at one another and said nothing.

In the midst of the chaos, Liza was returning to the table with large trays of food. She navigated her way through the maze of armed men and arrived at Dante's table to see it wet with spilled mead.

"Looks like we've had a bit of an accident." Said Liza sounding a little flustered, "Not to worry I've got your supper here, I'll just sit this down and then I'll grab something to clean that up."

"Oh, my darling Liza!" said Danger Duke, "To think they said the perfect woman doesn't exist, and then I laid eyes on you, why don't you let me take you away from all of this?"

"Oh, now what would be the fun in that?" Liza replied.

"Let's you and I discuss that part later for now another round of drinks for me and my friends!" shouted Duke, and cheers went up from the others as if the halfling had done something of note and not simply placed a drinks order. Liza sat down the trays of food and quickly shuffled away, the adventurers all hungrily ogling after her as she did.

"I thought there were supposed to be four gamers per group, but there are only six of you, what happened to the rest?" Dante asked.

"They're over there at the bar being anti-social." Danger Duke pointed at two humans sitting at the bar. One of the two men wore a shabby cloak with chainmail underneath it and had a heavy mace hanging from his waist, the other was wearing a rapier on his waist and strapped to his back was a lute.

"Mandrake's the bard, the other one is Orion, he's a cleric, but he's old school though, front lines heat of battle type of guy like a combat medic. Hey Mandrake, come over here and meet the guys from team 25!" Danger Duke yelled out across the tavern. The two men at the bar along with nearly everyone else in the tavern turned to look at the halfling, but without a word both Mandrake and Orion went back to their previous conversation seemingly showing no interest in fraternizing with Danger Duke or Team 25, and in all honesty, Dante couldn't blame them.

"Another round of mead as requested." The frazzled old man who had first welcomed Dante and the others into the tavern had arrived at the table with six mugs, all of them filled to the brim with mead.

"Hey, you're not Liza!" said Danger Duke.

"Wow nothing gets past you, does it?" Morrigan quipped.

"Apologies mi lord, but we are quite busy tonight, stretched thin you might say. So tonight, me and the wife and dear Liza we are all working hand and hand."

"Hmph," grunted Danger Duke only half listening, "Well why is it that you only brought out six mugs, I said a round of mead for all of my friends, four of us here don't have refills."

"Oh, yes sorry that is my mistake I'll be right back-"

"No, no that won't be necessary." Dante interrupted "We actually were not drinking mead we were drinking grog. But we're fine for the moment. Believe me the food is quite enough."

"Oh yeah," shouted Duke, "Let us get six orders of that food as well, adventuring is hard work, you work up quite an appetite. Am I right boys?" There was a look in the halfling's eye, that of a mongoose, small and unassuming at first sight but in reality, a vicious and dangerous animal under the right conditions.

"Oh me, I am deeply sorry mi lord but as I tried explaining to you yesterday, while we are grateful for your patronage we are not truly equipped to feed so many and well, I hate to inform you but we... we are out of food for the evening."

"You're what?" replied Danger Duke sounding surprised. The halfling hopped up from his chair and stared up at the tavern owner who though he was nearly a foot taller than the adventurer still seemed to shrink back as he approached. "So you're telling me that you come out here and for one, you're not Liza, and then you don't bring enough mead and then on top of that after me and my friends bust our butts fighting monster and saving villages we can't even get anything to eat?"

"Well with all due respect sir you all saved Bexby Parva from a goblin raid, not Black Water but still we were grateful that you aided our neighbors that's why we offered a free round of mead for your party, but that was two days ago mi lord."

"Free mead...you think I became an adventurer for free mead?"

"Well no, I was just-"

"Here is what I think of your free mead." And lifting up on the tips of his toes the halfling turned the mug of mead upside down emptying its contents onto the tavern owner's head.

The adventurers of team 17 and team 12 erupted in laughter, but Dante did not. He jumped to his feet and snatched the mug from the halfling's hand.

"What are you doing?"

"What's the matter?" asked Danger Duke with a genuinely surprised look on his face.

"Dude you are tripping right now, you need to chill!"

"Buddy, relax. We're just having a laugh with some NPCs."

Dante turned to the tavern owner. "I'm really sorry about that sir, I think he's had a bit too much to drink already. You know how halflings get when they've had too much. Please, forgive me on my friend's behalf-"

"It's fine young master." Said the old man in a low voice, "it's been like this for a couple of days here now. But I do thank ye for yer concern." His eyes drifted off aimlessly towards the back of the tavern, "I'll go get something to clean all this up." He said, walking away, humiliated.

Dante shook with anger. He looked over at Duke, who was now in conversation with Cyanide and Mr. Wuddlekins as if nothing had ever happened. He retook his seat in silence. Alex stared at him from across the table, and immediately Morrigan and Robyn leaned in close to speak in low whispers.

"What are we going to do? Asked Robyn

"I don't know." Dante replied.

"This is typical of a lot of gamers when they assume there are no real consequence to their actions," said Morrigan, sitting to Dante's left with the rest of the tavern to her back. "We have to somehow let them know that there *are* consequences to their actions." She whispered.

"Hey, I need to know what's going on too." Said Alex who had gotten up from his seat and come over to join in on the whispering.

"We're trying to figure out what to do about these other gamers,' Dante replied, "they're out of control."

"We have to tell them the truth about Deos, that its real." whispered Alex.

"What about Pope?" asked Robyn.

Dante looked over his shoulder to the corner of the room where Pope and his men sat only to find Pope looking back at him, his eyes his eyes accusatory and distrustful.

"Crap, he's looking dead at us." Dante reported.

"What?" asked Alex about to turn his head to see for himself.

"Don't look over there," Dante said in a loud whisper, "We already look mad suspicious over here huddled up and whispering. Alex go back to your seat. Robyn you keep an eye on Pope you have the best natural view of him."

A small commotion was building near Liza, at the back of the tavern. She stormed out in a huff and then marched right up to Dante's table. "You all need to settle your debts and leave!" she said loudly.

At the sound of her voice Danger Duke spun on his heels and began to put on his usual show. "Liza my love, you have returned at last."

"I said settle up and get going," Liza said again, but the fire had gone from her voice.

Danger Duke sat back down in a chair and propped his feet up on a table. "Now why would I do that, we're in love I was actually planning to move in."

From the bar Mr. Arnum, Mr. Bailey and Sir Gus stood from there stools and then Mr. Arnum spoke. "If Liza is asking yer to leave then I think ye outta oblige her and leave."

"Who asked you, you old drunk!" snapped Duke.

"Pope's watching," whispered Robyn. "Everyone at his table is watching."

"Yes we will leave," Dante said, looking from Liza to Mr. Arnum while making his way over towards Danger Duke.

"I'm not lea-" started Duke but Dante cut him off.

"We'll leave, and to show that there are no hard feelings, a round of grog for everyone, on me!" a rabble of cheers went up from everyone not in the immediate vicinity of the tension. "Liza how much would that be, for a round of grog for everyone." Dante asked.

Liza looked around the tavern doing what appeared to be a quick tally of the number of patrons inside. "It'll be roughly 250 copper pieces." responded Liza.

"250 copper, what's that 25 silver, which is 2 and a half gold," Dante reached into his coin pouch, "Look how about we make it 3 gold even and here is another 2 gold for the food and drink that me and my friends ordered and for any trouble that we caused." Dante held out the coins extending them towards Liza, a literal peace offering. She seemed hesitant but took a step towards him.

"And you all agree to leave as well?" she asked.

"Yes, we'll leave," said Dante, "I'd just prefer to leave on decent terms."

Liza softened, she extended her hand and took the five gold coins.

"Your friend poured mead on my father's head, humiliating him in his own tavern after he has been nothing but kind to him even after everything else him and the others have done to this town for the past couple of days. You should know neither our dignity nor our pride is up for sale."

"Of course not." said Dante "Like I said I just prefer to end on decent terms."

"What's your name Urth Lander?" Liza asked.

"Dante."

"Well, Dante, thank you for your consideration. But now I think it's time for you and your companions to go."

"Yes, I think it is." Dante turned to the halfling. "Duke we need to leave."

"Leave for what? Because some NPC's are offended, where would we go?"

"We can go to another tavern." Dante replied.

"This is the only tavern in town!" said Danger Duke annoyed.

"Are there no other inns" Dante asked.

"This is the one and only place to stay in Black Water." said Cyanide from near the bar.

"And you just paid five gold for us not to stay here." said Mr. Wuddlekins with a smirk.

"Well there has to be somewhere else we can go. I have something very important to talk to

you all about and we can't discuss it here." Dante said looking back at his friends for support. Alex, Robyn and Morrigan nodded encouragingly.

"Discuss what-" Duke began to ask but was cut short.

"We don't just want you out of the tavern." Said Mr. Arnum who was still standing and still looking rather riled up. "We want you to leave Black Water altogether. You Urth Landers have been nothing but trouble since you've got here."

"You see!" said Danger Duke looking at Dante but motioning to Arnum, "you give these computer programs an inch and they take a mile. I'll tell you what, how about we don't leave. How about you leave. Gentleman can you show these good fellows to the door." At the halfling's behest Mr. Wuddlekins, Saber Lord, Cyanide and Thorn all grabbed hold to Arnum, Bailey and Gus and dragged them forcibly towards the tavern's open door before violently shoving them out. The adventurers then turned around and strutted back towards Dante's table laughing and smiling at themselves proudly. By now the entire tavern had turned its attention to Dante's section of the room, and never being one to miss out on the opportunity to be the center of attention, Danger Duke leaped up on to the top of the table with the look of someone who was about to start shouting.

"What are you doing?!" said Dante, grabbing a hold to Duke's arm.

"I'm about to confess my undying love to Liza and maybe sing a song to liven this place up after you killed the momentum I had going earlier."

"You idiot get down off that table and act like you have some sense! You guys can't run around this place acting any way you want."

"That's kind of the point. It's a game, we can do whatever we want, and more than that, it's a beta, you're supposed to try and break it, so the developers know what bugs to fix. So, let go of my arm so I can sing my solo before the spotlight turns cold." Duke tried to pull away, but Dante's grip was too strong.

"This isn't a beta," Dante hissed, twisting Danger Duke's arm.

"What?" replied Danger Duke looking confused.

"Listen to me, we're not *in* a game. We've been sent to an alternate world, a real Deos with real consequences. These aren't NPCs, they're *people*." Dante didn't want to spring the information onto Duke this way, but he hoped the shock would calm him down a bit so he and the others could regain control of the situation. Then they just had to tell the others, keep Pope from finding out and then together maybe they could all figure out a way to get home. At least that was the plan.

Danger Duke looked at him. Stared him in the eyes as if searching for some sign or validation of the truth that he was telling. And then without saying a word, he burst out laughing.

"Wait a minute, you think this is real?" he said loudly.

"Keep your voice down." Dante hissed.

"And get off of our table." Added Robyn, "I can't see." She said as she tried looking around him to Pope's corner of the room.

"All of you believe this nonsense?" Danger Duke asked looking at Morrigan and then over to Robyn.

"It's not nonsense, it's the truth," said Morrigan.

"Aw man this is too rich." Danger Duke said and in a quick movement ripped his arm free of Dante's grip and began to yell from atop the table. "Hey guys, you gotta come hear this. These guys think we're really in Deos!"

"They what?" said Mr. Wuddlekins a large grin already spreading over his feline face. Dante looked over his shoulder toward the bar and saw a number of Duke's friends coming closer and now even Orion and Mandrake seemed to be intrigued by what was going on. Then he looked over to Pope side of the room and saw the captain shaking his head disapprovingly. He cursed to himself and immediately the thought occurred to him to simply reach up and rip the halfling down from atop the table but before he could act, he felt someone hovering to his left.

"What is going on here?" said the low baritone voice of a woman. Dante looked over to see Corrine, or at least the woman that had been pointed out to him as Corrine standing behind Morrigan's chair, and behind her was Robyn and behind Robyn was Alex.

"These guys are convinced that we've been sent to another world. They think this is the real Deos. They think the NPC's are real people." He burst out laughing again "I think they've been in the game too long; they're losing touch with reality." Danger Duke's adventurer friends burst out into fits of laughter.

Corrine did not, her face merely went stone white and then she turned to look at Pope, who was now standing. Dante's mind exploded. The laughter of Danger Duke and his friends turned to an echo in the back of his mind. Pope's words just outside of Black Water replayed themselves in his head over and over again, "...Do not tell anyone the truth about Deos... Insubordination will not be tolerated..." The images of their fight, if Dante could even call it a fight replayed themselves over and over in his mind's eye. Pope's sidestep, the lighting fast knee to the gut, the elbow to the back and then how his face smacked the ground. It had taken days for the bruising to fade, he could still feel tingling in the places he had been hit. He could still feel the fresh sting of humiliation.

What would be the humiliation for this? What did zero tolerance for insubordination look like? Back in Illdershire Pope had somewhat needed Dante and the others. Now he had 8 combat consultants, 2 game guides and 8 gamers to help him navigate his way through Deos. Now Dante was expendable, now maybe they all were.

"I thought you said they were under control?" Corrine called out to Pope as he approached.

Dante didn't have another moment to waste. He looked over to Morrigan, Robyn and Alex. "We have to go!" he yelled.

"What?" asked Robyn.

"What do you mean? Go where?" replied Alex.

Morrigan who was the closest to Dante did not respond at all, as she had just shoved Danger Duke off the top of the table and into a crowd of laughing adventurers and appeared to have not had heard him. Without thinking Dante reached down and grabbed Morrigan's hand and pulled her along with him. "Come on!" he said, rushing toward the door.

Robyn and Alex both realizing what was happening pushed pass Corrine and followed him toward the door.

Robyn bumped hard into a confused and bewildered Dwight as she passed him, almost knocking the game guide to the floor. Instinctively Alex almost stopped to help him up until a harsh rebuke of "Alex come on!" from Robyn kept him moving passed the game guide with nothing more than half mumbled

"Sorry."

The four of them weaved their way through the crowds of the Sipper and the Sapling, making it to the door before most anyone else knew what was going on. Dante looked over his shoulder to see Pope giving chase. The four of them burst out the saloon style doors of the tavern. It was still daylight, but the sun was already beginning to slink towards the western side of town. It would be dusk soon, and dark soon after. Dante had hoped the town of Black Water would be empty and free of people as it was when they arrived. It was not. In the town street, in front of the tavern a makeshift mob had begun to form, but instead of being made up of unruly adventurers it was composed of what looked like angry town folk, and there standing squarely in the front of the group were Mr. Arnum, Mr. Bailey and Sir Gus.

"For the past two days these so called 'adventurers' have been harassing us, abusing us and humiliating us," screamed Mr. Phineas Arnum.

"Yea!" the crowd of townsfolk screamed back.

"Well I say we don't take it anymore! I say we run'em out of town on a rail!"

"Yea!" the town screamed back.

"There some of'em go right there!" someone from the crowd yelled when they spotted Dante and the others.

Mr. Arnum spun around. Dante could still see the extra thick smattering of dirt on his face from where Mr. Wuddlekins threw him out of The Sipper and the Sapling just moments before.

"No," said Arnum holding up his hands to the crowd. "These are adventurers that were just passing through, they were already about to leave... weren't you?"

"Yes!" Dante said quickly, "Yes we were just about to leave!" And still holding on to Morrigan's hand, Dante stepped forward, and as he did Mr. Arnum stepped aside giving Dante a silent nod. The townspeople made for Dante and the others a small path amongst the mob allowing them to pass through unhampered. Once they made to the other side of the sea of people Dante heard the tavern doors swing open again, and he turned to see a number of adventurers spill forth, Pope among them. At the sight of the adventurers the crowd went into uproar.

"It's them!" someone from the crowd screamed. "They destroyed my shop."

"They killed my livestock."

"Run'em out of town!"

"Now's our chance, let's go!" Dante called out, and without looking back he ran.

"Dante!" Pope yelled from the other side of the crowd, but when he tried to move forward a sea of yelling, screaming dirty-faced town folk blocked his way. Desperate, Pope reached around his back for his crossbow but a hand on his arm. It was Corrine.

"Captain," she said in a low voice. "I think it would be best if we refrain from using lethal force here. A massacre of the local populace will undoubtedly attract the attention of the authority figures of the larger city-states and surrounding towns, more than likely branding us as bandits and making it more difficult for us to move freely throughout Deos."

Pope released his grip on the large crossbow. "Point made." He said. "Tell the men the use of lethal force is not permitted. Lansing."

"Yes sir," said Lansing appearing at Pope's side out of nowhere.

"I want at least two men to squeeze through this crowd and get on their tails. Do not let them get away."

"Right away sir,"

"Go ahead Dante!" Pope yelled out over the crowd. "Run Away, but I'll be right here when you finally decide to stop! Once you realize that you can't run forever!"

Dante could hear Pope yelling over the roar of the mob, but he wasn't interested in anything that he had to say. He led the others south, directly away from the tavern past a row of crooked buildings and towards the tattered wooden fence that marked the border of Black Water. They climbed the waist high fence and a few steps later found themselves in the forest that surrounded the town. Faster and faster through the woods they moved desperate to put the town and everyone in it and anyone who may have come out of it behind them.

The forest was thick and wooded and the vines and branches seemed to reach out to grab at them, slowing their movement and attempting to tear at their clothes and armor. Every time slowed, the threat of distant footsteps and snapping twigs urged them on. It was only when the sounds of Black Water had become faint did they relax. They were at least a mile into the forest and away from the town before they stopped to catch their breath. They sucked air, the four of them heaving and huffing, bent at the waist or kneeled down on one knee, each one trying to sate that desperate need for oxygen. And while they breathed, they listened, listened quietly. No distant footsteps, no snapping twigs, no hurried footfalls. They smiled at one another and soon the smiles turned to laughs. They had done it. They had run off. They had gotten away. And then the laughter faded. But where to? Run off to where? Dante looked up at the sky. It was dusk, and it would be dark very soon.

"Ok," he said, still trying to catch his breath. "We are in the Black Wood. Which traditionally in the Dragon Dale games is a very dangerous area filled with very dangerous predators."

"What?" said Robyn "Well if that's the case then why did we run in here as opposed to a direction that was a very safe area filled with very safe predators?" Robyn asked.

"It's about to get dark," Morrigan said. "I don't imagine the Black Wood is known for becoming friendly when it gets dark?"

"Why did we run so far if we were just going to get killed in the woods?" said Alex.

"No listen," said Dante, "We came into the Black Wood to avoid being followed, and yes this is a dangerous area, but the general rule is the deeper you go into the forest the larger and more aggressive the predators get," said Dante.

"Well, you should have led with that," said Robyn, "Why didn't you lead with that?"

"Relatively speaking we are not that far into the forest, but we don't have much daylight left, now if we just keep heading west we'll come out in the Illder Plains, which is a lot safer then where we are now."

"Ok great," said Alex, "let's do that."

The four gamers began to trek west, towards the setting sun, but as they moved cautiously yet quickly through the forest, Dante began to experience the indescribable feeling that they were being watched. He couldn't hear anything out of the ordinary, there were birds and bugs the usual sounds of the forest. And when Dante looked over his shoulder, he saw nothing behind them, not even the flutter of a shadow or an isolated falling leaf. Nothing to really even reaffirm his suspicions, but he knew something was there. It felt almost as if the trees themselves were stalking them.

"What?" asked Alex as they walked.

"What?" responded Dante.

"What are you looking for?" Alex asked.

"I'm not looking for anything?" Dante replied beginning to walk a little faster.

"You were definitely looking for something." Inserted Morrigan.

"If you're looking for something then just tell us, and we can help you look for it." cried Robyn.

"I can't tell you what I'm looking for, because I don't *know* what I'm looking for, I'm actually more concerned that something is looking for us." Said Dante increasing his walking speed to 'brisk' as they forced their way through the foliage.

"Let's just pick up the pace and everyone keep a look out." said suggested Robyn.

"If someone else says the word 'look' one more time I'm going to explode." snapped Morrigan.

The group increased their stride from march to a trot and though the forest seemed to resist their passage, blocking their way with more bushes and brambles that they had to step over or around they moved at a much greater pace than before. Around them Dante noticed that the birds had gone silent, and his stomach lurched. He looked over his shoulder and saw a large group of leaves falling from what looked like an otherwise empty tree, and then from one tree to another he saw a shadow flutter and his heart sank.

"Run." Dante muttered just loud enough for everyone to hear.

"What? What happened?" asked Alex confused.

"Just run!" Dante shouted breaking into a sprint.

And as they did the trees behind them came alive. They shook and shuddered dropping leaves and twigs and small branches. Dante couldn't tell if it was the trees themselves that were after them or something in the trees, but every time he looked up, the trees looked empty and it was only the trees behind them that shuddered, meaning that whatever it was, they were ahead of it, and he intended to keep it that way. So they ran, Alex, Morrigan and Dante sprinting through the forest, racing against the setting sun and being chased by some unseen and unknown threat.

"I see it!" called out Robyn between desperate breaths for air. "The edge of the forest. We're almost there!"

"Keep going!" Dante called back. He could hear the shuddering trees getting closer and closer.

And then he too could see it, the wide-open fields of the plains beyond the black barked trees of the wood. Robyn was in front of him, he could feel Morrigan close behind him and could hear Alex struggling in the rear. Whatever it was that was chasing them was getting closer and though they were near to the edge of the forest Dante wasn't sure if they all would make it out before the trees caught up to at least one of them. For reasons he couldn't fully comprehend Dante stopped and pulled out his sword and turned around.

"What are you doing?" asked Morrigan as she ran towards him.

"Just keep going," he huffed, "Head for the clearing!"

Behind her Alex was struggling to keep pace. He was about twenty yards behind and Dante could see the shuddering trees right on top of him.

"Alex come on!" Dante yelled, reaffirming his grip on his sword.

The dwarf tried. Dante could say that, he genuinely tried, but the Black Wood is an auspiciously sinister place and he was convinced that the plants moved of their own volition in an effort to spite any would be travelers. As in that exact moment, as Alex picked up speed, his foot caught itself on a particularly gnarly root and he tumbled face first into the dirt. That's when Dante saw the creature. It was in the trees, or rather it was moving among the tree branches, and even to say he saw it in that moment would be a bit of a stretch, mostly because there was little to see. The creature was, not merely camouflaged, and not completely invisible, but more so translucent. It was like a mass of distorted and misplaced light that moved and acted of its own accord. It was to Dante as if the creature did not want to be seen and therefore could not be seen, regardless of the wants or desires of the onlookers. It bound from tree branch to tree branch causing the tree tops to shake every time it leapt and landed and then once Alex had fallen it had apparently found its opportunity to strike because Dante watched as the large translucent mass hurtled down from the trees and on to the back of the fallen dwarf.

unpredictable movements or at the very least buy Alex some more time. Just as his arms begin to tire and his sword swings to slow, the treehugger cat let out a loud and painful howl.

For a moment Dante thought that his sword had made contact, but then he saw the small wound in the treehugger's left flank, a wound from what looked like a crossbow bolt. Dante swung his sword again, the cat dodged, and then he heard it. The whistling sound of a flying cross bow bolt, it came from behind him and pegged the cat in the leg. It let out another howl and immediately bounded into a tree.

Dante turned to see Robyn, Morrigan and Alex about thirty yards out, and just beyond them, the clearing. He took off, running as fast as he could. He could hear it in the trees, behind him leaping from branch to branch, tree to tree, he could hear the leaves rattling and shaking and he could feel it getting closer and closer. The others were just twenty yards away. His sword was still in his hands as he ran, the weight of seemed to have tripled after the continuous swings. His blood burned like acid. His arms, legs and lungs felt as if they would burst. But his friends were now only ten yards away. Robyn lifted the small hand crossbow and shot it into the trees, but the expression on her face told Dante she hadn't hit anything, and the lack of pain filled howls confirmed it. He could still hear the growling though, angrier than ever.

Dante was on top of them now. "Go!" he shouted, and they did. They ran. The trees rattled and shook, the cat roared and they simply ran faster. The plains were right there, not more than ten yards away, practically in reach. But then Dante felt it. Time itself slowed to a crawl. He could see them, his friends so desperate to survive, the pained looked on their faces the panicked looks in their eyes. Running because he'd told them too, running because he's led them into the Black Wood.

Leaves fell from the sky like snowflakes, and in that moment, Dante could hear nothing but his own ragged breathing in his ears. He knew without looking up that the Treehugger Cat had gotten not only ahead of them, but above them and now was in the perfect position to pounce. They would escape, they would be free of the Black Wood, but one of them would die, one of them would be claimed by the Treehugger Cat and would never leave the forest. The burning in Dante's veins changed from acid to magma. They had come so far, were so close. They could not fall short now. He had to do something. His sword was still in hand, the cat was overhead and at any moment the world might speed back up and it would be throwing itself at one of them. If only he could strike it, slash at it the way he had done the wolf and even the illder stag. But he no way of controlling those attacks and besides the damn cat was too fast for him anyway. Or was that true? He heard tree limb creak and immediately knew, this was it, this was the pounce, it was now or never.

With his sword in his right-hand Dante bound out on his left leg, still in full stride of his run, he flexed into his step and pushed himself into the air, jumping to meet his doom head-on. He twisted his torso, turning mid-jump and saw it, the Treehugger cat, claws out, fangs raining down upon them like death. At the

Dante rushed forward, sword overhead screaming but it was too late. T creatures landed on top of Alex pinning him to the ground and in the proce the odd reflective light barrier surrounding the creature faded revealing a lar predatory cat poised on the back of the dwarf. Its body was covered in da stripes like a tiger, only, because of its green fur, it looked like it was covered a patchwork of leaves and foliage perfect for hiding in the canopy even wh it wasn't surrounding itself in a shell of distorted light.

The large green cat lifted a heavy paw resplendent with razor sharp clav Dante was close enough to strike and swung his sword. It nothing but air. T cat was fast, it was on the ground now and it growled and roared at Dante he stood sentinel over its fallen prey. Alex crawled up to his hands and kne and then up to a kneeling position.

"Alex, you're alive!" Dante said surprised but careful not to take his eyes the large cat.

"Yeah," coughed Alex, "it landed on my shield." He pointed to his back and t round circular shield strapped to it. "Still knocked down half of my HP thoug He coughed and then spat a mouthful of blood.

"Okay, well we need to get out of here. The edge of the forest can't be mo than fifty yards away, think you can make it?"

"I don't know, is that a giant dwarf eating monster still growling behind m Alex asked.

"Sure is."

"Then I highly doubt it."

"Look, Alex on the count of three I want you to run for the clearing, Morrig and Robyn should already be there. I'm going to hold it off so you can ge head start and then I'll be right behind you."

"Dante, man, I don't think you can survive a direct hit from that thing, y should just go."

"Listen! On the count of three... you run. Got it?"

"Yeah bro," said Alex softly "I got it."

"One." Dante watched as the predatory cat stalk back and forth looking fo way around the sword. He looked for and found the status box hovering abo its head.

"Two" Dante focused, revealing exactly what it was that he was dealing wi Treehugger Cat, level 9. They were fast, they were deadly, and they were stro Alex was right, there was no way he would be able to take one on by hims They would probably not even be able to take it together, but then they dic have to take it, they just had to get away from it.

"Three." Dante called and when he did Alex shot off as fast as he could. T treehugger cat, responding to fleeing wounded prey, sprung forward, but Da was there, and he swung the sword again, this time almost hitting the cat w narrowly jumped out of reach of the blade. The cat roared in anger, baring la sharp fangs and flashing bright glowing eyes of a ferocious predator.

Dante swung the sword again and again, wildly and recklessly, hoping either catch the treehugger by sheer luck, scare it away with his wild sight of it the heat within him surged, the magma in his blood shot out in every direction and he pulled his sword arm around him so incredibly fast that time twisted.

"Lightspeed Slash!" Dante called out loudly, and without hardly realizing as the shimmering metal blade blurred in an amorphous grey cord and made the sound of a snapping whip, slicing itself through the falling Treehugger Cat. The momentum of Dante's swing brought him around full circle, landing him clumsily on to his foot and knee, his blade outstretched for balance. The Treehugger landed and let out a loud yowl of pain.

The others stopped mystified and confused by what had just happened. One third of Dante's MP bar had disappeared while the Treehugger Cat still had two-thirds of its HP left. Regardless the strike had caused it concern and for a moment it looked at the four adventurers from a safe distance, then it growled, then roared, and then rushed toward Dante, still on the ground, ultimately deciding the meal was worth the fight.

Dante struggled to get his bearings. He stood but then faltered, nearly dropping his sword. The cat bound toward him finally able to close in on a target and just as it seemed to have him within its grasp, a spout of flames burst forth, forcing the cat to jump backwards again. It roared in frustration as burning black trees blocked its path, if only momentarily. The highly resilient trees of the Black Wood seemed to fight back the blaze, but by the time the flames died down, the four adventurers had already pulled themselves from the grips of the Black Wood.

On the other side of the trees on the open fields of the Illdershire plains Dante, Alex, Morrigan and Robyn could still here the Treehugger Cat roaring in rage. The sun had all but set now, and only a few rays of twilight persisted. The four of them breathed heavily as they looked back at the dark and intimidating woods.

"Think it'll come out after us?" Robyn asked.

"No," said Dante "they use the cover of the trees to ambush their prey, I don't think they hunt outside the boundaries of the forest."

"Do you think I started a forest fire?" asked Morrigan.

"I think you saved my life." Dante replied.

"Unfortunately," said Morrigan, "But presently I'm more concerned with the fact that I just jump-started a wildfire."

"I don't think so," replied Alex looking into the woods, "It looks like the fire has gone out and I don't see any smoke."

"I'm pretty sure the Black Woods are either enchanted or alive." Dante said, "I don't think your fire is strong enough to burn them down."

"It was strong enough to save your life," snapped Morrigan.

"Unfortunately." Dante replied.

"Guys, I hate to interrupt, I really do, but it's getting dark and in case you haven't noticed we're stuck out here alone, just the four of us. What are we going to do?" Robyn was peering into the dark coming over the plains from the west with concern on her face.

"Well, we definitely can't go back to Black Water," said Alex.

"And Pope will probably be sending someone after us so we can't stay here," said Morrigan

"Yeah see, you guys are telling me things that we can't do, I said what are we going *to* do?" said Robyn impatiently.

"We're going to have to head to Illdershire," said Dante,

"Illdershire is a day and a half walk away. That leaves us in the wilderness for at least two nights with nothing but the clothes on our backs. Once again just the four of us surrounded by who knows what," said Robyn.

"Maybe not," said Dante, who then cupped his hands around his mouth, took a deep breath and began a deep and mournful wolf howl that echoed across the plain.

"Uh, Dante, what are you doing?" asked Alex.

"Why are you doing that? Why is he doing that?" Robyn asked starting to sound panicked.

In the distance a wolf howled back. Prompting Dante to cup his mouth and howl again.

"He's talking to them, why are you talking to them, they're going to come over here and I'm out of crossbow bolts."

"I think he's finally lost it," said Morrigan dryly.

"No, I haven't lost it. I told you all before I talked to the Alpha wolf, and after we killed the Raptor he and I entered into an understanding."

"An understanding? What type of understanding?" asked Morrigan.

"Well... he adopted me into their clan."

"He adopted you..." said Alex.

"I'm done." Said Robyn throwing up her hands in the air.

"Look guys I don't make the rules. This is Deos. We've all played Dragon Dale we know how these things go. Now the wolves of the Illdershire plains offered me an alliance, which included assistance and safe passage whenever we were in the plains, and personally I think it would be silly not to use it."

The group was quiet for a short moment, then Morrigan looked up and spoke. "So, would it be correct to call you a cub scout."

"Ha," said Dante sarcastically, "that's very funny, but I'll have you know I am a full-fledged Black Wolf with all right and privileges thereof."

"Well, I definitely know you were raised by wolves." said Morrigan.

"I should have just let the tree cat eat me." said Alex in despair, then regret when he heard a loud throaty growl and turned to see a trio of large black wolves approaching them with their hackles raised and their fangs bared.

"Um Dante, there are wolves here and they don't look friendly... the actually look very hungry," said Alex in a panic.

Dante, who had sat down in the grass, rushed to his feet and threw himself in front of Alex who the wolves seemed particularly taken with. Dante threw his hands up to show that he wasn't holding any weapons and then remembering that the wolves themselves were very formal, decided to bow and announce himself.

"I am Dante Battle servant of Canis Romulus, I seek an audience with the Lord Alpha." At this the wolves seemed to calm themselves and then one after taking a few steps backwards turned and sprinted away.

"Do you think it's working?" asked Robyn. But when she spoke one of the remaining wolves growled loudly.

"I think they want us to remain here quietly until the other gets back," Dante whispered.

It did not take long before the other wolf returned and when it did, following behind it was the largest, blackest wolf that either Robyn, Alex or Morrigan had ever seen. It trotted up to them leisurely and as it did Dante not only relaxed, but approached it as if approaching an old friend. He stepped toward the wolf, which seemed big enough to bite him in two, and then swallow him in a single gulp and kneeled like he was greeting royalty.

"Lord Canis," said Dante, bowing deeply.

"Black Wolf Dante." Canis responded in greeting. "Your journey has brought you back to the Illder Plains with allies."

"Lord Canis I once again am in need of your help."

"You say once again young wolf, but your first request for aid ended only in counsel, which I give to you freely and without restraint, yet it appears to me, on the issue of pack leadership that you have resolved that concern on your own. It appears you have decided to split the pack."

"Well.. I hadn't originally thought about like that but, yes sir, I guess so."

Canis looked around Dante to the adventurers standing behind him. "It looks as if you have chosen well, you have brought strong warriors to create you pack. And it is also a good sign to start with two males and two females."

"Umm thank you sir."

"Tell me Dante, is one of these females your life mate."

There was a loud cough and then choking sound from behind Dante.

"Um no Lord Canis we are all just friends, simply pack mates that's all."

"Yes, well I can see that you all have the making of a strong new pack and many warriors will come to join you in due time, either that or you all may breed your own."

More choked laughter. Then in the midst of their conversation the great wolf began sniffing the air, his large nostrils taking in great wafts of air until it slowly led him back down to Dante. He looked at the boy and then beyond him to the dark woods.

"You smell of battle Dante," said the alpha.

"Yes sir, that is why I called you, our new pack need to get back to Illdershire, but when we split from the large pack, we left all of our supplies and we simply have a difficult road ahead, any assistance you could offer us would put me firmly in your debt my lord."

"Nonsense!" the great wolf said in a loud and strong voice that almost knocked Dante off of his feet. "You are a member of the Black Wolf Clan, you have no debts." and with that the great wolf barked and out of the dark three more large wolves appeared, bigger than Dante was used to seeing. "We shall carry you to Illdershire, your companions will ride on their backs, and you will ride with me."

There under the twin moons of Deos, Alex, Morrigan and Robyn climbed on the back of dire wolves as Canis Romlus kneeled down and allowed Dante to pull himself up on to his large broad back, and together they rode off into the darkness of the Illder Plains.

PART II

Chapter 17: Visitation Day

"Battle. You have a visitor," said the guard.

Malcolm looked up from his book at the female guard standing at the open entrance of his cell. Malcolm Battle, ruggedly handsome, dark-skinned and in his late twenties, looked like an older version of Dante, only more weathered and more dangerous. Dante would say it was the facial hair. Malcom always kept a relatively short but otherwise expertly manicured beard and mustache that Dante reasoned his brother had only grown in an effort to look more handsome, more dangerous, or both. Malcom, who had never taken the time to confirm or deny these allegations, instead simply countered with the argument that everything about him was expertly manicured. If the obsessive-compulsive level of neatness in his prison cell was anything on which to base his argument, then Malcom Battle had an open and shut case.

Malcom rose from his bed and slid the small paperback book he was reading back in its place among the others in his private makeshift library. The small collection was shelved alphabetically, by author and as a result Malcom was sure to put the book, 'The Souls of Black Folk', by W.E.B DuBois in the D section under Dubois and not in the S section under 'Souls' as he was sometime prone to do when he was in a rush. It was when he made such mistakes that he had to remind himself that success was the result of disciplined and deliberate focus, a lack of focus led to disorder, disorder led to mistakes and mistakes led to 12 to 15-year prison sentences.

"Sometime today, Battle," droned the guard.

Malcom presented his hands to the guard. She pulled out a pair of handcuffs and gently placed them onto his wrist with a metallic click-click-click.

"You just had to put the book on the shelf huh? Couldn't have just... left it on your bunk... until you got back?"

"Everything in its place," Malcom replied with a wink, to which the guard replied with an eye roll and then turned and led the prisoner out of his cell, through the cell block and a series of heavy, remotely operated security doors, ending in a large open room filled with seven to eight round tables and a corner of poorly stocked vending machines. Three of the tables, Malcolm noticed, were already occupied by other inmates all sitting alone apparently waiting for visitors.

"You're at table three Battle, see you in a few," said the guard, unlocking Malcolm's cuffs.

He rubbed his wrist, sat down at the table, and began to wait. After about fifteen minutes had passed, the security doors on the opposite side of the room buzzed, then opened and a white woman walked into the room and sat at one of the tables with one of the other waiting inmates. Five minutes later there was another buzz, and then another visitor for another inmate. Then ten minutes later another buzz. For about thirty minutes, by his account, Malcom sat at his table alone watching other visitors come in to visit other prisoners when the door buzzed again. It opened and this time a brown-skinned woman walked in. She was the color of caramel, with full thick lips, bright brown eyes and an uncommonly gorgeous face, so much so in fact that a number of the other inmates seemed somewhat mesmerized by her as she walked by their tables.

The young woman walked oblivious to the conversations or arguments taking place around her and sat down with a smile at Malcom's table.

"Hey you..." the young woman said, smiling to reveal perfect white teeth.

"Hey yourself." Said Malcom with a smile of his own.

"It's good to see you..." she said her smile fading a bit as if she had been expecting a slightly warmer welcome.

"It's good to see you too babe, you know your visits are the highlight of my week," Malcom said, reaching over the table and grabbing the young woman's hands within his own. "Where's Dante?" he asked.

"I was going to ask if you had talked to him. He was supposed to meet me in front of the prison this morning, but he never showed."

"Never showed?" Malcom looked confused.

"I called the cell number you gave me, went straight to voice mail. I texted it too, no response. You see Malcom this is why you should have let me just go pick him up from his hotel, it would have been less confusing. He may have gotten lost or nervous."

"Nah-nah-nah, Dante's not like that." He cut her off mid-speech, removing his hands from hers. "He doesn't get confused or lost, or even nervous, not when it comes to something like this. He's precise and methodical, you give him directions and he executes. I told him clearly, San Marcos State Correctional Facility, 8am. Then I gave him your number and told him to call you if he had any issues and that you would do the same if anything changed. And now you're telling me he never showed up and he's not answering his phone?" Malcom looked down at the table as he spoke now, halfway lost in thought.

"Maybe his videogame thing went longer than expected and he got caught up in that. You know how *you* get when you get into those games."

He cut his eyes at her. "Nah, Dante would have called. Something's wrong."

"Babe, I'm sure he's ok."

He looked up again this time with a small glint in his eye. "Can you go by his hotel, maybe check and see when they saw him last?"

"Malcom." She said in a tone that implied that he was overacting, being overprotective which she knew he was prone to do, especially when it came to his younger brother.

"Kiesha please, could you do it for me, it would just really make me feel better."

Kiesha let out a sigh, "Of course, babe, I'll look into it for you."

"Thank you Keesh, I'd be lost without you."

"I know." Kiesha smiled. "Oh, I also talked to your lawyer."

"Yeah, what does he want?" Malcom asked, suddenly appearing to lose interest in the conversation.

"More money."

"Of course, he does," said Malcom with a slight roll of his eyes, "Alright, whatever he's asking for give it to him. I know he had to pull a few strings to get me escorted to my mother's funeral."

"Aw babe I'm still so sorry about that." Kiesha said reaching out a hand and caressing the side of Malcolm's face. He reached up and grabbed a hold to her hand and held it there.

"What about you?" he asked "Are you ok? Do you need anything?"

"Babe I keep telling you I'm fine. I'm still in the condo, your safe is still looking very full and very healthy," she smiled and kind of chuckled but at the same time her eyes begin to tear up betraying the brave face she was attempting to put on, "and the shops are still doing well, but Malcom I'm more concerned about you. What do you need?"

He reached his hands across the table from his face to hers, caressing her cheek and wiping away the tear streaming down the side of her face. "As long as I have you, I have everything I *need* in this life. But do you want to know what I'd like?" he asked with a smile, and then even found himself holding back a chuckle. "What I would really really like?"

What's that?" Kiesha asked beginning to hold back a giggle of her own.

"I would really like you to go by my brother's hotel and check in on him for me." Malcom said breaking out into a laugh.

"Oh my God!" said Kiesha laughing as well, "I said I'd take care of it didn't I?" and she pushed back her chair to stand from the table.

"I know you did, I'm just... I'm concerned," Malcom said solemnly.

"I know you are babe, that's what makes you such a good big brother."

"No... if I was a good big brother, I wouldn't be sitting in here."

Malcolm we both know that's not true... I'll go see what I can find out for you okay?"

Malcom simply smiled and watched as his girlfriend walked away. Once the Security door closed behind her, he stood, and the guard returned, placed the handcuffs back on his wrist, and escorted him back to his cell. Once he had the cuffs off, he didn't bother removing the book from its place on the shelf. Instead he laid across the bed and replayed in his head the last conversation he'd had with his younger brother, desperate to try and figure out, where in the world he could possibly be.

Chapter 18: The Observation Room

Deep within the Last Legend Games Headquarters Building, in the heart of the labyrinth like corridors of sub-floor one, there is a large room that holds over thirty employees of the Dytorus Corporation.

The room in which they sit, stand, or run back and forth for coffee, water and office gossip, all to help see them through the day, is structured like an amphitheater and segmented into three parts.

The topmost balcony level holds the only door in or out of the room and is the level through which all employees must enter and exit the Amphitheater. The balcony also serves as the management employee work area and hosts a series of desks, each with its own computer monitor and phone, a sitting area with a view of the bottom two levels and also an additional door, that when opened, leads to a meeting room with a large oval table.

The next section of the Amphitheater, separated from balcony level by thin metal railing and four small steps, is the mid-level. Most of the employees that worked in the Amphitheater sat on the mid-level. The walls of the level were lined from floor to ceiling with computer servers which hummed and blinked twenty-four hours a day, seven days a week, even when the employees were not present. They computers worked unceasingly, feeding off a power supply separate from that of the rest of the building, processing complex computational equations, and analyzing over a million data points per minute. That data was then fed to computer monitors in the form of readout reports, or to printers in the form of printout reports. The employees on mid-level watched the monitors for the readout reports and watched the printers for the printout reports, to then summarize, categorize and archive each file and report to middle management up on the balcony level any report or printout that seemed out of the ordinary, which could sometime be difficult when studying the finer points of interdimensional travel and the laws of physics that govern extraplanar realms of existence.

Below the mid-level was one remaining segment to the Amphitheater, separated by another four steps and a ceiling high wall of bullet proof glass.

The ground level, more commonly referred to by the Dytorus Employees as the Stage, was a level on which no one worked, and no one entered.

There was also one additional door on mid-level, which led to a small square shaped room that sat off to the side of the Amphitheater. The small square room was split into two distinct halves, and on one half of the room sat a man and a woman.

"I still can't believe we're working with technology that sends people to another world," said the woman, who in actuality, happened to be Sara, who, up until very recently had worked in the character creation department but now found herself in the Player Correspondence Monitoring Department.

The man with whom she sat, Frank, had always worked in Player Correspondence and seemed neither interested nor impressed by the technology which dazzled Sara. Instead, he slurped loudly from a cup of lukewarm coffee and stared lazily into the other half of the room and then back again to a computer screen that sat before the two of them.

"If you had the opportunity to go over, would you?" Sara asked.

"Absolutely not," said Frank, almost spitting out his coffee in the process, "Going over there is suicide. Ninety-five percent of the people who go in never come back."

Sara seemed to sink down a bit in her chair in reaction to this response. She was normally a very upbeat young woman, cheerful, which most people found pleasant but secretly she suspected it annoyed Frank.

"A friend of mine went in," she said solemnly, "Stephen Choi..." she said the name as if in the hopes that Frank might recognize it, but his facial expression showed no signs of such recognition. "He went in as a game guide, so I'm sure he'll be fine," she let out a chuckle, forced, insincere. "He's too stubborn not to make it back. It's the gamers I feel sorry for, they really didn't have any idea what they were getting into."

"Yeah, but if you're right about your boyfriend then those gamers will also come back and when they do, they'll go down in history as the new explorers and astronauts of our generation. They'll be rich, famous, and, in the end, no one will remember how their little adventure started, heck they'll be say they volunteered for it, that it was their idea. It's like when they shot monkeys or dogs into space, the animals never had any say in it, but whenever the animal came back, they were like rock stars."

"And when they didn't?" asked Sara, "...Come back I mean."

"Sacrifices must be made for the advancement of science or 'the advancement of humanity' or whatever it is this company is always spouting on about." Frank spoke as if he were reading off a brochure.

"Yes, sacrificing our humanity for the sake of humanity," Sara mumbled under her breath.

Frank looked at her curiously, one of his eyebrows raised in apprehension. Sara caught his eye and blushed uncomfortably.

"Let me guess," said Frank. "You were the type that set the frogs free in science class in order to save them from dissection, am I right?"

Sara laughed. "No not exactly, I just think it's funny how we use words sometimes. That's all."

"Well, don't let anyone in middle management hear you using words like that," Frank replied.

"If anybody gets a whiff that you are the slightest bit squeamish about what's going on here, you'll be off the project, out of Dytorus Corp and unemployable by anyone with so much as a pot to piss in before you can say 'ribbit'. And that's if you're lucky." Frank stared at Sara for a moment, his placid skin and droopy eyes lingered in her direction for longer than she thought necessary, she imagined in an effort to punctuate just how serious he was about middle management and the zero-tolerance policy they had for the faint of heart.

She let out another uncomfortable laugh in an attempt to lighten the mood. "No, of course. This is a good job. I don't want to lose it."

Frank looked away from her and turned his attention back to the computer monitor.

"This is a good life; I don't want to lose it." He said.

Sara was quiet, unsure what Frank meant. She couldn't tell if he was saying that his job was his life and livelihood and he didn't want to risk his career, or if he was saying that his actual life, and by extension her life, were in danger. She thought about asking for clarification but before she could say anything else the monitor in front of them beeped.

"Heads up Frog Princess, we've got action," Frank called out.

Sara frowned at the new nickname but found herself excited all the same by the activity. She came over from the 'Deos Diver Prep Team', where she would help the game guides, combat consultants and then eventually the gamers themselves prepare to go into Deos. Her specialty was helping to develop the character creation technology that built the new bodies the players inhabited while inside Deos.

She was recruited by the Dytorus Corporation for her talent in the field of bio-prosthetics, the replacing of damaged or missing limbs and organs with biologically cultivated ones. Rebuilding the human body piece by piece to make people whole again. That had been her life's ambition, instead she had been roped into a company that was sending people to their doom by telling them they were going to play a video game. It was about then when she had met Stephen, the one other person at Dytorus Corp that seemed to have a conscious about what they were doing. Together they decided that he would go in game with the players, keep them safe, get them back home and then with 200 witnesses they would blow the lid off of this whole thing. They'd set the frogs free once and for all, no more science class, no more dissection.

But for now, it was a waiting game. Everyone going into Deos was already in. No one needed a new body, so she had been reassigned from Deos Diver Prep and Character Creation to this new role in Player Correspondence and with this, her first experience in receiving a live correspondence from the players in Deos. She was admittedly a little excited.

In front of them, dividing the room into its other half was a large glass window that allowed Frank and Sara to look in on the second half of the room. Through the window they could see a small round fire brazier. It looked like a medieval circular waste basket, only shorter and squatter and burning with an unending bright orange fire. It was always burning. But now, not only was it burning it also had begun to emit smoke, something it clearly had not done before. Slowly, thick white smoke had begun to rise from the flames, but instead of drifting up to the vents in the ceiling the smoke hung just a few feet above the small fire ring. It gathered in place like a small raincloud, slowly growing thicker and thicker until it began to coalesce and solidify into a single object, forming itself into what looked like a sheet of paper, or more accurately by Sara's estimation, a sheet of worn parchment.

"What's happening in there? What are we looking at?" Sara asked.

"Magic." Replied Frank.

The parchment finished forming and then just as miraculously as it had appeared from the flames, handwritten script formed across its face. Sara gasped. As the writing stopped a thin green light flashed across the face of the page and there was another beep from the monitor then an electronic voice chimed the words "Scan complete" and the parchment rolled itself up into a tube and fell to the ground as if released from an invisible grip.

In the observation room, words populated across the computer screen:

"Cpt. Marcus Pope reporting--

We landed safely on the Illder Plains of Deos, all players, game guide, combat consultants and gamers intact. We made contact with 2 classes of local fauna, both hostile. Both have been dispatched. Upon making contact with the locals in a nearby town we were hired to exterminate the invasive predator species in area.

Team agreed. Gamers enthusiastic. Team was accompanied by one local, referred to by gamers as a Half-Orc Cleric. Mission successful. En route back to town, team was ambushed by native flora, a man-eating plant, game guide gravely injured. Death imminent. The local escort performed life saving measures that placed game guide in suspended animation. The escort states that game guide can be resuscitated by 'healer' with proper skill and knowledge.

If true, this means a person can be brought back from near death state. Ability to stabilize gravely injured soldier and place in suspended animated state has limitless application on battlefield. I will continue to monitor situation.

I have made contact with team 17 and 12, we have had an incident with the townspeople in the city of Blackwater due to the gamer's erratic behavior. As a result, we have been forced to make camp outside of town to avoid further conflict. I will bring order to the group at dawn, incidents like these should be avoided in the future.

We shall proceed to the city of Abilene Bay to continue pursuing our original objectives. Advise other captains to rendezvous with us there.

Gamer Dante Battle has broken away taking with him three additional gamers. I have reason to believe that gamer is either aware of multidimensional travel, or that exposure to Deosian atmosphere has caused severe mental break. Either way he is to be considered hostile and a danger to mission.

Pope out."

"Is this what I think it is?" Sara asked astonished but what she had seen and what she was seeing.

"I'm not sure what you're thinking," said Frank who had begun punching commands into the computer, "but what you are looking at is a correspondence from Marcus Pope. The Captain has a fire ring like the one that in that room, he lights his ring, writes a message, burns it in the ring on his side and then the letter reappears out of the fire ring here on our side. This is fairly sophisticated Deosian technology, a high-level magical item. Aside from Pope there are four other people that have a fire brazier each one able to talk to the one in that room, and all of them are combat consultants."

When he was done typing Frank stood from his seat and walked through a door that let him into the other half of the room. Sara could see him through the window as he picked up the rolled-up piece of parchment and brought it back. "When a message comes through, the system scans it, creating a digital copy that is automatically saved on the system hard drive. We file it, log it, forward it to middle management and then archive the original." Frank opened a large file cabinet in the corner of the room near the door and slid the roll of parchment into a drawer with a number of others. "And that's the job." he said.

"This is extraordinary," Sara said. "How does it work? I've- I've never seen anything like this before."

"The braziers were brought back from a previous expedition to Deos, that's actually when we found out that the magic of Deos still works here on Earth, but it's tricky," Frank said, finally looking interested in the conversation. "Deos has a lot of rules, and the magic comes with those rules even when it hops to a different world. The fire ring is a rather straightforward magical item, so we are able to use it pretty easily, and as you see it works just fine between worlds. It's not nearly as complex as say, the full character creation process, or even the portal technology which is a combination of both Earth science and Deosian magic. That's where things get really difficult to understand, its like staring at the source code of the universe, that stuff will drive you insane. So, to tell you the truth, I try not to really think about it too much." Frank sat down and leaned back in his chair, tucking his hands behind his head. "Receive the correspondence, forward the correspondence, file the correspondence away, that's pretty much the job and that's what I try and stick to."

"Yeah," said Sara, looking back through the glass window at the small iron brazier and its bright orange flame. "That's one hell of a job."

CHAPTER 19: THE COMPANY MAN

Admittedly, the first time you take a life can be quite difficult. The first kill is the hardest, but surprisingly, each one after that becomes exceedingly less challenging than the last, and before long, taking a human life becomes as common as seeing a sunrise or a sunset. The human psyche is incredibly adaptive in that way. This works well for the soldier, who has taken war as his craft and killing as his profession. Marcus Pope was one such professional, a talented soldier with a career steeped in violence and pain. For him, every sunrise reminded him of a kill, every sunset a death.

The morning sky over Deos was clear, blue and dazzlingly bright. He had watched the sun rise over a crest of dark trees to the east and knew that at one point in time he would have considered such a sight beautiful.

He had no time for trifles like beauty these days though. At least, that's what he told himself. He reached up and touched the small golden locket that hung from his neck. In truth, it was not that Marcus Pope did not have time for things like beauty, but more or less that he no longer had the capacity to comprehend things like beauty. Beauty, compassion, affection, love, the very things that most men craved, Marcus Pope saw as pointless emotions that hindered a soldier's ability to complete a mission. He could spot them, emulate them, use them to manipulate the weak-minded and soft hearted, but he did not feel them. Not since Tabitha.

He released the heart locket and casually tucked it beneath his clothes and armor.

He grabbed his waterskin, doused the flames of the small fire and once the heat waned, he picked up the brass fire ring that had, mere moments ago, confined the enchanted flames that he used to send messages back to the Dytorus Command Team on Earth. He placed the ring carefully into his pack, then stood and turned his back on the rising sun, only to find himself staring at a gathering of poorly constructed tents, dwindling fires and a random scattering of supplies. Weapons and armor lay scattered, while also, among the rubble, were a large number of adventurers, strewn about the place in varying degrees of sleep, drunkenness and hangover. The entire scene brought to Pope's mind the idea of a medieval fraternity house, an idea which brought along with it, a teeth baring level of disgust. These fools.

They had made camp a mile and a half northeast of the town of Black Water, but only after a village wide brawl with the local townsfolk had forced them to withdraw from the city itself. They were now wedged in a small clearing that sat between the town and the forest of Black Wood. There were 19 of them in all. Including himself, Pope now had 9 Combat Consultants, 2 Game Guides and 8 Gamers under his command. The Combat Consultants were all ex-military, professional soldiers handpicked by Pope and trained to carry out any objective. They were consistent, dependable and reliable, well-honed tools vital for the completion of the mission in Deos. The two Game Guides, who were both direct employees of the Dytrous Corporation assigned to the mission by the company and not Pope, they were more like intelligence agents, or science officers. They were practically useless in combat, although their thorough knowledge and understanding of the surrounding area and its local inhabitants and customs did prove useful. Lastly were the gamers, by far the most ill-conceived addition to the entire Deos Diver Operation. Civilians with absolutely no military experience, unknowingly sent into an extremely hostile environment with no training other than a lifetime spent sitting on couches, staring at television screens and mashing buttons on a video game controller like a bunched of trained monkeys. Somehow the Dytorus Corp found it reasonable to consider this brain melting recreational activity simulated training for the mission at hand.

The gamers were considered by HQ a well-balanced middle ground between the soldier and the science officer, an idea so bad that it had to come from the private sector. Pope spat on to the ground in repugnance as he surveyed his "men". Never in a hundred years would any real military outfit worth its salt employ such a tactic. But as he was well aware, this was not a real military outfit. He was not in the military anymore, he was a mercenary, and this mission was a business venture.

Yet and still, regardless of who was passing down the orders one thing remained the same, Pope was a soldier, and a soldier's job was clear: Complete the mission, at all costs.

"Lansing." Pope said in a voice barely louder than a mumble, yet without fail his second in command appeared as if he had been anticipating the call.

"Captain Sir," responded Lansing, standing at attention before Pope, straight faced and rigid. His long, silver hair was pulled back into a tight ponytail, his thin sharp nose was pointed toward the bright blue sky while his pale eyes zeroed in on the captain with a ferocity that begged for an order of violence or mayhem.

Lansing had served under Pope before. They had been in the same U.S. Army, Special Forces unit. Delta Company, tried, tested and true. David Lansing was the perfect subordinate, when he was given an order, no matter what it was, he carried it out without question. The perfect soldier.

Pope squatted down before the blackened embers of the now extinguished fire and then toward the glowing Deosian sunrise, "Find Hernandez," said Pope in a cold and emotionless growl, "Then the two of you go and round up the men. I need to meet with them... now."

"Right away sir," replied Lansing, who then turned on his heels and disappeared into the camp without another word.

One competent subordinate amongst so many useless ones. Even most of the combat consultants were expected to die during the course of the mission, and the gamers, well, every game of chess has its pawns, and pawns were meant to be sacrificed. In the past all operation into Deos had ended in utter failure, hardly any of the volunteers that have traveled into the land of Deos previous to Pope's team had returned alive, and all of them were trained soldiers. But now things were different, now they had soldiers, they had experts, and they had these... pawns, pawns that were meant to be used as both soldiers and experts, as combatants and guides, as distractions and as backup, as scouts and as reinforcements, pawns that were meant to be used however Pope saw fit, just so long as he completed the mission.

Over his shoulder he could hear Lansing and Hernandez gathering the members of the camp. He could tell easily enough without looking that some of the men complied to the summons without complaint, the combat consultants no doubt, while others, the gamers, resisted the request, complaining of needing more sleep, or wanting more breakfast, or simply muttering that they did not see any reason as to why *they* were expected to come to a meeting in the first place. Insubordinate, undisciplined, useless and weak. Most of them would be good for nothing other than cannon fodder. Out of all of the basement dwelling button mashers they sent across the dimensional rift it would be a miracle to find even one that was worth the effort.

Well, but then again, there was one. Dante, our junior soldier in training who decided to go AWOL, yes, they would have to remedy that... if he was still alive at least. After all, good help was so hard to find in these trying times, and when resources were scarce, not even a single pawn could be wasted.

"Captain Pope," said a female voice from behind him. "I understand you wanted to meet with everyone."

Pope stood, unfolding himself from his squat and standing to full height. He turned to see Corrine and Dwight, the two Dytorus Corp game guides, standing alongside a host of disenchanted looking gamers.

"Yes," said Pope, "but not until everyone is here," said the captain looking down his nose at the woman.

Behind Corrine more gamers straggled in but apparently only at the behest of some rather determined and stony-faced combat consultants. Pope observed as Hernandez seemed to be having a particularly tough time explaining to a gamer, roughly the size of a child, why it was in his best interest to attend the meeting.

"I don't understand why I have to attend a meeting. I don't work for Dytorus Corp or Last Legend Games, I'm here to play the Dragon Dale Beta, not sit through staff meetings," complained the child-sized man.

"Yes, well the meeting is *about* the game so if you would just come along. The quicker, we can get together then the quicker we can get the meeting over with," replied Hernandez.

Pope recognized the gamer from the previous day, in the tavern he had been one of the last people to speak with Dante before he had fled, and judging from the reaction of the townspeople when he stepped outside the tavern, it might have been safe to assume he was one of the main reasons why their entire group was making camp outside the city as opposed to sleeping at the inn. As Hernandez ushered him along, a small band of gamers followed in their wake, a cat man, a lizard man, and a pointy-eared female, they laughed at the tiny adventurer's every wise crack and snide remark, so obscenely blissful in their ignorance and confident in their weakness. The sight of it all enraged Pope and silently he decided that he very much hated each of them.

"Captain, everyone is present and accounted for sir."

"Thank you, Lieutenant."

"Captain? Lieutenant? What is this? Boot camp?" said the small adventurer to which the cat man, lizard man, and pointy-eared female laughed heartedly.

"What's you name, son?" Pope asked twisting his head so that he could make eye contact with the small man.

"Danger Duke," said the tiny adventurer.

"You know what, Danger Duke? You have a big mouth for a runt," said Pope calmly.

"Wha-what did you say?"

"You're obnoxious and you behave as if your actions have no consequences. All of you do. That's why we're here." Pope motioned to the surrounding camp. "That's why we're sleeping in the dirt instead of beds." Pope looked back to the tiny gamer. "Because of you, because of all of you. Up until now you have been operating with complete autonomy, doing whatever you've pleased. Acting with a complete lack of leadership."

Corrine cleared her throat.

"That ends today," Pope continued. "From this moment forward you fall under my command."

"Your command? Dude, we're in a video game, not the army. This is an MMORPG, not some Real-Time Strategic War Game. The best part of these games is the freedom to make choices, especially the wrong choices, I didn't sign up for this Beta to come follow orders. I would have just let my dad send me to military school for that." The adventurer's band of cohorts giggled. He looked around at them reassuringly. "I mean who is this guy?"

"This," interjected Corrine, "Is Captain Marcus Pope, he is the head of Dytorus Corp Mobile Security and the lead combat consultant."

"Combat consultant? Shouldn't he just consult? What's the deal with calling these meeting and talking about taking command?" Danger Duke's retorts were met with murmurs of agreement from the gamers.

A smile crept across Pope's face.

"When are we going to logout and take a break?" asked a human male wearing chainmail armor and a mace.

"When are we going to split into smaller groups and go off on our own?" yelled out the cat-man.

Then another human male spoke up, this one with a small musical instrument strapped to his back and a rapier on his belt. "In the tavern, one of the players seemed convinced that we were not in a video game at all." The murmurs and complaints of most of the other gamers grew quiet as the human continued. "He said we'd been sent to another world altogether, then he ran out of the tavern and disappeared into the forest... Do you have any idea why a player would do something like that... Captain?"

Dwight had started sweating and Corrine moved forward as if she might say something, but Pope raised a hand to silence her.

"You won't be logging out, and we won't be splitting up because the player in the tavern yesterday was telling you the truth. This is *not* a game."

"Pope, stop!" said Corrine in a panicked voice. He turned and looked at her with cold dead eyes that had seen a hundred sunrises and sunsets. Instantly Corrine grew quiet and stepped backwards.

"Its time they know," he said with a tone of growing concern, before turning back to the rest of the group.

"You all *have* been transported to an alternate world, one that mirrors the video game world of Dragon Dale. The games you have been playing for most of your lives are based off of past missions into this world, Deos. Only the *real* Deos is much more dangerous, hostile and unpredictable than anything you've experienced in your mother's basement. You have been brought here because you are the best of the best, and we need the best because the Dytorus Corporation and Earth are here to tame this wild world."

"Tame this world?" began the adventurer in the chainmail armor.

"Deos is a world of magic, power and treasure," Pope's voice seemed to tremble with excitement, and he leaned forward as he spoke, drawing everyone within the sound of his voice closer to him. "All its riches are yours for the taking, all of which equate to a veritable fortune when you return to Earth. Here you all have a chance to forge a path into a new world and make yourselves extraordinarily wealthy while doing so, but I assure you, you cannot do it alone, but together with me, we can conquer this land."

"You've gotta be kidding me. Mandrake, Orion, don't tell me you guys are buying this?" Danger Duke turned to his compatriots with a pleading expression. "This is a video game. You all have health bars floating over your heads for god's sake. What is wrong with you people? There's no way I'm following this whacked out army nut with PTSD."

There was a resounding *thawck* as the bolt from Pope's crossbow zipped across the clearing and buried itself firmly into the tiny adventurer's thigh with the back half of the bolt protruding outward like a half-bored nail waiting to be driven into a post. The small adventurer looked down for a moment in silent disbelief, before the shock of pain prompted him to grab hold to his thigh howling in agony as blood streaked the length of his leg.

"He shot me! He shot me with a crossbow!" he screamed, and over his head one third of his health bar faded into oblivion.

"That pain you're feeling is real and that's because this world is real and the most important thing you need to remember is that if something can hurt you, then it can kill you, and if you die in this world, you're dead. Just like on Earth." Pope looked around at the group in front of him, the gamers looked uncomfortable, scared, confused. They looked just as weak as they were. The tiny adventurer that had been so loud and boisterous all morning was now holding his leg, sobbing in pain. His band of sidekicks were no longer laughing, instead their eyes shifted nervously back and forth from Pope's crossbow to their wounded defacto leader. Pope's smile grew wider and he found himself holding back a chuckle of his own. Pawns were always so easily broken by fear of pain.

"I'm sorry I shot you," he said "but we don't have all day to debate. A small amount of pain now, is a small price to pay if it saves your life later. Let's have a healer fix that wound, you'll be good as new in no time. Everyone else let's breakdown camp and prepare to head out in 30 minutes."

"Where are we going?" asked the cat man.

Pope shouldered the crossbow, a movement that made the cat man flinch. "Our mission is to establish a base of operation in Deos and as I understand it the best place to do that is Abilene Bay, roughly a 3-day march through the forest. Once we get there we'll meet up with more gamers and more combat consultants and together we'll take from this land everything we desire, returning home true heroes. *Real* adventurers. Now who's with me?"

The combat consultants let out a cheer. The gamers looked uncertain.

"I said who's with me?!" Pope asked again louder and this time thrusting this crossbow into the air. Both the combat consultants and the gamers let out an obligatory cheer in unison.

"Now," said Pope, "Break camp, we march in thirty."

With nervous reluctance the group dispersed. The lizard and cat-man carried Danger Duke off toward an open tent, where the adventurer in chainmail followed, his hands already glowing with the golden light of restorative magic.

"Captain Pope. A word?" Corrine kept her voice low.

Pope turned to her, his crossbow now once again slung across his back and his hands held discreetly behind him. He stood tall and erect, with his chest out and his head high. Corrine seemed to shrink in his presence.

"What can I help you with Ms. Weathers?" Pope asked in a cold and stony voice, daring her to question his behavior.

"It seems Dwight may have misplaced his pack. He believes he lost it in the chaos and confusion of yesterday's riot."

"And why Ms. Weathers are you telling me this?" Pope asked.

"Well, he had some very important information in that pack. Information vital to the nature of our objectives here in Deos." Corrine looked embarrassed.

Pope let out a long-labored sigh.

Just as he expected... useless.

Chapter 20: The Wolf Rider

Ali Vishna was a merchant returning to the city of Illdershire after a short trip into the Bleekmore Hills. He was traveling alone. Well, mostly alone. The roads outside the towns and cities could be dangerous, especially considering that Ali Vishna often veered off of the Merchant Road in order to take alternate paths and shortcuts, a behavior his wife deemed as foolish. For a married man with children and a demanding business to go off galivanting into the wilderness, running along some imaginary trade routes to some tiny towns that no one had ever heard of, just so that he could make a few extra coins at market, and then brag to his merchant friends on how he does not have to wait on the traveling trade caravans to resupply his stocks, it was obvious to her and everyone that knew Ali that the trips were more for his ego then his shop. But Ali Vishna saw things differently. Ali knew that in order for any merchant to become a great merchant he must be willing to do things that others were not willing to do. He *must* take risk, but the key was to take *calculated* risk.

So, Ali Vishna traveled alone, with the exception of his pack beast, a shaggy bison named Winruff. Shaggy bison are big lumbering beast that walk on four legs and that, for the most part, look like large fur-covered boulders. They are grazers, plant eating bovine covered from head to hoof with long and coarse brown hair and it is difficult, in most cases, to tell one end of the bison from the other. An occasionally swishing tail to shoo away flies is the sole indication of the shaggy bison's rear end, while two short curved and sharply pointed horns are the only distinguishing feature of the bison's front. It's eyes, nose and mouth are completely concealed by its overgrown coat of fur. Shaggy bison are incredibly strong and exceptionally intelligent creatures. This makes them ideal as pack beast, able to pull large carts and wagons, as well as carry tied on goods and even a rider over great distances, with little trouble. They are not the fastest steeds, but they are reliable, do not spook easily and their large size and strength stave off all but the most vicious predators.

It was Winruff that made Ali Vishna's trading expeditions possible, Winruff, and Ali's own intricate knowledge of the Illder countryside, all of its hidden roadways, secret paths, game trails and short cuts. His wisdom, his Winruff, and of course his Blunderbuss, a handheld weapon made of metal and wood by the dwarves of Oningrad, or the Gnomes of Hemera-Balgrad, or perhaps a combination of the two, no one really knew. He had purchased the Blunderbuss some years ago from a half-elf traveler who was passing through Illdershire desperately in need of gold. The weapon was activated by pulling a trigger mechanism similar to that of a crossbow, but instead of launching a bolt at a target, the cylindrical opening of the Blunderbuss exploded in a ball of fire and smoke and flung from its burning mouth a number of small metal pellets that spread out and ripped through anything in their path. The thunderous sound that it made was nearly as scary as what it did to anything foolish enough to be standing in front of it when its trigger mechanism was pulled, and every time Ali Vishna fired it, he struggled not to drop it, or allow it to go flying out of his hands. Ali Vishna was confident that whatever the blunderbuss couldn't kill, maim, or mortally wound, it could at the very least scare away.

It was on the tail end of a recent trip across the plains that Ali Vishna noticed something curious. Across the plains, from some distance away, Ali saw a pack of wolves racing toward Illdershire. He found this as particularly odd, considering that wolves were a rare sight during the daylight hours. He fumbled for the blunderbuss. The wolves were easily over a mile away, but their sense of smell was powerful, and hadnt bathed in days, nor had Winruff. But quickly, Ali relaxed. The wolves hadn't noticed him.

He, however, couldn't tear his eyes away. They were abnormally large wolves running incredibly fast. They chased no prey; but instead were concerned only with arriving at their predetermined destination as soon as possible. He'd likely never see wolves like this again in his life. It would make a great story to tell his wife and children later. And then a dark shadow at the back of the pack became clear and Ali had to stifle a scream. It was without a doubt, the biggest wolf Ali had ever seen, at least ten feet tall with fur like a midnight sky. Ali sunk behind a rock and pulled Winruff with him. Suddenly, neither 1 mile nor 10 miles would be enough distance between himself and this great beast.

From his now hidden position in the grass Ali continued to watch the great wolf bound across the plain from the back of the pack, pushing the rest of the wolves onward. The merchant clenched his chest attempting to settle his pounding heart for fear that even the sound of it would soon give him away, for he realized now that he was not merely observing some ordinary pack of wolves roaming across the plains, but that he had instead somehow stumbled across and managed to lay eyes upon a beast nearly as glorious as Canis Romulus the Legendary King of Wolves.

"By the Gods," Ali whispered to himself, "wait until the boys in the market hear about this." And then Ali Vishna spotted something even more peculiar. On the back of the giant wolf, arms outstretched and clinging to his man, appeared to be a person. Still lying on his belly, Ali reached up into one of the saddle bags strapped to the side of the shaggy bison and felt around until he pulled out a spy glass, a telescopic lens with which he would use to take a closer look at the wolf king and the rider he bore, however once he had extended the spy glass and aimed at the direction of the great wolf, he found that not only had it stopped running but its rider was now dismounting. The wolf lowered itself and the tiny figure upon its back slipped to the ground. A human, clad in dark leathers.

He focused the spyglass in on the rider, a dark-skinned, dark eyed youth with a sword on his belt. "Hathor's Nightdress," Ali mumbled under his breath. "The Wolf Rider is a bloody adventurer." Ali scanned the spyglass both left and right of the rider looking to get another view of the King of Wolves, and was shocked to find the wolf's large predatory eyes staring back at him. The wolf licked its thin lips revealing for only a brief instant terrifyingly large white teeth, a sight which made Ali throw the spy glass from his face as if it had suddenly grown hot to the touch. The lens dropped over the edge of the precipice and tumbled down the side of the cliff, clittering and clattering the entire way down. "Hathor's Petticoat! Come Winruff we have to move now."

The shaggy bison groaned in defiance at the thought of getting up, now that he was on the ground and comfortable.

"Move your great big dolt or by this time tomorrow you and I both will be nothing more than wolf excrement fertilizing the Illdershire grass!" Ali shouted in a whisper, and begrudgingly enough the bison obeyed, climbing back up to a stand in a series of moos and groans, all of which Ali Vishna attempted to quiet as best he could. Once Winruff was back up on all fours Ali flung himself into the saddle amongst the overpacked goods and slapped the reigns, in an attempt to urge the pack beast down the back side of the cliff and through a path that would deliver them safely to the North Gate of the city of Illdershire, hopefully before the wolves could close the distance between them. He slapped the reigns again, and Winruff moo'd in frustration, and began a slow but determined trot toward the backside of the cliff. Ali cursed the bison and threatened to sell him to the butcher once they got back to Illdershire, a threat which apparently fell on deaf ears as the bison's speed did not change. Ali Vishna looked back over his shoulder, half expecting to see wolves sprinting towards his direction, instead he found that the beast had not moved, the great wolf was now sitting and appeared to be talking to its former rider. Could the wolf speak? Was this in fact Canis Romulus he was seeing? And even more puzzling, who was this dark-skinned dark-eyed swordsman, who rode wolves across the Plains of Illder and spoke with the King of Wolves as a father speaking to a son? Winruff trotted on carrying Ali down the backside of the precipice and taking the wolf and his mysterious rider out of sight.

Chapter 21: Return to Illdershire

Dante and his team rode clear through the night, across the Illder Plains atop the back of Canis and his wolves. They stopped a few times, but only for a couple of minutes at a time and always for the sake of the adventurers, never for the sake of the wolves. In the end no one slept, but as the moons fell and the sun had begun to rise again, Dante could see the dark silhouette of Illdershire take shape in the far-off distance and doubted if even horses could have traveled half as fast.

Canis Romulus moved with the speed and grace of a formless shadow dancing across the face of the grassland. Dante clung to the wolf's huge dark body, tufts of shiny black fur gripped tightly in each hand while his legs and thighs did the best they could to clamp down on the wolf's constantly moving frame. They bounded over the plains in great leaps, padded paws barely making a sound on the soft grass. Dante realized early on that they were moving so fast that the plains had become a blur. The tussling and jostling of the dashing wolves made it hard to see, hear or even think clearly. Once he learned to lean into the run, becoming one with the great wolf king, his vision cleared. His eyes narrowed and focused on the wolf that ran ahead of them, and suddenly the ride became not only bearable, but the entire thing begin to feel natural and right.

Before long the sky turned an early morning blue. Illdershire loomed in the distance, now only a few miles away. Dante could feel Canis slow, his sprint dropping to a trot and shortly thereafter stopping altogether.

"We are here," the great wolf said, allowing Dante to dismount and land in the grass on shaky legs. The other wolves that had been running ahead of them had also stopped and Dante could see each of his friends sliding off of the back of the large bulky wolf that had carried them through the night.

"This is as far as we go, young one." Canis said, now looking back at Dante, and now in a seated position, his large hind legs tucked underneath him. He looked down at the adventurer with an expression of fatherliness, a kind yet stern nurturer, and Dante wondered if there was even more to the Great King of Wolves than appeared.

"I dare not lead my wolves any closer to the city," continued Canis, "so we must part ways here, the remainder of the journey, you and your packmates can safely travel alone."

"Yes, of course," replied Dante, "Thank you Canis. I'm not sure what we would have done without your help." Dante stared up at the talking wolf and suddenly felt himself overwhelmed with emotion. He was trapped in an alternate world, with little to no hope of escape and his only source of comfort and safety was a giant talking wolf. It was quite possible, Dante realized, if not more logical and more likely that he had actually gone insane and everything that he was experiencing was all really no more than a very lucid, very realistic dream. He felt the urge to weep, and then wake up with a start, in the dark, in his childhood bed, in his childhood room with the television blaring and one of his old consoles running one of his old Dragon Dale games, and then suddenly this nightmare would finally make sense.

But as Dante stood there on the open Plains of Illder, he felt the Deosian sun bearing down upon him. He felt a gentle breeze blow in from the east, cooling his skin and carrying with it the scent of sweet grass and distant civilization. The chittering of unseen insects and the chirping morning birds filled his ears and no matter how hard he willed it, he could not wake up and that overwhelming urge to weep threatened to overtake him once again.

"Dante," said the wolf in his deep rich voice that by its timbre alone snapped him from his daydream. "I must tell you that I find myself quite proud of the honorable path you have taken."

Dante blinked the tears out of his eyes as he looked back up at the wolf.

"In your issue of clan leadership, you could have forced me and my wolves to aide you against your rivals, or you could have simply accepted your role below an unfit and unjust alpha, but instead you did neither. You made the most difficult of all choices, you took a stand and did what was right, you did what was best for your pack."

"I don't feel very honorable," Dante contended. "I feel defeated. In fact, it seems like I've suffered a defeat at every turn. Pope, the Tree Hugger Cat, even coming to Deos was..." Dante felt a catch in his throat. "It's just been one bad decision after another and every time I step up, I just get knocked back down."

"You are young and have much to learn," said the wolf. "Unfortunately, I have no doubt your travels will take you far beyond the reach of both my assistance and my counsel, but before we part, I will leave you with at least one lesson. You must remember this above all else if you are to lead this new pack you have created. For a wolf, failure and defeat are not the end, but instead, steps on the journey. Never be ashamed to take time and lick your wounds and learn from your mistakes. Only then may you return to the battlefield stronger and fiercer than before. To help you remember this ideal and to always remind you that you have a place here among the Black Wolves of Illder, I bestow on to you a boon."

"A boon?" repeated Dante. A boon, in the world of Dragon Dale, was a blessing or special ability, usually given to adventurers by beings of extraordinary power. "But boons are for-"

Before Dante could finish the thought the wolf's large front paw lifted from the ground and planted itself into his chest, knocking him on to his back. He hit the ground with a thud, the wolf's heavy paw pressed down upon him. Canis's weight squeezed the air from his lungs and his thick black claws dug deep into Dante's torso. He struggled to free himself, but he might as well had been pinned down under the rubble of a fallen house. He thought he heard from his far left, someone call out to him, but he couldn't be sure. Everything around him had suddenly become distant, muffled. He struggled for breath. Pushing with every ounce of his strength, he tried to lift the wolf's paw from his chest, as now breathing was nearly impossible and the spear tipped claws were drawing blood. He looked up to see the king wolf looming over him, his great mouth gaping open as hot breath beat down upon him and a black tongue flashed over white teeth nearly large as swords.

Then he heard loud howling that resonated with his soul. The world spun, and Dante could feel his eyes cross in an attempt to keep up. His vision blurred and the image of Canis that loomed over him doubled. One continued to stare down at him as if he were cornered prey, the other reared back his large head and sung the chorus of wolves, howling in a frequency that latched onto a part of his consciousness that he didn't even know existed. He closed his eyes, fearful that his mind was on the brink of collapse as it tried to reconcile what he was seeing, feeling and hearing all at once. The howling reached a crescendo within his skull, growing so loud that he thought he would scream. And then, almost as suddenly as the ordeal began, it ended. The howling stopped and the pressure against his torso lifted. Dante opened his eyes to find himself standing once again and Canis still sitting in front of him seemingly unmoved, with the exception of one forepaw that appeared to be moving back to its original place upon the ground.

"What jus- what just happened?"

"I have bestowed unto you the Boon of the Black Wolf. It is a minor boon, but in a short time you have shown yourself more than worthy. This is my gift to you, may it serve you well, and may it grow with you as you journey fourth."

"What does it do?" Dante asked, holding his chest, still recovering from the effects of receiving the boon.

"It will serve as a reminder of what is important to a wolf." Canis sat up to what Dante imagined was his full height, and for the first time, in the full light of day, Dante could see the numerous scars covering the great wolf's body. "There is no such thing as failure, only survival, and every day that we survive we grow stronger in order to survive another day."

Dante stared up at the gigantic wolf and wondered who or what could have threatened, let alone wounded, such a large and terrifying creature.

"Fare thee well young wolf, I look forward to the day our paths cross again," said Canis, who stood to all fours and then as if carried off by a black wind disappeared from sight with a flash of movement as he and his wolves dashed back into the depths of the plains.

"Dante..." said a voice from behind him. The pounding sting in his chest faded as he looked over his shoulder to see Morrigan, Alex and Robyn standing together, waiting for him.

The town of Illdershire had seemed an ominous place only a few days prior, but now after their return from the wilderness of Deos and their experience in the town of Black Water, Illdershire seemed like a safe haven, and still the group found themselves ill at ease even within the safety of the towns walls. After all, though seemingly safe at the moment, they were still trapped.

"I guess the question now is, what do we do next?" said Morrigan in a low voice as they wandered aimlessly through the city streets. She didn't seem to be talking to anyone in particular, but more so merely posing the question to the group.

"Well we could just stay here right? I mean at least in the city we know we're safe." suggested Alex

"Yeah but for how long?" asked Dante. "The wolves got us here fast and may have bought us some time, but if Pope and his men are still looking for us, we have to assume we only have one day maybe two before they could possibly stroll into Illdershire. And then suddenly we're not so safe anymore."

"Do you really think they'd come all the way back here looking for us?" asked Alex. "I mean, they may not even know where we are. For all they know we died in the Black Wood, or are lost on the plains."

"That's a big 'If'," said Morrigan, "One we'd have to be willing to stake our lives on."

"And even if they're not looking for us, that only solves one of our problems," said Dante, "We still have to figure out a way to get back home. We can't stay in Illdershire forever."

"Which brings us back to *how* do we get back, when our only ride is a megalomaniac that we're purposely trying to avoid?" asked Morrigan.

"A megalomaniac with a small army," said Alex.

"Oh that reminds me," said Robyn, who then dropped down to one knee and began shuffling through one of the packs she kept on her hip. Which was odd, seeing as Dante did not recall her having two packs. They had all started with only one.

Dante took a deep breath while simultaneously running his hands down the length of his face. He was tired. Exhausted. They hadn't slept at all during the night and now it seemed to be catching up with him. His thoughts were scattered and disorganized, he felt like he could barely keep his eyes open let alone figure out a plan of escape from one world to another.

"We're screwed," Dante muttered.

"What? Why would you say that?" Alex asked in a bit of a panic.

"Guys I may have found something," mumbled Robyn from her position on the ground.

"Pope has nearly every possible advantage. He has us outmanned, outgunned, and he has the only known ticket back home." Dante rubbed his forehead again. "Our only leverage... and I mean maybe the only thing we could have going for us is if Pope thinks we can't survive in Deos on our own. If he assumes we're as good as dead after running into those woods-"

"Which we almost were," added Morrigan.

"If Pope and the others are not looking for us, that would at least give us the element of surprise. But there's not really much we can do with that alone. We need more. We need to know something that they don't, or I mean, at least know why they really brought us here."

"We do." Robyn said again, still not looking up from her scroll. Suddenly the others turned their attention to her.

"What do you mean 'we do'?" asked Dante.

"I mean we have details of exactly what they are trying to do in Deos." Robyn held up the scroll. "I stole this off that weird guy in the Tavern. Dwight."

"How?" asked Alex. "When?"

"I bumped into him as we were making a break for it." Robyn answered matter of factly, "Took it as we were running out. Figured it might be useful and would at least piss him off. Hadn't had a chance to go through it until now. It's mostly gold, a few potions and then this." She handed Dante the now unrolled piece of parchment.

"What does it say?" asked Morrigan.

Dante's eyes grew wide as they danced over the surface of the thick yellowish-brown paper. He started smiling, and then he chuckled.

"What does it say!" Morrigan asked again, this time slightly more fervent than before.

"Well one side of it is a map," Dante said holding up the scroll so everyone could see. "A map of Deos. Looks similar to the type of map I saw Stephen reference a couple of times before, only," Dante's smile grew even wider. "on the other side," Dante turned the map over revealing the back, upon which a litany of script was scrawled in neat cursive handwriting, "It's a breakdown of their objectives. Their *real* objectives."

"What?" Morrigan look astonished. "How?"

"Each of the game guides must have one of these scrolls," Dante reasoned. "A map on one side and their "mission" on the other. Oh my God I can't believe this. Robyn you're a genius. I'm so happy I could kiss you!" Dante said excitedly.

"Hey there cowboy, don't you go threatening me with a good time."

"Well before you start kissing people," Morrigan interrupted "what exactly does the scroll say, what's their mission?"

Dante turned the scroll over in his hand once again, his face stuck in a grin. "Well, they have three main goals. One is to determine the source of magical power in Deos and then determine if it can be monetized or weaponized."

"Well that doesn't sound like something we should be happy about," Morrigan said dryly.

"Two." Dante continued, ignoring her remark. "Is to determine the status of the political climate in the region and to determine if there is an entry point for the Dytrous Corporation."

"None of this sounds reassuring," said Morrigan.

"No it doesn't." Alex chimed in.

"Wait for it," said Robyn.

"And three," Dante now began to read directly from the scroll, "One of the original game designers, Benjamin Sandberg, is believed to be hiding in Deos. It is also believed that he possesses the knowledge to move freely between worlds. If possible, he is to be located and questioned as he is suspected to have valuable information pertaining to objectives one and two." Dante lowered the scroll from his face and then passed it to Morrigan so she could read it for herself. "Do you know what this means?" he asked and she scanned over the document with Alex reading over her shoulder.

"That corporate greed has taken over Earth and now they plan to expand their dominion to other markets?" said Morrigan.

"This means," he continued, "that we now have a chance. They believe that Benjamin Sandberg, one of the original creators of the Dragon Dale games is somewhere here in Deos. They're looking for him. If we can find him first..."

"He might be able to send us home," said Alex, looking up from the scroll with a new glint of hope in his eyes.

"Yes," said Dante feeling for the first time in what felt like a long time an emotion other than despair and disappointment. Perhaps Canis had been right, maybe there was no such thing as failure, not as long as at least a little bit of hope survived.

"This says that they 'believe' he may be here. They don't actually know," said Morrigan, flipping over the scroll to now look at the side with the map drawn on it. "He may not even be in Deos, and even if he is here, he could be anywhere. For all we know he could be dead."

"Benjamin Sandberg disappeared five years ago right around the time that Dytorus Corporation acquired Last Legend Games. He had a major falling out with the game's other two original creators, Arthur Hirsch and Michael Edwards, all because they wanted to sell and he didn't. He held a press conference, made a big fuss about the merger and then disappeared from public life. I remember people joking on the internet saying that Dytorus Corp had either had him killed or drove him insane. But I'm willing to bet the truth is he came back to Deos and went into hiding. Don't you get it, that's why he didn't want to sell. He didn't want to let Dytorus get their hands on Deos. Hirsch, Edwards and Sandberg must have been the first people to discover a way here, then they went back to Earth and built a game based around their experiences. Benjamin Sandberg has been coming back and forth to Deos for the past twenty-five years. There's no way that he's dead. We just have to find him. We have to find him before they do."

Morrigan stared at Dante. His eyes were shimmering, almost as if he was on the verge of tears. He spoke with so much conviction, so convinced that they were on the right track. He spoke as if he didn't have a solitary doubt that this one chance could lead them out of their nightmarish situation and back to a world that made sense.

"Ok,"said Morrigan, looking back down at the map,"Say you're right, say he is here. How do we find him? How do we find one person in a place this big? He could be anywhere."

For a moment the group was silent, the four of them taring at the map in quite contemplation. She was right, Dante thought. Sandberg could be anywhere in Deos and tracking down one person in a world of God knows how many people would be literally like finding a needle in a haystack.

"Abilene Bay," said Dante still looking down at the map.

"But that's where Pope is headed, why would we go there?" Alex asked.

"It's our best shot." Dante replied. "Traditionally in the Dragon Dale games Abilene Bay is a hub of activity, commerce and information. The best chance we have of finding Sandberg starts in Abilene Bay."

"The quickest way to Abilene Bay is to head east," said Robyn running her finger along the map, "We'd have to go back to Black Water, cut through the Black Woods and pop out right in front of the city. Only thing is, if we go that way, there is a pretty good chance we'll run into Captain Crazy, especially if they're coming back this way looking for us."

"Yeah, and we probably shouldn't head back to Black Water anytime soon, we didn't exactly leave there on a good note," said Alex.

"We'll have to go around." Said Dante. "See here?" he pointed to the city of Illdershire labeled on the map, then slowly moved his finger upwards. 'We leave Illdershire and head north, take the Merchant Road to the town of Bleeksborough, up here in the hills. Then we leave the Merchant Road and head east until we hit the Erebus Lake, in Dragon Dale 4, 6 and 9 there was a ferry that would take you across the lake to the city of Midell. From there we can walk the rest of the way to Abilene Bay. This way we avoid the Black Woods altogether and we pretty much eliminate the risk of running into Pope."

"If we use our first trip to Black Water as a reference for time and distance, it'll take us roughly five days to make the trip going that way," said Morrigan. "We'll have to spend a couple of nights camping outside, but most nights we should be able to rest in the towns. That's considering we don't run into any hiccups. If we can buy or rent some horses or something along the way, we maybe can get there even faster."

"This could work," exclaimed Alex.

"We just have to find Benjamin Sandberg before Pope finds him," said Dante.

"Or before Pope finds us..." added Robyn.

"And all while trying not to get killed by a very dangerous world where everything with a mouth wants to eat you," added Morrigan.

"Umm yeah..." said Alex now looking a little doubtful.

"Don't worry Al," said Robyn slapping Alex on the shoulder, "We got this, it'll be easy."

"We need to go shopping," said Morrigan. "We need to grab supplies for the road, rest here in Illdershire tonight and head out first thing in the morning." She rolled up the map and handed it back to Dante who took the parchment with an approving nod of agreement.

Dante knew the journey to Abilene Bay would not be easy, but that was okay with him. He didn't need easy. All he needed was a chance, and lucky enough a chance was all he had.

Chapter 22: Ali Vishna's Trinkets and Treasures

Ali Vishna was stocking shelves in the back of his shop when a group of customers walked in through the front door. They were dusty, road worn, adventurers most likely, definitely not townsfolk. For Ali Vishna this was normal. A lot of travelers passed through Illdershire, merchants, traders and especially adventurers.

Ali's shop was small, clean and well lit. The open windows allowed for plenty of natural light, which gleamed on the polished wooden floors. The air of the shop was filled with the faint yet lingering smell of lemon oil, which Ali used on, not only the floors, but the counters and shelves as well. It was a widely known fact that Ali's shop was his pride and joy and everything he did was meant to make it the best in all of Illdershire and eventually all of Deos.

Ali Vishna stood to better greet his customers and gasped.

The face was unmistakable, one he could never forget: the Wolf Rider. It was the same swordsman that he had seen earlier that morning, riding across the plains on the back of a gigantic wolf. Just for a moment he froze. Part of him, the sane part, wanted to bolt out of the back door of the shop. Then another part of him, the merchant part, wanted his autograph, to frame it and tell everybody that walked by his door of the dangerous and mysterious customers that visited his modest shop. Three other adventurers stood in the company of the Wolf Rider and Ali was struck by how young and good natured they seemed. They were just kids.

Dante jumped when the shopkeeper emerged from the shadows of the shop, loud and boisterous, his finger pointed at Dante as if prepared to accuse him of something.

"It is you!" he said, hand still shaking from either nervousness or excitement, Dante could not tell which. "It is you! You are he! He is you!"

"I don't know what you mean?" Dante said wearily.

"This morning, on the plains. I saw you. YOU ARE THE WOLF RIDER!"

"Oh..." Dante's mind raced, he hadn't thought about the fact that he might have been seen during the morning, nor did he know what the consequence of such a thing would be. "You mean Canis."

"You are on a first name basis with CANIS ROMULUS THE LEGENDARY WOLF KING! By the Gods this is even more magnificent then I thought." The shop owner was speaking fast and was visibly shaking, "To think I, Ali Vishna, witnessed with my own eyes the vestige of Canis Romulus, the King Wolf of the Illder Plains. Ha! That is like- that is like seeing a dragon." Ali Vishna seemed to be talking more to himself then to Dante, Ali slapped himself on the forehead in disbelief. "And now in my shop, his rider!" The shopkeeper's eyes grew wide, so wide that Dante thought for a second they may overtake his entire face.

"No, I'm not his rider, he was just giving me a ride, just the one time. It's not like... a regular thing." Dante tried to explain while Alex, Robyn and Morrigan exchanged glances, all trying to figure out if the shopkeeper's obvious excitement was going to make it a good or bad day for them.

"Oh my young friend you are being too modest. He could have eaten you, but instead he carried you upon his back. The King of Wolves!" Ali's eyes gleamed, "He must accept you as one of his own."

"Yes," Dante answered reluctantly, looking to his friends for help as to how to navigate this conversation. They responded with shoulder shrugs. He was on his own.

"I knew it!" Ali Vishna burst with uproarious laughter. "I," he gestured to himself "am Ali Vishna greatest merchant in all of Illdershire, and this is my humble shop. What is your name my young friend?"

Dante replied quietly, immediately regretting using his real name.

"Oh-ho-ho so much modesty. No, not *just* Dante." The shopkeeper began to circle Dante looking him up and down like a butcher would a prime cut of meat. "No, I see you, and I see you for who you really are... *Black Wolf* Dante."

"What?" Dante responded, partly confused and partly amused.

"I can see it now, dark skin, dark eyes, even darker past. Taken in by the wolves because they sense his wild and feral nature." Ali Vishna balled his hands into fist and stared up towards the ceiling as he spoke in a low and dramatic whisper.

"Who says I have a dark past?"

"All adventurers have a dark past my friend," Ali said dismissively "Where are you from?"

"Earth."

"A wandering swordsman from a faraway land that no one has ever heard of, struggling to escape a tragic past," Ali then pointed at Robyn and Morrigan, "Caught in a love triangle with two beautiful women, its daring, it poetic-"

"Alright now sir," Dante interrupted. "I think you're getting carried away."

"Okay perhaps the love triangle is too much, we will wait and see huh? Give it time to blossom. Either way, Dante, Black Wolf Dante, I am honored to have you in my shop. Come you must buy something; it will be a great endorsement for my business."

"Is that what this is all about, drumming up promotion for your business?" asked Robyn, looking a little redder than usual.

"It is not every day that the envoy of a legendary Beast King comes into my shop. It is my duty as a Deosian to mark the occasion with the proper acknowledgement and to also ensure that he and his friends all receive a 10% discount on first-time purchases. Come Black Wolf, what do you think? You must purchase from Ali Vishna, it will make me the envy of all my friends, my children will think me a hero, my wife will love me again."

Dante sighed. There was no way out of this. "We are traveling north to Bleeksborough tomorrow and need all of the essentials for two days on foot."

"Why Black Wolf, you shall be the most prepared any adventurer has been for any adventure that there was."

"In addition, do you," asked Morrigan somewhat reluctantly "have anything in the realm of spellbooks?"

CHAPTER 23: HEAD FOR THE HILLS...

The following morning at dawn, Dante, Alex, Robyn and Morrigan exited the city of Illdershire. They left through the North Gate and began their trek on the Merchant Road to Bleeksborough.

"You know what this kind of reminds me of?" said Alex, speaking to no one in particular. "Wastelander 3 in survival mode. You guys ever played Wastelander?"

Dante had of course, but he kept silent.

"Wastelander 3 is a sci-fi game about roaming a post-apocalyptic landscape without being killed by giant radioactive bugs or mutated human cannibals. How does this, even remotely remind you of that?" asked Robyn.

"Well because when you play Wastelander *in survival mode* you can only save your progress when you rest in the settlement camps. Then when you die in the game you restart from your last save point, but that means you basically lose any progress you've made since you left the last settlement, which could mean losing hours of gameplay. So whenever you leave a settlement you have to pack enough supplies to last until you reach the next settlement. Otherwise you could end up in pretty bad shape in the middle of the wasteland."

"This is nothing like that or any video game, because if we die here we're dead. End of story," snapped Morrigan.

"I know that," said Alex both sounding a little hurt. "I was just trying to lighten the mood with a little bit of conversation."

"Well don't," said Morrigan coldly. "Who said the mood should be light?"

Alex sighed, muttered something unintelligible under his breath and looked over to Dante for support, but instead found staring blankly ahead like he was in another world altogether.

Dante carried over one shoulder, a pole, or more accurately, a long, well-made stick, at the end of which was crossed another smaller much shorter stick, so that together they formed a very large, very thin, nearly man-sized lower-case letter 't'. The t-shaped pole was called a Furca, and on the "t" shaped end there was a large roll of canvas tied securely to the protruding arms of the pole, while hanging from the arms were an assortment of tools, a pickaxe, a small shovel, a cast iron pot and a long machete like blade that Ali Vishna had called a faix and explained was meant to help cut corn from fields, or to clear paths of thick vegetation that may happen to find its way into an adventurer's path.

Ali Vishna had not had any spell books in stock, but had sold them the Furca. In addition to the roll of canvas and the assortment of tools, the Furca also included a large leather satchel nearly twice the size of the hip packs the group had started out with. He had assured them that they would want the additional storage for their supplies, health potions, healing salves food stuffs and the like. He of course had bags, and sacks that he could have sold them, but the beauty of the Fucra, Ali had explained, was that it could be easily dropped at a moment's notice. If any adventurers had ever found themselves ambushed by goblins, set upon by gnolls, or waylaid by bandits, they didn't want to be caught lugging around a sack, they wanted a Fucra, that allowed them to drop their junk, draw their weapons and die with dignity. As it turned out Ali Vishna was a very good, very convincing salesman and as a result, they bought the Fucra, among other things.

Dante gripped the Fucra in one hand, and in the other held tight to his open spirit tome.

- You have unlocked a new ability! 'Lightspeed Slash'
- 'Lightspeed Slash' has been added to the skills and abilities list.
- You successfully escaped the Tree Hugger Cat
- You have gained 200 experience points!
- Congratulations! You have been gifted a boon!
- Canis Romulus has bestowed unto you 'The Black Wolf Boon of Recovery'
- 'The Black Wolf Boon of Recovery' has been added to the features and traits list.
- You have abandoned the quest, "The Long March Home"
- You have been issued a new quest, "Searching for a Stranger in a Strange Land"
- Congratulations! You have been given the title 'Black Wolf Dante'
- Your Reputation Rank is currently listed at 'Unknown Unknown'
- You have a total of 8200 Experience Points

So much had happened since he last checked the book. He had broken away from Pope, escaped the Black Wood, learned a sword skill, received a boon, gotten a nickname, found out one of the original Dragon Dale game creators was hiding in Deos *and then* decided to find him, and the spirit tome had recorded it all. It was so odd, Dante thought, how this little book captured everything the way that it did, and how everyone, every resident of Deos, just happened to have one of these magical recording devices, transcribing the highlights of their lives and then quantifying it all. The world they were in was so visceral, so dangerous, so real, but then there were these other elements like the spirit tomes, and the status boxes that were so incredibly game-like. It was one world, with two perspectives of reality in conflict with one another. He felt like he knew so much about Deos, and yet there was so much he didn't understand.

He put the spirit tome away and pulled out Stephen's rose-colored spirit crystal. Back in Illdershire, he had gotten Ali to attach the large jewel to a thin but sturdy piece of black cord. Ali had assured Dante that the cord was not only sturdy, but that it was in fact Bark Spider cord, and supposedly unbreakable, seeing as how it was made from the webbing of the rare and elusive Coto-Coto Bark Spider whose webs were said to be as light and flexible as silk, but as strong as iron. He'd attached the cord to the rose colored crystal, forming a necklace that he now pulled down over his head and around his neck, tucking the glimmering jewel deep beneath his leather armor. It made more sense to have Stephen's spirit crystal closer, safer, at least until they could figure out how to restore him. Yeah, Dante thought to himself, bringing Stephen back, one more impossible thing for him to figure out.

"Dante?" Alex spoke in a voice much louder than normal and in an alarmed tone that signified that he had probably called out to Dante more than once.

"Huh?" said Dante snapping back to reality. "What was that?"

"We were saying that maybe we should stop and rest, it looks to be about noon and we've been walking all morning."

Dante shielded his eyes and looked up towards the bright Deosian sky to find sun directly overhead. "Oh," said Dante hesitantly, "I thought you guys were talking about Waterlander 3?"

"Um... That was like four hours ago." Alex said with a concerned chuckle. "You okay man, you've been quiet all morning."

"I've just been thinking of how to find Sandberg, get Stephen restored and then get us all back home."

"And what do you think we've been thinking about?" said Morrigan snidely.

"What?" said Dante taken aback by the sudden accusation. "I wasn't implying you're not..."

"Lunch," She said, cutting him off mid-speech. "We've thinking about lunch." Morrigan said. Her eyes seemed to pierce through him. Her face, her skin, Dante noticed, seemed to almost glow in direct exposure to the sunlight. The small gold studs in her ears and her nose, sparkled in the day light, her brown eyes flashed. She was both striking and at the same time, intimidating.

"Leave him alone Morrie," Robyn said, giggling.

Morrie? Dante thought to himself before looking back to Morrigan, only to find that her serious expression had broken into a large bright smile punctuated by a lighthearted giggle.

"You're going to give yourself an ulcer with all that thinking." Morrigan's smile widened and Dante realized, embarrassingly enough, that she was joking with him. There was the undeniable feeling of electricity in the air, happiness, a small semblance of normalcy.

"Yeah," Dante responded attempting to regain his composure and at least some of his dignity, "well I didn't know that we were allowed to make jokes, *Morrie*."

"There's a lot that you don't know kiddo, and that's Morrigan to you." And once again, Dante had no idea if she was kidding.

The party made their way to a shady tree slightly off the Merchant's Road, and it wasn't until they'd all sat in the soft grass that they realized how much they needed the rest. A stream wound beside their path before passing beneath a small bridge. The rolling hills of Bleekmore loomed before them and the lush green plains of Illdershire spanned out behind them, making their shade tree as good a place as any to stop and have lunch. From the satchel on the furca they pulled parcels of bread, cheese and slices of dried meat, all wrapped tightly in individual swaths of cloth. They sat nibbling their rations, all trying to imagine that the bread wasn't as stale, the meat wasn't as tough, and the cheese wasn't as bad as it all really was.

By Dante's estimate, they had traveled 15 miles since dawn, and could, if things went well, travel another 15 miles before sunset. They'd spend one night in the Bleekmore Hills and by the end of the next day be in Bleeksborough. Once it appeared that everyone had finished gnawing on their food, they all agreed to continue, Alex insisting that he carry the Furca for the second half of the day in order to give Dante a break.

In Bleekmore, the Merchant's Road twisted and curled at what seemed like every few hundred feet unlike the gently undulating, open paths of the Illdershire plains. The party found themselves trudging sharp inclines and then slipping down equally steep slopes. The casual chatter that Dante had "blanked out" on in the Illdershire plains was now notably absent, and had instead been replaced with heavy breathing and the occasional harsh swallow as every few hundred yards caused muscles to ache and mouths to dry. Alex, oddly enough, considering that he was carrying roughly fifty pounds of extra weight in the form of the Furca, seemed to have the least trouble, but then dwarves possessed extraordinarily high physical endurance and mental fortitude. Alex's limbs were as thick as tree trunks and twice as strong, yet he carried himself the exact same way as he had in the Last Legend Games building lobby despite looking as if he'd lost three inches of height and packed on about 20 pounds of solid muscle.

"We should think about making camp," said Robyn, looking up at the sky and then down at the map. "We're still quite far from the town, and it looks like the sun could be setting soon. We don't want to get caught out here in the dark unprepared."

They found a clearing nestled between three hills and a bend in the Merchant's Road that would not allow anyone traveling on the road to see them until they had already rounded the hills that jutted out on either side of their clearing. After they all agreed upon the spot, they unfurled the roll of canvas from the Furca and laid it out to form the basis of their tent. The pole which they had used to carry everything, served as an essential piece to the tent's framework and was supplemented by a number of stakes and poles that had been stored inside the satchel of the Furca.

Dante and Alex worked hard to feel their way through the process by arguing with each other about what piece went where. At the same time Robyn and Morrigan walked around the clearing collecting sticks, twigs, logs and stones to make a fire pit, which Morrigan lit with her bare hands.

They had finished just as the sun was setting, a glowing orange fireball drifting slowly below the hills of the western horizon and in the process turning the sky from a shade of pale robin's egg blue, to a mournful lilac purple. The campfire crackled softly, Robyn passed Dante a chunk of bread and a slice of dried meat, salty and tough like mummified beef jerky. Dante thought for a moment about putting the dried meat back under the fire, but the idea attracting any nearby predators made him think better of it.

"You know what I really miss about the real world?" said Alex out of nowhere. "The internet. We used to be able to look up anything. GPS directions to the nearest town, tomorrow's weather forecast, edible plants in the area. We had access to everything. Now, we don't even know what time it is."

Alex let out a sound that was somewhere between a sigh and a laugh. "The internet made the world *seem* so small. But *here*," Alex paused and made a sad sigh, "even aside from the magic and the monsters, aside from the fact that we're trapped inside a killer video game, the really scary part, is just how incredibly *big* it all is, how big and wild and truly inconceivable the world really is and how the only things we know for sure are the things we can see right in front of us."

"You know what I miss from the real world?" said Robyn.

"Police stations?" said Morrigan.

"Your bail bondsman?" Dante added.

"... Holding cells?" asked Alex.

"No, no, no," replied Robyn, ignoring their comments, "Public transportation."

Dante didn't look up, but he was sure he could hear Morrigan's eyes roll.

"When I was younger, I grew up in a lot of different foster homes and I used to run away from them all the time." Robyn continued very nonchalantly, "And every time I'd run away, I'd go hop on a subway train, or a metro bus, or a city trolley, anything that I could sneak on to for free or cheap and then I'd just ride around whatever city I was living in at the time. I used to move around a lot and to just sit on a bus and stare out the window and watch the world pass by made me feel like I had agency. Somewhere to go. Of course I just ended up at an arcade or a mall, picking pockets, playing games and shoplifting until I was caught by the police and sent back to my foster home." Robyn smiled as she remembered.

"Eventually my social worker got smart and put me with a foster mother who was also a bus driver. That made running away difficult, but my foster mom did let me ride with her during her shifts and gave me money for the arcades. She was the one who bought me my first Gamestation console... it came with Dragon Dale 4. I still have it." Robyn leaned back on to her elbows in the grass and tilted her head back, her blond hair seemed to reflect the flickering flames of the campfire and her eyes shimmered as she stared up at the darkening sky. "I haven't ridden on a bus or a subway train in years, but here suddenly I just really miss them."

"Robyn wow... that was deep," said Morrigan.

Robyn shrugged her shoulders and smiled. "I'm full of surprises." She tossed a stick into the fire and a plume of ash and smoke wafted into the air in protest.

"I miss running water," said Morrigan. "Baths, showers, modern plumbing. I miss my cat. But mostly I'd say I miss not having to worry about the constant threat of death hanging over my head at every turn."

"You have a cat?" asked Robyn perking up at the idea of Morrigan and a pet.

"Yeah, an Egyptian Mau, she's gray with black spots like a little leopard. She's more of a roommate then a pet though, just kind of comes and goes as she pleases."

"Sounds like my kind of girl." Said Robyn with a giggle.

"Yeah, you'd like her," Morrigan said with a smile. "She's a real sweetheart. We really took care of each other."

Slowly all heads turned towards Dante. He knew what was coming next. What was it about high stress situations and campfires that made people want to share their innermost feelings?

What did *he* miss most about Earth? He missed his mother. He missed his brothers. He missed his father, but his father had died years ago, his brothers not only hated each other but were secluded to two different parts of the country and now even his mother was gone. The word "Alone" popped into Dante's mind and he felt a lump catch in his throat but then he pushed it back down, deep into the pit of his stomach and forced it to stay there.

The sound of the crackling campfire filled his ears, and he could feel its warmth. The light from its flames, was now all the light they had. That's when it began to make sense to him, the way an open fire affected people the way it did. The popping of the burning wood was like a balm against the deathly silence of the night, the fire's warmth, a comforting blanket against the cold, and its flickering light was the last line of protection against an all-consuming darkness. It only made sense for them to cling to it, to gather around it, to share their stories with it and with anyone else who may be near, in the hope that those stories gave reason to linger just a little bit longer by the fire's warmth and light and sound and safety.

He heard someone take a heavy breath, and knew immediately that it was Morrigan and he was taking too long to answer.

"Pizza." Dante replied. "I miss pizza. There was this great little pizza place called Angelo's over by Milgrad University me and my teammates used to go there all the time."

"Milgrad? Isn't that one of those high society private schools?" asked Robyn.

"Yep." Replied Dante taking a big bite of the dried meat.

"And you went there... how?" asked Morrigan in what sounded like disbelief.

"Scholarship." Dante answered. "Academic and athletic. Lacrosse."

"I don't think I've actually every met anyone who plays lacrosse. How did you get into that?" Alex asked.

Dante took a deep breath, "I grew up playing football, but in my second year of high school I decided that I wanted to go to Milgrad for college. Only problem being, Milgrad didn't have a football program at their school. So," Dante shrugged, "I switched from football to lacrosse so I could get into Milgrad on scholarship."

"That's pretty impressive man," said Alex. "I mean to switch sports like that, in high school. That's kind of amazing."

"Yeah, its okay." Said Dante solemnly. "Look guys, it's getting late. We should probably try to go ahead and get some sleep so we can get an early start in the morning.

"Not a bad idea Ivy League," replied Robyn. "Personally, I'm bushed."

They agreed to leave the fire burning as they all migrated to the tent. Morrigan had been staring at Dante since he'd offered his comment about pizza, and now she passed by unusually close to him on her way to the tent. So close that Dante couldn't help but to notice the smell of her, it was warm and sweet reminding him faintly of white nectarines and peach blossoms in spring.

"Pizza?" said Morrigan, arching an eyebrow. "That's all you miss?"

"Yep," replied Dante coldly. He took a deep breath, in and out of his nose, as if now he was the one growing impatient. "Pizza."

Inside the tent it was cool and dark, and the chattering that had taken place outside around the fire was replaced with silence, and before long the sound of the heavy breath of sleep.

Dante lay near the tent entrance, one hand on his sword pommel, listening for anything to disrupt the perfectly layered harmony of night sounds, hoping that morning came quickly.

Dante could not remember falling asleep, but the sounds of shuffling, scratching and then crashing forced his eyes open with a start. He rose in a panic, only to see Robyn already awake and on high alert. She placed a finger to puckered lips, motioning for him to stay quiet.

"Is it morning?" Dante asked quietly.

"I'm not sure, it's still dark out," Robyn replied.

In the distance Dante heard a distinctive high-pitched screech followed by a trembling boom and he could have sworn he felt the ground shake. He looked at Robyn, but she merely shrugged her shoulders in confusion.

"Let's wake the others," He said, stirring Morrigan and Alex from their sleep alerting them to the fact that there might be something dangerous outside.

"What do we do now?" asked Morrigan.

"I'll go take a look, you guys stay here, and I'll be right back," said Dante.

"Don't be stupid," replied Morrigan, "We'll all go. Never split the party that's RPG 101."

Dante shrugged, he didn't see any point in arguing with her, primarily because he didn't think he could win and secondly because she was right about keeping the party together. It was an age-old idiom from the tabletop RPG days. You never ever broke up the group if you could help it. When he thought about it, they had already separated themselves from one group and really couldn't afford to divide themselves anymore.

Together the exited the tent. It was just before daybreak. The sky was still dark, but the edges of the horizon glowed with what was soon to be the rising of the morning sun. Their camp itself was clear, but a series of screeches, grunts and the assorted sounds of a scuffle could be heard coming from the other side of the hill that sat just north of their clearing. They looked at one another. The other side of the hill was directly in the path of the Merchant's Road and their path to Bleeksborough.

Dante removed his sword from its sheath and began to move around the side of the northern hill, the rest of the party behind him. Dante saw it first, though, he wished that he hadn't, he actually wished that he hadn't seen it at all. Standing there in the middle of the Merchant's Road surrounded by at least five cockatrice raptors was a large lumbering ogre. The ogre was big, over nine feet tall, with thick muscular limbs, a small head and an exceedingly large and rotund stomach that protruded out and over its dirty and tattered Lyon cloth. It was covered in pinkish-brown dust colored patchy dry skin that reminded Dante of an elephant or a rhino. It wielded in its right hand, a large battered tree branch, that is used as a club which it swung wildly and chaotically at the surrounding raptors.

The raptors leaped toward the hulking mass with teeth and claws, though for all their effort it seemed to do little good. Their attacks barely scratched the ogre's thick skin and their stone-paralyzing venom appeared to have no effect on the ogre at all. One by one the ogre captured each of the raptors with an attack of his own, either crushing them under the blows of his club, or grabbing them with his free hand and biting off their heads or simply slamming them into the ground until they stopped moving. It was hard to watch, even for Dante, who didn't necessarily feel any sympathy for the raptors, but realized in seeing the things die in this way he wouldn't wish death by ogre on anyone, not even his worst enemy.

"We have to get out of here." Morrigan whispered.

"I think that's a good idea." Agreed Alex.

"Well, that thing is standing in the middle of the road, which just so happens to be our path to Bleeksborough." Robyn whispered.

"Maybe now that he's killed the raptors he'll just move along," suggested Dante in a low voice.

The ogre's health bar changed from solid white to red, to yellow to green. The raptors had only managed to take down about ten percent of its total health.

"It's a level 10 Ogre." Dante said, cursing under his breath. "And it's nearly still at full health."

"That's it." Said Morrigan, "We have to go back to Illdershire."

"We can't go back to Illdershire, we have to go to Bleeksborough." Argued Robyn, "Pope could be right behind us."

"There is an ogre right in front of us!" said Morrigan in a loud whisper.

"Shhh!" said Dante "Be quiet and give it a second maybe he'll just leave."

"Maybe we should just wait him out at the camp?" Alex suggested.

"Then how would we know if he left or not?" asked Robyn.

"Guys be quiet."

"Hey! Who's there?" the ogre called out in a deep voice. "Wallace, is that you?"

The party froze in horror. Before they could act they were further startled by a second voice.

"Yeah, it's me mate." The other voice was just as deep and just as gruff as the first one. Another ogre. Dante's heart sank into his stomach. He peered back out from his hiding place to see a second ogre walk up to meet the first.

"I killed these lizard bird thingies, these oughta be good eating eh?"

"I suppose so. These ought to be good eating indeed. What do you think Virgil?" said Wallace, to which a third even larger ogre appeared.

"Well not as good as dwarf, or Elf, or even Human. But it's better than nothing I suppose. Well Let's start cooking'em then. I'll start the fire, Wallace you grab some firewood and Byron you rip the heads off those birds."

"Are we going to cook them right here then Virgil?" the ogre who had killed the raptors and was apparently named Byron asked.

"Well, we're not going to take them back to bleeding Dalgonia Castle are we Byron? Here is just a good a place as any, unless you have somewhere you need to be quick fast and in a hurry."

"Well, no Virgil, I suppose I don't."

"Then quit yer yapping and get to ripping the heads off them birds." And with a large meaty fist Virgil bonked Byron over the head, then plopped down in the middle of the road with his back to the party and begin to setup a stone ring in order to build a cook fire.

"Now what do we do?" Alex asked, looking at Dante.

"How am I supposed to know?" Dante whispered, a little frustrated.

"Can you call the wolves for help?" asked Morrigan.

"That only works in the Illder Plains, we're in the Bleekmore Hills now. They can't help us here."

"Did you scan all of the ogres?" asked Robyn.

"I did."

"Are they strong?" asked Alex.

"For reference the one that killed the raptors is by far the weakest."

"Dude we are so dead." Alex mumbled.

"No, we're not," said Robyn attempting to sound whisper determined. "this is where my area of expertise comes into play. We're going to sneak past them."

"Sneak?" repeated Dante.

"Yes, I am a rogue after all. This is what I do. . I'll sneak over to the left side of the road and distract them. You guys sneak pass them on the right side of the road and get to safety. We'll meet you on the other side of the ogres and head to Bleeksborough. It's a foolproof plan."

Dante frowned. He was almost convinced, right up until her last statement.

"Robyn, this is not a game, being a rogue doesn't-"

"I know we're not *in* a game, but this world still follows the same rules and laws that a game world does. That's how you've been so successful up till now, you've been sticking to your gamer instincts. Well, it's time for us to start doing the same."

"Successful?"

"Just trust me." Robyn said, before disappearing into a clump of overgrown vegetation near their hiding spot.

"Where'd she go?" asked Alex

Shuffling and movement of a small bush could be heard from a few feet away, and then again just as quickly, more movement slightly further away. Robyn was moving stealthily and speedily across the landscape and was soon positioned behind the ogre named Wallace who was quite consumed in his task of collecting firewood. A few more bushes moved, all in close proximity to Wallace and then suddenly and without warning the ogre yelled out.

"What's your problem?" asked Virgil.

"Something bit me... or stung me." Wallace said rubbing his large and dirty buttocks. "Do you think there's snakes around here?"

"I don't know but if you don't quite yer whining and get back to collecting that firewood I'm going to pop you one much harder than any old snake bite, I can promise you that." Replied Virgil impatiently.

"Alright, alright, no need for violence." Wallace went back to his search for firewood. But after a few more seconds he let out another howl. "Owwww, it bit me again! This time in me other cheek."

"What in the bloody blazes is going on over here?" Virgil went over to take a closer look at what was going on with Wallace. Byron dropped the raptor carcass he was holding and made his way over to his yowling comrade.

The right side of the road was now clear and as long as they moved quickly and quietly, they could sneak by without being seen. Dante Alex and Morrigan crept from behind the crumbling rock wall that had been their hiding place and moved along a small embankment between the Merchant's Road and the neighboring hill. They stooped low, their bodies hunched over themselves like cat burglars as they scuttled through the grass like field mice.

On the other side of the road Virgil and Byron were helping Wallace search the firewood gathering area for signs of a snake or insect large enough, strong enough or bold enough to bite an ogre.

"What was it Virgil? Do you think it was a hellfire snake?"

"No you idiot, what would a hellfire snake be doing in the middle of the hills."

"Maybe it was a panther wasp," suggested Byron, "Or a Bark Spider!"

"Panther wasp, and bark spiders live in the Coto Coto forest you moron they wouldn't be in the hills niver."

"Well these little lizard-bird things aren't from the hills but they're here, so I don't think it make me a moron to think there could be a panther wasp that done made its way to the hills as well." Byron said defiantly.

At this comment, Virgil turned and stared at Byron out of what appeared to be his one good eye. His sudden movement caused Dante to freeze. Virgil stuck out his chest and the already large ogre seemed to grow in size, proportionally Byron seemed to shrink before him.

"You listen here baby Byron," said Virgil beginning to froth at the mouth, the large tree trunk of a club gripped in his right hand beginning to waver in the air slowly. "If I say you're a moron, then until Grendell himself comes out of the bloody sky and says something different, you are without a doubt a bleeding moron. And if you don't like it-"

"OWWWWWWW!" cried out Wallace for a third time, his howl almost but not quite masking a girlish giggle at the sound of which Virgil froze.

"Wallace shut yer hole. And Byron you get yer mitts ready, I'm about to flush out a mouse." Without another word Virgil turned and began slamming his club in the area that Robyn had been hiding in. The chunk of tree he wielded as a weapon hit the ground with resounding slams, obliterating everything it touched. Robyn dove from her hiding place and spilled out onto the road in order to avoid being crushed and as soon as she did, Byron's large meaty hands grabbed hold to her by one leg and lifted her from the ground.

"What have we got here? A little golden haired field mouse?" said Byron with a chuckle.

"Careful," said Wallace still rubbing his backside, "That one there has teeth it does, likes to go for the meaty parts too, if you know what I mean." Simultaneously the ogres burst into laughter as they dangled Robyn aloft over the Merchant's Road. Dante watched everything unfold from the embankment on the side of the road some ten feet from freedom. Instinctively, without being fully aware of what he was doing, He bolted from his hiding place and ran out into the middle of the road with his sword in hand.

"Look there's another one!" the ogre said as it lifted its large arm and tried to swat Dante with its club. With a dive and a roll Dante dodged what felt a speeding bus. He tumbled back up to his feet, only to find himself snatched off of them again by Virgil.

And like clockwork, Alex and Morrigan came running out onto the road next, both with their weapons drawn, but before either of them could launch a single attack Wallace had grabbed them both from behind in a bear hug.

With all four adventurers now captured, the ogres tied them up and begin casually discussing how delicious they would be eaten along with the lizard-bird things they had killed earlier.

"A dwarf, two humans and a half elf. It's a feast!" said Byron merrily.

"How should we cook them?" asked Wallace.

"Should I debone them?" asked Byron

"I was thinking we could leave the bones and roast them, gives them a good crunch, especially the dwarf." Said Wallace

"I think I'm going to be sick," said Alex.

"Don't you go being sick, because if you're sick then I'm going be sick next," said Byron

"It's true" said Wallace "he has a weak constitution."

"Will you two quit talking to the food," said Virgil.

Dante looked over at Robyn and saw her slowly undoing her ropes and he had an idea.

"Anyone who knows anything about cooking dwarf knows you have to leave the bones in," said Dante smugly.

"What!?" said Vergil, Byron, Wallace, Alex, Morrigan and Robyn all in unison.

"What would you know about cooking dwarf, human?" said Virgil.

"Oh I get it, he's one of them cannonballs." Said Wallace enthusiastically.

"What's that?" asked Byron.

"You know, it's one of them men-folk that eats other men folk, human that likes to eat dwarf-men, or elf-men or even other humans. You know a cannonball."

"Ohhh." Said Byron, "A cannonball."

"That's right,' said Dante, "And every self-respecting *cannibal* knows that you always cook a dwarf with the bones in."

Robyn struggled vigorously to free at least one hand from her bonds.

"Yes, listen to him," said Alex, "he's a cannibal, he knows what he's talking about. Don't take my bones out."

"Leave the bones in," Dante continued, "but you have to be sure to take out the guts."

"Ok, nevermind. Don't listen to him, he doesn't know what he's talking about he's crazy," Alex said.

"Now that you mention it, I think my mother you used to have an expression about cooking dwarf. 'Bones in, Guts out' she used to say," said Byron.

"Leave the bones in the dwarf but be sure to take them out of the half-elf," Dante said. "Half-elf bones are thin and delicate like fish bones; you wouldn't want to choke on them. You're definitely going to want to fillet the half-elf."

"I'm going to roast you like a marshmallow the moment we get out of this Dante. Just you wait." Morrigan muttered through gritted teeth.

"Well tell me cannonball, what's the best way to cook human?" Virgil asked, pushing his big ugly face close to Dante's. His teeth were sharp yellow and jagged and his breath smelled like raw sewage.

"There is only one way to cook human. Low and slow," Dante said without blinking.

Virgil's face pulled back into a hideous grin as goblets of drool begin to drip from his salivating mouth.

"Put'em on a spit and cook'em slowly over low heat until the skin starts to crackle and the meat starts falling off the bone."

Virgil licked his lips, sat back and seemed to consider this, and after a moment when it seemed he could find no issue with Dante's suggestion he seemed to accept it as a good idea.

"Alright Mr. Cannonball, who do we cook first?" He asked, turning away from Dante and going back to build his cook fire. "The dwarf of the half-elf?"

The moment the ogre turned away Dante looked over to Robyn with wide eyes and a series of odd facial expressions, trying to motion her to hurry up and free herself from her ropes. "Oh no," he said in a steady and calm voice, "If you want to have a feast, you have to cook the humans first, that way, everything is done at the same time." Dante explained.

"Well, I suppose that does make a wee bit of sense," said Byron

"How about we don't cook anybody, and instead, you untie them, let them go, and we all walk away without anybody getting hurt?" suggested a new voice.

Chapter 24: 3 Ogres and a Half-Orc

"Who in the twelve Hells are you?" roared Virgil.

The bulky figure in a dark cloak and hood stood in the middle of the Merchant's Road, his path blocked by three hungry ogres.

"Why Virgil, I think that's one of them orcs." Said Byron.

"Orcs? Blah!" said Wallace sticking out a cracked and gnarled tongued. "Orcs taste horrible."

"Orcs don't taste very good but salted and smoked, orcs do well as travel rations," said Virgil scratching his chin.

"I," said the cloaked figure, "am a half-orc, and my taste is inconsequential because neither I, nor anyone else on this particular stretch of road is going to be cooked or eaten this morning."

He removed his hood to reveal pale green skin, dark green hair, a bearded face and a pair of boar-like tusk that protruded upward from his bottom jaw and peeked out over his upper lip like reverse set fangs, only thicker and more round, as if they were made for crushing bone as opposed to puncturing skin.

"Shinto?" Dante was just as confused as the ogres were by the half-orc's sudden appearance.

Nearly simultaneous to Shinto's appearance, the sun peeked over the top of the eastern hills, brightening the morning sky and sending gentle rays of sunlight pouring onto the Merchant's Road.

"Virgil, the sun's coming up. Do you know what this means?" asked Byron.

"Yes," said Virgil, picking up his club and slamming it into the ground "it means we're late for breakfast. Curse the fire, kill the orc, we'll eat them all raw!"

At Virgil's command, Wallace lunged at Shinto and Dante's hopes of rescue sunk. Shinto was big, but he was no match for a nearly 10-foot-tall 1,000-pound ogre, let alone three of them. Wallace charged like an angry bull. Shinto held his ground, his right hand became engulfed in translucent purple flames that flickered wildly for a brief moment before solidifying into a shimmering purple blade a foot long, twice the length of Shinto's already large hands. The ogre reached for him, but missed by a hair's breadth when Shinto side stepped the charging ogre, maneuvering himself out of the monster's path. Before Wallace could recover, Shinto took his purple bladed hand and plunged it violently into the ogre's thigh.

Wallace screamed out in pain as Shinto's hand buried itself wrist deep into his leg. Large black veins began to pulsate and bulge around the wound. In one fluid motion, Shinto removed his hand from the ogre's thigh, and as he did, the shimmering purple blade vanished and Shinto bounded backwards, out of reach of the wounded ogre.

"Virgil!" Wallace screamed, "he's poisoned me!"

"Hehe' he stung you good Wallace, you're bleeding like a stuck pig you are."

"Great Grendell's balls it hurts! Must be some type of orc venom."

"Orcs don't have venom you twit, now quit your blubbering and put some dirt on it," shouted Virgil from the middle of the road.

As instructed Wallace reached down and grabbed a handful of mud and dirt and smeared it all over the open leg wound, attempting to stop the bleeding by simply plugging the hole in his thigh with dirt, standard practice for ogres, as their extraordinarily high constitutions allowed them to heal wounds in the most rudimentary manners and still stay free from infection. This time it didn't seem to be working.

"Virgil, it's still bleeding." Wallace groaned. A combination of dirt and blood was now pouring down his leg just as much as before, perhaps now even more. And from Dante's point of view, he was even starting to look pale. "I feel woozy."

"Yer just hungry, that's all!" said Virgil, "Come on let's smash this little half-orc, that'll make you feel better."

Virgil stood to his feet, grabbed his club and stretched, almost as if he was excited at the opportunity to smash something that did not run screaming in terror at the sight of him. At the same time, Robyn had finally managed to free herself from her bindings. Slipping free one hand and then the other.

"You don't have to do this," said Shinto calmly. "It won't end well for the lot of you."

"You are quite the cocky little snot, aren't you?" replied Virgil, spitting into his hand and regripping his club. "I'm planning to enjoy this."

"Aye now Virgil, be careful with that one, he's a tricky little blighter, he is." said Wallace, still attempting to slow the bleeding from his leg. All three ogres, preoccupied with Shinto, completely failed to notice that Robyn had not only freed herself but was quickly and quietly untying the others. Dante felt the ropes holding his arms behind his back slacken as she undid the surprisingly well constructed knots that the ogres had used to bind his wrist to his ankles. Dante found himself able to move once again while Robyn helped Morrigan, and he took it upon himself to free Alex. Using the knife that he had received from Pope he cut Alex's ropes, releasing the dwarf.

"I'll take the two on the right," said Shinto, "you all take the one on the left." his hand shone bright with purple flame once again only now it was bigger and brighter than before.

"You? Take the two of *us* you say?" said Virgil, his dirty pink face turning red with anger. "Why you puny little bug, you'll be nothin' more than a fine green paste when I'm done with you!" his club raised high over his head Virgil dashed forward in a fit of rage, moving with the speed and power of a runaway freight train. he brought his club down hard on the spot where Shinto had been standing, but another well timed sidestep had once again taken the half-orc out of harm's way. Virgil, however, was much faster and combat experienced than Wallace, and missing one attack did not leave him unguarded enough to have a shimmering purple blade jabbed into one of his limbs. He followed one attack immediately with another. A powerful backhanded swing brought the club flying back toward Shinto at such a high rate of speed that the half-orc had to bend backwards, but then immediately snapped back upright and stabbed the now wide-open ogre in a very precise spot, just left of the chest and slightly below the shoulder, a space left exposed by the wild and ferocious backhand swing. The purple shimmering blade went in and out of the monster's flesh like butter, and when it did Virgil's weapon arm faltered. Shinto's blade shimmered, but before he could prepare for a counter attack, Wallace appeared behind him, lifted his own club. He was no match. In his continued expression of unparalleled grace and speed, Shinto stepped backward, ducked under Wallace's large arms and gently removed himself from between the two ogres and instead of hitting Shinto, Wallace's, club came down hard into Virgil's face.

"Oh, wow sorry about that mate."

"Watch where you're swinging that thing, twit!" Virgil said swinging around his own club and smacking Wallace in the face with it so hard that he spun around and found himself facing Shinto, whose shimmering hand blade had now been replaced with a hearty mace. Shinto swung the mace in an upward arc, catching the ogre hard on the chin. There was a loud crack, the monster's head snapped back and for a moment he tottered on both feet as if he were still standing, before falling forward like an old tree in a forest. He slammed into the ground face first and lay there unmoved. Virgil who was standing behind the now prone ogre looked down at Wallace's limp body and then back up at Shinto.

"You killed my mate?" Virgil said, surprised.

"To be fair," Shinto responded. "I did warn you." He said, attaching his mace back to his waist.

The orgre screamed, rushing forward once again, only this time his club arm dripped blood from the shoulder joint. Virgil swung the weapon around, his arm doing little more than gripping the club as it mostly hung limp from his disabled shoulder. The ogre's weapons arched out wide and high and came toward Shinto in slow motion. Shinto made no efforts to dodge, he simply raised his left arm, which produced a radiant golden shield. The ogre's club bore down and when it hit the shield it bounced away, as though the club were a balloon filled with air.

The deflected attack left the ogre vulnerable. Shinto stepped forward, not wasting the opportunity and plunged his shimmering bladed hand directly through the ogre's chest and into his heart. The monster's body went limp, and the lights in his eyes dimmed.

Dante watched Shinto in amazement, he found himself nearly hypnotized by the half-orc's mastery over magic, movement and his expertise in combat. He was so in awe in fact, that he completely forgot that he had an ogre problem of his own to contend with.

Byron lunged himself at the adventurers with his club lifted high up over his head. By the time Dante spotted the charge it was too late to react and instead he simply braced for impact. But it never came, before the ogre made it to him Alex dashed out into its path, his shield raised in front of him. The ogre swung his heavy club knocking Alex off of his feet and sent him tumbling back some 10 feet across the road. Dante watched as half of Alex's health bar disappeared. He panicked, knowing full well that if Alex took another hit like that, he wouldn't survive. Dante rushed in with his sword drawn slashing the ogre across his large stomach. The blade hit with impact and then slid across the monster's thick patchy skin barely leaving a mark. Byron, looked down at Dante, smiled an ugly jagged tooth smile and raised his club to swat Dante as if he were nothing more than a very large and very pesky gnat. Dante dived and rolled narrowly dodging his second ogre club of the morning. It dawned on him the only way he could get away from the ogre's extremely fast and extraordinarily powerful attacks was to fling himself out of range, the realization of which made the fact that Shinto dodged those same attacks with such ease all the more amazing. Dante rolled back up to his feet, only to see Alex now rushing toward the ogre once again. The dwarf hacked at Byron with his axe, but the attack did little more than Dante's had done and seemed only to give the monster a better idea as to who he should attack next.

Byron cocked back to strike at Alex, a blow which Dante was sure would kill the dwarf, when a bout of flames burst forth and caught the ogre in the eyes. Byron howled, grasping at his face and flailing his club around wildly as he blindly searched for the source of the magic fire.

Dante looked up to see Morrigan slowly walking backward, spewing fire from her hands while at the same time keeping herself as far from the ogre as possible. Byron continued to swing his club chaotically from side-to-side attempting to destroy any and everything in his path. Alex was pinned in by the ogre's wild swings, unable to do much more then hide behind his shield and attempt not to be clobbered into smithereens, while behind the ogre Robyn moved stealthily with her daggers. Unseen and undetected Robyn jabbed both of her dagger points into the back of the ogre's knee. Byron screamed out in pain and then began to flail around wildly in a circle, stomping and thrashing about, pounding the ground around him in what looked to Dante like a deadly and rage filled temper tantrum. Byron was still blinded, or at least his eyes were still closed, even though Morrigan had stopped the fire stream.

Dante looked at Byron's health bar, they had whittled it down to about half, about as much as the raptors had, however Dante noted that the largest reaction came from Morrigan's fire attack and Robyn's dagger attack. Morrigan's attack targeted the eyes, and technically blinded the ogre making it more of a status effect, but Robyn's attack had actually been the only one to genuinely hurt the ogre, even if it did only do a few points of damage. Then Dante thought about Shinto's magic-based attack with the purple flame blade and how extremely effective they had all seemed to be, and that's when it hit him, an idea. Dante scrambled on his person for a water skin, and then with his sword blade sliced off the top of the container.

"Morrigan!" Dante called out. "Freeze this!" and in one big motion he slung the water into the air. Without question or hesitation to his odd request Morrigan reacted on his instructions and blasted the column of water with cold air, instantly freezing it into a gigantic white icicle.

"Now!" Dante called out, before the icicle could fall to the ground. "Throw it!" he said pointing at the ogre. Morrigan eyed him, and then through concentration of will, switched her magical element from cold to wind and used it to propel the ice through the air like a javelin. The makeshift spear hit Byron in the shoulder, puncturing through his thick skin and forcing him to drop his heavy club.

"Now's our chance!" Dante yelled, running toward the ogre with his sword held out directly in front of him like a knight on a charging horse. The moment he got within reach Dante thrust the sword forward with all his strength, plunging the blade into the ogre's stomach. The sword punched through the hard outer skin and then sank in all the way to the hilt, forcing a loud pain filled roar out of the ogre. Byron stumbled backward, then looked down at Dante, his large hands now empty. But just as he looked as if he was about to muster up enough strength for one more attack, Alex and Robyn flew in laying into the ogre with axe swings and dagger stabs. The monster roared in misery, flailed his arms in a desperate attempt to stay on his feet, but then stumbled backwards one, two steps, and then fell dawn dead flat on his back, his health bar drained down to nothing.

"We- we did it." Alex said from beside Dante. "We killed an ogre!"

Shinto sat a few feet away beside the overlapping carcasses of the two ogres that he had killed by himself. With a cold and stony expression of indifference, or perhaps disdain, the half-orc rose to his feet, his green eyes trained on the four adventurers. Dante opened his mouth to speak but before words came to him, Shinto spoke instead.

"I thought I told you all to go home."

Chapter 25: Explanations and Allies

"Well, it's good to see you too," Robyn muttered under her breath.

Shinto looked around Dante and the others, focusing his eyes further down the Merchant's Road, as if he was expecting someone else to come running up from the southern end.

"Where are the other of your group?" he asked. "Don't tell me they returned home, and you all choose to stay behind... Or worse." Shinto eyed the rose-colored spirit crystal hanging from Dante's neck.

"No," Dante said clutching the crystal in his hand and then looking down at it thoughtfully. "No one has returned home and it's not by choice." The half-orc's expression remained unchanged., awaiting an explanation.

"The truth of the matter is we're trapped here. We can't go home," Dante began.

They moved to the shade of the tree and sat, and Dante explained everything. From the existence of the Dragon Dale games on Earth and the special invite they all received to play the Beta, all the way up to the Dytorus Corporation's Games Guides and Combat Consultants and the Gamers themselves being transported into Deos under false pretenses. They barely knew Shinto, but at the same time he was the closest thing in Deos that they had to an ally. He'd already saved their lives twice.

"So, if I understand this correctly, your Land of Urth is not just some foreign continent across the Tethys Sea, but it is actually another world, on another plane of existence?"

"Yes" said Dante, relieved to see Shinto following his logic.

"And in your world, they have a children's game called Dragon Dale where Urthlanders pretend to be adventurers in Deos?"

"Well, it's not for children, actually," huffed Alex. "Lots of adults play it, too."

"But then a corrupt merchant's guild tricked you and a host of other gamists?"

"Game-ers" corrected Robyn.

"From Urth Land" Shinto continued ignoring her correction. "Into coming to the real Deos with a large group of spies and hired mercenaries?"

"Correct," said Dante.

"And now in order to get back home, we've fled from the 'Mercenaries'" said Morrigan "and are currently in search of an old Urthlander named Sandberg who we believe came here years ago and still knows of a way that can get us back home."

"That's why we're heading to Abilene Bay, we figure if we're looking for someone and have absolutely no clue as to where they are, that's the best place to start," said Robyn.

Shinto's cold expression of indifference had now been replaced with one of thoughtful contemplation. His large green hands stroked at the thick coarse hair of his beard as he stared insightfully at the ground, deep in thought. "First and foremost, I must apologize to you all."

"What?" said Alex, "Why would you be apologizing to us? You just saved us from these ogres, we should be thanking you."

"I apologize for our previous encounter. I should never have had you all accompany me to the Raptor's Nest, it was too dangerous. I knew you all were not from the adventurer's guild, but I was curious, and wanted a better idea of who you were which is why I proposed we travel together. I assumed I could keep you all safe, but." Shinto looked at the spirit crystal around Dante's neck once again. "It is my fault that your friend is in that state. I should have gone to hunt the Alpha Raptor on my own."

"Well, wait," said Dante, "You can't really blame yourself for that, I mean we were planning to go after it anyway."

"Yeah, and it's not like you had much choice. There's no way you could have killed that thing by yourself, it was the size of a dinosaur." Alex added.

Dante looked pass Shinto to the two dead ogres laying behind him and then back to the half-orc realizing he really wasn't sure what Shinto was capable of.

"You're traveling alone? Dante asked curiously.

"Yes, I had been," said Shinto, his face no longer cold and foreboding as it was before but now much more thoughtful and expressive. "I had been heading to the far south on an errand, but now, if you'll have me, I'd like to accompany you all to Abilene Bay. As you can see, travel through Deos can be quite perilous for the inexperienced and I feel it is my obligation to assist you all in your plight."

"You're going to come with us? All the way to Abilene Bay?" Dante asked.

"If you'll have me."

"I thought you were on your way south?" said Morrigan.

"My business can wait. Besides between here and Abilene Bay you all are liable to run into things far more dangerous than ogres, and I fear without proper guidance the chances of you reaching your destination are low. I can't have your deaths on my conscious."

There was no need for the group to discuss. "Well, that's settled," Robyn said. "We are now officially a party of five."

"We should go back and pack up our camp," Alex suggested, "and hit the road."

"I think that is a good idea," Shinto said in agreement.

The newly formed party begin to head south on the Merchant's Road, back toward the makeshift camp Dante and the others had scurried away from just before daybreak. In the midst of the short walk back Dante found himself in the rear, a few steps behind Shinto, with Alex in front leading the way back to camp and Robyn and Morrigan on either side of him. He was reminded of their trek out of the Raptor's nest, and immediately felt on guard. He had been right on Shinto's heels that day too. That was actually twice now that the half-orc had saved his life. He thought about how easily he had handled two ogres at once, how he had apparently kept the Stephen from outright dying and how he appeared to be traveling across Deos alone and with little trouble. Dante looked up at Shinto's large broad back, his hood was back up covering his head, and he moved like a large lumbering shadow across the Merchant's Road, smooth and quiet, uncharacteristically so for someone of his size and build.

By the logic of Dragon Dale Games and all video games for that matter Shinto either had to be a potential mentor and ally, or an extremely powerful enemy disguising himself as a friend. If he were the first, then Dante and the others had finally gotten a lucky break, but if he turned out to be the latter, than they may have been better off staying with Pope.

Perhaps if there was a hint, some type of clue as to the half-orc's true intentions. Dante looked up at Shinto's status box which hovered discreetly overhead, practically invisible until he had decided to look for it. A lot of things in Deos were beginning to feel that way, inconspicuous, subtle, nearly nonexistent until a certain amount of focus was placed upon them. But even when focused upon Shinto's status box only gave so much information.

Shinto Mongore MercifulLv??Half-Orc Cleric

No subclass, no level, and his HP and MP didn't even populate, not even when Dante used his scan ability. The only information available to him was information that Shinto had already previously given them. His name, race and his job class. Dante thought for a moment. His job class. Shinto was a cleric, a healer, in effect a priest and in the world of Dragon Dale clerics were always associated with gods or deities. If Dante knew what god Shinto drew his power from then he would have an idea of what his intentions were. If Shinto worshipped a god of justice or life, or one that believed in protecting the innocent, then they were probably in good hands. On the other hand if he worshipped a god of deceit and deception who reveled in destruction and the sacrificing naive and vulnerable adventurer wanna-be's then they were screwed.

Dante looked the half-orc up and down, searching for some sign of symbol of his god. There was not much to see, at least from behind. Shinto wore a large brown cloak they lay draped over his shoulders covering and concealing most of his bulky upper frame, however, hanging from his waist from a set of leather straps, peeking from just beneath the edged of his cloak was a book. It was a large thick tome of a book, at least 4 to 5 inches thick by Dante's estimate, bound in leather as well as a two-metal clasp to help keep it shut. It hung from his back, nearly unnoticeable at first, but now that Dante had spotted it, he didn't understand how he could have ever missed it to begin with, even in comparison to Shinto's large frame, the book was huge. Its leather cover was cracked and weathered from either age or use reminding Dante of the old family bibles he used to see when he would visit his grandmother's house and immediately, he knew that this had to be Shinto's holy book.

Dante craned his neck, attempting to get a closer look at the book's cover. It was embossed with a large tree whose exposed roots and crooked branches seemed to spread out in every direction. Dante recognized it immediately.

"Shinto, your book, is that Yddgrrsil on the cover?" Dante asked.

"It is." Shinto answered without turning around.

"Is that the symbol of your god?" he asked, thinking to himself that perhaps these questions should be saved for later, that now, in the middle of nowhere was not the time to possibly antagonize the only friend they had, especially if he wasn't really a friend. Dante probably should have just gone along with the charade at least until the got to a city, some semblance of safety, but he couldn't help himself. He couldn't bite his tongue and allow himself to be led quietly like a sheep to slaughter, not after they'd come so far.

"Not exactly," answered Shinto.

Dante felt his hand drift toward the hilt of his longsword. In the Dragon Dale games Yddgrisil was the symbol of the lost city of Dragon Dale and did not represent any particular god, at least that Dante knew of, and an answer of yes would have been concerning, but for reasons Dante did not fully understand, Shinto's answer of "Not exactly" was just as concerning. He did not trust him, he realized. The half-orc had saved his life twice and still, he did not trust him. Dante gripped the hilt of his sword.

"So, who is your god then? Orcan? Mylon?" Dante asked, a bite in his voice, a growl in his throat, he tried to downplay it, but his paranoia had worked his mind into a frenzy and now he was having a hard time hiding it. Orcan was the orchish god of war and the hunt. Mylon was the god of death. It was all or nothing now.

Shinto looked back over his shoulder, his tusk and teeth shone in what Dante recognized as a small smile.

"Your Urthlander games have given you all knowledge of the gods of Deos?" Shinto asked.

"Somewhat," Dante responded, still very much on guard.

Shinto chuckled within his throat. "No, I'm not a cleric of Orcan, or of Mylon. My relationship with the gods is... complicated and my position is unique. I can assure you however, my intentions with you and your friends are pure." Shinto's eyes caught sight of Dante's hand on his sword. He looked back up at him. "I am a cleric of knowledge, and the preservation of the Land of Deos is my charge and ultimate priority. That is all I can tell you for now. I hope that that will suffice."

Expecting a veiled threat or some display of power Dante found himself taken aback by Shinto's show of humility and felt a pang of guilt for his unwarranted suspicion and interrogation.

"Oh, well, thank you for that... and thank you for your help with the ogres as well. Thank you for everything actually."

"Don't thank me yet." Shinto replied. "The journey is far from over."

Chapter 26: No Good Deed...

The Black Wood was lush. Alive and living with unruly; unchecked vegetation. The land beneath it lolled and rolled like a wave frozen in time. Trees jutted up from the ground like the dark skeletal fingers of giants, leering and looming over the Merchant's Road with hungry anticipation.

Pope and his crew had been in the Black Wood two nights and three days and had lost three men. There had been 19 of them to start. They marched into the forest arrogantly, confident in their numbers. Convinced that they could overwhelm anything that they might come up against, considering they looked, to the untrained eye, like a small army.

They grew in violent spurts, the trees. Some were thick and tall like hickories and oaks, with dark colored barks and dark green leaves. Others were small and thin like Cedar trees, their low hanging branches obscuring anything at eye level a few dozen yards beyond the road. Lastly were the enormous Redwood-like trees. They were as wide as houses and as tall as buildings and all apparently grew deep in the heart of the forest.

On the first day, a number of the men armed with ranged weapons had taken to shooting small game as they could spot it, antlered rabbits that scurried along the forest floor and squirrel like rodents that bound through the trees. They'd shoot from the road and whenever they scored a hit, would run into the forest and grab their fallen prize. Pope did not care to participate in the game, nor did Lansing, but both the gamers and combat consultants seemed to enjoy it greatly and upon every shot they let up a cheer, and so, imagining that it was good for morale and that the men were, in effect, gathering food, Pope allowed it to continue. It was during a high point in the game that Gordon spotted a particularly plump antlered hare. He drew his bow.

In the hours that they had been marching, they group had hit four of these "jackalopes" as the gamers had called them, and two of them had been scored by Gordon. Roberts, a half-orc combat consultant and Wuddlekins, the cat-man, had nabbed the other two. If Gordon could hit this big one, it would give him a clear lead in the game and arguably put him in competition for best shot in the company, perhaps even over Lansing.

Gordon loosed the arrow and caught the jackalope in mid-air as it attempted to dash away. The arrow hit the creature with force and carried it another five yards into the forest and away from the road.

"What a hit!" said Mr. Wuddlekins the Kalgari cat-man who had seen the jackalope only a split second after Gordon had, but a split second too late.

Gordon smiled. Let's see Lansing top that.

"Now I just have to find it." Gordon said, placing his bow on his back, and stepping off the road.

"I'll go with." Offered Wuddlekins and together the two of them left the Merchant's Road and walked deeper into the forest than anyone had before.

Pope lead the group, he set the pace for the march and the company followed. He did not slow or stall his speed to accommodate those playing the game. He operated quite plainly in a keep up or be left behind philosophy. As a result, whenever someone left the road to go and claim a successfully hit target a number of others had to wait around for them to rejoin the group in order to avoid anyone getting left to far behind.

The others watched with murmmers of excitement as Gordon and Wuddlekins disappeared among the trees. They surveyed the tree line anxiously, expecting that at any moment Wuddlekins and Gordon would come bursting forth with a large jackalope in hand, at which point they would let out a cheer and then would begin their search anew for an additional target for which to test their skill. But after two minutes passed, then three and still neither adventurer had reappeared the men begin to eye each other with concern.

From within the forest there was a loud crash, a scream, and then a distinct and awful crunching sound that echoed throughout the woodland. Wuddlekins came sprinting out from among the trees. The fur that covered his body was frazzled and standing on end, with small sticks, twigs and leaves caught in its tangles. His face and hands were covered in scratches and bruises as he hastily stumbled forward, falling over himself and looking back over his shoulder in a panic. He spilled onto the Merchant's road in a heap landing flat on his stomach before clamoring back up to his hands and knees and then turning to face the woods from which he ran so desperately away, still crawling backwards, attempting as best as he could to continue to put distance between himself and the dark clump of trees. He stopped only when he hit the wall of adventurers that had been standing on the road waiting for him and Gordon to return, and even then, he didn't notice they were there. It wasn't until someone said something that he seemed to acknowledge their presence.

"What happened? Where's Gordon?" asked Roberts, the deep voiced half-orc.

Wuddlekins looked up, his cat like eyes wide and wild with fear. "It got him, in the woods, something got him. I had to run. I had to!"

With a rough hand the half-orc grabbed hold to the cat man by the scruff of the neck and held him at arm's length.

"What are you talking about? What got him?"

"THE FOREST! The forest got him!" Mr. Wuddlekins, seemingly still desperate to place more distance between himself and the woods, struggled to free himself from Roberts's grip, but it was no use. The Half-orc's hands may as well have been iron shackles.

"What's going on here?" asked Pope. The noise and commotion had prompted him to turn around and investigate. A hush fell over the members of the company as the captain pushed his way through the crowd and upon seeing him even Mr. Wuddlekins seemed to calm down a bit. His eyes darted around the crowd until they fell upon Danger Duke, the halfling Barbarian, who at the sight of Pope appeared to try and make himself even smaller than he already was.

"This one ran into the forest with Gordon," Roberts explained. "a few minutes later he came back out, alone, spouting some gibberish about how there something out there in the woods."

Mr. Wuddlekins wore the face of a cornered animal. He trembled with fear.

"Son, I know you're scared, but I need you to calm down and tell me exactly what happened," Pope said, placing a hand on the cat-man's shoulder. At the same time Roberts released his grip, and the combination of being set free in addition to Pope's powerful authoritative presence calmed the irrational gamer.

"We-um went into the forest for the jackalope that Gordon shot. The woods get darker the further you get from the road, we couldn't see well but then spotted some antlers near the base of a tree." Mr. Wuddlekins eyes begin to well up with tears. "When we got closer, we could see that the antlers belonged to some creature that had already found the jackalope. It had its back to us, it was hunched over and squatting." He swallowed hard. "It was eating and making these god-awful sounds. I figured we should just back away, but before I could say anything the creature heard us, smelled us, because it turned around and looked at us... and its face." He whimpered. "Its face was just bone... and it had these glowing red eyes. It leaped, so fast I didn't see it move and just all at once it was on top of him..." Wuddlekins looked at Pope as if pleading. "It had a skull for a face and it got him. I had to run. I had to."

By now everyone in the company had gathered around to hear Wuddlekins' story. Corrine, Dwight, Danger Duke and Roberts all looked at Pope for direction.

"Captain, would you like me to organize a group to go back in after Gordon, sir?"

"No." replied Pope coldly. "We press forward, double time, and stop this silly game."

"Aren't we going to try and save him?" asked Danger Duke aloud, but to no one in particular.

"There's no point." Replied Wuddlekins solemnly, "he's dead."

The company marched on through the day in contemplative silence. Members of the company who had previously played the hunting game now watched the trees with veiled anticipation, expecting that at any moment Wuddlekins' monster would come rampaging out of the forest, ready to launch itself at them in much the same way it had Gordon. But after a few hours without so much as a hint of danger, a number of the men found themselves wondering if their fears were unfounded and some begin to doubt if there was ever even anything to fear at all. Whispers of disbelief spread through the company and as the sun set most of the men believed Wuddlekins had simply lost his nerve, left Gordon alone in the woods and at any moment the combat consultant would come stomping back up to the group, angry and put out by the entire ordeal. Wuddlekins did little to combat the whispers and rumors of cowardice. In fact, his main focus seemed only to be walking within the middle of the group and constantly keeping as many men as he could between himself and the trees that lined the road.

By night fall of the first day Pope ordered the men to set up camp in the middle of the Merchant's Road. If they should be fell upon by thieves, opportunistic cutthroats, or a roving group of bandits traveling under the cover of night they would be sitting ducks, sleeping there in the middle of the road, but both Dwight and Corrine had assured him that all previous intelligence reports coming from Deos showed that no one ever traveled through the Black Wood during the night. The probability of anyone meeting their camp on the road was impossible, and the forest was not an option.

The men setup the tents and a series of campfires on the road and then, under the instruction of Hernandez, drew lots to determine the order of the watch. Pope ordered two combat consultants on watch duty at all times through the night. Hernandez split the night watch into two 4-hour shifts, and then after 8 hours they would break camp and prepare to resume their march at the first sign of daybreak. Hernandez volunteered himself for first watch after which Roberts, the half-orc, volunteered to sit-in along with him. The lots drawn afterward put North, an elf Ranger and Shane a human Battle Guard, and the only female combat consultants, on second watch, leaving the other consultants to rotate in on the coming nights.

For the first four hours, Hernandez and Roberts sat in front of a fire, listening intently to every cracking twig and chirping insect. They imagined, that perhaps, it was here in the dead of night, when the forest trees seemed to be shrouded in an inconceivable darkness, that Gordon would finally stumble his way out of the trees and find his way back to them. But much to the dismay, or perhaps relief, of both Hernandez and Roberts nothing stumbled from the trees.

At the arrival of the second watch Hernandez and Roberts stood, ready to depart to their own respective tents, anxious to sleep off the weariness of a long and exhausting day.

"It's been quiet," said Hernandez as the two new combat consultants approached. "Just stay alert and come and get me if you hear or see anything out of the ordinary."

"Will do," replied North with a curt nod.

North and Shane took their positions, both still dreary eyed and yawning from the short rest they had just received. Shane sat down on the ground and propped her back against a stack of firewood. She sat her sword to one side, her shield to the other and then buried her face in her hands.

"I can't believe we drew second watch on the first night," She rubbed her eyes, trying hard to brush away the drowsiness. "Those few hours of sleep felt more like a tease than anything else."

"Tell me about it," North replied. "I spent half the time laying there thinking about how much sleep I *wasn't* going to get tonight." North sat down across from Shane on a large log that the men had pulled over in front of the fire, he placed his longbow and quiver next to him. "Tell you what," he said. "Hernandez said it's been quiet all night and it doesn't really take two of us to look out for nothing, so what do you say we take turns getting some extra sleep. You can even go first if you want."

Shane looked up at North with an expression of smirking amusement. "You're kidding right?"

"No, I'm serious. You take a couple of hours and then I take a couple of hours we both get a few more winks. It's a win-win really."

Shane let out an audible laugh. If Captain Pope caught either of them sleeping while on watch duty, she couldn't even begin to imagine what the punishment would be. But the promise of a couple of more hours of sleep was tempting. Shane closed her eyes and rubbed her fingers through her hair. She held it there for a moment, her eyes still closed, fantasizing about the idea of a few extra moments of sweet blissful sleep.

"Are you sure you're not going to fall asleep while I'm asleep?" Shane asked.

North did not respond.

"Because if morning comes and the two of us are caught napping by the fire, we might as well run off into the forest and get lost like Gordon did."

Nothing.

"North did you hear me?" Shane opened her eyes and looked up, expecting to see North had already dozed off. Instead, she saw no one. North was gone and the log on which he had been sitting was empty, with the exception of his longbow and quiver which lay leaned casually up against it.

"North?" Shane scrambled to her feet and hurried over to where her partner had been sitting. She picked up the bow and quiver then looked around the log for some trace or sign of the elf. She thought for a moment that he may be hiding, attempting to play some type of trick on her but when she examined the space around the log there was nothing to find but darkened road and the even darker forest beyond. There were no hiding places for a six-foot 4-inch elf to hide. "North, where are you?" Shane stepped closer to the edge of the road, toward the dark forest tree line, as she did, her boot slipped. She looked down to find she was standing in a splattering of dark red blood sprayed out across the stone road like spilled paint. At the sight of it Shane's eyes grew wide and before she even realized it, she had opened her mouth and began loudly calling out for Hernandez.

Shane's yelling brought a number of gamers and combat consultants out of their tents and spilling back out onto the road. The found her in front of the campfire, huddle against the wood pile, staring unflinchingly at the spot that North had been sitting in just moment ago.

"Shane," said Hernandez who was now standing over her, "what happened?"

"I-I don't know, he was just sitting there, he was just sitting right there, and then all of a sudden he wasn't."

"What do you mean?" Hernandez asked. "Did he get up to patrol the perimeter, to take a piss, what?" his voice was becoming more forceful as he pushed her for information.

"No, he was sitting right in front of me, we were talking, I closed my eyes for a second, and when I opened them again, he was gone?"

"You closed your eyes? Shane, did you fall asleep?" The other members of the company gathered, but Roberts held them back from coming to close.

"What...? No... At least...I don't think so."

"Christine, this is not an issue of blame, it's an issue of safety. The entire camp could be at risk. I need to know what happened in order to know what we're dealing with. Now did you fall asleep on watch duty?"

"No!" Shane responded loudly "North and I were in the middle of a conversation. I closed my eyes for two seconds, and when I opened them again. He was gone. I don't know what happened. I don't know where he went. I don't know what's going on."

"It was the creature," Wuddlekins had pushed his way up the front of the crowd. "The same creature that got Gordon, it's gotten North. It's hunting us now."

"Get him out of here," said Hernandez.

"Get everybody out of here," cut in another voice. Pope. The members of the company turned around to see him standing there with his heavy cross bow in hand and Lansing and Corrine at his side. He looked like he hadn't been to sleep at all. "Everybody get back to your tents, rest up, we're moving out at first light."

At the sight of the captain Hernandez hurried over towards his direction. "Sir, North has gone missing sir, Shane said it happened right in front of her. I think our position has been compromised."

"I heard the whole thing Hernandez. Lansing and I will take over the reminder of watch duty for tonight. Everyone else to bed." Lansing stared at Hernandez with his signature cold and stony expression.

"But sir, you placed me in charge of night watch, and besides that we've just been attacked. Don't you think we should break camp and start moving now-"

"Hernandez. I said to get these men back to their tents and see to it that they get rested up so that we can head out at first light. *That* is an order soldier. *Do not* make me repeat myself again. Is that understood?" Pope's voice never rose higher than the volume of a whisper but at the sound of his words Hernandez's back straightened as if someone had poured cold water down the length of his spine.

"Sir, yes sir." He responded and with a nod to Lansing, he stepped past Captain Pope and began ordering gamers and combat consultants back to their tents. Under Hernandez's direction Corrine and Cyanide helped Shane to her feet. Pope and Lansing took their seat in front of the campfire and with longbow and crossbow in hand, stared out into the dark trees until the early morning sun began to brighten the sky, marking the start of a new day in Deos.

James North was well liked by most of the company, and his sudden disappearance right from under the nose of another combat consultant squashed any suspicions that Gordon was simply lost and destined to make his way back to the company sooner rather than later. There was no longer a question. Danger surrounded them, unseen and lurking in the shadows just beyond the edges of sight. They marched, stopping only once to rest and eat, before starting up again. Wuddlekins who had become somewhat validated in the disappearance of another member of the group, found himself back in the company of his old friends Danger Duke, Saber Lord, Thorn and the other gamers, now curious about what he had seen in the forest.

Sunset came quickly on day two. As dusk rolled in and the company set camp, Pope ordered four men to watch duty per shift, no one was to be alone for any amount of time and no one was allowed to sit while on watch. Previously Hernandez had taken volunteers, now Pope assigned the guard. Eliot, a dwarf battle guard, and Kurt, a human battle guard, were the two combat consultants chosen for first watch and in order to supplement the consultants that had been on watch the night before Pope selected two gamers. Orion the human cleric, and Danger Duke, the halfling barbarian.

"But why, why me?" Duke asked Hernandez later after Pope had left the men to their own devices for a short time before lights out. They were in a tent with Torrent, Thorn and for reasons none of them really understood, Dwight.

"What do you mean?" Responded Hernandez. "Why not you?"

Danger Duke motioned to himself. "Um in case you haven't noticed I'm not exactly built for combat, meanwhile there is a monster out there murdering highly trained soldiers like something out of a horror movie. Pope hates me doesn't he, he's doing this because I said he had PTSD, he's trying to get that thing to kill me isn't he?"

"He doesn't hate you... at least not any more than he hates anyone else. Everyone simply has to pull their weight, that's it. Just stick by one of the consultants and you'll be fine."

"A consultant stuck by one of the consultants and he wasn't even fine!" Danger Duke said in protest. "What chance do I have?"

"You're a gamer aren't you? Use your knowledge of the game to your advantage. That's what Dante used to do." Hernandez stood up and removed his sword and stretched out.

"Dante? Who is Dante?"

"The guy that ran off. Back when we were in town."

"The guy that ran off? He's dead for sure! Nothing survives in those woods for more than fifteen minutes alone and he ran off into them two days ago."

"He wasn't alone," said Hernandez, placing his hands behind his head like a makeshift pillow.

"Okay, so maybe they lasted an hour, but I'm pretty sure by now they're dead! Just like I'm going to be dead if I have to go out there on watch duty tonight."

"You're being dramatic, just stay alert, keep your eyes and your ears peeled and you'll be okay." Hernandez closed his eyes and drew in a deep breath. "Now clear out of here I need to rest up while I can, the rest of you should do the same. Danger Duke. Report to watch duty. That's an order."

Danger Duke grimaced and left the tent mumbling "I'll tell you where to stick those orders" a comment which Hernandez heard but chose to ignore. The other gamers, Torrent and Thorn left along with him, leaving no one else in the tent but Hernandez and Dwight, who sat quietly in the corner curled up on a bedroll of his own.

"Do you think they're still alive?" Dwight asked in his nasally voice.

"Who, Gordon? North? No unfortunately not. I don't think so."

"No, not them.... I mean the gamers from team 25.... You didn't seem as convinced... as Danger Duke that they hadn't survived their ordeal... in the Dark Woods."

"Oh, you mean Dante. Honestly, I don't know. That kid is almost too stubborn to die, he's kind of like the captain in that way. Nothing that he'd do would really surprise me. Hernandez rolled over onto his side turning his back to Dwight. "Now get some rest... you're going to need it."

Outside the tents, the night watch roved the perimeter of the camp, walking along the edge of the road, eyeing the forest. Danger Duke jumped at every sound he heard. The chirping of insects, the crackling of the fire, the distant hoot of some strange Deosian bird all served to only make him more and more uncomfortable. He made his rounds with Eliot, a hearty and thick dwarf that carried a heavy shield and an even heavier hammer.

Kurt and Orion circled the tents on the other side, always in sight, and since Danger Duke refused to walk on the side of the road closest to the forest he was for the most part, covered on all sides . As they passed the campfire for what Duke assumed was the one hundredth time that night and after about what he assumed to be about two hours into their shift, though he felt it was impossible to tell for sure, Eliot looked over to him and said, "Wait here."

"Wait? What? I thought we were never supposed to split up? I thought we had to stay in groups of two at all times?"

"Wait here." Eliot said again but this time more forcefully.

"I can't-? But we-? This is where North disappeared!" Danger Duke said loudly in protest.

"Wait! Here!" Eliot repeated, this time raised his hammer in a threating manner.

"Okay!" Duke replied, defiant in his tone but obedient in his action.

The dwarf turned and slowly walked away from Duke leaving him alone by the campfire. The halfling clung tightly to his broadaxe attempting to hide behind it as he knees trembled and shook under the weight of his fear. The small fire to his right crackled, calling out to anyone who would listen to throw another log onto the blaze. Insects chirped out a harmony that, if listened to while looking up at the night sky, almost seemed as if it was perfectly in-synch with the twinkling of the stars. Danger Duke however was not listening to the crackling of the campfire or the chirping of the insects nor was he looking at the twinkling night stars. He was looking and listening only and wholly for any sudden movement in the forest. He strained to hear or see any fluttering shadow, or glowing eyes or any single thing in the forest that would give him reason to scream out for help.

"Keep your ears and your eyes peeled and you'll be fine," he said to himself. Eyes peeled. He thought. Peeled eyes. His mind wandered. "I wonder if the monster peels the eyes before he eats them?" Duke's heart sank. as if he wasn't terrified enough, now his own mind had turned against him and was sending him into a downward spiral of imagined horrors possibly more terrifying then the real ones. He let out a low whining moan and desperately wished Eliot would come back from wherever it was that he had disappeared.

Danger Duke was so preoccupied with his thoughts, imaginings and wishes that he hadn't noticed the creature crept from the shadows of the forest and onto the Merchant's Road. It moved with supernatural silence, its hooved feet soundless. Danger Duke never turned, until he heard it. The broken raspy breathing of something otherworldly and large.

Duke froze. He held his breath in attempt to ensure that he wasn't somehow scaring himself once again. But even as he stood there, heart thumping in his chest, lungs burning from a lack of oxygen, he heard the crooked raspy breathing of something evil and hungry behind him. He turned.

The light shed by the flickering orange blaze gave Duke a clear view of the thing that had been stalking their group for the past two days. Hooved feet led up to thick and powerful deer-like legs that bent backwards like reverse-set knees and then folded back in upon themselves with regular legs and muscular, humanoid thighs. The entire creature's body was covered in dark brown fur with the exception of its head which shone in the fire light as nothing but a bone white deer skull complete with a large set of antler protruding from its crown. As the thing stood slowly, the sounds it made changed from broken raspy breathing, to a blood curdling rattle that sounded like a combination of grinding teeth and crackling bone. Human eyes peered from the deep dark sockets of the skull like face and in that moment Duke couldn't tell if the antler crowned head was a mask or the creatures real face, but as it unfolded itself larger and larger stopping finally at what had to be at least seven feet in height, he knew that it definitely was not human, or elf, or orc or anything common to the natural world.

Danger Duke opened his mouth to scream, but only a dry hoarse gasp came out in its place. The creature, tall dark and terrifying, raised a gnarled and twisted claw in his direction, but then winced and pulled it away quickly when it got close to the fire. The monster stopped for a moment, examined the flames and before either it or Duke could think of what to do next there was a defining 'thunk.'

The monster looked down, considered the crossbow bolt protruding from its chest, opened its mouth and let out an ear-splitting roar, revealing a mouth full of elongated teeth and a forked tongue. Danger Duke stared up at the creature slack-jawed and blinked dumbly as he watched a small health bar pop into existence above the monster's head.

"Move out of the way you idiot!" shouted someone from behind Duke, and at the same time he heard two more 'thunk' 'thunk's and this time saw two crossbow bolts slammed the monster again. The thing's health bar dropped by only a slight margin. It roared again and then leaned back as if preparing to lash out, but just then two people ran up on either side of the halfling. Eliot the Dwarf on one side and Hernandez on his other. Both had their shields and weapons drawn.

"Job well done Duke! Now fall back, we'll take it from here." Hernandez said. He was bouncing on the balls of his feet with his shield in front of him and the tip of his sword pointed toward the monster.

"What?" said Danger Duke, confused and bewildered.

"Move out of the way kid!" Eliot shouted before pushing Duke backwards away from the fire. The dwarf was strong and the force of his push sent Danger Duke stumbling backwards and ultimately landing on his butt, but the jolt of the fall knocked the halfling out of his stupor.

"Are you hurt?" asked Orion who had rushed to his side and was now helping him up to his feet.

"Um no." said Duke. "I don't think so."

"Good. Get up, let's move back out of the way."

Orion took hold of his arm and Duke saw Captain Pope, Lansing, Shane, Corrine and Dwight, none of them seemed at all surprised to see the monster in the middle of camp.

"They're clear. Fire arrows," commanded Pope. As directed Lansing and Shane lifted their longbows and released an arrow each in the monster's direction. One of the arrows hit, the other went wide and missed the monster altogether.

"What's going on here?" Danger Duke asked, still feeling a bit disheveled.

The commotion of the monster in camp had begun to bring gamers out of their tents, each of them looking just as confused as Danger Duke had been. They were looking at the monster fearfully, all careful to keep their distance.

"They call it a Wendigo." Pope called out; his voice boomed as if addressing the camp in its entirety. "It's already claimed two of our lives and if we don't kill it now, it will kill us all before we leave this forest.

Danger Duke looked back toward the campfire where the monster stood. Hernandez and Eliot flanked it on either side and now somehow Kurt had maneuvered himself behind the thing so that the three of them had encased the monster in a kind of triangle formation.

"Grab your arms! Prepare to attack on my command!" Pope yelled out, and at his words the gamers scrambled back to their tents and then begin to come back out reluctantly with weapons in hand.

The Wendigo was still trapped within the combat consultant's triangle. It looked to be a combination of both surprised and frustrated. It rattled and roared in multiple directions, as if trying to decide who it would attack first and then suddenly, without warning, it launched itself forward and slammed Eliot's shield with a heavy claw. The force of the blow knocked the dwarf off his feet and sent him rolling back to the edge of the road.

Immediately Eliot took the hit and Hernandez bellowed out a scream that echoed through the whole of the wood.

"Beast! Come, Fight Meeee!" he screamed with such fervor that his body lifted off the ground and wisps of smoky white steam begin to briefly emanate from his person.

The Wendigo which looked poised to attack the dwarf a second time seemed now unable to resist turning around and focusing his attention on Hernandez. Hesitantly it turned its skull-covered face away from the dwarf and aimed it at the human battle guard.

"Come!" Hernandez screamed. In a flash the Wendigo bolted. Hernandez lifted his shield in front of him and allowed the tip of his sword to point towards the ground and in the instant before the creature made contact, he uttered the words.

"Sword Dance." The blade of his sword glowed bright red. The Wendigo's foreclaw slammed into the shield and in anticipation of the blow Hernandez dropped down to one knee and brought his sword thrusting into the creature's torso. The Wendigo let out a roar of pain. At the same time, Hernandez screamed in agony. The monster's attack, which had been partially deflected, still managed to somehow destroy a portion of his shield, grazing his arm and dislocating his shoulder in the process. Something warm and wet poured down the length of his arm and even through the pain the tip of his fingers tingled and turned numb.

"Kurt! Pull it off of him!" Pope yelled.

"Over here, beast!" Kurt yelled in a loud voice that lacked the conviction Hernandez's had just moments before. The Wendigo pulled itself off of Hernandez's blade, looked at Kurt but did not seemed convinced that he was worth attacking.

"KURT! PULL IT NOW!" Pope yelled.

"Fight me! Fight me you demon!" Kurt screamed at the top of his lungs and banged his sword against his shield. The Wendigo raised a clawed hand for one more attack against a kneeling Hernandez.

With his sword still in his right hand and a broken shield still attached to his left, Hernandez could do nothing but look as the Wendigo slowly raised one of its long thin arms and swung it down fast and hard.

The blow sent Hernandez skidding across the road and careening into the side of one of the tents, collapsing it around him. He lay there, unmoving.

The Wendigo trudged slowly toward Kurt now. Black blood poured from the wound in its torso. The thrust that Hernandez had made to it's abdomen had hurt it, knocking off a considerably chunk from its HP but even so, it still had well over half of its health bar remaining.

"Orion see to Hernandez." Pope ordered. "Roberts... hit it."

Orion had been helping Eliot. The dwarf was wincing and holding on to his arm, which judging from how it bent at the forearm as if he had an extra elbow, looked obviously broken. Orion was holding a hand over the crooked limb, infusing it with a radiant golden light. Slowly and much to Eliot's discomfort the arm began to right itself and anyone close enough could hear the bones cracking and popping as they reset and mended themselves back together doing in a matter of seconds what normally would have taken months.

"I don't think it's completely healed but that should at least hold you over for now." Orion said.

"I'll be fine," said the dwarf, still squeezing his arm tightly and grimacing at the pain "Go check on Hernandez."

Meanwhile, Roberts marched down the center of the battlefield. He had come from behind that Captain when commanded and had answered his order with a simple.

"My pleasure."

He advanced with a brisk strut, his steps determined, he cracked his neck as he walked and then snorted a hard breath out of his nose that came out as steam. A feral growl began to rumble deep within his throat. His strut turned into a jog, and then quickly his jog became a sprint. The half-orc ran with large double-bladed axes in each hand. His growl turned into a guttural roar as he closed in on the Wendigo. The creature took no notice of the half-orc running up behind it, and as such was blindsided when Roberts raised his two axes overhead and brought them crashing down with such savagery that onlookers were unable to tell which of them was the monster. The Wendigo roared and flailed, while Roberts' massive arms swung and ripped, violently ending with him pinning the thing to the ground. Roberts had a knee in the Wendigo's back while one of his axes nailed its left arm to the ground and luck had seen to it that its right arm was pinned under its own body. Robert's other axe secured one of the Wendigo's legs and with a free hand the half-orc had grabbed the monster by the antlers to keep its head from thrashing.

""Now, while we have the advantage, everyone, attack!" shouted Pope.

The gamers flooded the battlefield with weapons raised. Wuddlekins lead the charge, a shortsword in each hand. He was the first to make it to the Wendigo, jamming both blades into the thing's neck and staring deep into its cold dead eyes, his cat like face pulled back into a sneer, revealing nearly all of his own long and pointed fangs. After Wuddlekins struck, Saber lord and then Cyanide followed, then Thorn and Mandrake. They hacked and slashed at the Wendigo ferociously, like angry ants tearing at the body of some larger much more dangerous insect that made the mistake of becoming wounded on the wrong part of the forest floor.

Danger Duke, who had yet to join the fray, watched as his friends tore into the monster that had almost killed him a few moments earlier. The Wendigo's health bar had been depleted by a considerable amount at this point and by all means the fight looked to have swung completely to their advantage. Duke, feeling that there was no better time than the present, regripped his axe and began running toward the restrained Wendigo. The monster only had a third of its health bar left and at the rate they were going that wouldn't last very much longer. He only needed to get in a few slashes and he would have pulled his weight, and that's all that mattered. Danger Duke kept running and soon found himself right in front of the monster, but found the battle looked drastically different up-close then it did from afar.

The Wendigo's brown fur covered body was now covers with countless cuts and wounds, all of them oozing thick black blood. The creature's skull covered face was now riddled with cracks and covered with dirt and grime. The gamers as well as Roberts were all splattered with the black ichor that spilled from the Wendigo's body. They all grunted and growled through gritted teeth as they chopped and stabbed at the monster in front of them, all simultaneously willing it to die.

"Get back!" grunted Roberts from on top of the creature. "I can't... hold it... anymore!" he struggled to speak, and even as he did the Wendigo's movement increased.

As instructed the gamers begin to pull away, but not all of them.

"Wait? What? But I haven't- I mean we almost have it." Muttered Duke, axe still in hand.

"Fall back! We'll regroup and finish it off." Pope commanded from his position on the back line.

Danger Duke and Wuddlekins were the only ones who had yet to retreat. Wuddlekins stabbed the monster in the neck over and over again with so much fury and rage that he seemed possessed. Black blood poured from the wounds in spades, but now the Wendigo freed the arm from underneath itself and slammed it into the ground before it as if preparing to do a one-armed push-up. With the added leverage of a free hand, the Wendigo ripped its head free of Robert's grip, breaking off the antlers on the right side of its head in the process, but then using the remaining antler on the left to come down hard across the front of Mr. Wuddlekins, slashing him across the face and chest. A spray of red blood splattered from the rage possessed Kalgari and he fell backwards both blinded and surprised by the attack. In a fit of panic Danger Duke took his axe and slammed it into the Wendigo's arm and left it there, pulled Wuddlekins to his feet and tried as best he could to lead the Kalgari ranger to safety.

The Wendigo roared as another blade hit its forearm, but the pain did not slow its ascent. Pushing into the ground to lift its body up it freed its other arm from the axe blade. Now with both arms free it was able to lift its entire torso and regain its footing on the road. It kicked its left leg free of the blade that had it pinned to the ground and then with a long and slender arm reached around and grabbed the half-orc from off of its back and slammed it into the ground. The Wendigo lifted a claw to attack the half-orc again but before it could bring down its fist, Pope gave a command.

"Burn it."

Corrine and Dwight chanted in low ominous tones and waved their arms in front of themselves in tight circles as if stirring the air. Bright orange spheres of fire burst into being. Corrine's was larger and burned slightly more intensely than Dwight's but in the darkness of the forest the two orbs looked like miniature suns blazing in depths of space. The mages began to churn their arms even faster and the fiery orbs began to throb with heat and power. Then right when it seemed as if the bright orange spheres were about to explode and overtake everything in their wake, both Dwight and Corrine thrust their arms out toward the Wendigo.

"Ignis!" they shouted in unison, and all at once the glowing balls of fire hurled themselves at the Wendigo slamming into its chest and stomach. On contact the fireballs engulfed the entire creature in a bright orange blaze, filling their area of the forest with blazing light as well as the painful roars of the burning Wendigo. The monster flailed wildly on the Merchant's Road. It swung around blindly trying to hit anything within its reach.

"Hit it again." Pope commanded.

Again, Corrine and Dwight manifested the fiery orbs and sent them careening into the Wendigo. Again it howled in pain as flames burned anew.

"Again." Commanded Pope.

The next volley was smaller and less intense then the first. The Wendigo continued to burn, and its movement slowed, but it maintained its position. Its health bar had dropped to a sliver.

"Hit it again!" Pope growled, frustrated at the creature's persistence.

"I'm out of mana," said Corrine.

"So am I," said Dwight.

"Stand me up." Hernandez spoke from the rubble that used to be a tent.

"I don't think that's a good idea," said Orion.

"I said stand me up!" Hernandez shouted.

Reluctantly, Orion helped the bloodied battle guard to his feet. His body was a mangled mess of tattered armor and broken limbs. He still held the broken shield, though the arm attached to it looked useless.

Hernandez groaned in pain through gritted teeth and Orion sent golden arcs of energy across the combat consultant's spine. Hernandez grunted and spasmed as the magic healed his broken body. After a few moments, Orion moved the healing light to Hernandez' ribs, then down to a leg, repairing it, then back up to his head, but no matter how much he did it never seemed to be enough. Hernandez had more injuries than what one mage could heal.

The creature now stood on the merchant's road covered head to hoof in agonizing burns. Its body and mask were blackened and charred and the cracks, cuts and wounds that once spewed black blood now seethed with an orange glow..

Roberts was laid out flat on the road, knocked unconscious from the body slam that the monster had inflicted. Straight ahead stood Pope, the wizard and bowmen, a clear line of sight for the Wendigo yet still some distance away. To the right were two much closer targets, a halfling and a half-blind Kalgari who hadn't gotten nearly as far away as the others. Wuddlekins could barely see or stand and was much too heavy for Duke to carry.

"Hernandez be still," said Orion

Everyone saw it, all at once.

"Shut up," said Hernandez.

"Don't move, you shouldn't move. You're in no state to move."

The creature honed in on Danger Duke and Wuddlekins with pained and hungry eyes. It hunched down to all fours, the monstrous rattle reverberating from behind its mask.

"You're going to reopen your wounds, refracture your bones, not to mention the things I haven't even been able to heal. Don't you get it. If you don't stop you're going to kill yourself."

Pope fired volley of crossbow bolts at the Wendigo, all of them finding their mark. The three shots hit the creature in quick succession and sunk deep into its charred flesh, eating into its remaining health bar more than they had before, but even then, it did not seem to deter what was to come. The Wendigo was on the verge of death and determine not to go alone.

"I told him no one would die. I told him it would be okay. I have to make it... okay. What...? What would my father think?" Hernandez tore himself from Orion, babbling incoherently in his shock.

The Wendigo launched itself forward cutting through the air with uncanny speed. Danger Duke watched in horror as he and Wuddlekins stood defenseless. The monster raised a giant claw and roared as it flew across the battlefield, thrilled by the promise of blood.

"Sword Dance," said Hernandez, softly but with conviction.

The Wendigo's foreclaw stopped short only a few inches from Duke's face. It was frozen in place. Hernandez had thrust his sword into the creature's chest and the Wendigo, moving so fast and so focused upon its prey, had impaled itself on the warrior's glowing blade. The sword sank in to the hilt, stopping the monster dead in its tracks and in the process shearing away any remaining hit points that the Wendigo may have had left. The monster went limp over Hernandez's shoulder then dropped to the ground in a lifeless heap.

Hernandez stumbled backward and fell. Orion and the others rushed to his side.

"You did it." Orion was laughing. "It was dangerous, and it was dumb, but you did it."

"Yes," said Hernandez, "I guess I did." He took a slow and labored breath. Orion looked down and saw a large gaping hole in the battle guard's abdomen. The Wendigo's other claw had pierced his stomach when they collided.

"Oh no." Orion muttered.

"What is it?" said Danger Duke dropping down beside Orion. "Oh no."

Hernandez looked over at Duke. "You did it." He smiled weakly. "You pulled your weight."

"Hey man, don't talk. Just um... try not to move. Orion, don't just stand there. Heal him."

Orion placed his hands over the wound and radiant light begin to reknit the wound, but the progress was slow.

"Come on man, faster!"

"I'm trying, let me concentrate."

Hernandez grabbed Danger Duke's wrist. "When you find him, tell Dante he was right." He whispered. "I'm sorry... for my part in this... I'm sorry. Keep your eyes peeled, ears peeled... you'll be okay." He smiled and the light faded from his eyes.

"Orion heal him. Orion... hurry up man, heal him. Orion."

"I CAN'T!" Orion yelled. "I'm nearly out of mana... and I think, it's too late."

Pope pushed his way past the crowd that had gathered around Hernandez's body started down at the broken and mangled body of one of his former men. Then he folded the soldier's arms gently across his chest and closed his eyelids. The captain bowed his head, then raised it to look at the others.

"Orion see to Wuddlekins, have Mandrake and Thorn help you, they have some minor healing magic. Lansing, you and Corrine see to camp and make sure that everyone is accounted for. Roberts, Kurt, start digging a grave." Pope looked up and Danger Duke who was staring at him from across the body of Hernandez. "You. Come, help me bury him."

"Yes- sir, yes, sir." Responded the halfling with tears in his eyes.

They buried Hernandez on the side of the Merchant's Road just outside the shade of the forest trees. They marked his grave with his sword and his broken shield and then they marched on for a full day, not even stopping to rest. Almost immediately upon clearing the woods the men's spirits began to pick up. The losses that they suffered weighed heavily upon most of them, but the fact that those who remained had survived the worst of it filled them with an odd sense of camaraderie and pride. A number of the gamers and the combat consultants began to look at and treat each other differently. The sense of separation that existed among them before was all but gone, they were no longer gamers and game guides and combat consultants, but instead they were now adventurers, soldiers and survivors all one in the same.

Roughly an hour's march outside of the of the forest, Pope could see in the distance an altercation unfolding. Some fifty yards ahead of them, two men were becoming exceedingly rough with what looked to be an elderly woman. The woman had been holding a basket of fruit and flowers until one of the men knocked it from her hands, spilling her goods onto the road, the other man then grabbed her briskly by her hair and threw her face down to the ground.

Wuddlekins didn't hesitate, he ran forward to aid the woman, but Pope's arm shot out, blocking his path. The cat-man looked questioningly at Pope through his one good eye. His head was wrapped in bandages most of which concealed his right eye and left ear from where the Wendigo's antlers had caught him. The healing magic had restored all of his HP but the wound to his eye had been so extensive, that even once fully healed they found that he still could not see out of it, and though his hearing was fine his left ear was split down the middle. Now he simply wore the bandages in the hopes that time would offer more healing than the magic.

"Aren't we going to help her?" he asked.

"In due time." Pope said calmy. "Ready your weapons, but do it subtly."

"But there's only two of them."

"Consider that an order," chimed in Lansing in a low voice.

Wuddlekins looked over at Lansing and then back at the Captain who hadn't bothered to look back at him but instead was still walking forward at the same pace as he had before.

"Yes, sir, I'll tell the others." Wuddlekins replied in a whisper.

"Good man," Lansing said.

As Pope and his men continued to march forward, the men's attack on the old woman became more vicious. As she attempted to gather up her fruits and flowers, one of the men stomped the items beneath their feet, purposely coming down on her fingers in the process. The second man offered swift and aggressive kicks to the abdomen as she crawled around on the ground at their feet.

"You insolent old witch!" another swift kick to the gut. "You'll learn one way or the other!"

"Could you stop that?" asked Pope calmly. "And move out of the road while you all are at it."

"What's that?" The man that had been doing the kicking looked up as if he hadn't noticed the group of sixteen people marching towards him.

"Could you stop kicking that woman and move out of the road so we can pass?" Pope asked again.

"Well, no I can't." said the man. The old woman now lay at his feet curled up in the fetal position.

Pope let out an exasperated sigh. "And why is that?" he asked.

"Because in order to travel this road, everyone has to pay a tax, and this old crone has yet to pay up." He kicked the old woman again. "And if you want to pass, you'll have to pay as well."

"How much?" asked Pope.

"How much have you got?" asked the man who had done the kicking and immediately he and the man that had done the stomping burst out laughing.

Pope let out another sigh, "I see there is no way we can be reasonable about this."

"You want reasonable? How is this for reasonable?" The kicking man let out a shrill whistle, and a number of other men with crossbows and short bows stepped from nearly every available rock and tree. "Now ye might have felt pretty high and mighty when you thought you had the numbers but now me and my mates obviously have the jump on ye. Now if you don't want to be turned into Dalgonian goat cheese, you'll spill out all yer gold and drop off all yer valuables. Real nice like."

"Yes, of course." Pope responded lifting his right hand into the air to show he was not holding a weapon. And then with a quick and decisive action his open palm turned into a tightly clenched fist. "Kill them." Pope commanded. Pope's team reacted, longbows and crossbows flew out with blinding speed firing into the direction of the bandits before they could understand what was happening.

The man who had done the kicking jumped in reaction to the Pope's men violent and immediate response to his threat. Even with the advantage of numbers, travelers rarely put up much of a fight when they had a dozen arrows and crossbows aimed at their party. Not to mention this was the road from the Black Wood, a journey that often-left travelers weary and exhausted. These jobs were usually easy pickings, but today however, things had gone oddly wrong, first the weird old lady almost messed up their ambush, and then... then this.

The bandit looked down and saw two very large crossbow bolts sticking out of his chest. He looked back up toward the man he had been speaking with and saw that he was now holding a very large, very menacing looking crossbow. He looked over to his partner, who also had a crossbow bolt protruding from his chest as well. He tried to say something, but the words seemed caught in his throat. His vision blurred, his knees buckled and before he could figure out which of the Gods to call out to, everything went black.

Pope watched as the bandit spokesman collapsed to the ground after taking two bolts to the chest. Low level highwaymen attempting to rob weary travelers on their way into the city. Unskilled, undisciplined, and now dead. Not much of a surprise really, with the proper leadership and training such men could be a threat in this world. But in Deos just like on Earth one fact remains true, only hell awaits the undisciplined.

"Check them for any weapons that are in decent condition, and let's keep moving. We've almost reached the city," said Pope, and after only a few moments of rummaging through the bandits' belongings, the company prepared to continue their march.

"My lord," said a humble and meek voice.

Pope looked down to see the elderly woman back on her feet and bowing in front of him.

"You're still alive," said Pope with surprise.

"Yes, thanks to you my lord. Why if not for your aid, I am afraid to think what would have become of me. By the grace of the Gods you have saved my life this day."

"Thanks to me?" Pope smirked. "You mean to tell me you weren't a part of the bandit's ambush? A part of the plot to lure us in?" Pope could see the bruises and scratches across the old lady's face and hands. If they had been play-acting, they had been dedicated in playing their roles, she looked badly hurt.

"No, my lord, not at all. I am an old woman traveling out near the edge of the forest to collect flowers and fruit to sell in the marketplace. I have no place in the plots of bandits and criminals."

"Yes," said Pope coldly, "So you say." he eyed the woman curiously. Up close, she looked much older than what he had originally thought her to be. She had a long narrow nose that had grown crooked over time. Her face was wrinkled and cracked, her skin pale and thin. Long stark white hair covered her head and lay draped messily over pointed ears and sharply angular facial features the last of which lead Pope to deduce that she perhaps was an elderly elven woman if he had been forced to guess. "Please do try and be more careful in the future."

"Why yes, my lord of course, but might I say." The old women bowed her head even more humbly. "A noble deed such as the one you have done is worthy of compensation. Aside from peddling flowers and fruit I am also a teller of fortunes, a seer of destinies. I do not have gold my lord, but for your heroism I shall reward you with a glimpse into your future, knowledge of your fortune, insight into your destiny."

Pope chuckled at the old women's offer. "That won't be necessary. My men and I really must be on our way."

"But my lord, I must insist. You see I am an elven woman of the old way. We have a saying. 'No good deed must go unrewarded.' This is one of the oldest and most sacred traditions in Deos. It would dishonor the Gods if I do not repay the kindness that you have shown me on today."

Pope let out a heavy-hearted sigh. "Fine, but make it quick, we have to get to Abilene Bay before night fall."

"Yes, my lord of course." The old woman took Pope's hand and began to stare intently at his palm, her long thin fingers tracing the lines and subtle creases in his hand. "Ah yes, how very interesting. You are a warrior and a traveler yes, but a warrior of a different type I see, and one that has traveled from a very faraway land. A land of mystery. A land to which no ship has sailed." She pushed her face closer to his palm, as if straining to see something that was unclear. "You have come here on a mission of great importance, a mission that you mean to see done by any means at your disposal." She looked up at him with a wrinkly faced smile of a proud old grandmother. "You are a resourceful man, disciplined, focused, strong of both mind and spirit, success does not always come easy to you but it comes because you do not abide by failure. These are good traits to have." She looked back down at his hand once again. "Ha that is interesting." She said with a slightly different tone. Pope did not take the bait. "Not something that we see often with men of your caliber, but it is to be expected even with the best of them." She looked up again. "The one that got away." She said and gave him another smile, this one somewhere between smugness and sympathy. She looked at his hand again, this time holding it up to the light of the setting sun. "Yes, it is all there. The destiny in store for you is unlike any other, I see that you shall achieve great things in the land of Deos. Things that few people could have imagined."

She held his hand aloft, as if a contest had just taken place and she was announcing him as the winner. Pope slowly allowed his hand to drop from the air.

Pope smirked dismissively, when without warning the old woman grabbed Pope by face and looked deeply into his eyes.

"I can see it in your eyes my lord. The pain of a man who has suffered great loss," her voice seemed deeper, more penetrating than before. "The one loss none of us should be made to suffer, but I see something else in those eyes as well, determination. The determination of a man that would do anything to make right what the universe has made wrong. The determination of a man who would fix it all, if he only had the power."

Pope found himself frozen for a moment, but then after a brief second, he snapped back to reality and forcefully knocked her hand away from his face.

"I can help you find that power my lord, old mother knows many great things." She looked down at the road as she spoke, oddly avoiding eye contact with him now, as she nervously rubbed the back of her hands and mumbled under her breath almost as if talking to herself. "Old mother knows many small things as well, knows many secret things, hidden things, forbidden things."

The woman looked so frail and weak standing there now, but when she had grabbed him, he felt and heard something altogether different than what he was hearing and seeing at the moment. "Stand aside old woman. I won't ask you again." Pope pushed the passed her and began to continue down the Merchant Road.

"Proof then? Yes, a man of your reasoning is a man that needs proof. Your fallen friend, crystallized by the green one, yes? Well, I know of a way to restore him, back to full health, to full life. That would be proof enough for you?"

Pope stopped where he stood. "What did you say?"

"I know of a way to restore your friend, the one in the crystal?"

"How did you know about?"

"I am an old woman, an old mother, I am prone to worry. The only time I do not worry is when I know, therefore I know things, that way I do not have to worry." the old lady blushed and appeared bashful which was an odd and curious thing to see.

"But... I don't have the crystal." Pop responded, cutting his eyes at the old woman, partly testing her and partly himself still confused by how she could have known about Stephen.

"No, you do not, but the boy does. He comes quickly to Abilene Bay. He is not far behind. Speak with him. Your goals do not differ that much, to have your friend restored, to have your proof, to what lengths would you be willing to go?"

"Once I get the crystal how do I find you?"

"In the market, I peddle my wares, I read fortunes, sell flowers, you can find me there. Bring the boy. I will tell you all how to restore your friend, how to have your proof."

As Pope slowly walked away, the old woman stood staring, smiling as he left with his men following behind him. She stood there, alone in the road, and as they got roughly some thirty yards away, he looked back to see her crouched down, going through the pockets of the bandits that they had left behind.

Chapter 27: The Eldest Battle

"Sergeant Battle. The Colonel will see you now."

"Thank you, Linda." Bryan rose from the small chair in the waiting area and made his way through a set of heavy wooden doors into a large and spacious office. A middle-aged, mustached man sat behind an ornate oak desk. A flood of natural light poured into the room from the direction of two different walls. The glass windows, through which the light was filtered, were so clean, clear and utterly spotless, that aside from the occasional crystalline glare, it was difficult to determine if they were open or closed. The room itself was sparsely decorated: A tri-folded American flag, a globe, an antique pistol and some books, shelves and shelves of books and all of them on military history, or military tactics or military figures, and the tactics those figures used throughout history. Bryan noticed a clear-cut theme.

The man behind the desk had not bothered to look up from his work upon Bryan's entrance. He looked from one sheet of paper to another, and then back to the original again, and then, after making the determination that his strict standards had been met, placed his signature in the appropriate field.

"Colonel, I understand you wanted to see me sir." Said Bryan straightening out to his full height as he spoke.

"Ah yes Sergeant Battle. At ease." The colonel placed his initials on two more pages before looking away from his work. He looked up to meet eyes with Bryan Battle and smiled. Bryan was tall and brown, with short cropped hair and a clean-shaven face. He was leading man in an action film handsome, and somehow even though he was in his early thirties, he still had the look and feel of a collegiate quarterback. In a lot of ways, he looked like the prototype of the ideal man, and because of this, older men would often look at him and picture their ideal son, either that, or an ideal version of themselves.

The colonel had a thick white mustache, a head of silvery white hair, and a chest full of medals, though he wore his service on his face. You could see in his eyes and in his facial expressions that he was bred for military duty. Bryan had heard that the colonel could trace his ancestors back to the revolutionary war, maybe even further, back to England, his majesty's royal navy, maybe even all the way back knighthood. Bryan wouldn't be surprised.

"Sergeant, I want to thank you for meeting with me today." The colonel placed the documents he was reviewing into a folder, closed it and set it aside, giving Bryan his full attention. . "As I'm sure you are well aware, a position has come open in upper management, and your name has come up in a number of conversations in regard to filling that position."

"I must admit I was not fully aware of all of *those* details sir."

"Yes," the colonel opened another folder and begin to skim over the contents. "It seems that you have developed quite the resumé. Says here that you graduated from Northfield University up in Vermont then joined Air Force Special Operations Pararescue. Pararescue training is tough." Said the colonel looking up from the papers that were apparently Bryan's resume. "They call it 'Superman' school."

"Yes, colonel, I've often heard it referred to as that."

"Let's see... says here you served in Pararescue for four years before leaving the Airforce for the Navy." The colonel flipped to the next page. "Entered into BUD/S training. Graduated and became a Navy Seal. Team nine it says here." The colonel smirked at the page. "You served in Afghanistan, Iraq, a little time in Pakistan, and then, look here, what a surprise. You leave the Navy and go and graduate from Army Ranger school, with the distinction of Top Honor Man no less." The colonel looked up from the folder once again. "Then that's when you popped up on our radar and got yourself recruited by the agency. That is what you were trying to do correct, with all of this branch hopping, and accolade hoarding, you wanted to get the attention of the agency?"

"Sir, back then I wasn't even sure if the agency wasn't just a rumor. I was just trying to serve my country in the best way I knew how."

The colonel let out a snorted chuckle at this response. "Good answer, because as you now know, as far as the world is concerned, we don't exist. I'll be frank. I like you Sargent Battle. You've been with us two years and it's obvious that you do good work. You're thorough, you're precise and you leave nothing to chance. You're an exemplary soldier, and agent."

"Thank you, sir." Bryan attempted to hold back a smile.

"However, this new position that you are being considered for is one of such... sovereignty, that the consideration for it encompasses far more that simply a candidate's military and work history."

Bryan tried not to let his confusion show on his face. The colonel looked back down at his stack of papers of Bryan's personal history.

"I see that you have a younger brother. An ivy league scholar, an athlete, quite the accomplished young man."

"Yes, sir my brother Dante. He attends Milgrad University on a combination academic and athletic scholarship. He is a major point of pride for me sir." Bryan wasn't exactly sure where this conversation was going, but he had an idea, and it filled him with unease.

"I bet he is. As I understand it, your father died when you were fairly young, I don't think it would be a too much of a stretch to say that you had a hand in raising young Dante, and that in a way, a large part of his success is, in fact also your success."

Clever, Bryan thought, but he hadn't made it as far as he had in his military intelligence career by falling for such obvious traps.

"Dante is an extraordinarily bright kid, and a hard worker, much of the success that he has achieved can be attributed to our mother's positive and reaffirming influence, sir. If I've tried to teach my brother anything, it's to lead by example and always take responsibility for your actions."

"Admirable. And your other brother? The one currently in prison for grand larceny, forgery, fraud and robbery. Malcolm is it? He was apprehended attempting to pull off a rather complex robbery of a diamond exchange."

Bryan suspected this was coming.

"Sergeant Battle if I'm being honest this *other* brother of yours is the only black mark on an otherwise flawless resume. And while you of course can't be held responsible for the actions of your brother, when one considers the levels of exposure, security clearance, and even influence that you would have in this new position, well let's just say things like this have to be taken into consideration. If only to ensure that our agents are in no way compromised." The colonel looked up at Bryan. It was now his turn to speak.

"I understand wholeheartedly colonel, and I can assure you that won't be a problem in the slightest. Due to his poor decision making ever since our teenage years, my brother Malcolm and I have not seen eye to eye for quite some time and I can honestly say that currently we have little to no relationship."

"Glad to hear it Battle because for the position in question an agent's loyalty to duty and country must be uncompromising."

"Sir, as far as I am concerned, I only have one brother, his name is Dante and honestly it's been like that for quite some time."

"Well, in that case, I think I've learned everything I need to know. Thank you for your time and your candor Sergeant Battle. We'll be in touch about the position, there are still a few other candidates to consider but at present you're at the top of the list. Dismissed."

Bryan let himself out of the office, closing the doors behind him. He began making his way down the hallway back to his own office, all the while replaying the conversation he'd just had with the colonel in his head. He was looking at a possible promotion to upper management, which of course really just meant he'd become a Senior Field Agent with agents of his own under his command. He'd probably be the youngest Senior Field Agent in the history of the agency. As Bryan pondered his ambitions, he noticed Sims, a junior agent, coming down the opposite side of the hallway.

"Battle, a letter came for you. I dropped it on your desk." Sims announced cheerfully.

"Thanks" Bryan replied, a little curious as to who would have possibly sent him a letter as opposed to having sent him an email or just as easily called him.

Bryan walked into his office. It was much smaller than the colonel's and didn't have nearly as much natural light, but it was immaculately well kept and neat, and the cleanliness of it helped maximize the small amount of space making it much more comfortable. Besides he wasn't there that much. He spent most of his time in the field anyway. He sat down at his desk and as promised there was a letter waiting for him. It had a handwritten address on the envelope but no return address.

Bryan,

While I know I'm not your most favorite person in the world right now, and to be honest you're not really mine either, I am writing you this letter because we are in an emergency situation.

I believe Dante has gone missing.

I last spoke to him about a week ago. He was coming out to California to play a demo of a new video game and his plan was to come to the prison for a visit while he was out here, but he never showed up. I had my girlfriend go check on him at the hotel and they said he had already checked out.

Everything about the situation feels wrong. I've been calling him every day for the past week and he hasn't answered once. I've had Kiesha call, he hasn't answered. I had her text him and he responded one time and said he didn't feel like talking. That doesn't even sound like Dante. I know it sounds crazy, but I think someone has his phone and they're responding to his text messages posing as him. I could be wrong. Please try contacting him and see if he'll answer.

I really just want to know that he's okay.

Needless to say, I'm worried and I thought that you should know what was going on. Whenever you get a chance write me back or give me a number that I can call.

I'm concerned for our little brother.

Sincerely,

Malcolm

Bryan let out a deep sigh as he folded the letter and slid it back into the envelope.

"Malcom, what are you up to now?" he mumbled to himself.

Part III

Chapter 28: Under Shinto's Wing

"It felt so nice to sleep in a real bed, even one stuffed full of hay. Do we really have to leave already?" Robyn stretched her arms and back as she walked toward the town's eastern gate. Morrigan, Alex and Dante walked alongside her.

"If we want to get back home then, yeah, we do." Dante responded. "We have to find Sandberg before Pope does, otherwise we're going to be sleeping on hay beds for the rest of our lives."

The party had reached the town of Bleeksborough the day prior and slept the night at the Hollow Hill Tavern. It had been nice enough. There had been hay stuffed mattresses, hot food and a refreshing lack of ogres. Now they were heading east towards Abilene Bay. Shinto waited at the town gate. He too had stayed at the Hollow Hill Tavern, but while Dante and the others rested, Shinto had awakened before dawn to scout the road ahead.

The party approached the eastern gate to see two human guards standing nervously near a calm Shinto. The guards gripped their long spears and shifted restlessly, eyeing each other and then the half-orc to determine if one of them should say something to him. Shinto, for his part, stood with his back against a tree apparently unbothered by the guard's discomfort.

"Morning Shinto!" said Alex cheerfully, completely oblivious to the dynamic between the stoic cleric and the gate guards.

"Good morning." Shinto replied. "Are you all prepared to leave? We should head out as soon as possible."

Dante noticed the guards let out a sigh of relief.

"Aren't we going to stay in town a little longer? Let the shops open up maybe resupply on some of the essentials?" asked Robyn.

The guards tensed.

"No." said Shinto, "Harrington is only a couple of day's journey, we should be fine with what supplies we have. It's better to get the expedition underway."

The guards relaxed again. Then discreetly one of them cleared his throat.

"Adventurer." The guard said in a low voice, but one loud enough for Dante to hear. Dante turned upon hearing the guard's call and in doing so, the pot, pickaxe and shovel hanging freely from the Furca banged into one another lightly, making the sound of a cast iron wind chime. The guard winced as if sound caused him pain, but the annoyed expression on his face afterward told Dante he had simply been trying to keep a low profile. "Are the four of you traveling with that orc?"

"We are."

"Well, a little word to the wise, from one human to another, be careful. Those orcs should never be trusted." The guard's face pointed in Dante's direction, but his eyes cut suspiciously toward Shinto.

"Is that right?" said Dante, unsure how he felt about this advice.

The guard continued. "I'm guessing you all hired him as some sort of guide or mercenary. Maybe to help you traverse the hills or perhaps cross plains from here to Harrington. But their type would just as soon lead you into an ambush of orcish raiders then to take you to your destination. I'm telling you for your own good friend, be on your toes around that green skin, if he tries anything funny, you'd best get the jump on him before he and his savages get the jump on you." The guard looked at Dante and winked as if he had done him some great favor. Then leaned back into position and stood at his post, face forward, mouth closed as if he had not just spoken a word. Dante stared at the guard for a moment, then scanned him.

Name: Unknown Lvl: 8 Job Class: Bleeksborough Town Guard

Level eight. Even after receiving 1,200 experience points for killing that ogre they faced in the hills, Dante was still only level 5, giving the guard a solid three levels on him. That was strong, but there wasn't a doubt in Dante's mind that Shinto, green skin and all, could obliterate both of these gate guards with the slightest effort. With a band of orcish raiders, even if they were merely half as skilled as Shinto, they could probably raze the whole town in an afternoon. It would be silly, not to mention inefficient for them to do something as counterproductive as pose as guides and lure low-level adventurers into an ambush. Then Dante remembered something.

Early in the Dragon Dale series, particularly in games 1 through 4, orcs had been reduced to an overtly evil race of beast men. They roamed Deos in hordes, terrorizing towns and villages as they went, often forcing the players to intervene in order to put a stop to their raiding and pillaging. Either that or they were in the employ of some dark lord, playing the part of ruthless and merciless soldiers in a great black army threatening to consume the entire land in blood and chaos. Even when they were neither of those, they were still at least always dumb mean brutes that delighted in violence and the suffering of others, yet somehow were never smart enough to rub two copper pieces together. It wasn't until Dragon Dale 5 that Dante could recall an orc NPC that didn't speak in grunts, and in Dragon Dale 6 there was actually a half-orc that joined your party as an ally. Then in Dragon Dale 7, the online multiplayer version of Dragon Dale, half-orcs were a playable race during character creation, and even then, every orc or half-orc that was not a player character fit a very specific stereotype, either a bandit, a barbarian, or generally untrustworthy.

It was odd, because Shinto seemed to be none of these, in fact he was the total opposite, and that made Dante wonder, had the perception of orcs in past Dragon Dale games all been some type of demonization, or exaggeration, or was Shinto simply the exception.

"Thanks for the advice... friend." Dante replied to the guard with a grimace and a hint of sarcasm as he turned to leave and join the others who had already begun walking east. The guard looked at him with bewilderment, confused as to why he had seemingly taken offense to such sound advice, but that was adventurers for you. They were arrogant, thick-headed, impulsive, and they couldn't be reasoned with. The guard shrugged his shoulders, that's probably why they died by the cart load.

Dante picked up his speed so that he could catch up with Alex, Robyn, Morrigan and Shinto. Alex had been dawdling in the rear, waiting for Dante. "What was that guard talking about?" he asked.

"Nothing worth repeating," Dante replied, "what are they talking about?" Dante indicated Shinto, Robyn and Morrigan, deep in conversation.

"The fight we had with the ogres yesterday," Alex answered nonchalantly.

"Really?" said Dante, his interest piqued.

"I noticed you chained together quite a combination of spells in quick succession. Elemental manipulation of cold, followed by an elemental conjuration of wind. It was impressive." Shinto was speaking to Morrigan.

"Honestly it all happened so fast I was more so acting off instinct than anything else." Dante saw her brown cheeks flush red with embarrassment. He averted his eyes, if she caught him catching her blushing, he knew he'd be the one in trouble.

Shinto let out a hardy laugh. "Well, I think that shows that you have really good instincts." He said. "Have you had any formal training?"

"No," Morrigan scoffed. "I barely even know what I'm doing. Half the time it feels like I'm fumbling around in the dark."

"I understand. Well, I have studied some magic and if you like I could advise you on some of the fundamentals. Perhaps get you started on some of the basics from which you can build."

"Really? That would be great," Morrigan replied.

"Good." Said Shinto. "Shall we begin?"

"Oh, we're starting right now!"

"Of course," Shinto replied, "there is nothing else to do between here in Harrington aside from walk."

"Yes. Yes, of course. Let's walk, talk and learn magic." Morrigan responded in the sarcastic and subtle dry tones Dante was used to.

"First lesson." Shinto smiled. "Magic is a craft, a system of creation based off the manipulation of raw materials. In the case of magic the raw material from which you craft is mana."

"Simple enough."

"But that poses the question. What is mana?" Shinto looked at Morrigan and then Robyn. They both shrugged. "Mana is the life blood of Deos."

"Life... blood." Mumbled Robyn quietly sounding a little concerned.

"Mana emanates from every part of Deos. It's in the air, the water, the land itself. Every living thing and even some dead things secrete this nearly imperceivable energy. It rolls over and encapsulates the world, like a great pulsating tide, currents and waves of raw magical force, spinning and churning all around us. A Deosian, or in this case an Urthlander, posing as a Deosian, is constantly absorbing this energy from their surroundings and processing it through what we call their Mana Core. Mages as well as skilled warriors are able to harness and manipulate the mana that their bodies accumulate, storing and pulling it from an inner reserve called a Mana Pool. Once a magic wielder's MP has been exhausted, they are forced to wait for their body to process more raw mana, and fill their bodies reserve of magical energy once again. These all may be concepts you are well familiar with."

"Somewhat," responded Morrigan. "I know what MP is." She said, looking a little overwhelmed.

Shinto laughed. "To put it simply, the mastery of mana allows a mage to manipulate, generate, conjure, manifest, create, enhance, diminish, restore or alter the world and environment around them via the crafting of spells."

"Now *spells* are familiar territory." Said Morrigan hopefully.

"That's very good. Lesson two begins there. Using mana to carefully and deliberately craft spells."

"Lesson two?" Morrigan said starting to look concerned once again.

"All spell craft is based on four steps. Focus. Shape. Charge. Release."

"Focus. Shape. Charge. Release." Morrigan recounted the steps on her fingers in quick succession.

"In basic spell casting, a mage focuses mana to a point, usually in the hands, then shapes it into the desired spell, the mage then charges the spell with additional mana and releases the spell once it's reached the chosen intensity. Similar to how an archer fires an arrow."

Shinto held his left hand toward the sky, his large green palm facing up, and with his fingers slightly bent. He flexed his hand into a fist and then released it and when he did a ball of brilliant gold fire sat dancing in the palm of his hand. He brought up his right hand, two fingers pointing at the spinning ball of golden flames. His right hand started close to the magical fire dancing in his left but as he slowly pulled his right hand back toward his face, the fiery sphere in his left began to grow larger. When it was bigger than his hand, Shinto thrust the heel of his right hand forward and the golden ball of fire shot into the air like a rocket on the fourth of July. The half-orc looked over at Morrigan and smiled.

"Focus. Shape. Charge. Release. Now you try."

"What? No I can't do that. I can thrust both my hands forward and spit out flames, or blasts of cold, or a gust of wind. Basically, whatever my spirit book told me I'd unlocked as a spell, and it hasn't yet mentioned anything about golden fireworks."

"Based iff what I've seen, you've been using your magic effectively but inefficiently. I imagine you've also been running out of mana extraordinarily fast. This process will help. You don't have to make golden fire, see if you can make another ice javelin, like you did yesterday. Only this time let's try a smaller one and we'll do it without the aid of water."

"I don't know..." Morrigan said hesitantly.

"What is there to be afraid of?" Shinto sounded genuinely confused.

"Well at the moment everybody is watching me. I don't want to... you know, get it wrong. I feel like I'll never be able to live it down." Morrigan said with a mixture of embrassment and nervousness at suddenly being thrust into the center of attention.

"You get it wrong until you get it right, that is the essence of learning," Shinto said gently. He looked at her with unwavering green eyes that beamed in the morning light.

Morrigan lifted her left hand. They all stopped walking to watch.

"Breathe in deep," Shinto said in a low voice. "Focus your mana into the palm of your hand, close your eyes if you have to, that may help you concentrate."

Morrigan closed her eyes and took a deep breath. She felt an energy swirling about inside her. It felt kind of like a strong wind blowing about the boughs of trees. She grabbed hold to it and pushed the wind toward her open hand. The wind obeyed, gathering in a swirling mass beneath the surface of her palm.

"Now, use your will to shape the mana into the form you desire. Imagine cold temperatures, fresh snow, water turning into ice."

Morrigan did, and a small crystalline globe of ice and snow formed in the palm of her hand. It was the size of a golf ball, but with every passing second it grew bigger.

"Good, now open your eyes. Stay calm, you're halfway there, now bring your other hand about, you need to charge the spell with mana."

Morrigan brought her right hand up and almost as if drawn by some type of magnetic force her hand was pulled toward the small swirling orb of ice and snow. She could feel the mana coming off her right hand and feeding into the spell sitting in the palm of her left. She spread her fingers, twisted her wrist, and began to pull her hand back slowly, each movement releasing a different amount of mana into the spell. It felt like trying to tune into the right radio frequency. The proper manipulation of her right hand could send large amounts of energy into her left making the difference between a heavy and condensed sphere of magical energy, or a hollow shell that was more like a magic bubble. She understood what Shinto meant about this method being more efficient. A spell could be more or less powerful not only depending on how much it, but also depending on how well you charged it.

"Now release it!" Shinto shouted, on command Morrigan clenched her right hand into a fist and slammed it forward. Partly because she had seen Shinto do something similar and partly because it simply felt like the right thing to do. In concert with her movement the orb, which had looked like a small spherical blizzard, formed into an icicle the size of a dagger and then went flying forward with incredible speed, plunging itself into the ground and covering everything within three feet of where it landed in a thin layer of frost.

"I did it!" Morrigan yelled gleefully.

"Well done," said Shinto approvingly. "It looks like you have the gist of it quite well. With time, knowledge, practice and experience you can learn and develop a wide variety of spells from a wide range of magic disciplines."

Morrigan had only used one tenth of her MP in the ice spell. She was beaming with excitement.

"Sometimes, magical words, chants, even the right movements can help increase the power and efficiency of a spell." Shinto explained. "Some wizards might use items, such as a special staff, or magic crystals, to assist in focusing, holding and shaping their mana. Any advantage they can find to enhance their spells. More advanced mages can complete all four steps with one hand, which with the proper training allows them to cast individual spells with both hands simultaneously. Then there are the greatest mages, true masters of spell craft who cast magic merely with thought.

"There is a general rule of thumb that says you can tell the true skill of a mage based upon how much they physically move when casting spells. Hands movements, magic words, even focus items are all aids to help a mage harness the mana around them. The most advanced mages launch spells without seemingly moving a muscle, and instead perform all four steps purely with their will, in the process of casting, magic simply forms around them and launches itself at its target." Shinto stared off into the distance as he spoke about this high level of spell casting, as if here were recalling long-forgotten memories. "But mages with that level of skill are rare," he said coming back to himself.

"Are you one of those?" Dante asked inquisitively. "One of those rare mages I mean."

Shinto looked back at him, silent for a brief moment, then gave a weak smile. "No, not by far." I would need to study magic for another one hundred years to consider myself a mage of such caliber. There is far too much I don't yet know, still so much left to learn." Shinto turned and began walking again, and the rest of the party followed. Morrigan turned and gave Dante a sharp look of rebuke for asking Shinto such a personal question.

"So one day I can develop my own spells?" Morrigan asked, catching up to Shinto.

"Yes," said Shinto. "Mages pass down and trade spells all the time, like chefs with favorite recipes. And of course, once a mage gets comfortable enough with her own magic, she will start to develop her own spells. In most cases it's just a matter of inspiration, imagination and necessity. Ah here is a perfect demonstration. Take this for example."

As they walked through the open grassland, Shinto pointed to a small creek off to the right of the path they were following. On the edge of the water near a clump of reeds sat a pudgy toad. Shinto squatted beside and waved Morrigan over.

"Inspiration, imagination and necessity," Shinto repeated. "Here we have one of the three. Inspiration. The toad is big, slow and clumsy and by all accounts has no hope of catching the dragonfly." As Shinto spoke a winged insect buzzed and hovered roughly a foot from the edge of the stream. "But as fate would have it, nature have blessed the toad with a solution to his problem." Just then the toad whipped out its tongue and snapped up the dragon fly right out of the air. "Ha you see. Just as nature delivers a solution to the toad, magic delivers a solution to the wizard."

"I'm not sure I get it," said Morrigan.

"Imagine you are the toad. Better yet, imagine you are you, right now and you are starving. Imagine that toad is your dragon fly. Imagine you needed to capture that toad right now from where you stand, otherwise you'll die of starvation. Using your mana, I want you to reach out and grab hold of that toad." Shinto said.

Morrigan looked at Shinto and then at the toad then held out her right hand in the direction of the small creek. She took a deep breath and just like last time grabbed hold to the mana she felt swirling around within her guiding it toward her extended arm and in her mind pictured the lashing tongue of the toad flying outward to grab hold of the dragonfly, only now she imagined that the tongue that lashed out flew from the end of her hand and that it would instead grab hold to the toad and with one fluid motion pulled it back to her. She replayed the four steps in her mind. Focus. Shape. Charge. Release.

With a sudden burst of will an arc of energy lashed out and hit the edge of the bank with a splash. Dust, dirt and grass flew towards the party, splattering mud and creek water. When the adventurers looked up, brushing splatters from their eyes, Morrigan opened her hand to find not a toad but a palmful of grass reeds. Ahead, they heard a croak and saw the squat fat little toad hop into the air and plop into the stream with splash.

"I missed," Morrigan said, still looking down at her hand.

"Yes," said Shinto, wiping muck and mud from his face. "But you performed the spell, nonetheless. I'd say that's a job well done. That spell is called Magician's Reach. It's one of the first things wizards teach their apprentices in a formal training situation. It takes a lot of practice to master but you did very well for a first attempt."

"Speaking of wizards," said Morrigan, wiping dirt from her robe. "Do you think you could take me on as your apprentice. I mean officially oversee my magical training, just up until we find our way back home, that is?"

"Well, I am flattered that you think that highly of me, but I am not qualified to take on an apprentice. I am however glad to help you as much as I can with what little I do know of magic. As a matter of fact, I have one more thing to show you."

Shinto held his hand palm up and as it did before a sphere of brilliant golden fire burst into existence there in the center of his hand. Shinto held the magical sphere aloft in front of his chest, then gently placed his right hand over his left slightly above the sphere.

"This exercise harnesses modified aspects of spell craft. Just as I showed you earlier. Only here, you focus the mana into your hands and give it merely the rough shape of an element, not the fully fleshed out shape of a spell. The objective is to form energy into a sphere and charge it." The golden fire ball began to spin and churn within Shinto's hand, only this time it twisted and spun much more violently than it had before. It looked like as tiny firestorm in the palm of his hand.

"The idea." Shinto continued "is to continuously feed more and more mana into the sphere, intensifying the churning and potency of the chosen element while at the same time maintaining the integrity, shape and control of the sphere." Shinto relaxed his hands and the sphere of fire simply dissipated into thin air. "It's an exercise that teaches mana control and mental fortitude. My old master used to say it mirrors the constantly churning mana core of Deos. Doing it for at least an hour a day will give you a better of understanding of magic. It also helps develop your magical power and stamina."

Morrigan held her hands in much the same way Shinto had and with a little concentration there was a flicker of flame and then a small orb of orange fire burst to life between her hands.

"Very good. Very good indeed." Said Shinto. "I must say, If I was taking students, I could not ask for someone more talented." The half-orc laughed.

Chapter 29: Harrington, The Ferryman and the Great Erebus Lake

The party traveled for two full days with no trouble. They no longer traveled by the safety of the Merchant's Road, but instead followed a worn dirt road through the Jua Valley, a small strip of grassland nestled between the Hathorian Mountains and the Bleekmore Hills. They walked during the day and made camp at night. The weather in the valley was pleasant, warm without being too hot, and even when the excessive walking and the heavy furca that they passed between them made it seem hotter than it was, a cool wind blew in from the west, chilled by the mountains, cooling their back and making the tall blades of grass sway in its wake, sweeping over the green landscape in such a way that it seemed as if the land itself was pointing them in the direction that they should go. This cross breeze made the valley tropical in temperature, and alive in nature.

The only animals the party came across were grazing herds of wild mouflons, and zebu. A mouflon was a medium sized herbivore with long curling horns that looked like a cross between a sheep and a goat. A zebu was a larger herbivore that looked a lot like a cow, only they had large droopy ears, an excessive amount of loose skin hanging from their necks, and a large fatty hump on their front shoulders like a camel. The zebu also had menacing horns that grew in a large circular arc, ending in two sharp points.

For two days and nights the party traveled in peace, most of which Dante attributed to Shinto's presence. The half-orc was a wealth of knowledge on everything from spell casting and shield craft to all things Deos, and he never hesitated to share what he knew. In a number of ways, when he looked beyond his incredible bulk and pale green skin, Shinto reminded him of a young and enthusiastic college professor, eager to teach anyone eager to learn.

Dante noticed that during the day the cleric took great joy in plants. As they walked Shinto was constantly pointing out plants with medicinal qualities, or roots that were edible in a pinch, or wild growing herbs that made for strong teas. It seemed a passion. He carried with him, seemingly at all times, a mortar and pestle and anytime they stopped to rest, he'd pull it out, and then rummage through his pack and pull out any and all of the plant clippings, leaves or roots that he had collected from the random assortment of flora that he'd spotted along the way. He would then spread them out carefully and neatly in front of him and begin to toss different combinations of things into the mortar and use the pestle to grind them into either a fine powder or a thin paste, ingredients to a new potion, healing salve or one of his latest pungent and aromatic teas.

"This is yarrow," said Shinto, referring to a small green plant who's one distinguishing feature was a cluster of white and yellow flowers at its crown. "If you find yourself in a bind and don't have access to restoration magic, or healing potions, you can crush or chew some clean yarrow and apply it to your wounds. It will help reduce bleeding and encourage healing." He then repeated similar advice for three other medicinal plants, two edible roots, and a number of wild growing vegetables that he claimed and then aptly proved could be boiled in water over a campfire to easily make a passable and arguably delicious vegetable soup.

At night they camped by the light of two moons and the gentle twinkling of the Jua Valley's iridescent fireflies. The glowing insects sparkled in a variety of colors, soft pale hues of blue, green, orange and purple that dotted the darkened valley floor. Morrigan and Robyn slept in the tent, while Alex and Dante along with Shinto slept on bed rolls laid out under the stars and open sky.

By noon of the third day, they found themselves approaching Harrington village, a small settlement on the western edge of the Great Erebus Lake. Harrington was tiny and meek as far as Deosian towns went. The solitary dirt road they had followed all the way from Bleeksborough led directly to a long wooden pier that extended into the lake. Huddled strips of one and two-story wooden buildings had sprung up on both sides of the old dirt road stretching some few hundred yards from the lake shore back out towards the heart of the valley.

The town wasn't abandoned, but it wasn't bustling either. As they approached, they could see people meander from building to building, no one seeming to be in any particular rush to be anywhere else within the small settlement, and no one seemed to be concerned with a group of approaching strangers coming in from the valley. They entered the town through an open and unguarded wooded edifice similar to the one that stood at the entrance of Black Water.

As the group of adventurers crossed the threshold into Harrington they were greeted by a small voice that was heard well before it was seen.

"Hello." Said the small voice.

Dante looked around to find the source of the voice was a small girl looking up at the five of them from the porch of a nearby building. The girl was human, no older than eight or nine years of age and she was holding in her hands a small stuffed zebu.

"Hello." Dante replied.

"My name is Allie, what's your name?" the girl asked.

"My name is Dante, this is Morrigan, Alex, Robyn and Shinto." He answered pointing at each of his party members.

"Welcome to Harrington." Said the little girl bashfully. She swayed from side to side, her stuffed zebu tucked under her arm and her tiny hands twiddling the hem of her blue and white stripped dress between her tiny fingers.

"Why thank you," said Robyn, overtaken by the little girl's cuteness. "Are you from the welcoming committee?" she asked.

"No ma'am," replied the young girl "I was being polite." She said dipping in a small and quaint curtsy. "My father said it is important for a young lady to always be polite."

"Wow," said Alex in surprise. "Robyn, I think she could teach you a thing or two."

Robyn frowned and punched Alex hard in the arm. "Who said I was trying to be a lady?" she said sternly.

The small girl giggled, then hopped off the porch and came skipping towards the party. "You all are funny. What brings you to Harrington? The fish or the ferry?"

"I'm sorry, what?" asked Morrigan taken aback by the child's direct and rather eloquently posed question.

"Harrington is a fishing village," explained Shinto. "This town sits on the western edge of the Erebus Lake and most visitors only come here for one of two things. To buy at the famous fish markets of Harrington or to ride the ferry across the lake to the larger sister city, Midell."

"Hey, that's right Mister. Are you from Harrington?" the little girl asked.

"No," answered Shinto. "but I have visited a time or two."

The little girl's eyes grew wide. "Are you all adventurers?" she asked gleefully.

Shinto kneeled down to eye level with the young girl and removed his hood, revealing to her and the cresting sun his dark green hair, pale green skin and large jutting tusk.

"We *are* adventurers," he said, in a voice that Dante hadn't noticed up until then sounded as rough as sandpaper. "And we've come for the ferry," he said gruffly.

Dante couldn't tell if Shinto was trying to scare the little girl or if he simply had forgotten how intimidating he could be. He was reminded of the guards outside Bleeksborough, and the unquestionable fear, loathing and contempt they held for the half-orc.

The girl stared at Shinto and then reached up with a small hand and gently stroked his face. "I like your beard," she said.

"Thank you," said the Cleric. "I am rather fond of it as well."

The small girl giggled. "Some other adventurers came yesterday, they want to take the ferry too."

"Other adventurers?" said Dante alarmed. "Were they Urthlanders?" he asked.

"You're an Urthlander? I've never seen an Urthlander before. The other adventurers didn't say where they were from, but they were not from Urth. I would have remembered that."

"I bet you would have," said Dante.

"The other adventurers are still here if you would like to meet them," said the girl.

"They haven't taken the ferry yet?" asked Dante.

"No." replied the girl. "No one can take the ferry right now. It's not running, my father says it's too dangerous."

"Your father?"

"Yes," said the girl. "My father is the ferryman."

"Kids." mumbled Morrigan under her breath. Allie looked up at her and frowned.

"Little one," said Shinto patiently. "We need to cross the lake. Can you take us to your father, perhaps we can convince him to help us?"

Allie thought for a moment, her tiny finger poking her chin. "I'll take you to my father, but in return you have to promise to tell me about Urthland."

"A fair trade," Shinto said with a chuckle.

Allie led the party deeper into the village of Harrington. She walked with her head high, her arms swinging and her short little legs making long, proud strides. She looked like the grand marshal of some odd and miniature parade as the adventurers followed her past building after building, moving ever closer to the large wooden pier at the furthest edge of town. As they walked, she asked random questions about Earth that she had chosen to Dante to answer.

"Are there kids there? Are they nice? Do they eat fish? What else do they eat? What types of games do they play?"

"Yes. Sometimes. For the most part. A bit of everything. They play all types of games. Pretend, hide and seek, tag."

"Tag?" interrupted Allie. "What's tag?"

"You know, tag. One person is 'it' and they chase everyone else around until they catch someone and when they do they touch them and yell 'Tag, you're it!' and then that person has to do the chasing and the game starts all over again."

"Oh," she said realization dawning. "How do you win?"

"You don't win, you just play."

"Oh. Well, how do you know when the game is over."

Dante laughed a little. "It's just over once everyone gets tired of playing."

"Urthland is strange... but 'Tag' sounds fun."

"Are we really doing this?" Robyn asked Morrigan. "Taking advice from a kid?"

"Maybe it's more of the golden boy's gamer logic." Morrigan answered. "Either that or he's finally lost his mind. Besides, Shinto seems to know what he's doing."

Robyn shrugged. "Where'd Alex run off to?" she asked, and just as she did, the dwarf reappeared behind them eating what looked like a fish popsicle.

"What is that?" Robyn asked a look of disgust on her face.

"Steckerlfisch, Smoked mackerel on a stick, they're selling them over there at that food cart, only cost three copper." Alex took a bite of the fish whose crispy skin and flaky white meat broke away with ease.

"What's wrong with you?" asked Morrigan more annoyed than concerned.

"What?" Alex asked with a mouthful of fish, "I was hungry."

On the western side of town, they passed a number of large wooden racks that at first glanced looked to Dante like crudely constructed clothing lines, only these structures instead were draped with large fishing nets made of thick dark rope, hung up apparently for repairs and detangling. The air was thick with the smell of fish and lake water, as the nets sat drying in the warm sun.

The party soon found themselves standing on the dock. In front of them was a large wooden boat with a smokestack at its center. Near the rear of the boat, directly behind the smokestack was a large paddle wheel, followed by a small wooden surface area that served as the ship's rear deck. On the other end of the boat, in front of the smokestack was a small wooden cabin meant to serve as the wheelhouse. The man inside wore a sailor's cap, clenched a pipe between his teeth and seemed to be deeply preoccupied with a number of maps and charts that were stretched out in front of him.

"Papa!" yelled Allie. The man looked up in surprise, pulled the pipe from between his teeth saw his daughter and smiled. Then he saw her company and his smile became a frown.

Allie ran onto the boat, the wood of the ferry slip dock creaking beneath her feet.

"Hello sweetie." Said the ferry boat captain, "What trouble have you brought Papa today hmm?" Allie jumped into her father's arms.

"I assure you sir, there is no trouble," said Shinto calmly.

"When my daughter comes home with adventurers in tow that normally spells trouble for me. I assume you all are adventurers, aren't you?"

"We are," answered Shinto.

"And I suppose you want to take the ferry across the lake."

"That was our hope."

"Yes, well then we do have trouble after all. The ferry is not running, you'll have to find another way to Midell."

"Is there something wrong with the ship?" Dante asked.

"No, of course not. The ferry is fine, it's in perfect working order." The ferrymen paused for a moment then looked at his daughter who he was still holding in his arms. "Minnow, be a dear and go get Papa's tobacco pouch, will you? I'm running low."

"But papa, these are my new friends. I'd told them I'd bring them here to meet you."

"And you did Minnow. Now I need you to go and get my tobacco pouch, go on now. And stop by Mary's Tavern on your way back and tell her I'll be coming by for some of that fish head soup."

"Yes papa." Allie jumped out of his arms and ran off toward the town, leaving the dock and the adventurers behind her.

The ferry boat captain pulled out a match, struck it and used the small flame to light the pipe he held clenched between his teeth. He took short shallow puffs on the pipe until the match flames began to flare up from within the chamber and plumes of white smoke followed behind them.

"There have been some strange occurrences on the water," said the ferryman, taking a long pull of his pipe, the pungent smell of tobacco permeating the air. "It's too dangerous to cross the lake right now."

"What do you mean dangerous?" asked Robyn.

"Well, first vessels stopped coming over from Midell. It's been nearly ten days since we've had a ship from across the lake to dock here at Harrington. Then around three days ago one of our fishing boats, the Pericles, went out chasing red-tailed caitfish and the whole crew just disappeared. The ship came back, but it didn't have a single soul upon it. Drifted in empty, almost crashed into the pier." He took another long drag of his pipe. "We formed a search party and went out looking for some sign of the crew. Ran into a thick fog near the middle of the lake, search party got separated and when the fog cleared, another one of our ships had gone missing." The ferry boat captain reached down near where he was standing and picked up what looked like a piece of driftwood from off the deck. He tossed it onto the dock where it landed with a loud clattering thud. The shard of wood had a large white "S" painted on its face. "That's from the fishing vessel the Sundial. The missing ship from our search party. That's all that's left of her, washed up on the shore yesterday." The ferryman pulled the pipe from between his teeth and a column of smoke escaped his nose. He let out a heavy-hearted sigh, then looked back up at the adventurers standing around him, his eyes darting from once face to the other in quick succession. "As I said, I can't take you Midell, it's just too dangerous. I hope you understand."

"We'll pay you one hundred gold to take us across." Robyn blurted out, catching everyone by surprise.

"What?" The ferry boat captain's eyes were wide with surprise but then swiftly narrowed in on to Robyn.

"We'll pay you one hundred gold to take us across," Robyn pulled out a coin purse, it bulged with the weight of the numerous coins inside.

"You bloody adventurers and your obsession with gold. People are dead. You can't just wave a coin pouch in my face and expect me to do whatever you ask. My daughter has already lost one parent. I'm not going to let her lose another over something as silly as one hundred gold."

Just then Allie came running back on to the dock, a small leather pouch in her hand.

"Papa, I have your tobacco! Hey – Papa, you already have tobacco in your pipe."

"Oh yes my dear, right after you left, I found a wee bit," The grisly old sailor bent down and scooped the little girl up in his arms once again. "but I do still need the rest of this so you my darling minnow have made my day. Now what do you say we go over to Mary's and get us something hot to eat eh?"

"Yes papa, I told Mary to prepare you some fish head soup just the way you like it, extra spicy!" Allie said with a large and excited smile.

“Oh, ho ho, now that is my girl! Off to Mary’s we go!” The ferrymen stepped off the boat with the little girl still in his arms. He smiled brightly when looking at the little girl, but his facial expression changed when he looked away from her. “I’m truly sorry I couldn’t be of more help to you all. Please, if you’ll excuse me.” He said in a low voice as he walked pass Dante, Shinto and the others. He left the dock and walked back towards the town of Harrington, Allie yelling out over his shoulder as they went.

“Goodbye Urthlander! Let play ‘Tag’ later okay?”

“Well, this is quite the conundrum,” said Morrigan. She held the broken piece of wood from the Sundial as the party stood silently on the Ferry Dock.

“I really thought offering him a hundred gold would have worked,” said Robyn.

“A bunch of his friends just died, and you thought you could just pay him off and he’d forget about it,” said Alex.

“Well, I didn’t see you coming up with any ideas” Robyn snapped.

“You didn’t give anyone a chance to before you started pulling out bags of gold!”

“Oh, and I suppose right before I said something you were about to swoop in and save the day?”

“Guys, we don’t have the time to argue, we have to find a way across this lake.” Dante interrupted. “Maybe we can try and hire a fishing boat, maybe one of those guys will be more willing to risk it.”

“That might work.” Said Alex. “I can see a few fishing boats still out on the water.”

“The ferrymen said the danger lurks near the center of the lake. The fishermen may feel wary when we ask them to venture further from the coast,” Shinto added.

“What about the ship that drifted in... maybe we could buy that boat and take it across the lake ourselves.” Dante suggested.

“Not such a bad idea. Also, this strange fog, the disappearance of people and ships, these all sound like issues that get worse before they get better. This is a job that requires a special set of skills from a group of people willing to accept a certain amount of risk.” Shinto placed a heavy green hand on Dante’s shoulder.

“Sounds like a job for an adventurer!” said Dante.

“Yes, adventurers that are not only willing to investigate the town’s concern at no cost and with no contract, but who ones who are also willing to pay gold to anyone willing to help get them to the source of the problem and then to the other side of the lake once the situation is resolved.”

“Ah great point,” said Dante. “But wait, what if we come across this thing in the middle of the lake and it turns out to be more than we bargained for?”

“At this point the only way we are going to make it to Midell is to help Harrington with the issue it’s having with disappearing people and ships. This my friends is the moment every Deosian has to face at some point or another, the moment when they must choose the warmth and safety found in the confines of the towns and cities or the unknown danger and mystery of adventures that await you out there.” Shinto motioned to the open water and the wilderness that surrounded. "It's all or nothing really. I'm sorry but this is not Urthland, you cannot *play* adventurer here. If you want to make it to Abilene Bay, you must choose. Either you all can stay here in Harrington and build a new life as perhaps Zebu farmers or you can do what others are not willing to do and truly become adventurers."

"I'd rather be an adventurer than a zebu farmer," said Alex quietly.

"Yeah, I agree, I don't think this is the place I want to settle down, I'd rather take my chances on the water," said Robyn.

"I doubt zebu farmers have much use for magic, so I vote adventurer," said Morrigan.

They all looked at Dante who had not said anything but was wearing a large grin.

"Thank god," he said with a laugh, "I was hoping I wasn't going to have to go out on that lake by myself."

The four of them laughed and Shinto smiled.

"Perhaps we should go to Mary's Tavern. Dante, I want you to do the talking. No offense to anyone else but I believe the daughter has taken a liking to you and that may be something that plays to our advantage."

They walked back into town and found Mary's Tavern, an open room with men and women with the same sun-burned patina as the ferry boat captain. There was however, a table of three individuals nursing bowls of soup and glasses of ale that did not have the sunburned marks of the Harrington townsfolk. An older man wearing a black tuxedo and a top hat sat beside a woman draped in white and gold robes, a hood covering her head and concealing most of her face. The last of the trio was Kalgari cat-man, who sat to the right of the man in the top hat. He had jet black fur and bright yellow eyes and didn't bother looking up at Dante and the others as they walked into the tavern.

The ferrymen and his daughter sat at a table in the corner of the tavern while a barmaid was setting a bowl of steaming liquid in front of the two of them. Dante made a b-line for their table.

"Captain?" said Dante approaching the table with Shinto, Morrigan, Alex and Robyn behind him.

"Khinum curse me, I've always heard you adventurers were a persistent lot but now I see it first-hand. Look here boy, my answer is the same now as it was ten minutes ago and the same as it was yesterday when your other adventuring friends over there asked me about the same thing. The ferry is not running, it's too dangerous, and no amount of gold is going to change my mind."

"Captain, I'm not here to try and change your mind." Dante said. "But I do still need your help. You see you're right about one thing, us adventurers are persistent and determined. We noticed that a number of fishing boats were still on the water, despite the danger. We were hoping that you could perhaps point us to a fishing vessel that may be willing to take us across. We'd pay, of course."

The ferry boat captain dropped his spoon into his soup with a loud clang, causing some of the other patrons to look up and over in their direction. In particular the trio of adventurers sitting at a table of their own.

"A fishing vessel? You kids just don't get it. We've already lost two fishing vessels to whatever is going on out there and now you want us to risk another so you can get across the lake. I can't be party to that. The men and women that are on that water are out there because they have to be. The work they do keeps this town fed. Keeps it alive. I won't ask anyone to risk their life for anything less than that."

Dante let out a breath through his nose. He understood the ferry boat captain's position of course, the issue was the captain did not understand his position, but then how could he, how could Dante explain to this man that he was from another world and getting across that lake was vital to him getting home. How could he explain that the same responsibility that the ferrymen felt toward Harrington, Date felt towards his friends?

"Perhaps we could rent or purchase a boat, one that no one is using? That way we could go out on our own and not put anyone else into any type of unnecessary risk–"

"Do any of you know how you operate a ship? Do any of you even have a single level in sailing?" Dante froze at the mentions of levels, it was the first time he had heard a Deosian openly acknowledge the existence of either levels or job classes in the traditional sense.

"I didn't think so," the ferry boat captain continued. "Look, I'm sure whatever your reasons are for traveling to Midell that they are important to you, but I assure you son they are not worth your life. Whatever it is, it can wait a few more days. Travel south from here, go *around* the lake, it'll take longer but it will be safer."

"I'm sorry but we can't do that. Whatever it is that happening in the middle of the lake, whatever it is making ships disappear and crews disappear, there's no reason to believe it's going to stay out there, eventually it's going to spread, or move, or possibly even set it sites onto Harrington. But right now, in this moment, you have in front of you five adventurers, who are ready and willing to sail out into the middle of that lake and solve the mystery of what's plaguing your town before it has a chance to claim any more lives and we're willing to do it even if we have to purchase a rowboat and paddle ourselves out. We *are* going to cross this lake, and from the look of things, it just so happens that we can help your town in the process. So, help us, help you and point us to a boat that will get us on our way. We'll take care of everything else."

Before the ferryman could reply, a voice spoke from behind. "Make it eight adventurers."

Dante turned to find the man in the top hat.

"You have eight adventurers ready to sail out at a moment's notice to confront whatever is lurking in the middle of the lake, although we would prefer something larger than a rowboat, but then beggars can't be choosers now can they."

The ferryman looked as if someone had put their face in his bowl and started blowing bubbles in his soup. "Alright, if that's the way it's going to be," he said and sighed. "Come first thing in the morning, I'll take you across the lake."

"You don't have–" Dante began.

"I'll hear nothing else of it!" the ferryman said forcefully. "None of you know how to operate a ship well enough to get across the lake on your own, and I'll have no more of this rowboat nonsense. I'm afraid you lot might just be crazy enough to try, so the easiest and simplest thing to do is to just take you myself. And besides you were right about one thing, whatever is going on out on that water, it's just a matter of time before it comes creeping closer to Harrington." The ferryman looked down at his little girl. "If I can do anything to stop it before it gets closer and starts to threaten the town, I have an obligation to do that."

Dante felt a quiet tap at his arm, he turned to see Robyn with a coin purse in her hand she passed it to him. Dante took it and begin to place it on the table.

"Keep your bloody coin," said the ferrymen.

"No" said Dante, he looked down at the small girl. "I understand that we're asking a lot of you. We insist that you take this." Dante placed the bag of coins directly into the ferrymen's hands.

He looked up and over at the bar where, standing behind the counter, a woman, much like everyone else in the tavern, was watching and listening intently to the conversation between him and Dante. "Mary." The ferryman called out to her. "Can you keep an eye on Allie tomorrow morning while I make a run over to Midell?"

"Of course, Isaac," she answered solemnly. "Whatever you need."

He tossed the coin purse across the room and it landed on the bar with a loud crash as the coins banged against both the wood and one another.

"And can you hold on to that for me, just until I get back?" he asked.

"Sure Isaac. Until you get back," Mary replied.

"Papa?" Allie looked up at her father with an inquisitive and curious smile, "Can I come along? I want to be an adventurer too!"

Chapter 30: Fog on the Lake

"I'm sorry, but I don't think I caught your name." said the man in the top hat. His hand was extended out in front of him and he wore a large disarming smile across his face.

"Oh, um... its Dante."

"Dante! It's a pleasure to make you acquaintance." The man in the top hat's arm shot out and grabbed Dante's in his own, shaking them both vigorously. He wore white velvet gloves that felt soft to the touch, but concealed a firm grip that Dante wasn't sure he could have pulled away from if he tried.

"I am Carlyle the Magnificent, but please, just call me Carlyle." Said the man in the top hat.

"Carlyle." Dante repeated.

"The magnificent, yes but please, just Carlyle will do.I must say old boy, that was a roaring speech you gave in the tavern yesterday, you are quite the orator." Carlyle released Dante's hand then proceeded to remove his top hat, revealing a head of sandy brown hair slicked sleekly backwards. "My colleagues and I were at a complete loss as to how were going to traverse this lake. Needless to say, we are in your debt."

"Um sure... don't mention it." Dante replied, unsure of what else to say.

"Ha, a modest man of few words, except of course, when more words are necessary. I like it. I'm the same way really. 'Never a wasted word' I've always say."

"Carlyle stop pestering the boy," said the robed woman said, pushing past the man. "Pay him no mind, he'll talk your ear off if you let him."

"Ah yes, how rude of me. Dante this is Lin. Clerical priestess of the sun goddess Hathor. Here to offer succor in the name of the divine mother and so on and so forth." Carlyle's white gloved hand danced in the air in playful discontent.

"Oh, be quiet, heathen." The woman's voice was clear as a bell radiating warm and reaffirming energy that washed over Dante like waves of light. Lin looked over at him through thin eyes. Delicate features and jet-black hair peeking out at him from underneath her hood.

From behind the woman appeared the large Kalgari cat-man. He was almost as tall as Shinto and his dark black fur made him look like a living shadow moving in three-dimensional space.

"Hoku," said the Kalgari. He gazed down at Dante with piercing yellow eyes, seemingly scanning him for weaknesses. His nose twitched as if subtly sniffing the air, capturing scents and recording them to memory, an idea that did not bode well with Dante. "We are indebted to you for convincing the ferryman to transport us across the lake. You have my thanks." The Kalgari nodded respectfully, a slight, barely perceptible nod, and Dante released the breath he was holding.

"Glad to help... Hoku." Dante replied assuming that the Kalgari had led with his name. Without a word the cat-man turned and walked away. "Alright then, nice to meet you." Dante mumbled

Carlyle and Lin stepped past Dante and introduced themselves to the rest of the group. Lin and the girls were engaged in a casual conversation that left them all smiling as if they had always been lifelong friends. Carlyle was talking to Shinto and Alex but his focus at the moment seemed to be exceptionally preoccupied with Shinto.

"I'm sorry, did you say your name was Shinto? As in *the* Shinto? Well... I must say, I'm honored not to mention a little embarrassed that I didn't recognize you before now. Not that I suppose I really could have, you are somewhat of a myth–"

"I'm afraid you may have mistaken me for someone else." Shinto said briskly.

"Shinto Merciful, Half-Orc adventurer, The Green..."

"It's just Shinto. A common name among orcish males."

Dante looked from Shinto to Carlyle and back to Shinto again.

"Oh yes of course," said Carlyle, looking confused. He cut his eyes over towards Alex and then Dante before zoning back in on Shinto. "My mistake. Pardon my ignorance."

"No need for apologies." Replied Shinto. "Happens all the time."

"Stop your dilly-dallying and come aboard." The adventurers stood on the Harrington dock in the dim light of early morning. The water of the lake was calm before them, a large shimmering mirror reflecting a hazy sky, distorted only with the occasional ripple. "It takes two hours to get across the lake to Midell and I want to shove off as soon as possible." The ferry boat captain called out.

"Welcome aboard the Nimue, I'm Isaac, the ship's Captain. Right now, the water is calm, and the weather clear, but we can't know what to expect once we get out there. But you all are adventurers, so I imagine you are prepared for these types of things. Well hold on to something, I'm going to start her up and we'll be on our way."

Puffs of thick blue smoke spewed from the stack. Captain Isaac reappeared from below deck and made his way into the wheelhouse. With both hands he pulled forcefully on a couple of waist high levers that protruded from the floor then quickly grabbed hold to the helm, at nearly the same time the ship lurched forward and begin to slowly move itself through the water. Dante looked toward the rear of the ship and saw that the large paddle wheel had begun to turn, propelling the Nimue and everyone onboard away from the dock and into wide open mouth of the great Lake Erebus.

The ship moved smoothly through the water at surprising speed. Dante had grown so used to walking that he forgot how much he enjoyed watching the world pass at pace. He took a deep breath, the early morning lake air was cool and brisk, he felt it fill his lungs and a chill his skin.

"Captain. I just wanted to say you have a really beautiful ship here," Dante said.

"Yes well, let's just hope she doesn't go the same way as the Sundial," replied the Captain not taking his eyes off the water.

"Do most ships operate with paddle wheel like yours? Most of the other fishing vessels looked like sail boats."

"That's because they were," said the captain. "Fishing vessels are run by crews, this is a ferry, it's a one-man show. I can't be expected to operate a sailboat of this size by myself now can I?"

"No sir, I suppose not," Dante replied. "So what's turning that paddle wheel... if you don't mind me asking."

"Well it's a mana engine of course."

"A mana engine?" Dante felt like someone set off a firework within his brain.

Aye, same basic principle as what they use for air ships, just much older, not nearly as powerful, but it's a mana engine none the less."

Dante was familiar with the concept of airships within the Dragon Dale game world. At least his player characters had ridden on them before. And he had heard of mana engines in passing, as a sort of blanket technological term that he assumed was being used in place of a standard engine. He had no idea they were real.

"I'm sorry, I'm not familiar with mana engines. How... how does it work? What does it use for fuel? Did you build it."

Captain Isaac looked at Dante and saw the excitement on his face. And the Ferryman's scowl softened.

"Allie said you were from some far-off place; I guess I shouldn't be surprised if your technology hasn't caught up to ours here on Deos yet. A mana engine runs on mana crystals of course and as for how it works... well, it takes magic energy and converts it into mechanical energy in order to do some basic task. In this case, it spins that paddle wheel which pushes this boat through the water. In the case of an air ship, it lifts the ship into the sky and helps navigate it through the air. As you could imagine, my engine is much less complicated then the type you'd find in an airship. But even then, its still pretty rare. And no I didn't build it, but I've fixed it so many times I've practically rebuilt the thing twice over." As the captain spoke Dante could notice a sense of pride bleeding through his words. "Yeah, I know that engine backwards and forwards by this point. Every bolt and screw, I know it like the back of my hand."

"You said it runs on mana crystals?" Dante repeated still hung up on the first portion of the ferryman's explanation.

"Yeah, good ole mana crystals," Captain Isaac threw something in Dante direction. The adventurer reached up and snatched the item out of mid-air, more by instinct then by choice, when he opened his hand to see what it was, he found himself staring at a small blue gem the size of a marble. It was just like the mana crystals he had been collecting since arriving in Deos. "They accumulate at the bottom of lakes and rivers all the time. We dredge the lake ever so often and find enough to keep the Nimue fueled up for a few moons at a time. They're pretty strong so it doesn't take much to keep her going."

Dante looked up. "You find these by at the bottom of lakes and rivers?"

"That we do. You could dig for'em and find them underground if you knew where to look, but I leave that to the dwarves, the water is much easier."

"We... adventurers collect these, from the creatures we hunt. They drop them and we gather them up."

"Hmph... is that so? To each his own I guess."

"Can I see how the mana engine works?"

This time the Captain's scowl didn't fade. "I don't think right now is the time for me to be giving a tour. In case you forgot, we're expecting to run into a spot of trouble at about the halfway mark of this trip which is easily three leagues out."

At that moment Robyn burst into the entry way of the wheelhouse. She looked wild eyed and frightened as if she had just seen a ghost.

"I think we have a problem." Robyn said, out of breath.

"What's the matter?" asked the captain.

Robyn stepped aside. A small girl shuffled forward, her fingers fiddling at the hem of her dress, she looked up at the captain and then swayed from side to side.

"Hello papa," Allie said.

"Allie? Khinum's cursed me! What are you doing here child?" Isaac screamed. "You're supposed to be with Mary!"

"I was with Mary when you dropped me off this morning, but then I told her I wanted to go down to the dock and see you off as you departed, and she said it was okay as long as I came back straight away, and I went down to the dock and you were busy prepping the ship and you didn't see me so I snuck on board and hid in one of the barrels so I could come along too. Papa I don't want to stay behind with Mary. I want to be an adventurer!"

"Allie this is no game!" Isaac said in a forceful tone that only a father could muster. "We are headed into danger. You should not be here!"

By now the adventurers had begun to crowd around the wheelhouse forcing Dante inside the relatively small space with the contentious father and daughter duo.

"Perhaps we should simply turn around. Take her back to Harrington and just start again before we get too far." Dante suggested.

"Oh, you bet we'll be turning around. We're turning around right now." Isaac said almost more to Allie than to Dante, yet Dante felt as if he was being scolded as well.

"Captain," called out Hoku who was still standing on the front deck, as he seemed to be the only person on the ship uninterested in the conversation taking place in the wheelhouse, "We have fog ahead."

"What?" shouted Isaac, "We're still another three leagues from lake's center."

The adventurers spilled out on to the front deck. Hanging just above the surface of the water, a thick cloud like fog, so dense that it almost seemed solid. At least it did momentarily, right up until the bow of the ship penetrated the ghost-like veil and they felt themselves being swallowed up by the all-consuming mist.

The inside of the fog was odd. The air itself was thick, humid and viscous. Dante could see across the deck of the ship easily, and he could even see the water beneath them, but if he looked out any further at what used to be open water or blue sky, he saw nothing but dense gray fog. The ferry itself had been completely engulfed. Dante barely could see more than 20 yards in any direction, and doubted at all if Issac could see well enough to still turn the ship around.

"Visibility down to zero," said the ferry boat captain from the wheelhouse, "I can't even spot the sun. I'm going to have to steer her blind using the compass. Hold on to your butts."

He was right Dante thought, even thought light still filtered in through the mist, it was impossible to pinpoint the sun's position in the sky. Now it made sense how the rescue boats had lost each other, if they weren't tied together it would be hard to tell if there was another ship sitting right next to you until you were nearly crashing into one another.

"The fog is magical in nature," said Shinto. "Someone or something is conjuring it."

"Look!" shouted Morrigan. "There something in the water."

Dante looked over the edge of the boat. Large black shadows were racing alongside the Nimue, moving at incredible speeds. The shadows grew larger as whatever it was beneath the water rose closer to the surface. There were a dozen of them, moving as fast as the ship itself, and some even faster.

"Are they fish?" asked Robyn, a slight panic in her voice.

"Sharks?" suggested Alex.

"Why would there be sharks in a lake?" snapped Morrigan .

"Whatever they are they have us surrounded. Prepare yourselves!" shouted Hoku.

At that exact moment one of the shadows to the left of the ship burst forth from the water and shot into the air like a missile. At first it was a blur, moving through the fog as if something had catapulted it up from underneath the water, and then all at once it landed hard on the port side of the deck. Heavy and wet, it took shallow raspy breaths and stared menacingly from one adventurer to the next.

It looked like a creature from a nightmare. It was almost seven feet tall. Its large bulbous eyes were completely black and stared unblinking across the deck at the stunned adventurers. It had only two slits for nostrils and a large open mouth filled with rows of needle like teeth. Water dripped from its body, and its wet bluish-green skin shimmered and glistened in the light of day. Random parts of its body were covered in pieces of old and corroded metal armor, leather straps and large seashells, while its muscular arms and webbed hands gripped tightly to a long and rusty trident, whose crooked and jagged edges looked dangerous in more ways than Dante could imagine. A thick piece of string attached to a conch shell hung from its neck while around its waist was a makeshift loincloth, soaked and dripping lake water. It stood on two legs, poised and balanced like a seasoned warrior on large feet with long webbed toes. It had a fin on the top of its head and three long slits on either side of its neck which opened and closed all in rhythm with its shallow raspy breaths. Behind it swished a long thick tail which slowly whipped about, like a fish out of water, thrashing for life.

"It's a fish-man?" said Robyn bewildered by what she was seeing.

"No," Dante mumbled. "It's a sahuagin."

"Sahuagin?" Carlyle repeated after hearing Dante mutter. "It's a Sahuagin!" he shouted at the top of his lungs.

At nearly the same time Dante watched as the sahuagin took what looked like a deep and painful breath, the gills on the side of its neck opened wide as it attempted to suck in both air and moisture from the thick fog that surrounded them. It made a terrible squelching and sucking sound as it did so, almost as if it were drowning on dryland, and then in one fluid motion it grabbed the conch shell that hung from its neck held it up to its hideous mouth and blew. A deep bellowing drone resonated from the open end of the shell, like that of an old ancient whale that swam up from the depths of a forgotten ocean, or the foghorn of some haunted light house, operated only by the ghost of drowned men.

Dante's blood ran cold.

"It's a raid!" Shouted Hoku. "Grab your weapons!"

As the sound of the conch shell horn faded three more shadows erupted from the water, then three more after that and soon lake water and fishmen were raining down onto the deck of the Nimue. They all landed on the ship with the same type of jagged multi-pronged harpoons as the first and when he looked back to the original horn blower, Dante found the shauagin charging directly toward him, its rusty spear-like weapon aimed at his chest. He moved without thinking, partially unsheathing his sword and blocking the sahaugin's trident with the flat of his exposed blade before the fishman could impale him.

Angry at its missed opportunity the sahaugin leaned forward placing its weight and strength onto the spear. In a panic, Dante ripped the sword upward, pulling it free of its sheath and completely deflecting the fishman's spear attack. Then grabbing the hilt of the longsword with both hands, he forced all of the hot magma like energy he could muster inside him into the blade of the sword. The weapon began to glow as if it had just been pulled from the heart of a hot and fiery furnace and immediately Dante knew it was ready.

"Lightspeed Slash!"

Almost more off instinct than anything else, Dante moved the sword hilt across the sahaugin's chest and back again as fast as he could and as he expected the handle moved through the air with little to no resistance, the blade flexing and bending in a near liquid state. He had dragged the sword handle in front of the sahaugin's chest once, twice and then a third time before he realized that time itself had seemed to slow down around him and had somehow managed to capture the fishman within its effects in the process. The Shaugin had not reacted in the slightest to a single one of his attacks. It had not attempted to defend itself, dodge the attack or even reel back in pain. The creature, he realized, was momentarily trapped in a state of slow motion. An aftereffect, apperantly, of his activated ability.

By the time Dante finished his third slash, he watched as his sword rematerialized into a solid object and three large gaping wounds formed across the sahaugin's chest out of nowhere. The creature stumbled backward hurt and confused clenching it chest but still upon its feet.

Dante did a quick assessment. He had drained nearly a third of his own MP with that attack, but he had taken more than half of the sahaugin's HP in the process. It was amazingly effective but not enough to outright kill the creature in one shot. He scanned it. Hmph. That was why, it was a level seven Sahaugin Raider, two levels higher than him, the chances of killing it in one hit were slim to none. Even then, taking more than half of its HP with a single ability was pretty impressive. Atleast Dante thought so, the Shaugin, however, disagreed. No longer disoriented from Dante's lightinging-fast attack the fishman charged him.

Dante's mind raced. He could use the Lighspeed Slash two more times before his MP was completely depleted. He could activate the ability again and undoubtedly kill the Shaugin infront of him but he had no way of knowing how many sahaugin there really were and if he needed to conserve his MP for a long drawn out fight or if he should hit the one in front of him with everything he had and worry about the next sahaugin when the time came. But before Dante could make a decision it appeared to have been made for him, the charging Shaugin had quickly closed the distance between them and was now so close he found himself with little time to defend himself let alone activate an ability. He had spent too much time thinking and not enough time acting. He cursed under his breath. And then, before the fishman could attempt to impale him a second time, a large chunk of jagged ice slammed into the sahaugin's torso. *Twick!* The ice shard hit the creature with force, flash freezing the wet and slimy flesh upon contact. The sahaugin's body stumbled backwards and fell over the railing of the ship, an ice shard prtrouding from its stomach, its HP zero. Dante looked back over his shoulder to see Morrigan standing there a swirling sphere of ice magic dissipating from between her hands.

"Thanks," Dante choked out between labored breaths.

"Lookout!" Another Sahaugin had burst from the water and was now flying through the air coming down towards the deck with its crooked spear aimed at Dante head.

Reacting quickly this time Dante swung his sword upward, knocking the new sahaugin's trident off course. He followed up with a hard slash downward and caught the fishman across the front as it landed on the deck. The longsword slid across the sahaugin's chest, shearing through soft skin and tearing through firm muscle as it went. Dante raised the sword to chest height, turned it flat and thrust it directly into the heart of the wounded sahaugin. The creature let out a gurgling, gasping roar and yanked the sword from its chest. The fishman dropped down to one knee holding its wounded chest, and then without warning thrust itself forward slamming a shoulder into Dante, knocking him off his feet. The wounded sahaugin closed in when it was blasted with a flash of crackling yellow energy. Dante looked back half expecting to see that Morrigan had saved him yet again but instead saw Carlyle levitating at least an inch off the deck and casting arcs of yellow lightning from the end of a stage magician's wand.

The deck was in chaos. Twelve sahaugin were aboard the ship, each on the attack. Alex used his shield to deflect the spear attack of one sahaugin, and then stepped in close to deliver an axe blow to the thing's gills, a wound which left the fishman riving on the deck in pain, but before Alex could finish the creature off, another sahaugin appeared, anxious to spear the dwarf through the back. Out of thin air Robyn appeared and stabbed two daggers into the gills slits of the offending sahaugin. It died instantly.

Morrigan, who had just helped save Dante moments before, stood back to back with Lin. Lin's hands were together as if in prayer, but when she lifted her head and parted her hands only slightly, she released a concentrated beam of heat that scorched a hole clean through a sahaugin's head.

Then there was Shinto. A sahaugin tried to throw its trident at the half-orc, only for him step out of the path of the weapon, snatch it from mid-air, and thrust it into the torso of another sahaugin. Shinto thrusted his hands back towards the fishman, covering him in golden flames that sent the sahaugin into a desperate panic. At least until Shinto pulled out his mace and with a sinle blow stroke the burning fishman in the head, dropping it instantly and extinguishing the flames on contact. The sahaugin lay at Shinto's feet, a crumpled smoldering heap, barely recognizable as anything other than a large, charred fish. The other sahaugin seem to avoid Shinto after this, focusing their attacks more on the others instead.

Dante turned his attention back towards the direction of the sahaugin that had been struck by Caryle's yellow lighting only to find Hoku now standing over him, two blood covered scimitars in his hands and the body of a sahuagin in two distinct pieces at his feet.

"On your feet. We must see to the captain and his child," said Hoku.

"Right." said Dante who then grabbed hold to Hoku's outstretched hand and pulled himself back to a standing position.

Dante and Hoku burst into the wheelhouse only to find it empty. At the rear, two sahaugin were attempting to escape, each with a person over their shoulder.

With a burst of speed Hoku gave chase and within seconds was within arm's length of the second fishman, the one holding the larger heavier ferry boat captain. Hoku grabbed the sahaugin by the tail and slid a scimitar into its torso, the fishman faltered and dropped the captain. Hoku pounced on to the creature like a predator on wounded prey. Dante rushed to the side of a disoriented Isaac, stunned by the sahaugin as they stormed the wheelhouse but now, coming back to his senses.

"Allie." Isaac mumbled. "they took Allie."

"I'm going to get her back," Dante said.

Isaac gripped Dante by the forearm. "You *have* to get her back. No matter what." Isaac looked at Dante with the glistening eyes of a desperate man. The strength had drained from his face and all that was left was the weakened and fragile frame of a soaked and salty old sailor clinging to one last hope. Dante.

"I promise." The captain released his arm and Dante broke into a sprint.

Sahaugin are not naturally fast runners, mostly due to their oversized feet and long webbed toes. With every step Dante felt himself gaining on the fishman, but the ship was not very long, and before Dante could get close enough to grab the sahaugin's tail, the fishman had reached ship's stern. And while sahaugin are not natural sprinters, their strong frog like legs, do make them natural leapers. The moment the fishman reached the back of the ship, with Allie strewn over its shoulder, it launched itself into the air and dived into the cold lake below.

Dante's heart dropped into the pit of his stomach as he watched the creature and the young girl go overboard. His arm was still outstretched reaching for the sahaugin's tail before he realized he was grasping at nothing but air. He watched the monster crash into the water while Allie looked up at him, her small hands reaching out to his for help, he hadn't realized up until that moment, but she had been aware the whole time, watching him give chase, calling for him to save her, but instead she had slipped through his fingers and now he was watching her face disappear beneath the waves. Immediately Dante realized what he had to do. He ducked his head and charged forward even faster than before.

"Dante wait!" he heard a voice call out from behind him, but he could not wait. Every moment that passed could mean the difference between them saving her and losing her forever. Without hesitation, Dante hit the rear of the boat stepped up on to the ship's railing and dived headfirst into the Erebus Lake after Allie and her sahaugin captor.

The lake water was colder than Dante could have imagined. It struck him all at once draining the warmth from his body and siphoning off some of his HP. Once he was underwater, he began to look around frantically for a sign of the sahaugin that had just jumped from the ship and then he spotted it. The creature had swam roughly 30 yards out, plain as day in the surprisingly clear depths of the lake. It was still holding Allie in one arm and one of the signature tridents in the other. Although now the sahaugin no longer retreated. Perhaps it was Dante's boldness to follow it into the water that had caught its attention, or perhaps it was being back in an element in which it felt more well suited, either way the fishman seemed to be done running away and now merely floated there in the lake, its large tail swishing from side to side treading water while it watched Dante thrash about in a panic, searching desperately for it.

Once Dante spotted the sahaugin, they locked eyes, and immediately he realized that the fishman had suddenly resolved to have two victims on that day as opposed to just one. The monster cocked back one arm and with incredible strength heaved its trident at Dante. The spear flew through the water like a torpedo. Dante turned and twisted his body, trying as best he could to move himself out of the projectile's path, but the agility and speed that he enjoyed on land he sorely lacked underwater. His attempt to dodge the trident ended with him being speared through the thigh by the jagged tips of the sauaugin's harpoon.

A feeling like hellfire coursed through Dante's leg, a burning pain like he had never felt before. He screamed, and a cloud of white air bubbles escaped his mouth. His sword still gripped tightly in one hand Dante yanked the crooked spear from his leg, releasing a flurry of red mist into the water around the wound. His leg throbbed with unimaginable pain and suddenly he was reminded of his own HP. The shoulder tackle, the sting of the cold lake water and now a trident through the leg had drained Dante for more than half his points, and an intense burning in his lungs let him know that he was now also slowly losing HP due to a lack of oxygen. With a bloodied leg and a desperate need for air Dante began swimming for the surface, if only to get a quick breath and gather his wits. But as he scrambled upwards toward the open sky he glanced down and saw the trident throwing shauagin swimming in his direction at unbelievable speed, a trail of small bubbles following in its wake. Within seconds the fishman was upon him, Allie still tucked tightly under the thing's right arm. With the force of its speed and a long strong arm the sahaugin tackled Dante hard, with a powerful swish of its tail and kick of its frog-like legs it went into a dive, dragging both him and Allie deeper into the cold depths of the lake.

It was going to try and drown him. He thought. If he didn't do something, it was going to drown the both of them.

The tackle had knocked away another chunk of his HP and the desperate need for air was sending him into a panic. Dante watched as the water's surface above him retreated, and felt himself growing dizzy from a lack of oxygen. His vision started to blur and holding his breath had become painful. If he didn't take a breath soon, he would blackout, and both he and Allie would die.

He struggled to free himself from the sahaugin's grip but the fishman's hold was too tight. The sahaugin's strength and speed underwater had doubled, while his had only waned. It took Dante a moment to realize it but he was still gripping his sword in his right hand, not that the blade would do him much good, the sahaugin was to close for him to get a good swing at it and even If he could, fighting against the water resistance made his attacks slow and clumsy. It was no wonder the sahaugin had charged him the way that it did, it was obvious it hadn't considered the sword a threat now that they were underwater. The fishman took the equivalent of a breath, expelling a mass of small bubbles from its gills as it prepared for another powerful thrust forward.

Almost immediately an idea forced itself into Dante's hazy mind. He thought about the sahaugin's raspy shallow breaths outside of the water. He thought about the effective attacks landed by both Alex and Robyn that had dropped two other fishmen near instantly. And that's when he realized, the sahaugin's perhaps one and only weakness now that it was underwater, and his only chance of getting himself and Allie back to the surface, were it gills. Dante gripped his sword tightly with both hands and brought the pommel down hard onto the fishman's gill slits, twisting and digging as viciously and as forcefully as he could into the sahaugin's soft neck.

In the instant Dante started his attack, the Sahaugin stopped diving and let out a choked gargled roar. The creature released both Dante and Allie and waved itself backwards, one webbed hand gripping its now red and inflamed gills.

Dante's chest ached, his eyes blurred as he began to lose consciousness. The sahaugin lashed out at him and nearly half blind Dante poured his will into his sword and time slowed to a crawl. He couldn't say a word but within him his mind screamed it. Lightspeed Slash.

Underwater and being dragged along by only one arm, the sword fanned out leaving a hazy after image of itself as it cut a swath through the water. A slowed and suffocating Dante was only able to make two strikes as opposed to three, one across the gill slits on the left side of the creature's head and the second after he grabbed the sword with both hands, reversed his grip and thrust its pointed tip violently into the gills on the right side of the creature's head. Immediately time came thundering back into being and the incredible high-speed movement of Dante's sword sent shockwaves resounding through the water. The sahaugin let out another gurgling roar as Dante pulled his blade from its neck. Its mouth filled with a sickly pink foam of air bubbles and blood as it gargled and choked gripping its throat and sinking to the bottom of the lake.

Dante grabbed hold to a limp and unconscious Allie and began frantically swimming towards the lake surface. His sword slipped from his hand but due to his desperate need for air and the desire to hold tightly to the young girl he didn't even look back. Dante kicked his legs to try and speed them along. He could see the light of day just above the waves, but also between him and open air, there were at least three more armed sahaugin swimming just beneath the surface of the water. He didn't know if they had spotted him. He didn't care, the only thing that mattered was getting to the surface and getting air even if that meant taking a chest full of tridents. And then, right before his vision blurred to nothingness and the world around him disappeared, a large humanoid figure broke the surface of the water and a flash of purple sheared one of the sahaugin in two. Dante kept kicking, forcing himself up towards the light. A scorching red beam shot through the waves and incinerated another of the sahaugin in its tracks, while arc of yellow energy slammed into the last remaining sahaugin sending it sinking lifelessly to the lake bottom. Through it all Dante stretched and reached upwards, yearning for the light that was only just above him, the last bastion of hope for his survival as all around him everything else had faded from view and then, when he realized he could go no further, and he would undoubtedly die beneath the waves of the Erebus Lake a massive green hand reached out to meet him, yanking him forcefully upwards allowing his head and shoulder to break the surface of the water. The moment crisp cold air blew across his wet face Dante threw his head back, opened his mouth and took the deepest most satisfying breath he had ever taken in his life.

Chapter 31: The One that Didn't Get Away

"What are you? Crazy?" Morrigan yelled at Dante. "Are you *trying* to get yourself killed?"

"You did it!" chimed in Alex, "You really did it, you saved her."

"How did you survive an underwater battle with a sahaugin?" Carlyle asked more to himself then to Dante.

Back onboard the Nimue there was a flurry of excitement. Questions, comments and statements flew in from every direction. Dante didn't respond. He sat on the deck with his back propped against the wheelhouse, shivering, soaked and bleeding.

He watched intently as Shinto, who had pulled them near lifeless from the water, lay the young girl down gently on the deck a few feet away from him. Isaac was by her side, panic and desperation stricken across his face. Allie was dripping water, limp and unresponsive, her head lolled as Shinto lay her down. Her eyes were closed, her skin pale white and her lips a frighteningly dark shade of blue that made Dante's stomach twist up in knots.

Isaac's mouth was moving he was saying something, screaming something, either at Shinto or at Allie. Dante couldn't tell, he couldn't hear anything, or anyone, all he could do was stare at the little girl that lay there pale, blue and unbreathing. He half expected the cleric to sit her down and then immediately begin to perform CPR in an attempt to get her breathing again, but instead Shinto simply laid a gentle hand on the young girls unmoving chest. Golden light radiated from his palm and pushed its way into Allie's torso. Her small body slowly heaved upward as if her chest was filling with air and then suddenly all at once, the young girl coughed up a mouth full of lake water, and Shinto turned her to her side where she continued to spit out more and more of the thick clear liquid, purging all the fluids from her lungs and at the same time taking in deep gasping breaths.

Sound came back to Dante's ears, and he realized that he too had been holding his breath as well, which was odd considering a few moments ago air seemed to be the most precious thing in the world to him.

A sudden wave of confusion hit him. His mind raced in an attempt to makes sense of the last few moments.

A sahuagin had grabbed the girl. He jumped into the lake to go after them. Jumped into the lake? What had he been thinking? *What are you? crazy? Are you trying to get yourself killed?* Morrigan's words replayed themselves in his mind. Morrigan's words? Had Morrigan said that? Had he said that to himself?

"What are you?... Crazy?... Are you...trying... to get yourself... killed?"

"Well?... Are you?" a voice familiar, yet foreign whispered into Dante's ear. As it faded, he swore he could have heard laughing echoing in the distance, and then all around him the world began to go black.

The pain in Dante's leg throbbed him back into consciousness. He winced and a low moan escaped his throat. His surroundings flashed back into view as if he had just taken a shot of caffeine directly into his veins. The hand that lay flat against the deck of the ship, the one that he had been using to keep himself upright, clenched shut in reaction to the pain shooting through his body, but instead of gripping the deck he felt his hands close tightly around the hilt of his sword. His eyes drifted towards the blade, confused as to how it had found its way back into his possession. He was sure he had dropped it underwater and had lost it to the bottom of the lake.

"Dante are you alright?" Alex asked, a look of concern across his face. "Morrigan, does Dante look ok?"

Morrigan looked at Dante's face and frowned "Hey someone, Dante needs help." She called out with panic in her voice. Dante could hear it, he could see it, though he didn't feel that there was much he could do about it.

Lin dropped down to Dante's side, "His HP is nearly at zero, he's blacking out." She placed both hands over Dante's wounded leg the priestess began speaking in a low rhythmic voice. "Hathor, goddess of the Sun, Mother of divine light, I asked that you lend me your strength so that I may offer respite to this your weary and wounded child. Succor!" she announced and with glowing orange energy and extreme warmth. The pain in Dante's leg subsided as the lacerated flesh stitched itself back together. At the same time his mind cleared, and his HP bar begin to slowly fill, bringing him back to a state of normalcy, allowing him to reorient himself and shake away his confusion.

He blinked a couple of times and looked up to see Lin smiling at him, her hands still glowing bright orange. She waved them slowly over his body, as the light shone upon him its soothed and warmed his aching and stiff muscles.

"You heal fast," Lin said to him with a smile. "Your body absorbs Hathor's healing light well. The goddess smiles upon you."

Dante knew that the Black Wolf Boon of Recovery bestowed on him by Canis Romulus, had been at play in the course of his healing and he recalled the wolf's words from that moment.

"Every day we survive we grow stronger in order to survive another day."

"Thank you for healing me," Dante muttered in a hoarse and whispered voice apparently sore and damaged from his time in the water.

"That was a brave thing you did," Lin said her face fading from the comforting smile to an expression of sincere gratitude, "A very brave thing indeed."

"Dante!" Isaac came running toward Dante and Lin, he had Allie cradled tightly in his arms she was awake, but she looked exhausted and still a little cold, but otherwise unharmed. "Dante, I want to thank you. You saved my daughter. You saved my little girl." Isaac's eyes welled up with tears.

"Mr. Dante," said Allie, her little voice squeaking out like a small mouse from the cradle of her father's arms. Allie suddenly talking stirred emotions within Dante that he did not know he had, he felt his own eyes begin to water simply from hearing the sound of her tiny voice. "Mr. Dante... was that tag?"

"What?" Dante asked slightly confused but somehow found himself smiling at the mention of tag.

"You the monster and I. Did we just play a game of tag? Like they do on Urthland?"

"No, not exactly." Dante replied. Suddenly it was clear why he had jumped into the lake after the sahaugin and the young girl. There was no part of him that could have allowed such an innocent life to be lost while he had the power in him to at least try and prevent it. That's why he jumped, because if nothing else he had to at least try, even if it seemed foolish, even if it seemed crazy, even if it killed him. "Tag is a bit more fun."

"Good." Allie replied. "because I didn't like that game at all, and I really want to like tag."

Dante pulled himself up to his feet. "Yeah, I didn't like that game either, but I promise you'll like tag a whole lot more."

Allie smiled and then nuzzled her face into her father's chest.

"I'll take her to get some rest and then I'll get us across this water and docked at Midell." Isaac said enthusiastically.

"Thank you, captain," said Dante.

"No son, thank you." Said Captain Isaac with a nod, and he made his way into the wheelhouse with Allie in his arms.

Dante felt a heavy hand grip lightly on to his shoulder and immediately he knew who it was, "Glad that you're back on your feet, but you should get some rest as well." Shinto released his grip on Dante's shoulder and begin walking briskly toward the front of the ferry. "I'll be back to check on you in a moment."

"Wait, what? Where are *you* going?" Dante asked moving after Shinto in an attempt to keep up. He walked with a limp, his leg had been healed but it was stiff and sore. He was back up to one third of his total HP but he could still feel the effects of almost being knocked down to zero.

Dante picked up the pace in order to catch up with Shinto. Robyn stood with a coil of rope in one hand and a dagger in the other and in front of her Hoku was crouched over a captive sahuagin, bound and tied in ropes and laid out on the ferry deck like a fish pulled fresh from the sea.

"Dante you're alive!" said Robyn enthusiastically. She holstered the dagger, dropped the rope and ran pass Carlyle and Shinto toward Dante, throwing herself into his arms. He struggled to keep himself from falling over. She squeezed him tightly and he could feel her tremble within his grip. Then suddenly she released him and without warning slapped him briskly across the face. He was overwhelmed by an odd sense of déjà vu.

"We thought you were dead. You were under water for a full five minutes." She said, tears in her eyes.

"Sorry." Dante said, his cheek stinging slightly, "I didn't mean to make you worry."

"It's fine, golden boy." She sniffed. "Just don't let it happen again."

Dante smiled, a warm yet somehow insincere smile.

"It looks like you've captured one of the sahuagin." He said nodding his head passed Robyn toward the restrained fishman that was now surrounded by Hoku, Carlyle, Lin and Shinto. Alex and Morrigan were standing next to Robyn and Dante as they all tried to determine what to do next.

Robyn wiped her face. "Hoku and Carlyle managed to disable this one as it tried to get away, and they asked for help tying it up and well... I had rope." She said with a smile and a shrug. "I think they're going to try and question it, figure out why they have been attacking ships on the lake."

"Question it? Do they really think it will cooperate?"

"Can it cooperate?" asked Alex. "Can it even talk?"

"In the Dragon Dale Games the Sahuagin spoke their own language." Dante replied. "So if someone speaks Mer they can talk to it. Personally, I want to see what they were doing here." Dante said with a determined look in his eyes and together with the others they made their way towards the restrained fishman.

As they approached the bow of the ship Hoku was grabbing the restrained sahuagin by the ropes and pulling it upwards so that it now sat with its slimy back propped up against the Nimue's bulwark. The creature was bloody and bruised, its body covered in a number of scratches, cuts and scorch marks, souvenirs from the encounter it had with Hoku and Carlyle on the deck. One of its legs was suffering from what looked like a particularly nasty burn and involuntarily it twitched and jumped of its own accord. Dante assumed this specific wound was the result of a well-placed blast from Carlyle and his magic wand, and was more than likely the primary reason the sahuagin had not been able to escape to the water. The sahuagin took deep raspy breaths, gills flaring as it dealt with the pain from its wounds and the difficulty of breathing outside the water.

"Is it going to live long enough to answer any questions?" Morrigan asked aloud. "Looks like it's in pretty bad shape."

"It'll live," said Hoku coldy, "long enough for our purposes at least."

Dante scanned the fishman, its HP was in the red, only at a tenth of its total health bar remained, but it didn't appear to be in immediate danger of death and Dante knew that the amphibious Sahuagin could survive for hours outside of the water despite their raspy and labored breathing.

The fishman looked from adventurer to adventurer with cold eyes.

"Heal it," said Shinto calmly.

"What?" replied a number of the adventurers in unison.

"I need to get information from it and I cannot do that if it's not in the right frame of mind. We need to heal it, in order to calm it down enough for me to get the information that we need. Lin if you could please?" Shinto motioned to the sahuagin. Reluctantly Lin stepped closer and then crouched down near it raising her hands the same way she had done over Dante, the fishman jumped as she approached but Hoku pulled tightly on the creature's ropes slamming it back against the bulwark.

"Hathor, goddess of the Sun, Mother of divine light, I asked that you lend me your strength so that I may offer respite to this your weary and wounded... child. Succor!" Lin repeated the prayer that she had said over Dante's leg and just like before her hands begin to glow a bright orange. She waved them slowly over the battered sahuagin and slowly a number of the cuts and bruises that covered its body begin to recede. The fishman struggled under the light of Lin's hands and Hoku held on to it tightly. Dante noticed that the sahuagin recognized that it was being helped and yet, it still resisted the aid. Perhaps it assumed they were only healing it so they could then torture it, perhaps that is what the sahuagin did to their prisoners. Lin avoided healing the sahuagin's badly damaged leg but after a few minutes of bathing it in orange light, Shinto called for her to stop. Dante looked to the creature's status box and saw that it had been brought up to one fourth of its total health, not exactly fighting form, but a lot better than it had been moments ago.

"I'll take it from here." Shinto said, stepping forward toward the sahuagin, the wooden boards of the deck groaning under his massive size.

Shinto loomed over the sahuagin like a pale green harbinger of doom, the fishman looked small and frail by comparison and right as everyone sort of braced themselves for what was expected to undoubtedly be the first blow of many, Shinto instead crouched down to a squat, dropping down to eye level with the restrained fishman.

Yet instead of speaking in Mer, Shinto took a deep breath and reached out his left arm pointing two fingers at the sahuagin's forehead. Dante watched in a mixture of awe and confusion as Shinto's extended hand became encircled in softly glowing rings of purple light, each one a different size. At the same time the Fishman's dark eyes had begun to glow the same color purple. The rings encircling Shinto's hand spun in alternating directions, each one moving of its own accord and speed, and at what seemed like random intervals the rings would stop, change direction and then spin again until soon each of the rings were spinning in unsion. Dante looked back to Shinto and saw that his eyes had too flashed a bright purple and all at once the rings around his hands vanished and the sahuagin's body went limp. When Dante looked to its status box it still had the same amount of HP as it did before Shinto did whatever it was, he had just done. The creature, it appeared, had fallen into a deep sleep.

"What was that?" Dante asked out loud unable to hold the question back.

"That was a Mind Penetration spell," answered Hoku, still positioned beside the sahuagin and still pointlessly holding onto its ropes which he released now that the fishman was completely unresponsive.

"There had been about 25 of them to start," Shinto began, "A small sahuagin raiding swarm. They swam up from the Sunblind Coast moving west through the Alder Guard River and then north through the Erebus River before they stopped and began nesting here in the Great Erebus Lake. They setup the water fog trap and begin preying on fishing vessels that passed through the center of the lake. Their goal was to capture as many surface dwellers as they could so they could then sacrifice them in a sahuagin ritual that would allow them to harvest spirit crystals."

"Harvest spirit crystals?" said Hoku, "You mean in the same way adventurers collect mana crystals from monsters and wild beast?"

"Yes," answered Shinto, "Advanced races, such as humans, elves, orcs, Kalgari, we do not naturally create mana crystals upon death like other creatures. Instead, we form spirit crystals, but even this is not considered a natural process and the formation of such crystals must be forced via either a ritual, or by a spell cast at the time of death." Shinto looked over at Dante as he mentioned the last point and instinctively Dante reached up and felt for the rose-colored jewel that lay tucked snuggly underneath his armor.

"But why would sahuagin be harvesting spirit crystals, what would they be doing with them?" asked Hoku.

"This sahuagin was merely a low-level warrior, he did not know the reason for the task, only that they were to capture as many surface dwellers as possible, but based off what we know, spirit crystals are really nothing more than very potent, very concentrated forms of mana crystals, and we know mana crystals are used to make ether potions, power mana engines, and make magic items, so I would assume the sahuagin are stockpiling spirit crystals for some purpose that requires very large amounts of magical energy."

"So, a spirit crystal is like a mana crystal multiplied by what? Ten?" Robyn asked.

"More like multiplied by one thousand," said Lin.

"This sounds very bad," said Alex.

"It is," added Carlyle, "While a spirit crystal may serve a number of purposes they are most often sought for only one reason."

"Necromancy," said Lin.

Necromancy, Dante knew, was magic involving the manipulation, control and most often reanimation of the dead. In all past Dragon Dale games necromancy was almost always exclusively frowned upon and oftentimes viewed as something both unholy and unnatural. It wasn't until the more recent iterations of the franchise did Dragon Dale begin to allow players to even dabble in the dark art of necromancy with simple spells like raise zombie and drain life which allowed players to feel like dark wizards. Dante, however, a long time student of Dragon Dale lore, always knew these small magic tricks paled in comparison to what a true necromancer was meant to be.

"We need to report this to the Adventurer's guild," said Hoku. "They will need to open a quest and send more adventurers here to sweep the lake and ensure that the area has been cleared of sahuagin. And if what you say about the spirit crystals are true, I imagine there will need to be an investigation into the Sunblind Coast as well."

"I agree," said Shinto, "the four of us are headed to Abilene Bay, we shall make a report when we arrive, but I think you all should send word from Midell as well. In my experience the Guild is more likely to act if they have heard a similar account from multiple sources. Convincing them that the sahuagin are turning people into spirit crystals may be a hard sell but informing them that there are sahuagin at Erebus Lake should be enough to get their attention."

"And shall we tell them how we found out the sahuagin were using the captured fishermen to harvest spirit crystals?" asked Lin aggressively. "Advanced telepathy like that Mind Penetration spell you cast is forbidden magic in each one of the major four city-states." She stared up at Shinto with a cold and stony expression.

"Yes, well I suppose that it is a good thing that we are in the middle of a lake and not in any of the four major city-states," Shinto replied coolly.

Lin's face went flush with color, "You are a cleric of some considerable knowledge and skill, proficient in the ways of magics that are supposed to be deemed unsuitable for the civilized world, you bear no marking from any temple that *I* recognize, and you have yet once to evoke the name of your god. Master Shinto, as a priestess of Hathor I demand to know what deity you serve?"

The half-orc took a deep breath. He looked annoyed. Dante was reminded that he took Shinto through the exact same line of questioning and found it funny that he was already going through it again only a few days later. Dante looked over at Lin, she had her hands to her sides, but she flexed her fingers nervously as if she was mentally preparing to cast a spell. Hoku had lifted himself up to his toes, his hands drifting down toward the hilt of his swords, and suddenly Dante realized that they were on the brink of combat. Just as he had been prepared to pull his sword if Shinto had named the wrong god all those days ago, it appeared that Hoku and Lin were of the same mindset, and from the look of it, her position as a priestess of Hathor was a formal request. Shinto had no choice but to answer.

"You mean to say you don't know?" interrupted Carlyle, "Oh my dear Lin, you have spent far too much time in the local temples and not nearly enough time in the local taverns. You really don't know who we have been sharing this ferry with?" Carlyle laughed. His attitude seemed to lighten the tension onboard the deck and everyone around him relaxed.

"What are you talking about now Carlyle?" asked Lin.

"Shinto serves Hassan the Merciful," said Carlyle without hesitation. "We have spent the better part of the morning with an adventurer of some renown, Shinto the half-orc cleric. If any of the stories are to be believed, *he* is a servant of Hassan the Merciful."

"Every day you spout new blasphemies. Hassan the Merciful is not a god."

"*Everyday* men and women still say a prayer to Hassan. '*A gold coin for Highender, a silver for Hassan, dropped in a body of water for a job well and done.*' It is a prayer of adventurers and mercenaries all over Deos. People have said it for years, if it is belief that gives the gods strength then if Hassan was not born a god he is undoubtedly one by now."

"I have heard that prayer before," said Hoku. "I have even said it myself a number of times."

"This is ridiculous, what does that have to do with Shinto?" asked Lin.

"I told you, Shinto is the cleric of Hassan, the one true cleric of Hassan. Blessed and chosen by Hassan himself. Not to be confused with the cults that used Hassan's name in vain. Shinto is the real deal."

"Cults!?" Lin said in a high-pitched voice.

"Yes, the Hassan Assassin Cults that emerged after Hassan disappeared. They claimed to be his disciples, but they really weren't." Carlyle's enthusiasm grew. "There were two of them. Two cults. They were engaged in a secret war with one another, until Shinto appeared and single handedly dismantled both of them."

"Yes, I have heard stories of the Shadow War, but I did not know it was Shinto who brought the peace," said Hoku. He crossed his arms and a look of concentration appeared on his face as if to suggest the topic of conversation had now begun to get very interesting to him.

"I can't believe I'm hearing this." Mumbled Lin.

"Hassan the Merciful, God of Adventurers, and his one disciple Shinto, Half-Orc Cleric. This meeting is about as rare as seeing a dragon I tell you. I mean, to think, we've fought side by side with Shinto the Green Dem-"

"That's not me." Shinto interrupted.

"What?" said both Lin and Carlyle in unison.

"I'm not the Shinto from the stories. I see why you would think that. Half-orc clerics are not exactly common, and we do share a name, but I'm not a cleric of Hassan, I serve Cassandra, the goddess of knowledge."

"Cassandra?" replied Lin "The goddess of scribes and scholars?"

"None other," said Shinto coolly.

"That's surprising... a cleric of your talents... I expected you to name someone else... someone more..."

"Important?" chimed in Carlyle with a grin.

"No, that's not what I meant, its simply that I never would have took you to be the cleric of a minor – err, a *younger* god."

"You see, this is why I ascribe to the idea that one should never discuss religion or politics while on a job," said Carlyle matter of factly.

"Yet somehow all you talk about is both religion and politics and your disdain for the both of them you... you deviant," snapped Lin.

"Yes, my dear but never on a job." Replied Carlyle with a wink.

Lin rolled her eyes.

"Ok, but what do we do about him? Or it? Or whatever it's called?" asked Alex, motioning to the sahuagin who was beginning to stir within its ropes. It moved its head from one side to the other as if trying to shake off a particularly nasty headache, or as if trying to wake from very bad dream.

"The answer to that is simple." Hoku unsheathed one of his swords with an alarming look of delight upon his face.

"Release him," Shinto said calmly.

What?" replied a number of the adventurers in unison, a reaction which was beginning to become a trend every time Shinto spoke.

"Are you suggesting we release this thing back into the lake to prey on more innocent people?" asked Hoku an edge of agitation in his voice.

"It won't be preying upon anyone else," said Shinto in his usual calm manner.

"Master Shinto, I must agree with Hoku on this one, while the beast man in some rudimentary way may appreciate our small mercy of releasing it *relatively* unharmed, once it reunites with its companions, I am quite sure it will quickly forget our benevolence and summarily resort back to its barbaric and violent ways."

"The sahuagin have met little to no resistance since they began ambushing ships here on the lake over a week ago, their fight with us here today has culled the numbers of their raiding swarm by half, after this they'll be in disarray, scrambling to reorganize and regroup, they'll be hesitant to attack another ship again for a while at first. By the time they get their wits about them once again, the Guild should have some additional adventurers out here to clean up any stragglers. Either way *this* sahuagin won't be attacking anybody else, the only thing it is concerned with is making the journey back to the Sunblind Coast."

"And how could you be so sure of that? Did it tell you that when you were digging through its mind?" asked Lin.

"Not exactly," answered Shinto, "I, more or less... made the suggestion, while I was inside. He was quite receptive, and I can assure you, now has no greater desire than to return to the Sunblind Coast as quickly as he possibly can."

"You're controlling its mind." Lin shook her head disapprovingly. "Hence why this type of advance telepathic magic is expressly forbidden, if you could do that to a sahuagin, imagine what this magic could do in the wrong hands, what if it was used against a guard captain, a royal advisor or even a senator, the results could be disastrous. That's why controlling the mind of living things is unethical, even sahuagin."

"More unethical than killing him?" Shinto asked with one raised eyebrow. "Besides, I am not *controlling* his mind, I have merely implanted an idea that will temporarily influence his way of thinking. After a few of days the spell will wear off and by then he should back to the Sunblind Coast, leaving one less sahuagin here to terrorize the Erebus Lake, and no one not even a beast men need die in the process. I think that is a result that both Cassandra and Hathor would find satisfying. Don't you?" Shinto looked at Lin through his unwavering crisp green eyes.

The priestess looked at the half-orc, then to the sahuagin and then to the half-orc again. "I suppose so." She answered after a brief moment of consideration. "Release it."

Hoku shrugged and with the same blade he had intended to execute the fishman with, he kneeled down and cut the ropes restraining it. Almost immediately the sahuagin scrambled up to its feet, looked from side to side at the adventurers that surrounded it, and then it tipped itself over the edge of the Nimue's railing and landed in the water with a splash, disappearing beneath the waves of the lake.

Lin turned back to Shino. "I have never seen an adventurer, cleric or otherwise, go out of there way to avoid taking the life of an enemy, especially a beast man. Exactly who are you Master Shinto?"

"I am but a humble adventurer, nothing more." Shinto answered plainly.

"Yes, but to what end?" inquired the priestess.

"To seek knowledge and preserve life," answered Shinto, "As is Cassandra's will."

"Yes, well... the goddess is fortunate to have such a faithful servant," replied Lin.

Shinto nodded silently in appreciation. As he did so, Lin looked at him with a peculiar look on her face. It was part admiration and part envy, like a talent scout that had gotten to the party a tad bit too late, and now had to watch the top recruit get picked up by another team. Carlyle, on the other hand, was smiling widely from ear to ear.

"This," said the wizard, "Has been a magnificent day for adventuring."

Chapter 32: Abilene Bay

Both minor and major deities graced the Deosian pantheon, each one believed to have influence over Deosian life. Chief among them was Hathor, goddess of the sun. She had more temples, more followers and more clergy than any other.

Mylon the god of death; Alsar, god of justice; Marthana the jealous goddess of hate, rage and desire also took their places beside Hathor. Some gods were worshipped by each specific race. Orcan, the orcish god of war and the hunt. Valshear, elven goddess of knowledge and magic. Onin, dwarven god of strength and the mountains. And those were just a few of the major deities, there were also the minor gods, like Highender a war god revered by mercenaries, assassins and sell swords, or Cassandra, a goddess of knowledge held in high esteem by sages and scholars across the continent, or Vagari, the patron god of bards and musicians. The lesser-known deities did not boast the notoriety or cultural influence of their larger counterparts, and were considered by most Deosians as lesser, or younger gods as opposed to the more prominent deities, who were thought of as elder gods.

In past Dragon Dale games, traditionally, the storyline of each new title was independent of the game that came before it. Which is to say, there were no sequels, no continuous plotline that carried over from Dragon Dale 1 to 2 to 3 and so on. Each new game started a completely new adventure with completely new characters and a completely new set of problems, the only thing that carried over from game to game was the setting, the lore and the gods.

Dante always assumed that this was a tribute to the old tabletop RPG days where players would sit down and play through a campaign and once it was complete, they would roll new characters and start a new story, each one with a few familiar faces or names thrown into the mix for nostalgia's sake. Certain popular NPCs were carried over from game to game like the cities and gods were, they became a part of the fabric of Dragon Dale, a part of the world's lore. Hassan the Merciful was one of those names. He had never actually appeared in any of the past games, only mentions of him. And often times he wasn't even referred to as Hassan the Merciful, for years he had been known as Demon Hassan or even Hassan the Butcher.

He was given the name Hassan the Merciful as a joke. In truth he was an adventurer and an assassin of such skill that he was rumored to eliminate his targets before they would even realize he was in the room. It was said to be a blessing to be a victim of Hassan, that way at least then you knew your death was guaranteed to be quick and painless… almost merciful.

As far as Dante could remember Hassan was one of the most prominent Sword Saints in the Dragon Dale lore. He was the prototype for the job class and a legendary warrior figure in the world. So popular in fact that when mercenaries and adventurers would pray to Highender before a notably difficult quest or mission, they eventually begin to ask for some additional favor from Hassan as well, just for good measure.

This superstition of praying to Highender for a blessing and then mentioning Hassan for luck spread the reputation and legend of Hassan the Merciful and soon it was no mystery as to why Hassan had begun to be regarded as a god in his own right.

A mortal made into a god… well at least in the eyes of his peers. There was nothing in the lore that supported the idea of Hassan actually achieving godhood, or that he even sought to. It was more or less a mantle thrust upon him by his men and men like him. Eventually, the mortal Hassan faded into obscurity, he either died of old age, or in battle, or went into hiding to escape the monstrous fame and inevitable jealousy that such things bring, yet regardless of what happened to the man, his name lived on, cemented in the thoughts and minds of countless Deosians as a man who made himself equal to the gods.

Needless to say, Dante knew everything that there was to know about Hassan, except for the fact that he apparently had a secret half-orc cleric devoted to him, whose name just so happened to be Shinto, however who also did not happen to be the current half-orc cleric that they were presently traveling with, whose name also, just so happened to be Shinto.

"So, you are saying that you are not *that* Shinto?" asked Robyn for what had to be the tenth time.

"That is correct." Shinto replied. "I am not *that* Shinto." He said, speaking with what seemed to be an endless amount of unwavering patience.

"What are the chances that you and this other guy are both half-orcs, both clerics and are both named Shinto? That's like three out of three. I mean, that's a pretty odd coincidence. Don't you think?" Robyn prodded.

"Yes," Shinto said dryly. "It is very odd."

The cleric, Dante noticed, didn't seem annoyed with Robyn's line of questioning, just uninterested.

The party was now outside the city of Midell. Issac had successfully guided the Nimue the rest of the way across the lake and docked in the port town that appeared to be a much larger and more impressive version of Harrington. Midell had been roughly the size of Bleeksborough, only it sat on the water, instead of in the midst of hills. Once they docked, Carlyle, Lin and Hoku informed the party that the three of them would be staying in Midell longer than they had originally planned. The Deosian adventurers decided to await a response from the adventurer's guild concerning the Lake Sahuagin. They all wished each other farewell, it was as if they had been friends for years as opposed to a few hours. As a lifelong athlete this intense but brief bond felt familiar to Dante. Weekend training camps, summer leagues, two a day practices, he knew firsthand that bonds were not truly built with only time but, with shared experience, and their experience on the lake had created within each of them a sense of trust no one had expected.

After a brief rest within the safety of the city's walls, Shinto suggested they continue forward to Abilene Bay, which was now only some ten to fifteen leagues from Midell, just roughly a full day's journey away.

On the other side of the lake, and outside of Midell, the local flora had begun to change. The grass had become thin, tall and reedy. Most of the trees had given up their limbs and boughs in exchange for long slender trunks topped off with patchwork bark that crosshatched upon itself as if it had been woven by hand. They looked like palm trees, and their presence, against the bright blue sky and along with the now oppressive Desoian heat, gave everything east of the lake a tropical feel.

They were about an hour into the journey and the question of the real and present Shinto versus the mythological and rumored Shinto kept creeping into the conversation, or rather, the party, particularly Robyn, kept forcing the issue as a topic of conversation.

Suddenly the real and present Shinto stopped walking. Then with the gentleness of an experienced gardener he reached up and plucked from a tree an oddly shaped, pumpkin colored fruit that looked like a seed pod, only covered in a thick and wrinkled skin.

"Pomona." Said Shinto, separating the fruit free from the tree with a decisive snap. "Almost forgot that these were in season. They have always been a favorite of mine."

"So Dante, what does the ole Dragon Dale encyclopedia have to say? Is Shinto, Shinto or is he *Shinto*?" asked Robyn with mischievous suspicion.

Dante hesitated. It really wasn't his place to say who Shinto was or was not, but Robyn seemed determined not to drop the subject until she found an answer that satisfied her curiosity.

"I've never seen anything about a half-orc cleric that acts on Hassan's behalf. I do know that if one cleric asks another which god they follow, they can't lie, they have to tell the truth, it's a competitive thing between the gods, a cleric can't deny their faith before another cleric, it's like a loyalty test. So if Shinto told Lin he follows Cassandra, then I believe him, he wouldn't have been able to lie to her about that." But what Dante didn't reveal is when he had asked Shinto the same line of questioning. Back then, Shinto had said only that, 'it was complicated', but what was so complicated about saying that he followed Cassandra? Could he have been ashamed because she was only a minor diety? No. Shinto, did not seem to care about such things, that meant that there was something else, something else that he hadn't shared with Lin. So he wasn't lying, but the question was, was he telling the whole truth?

"Shinto?" prompted Morrigan. The half-orc was still quietly and diligently plucking fruit from the nearby trees. The sound of his name jostled him out of the zen-like state that he had settled in as he thoughtfully felt through the low hanging tree limbs, discerning which pomona were ripe for picking versus those that needed more time to grow. He turned to meet Morrigan's eyes with his own, and from the look on his face, Dante knew he hadn't been listening to a word that had been said once he'd found the fruit trees.

"I had a question about magic, or maybe it's about mana. I'm not really sure," said Morrigan.

The only thing Shinto liked more than plants was answering questions. "I'm listening."

"Earlier you said magic is the manipulation of mana, that mages are skilled at using inspiration, imagination and necessity to shape mana into spells, well if that's the case, what exactly is a cleric. Why would a mage devote themselves to a god when magic is mastered through experience and experimentation?"

"That, is a good question." Shinto smiled like a proud professor. "And you're right, mages use mana to manipulate the world around them, mastering spell craft through experimentation, study and practice. A cleric who is in service to a deity is gifted spells that are often thought to be beyond the understanding of most mages. Their power is rooted in devotion and prayer. Clerics act on behalf of their deities, the idea being the more aligned the cleric is with the will of their god the more powerful the god allows their magic to become."

"So, mages learn their spells from books and clerics learn their spells from gods," said Alex.

"Yes, and as a result mages are often free to pursue whatever field of magic they wish, whereas clerics are often limited to the realm of magic bestowed upon them by their deities."

"So, in Deos, the gods are real?" asked Robyn, "I mean they come down from heaven and smite people and answer prayers and stuff like that?"

Shinto stared at her blankly, and for the first time Dante noticed that his face showed confusion.

"On Earth," Dante interjected, "religion is a point of contention. Our clerics don't get magic spells so there's no clear way to prove who's right, who's wrong, or if they even exist," said Dante with a smirk.

"I see," said Shinto. "yes well, similarly a majority of Deosians go their whole lives praying to the gods and most never receive a direct response, let alone actually encounter one. In fact, most clerics rarely even directly commune with a god themselves. The powers and spells that are bestowed to them are the remnant of divine laws set by the gods long ago.The gods don't actually have to interact with their servants to bless them, there is a system set in place that does that for them. It is considered a rare and wonderous event for a mortal to be contacted, let alone be in the presence of a god, those who experience such things are referred to as Godstouched. They are individuals that a deity has chosen to do a very specific task, they don't have to be a cleric, they actually don't even have to worship that god, they simply have to be chosen."

Dante's mind wandered for a moment, about when he first entered Deos, about the white room and the man in the eyepatch. "What about you?" Dante asked. "Have you ever spoken to a god, have you ever spoken to Cassandra?"

Shinto looked at Dante quizzically and then smiled.

"Yeah," said Robyn. "Can't you just call on Cassandra and ask her to send us back home?"

Shinto took one of the pomona he had gathered and twisted the bump on the top of the fruit and removed the waxy pumpkin-colored skin, peeling off the thick outer layer, "It doesn't exactly work that way." He responded. The heart of the pomona split up easily into neat symmetrically segments, one of which Shinto popped into his mouth. "Come, Abilene Bay is not far. Let us continue."

The adventurers once again begin to move along the road towards the direction of what they hoped and believed to be Abilene Bay. Twice they ran into roving packs of raptors as they walked. First a set of three, then a few hours later a set of four. In both cases Shinto culled the pack down until there was only two creatures left at which point, he stepped back and allowed Dante, Alex, Morrigan and Robyn to practice the tactics and strategies he had taught them, or that they had streamlined from previous encounters. They practiced corralling their enemies or separating them when necessary. Alex was the main tank, but Dante could distract a raptor by himself if the need arose. He was able to strike fast and then use his agility and dexterity to dodge or parry incoming attacks. Dante realized that his strength was in individual combat, whereas Alex excelled in taking on multiple enemies at once. With his shield and axe the dwarf had learned to fend off two raptors at the same time with little to no trouble. While he held their attention, Morrigan had grown rather skilled at hurling not only shards of ice from range but also motes of fire, which screeched as they flew through the air like small whistling birds. Robyn on the other hand had developed an uncanny knack for disappearing whenever fighting started, and then mysteriously firing her crossbow from one end of the battlefield, then moments later popping up behind one their enemies and plunging her daggers into their soft parts before somehow disappearing again behind some type of cover, or debris, or shrubbery or otherwise concealing her presence before the raptor could find her. They took turns attacking in waves, mastering their chemistry and cohesion in a fight and with Shinto's help they had in just the span of two battles become considerably more confident and efficient. With each victory, the defeated raptors dropped small blue spirit crystals and each one Dante collected and placed into his coin pouch along with the others saving them for some unknown means and some unknown time.

As the sun set, they found themselves at the edge of a small river. Marrowbone Creek marked the halfway point between Midell and Abilene Bay. If they set up camp for the night and got an early start in the morning, they would arrive in Abilene Bay before noon of the next day. They discussed it among the group, whether to press on through the night or simply wait until sunrise and unanimously decided to wait.

They setup camp for what they hoped to be one last time before reaching their destination. Abilene Bay was only six leagues away, roughly 18 miles by Dante's estimation. After one more morning of walking, they would be in a major city-state. Dante sat down in front of the fire and pulled out his spirit tome.

-You have unlocked a ranked skill, 'Forage'

-Your Forage skill has risen to a rank of 'F'

-You have unlocked a ranked skill, 'Herbalist'

-Your Herbalist skill has risen to a rank of 'F'

-You have been issued a new quest, "Mystery Fog over Erebus Lake"

-The Shaughin Raider has been defeated.

-You have gained 800 Experience points!

-You have been issued a new quest, "The Ferryman's Daughter"

-The Shaughin Raider has been defeated.

-You have gained 800 Experience points!

-You have fulfilled the primary objective for the quest, "The Ferryman's Daughter"

-You have gained 3,500 Experience points!

-You have fulfilled the primary objective for the quest, "Mystery Fog over Erebus Lake"

-You have gained 2,500 Experience points!

-Congratulations, your heroic deeds have earned you the recognition of your peers.

-Your Reputation Rank is currently listed as 'Unknown Adventurer'

-You have unlocked a new ability "Sword Summon"

-"Sword Summon" has been added to the skills and abilities list.

-You have obtained Level 6, Congratulations!

-Three Cockatrice Raptors have been defeated.

-You have gained 1200 Experience points!

-Four Cockatrice Raptors have been defeated.

-You have gained 1600 Experience points!

- You have a total of 19,800 Experience Points

Level 6. Not too bad, thought Dante. Now if he could just manage to stay alive and continue to gain a few experience points here and there, just maybe he'd have a shot at getting home. In addition to the level up he had also unlocked Sword Summon. Dante flipped to the skills and abilities section of the tome and found three abilities had been magically scrawled onto the pages, each one listed in the order in which he had unlocked them. He read the entry for the newest ability.

"Sword Summon – The Sword Disciple's most trusted and valued ally and friend is his sword. Some would even go so far as to say a disciple's sword is a representation of his soul. Whether that particular idea is true or not is hard to say however one thing is certain, a Sword Disciple and his weapon undoubtedly share a bond that cannot be easily broken or abandoned and as a result the two always seem to find one another should ever the need arise, a fact that appears to ring true for you as well. The continuous channeling of mana through your blade has especially attuned it to your spiritual energy and you are now able to summon the weapon to your side instantaneously if ever it is separated from you."

Impressive. Sword Summon had never appeared in any of the video games. It didn't have many combat applications, but then again, in a world like Deos where being separated from your weapon could mean the difference between life and death, the ability was both practical and invaluable.

Scan, Lightspeed Slash and Sword Summon, he had three abilities now, and still not the slightest idea as to how he was unlocking them. Some unknown criteria determined what abilities he unlocked and when. None of it seemed wholly dependent on level or skills, but instead seemed to take into account his physical and emotional state as well. This was a pain, he shuddered at the thought of having to have a near death experience every time he learned a new ability. Dante mumbled a curse under his breath. He was so used to knowing what came next, at least when it came to Dragon Dale, that suddenly not knowing what to expect for his own character, or rather what to expect for himself, made him anxious. He closed the tome and it vanished in a flash of light. He would, he resigned, simply have to learn as he went, just as he had been doing and hopefully that would be good enough to get them all home in one piece.

The girls retreated into the tent while Shinto, Dante and Alex made themselves comfortable on their bed rolls. They were in a more hostile area now, so it was decided that they would take shifts standing watch throughout the night. Shinto volunteered to take the first shift, and together the three of them agreed that he would wake both Dante and Alex after a few hours so that they could relieve him and take the second half of the watch together.

Dante lay on his bed roll with his pack tucked under his head like a makeshift pillow and stared up at the dark Deosian sky. The sun, which had beat down on them relentlessly during the day had now vanished behind the western horizon. The twin moons were concealed by a cover of clouds and the multi-colored fireflies Dante had grown used to while on the other side of the lake were absent. He peered endlessly into the inky blackness of the sky, searching for some type of reason or meaning as to why or even how he could have ended up in such a horribly fantastic and otherwise utterly unbelievable situation, but in the end, he found only more and more darkness.

Within minutes Dante fell into a deep and restful sleep. Hours later he and Alex were still deep asleep and Shinto decided, against his better judgement, not to wake them until morning. The half-orc removed the large and heavy book he kept strapped around his waist, opened it to a page marked with a ribbon and then, by the light of the crackling fire, sat quietly reading to himself.

Even from a distance, Abilene Bay was a wonder to behold. From miles out and in the unforgiving brightness of day the city could not only be seen clearly, but it shone and sparkled like a far-off glittering jewel. It sat on the shore the

Tethys Sea, jutting out of the land like a great monument. It shielded behind city walls the tops of countless buildings and burgeoning towers. The sparkling waters of the Tethys lay to the city's east, ships and boats dotted the calm sea. The Great Obelisk Lighthouse, the tallest structure in the city and a marvel of the Deosian world, towered above it all.

It was roughly midday when the party arrived at the Northern Gate of Abilene Bay's outer

Wall, bleached white due to constant exposure to the sun. The wall stood three stories high, twice as tall as the walls had been in Illdershire. From a distance Dante had somewhat been able to see past them allowing him to steal a glimpse of the city beyond. However, now that he was within a few yards of the wall's base, everything that they had been seeming to magically hold within their confines had all but disappeared, as the wall seemed to rise up like a stone tidal wave threating to crash down on Dante and the others, washing them away in one violent and fell swoop. The idea of this in general made Dante's stomach churn, though he did not share this sentiment with anyone else in the party. There was a sense of great excitement among the group as they approached. And they were not alone. Many others all made their way into the city of Abilene Bay at the same time. Merchants, travelers, adventurers, Deosians of all kinds jostled to enter Abilene Bay so many that Dante and the others found themselves in line awaiting their turn to talk to the gate guards and enter the city.

"When we get to the front," said Shinto, "the guards will ask you to state the nature of your business here in Abilene Bay. Do not worry, it is just a formality." He warned before any of the could offer protest. "Abilene Bay is a politically neutral city-state. Many travelers come in and out of their gates daily, but the city guard still keep tabs on who's coming into the city by asking this one simple question. All you need to say is that you have come to register at the Adventurer's Guild."

They were surrounded by a throng of people, some of them with large wooden wagons packed with goods pulled by large beasts of burden. Dante saw and smelled a zebu. It was being led via rope by a leathery skinned dwarf who had the creature packed down with bags and sacks filled with potatoes. He saw an old lady with a couple of moufflon. A couple of half-orcs. A large number of humans, more dwarves, half elves, high elves and even a few dark elves. All of them stood in line, clinging desperately to the shade of the city's looming white walls, waiting patiently to enter Abilene Bay.

It did not take long before Dante and the others did indeed find themselves in the front of the line. Which was good, because even in the shade Dante felt as if he were sweating away pounds simply standing there in dark leather armor. The gate in which they walked through was the equivalent of a large set of twin arches carved directly out of the limestone wall. Each arch, roughly fifteen feet high and nearly wide enough to fit a tank through. The two arches were being used, if perhaps not designed, to direct the flow of traffic in and out of the city.

Dante stood at the threshold of the arch on the left, designated for travelers who were entering, while the right arch was assigned for travelers leaving.

At the crest of the arch Dante could see a large wood and metal door ready to drop down at a moment's notice shutting off access to the city should the need arise. He assumed the same type of door was built into the structure of the other arch as well and a similar set up was undoubtedly implemented on each of the gates that allowed access into Abilene Bay.

"Name?" Said a gruff voice in a rather short and impatient tone.

Dante's eyes drifted towards an intricate and detailed decorative trim that ran along the border of the archway. It was a six-inch-wide raised stone relief mural which seemed to have been carved, by hand, directly from the limestone itself. The humanoid images within the relief transitioned smoothly from one scene to the next as if the mural was telling some type of story, either about the founding of the city or perhaps even the founding of Deos itself.

"Name!?" Said the voice again this time sounding much more impatient and much more gruff than it had the first time.

The suddenness of the voice snapped Dante to attention, and he looked down from the relief to see a surly and generally annoyed dark-skinned guard staring back at him.

The guard was a middle-aged human man with a stern expression and a clean-shaven face. He wore a bronze chest plate covering his torso and shoulders, but left his arms and legs exposed. Underneath the armor was a bright crimson tunic that easily reached to his knees, while bronze and leather greaves and vambraces covered his shins and forearms. On his head, apparently meant to serve as a helmet, was a leather and bronze faceguard that covered his forehead and ran down the sides of his jawline, leaving the guard's hair and head exposed to the Deosian sunlight that beat down upon them even in the threshold of the city gate.

"Hathor curse me, if I have to ask your name again I'll have you dragged out of line and thrashed." The guard held a scroll and quill, apparently adding names to it with every new entrant into the city. An elven guard, dressed in much the same manner as the dark-skinned guard with the scroll, placed one hand on the hilt of the short sword that hung from his belt. With sudden alarm Dante's mind fluttered into action.

"Oh sorry, yes, um, my name is Dante Battle. Sorry about that, it's my first time here..."

"What a surprise," growled the guard, his eyes dropping to his scroll. "And the reason for your visit?"

"I've come to register at the Adventurers' Guild."

"Of course, you have," mumbled the guard, "cursed adventurers, always holding up the line." He waved Dante further into the gate with an aggressive jerk of his head. "Go on inside and stay out of trouble."

Dante passed the threshold of the city gates and almost as if by magic the marvel that was the city was laid out before him. Abilene Bay was a sprawling mass of buildings and people. Intricate stone monoliths of limestone and sandstone stretched towards the sky. Stone boxes filled with thick and luscious vegetation lined the streets. Bright green bushes sprouted the most colorful and beautiful flowers Dante had ever seen, while tall slender trees stretched up towards the sun and out towards the ocean, their large, oversized palm leaves swaying in the breeze. The subtle scent of the sea lingered in the warm Deosian air. The overall effect was that of a coastal paradise; etched from stone and cultivated by hand.

The citizens of Abilene Bay were as impressive as its architecture. A myriad of races, made up mostly of dark-skinned humans moved hurriedly among the buildings and streets. Most of them dressed in brightly colored tunics, robes and an assortment of layered cloths. A combination of textured fabric and exposed skin appeared to be the standard form of dress among the locals, no doubt developed in part to combat the temperate ocean side city climate. Some among the crowd deviated with leather and metal armor, and others with the traditional cotton shirts and trousers, or perhaps skirts and dresses that Dante had seen more commonly in the smaller towns and cities back further west. In the near instant since entering through the city gate, Dante could identify Dwarves, Elves, Half-Elves and the most Half-Orcs, Saurians and Kalgari he had seen in one place. Not to mention the numerous amount of humans, the majority of which were all cascading shades of sun-kissed brown. It was clear that Abilene Bay was a melting pot of cultures and at the same time, a world all its own.

"Follow me," said Shinto, stepping out into the Abilene Bay street with the same amount of alacrity and sureness that he possessed in the Deosian wilderness. They walked on the sidewalk, while large animals that seemed to be a Deosian interpretation of horses, camels and hornless deer marched up and down the roadway pulling carts or holding riders.

"This is the main road through the city, it continues east, eventually leading to the Bay and as a result the Tethys Sea," said Shinto unprompted, once again reverting back to his professor like demeanor. "For the most part Abilene Bay is split into a few key districts. To the north," he said, motioning across the street to the left side of the road, "is the Sea Side District, it is the more affluent half of the city and is frequented mostly by Abilene Bay's wealthy and powerful merchant class. While to the south," Shinto looked towards his right momentarily facing the building that sat to the right of them and the countless others that lay beyond them, "is the River Side district, it is where the workers live. Each district is made up of its own wards but the easiest way to navigate the city is to remember that the further south you are off the main street the more seedy the area becomes and if you wander too far it can become dangerous, and likewise the further north you move from the main street the more opulent and expensive the area becomes and similarly if you wander too far north it also can become dangerous."

"Well, that's both interesting and alarming," said Robyn, staying close to the group.

The two sides of the street looked to Dante to be nearly identical, yet and still he had a clear understanding of the point Shinto had been making. Deosian cities it seemed, were not all that different from the cities of Earth, at least in some regards.

"If we continue east along the main road as if we were headed toward the bay, we'll eventually run into an area the locals refer to as Market Street. This is important only because the guild halls can be found there, specifically the Adventurer's Guild."

The party continued moving east along Abilene Bay's main road, flowing with the foot traffic of the city's residents, trying as best they could to not look like tourist from another world, but instead, young adventurers determined to register at the guild and begin their life as freelance heroes.

The group had been on the road for days on end with no real time to rest or regroup. They had spent nearly every day marching as far as their legs would carry them; fighting when they had to and spending their nights sleeping outside in the dirt, near an open fire. As a result, they now all looked worn-down, dirty and exhausted. The excitement of reaching Abilene Bay had washed away some of the feeling for them, but it had not washed away the look. They hadn't really noticed it themselves but as they walked down the main road, the citizen of Abilene Bay had formed a makeshift bubble around them, an invisible and imaginary boundary in which they would not pass, giving the adventurers a wide berth considering that they both looked and smelled as if they had been through hell and back.

Dante was only slightly aware of the extra space the group had been allotted. Most of his attention was focused on Shinto who he noticed played the role of a Deosian tour guide that could heal wounds, teach magic, forage for food and slay ogres all with relative and carefree ease, and he did it seemingly without expecting anything in return. He couldn't help but wonder as to why anyone would go so far out of their way to help anyone the way Shinto had helped them. If the roles had been reversed, he couldn't help but ask himself, would he had done the same.

"Abilene Bay is a very large city," said Shinto, still lecturing the adventurers as they walked, "It is rather easy to get lost here. I advise you all to stick together when possible and at the very least find a central location where you can meet should you get separated. People tend to believe that there is less danger within the confines of city, however that is not always the case."

For a brief moment Dante felt foolish for ever having believed the lie that he had been trapped in a video game, looking about the city he realized that there was no way that the world around him could be mistaken for anything other than a living breathing entity far beyond the scope of not only any modern computer program, but perhaps even beyond that of human imagination. All around him people of different races, fantastical races engaged in the activities of everyday city life in ways that he could recognize but never could have truly understood had he not seen it with his own eyes. Three Elven women, all tall and beautiful, carried on a conversation in a language he could not understand. Two large half-orc men passed them going the opposite direction almost trampling him in the process. A kalgari women that he made eye contact with winked at him prompting him to quickly look away. A human man in rags rattled a tin cup in the hopes that some passerby would drop a coin or two inside. A group of dwarves laughed heartily at a joke that Dante did not catch and in the distance, he swore he could hear the metallic ping of a blacksmith at work and smell the sweet aroma of fresh baked bread. He understood now why they had been dropped in the middle of the Illdershire plains, had they entered Deos here in Abilene Bay, there was no way they would have been able to swallow the idea of this place being a video game. No matter how much they would have wanted to.

The streets of Abilene Bay were littered with not only burgeoning green gardens but also large sculptures and statues, each one expertly carved from limestone. Most of the statues were of large animals, muflon or zebu, always in a seated or prone position and usually back-to-back and paired with another structure Dante recognized as an obelisk, a tall, four-sided pillar topped with a pyramid. Unlike the animal statues the obelisks were always made of a glassy black obsidian, each one was etched with a combination of gold lettering and pictographs.

It took a few minutes before Dante realized that the obelisks were simply road signs. The words etched into the stone were street names and their corresponding direction. The words "Atka Streetway" and a golden arrow pointed Dante to a road perpendicular to the one that he was currently on and if followed would have taken him further north into the cities Seaside district, while another arrow and the words "Bahl Croft Parkway" pointed him in the opposite direction and deeper into the Riverside district. The pictographs that accompanied words seemed to be some type of hieroglyphic language that Dante could not read or understand, but assumed it simply relayed the city's street names to its citizens that could not read the writing of the common-tongue.

Soon they came to the most arresting structure of all. Thick stone columns formed an entry way leading to a large distinctive building whose thirty foot tall double doors bore the image of a woman a painted bright caramel with high cheekbones, full lips, large eyes and long wavy hair nearly the same golden-brown as her skin. She was decorated with a golden crown shaped like the sun and had a number of golden rings around her neck as well as large gold hoops hanging from both of her ears.

"Who... who is that?" asked Morrigan awestruck.

"That is Hathor the Sun Goddess." Shinto stopped walking once he noticed that each of his pupils had stopped to gawk at the mural. "This is one of her many temples here in the city."

"One of many." Mumbled Alex.

"That's Hathor?" Dante was surprised at what he was seeing. Women, dressed in much the same manner as Lin had been in Harrington, could be seen passing in and out of the slightly open doors of the temple. From the partially open-door Dante could just barely see inside to a brightly lit and open hall at the end of which appeared to be a giant statue, another iteration of the mural only this time in all three dimensions.

"She kind of looks like you, Morrie," said Robyn looking up at the mural.

"Ummm... I don't know about that," said Morrigan.

Dante stared into the temple through the slightly open doors. The statue like the mural was draped in gold. The crown, the neck bangles, the earrings, all had been placed on the twenty-foot-tall idol, and it all glistened and sparkled under the light of the sun as if at any moment the statue would come to life and look down at him with real eyes. He had never seen an actual depiction of Hathor before and even in the form of a carved stone, she was beautiful.

"Let us continue on our way." Prompted Shinto ushering them along passed the temple and back onto the street. They walked on in silence for another ten minutes taking in the sights and sounds of the city before their half-orc guide stopped them abruptly.

"We're here." said Shinto, presenting the section of the city in front of him. "Market Street."

They stood before an enormous open-air bazaar where a large number of wooden stalls held the goods and wares of enthusiastic vendors, all of whom seemed to be in some stage of either display, negotiation, or trade with a nearby customer. The area was the size of a football field, crowded stalls covering every inch of it.

Outside the perimeter of the market were rows of buildings, some of them larger shops that could not be contained in stalls, but most of them were guild halls, large intricate buildings held by groups of specialized merchants or craftsman. Guild members worked together to determine the standards for their industries and help to influence the way trade was conducted on certain goods. In general, the guilds worked, first, in the best interest of its members, and then, the city-state in which the guild was based, but in the case of the Adventurer's Guild things were different.

The Adventurers' Guild did not act in the best interest of any particular member, nor did it act in the interest of any particular nation. It was the role of the Adventurers' Guild to act on behalf of all of Deos and in the best interest of all nations. For that reason the guild served more so as a centralized information hub that dispatched the mercenary like adventuring guild members all across the continent in an effort to assist any nation, city or town that was in need of a skilled warrior to come risk life and limb for the promise of coin and a little bit of glory. As a result, there was an Adventurer's Guild Hall in each of the major city-states, Dalgonia, Oningrad, El Arden Ka and Abilene Bay and while Abilene Bay had the largest of the four they all were interconnected which meant registering at any one of them made you a member in good standing at every Adventuring Guild Hall across the continent.

They stood at the steps of a large three-story building that reminded Dante of the old county courthouse buildings back home. Stone columns stood in support of a Corinthian style pediment which bore the relief of multiple figures, each one in the guise of a classical adventuring job class. A mage, a warrior, a bard, a cleric, an archer, and a rogue.

"The Adventurers' Guild," said Shinto, "inside you all can apply for an adventuring license, this will make it a bit easier for you to maneuver around Deos not to mention earn coin. Hopefully this helps get you one step closer to finding the person you're looking for and getting you all back home."

"Why does this sound like a goodbye?" asked Robyn.

"Because it is." Morrigan spoke before Shinto could reply.

The half-orc smiled displaying more of his bright white teeth in addition to his oversized tusk. "You are correct. Our time together *is* coming to an end, but before it does, I have an errand to run inside the city. I'll meet you all back here once you are done inside the guild hall and we can wait till then to say our goodbyes."

The first floor of the guild hall was mostly inaccessible to Dante and the others. They could enter the lobby but everything beyond that was locked behind great wooden doors that only opened for active members of the Adventurer's Guild. Dante noted that there were no guards that kept the doors closed, but instead they were all operated by magic. Evidently, a powerful enchantment had been cast on them that recognized active guild members and allowed them to pass yet stayed tightly sealed for anyone else. A number of more seasoned adventurers passed through the lobby at their leisure, the doors on the floor opening with ease at their touch, but when Dante or Alex or Robyn or Morrigan tried to pull open the largest set of double doors that sat directly in front of the halls entrance, they wouldn't budge. At one point Alex tried to piggyback on another adventurer entering the double doors. An olive-skinned female mage was even kind enough to hold the door open for him, but when Alex got close to crossing the threshold, his feet became heavy and his body started to lock up as if his muscles had become laced with concrete. The mage, upon realizing what was happening, rolled her eyes.

"New Adventurers must register on the second floor before you can enter the drinking hall." She said before letting the wooden doors swing shut behind her. Once the doors slammed close, Alex's body was released, and he found himself able to move once again.

The second floor of the guild hall looked a lot like the Dragon Dale equivalent to the Department of Motor Vehicles. Several long lines of people sectioned off by a labyrinthine series of ropes snaked their way to a room-length counter at the far end of the hall. Dante's heart sank, this had never been a part of any of the Dragon Dale games and he could see why. Everyone standing in line looked bored enough to turn to stone.

"Hi, welcome to Adventurer Affairs, how can I help you today?" said an upbeat female voice. It was a young red-haired dwarf standing at the entrance of the room. She held her hands behind her back and leaned up onto the balls of her feet as she spoke the word 'help'.

Oh hello," Dante responded a bit taken aback by both her initial presence, which he had failed to notice when he first walked in, and by her general cheeriness which seemed to be radiating from her in spades. "We've come to register as adventurers." He said reluctantly as if in the hopes of not saying it incorrectly.

"Outstanding, four brave new adventurers joining our ranks today, how exciting!" the dwarf said loudly.

Dante looked around the room, it was filled with people standing in line waiting to talk to someone behind the counter. He had no way of knowing what their issue of concerns were, but he imagined that at least maybe half of them were new adventurers as well. Had she gotten this excited every time someone announced they came in planning to join the guild?

"Well," said the dwarf, "My name is Ariana, and I am here to assist you. Are the four of you getting registered together?"

"Um, yes." Said Dante "We've been adventuring together for quite some time now."

"Yes, I can see that." Said Ariana cheerfully. "Well, if you all are already a close-knit group and you are here to register anyway, why not form an adventuring company?"

"An adventuring company?" said Alex.

"Yes," said Ariana just as excitedly as before, "There are so many benefits to registering as an adventuring company, greater access to the guild hall, access to quests with larger rewards and not to mention a higher probability of survival. You know what they say, 'Adventure with friends, see it to the end. Adventure unaided and only horrible pain and a gruesome death await thee.'"

"Well, that got dark fast," said Morrigan in a low voice.

"Is that really how that saying goes?" asked Dante.

"Oh yes very much so," answered Ariana with a smile, "It's in old expression coined by Magnar the Terrible back in the second age, they had such a way with words back then." Ariana giggled. "Adventuring history is a bit of a hobby of mine, but anyway, new adventurer registration and adventuring company registration starts with the line to my right, you can handle both at the same time for the sake of convivence and efficiency, just hand these forms to the clerk along with your spirit tome and they will get you all taken care of. Thank you for visiting the Adventurer's Guild I have greatly enjoyed speaking with you today. Happy adventuring!"

Dante took the rolls of paper that the young dwarf produced, seemingly out of thin air, and he and the others stepped into the designated line as directed.

"Look," said Robyn pointing to a pair of large signboards attached to the wall on the far side of the room. "It's a board listing the names of some of the adventuring companies."

There were two boards, one for top ranked companies and another for newly created companies. The top ranked board had ten names listed on it, each one numbered from one to ten, with the number one company, The Sword Hounds, sitting at the top. Beneath them was Alssariq and coming in third was a group called the Longfellow Adventuring Company. Near the bottom of the list in ninth place was a name that Dante was sure he had heard before, Myrmidon Adventuring Company.

There were also ten names listed on the newly created company board as well and while they were not numbered there was still one near the top that stuck out to the group above all others. The Dyrtous Adventuring Group.

"Guys, I think we should start our own Adventuring Company," said Alex.

"Why?" asked Morrigan, "we're already stuck together, and we don't plan on being here long enough to reap the benefits."

"I don't know," said Robyn, "I like the idea of starting an AC, it sounds pretty cool."

"Yeah, but we're not living in a world of cool any more, we're living in a world where its normal for people to die gruesome deaths filled with horrible pain." Morrigan responded. "This AC sounds like a distraction."

"Yes, but I had a thought," said Alex. "What if there are more people like us, what if there are more gamers that don't want to stay trapped under Pope and the Dytorus Corp, we could create an AC that kind of lets other gamers know that we're out here, I mean there has to be more than just the four of us trying to find a way home."

"That's actually a good idea," Morrigan admitted.

"I'd have to agree." Said Robyn, "I'm impressed."

"Well, it's not like it's the first good idea I've ever had," said Alex, embarrassed.

"So, we'll register as individual adventurers, and we'll register as a company as well." Dante confirmed. "I imagine that's what each of these scrolls are for." Dante unrolled one of the pieces of parchment and found what looked like a mostly blank character information sheet. There were open fields for entries such as name, class, level, race, age and a number of other fields that were standard fare for the run of the mill video game character. . Of all the things Dante had experienced since entering Deos, nothing he could recall, seemed more off putting then realizing that even fantasy worlds filled with monsters and magic still had paperwork and forms that had to be filled out and filed in order to get certain things done.

"Welcome to Adventurer Affairs how can I help you?" asked the clerk behind the counter once they finally made it to the front of the line. He was a half-elf male with slightly tanned skin and long chestnut brown hair. He used nearly the exact same words as the dwarf at the entry way, however his rendition came out far less enthusiastic then his dwarven counterpart.

"Hi, we would like to register as adventurers and go ahead and register as an adventuring company as well." Dante said this time with a bit more confidence and clarity then he had earlier. "Ariana told us we could do both here, she gave us these scrolls."

"Ah yes, Ariana," said the clerk, "Our very own little sparkling ray of happiness." He said flashing a smile, taking the scrolls then looking down at them all while speaking in a tone of unmistakable sarcasm.

"Um, yeah, she was great." Dante said a little confused.

"Names and Spirit Tomes please," said the clerk without looking up from the scrolls Dante had just handed over. A large feather quill began scribbling frantically across the parchment as the clerk filled in blank fields, even though Dante hadn't given him any pertinent information.

Dante and the others conjured their tomes into existence and sat them on the counter in front of the clerk each of them providing their names in the process. The clerk grabbed each of the booklets individually and thumbed through them referencing information from each book to fill in the remaining fields for the corresponding scroll. The clerk moved with unnatural speed, his hands moving over the scrolls and tomes with the dexterity and agility of Las Vegas card dealer, only faster. After only a couple of minutes he pushed the spirit tomes back across the counter.

"Each of you sign here, initial here and place your spirit signet here." The clerk pushed the documents forward and pointed to the specified points of interest.

"What's a spirit signet?" Dante asked.

The clerk took a deeply exaggerated breath. "It's the unique signature of your individual spiritual energy. You use it to seal contracts and agreements of a magical nature. Just take you thumb and press it against the parchment inside this box." The clerk pointed to a small box at the bottom of the scroll.

"Oh ok, I can do that." Dante replied.

"Yes," said the clerk rolling his eyes, "I'm sure you can."

Dante, Morrigan, Robyn and Alex completed the scrolls with their signatures, initials and thumb prints as instructed and then passed them back to the clerk.

"Well then, congratulations and all that, you all are now full-fledged members of the Adventurer's Guild with all right and privileges thereof. Now for the adventuring company." The clerk pulled out a large scroll from behind the counter and unfurled it Infront of the party, it rolled from the countertop to the floor, every inch of the parchment covered in writing.

"These are the Adventuring Companies currently active in Deos at this time, please take a moment to review this list and ensure that you do not want to join an already existing company before starting a new one."

Dante allowed his eyes to scan over the list, there were hundreds of names.

"Thank you, but I think we're going to stick with starting a new company."

"Excellent," said the clerk dryly raising his eyebrows in disdain. "in that case, before we go any further do you all have any crystals that you would like to declare? If you happen to have any, now I can count them towards both your individual adventuring ranking as well as your newly formed company rank."

"Crystals?" said Dante caught a bit off-guard.

The clerks eyes narrowed and he looked as if he were trying to stare daggers directly into Dante's heart in an attempt to either erase him from existence or to get him to spontaneously burst into flame right there on the spot.

"Mana crystals, the small blue gems that the monsters drop and that people like you turn into people like me for gold and prestige. It's the entire foundational basis of the adventuring economy. It's about to be your primary source of income outside of doing quest." Said the clerk, he now appeared to be obviously losing his patience.

"Ah yes, yes mana crystals, I'm sorry I didn't realize this is where we... declared them. Give me one moment we do actually have some crystals." Dante reached into his coin pouch where he had been keeping the mana crystals he had been collecting along their journey. He dropped a handful of small blue gems on the counter in front of the clerk, and then from his pack he pulled out and added to the pile a large blue gem from which had been pulled from the alpha raptor they had slain over a week ago. Dante held back only the wolf fang shaped blue crystal that he had found after their first encounter in Deos.

"Where did you get these?" The clerk seemed impressed for the first time. He pulled out a loupe, a cross between a monocle magnifying glass, jammed it onto his eye and bent down to take a closer look at the crystals.

"We've just been coming across them as we've been travelling, we got the big one from the Alpha Raptor outside of Illdershire."

"Exterminators in Illdershire, you're saying that was you?" asked the clerk looking up from the gem with the loupe still wedged into his right eye.

"Yes, well us, and a few others. No one else seemed interested in the mana crystals, so I've just been holding on to them."

"Yes, I bet you have," said the clerk. He removed the loupe from his eye, placed it into his shirt pocket and pulled from behind the counter a brass balancing scale. Into one tray he dropped all of the small mana crystals and into the remaining tray he began to add small brass weights until the two trays sat parallel to one another, both trays suspended in mid-air.

The large crystal the clerk raised up and down in his hand a couple of times, ballparking the weight of the gem in his head before scribbling a figure on to the fifth scroll that had apparently been reserved for registering new adventuring companies. Immediately afterwards, the clerk reached underneath his counter once again and pulled out small wooden box, which he filled with multiple stacks of newly minted gold coins.

"Your payout is 2,500 gold," said the clerk, pushing the box across the counter. Robyn shoved Dante aside and grabbed the box with both hands.

"This is ours?" she asked in disbelief.

"Yes," said the clerk, "I have already subtracted adventuring company registration fees and guild dues, everything that remains belongs to you."

"Great!" Robyn had a wide-eyed grin, "I'll ensure that this is distributed properly amongst the group."

"As much as I would love this interaction to linger on into eternity, we need to conclude our business with some final items. First, what would you like the name of the new adventuring company to be?"

"Uh huh, I'm sure you will." Responded the clerk disinterestedly, a false smile plastered across his face. "Now as much as I would love for this interaction to linger on into eternity, there are only a few more items left for us to discuss in order to conclude our business here on today. Firstly, what would you like the name of the new adventuring company to be?"

"The name." said Dante, looking over at the other members of the group. "Did we have a name?"

The clerk let out a loud and audible sigh. Dante ignored it.

"Oh yeah, I was thinking about that." Said Alex somewhat excited. "I figured we would want to name the company something that signifies to other gamers that we're from Earth, but that also says that we're clearly separate from the Dytorus Corporation."

"Should it be something with Dragon Dale in the name?" suggested Morrigan, "You know, to remind people of the game?"

"No, I don't think so," replied Dante, "Remember Dragon Dale is a famous legend here in Deos. Using it in the name of an adventuring company might attract more attention from the locals than from the gamers."

"Maybe we could put Earth in there somewhere," suggested Robyn, "Maybe something like Earthling Infiltration Force?"

"Seems a bit intense but okay." Said Morrigan.

"Wait," said Dante "maybe that's actually it. Have you all noticed how no one in Deos actually says Earth?"

"Yeah, they always say Urth instead, no matter how many times we try and correct them." Alex responded.

"And they call us Urthlanders instead of Earthlings. I imagine they simply assume we're from another continent," added Morrigan.

"That's our in, I say we roll with it. Any other gamers who see the name should notice it immediately," said Dante.

"Great, so Urthlander Infiltration Force?" Suggested Robyn.

"I was thinking something a bit more subtle," said Alex, "Maybe just Urthlander Adventuring Company."

"Ah yeah, the Urthlander Adventuring Company, that has a nice ring to it," Dante said with a smile.

"Do we *finally* have a decision?" asked the clerk, visibly annoyed.

"Yes," said Dante confidently, "The name is the Urthlander Adven-"

"Which of you is Company Leader?" asked the clerk abruptly, cutting Dante off mid-speech.

"Company Leader?" repeated Dante.

"Oh Mylon, sweet god of death, please just come and take me now!" The clerk pleaded in a low and desperate voice.

"I think it's pretty obvious who the leader should be golden boy," said Robyn.

"Who?" asked Dante densely.

"You, you nerd" said Morrigan.

"Yeah man, I mean we've been basically following you this entire time. You're the only choice." said Alex.

"No, we've been relying on each other this whole time and I've made more than a few bad calls."

"Don't make it weird. You're the leader because no one else has a better chance of getting us back home. You're the best man for the job, now just accept it," said Morrigan.

"Yeah, I mean look at us, The Urthlander Adventuring Company with Black Wolf Dante as our company leader, it doesn't get any cooler than that." Said Alex gleefully.

"Company Leader, Black-Wolf-Dante." Said the clerk, writing directly onto the scroll as he spoke.

"Oh wait, no, no he was joking. It's just Dante, or Dante Battle, not Black Wolf Dante, that... that's just a nickname, you don't actually have to put that down."

The clerk looked up with a halfhearted smile and the look of murder in his eyes. "Yes, well unfortunately submissions cannot be modified."

"Yes, but we weren't really making a submission in that moment, he was just making a joke."

"Yes, well you all have been sitting here chatting for some ten minutes and the joke was not very funny, so unfortunately, as I said, submissions cannot be modified. Not without an official Transfer of Leadership request form submitted in triplicate at the *next* window." In one fluid motion the clerk produced from behind the counter a small round bauble that he quickly slammed down onto the scroll with force, leaving upon it the impression of a sword, staff and shield a symbol that Dante recognized as the Adventurer's Guild official stamp and seal.

"As I was saying," continued the clerk, "The Black Wolf's Urthlander Adventuring Company has *officially* been formed.

Chapter 33: An Adventurer's Life

Dante, Morrigan, Robyn and Alex walked out the front door of the Adventurer's Guild to find a waiting Shinto standing at the base of the guild hall steps.

"Hail adventurers!" called out the half-orc, greeting them with a warm and friendly smile. As they approached, Dante couldn't help but notice how happy Shinto appeared to be, how proud he looked. "Registration went well I hope."

"Umm... yeah. As well as could be hoped I guess." Dante replied.

"We created an Adventuring Company!" shouted Robyn excitedly.

"Very smart," Shinto chuckled, apparently amused by Robyn's enthusiasm, "the guild tends to favor young adventurers who are in companies, they assume you have a better chance of survival."

"So, we keep hearing." Replied Morrigan as she looked over her shoulder at the numerous other adventurers that past by them coming to and from the guild hall.

"Were you able to run your errand?" Alex asked Shinto.

"I did," responded the cleric.

"So, I guess this is goodbye?" added Dante,

"Of sorts," said Shinto.

"Did you get your souvenir?" asked Robyn. She motioned to an object, wrapped in cloth, that Shinto was holding loosely in his right hand. "Is that... a seashell?"

"Well yes... this *is* somewhat of a souvenir I suppose." He reached down and removed the cloth from around the object revealing a large conch shell. "It's called a Sending Shell, it's a magical item used to communicate over long distances. They come in pairs. When you speak into one, your voice can be heard clearly emanating from the other, and likewise, if the matching shell is spoken into, you will hear those same words emanate from this shell."

"So it's like a walkie-talkie?" said Alex. "We have those on Earth."

"Good, so I take it you all are familiar with the operation of such items? That is fortunate. As I stated, the sending shells come in pairs." Shinto said, carefully wrapping the cloth back around the shell. "One of the shells is in my possession, and the other shell I am giving to you. Now that you all have reached your destination, I must take my leave of you, as I have business elsewhere, however, if you find yourself in need of help do not hesitate to contact me using the sending shell."

"Thank you," said Dante, "We couldn't have made it here without your help."

"Yeah, we'd probably be dead in a ditch somewhere if you hadn't come along." said Robyn, prompting Dante and Alex to turn and stare at her blankly. "Well, it's true," she said in response to their judgmental stares.

"Thank you for all of your help *Master* Shinto." Said Morrigan, with a tight-lipped smile.

"The pleasure has been all mine." Shinto reached into his pack and pulling out a weather worn book from his belongings and gave it to Morrigan. "I've noticed," said Shinto, "that you don't have a spellbook. An essential item for any young mage. I found this at the same magic shop where I purchased the sending shells. It apparently belonged to an adventurer who favored elemental magic, a good fit for you, I think. They only wrote a couple of spells inside, leaving plenty of space for you to make you own additions, I also added a few notes of my own. I hope you don't mind."

Tears welled in Morrigan's eyes and she stood and hugged the half-orc around the neck.

"Thank you. I've been looking for a spellbook since we got here. I tried to buy one before we left Illdershire but apparently they have to be made with a special paper and bound in a certain way, and according to everyone I've asked a real genuine spellbook is very hard to find."

"This should serve you well until you have one of your own commissioned, the best place for that is El Arden Ka, but perhaps you all will have already made it back home before that becomes necessary."

Shinto looked at each of the Urthlanders in turn. "Well, fare thee well young adventurers, until we meet again, may fortune smile upon you." Then with a gentle nod of his head, the half-orc turned and disappeared into the crowd of busy Deosians that filled the streets of Abilene Bay.

Almost immediately after losing sight of him Dante couldn't help but feel an overwhelming sense of vulnerability. The party suddenly seemed like a raw and exposed nerve in a large and unfamiliar city.

"So now what?" asked Robyn.

"Now we try and find Sandberg, right?" suggested Alex.

"Right," agreed Dante, "We should probably start in the Adventurer's Guild, we can probably get into those doors on the first floor now. It looked like some kind of tavern room. We can ask around inside and see if anyone is familiar with an Urthlander named Sandberg," said Dante.

"Yes, well before we get into that," Morrigan cut in. "Perhaps we should find somewhere to rest first. It would be nice to put down all of this stuff," she motioned to Alex who was holding the furca, which inside the city now looked exceeding large and out of place. "We need to get ourselves cleaned up a bit as well. In a world that functions like a game, we don't look like the most charismatic characters right now. We don't want to frighten off someone who could help us."

"What do you mean?" asked Alex.

Morrigan stared at the dwarf who had dirt smudged across his face and the muck stuck in his beard and didn't bother responding. Dante on the other hand could see what she meant. He imagined, that if they were to approach random citizens in their current state and begin to question them on the whereabouts of some little known Urthlander they would come off as both desperate and possibly a little deranged... neither condition being very conducive in helping them achieve their goal.

"She's right." Dante agreed. "We should find somewhere to get cleaned up and maybe rest a bit before we start looking for Sandberg."

"Wait, I thought we wanted to try and find the game designer as soon as possible." Said Alex. "Before Pope does."

"We do," Dante responded, "but I also think we have to be smart about it. We may be stuck here for a few days before we find any leads as to where Sandberg could possibly be and based off what we saw on that board in the Adventurer's Guild we know Pope, or at least someone from the Dytrous Corporation is wandering around here as well. I think it may be best to proceed with caution. We don't want to attract to much attention to ourselves, and a group of dirty stinky adventurers aggressively asking about another adventurers is bound to attract attention."

Alex scratched his beard reflectively in consideration of Dante's argument. "That's a really good point. I see why we made you leader."

"It was my idea." Argued Morrigan through narrowed eyes.

"Oh right, of course... Yes, well I think you would make a good leader too." Alex said nervously.

"Hey what about me." Robyn said staring at Alex expectantly as if she too were awaiting a compliment. "I'd make a good leader too, right?"

"Oh yeah," Alex eyes darted from side to side in a desperate panic, "well... naturally I just assumed you would be playing the part of the group's treasurer. You know, considering how good you are with money."

Dante found himself startled and impressed by Alex's quick recovery and apparently so did Robyn. She beamed at his suggestion and now seemed more than content with her official position within the party.

"So, I guess that makes you what? The sergeant-at-arms?" said Morrigan, a hint of annoyance in her voice.

"The what?" said Alex.

"Oh, never mind," Morrigan responded dismissively. ", let's just go find an inn."

"Okay, so next question, where do we find an Inn?" asked Robyn."

"So, glorious leader," said Morrigan, "which way do you want to go?"

Dante let out a sigh, he was already beginning to regret allowing them to name him leader of the adventuring company.

"Let's head back east the way we came, we're at least somewhat familiar with that part of the city. When we can, I think we should try and veer north, maybe find an inn towards the nicer side of the city, but its best we stay as close as we can to Market Street. We have to keep in mind we'll be using the Adventurers' Guild as our primary source of info to try and find Sandberg."

"Alright," said Alex. "That sounds like a good plan. Let's do it."

The four adventurers moved east along the city's main road, leaving the hustle and bustle of Market Street behind them. The foot traffic in Abilene Bay was unceasing, somebody was always going somewhere, but after being exposed to the crowds posed by the open air bazaar that was Market Street, the main throughfare, while busy, suddenly seemed a lot more manageable.

"You know what? When we come back out to look around, we should probably try and see if we can upgrade any of our equipment," suggested Robyn. "I bet this place has some of the best shops you could think of. We probably should have asked Shinto for some recommendations."

"I wouldn't mind visiting a blacksmith shop," said Alex.

Dante thought about what he'd replace or upgrade if given the chance, and then thought he'd be better off focusing on finding an inn for them to sleep in for the next few nights. It was then he noticed that Robyn had slowed her pace as she walked and as she did, a group of elves walking in the opposite direction slid past their group. It was a tight squeeze, both the elves and the adventurers had to turn sideways to pass. Dante, suspicious that perhaps the group's treasurer was looking for an opportunity to increase the balance of the company's gold coffers tried to keep an eye on Robyn's hands as the elves passed, but to his surprise Robyn moved pass the elves all while graciously seeming to keep her nimble fingers to herself. Then without saying a word, in the middle of the walkway, she stopped to reach down and tie her boot. Two city guards walking behind them had to split themselves up to narrowly avoid colliding into the back of the party. They passed by on either side of the adventurers, giving them dirty looks.

"Are you okay?" asked Morrigan.

"I am." Replied Robyn popping up from a freshly tied boot. "Sorry about that. What were we talking about again?"

"Upgrading our equipment," Morrigan said, a look of concern on her face as she looked over at Dante.

"Ah yes, shopping, we should definitely make time for that." Robyn said with a smile as if now the conversation had gotten back on track.

Dante stared at her for a moment, concerned that their time in Deos had finally caused irreversible mental strain that was now manifesting in this new strange and erratic behavior. He resolved to monitor her closely as well as to find them somewhere comfortable to rest as soon as possible.

They walked on for another few minutes before Dante spotted the familiar intersection and obelisk road sign from before. Of course, all of the intersection and obelisks looked the same for the most part, but this one in particular stuck out to Dante as it was marked with two prone muflon laying back-to-back and the obelisk road sign directed them to Atka Streetway on the Seaside and Bahl Croft Parkway on the Riverside.

"Guys, I think maybe we should try here," Dante suggested when Robyn swiftly and abruptly cut him off.

"We're being followed," she said in a low voice. "Someone has been following us since we left Market Street."

"Are you sure?" asked Alex.

"Of course I'm sure. I used to shoplift remember, I think I know when I'm being watched, and I definitely know when I'm being followed. Besides, I checked. I snuck a peek behind us when the elves past by and what do you think I was doing when I was pretending to tie my boots."

"I thought you were tying your boots." Said Alex.

"No you dweeb," Robyn responded sharply. "I was stopping short to see how the person following us would react, and as I expected when we stopped suddenly, they stopped suddenly."

"So they could maintain their distance." Dante said with sudden realization as to what Robyn had been up to.

"Exactly," she said in agreement with his comment, "any normal person would have just passed us by like the guards did, but a tail never wants to get too close to their target. That was when I knew for sure."

"Is it someone you recognize?" asked Alex.

"No, they're wearing a hood, so I couldn't get a good look at their face."

"We need to figure out who's following us and why." Said Dante. "It could be one of Pope's men, or it could be some local member of the thieves guild-"

"There's only one thing left to do," said Robyn, cutting Dante off. Without warning she dashed down Atka Streetway and then at the first opportunity ducked into an empty alley. The others followed. Moments later the adventurers found themselves in a narrow corridor that sat behind two sets of buildings slightly off Abilene Bay's main street.

"Robyn, what are you doing?" Dante asked once he'd caught up to her.

"I'm taking your advice." She replied turning around to face the way they had come to enter the alley. "I'm figuring out exactly who has been following us."

A few seconds later they heard approaching footsteps at the alley entrance. Dante turned to see a small cloaked and hooded figure step cautiously into the alley.

The hooded figure was the size of a child and moved forward slowly, approaching them with the calculated caution of one who had been found out but had come to the conclusion that it was too late to turn back.

"Who are you?" Robyn called out. "And why are you following us?"

Without responding the cloaked figure reached up and removed the hood from its head revealing a familiar face.

"D-Danger Duke?" Dante muttered, squinting at the halfling barbarian in front of them. "Is that you?"

"What are *you* doing here?" Morrigan had an edge of irritation to her voice.

"We spotted you all on Market Street." Danger Duke responded. "I was ordered to follow you... or rather approach you all with a proposition."

"Ordered by who?" Dante asked, although he was confident he already knew.

Before Danger Duke could confirm his suspicions, a number of other figures entered the alley. One by one they begin to fill the tiny space, outnumbering Dante and his friends two to one. Dante, who had been expecting to see some of the gamers that had been with Danger Duke back in Black Water, didn't recognize any of them, that is until a tall, sharp-featured elf made his way into the alley followed at last by a smug and ever-smirking Pope.

"So we meet again," growled Pope.

Chapter 34: Executive Decisions

“What’s the latest update from the Deos Diver Team?” The man was middle-aged and wearing a navy-blue sharkskin suit. The suit was tailored, cut to make him look taller and slimmer than he actually was. He had a head of perfectly coiffed, dark brown hair greying gently at the sides, just enough, he felt, to make him look seasoned and wise as opposed to old and weathered. His skin bore only the slightest signs of his age, a few modest wrinkles near the corners of the eyes, across the rest of his face however, his skin was suspiciously smooth and tight, especially around the forehead and cheek area.

Sara sat in the corner of the boardroom next to Frank, her coworker from the observation room, and wondered why they had been requested, or rather mandated to join an executive-level board meeting with the President and Chairman of the Dytorus Corporation in attendance.

“Mr. Chairman, based off Captain Pope’s latest communication, received from the black fire brazier.” The executive nodded toward both Sara and Frank who continued to sit quietly in the corner. “Pope has made contact with a number of other parties in the city of Abilene Bay. He has now brought together a total of five adventuring parties. He’s currently operating with roughly 32 divers under his command,” said the executive. He wore a dull grey suit and Sara knew him as the VP of her department, Player Correspondence. He undoubtedly was the reason she and Frank had been required to attend, in case any question arose concerning the messages that had come through the black fire brazier, the executives would be able to go directly to the source.

“Of the 50 teams we sent into Deos, over half of them are currently unaccounted for and at least 28 gamers, 9 combat consultants and 4 game guides have been confirmed dead,” said another executive, this one is a pinstriped suit, who Sara recognized as the VP of her previous department, Character Creation.

“So, you are telling me that our head of security has rounded up 32 men, we’ve loss 41, and we currently have around 200 people in the wind?” asked the Chairman.

"Yes sir Mr. President that is correct and might I say this expedition is proving to be a considerable improvement over our previous excursions into Deos. Why, Pope's contingency alone shows a 4% increase in the survival rate," said another slightly younger executive, this one in glasses and a navy-blue suit, but one not nearly as nice as the chairman's.

"A 4% increase?" repeated the Chairman. His nostrils flared.

"Yes sir, and that only accounts for the group under Pope's command." The young executive looked down at some papers that he had printed out in front of him. "If we take into consideration the confirmed losses suffered, and then the 14 additional parties scattered throughout the continent that are intact yet currently deemed ineffective, and then acknowledge that while we have roughly 25 parties unaccounted for yet only half of them may be dead, and the other half may very well be still at least somewhat functional, we are possibly looking at an increased survival rate of an estimated..." The young executive flipped over his page. "36%."

"36 percent?" repeated yet another executive this one slightly balding, rather overweight and wearing a black suit. "Unprecedented!"

The black suited executive's comment prompted the other executives in the room to begin eagerly talking amongst themselves, their chatter rising to a low hum that filled the boardroom like a hive of excited insects. Sara glanced at Frank and was about to ask what exactly all the fuss was about when the chairman cleared his throat and raised a hand and in response, almost immediately, the chattering of the executives died down.

"This 4% increase that Pope has secured is phenomenal," said the Chairman. "And the possibility, however remote, of a possible 36% increase in the survival rate of our Deos Diver Participants is no less than remarkable, and I must say, is a testament to the hard work of everyone that is currently sitting in this room. But we must remember, what Johnson has just quoted to us is an optimistic estimate. We aren't there yet. I want us to stay optimistic but focused."

"Well said Mr. President," said the executive in the black suit.

"What else do we have?" asked the chairman, ignoring the black suited executive's comment.

The first executive cleared his throat. "Pope has also reported that one of the game guides he was traveling with was gravely injured, the subject in question, I have him listed here as... Stephen Choi, was pronounced dead after withstanding multiple injuries from a category five, carnivorous flora."

Sara let out a small cry and covered her mouth with her hands. A number of the executives looked in her direction, saw that she was not wearing a suit, and turned their attention back to Johnson who still shuffled his papers.

"Pope's report states that he personally confirmed Choi's heart stopped due to sustained injuries, yet due to magical technology present in Deos his body was placed in a state of suspended animation. Upon further investigation, the captain believes he has now found a lead to revive him." Johnson looked up from his documents, a self-satisfied smirk on his face. "I believe it goes without saying sir, this could lead to tremendous advances in modern medicine and big profits for Dytorus Corp." The chatter of the executives grew once again.

"The remaining mission objectives are still underway," said a short-haired woman in a dark green pants suit. "No progress has been made toward finding Sandberg at this time, but we are expecting a new report soon."

"Good, very good," said the chairman, "Very promising."

The boardroom erupted in chatter.

"This is shaping up to be the best expedition thus far. We are forecasting the recovery of some highly rare and valuable Deosian artifacts," said the pinstriped suit.

"The communications department has done an excellent job managing the social media accounts of the gaming participants in their absence. Online engagement is up by 16 percent, most of them are more popular now than before they went in," said the grey suit.

"This Captain Pope was a good investment. His tactical expertise in addition to whatever it is those gamers are doing has shown itself to be very effective," said the black suit with a laugh. "I smell a big bonus in the upcoming quarters."

"Are we at all concerned about the ethical dilemma we'd face, not to mention the legal one, if our methods involving the gamers and their stated deaths were to somehow become known to the public," said a female executive in a burgundy pants suit.

The buzz of chatter stopped, and slowly all heads turned to the chairman.

"Ethical dilemma?" said the chairman, interlocking his fingers in front of his face and then leaning into his hands as if in deep reflection, "I think," he began slowly, "that everyone in this room would agree that we, with this Deos Diver Project and the access we have to this brave new world, stand on the precipice of human achievement, on the forefront of bold discoveries, the likes of which the world has never seen, better yet, never even truly imagined." The chairman spoke with a kind of tempered enthusiasm, he leaned forward in his chair pressing fingertips against the table. "Now knowing that, knowing what we as a society stand to gain should we be successful, as well as what we stand to lose should we fail, *I* actually believe it would be unethical of us *not* to do everything within our power to guarantee the success of this project." Sara noticed the chairman decided not to address the issue of legality.

The chairman leaned back in his chair now, surveying the room, taking in the faces of his executive team and in the process noticed the two non-executive employees sitting in the corner of the room. He ignored them. Standing from his seat he began to slowly pace the room, "And yes," he threw his hands up in mock surrender, "in the midst of it all, we as a company stand to make a profit, but I would argue we alone as a company have shouldered all of the risk. We as a company invested the finances, the research, the manpower, the endless resources needed to make this dream a reality, and yet it will be all of humanity that will benefit." His enthusiasm was no longer tempered, and he ended all of his statements with a pointed finger and extra emphasis. "Make no mistake people, we *are* breaking new ground, we *are* saving the world, we *are* etching our names in the annals of human history, but that doesn't change the fact that we are indeed a company. A company that is fueling the dream, that is driving this world into a better tomorrow, Yes!" his pointed fingers had become balled fist. "But in order for us to continue the important work that we are doing here we *must* remember that this company has demands. And no matter what obstacle may stand in the way, be it physical, technical, financial, or yes even ethical, the demands of the company must be met!"

Chapter 35: Reunion

"Dante," said Pope wearing his usual smug and arrogant grin. "I'm glad to see that you're still alive."

"Pope!" said Dante through gritted teeth. The adventurer stepped in front of his friends and placed one hand on the hilt of his sword. He never imagined Pope would approach them so soon or so boldly. Now they were outnumbered and surrounded in an isolated alley. They could, he imagined, cut a swath through the couple of men that lay behind them maybe make a run for it, or, if he moved fast enough, he imagined he could possibly take Pope's head with a few well-placed Lightspeed Slashes. He'd probably die in the process, but he imagined the surprise on Pope's face when his sword came flashing at him to fast to sidestep and the idea alone felt almost worth it. With the slightest movement Dante loosened his sword from its sheath, revealing perhaps no more than half an inch of its blade to the open air.

"Ah ah ah, I wouldn't do that if I were you." Pope said. "There are very strict laws against drawing your weapons inside the city. The guards don't approve of fighting, and they come down pretty hard on anyone they find breaking the rules. Besides, I've only come to talk." Pope lifted his hands above his shoulders as if to display that he held no weapons and as a result, no ill intent. Dante knew better.

"What could *we* possibly have to talk about?" Dante asked, his hand still gripped tightly on the hilt of his sword.

"A mutual friend in need of our help."

"All of my friends are standing behind me and the only thing any of us need from you is a way back home, so unless you've come to talk about that, we have nothing to say to one another."

"Well, that's not completely true. We have one additional friend here among us, but he's not exactly standing." Pope allowed his eyes to fall upon the rose-colored jewel that hung down from Dante's neck.

Dante upon realizing the focus of the captain's attention, released his sword and instinctively grabbed hold to the dangling spirit crystal.

"Our dear friend Stephen is trapped inside that crystal, and I have found a way to revive him."

Dante's eyes narrowed in on the captain. "How?"

"On our way to Abilene Bay we met an old woman, a fortune teller. We helped her out along the road and as a reward she offered to help us in return. Isn't that how things work in this world, complete quests only to be rewarded with new quests. Well, I've found a quest that will allow us to save Stephen, all I need now is the jewel. That's where you come in."

Dante took a step back and immediately felt Alex, Morrigan and Robyn standing behind him. Their presence prompting him to strengthen his stance and grip the crystal even tighter than before, determined to protect both them and it from whatever Pope was planning.

"If you think I'm going to just hand over this crystal, then you're crazier than I thought," he said narrowing his eyes at Pope. "You expect me to believe that some random fortune teller told you how to perform a resurrection spell? After everything you've lied about, why would I trust anything you have to say?"

"Dante, you shouldn't take things so personally, and besides you don't have to believe me, you can speak with the fortune teller yourself. She is here in the city; I can take you to her."

"We're not going *anywhere* with you!" Dante didn't necessarily say the words, as much as spit them like poison from his mouth.

"Am I to believe that you would let your disdain for me allow us to miss out on the opportunity to bring Stephen back? Especially when all you have to do is come and speak with an old woman in the market district? I'm surprised Dante, that seems extraordinarily selfish of you."

Pope's words enraged Dante to such a degree that he could feel his skin flush hot with the sensation of rushing blood. He released the crystal and regripped the hilt of his sword, bending his knees slightly and feeling the churn of a magma-like energy stir deep within his gut. Dante was sliding his sword from its sheath when he felt a hand touch his arm. Coolness interrupted the hot and angry energy he felt flowing through him and he looked back to see Morrigan's hand resting on his bicep, a look on her face that explained her every thought without words.

Don't said Morrigan's eyes, *Not like this*. And as if he had been plucked out of the heart of the sun, Dante felt his body relax, and without argument he released his sword hilt and stood back to his full height.

"We'll go to Market Street and we'll speak to this fortune teller, but if your story doesn't check out, you're not laying a finger on this crystal."

"Fair enough." said Pope with a smirk.

Captain Pope turned around and left the alley his men following suit, each of them exiting the alley one by one, disappearing back into the city. Most of them smiled and smirked as they departed from Dante's group, laughing to themselves as they turned their backs on the four ostracized adventurers. Dante noticed, however, a few of them looked distraught, particularly Danger Duke, who did not seem to be the same person he had been in the tavern. Nor was the adventurer standing beside him, who after a moment Dante realized was the Kalgari they had also met in Black Water, the one they had called Mr. Wuddlekins, only now he was wearing an eye patch and had a large slice missing from one ear. They had been, at least from what Dante could tell, through some trying times since he had last seen them.

As the last of Pope's men left the alley Danger Duke, who had been lingering near the group without saying a word and oddly avoiding eye contact, slowly approached Dante and the others.

"Dante," said the halfling quietly, "Hernandez wanted me to give you a message. He says you were right, and that he's sorry for his part in all this."

"Hernandez? Where... where is he?" Dante asked, suddenly realizing that he did not see him in the alley among the others. "Did he break away from Pope as well, is he willing to help us get back home?"

Danger Duke's eyes dropped to the cobble stone road that paved the alley floor. His small body appeared to shrink even smaller in size. When he looked up his eyes had filled with tears, which he seemed to be desperately holding back.

"Hernandez is dead. He was killed in the Black Wood after we were attacked by some type of monster. H-he saved my life. In the end he mentioned you, asked me to tell you that you were right and that he was sorry, so now my job is done." A single tear escaped Danger Duke's eyes and he immediately turned and left the alley where he was joined by an awaiting Wuddlekins.

"Hernandez is dead?" Robyn repeated from behind Dante, her voice cracking under the weight of her words. "That can't be true. He's lying. Dante? You think he's lying too, right?"

"No," replied Dante solemnly. "I don't think he's lying, not about this."

Dante, Morrigan, Alex and Robyn followed Pope and his group of gamers, game guides and combat consultants back to Market Street. Many of his men dropped off as they moved back through the city towards the open-air bazaar, apparently taking up post at random positions around their designated section of Abilene Bay. By the time they arrived back at Market Street only about three of Pope's subordinates still followed him, Lansing, Corrine and the large half-orc.

Together the adventurers moved speedily through the loud and lively market stalls. They passed by barking vendors selling everything from handmade carpets, to meat so freshly butchered some of it still moved. Pope walked with the steely determination that had become nearly as signature to his demeanor as his arrogant smirk. They weaved in and out of traffic sliding in between stall after stall until they came to a small section of the marketplace where the wooden booths had given way to a much more modest set of vendors. These less prominent merchants had been given retail space directly in the center of the bazaar and sold their wares more humbly from blankets or carpets stretched out across the paved road, as opposed to the well-constructed wooden booths, canvas tents, or brick and mortar buildings that spiraled outward from the heart of Market Street towards the large elaborate guild halls on its outer edge.

There were six ground vendors located at the center of the market, most of them selling jewelry. Necklaces, bangles and rings all adorned with colorful semi-precious stones glistened in the sunlight. Strands of thin wooden beads, a fashion accessory worn around the waist by the women of Abilene Bay, lay stretched out, side by side, near rows of hats and head scarves. However, among the vendors whose carpet laid storefronts held but simple adornments, there was one more space which held nothing but a basket of flowers and a withered and pale elven woman, older it would seem then the Market Street itself. She sat crossed-legged and alone, gently rocking back and forth, muttering and giggling to herself while shuffling and arranging a sheaf of small parchment cards.

Dante sighed loudly with irritation. Why did he even entertain the thought of following Pope back here when he knew beyond the shadow of a doubt the man was a liar? Perhaps now they should cut their losses and just turn and leave. He was sure it was at least true about the guards not allowing fighting inside the city, which meant as long as they were in Abilene Bay they were actually safe from Pope and his men. All he had to do now was find a lead on Sandberg before Pope did.

Pope cleared his throat in an effort to get the old woman's attention. She apparently hadn't noticed eight people had walked into her retail space.

"You have returned." She said without looking up. Her voice sounded like she had rusty piano wire for vocal cords, a sound that could not be clearly defined as either a screech or a hoarse whisper, but instead something that seemed to dance melodically among the two. In-between her words there was a sort of painful shriek and moan that was just barely decipherable amid syllables, the initial sound of it made Dante shudder, but the idea of being repulsed by an elderly woman's voice made him feel guilty, as if he was being rude, so he forced any feelings of uncomfortableness to the back of his mind until he could find an excuse to take his friends and leave. "You have brought the boy; you have brought the crystal."

"I have," said Pope. "Now tell them what you told me, about how you know a way to restore our friend back to life from inside the crystal."

"He is not *in* the crystal," said the old woman. "He *is* the crystal. And yes, I know of a way to restore him. I know of a way."

"You know a way to bring him back from the crystal state back to his original state. You know how to restore life?" asked Dante, talking slowly, pointing at the old woman every time he said "you" and pointing at the necklace when he said "crystal".

The old woman was standing now, looking at Dante from behind a crooked nose. "Yes," she said without hesitation. "I know many things. Many great things." The old woman smiled and her wrinkled and cracked skin which hung placidly from her face seemed to wrinkle and crack even more from the strain of her doing so. Dante pushed the feeling of uncomfortableness even further into the back of his mind and gave the woman a half-hearted smile in return.

"How do we know you just didn't put her up to this?" Dante said to Pope. "You want me to believe that you can walk into the city and bump into someone that can pull off a resurrection spell?" Dante turned to look at his friends who were standing behind him, "What's to stop us from just walking into a temple and asking some high-level cleric to do the same thing if it's that simple?"

"You are a smart boy," said the old woman, "smart enough to know that magics such as these are forbidden by the four cities. You will find no help in the temples, only castigation. But, you are correct, it is not easy. It is a very complicated ritual. But I see what you need is proof." The old woman looked at Alex, Morrigan and Robyn almost as if acknowledging them for the first time. "I see that all of you are in need of proof." The old woman smiled her cracked and wrinkled smile. "Shall I tell your fortunes? Yes? A fortune for each of you. That will be proof enough. That will allow you to have faith in what an old mother knows."

Ever since they had left Midell the temperature seemed to have increased dramatically. It was hot in Abilene Bay, and it felt even hotter in the marketplace and the last thing Dante wanted or needed was to stand around in the sweltering heat doing whatever *this* was. He felt himself losing his patience.

"No, I don't think that's necessa-" before Dante could finish his sentence, the old woman reached out with speed and grabbed him by the collar of his armor pulling him close to her with surprising strength. By the time Dante understood what was happening the old woman's lips were uncomfortably close to his ear.

"The boy has lost his mother, a tragedy for any child, but not only his mother but his brothers as well, for when the eldest brothers are at war where does that leave the younger? Ah, yes it leaves him alone. Alone and in the dark. In the dark, hoping and wishing that he was anywhere but where he was. So, the boy runs. Runs from what he has earned, runs from what he has made, runs from himself, the boy runs home. Runs home and sits in the dark, hoping and wishing that things could be as they once were. Hoping and wishing that he can escape to a world like the world of his youth, but the boy must be careful for that which what he wishes. For now, the boy has escaped one world for another and still he runs. Why? The boy does not know, but a mother knows. Yes, an old mother knows. It is because the boy yearns and he hungers. Like a ravenous wolf he hungers and will not stop running until he finds what he searches for, be it this world or the other, be it this life or the one after."

In a voice reminiscent of creaky metal and distant screams the old woman had just told Dante something that he equated less to a fortune and more to a series of dark secrets that he had, for the months, personally been attempting to avoid acknowledging let alone allow to be vocalized by a stranger. Dante's blood ran cold and suddenly the heat, the exhaustion, even the idea of being trapped in another world all seemed inconsequential. Instead the only thing Dante felt was exposed. Then, before he could respond, she moved on to the others, whispering in the ears of each of his friends. As she spoke to each of them in turn, he watched the color drain from their faces and a wobble set in their knees and he wondered if he had looked as horrified when she had been talking to him. He felt frozen in place watching the old woman, still stunned by her words. How could she have known to say such things? There was a chance that Pope could have known about his mother perhaps, it was public information, but what about his brothers? What about the feelings of loneliness, isolation, of desperation? How could she have possibly known all of that? Hell, those were things Dante still didn't understand himself.

The old woman hobbled back to her blanket, smiling innocently. When Dante looked over at his friends they were looking nearly as dumbfounded as him. Robyn, still distraught over the news of Hernandez had tears in her eyes, while Morrigan stared blankly at the ground. Alex looked up and made eye contact with him and nodded, he too looked shaken but seemed to understand that there was more at play here than Pope pulling a con. The world of Deos was filled with powerful and terrible magic of all shapes and kinds, and perhaps it was not too farfetched to think perhaps this old woman really was some type of fortune teller, and if she was telling the truth about that, then maybe she was telling the truth about being able to help Stephen as well. And if there existed in this world a chance to save a life that had been left in their hands, didn't they owe it to him to at least try?

Then Morrigan spoke up. "To bring Stephen back, what is it that you need to do?"

The old woman giggled, the same way she had when she thought she was alone with the cards. "No, my child, it is not what I must do, it is what you all must do. The ritual of restoration is complex. You must have the crystal, the knowledge, and the components for an elixir necessary to complete the restoration. You all have provided the crystal. Mother provides the knowledge as well as *most* of the ingredients for the elixir, however there is one component left that we do not have."

"You never mentioned a missing component before," said Pope.

"What's missing?" asked Dante, "Maybe we can fan out and find it here on Market Street, you're supposed to be able to buy anything in Abilene Bay."

"The last item we seek is something that can only be retrieved by the most capable adventurers. It is a flowering herb called a death's head rose, and it only grows deep within the heart of the Hell Hearth Swamp. You must journey there, collect the rose and bring it back here to me, with it I can complete the elixir of renewal and in so doing the ritual of restoration that will bring your friend back to life."

Almost immediately Pope turned toward the half-orc. "Gather the others and tell them to prepare to depart for the swamp tomorrow morning."

"Wait a minute," said Dante. "What are you doing?"

"I'm preparing to go on an expedition into the swamp to retrieve the flower. What else?" said Pope, annoyed, and perhaps for the first time ever from Dante's point of view, ill-prepared.

"The four of us traveling into the middle of the wilderness with you and all of your men seems like a great way for us to walk into a trap and get ourselves killed," said Dante. "Excuse me if I don't exactly trust you, but there is no way we are going into Hell Hearth Swamp with you and your lackeys."

"Then please, by all means feel free to stay here, we'll retrieve the flower and bring it back for the ritual."

"The crystal," interrupted the old woman. "The only way to find the flower is with the crystal, whoever goes to the swamp seeking the death's head rose most be in possession of the spirit crystal, it will lead you to the flowers."

Pope didn't say a word, he simply looked at Dante... expectantly.

"There is no way in hell I am giving you this crystal," Dante replied. "We'll go get the flower, you all can wait here."

"No. I can't run the risk of you changing your mind halfway through the mission and running off. Nor can I have you dying in the middle of the swamp and that crystal disappearing into the belly of a monster. No, I need to see Stephen restored to life. I'll tell you what. We meet in the middle, myself and one other member of my team will travel with the four of you. We'll journey into the swamp together to find the flower and bring it back. You'll have the advantage of numbers and I'll be there to make sure the job gets done right."

"And, the rest of your team stays here?" asked Alex.

"Everyone else will stay behind," said Pope.

"How do we know you won't try and ambush us once we get outside the city?" asked Robyn.

Pope sighed. "You just have to trust that I want to see Stephen brought back to life more than I want any type of retribution towards your group."

Dante looked at Alex, Morrigan and Robyn, but no one offered any additional objections or suggestions. They final decision, it seemed, was being left to him.

"Give us two days to prepare. We'll head out at first light." Dante said.

CHAPTER 36: THE FOOL

"I can't believe we're really going to follow Pope into a swamp, it seems like such a bad idea." Said Robyn.

The group left Market Street and ventured deep into the city in an attempt to distance themselves from Pope and his men.

"I agree," Said Alex, "but if we want to save Stephen, we don't really have much of a choice."

"We have a choice," Morrigan cut in, "we could not go."

"You mean not go with Pope?" Alex asked.

"I mean not go at all." She answered. "I'm sorry but have you guys forgotten that Stephen is one of the people that helped bring us here. He works *with* Pope. Why are we risking our lives to save him? In the Dragon Dale games Hell Hearth Swamp is a notoriously dangerous area and there is no reason to believe that won't be the case here as well. If we go there now, we're guaranteed to be out of our league."

She was right. In past Dragon Dale games Hell Hearth Swamp was filled with toxic mushrooms, poisonous plants, and venomous creatures. In some versions of the game, even breathing in the swamp was deadly, forcing players to use magic spells or find other workarounds to simply enter. But there was also another issue. In Dragon Dale 7, different regions carried different level requirements. The Illder Plains for example, which sat at the geographical center of Deos and held the starter town of Illdershire, was a low-level area and served as the launch point and learning area for most of, if not all adventurers in the game. In general, the further players traveled from the center of Deos, the higher the level required to safely navigate the world. There were a few exceptions, namely the Black Wood, which was unpredictable and dangerous regardless of level, but for the most part, players learned fairly quickly which areas were safe and which areas to avoid until they found themselves at a high enough level to travel without issue. By Dante's estimates, based off past games and taking into consideration what they had encountered so far, he imagined

Hell Hearth Swamp was for adventurers levels 10 to 12 and they were only level 6.

"You can't be suggesting we simply don't try and save him. We can't just abandon him here; he needs our help," Alex protested.

"We're the ones that have been abandoned! He lied. They all lied. They told us we were playing a video game and they sent us here knowing full well we'd probably die. Now we're going to risk our lives even further trying to help one of them, when we should be trying to find a way back home? It just doesn't make sense."

"You're right," said Robyn. "Maybe we should just give the crystal to Pope, let him take care of it."

Dante was torn. Stephen had led them into Deos under false pretenses, but Morrigan hadn't seen has face right before he died, she hadn't heard his last words. Stephen had told Dante the truth, and not because he was seeking some type of redemption but because he had wanted Dante to know, it was as if he had always wanted him to know. And then, Stephen's spirit crystal had been given to Dante, entrusted to him. His life was in his hands. That meant something. Didn't it? Could he so easily hand over another man's life without question? Could he cast aside the responsibility that Shinto had bestowed upon him? Had that been Shinto's intention? For him to be responsible for Stephen's life? For his soul? Or had he simply given it to him at random?

What would Shinto do? If he suddenly and inexplicably found himself responsible for the life of another that he held no obligation or loyalty towards, would the half-orc, as is his right, shirk a responsibility toward those in need of his help, or would he, regardless of inconvenience or difficulty, assist?

The highest difficulty, Dante thought. And somewhere deep inside he smiled to himself as a small part of him made the connection that somehow in some way, everything was connected.

"I'm not against giving it to Pope," Alex said, a bit of fustration in his voice, "I'm just saying that I don't think we can, in good conscious, not do anything to help."

"And I'm saying I don't care if we give it to Pope or not, I just want to make it clear these people you are so set on helping are the same people that sent you here as cannon fodder."

"Look, guys let's just give Pope the crystal, that will get him off of our back, he'll take his entire group into the swamp and that'll leave us free to find Sandberg."

"We're not giving Pope the crystal." Dante cut in, putting a stop to the heated argument. "Shinto gave the crystal to me, to us. He could have given it to Pope, but he didn't. He trusted us with it instead."

"I don't think you should read too much into that Dante," said Robyn. "I think he gave it to you because you almost died trying to save Stephen, but that was when you all still thought we were in a video game. We all did."

"No, it's more than that. When we met Shinto on the road and we explained our story, he could have kept going on about his way and left us to our own devices, but he didn't. He traveled with us for days, took us under his wing, gave us a step-by-step guide for how to survive in Deos. We wouldn't have made it here without him."

"Exactly and now you want to throw that all away," said Morrigan.

"Look, we could give the crystal to Pope and we could spend our energy on simply finding Sandberg, but I think we all know that would be a mistake. We have to unlock Stephen because it's the right thing to do, because he needs our help and because if it were any one of you locked inside that crystal, I hope you know I wouldn't even waste time having this discussion on if I were going to try and save you or not."

Morrigan stared at Dante for a moment as if weighing each of his words carefully. "You're asking a lot of us Dante. You're asking us to risk our lives for someone who obviously didn't care if we lived or died."

"I'm asking you to trust me," Dante said, his voice unwavering.

"Can you get us through that swamp and back out again?" she asked.

"I'm going to get us home." Dante replied.

Morrigan looked, in that moment, so extremely frail. She seemed like at any moment she would collapse upon herself and with a loud sniffle she attempted to use her hands to wipe her face clean of both tears and emotion but was only successful in one.

"I trust that you really believe that... I just hope that you can do it."

"Listen," Alex cut in. "we're all hot, exhausted and a bit on edge we just need somewhere to rest, regroup and collect our thoughts before we make our next move."

"Well, we've been trying to find somewhere to stay since we got here and haven't been very successful yet," said Robyn.

"Wait," said Dante remembering something, "In the Dragon Dale games, Abilene Bay is famous for three things, the Obelisk Lighthouse, the Citadel and the Agua Villa bathhouse. It's like the Desoian version of a high-end luxury spa," said Dante.

"I like the sound of that." Said Robyn.

"Yeah, but is it real, or is it something that just made up for the game?" asked Alex.

"Well, the lighthouse is real, and the Citadel is real, I don't see why the bathhouse wouldn't be real as well. We just need to find out where it is."

"You said its famous right." Asked Robyn.

"Yes." Replied Dante.

She turned around and called out to guard passing by. "Excuse me do you know where we can find the Agua Villa Bathhouse?"

"What do I look like? A tour guide?" said the guard gruffly. He looked the adventurers up and down and then let out an annoyed sigh. "A group like yours, I suppose I'll either be telling you now or arresting you later. Head north from here, then when you get to Valdameer Way make a left, its right next door to the inn, the Grand Opal, you can't miss it." The guard looked over the group again, then turned his nose up to the air and frowned. "I hope you have the coin for it. If you are in need of lodging, perhaps you all would be better suited at someplace on the southern side of the city."

"Oh no, we have coin, we just have been doing a lot of traveling and need to get out of our adventuring clothes. We actually clean up quite nice." Robyn replied.

"Yes, well, let's us hope that is the case. Alright now, move along then and stay out of trouble. I don't want any mischief out of you four especially not around Agua Villa."

"Sir, yes sir." Robyn replied with a salute, "And thank you for your service." She said as the guard walked away eyeing her suspiciously as he did. "So, it looks like it does exist!" she said turning back to the group "and it's not too far from here."

"You guys should head on over to Agua Villa and I'll meet you all there," said Dante.

"Where are you going?" asked Morrigan.

"I'm going to make a quick trip back to the Adventurer's Guild and see if I can find out anything about Sandberg."

"By yourself?" Alex asked. "I thought we agreed that wasn't a good idea?"

"Yeah, but that was when thought Pope didn't know we were in the city. I want to at least ask around the drinking hall once before we call it a day."

"Is this one of those, 'I need to be alone' moods that you tend to sink into from time to time?" Robyn asked unabashedly.

Dante didn't bother responding, and instead simply stared at her blankly.

"I'll take that as a yes." Robyn said after a couple of seconds of awkward silence.

"Come on guys," said Morrigan in a low voice, "let's head to Agua Villa."

Dante moved hurriedly through the streets of Abilene Bay. He only had a couple of hours of daylight left. The sun had already begun to drop towards the western horizon, and it would not be long before it set altogether and while he was looking forward to the respite from the heat, he did not think it was a good idea to for him to be wandering around the city after sundown by himself. That meant he didn't have much time to do what he needed to do and make it back to the others before dark. He knew that it was foolish, stupid even for him to split off from the group and run off into the city by himself, and to be honest, apart of him felt embarrassed, but then another part of him felt that it was necessary. Some visceral, primal, instinctual part of him deep in his gut told him that he must go back, and he must go alone. So he went, by himself clamoring through the city like a man on a mission, moving as fast as he could to get back to Market Street, back passed the guild halls, back passed the stalls, back passed the vendors and back to her.

She sat there in front of him, the old elven woman. She was alone, on her blanket, no customers, no clients, no one seemed to be showing the slightest interest in the old fortune teller, or the fortunes she told, no one expect Dante. She sat, piddling through the flower basket as Dante approached, rearranging the blossoms in attempt to make the basket look full and lively, but even from

Dante's distance he could tell the flowers that she was attempting to sell were either already dead or dying making her attempts seem, more than anything else, futile and sad.

"You have returned," she said the moment Dante got within earshot. She had not bothered looking up.

"I have," Dante said hesitantly. "I wanted to ask how you knew about those things you said to me. About my mother and my brothers... about me?"

"I am an old woman, an old mother. I am prone to worry. The only time I do not worry is when I know, therefore I know things, that way I do not have to worry." She looked up from her flowers and then slowly pulled herself up to her feet, she wore the same ragged and weathered smile that she had worn when she told Dante's fortune. A smile that she wore like a riddle.

"Do you know where I can find a man named Benjamin Sandberg? He is an Urthlander, like me. Only he came to Deos a long time ago."

The fortune teller stared deeply into Dante's eyes, and for a second, he thought she was going to begin spouting out the secrets of his heart once more.

"Such a young wolf," said the old woman with a smile and a motherly tone. "Such a *hungry* young wolf, *but* one that must understand that I am nothing more than a poor fortune teller who makes but a meager living telling people the deepest darkest secrets of the universe. Surely the boy understands that for old mother to tell you anything, there is a cost."

Gold? Was that all that she wanted was gold? "How much?" asked Dante, reaching for his coin pouch.

The old woman let out a laugh. A cracked and broken cackle that reverberated through his sternum.

"My dear boy, coins are not the only currency for which goods are exchanged."

Dante took a step backward and the same primal part of him that forced him back to the marketplace alone, sent a signal to his brain commanding him now to run away, ideally as fast as his legs would allow. He resisted the urge to flee and instead his hand unconsciously hover over the handle of his weapon.

The woman cackled again and then with uncanny speed took what had to be less than two steps and landed herself mere inches from Dante's face. She was there before he realized it and it was only after he registered what had happed did the sense of her movement actually hit him. A small gust of wind, the smell of withering flowers, the sight of pale wrinkled flesh so close to his face that he could see the thin blue veins hiding just beneath the surface of the paper-thin skin of the old woman's forehead. She was holding the spirit crystal gently in one hand, her long near skeletal fingers caressing the rose-colored jewel.

"The value of a thing," the woman began in that piano wire voice that made Dante's skin crawl, "is only worth what someone is willing to pay for it. I can give the boy the information he seeks, but only if he is prepared to pay the price."

"You want the spirit crystal?" he said, incredulous. He looked her up and down, scanning the woman intently now. Her status box populated in full color.

Name: Unknown Lvl:?? Job Class: Fortune Teller

No name, no level and no real information other than some generic line that reduced the old woman down to a general NPC nobody.

Slowly, Dante took another step back while at the same time tucking the spirit crystal underneath his leather chest piece. "I need the spirit crystal to restore my friend back to life, it's the entire purpose of me going to Hell Hearth for the death head rose that you asked for. Why would I give it to you?"

"Yes," said the old woman, releasing the crystal without resistance. "But if the boy could instead find the one that he seeks, then he can return home, return to safety and nothing in Deos would be of concern to him. You are a smart boy," said the old woman. "You will you not trade one life for four. Do not be foolish. Take an old mother's advice, for a mother is wise. Pay the price. Save the lives of those entrusted to you." The old woman held out her hand, her long thin fingers unfurling to reveal an open palm that quietly beckoned for the crystal that hung from Dante's neck.

He looked down at her empty hand. So, she did know about traveling between worlds. But how? Had Pope put her up to this? Had he tasked her with retrieving the crystal and had she said all of this to simply achieve that end? No. No that was unlikely. So what could she want with Stephen's spirit crystal?

Then he remembered the conversation he'd had onboard the deck of the Nimue with Shinto and the others. Aside from the life it represented a spirit crystal was in essence a highly concentrated form of compressed magical energy. Much like the mana crystals he had been collecting since arriving in Deos, these tiny gems were small items filled with tremendous reservoirs of power, something of incredible value to an experienced magic user. That's why she didn't want gold, perhaps she assumed that Dante did not know how valuable spirit crystals could be. They had just received a couple of thousand gold coins for a handful of mana crystals and spirit crystals were supposedly worth a hundred times as much.

So that was her proposal. The spirit crystal for the whereabouts of Benjamin Sandberg. Her hand lay before him, splayed out and open like a large white spider, her thin fingers tipped with fingernails dark and dirty. She offered him, in a single choice, everything that they were looking for, a way home, a way to save his friends, a way to save himself and all he had to do was give up the crystal. Stephen.

"Thank you," Dante replied, "that is a gracious offer, but I'm happy to find Sandberg on my own. I'm sorry, but I'm not willing to betray one of my friends just to save myself. Now if you'll excuse me, I have to get back, my friends are waiting for me." Dante turned to leave, turning his back on the old woman, even though he felt it was against his better judgement.

"Such devotion," cackled the fortune teller, "Such loyalty, such a sight truly warms an old woman's heart. Reminds me of my own son. Loyalty such as this must not go unrewarded. I offer to you boy as your reward, a name, Alabaster Floggins."

Dante stopped.

"It is said no good deed goes unrewarded, and what you have shown an old mother here today was good indeed." the old fortune teller said with another giggle.

Alabaster Floggins? Sandberg was operating in Deos under a gaming handle, under his avatar's name. Of course, how could he have been so stupid as to not realize that if they were going to find anyone hiding in Deos they would have to have their Deosian name.

Dante turned around to face the old woman once more only to find that she was gone. Her blanket was devoid of both fortune teller and flower basket and instead one of the stiff parchment cards lay face down and alone, like a note left just for him. Dante bent down and picked up the card. It was, much to his surprise somewhat familiar, though not completely what he expected. On the face of the card was the drawing of what looked like a young man. A rather carefree young man standing at the edge of a cliff with a small white dog at his heels and his face curiously pointed up towards the sky. He was illustrated as carrying a flower in one hand and in the other a stick with a bag tied to the end of it. At the top of the card was the number zero and at the bottom written quite plainly, were the words "The Fool"

It was, Dante recognized, a tarot card. The stack of cards that the fortune teller had been shuffling through earlier in the day had apparently been a deck of tarot cards. A tool commonly used by fortune tellers for divinations and reading fortunes, and somehow either intentionally or otherwise, the old woman had left behind, only one of her cards... "The Fool" card.

Fitting. Dante thought. Somehow, *this* is fitting. He slid the card into his pack and quickly began to make his way to Agua Villa to reunite with his friends.

Chapter 37: New World, New Name

"Welcome to Agua Villa, how can I help you?" asked a very pretty girl with coconut brown skin and curly black hair. She stood behind a counter near the front door of the very large and very opulent Agua Villa Bathhouse.

"Hi," said Dante. "I'm looking for my friends, a group of adventurers, they came in here not long ago, um, a dwarf, a half-elf and a human."

"I'm sorry sir but we have a very strict policy, that, for the protection and convenience of all of our guest, would not allow me to divulge any information about anyone who arrived outside of your own personal party. I'm sure you understand."

"Oh no, well that's just it you see, they are in my party, we just arrived at different times."

"Yes sir, well I am sorry, but, if you all arrived at different times, then I'm afraid that would mean that they are, by definition, not in your party."

"No, no, no, I'm sorry I must not be explaining this properly. We were already a party before any of us came here. Then we split up. I went somewhere on an errand, and they came here. We all agreed once I was done, that I would meet them here. You, see? All still one big party."

"So, you all were a party?" asked the clerk.

"Yes," said Dante feeling as if he had finally gotten somewhere.

"Then you left the party?"

"Ye- well, no I didn't really leave the party."

"Because if you left the party, that would mean you are not *in* the party and as I stated I cannot divulge information about anyone outside your own personal party."

"No, no, no, I didn't leave the party. I was in the party, I'm still in the party," Dante was beginning to lose his patience. ", the party is still a party, we just split up momentarily."

"So, you are saying *you* split the party."

"Yes, yes that's what I'm saying. We split the party."

"Well," she said still flipping through the pages of the logbook. "I've always heard that one of the most important rules for an adventurer is to never split the party. I guess the old rules just don't hold true like they used to."

Dante had heard that phrase before, 'never split the party' it was an expression from the original tabletop version of Dragon Dale, the game from which all successive video games were derived. How, he wondered, could a world like Deos be so familiar and yet still so foreign to him.

"Your name sir?" asked the girl behind the counter.

"Dante Battle."

"Ah yes, I have a reservation for you right here."

Dante let out an exasperated sigh.

"Looks like your friends have already made the basic arrangements, the details however are being left to you."

"Okay, and what exactly does that mean?"

"It means that preparations have already been made, by your party, for you to enjoy the relaxing and reinvigorating waters of The Aqua Villa Bathhouse. Now, would you like to make use of our public baths or would you like a private bath space."

Dante's eyes widened. "Private please."

"Not a problem, and would you like a private bath group space, or just an individual space?"

Dante's eyes got even wider, and he felt his face go flush with color. "Just a private individual space will be fine." He said, "hey wait, umm... what... what did my friends choose?"

The clerk looked up from her reservation book and flashed Dante a tight-lipped, smug, and slightly judgmental smile. He was beginning to think that she, in some small way, derived a type of joy watching him squirm and blush with embarrassment.

"They all chose private individual bath spaces as well." She replied with a self-amused grin. "but don't tell anyone I told you that."

"Oh no, of course not. Privacy policy," Dante said with a reassuring nod.

"And will you be needing any assistance today?"

"Assistance?"

"Yes assistance, some of our clientele request the services of an attendant to help scrub away the deeply ingrained dirt of the road."

"Oh, no, I think I'm good on that note. I don't need any assistance; I think I can take it from here."

"Well sir, in that case, you are in our Tranquility Suite, its down the hall and to your left please follow the aquamarine tiles along the floor to door number five. Thank you for choosing Agua Villa."

The Tranquility Suite was a lavishly decorated chamber etched out of marble and trimmed in fittings of brass. Shelves and tables of dark mahogany wood lined the room holding stacks of towels and an assortment of small, bottled oils and perfumes. Occupying the center of the room was a circular pool large enough to hold two to three people. A statue in the visage of a mermaid holding an overturned pitcher poured an unending stream of crystal-clear water into what appeared to be, the already full, bathing pool.

Reluctantly at first, almost for fear that the slightest movement might ruin the immaculate peace the room inspired, Dante removed his weapon, armor and clothing and slid himself into the water, which stopped at about chest height. Much to his surprise, it was hot, just a few degrees below unbearable, a stark contrast from the cool of the rest of the room. He could feel the heat from the water soak into his joints and achy muscles. The soreness that had been hiding within his limbs and his bones melted away. He closed his eyes and laid his head back, and for a moment he almost felt like he was back on Earth. Dante had spent most of his life on one field or another, a baseball field, a football field and most recently, because the college of choice had not had a football program, a lacrosse field, and in more ways than one sitting in a heated pool with a body full of sore muscles was like a home away from home for him. In his mind, the aches and pains, bumps and bruises that he felt after a long day had always inferred a since of accomplishment, those brief moments where he would sit in ice baths or hot tubs in an attempt to aid his body through the recovery process meant he'd just given all of himself on the field. It was the hard reset that was necessary for him to get up and do it all over again the next day. But that had been...

Dante opened his eyes.

That had been back when he was abusing his body, pushing his limits and beating himself up for sport. When the worse outcome for failure was that he would have to tally a hash mark in the 'loss' column as opposed to the 'win' section, but now, now failure undoubtedly meant death. Here losses were forever and winning... well winning just bought you a bit more time playing the game. He let out a sigh. It almost felt like being back on Earth, except for the looming threat of imminent death that is, that was a bit different.

Dante lifted his hands from the pool, shook the excess water from them, summoned forth his spirit tome and turned to the notifications page.

-You have fulfilled 3 of 4 primary objectives for the quest "Searching for a Stranger in a Strange Land"

-Congratulations! You have successfully joined the Adventurers Guild.

-Congratulations! You have joined an Adventuring Company.

-Congratulations! You are the founding member of an Adventuring Company.

-Congratulations! You have been appointed Leader of your Adventuring Company.

-Congratulations, your ambitious social climbing has earned you some status among your fellows.

-Your Reputation Rank is currently listed as "Fledging Adventurer"

-You have fulfilled the primary objective for the quest, "How to Resurrect Friends and Influence People"

-The primary objective for the quest, "How to Resurrect Friends and Influence People" has been updated.

-You have been issued a new quest, "A Fool's Errand in Hell Hearth Swamp"
-You have split the party

"Three of four objectives fulfilled?" "Stranger in a Strange Land" was the quest that he distinctly remembered unlocking after they figured out Benjamin Sandberg was supposedly hiding somewhere in Deos. Dante's eyes skimmed over the page quickly finding a section labeled 'Active Quest', there he found what he was looking for, the entry for "Searching for a Stranger in a Strange Land."

You're in a bind. You are trapped in the land of Deos with no visible way home. The people that brought you here weren't the most trustworthy and as a result you have broken away from their influence, the only issue being they were your only way back to the land of Urth. But alas there is hope, through a stroke of luck, or rather some would say skill, you have become aware of an old Urthland adventurer who is said to be hiding somewhere in the land of Deos. If you can find this mysterious stranger, he may be able to assist you in getting back home. This quest has four primary objectives.

~~*1. Arrive safely in Abilene Bay*~~
~~*2. Register at the Adventurers Guild*~~
~~*3. Ask around about information on Benjamin Sandberg*~~
4. Find and locate Benjamin Sandberg to determine if he can send you back home.

Dante looked down the page to another of the active quests listed within the same section. He noticed the entry for "How to Resurrect Friends and Influence People" and recognized that it had changed since the last time he had checked it.

A member of your party has fallen, as is usually the fate of most who call themselves adventurers, but by some mysterious stroke of destiny, your brother-in-arms has been given a second chance at life and has been turned into a spirit crystal. While in Abilene Bay you happened to cross paths with an old fortune teller who claims to know a way to restore your fallen friend, but before they can offer their assistance, you must present to them an item necessary for the completion of the resurrection ritual.

That was interesting, Dante thought. The 'Strange Land' quest line had four clearly defined, *predetermined* objectives that he and the party were able to address one by one. The 'Resurrect Friends' quest line however was not as neatly laid out. It did not have numbered objectives, but instead the entry appeared to be updating itself depending on their circumstances. Was that because they had discussed a pointed plan for finding Sandberg in Abilene Bay in a way they had not for restoring Stephen? Did the spirit tome simply notate the goal they had set for themselves regardless of the accuracy of their predictions? Could they use the tome as a compass to verify their decisions, or would that only lead them in circles, chasing their own tails?

Dante turned to the newest quest in the book. "A Fool's Errand in Hell Hearth Swamp".

"A Fool's Errand?" he repeated aloud, does that mean the book believes they were going on a wild goose chase? He read the entry for the quest.

Friendship has its benefits, and unfortunately it also has its drawbacks. Your desire to resurrect a fallen friend has brought you into conversation with a fortune teller who claims to be able to help you, but before she can, you must journey into the heart of the deadly Hell Hearth Swamp and retrieve the elusive Death's Head Rose, a key ingredient in the resurrection ritual. The swamp is dangerous, the rose is rare and on top of that you are not in the best of company on this trip. Survive the swamp, retrieve the rose and you just might be on your way to regaining an ally.

"Damnit," Dante muttered under his breath, the entry did a good job of not really giving anything away. It confirmed everything that he knew while staying vague on everything that he was unsure about.

"Survive the swamp, retrieve the rose and you just might be on your way to regaining an ally."

The conditions for completion were clear, "survive" and "retrieve", but the reward, the one that he "just might be on his way to", that was not guaranteed. Doubt was something that he could not afford at the moment. This was, he decided, not only a quest, but a test to determine if the information provided to him by the spirit tome could be considered trustworthy or if it was just a parrot of his own thoughts and ideas.

Just then there was a stern knock at the door of the Tranquility Suite. The sudden sound startled Dante and he dropped the spirit tome which immediately vanished before hitting the water, and almost instantly taking its place was Dante's sword.

"I'm sorry to disturb you sir," said the middle-aged man who'd just appeared in the door. His expression was stale but he seemed determined to enunciate every word as he spoke. "I am Broomfeld, the concierge." The man's eyes glanced down to the sword Dante was holding just outside of the water.

Dante looked at the man, looked down to his own sword and then looked back up to the man once again. "Well, hello, nice to meet you, but I told the lady at the front desk that I didn't need any help."

"I have simply come for your armor and garments, Sir. For cleaning. I also bring a message from your friends. They have secured lodging for your party at the Grand Opal and currently await your arrival in the parlor where they are at present enjoying both food and drink."

"Thank you Broomfeld. And sorry... for pulling a sword on you."

"Not to worry sir... happens all the time."

Dante left the Tranquility Suite feeling like a new man, or at least like a clean one. He wore a loose-fitting white linen tunic with a pair of matching trousers that had the feel and comfort of pajama pants. In the Grand Opal Inn he found Alex, Morrigan and Robyn sitting, eating and drinking all equally clean and all in an equal measure of comfort and newness.

"Dante! Bro, Welcome back!" said Alex through a mouthful of half chewed food. The dwarf held up a cup filled with sloshing red liquid that threated to escape the container it was in and spill itself all over Robyn.

"Hey, watch it!" said Robyn moving out of range of Alex's spilling drink.

"So," said Morrigan softly "Did you find what you were looking for?"

Like Dante, none of the other party members wore their original clothing, but instead were all wearing replacement white linens provided to them by the Agua Villa Bathhouse. Alex was dressed like him, white tunic, white trousers, but the girls, the girls wore full length dresses that were in essence a single piece of silk like fabric that had been folded and pinned in such a way as to make it wrap, hug, and hang from the body in a way that Dante had not previously imagined possible. Morrigan sat there, strewn across an overstuffed sofa, eating grapes and taking sips from a large silver chalice. Her braided hair was pulled up into a bun on the top of her head, leaving her slender neck and half-elven ears more exposed than they had ever been. Dante took a seat on the circular shaped sofa and sunk into its soft feather filled cushions. It felt like something out of a dream. He leaned forward a bit, found an empty chalice and poured himself a drink from a large pitcher filled with something sparkling, red and slightly translucent.

"I found a lot actually," Dante said. He took a sip from his drink and felt at first a sting and then a sweet warmth spread through his body. The liquids sweet nectar like smell hit his nose and tastebuds almost at the same time.

"Did you find a way for us to get that rose without us having to go through that swamp?"

"No," said Dante, "But I have been given that some thought. Morrigan was right about a number of things, Hell Hearth Swamp is dangerous, and we are going to be entering the area, under-leveled, not to mention even if we outnumber him two to one Pope simply cannot be trusted."

"What are you saying?" asked Alex alarmed. "You want to abandon the quest?"

"No that's not what I'm saying at all."

"Well, you're, not exactly doing a very good job of selling the benefits of this suicide mission," said Robyn.

"The point I'm trying to make is we have an uphill battle ahead of us so we'll need to prepare. We don't have a healer in the party, but if we stock up on healing potions and antidotes, upgrade our armor and weapons and keep in mind everything we learned traveling with Shinto I think we can increase our chances." Dante took another sip from his cup.

"So basically, you're saying we should spend all of our gold before going off to die painful horrible deaths?" replied Robyn with a straight face. A comment to which Alex spit out his drink in surprise.

"A hot bath and a cool head and that's what the best you can come back with?" said Morrigan chuckling.

"Well yeah," said Dante, "But that's because it'll work, I – I know it will."

"Well, if it's any consolation I believe in your bro!" Alex raised his cup in support.

"Of course, you do," said Robyn. "Men believe in anything."

"Right" agreed Morrigan. "It's us girls that need a bit more convincing." Morrigan and Robyn high fived each other and Alex rolled his eyes.

"I will say this, Mr. Wolf Whisperer. Though I do not in the slightest bit agree with this undertaking... at all, I must admit you have not led us astray thus far.

I can say with a straight face that I'm pretty sure we are still alive because of you."

Dante put a hand to his chest in mock surprise, "Do my ears deceive me, or does that sound like a compliment from Morrigan?"

"I'm not sure how much longer we're going to *stay* alive," she added quickly, taking another sip from her cup, "but thanks to you we're alive right now."

"Well, that didn't last long," Dante responded and together the group burst into laughter.

"I know things got a little heated earlier and it may have sounded as if I didn't trust your judgement but it's still important that you guys know regardless of which direction we take we are all in this thing together, so if you guys want to go into the swamp I am with you, 100 percent."

"Aww Morrie, that's so sweet, you're going to make me cry," said Robyn fanning her face.

"Well don't you start crying because then I'm going to start crying," said Alex to another round of laughter.

"No more crying. What we need is for Dante to come up with a better plan to get us through that swamp than 'Be well prepared' and I just might be able to *not* cry myself to sleep tonight."

Their smiles, Dante noticed, the laughter of his friends, was reaffirming, encouraging, and taking into account that he had only know them for a short amount of time, it still occurred to him how desperately he wanted to keep them all safe, to keep them smiling and laughing, to get them out of danger and back to the safety of home. No matter what.

"Well, I can't offer you a better plan than that right now, but I think I have something else. Alabaster Floggins," Dante replied.

"Who?"

"Alabaster Floggins." Dante repeated, "Its Benjamin Sandberg's Dragon Dale name, the name he's living under here in Deos."

"Wait, wait, wait," said Morrigan, "Where did you even find this information? At the Adventurer's Guild?"

"No, no not the adventurer's guild I got it from the fortune teller."

"The Fortune Teller!" they said in unison once again.

"When she whispered my fortune to me... it was... so accurate. It was like I didn't have a choice. I had to ask her." Dante stared into his cup, and watched as the shimmering red liquid rippled from the slightest movement of his hands. He took another sip, feeling the sting and warmth and sweetness all in quick succession. No one said anything for a moment and when Dante looked up he saw that everyone else was looking down into their own cups as well.

"So, she just gave you his name, just like that?" Morrigan asked.

"No, she didn't. Actually, she offered to tell me exactly where he was but for that information she wanted me to give her Stephen's Spirit Crystal as payment, but I said no." Dante immediately took a large gulp from his cup.

"Wait a minute, wait a minute, wait a minute!" Morrigan stood to her feet, "You mean to tell me she was willing to tell you exactly where we could find Benjamin Sandberg and you said no, without even consulting us?" she asked.

"She was only willing to tell me in exchange for the spirit crystal," Dante explained.

"What religion am I in this world?" Morrigan asked falling back on to the sofa with a flop "I need prayer."

"Why would she want the spirit crystal?" asked Robyn.

"I think the spirit crystal can be used as a magic power source for certain types of magic, I suspects she wants it for something along those lines." Dante replied.

"Wait so does this mean she really can't help us revive Stephen and she's just trying to get her hands on the spirt crystal?" Asked Alex.

"I don't know," replied Dante, "At least I don't hope so."

"Well while we're hoping," said Morrigan raising off of the sofa "Let's just hope you plan of preparation gets us through that swamp in one piece and once we do that, we'll all just have to keep a close eye on the old woman and the spirit crystal and make sure she doesn't try anything funny."

"Right," said Alex.

"And once we get Stephen back, we can all go track down Alabaster Floggings and get the hell out of this place and back home where the world makes sense," said Robyn.

"Now that," Dante said with a smile. "Sounds like a plan."

Chapter 38: Proper Preparation

Dante awoke the following morning in a large and comfortable bed with a splitting headache.

His armor and clothing were stacked neatly in the corner of his room but he didn't bother putting them back on. Instead he donned a fresh tunic and a new pair of trousers, provided to him this time by the staff of the Grand Opal. He washed his face and hands with fresh water from a bowl left in his room and then made his way out to the city street in front of the inn where the others waited. Together they made their way back to Market Street and began the process of preparation. Robyn, the group treasurer, allotted a budget of five hundred gold per person to be spent on goods and equipment for the journey ahead. Then, with a surprising amount of enthusiasm for the imaginary title that she had been given only a day prior, she distributed to each member of the party a pre-counted pouch of gold coins from which they could use to purchase whatever they needed.

It wasn't until mid-morning that the throbbing in Dante's head subsided and when it did, he found himself with Alex in a blacksmith's shop standing before a soot-covered dwarf with a long beard and a bright red nose.

"Ello's lads, welcome to the Orange Anvil." Said the dwarf over his shoulder, "How can I be helping you boys today?" he asked, somewhat busy stoking the flames of his forge with a large set of bellows, a dusty and dirty contraption that looked like a cross between an accordion and a set of bagpipes. The dwarf's large meaty arms made strong forceful pumps, up and then down again forcing air, and as a result, life into the flames of the forge. Imagining that the fire was to his liking, the blacksmith stopped and turned to face the two customers standing in the entry way of his shop. "Oy! Well don't you chaps look like a pair of fresh set adventurer's out to make your fortune in the world. What brings you in? Browsing or buying?"

"Buying... hopefully," said Alex quickly.

"Ay, that's what I like to hear. Gormith Ashbeard at your service," said the dwarf with a bow. One of his legs, from below the knee, had been replaced with a well-crafted and intricately decorated heavy metal rod.

"Dante Battle."

"Alexaldrin Oreheart, at *your* service." Alex replied with a bow of his own.

"Oreheart, you say, of the Oningrad Orehearts?" the shopkeeper asked.

Alex froze, and Dante could see a hint of mild shock spread across his friend's face. Dwarven family names were a big deal in Deos and never had it occurred to them that the name Alex was using may belong to someone else.

"Oh, yes." Alex replied, "One in the same, however, I'm not actually from Oningrad you see. I'm from a branch of the family that hails from Urth land. I am here in Deos traveling to Oningrad for the first time, to see the fatherland, meet my kin, all that good stuff."

"Ah it's a pilgrimage then! Now that is the type of noble quest every young dwarf should take at least once in his life. And who is this you have with you, a brother in arms to share the road and adventure? Not a dwarf but a brother is a brother I say, especially when the gnolls come nipping at your heels! Believe me I know!" The shopkeeper laughed and motioned to his metal leg. "Now I think it goes without saying, but you have come to the right place. I have the finest dwarven made weapons and armor this side of the mountain kingdom. Take a look and let me know if you have any questions."

Browsing the armors Alex and Dante came across a fully complete set of chain mail, scale mail, plate mail and half plate all of which had been made by Gormith from what he called dwarven steel, a metal that Dante knew based off past Dragon Dale games was said to be sturdier and more durable than iron or standard steel. The half-plate, Gormith told them, was spoken for, as it was a custom order for another customer who had already paid for the armor but who had yet to pick it up, the chain mail, scale mail and plate mail however were indeed for sale and items he was more than willing to part ways with, for the right price, of course.

"The plate mail offers you the best protection hands down," Gormith explained, "But, and I mean no offense lads, as far as warriors go the two of you still look a bit green in the gills and to be honest a full set of plate mail is something usually reserved for seasoned fighters. If you aren't proficient with heavy armor, this stuff might end up being more trouble than it's worth."

"That's a good point," said Alex staring longingly at the full set of glistening knight's armor.

"Say, where are you boys headed next? You taking the airship to Oningrad? Or are you taking a couple of horses and heading north on foot? Doing it the Dwarven way eh??"

"Actually we are headed to Hell Hearth Swamp first. We have business there to honor a fallen friend. Then we are heading to Oningrad afterward."

"Oy," said Gormith looking genuinely taken aback. "I guess what they say about you Orehearts is true, a dwarf amongst dwarves indeed. You're nothing but a wee tadpole and a foreigner no less but when you go on a bloody pilgrimage ye really make it one worth singing about. Hell Hearth Swamp is a might dangerous place for a young chap such as yourself. Lots of people worry about the poisonous plants and animals but it's the muck and the mud that really get you in a spot of trouble. Slows you down, tires you out, makes you easy picking for any beasties that may be roaming about. No, you don't want plate mail. You don't even want the scale; it'll only weigh you down. Go with the chain mail, it's the most maneuverable heavy armor you can wear and still will provide you good protection."

"Yes, but I already have chainmail." Alex said his removing his own armor from his pack and laying it across the shopkeeper's counter. Like Dante, he had not put his original equipment back on, but had brought it with him shopping, in the hopes of selling it when he upgraded to something more substantial.

"So, you do lad, but this here, this is only a chainmail shirt, and it is not dwarven steel, nor is it dwarven made." Gormith said looking over Alex's used armor with a discerning eye. "Go with the chainmail armor boy-o, it's a definite improvement over what you had but it'll still be somewhat familiar to you as far as fit and feel goes."

"How much is it?"

"Seventy-five gold." Gormith replied.

"Okay, I can swing that." Alex replied, "What do you have by the way of axes and shields?"

"Ay, going for the whole kit and kaboodle are we? Makes sense for what it is you lads are doing. I have a bearded axe, dwarven made of course, so it's a bit of an upgrade from what you may already be used to. I'll be glad to give it to you for 15 gold. That's the going price for a well-made longsword, only difference is this axe will last you a lifetime, two if I'm being honest. You'll be passing it on to your children's children and they'll be out slaying kobolds with it like it just came out of the forge."

Gormith hobbled behind his counter, reached down and came back up with a sturdy and dangerous weapon. "Axes like these are bestowed to Dwarven youth by their clan when a young boy reaches adulthood. At least, that's the custom here in Deos. Either way, even though it's not necessarily special it'll serve you well. But, when we are talking shields I do have something special." Gormith disappeared into the back of the shop and came back out a few seconds later with a circular metal shield with the image of a large snowcapped mountain painted on the face of it. "This, I call the Shield of Onin. It's my crowning jewel. A regular masterpiece, best thing I've ever made it is."

"Excellent," Alex responded with a grin. "Dwarven made from dwarven steel I assume."

"Of course," Gormith, responded, "but it's not just that. This here shield... its perfect."

"Perfect?" repeated Alex, a hint of disbelief in his voice.

Dante looked at Gormith's Shield of Onin, it seemed, for the most part like a regular shield. It was well made, nicely constructed and obviously in pristine condition, but there was really nothing about it that would indicate that it was perfect. Then he scanned it.

Shield of Onin

Quality: Exquisite

Condition: Flawless

A dwarven shield of exceptional quality crafted by a master smith of remarkable skill. It appears to have no visible weak points.

"Wow it is perfect," Dante mumbled under his breath.

"See your friend here has the eye for it. This shield is the culmination of every smithing technique I've ever learned all brought together in one item." Gormith brought himself down to eye-level with the shield and slowly rubbed his fingers across its smooth surface. "It's unbreakable," he said in a low voice. "The metal ore I used to make the steel came from the heart of the Onin mountains. Ore so pure it had to be blessed by the god of the mountain himself. I had to feed the fire mana crystals just to get the forge hot enough to shape the metal properly. The shield is resistant to heat, to cold, and it can withstand nearly any attack thrown at it short of a dragon blast at point blank range, even then there's a chance you'd be burned to a crisp and the shield would still be there, looking just as bloody immaculate as it does today."

"How much?" asked Alex, apparently convinced by Gormith's sales pitch, or rather his admiration of his own work. Alex lifted the shield from off the counter and slide his hand firmly into place within the grip. He smiled to himself, seemingly impressed by both the shields heft and balance.

"How much?" repeated Gormith almost as if he had forgotten that he was talking to a potential buyer. "Well, for you, a young dwarf looking to make a name for himself, on a quest of honor and glory and all that, one who still respects the old ways. I suppose I could part ways with it for, I don't know, I'd have to say no less than once hundred and fifty gold. Which is a steal considering that's my life work."

"I'll take it." Said Alex without hesitation. "I'll take it for one hundred and fifty gold."

"I guess even you foreign Orehearts are bloody bleeding coin too then aren't you."

"I don't know about that." Replied Alex, "It's just that, if it's a good as you say it is then, well, it's worth it."

"Of course it's worth it! It's worth three times what I'm charging you for it, just so happens that you remind me of a younger version of myself is all. So... no point in it sitting in here collecting dust when it could be out there adventuring, going on pilgrimages and the like." Gormith said with a dismissive wave of his hand, he seemed somewhat sad to see the shield go.

"No, I really appreciate it and I promise to take care of it as well."

"Promise to take care of yourself lad, I've seen a lot of good dwarves die for honor and glory. Use the shield as a shield. Protect yourself, protect your friends, and try and comeback in one piece if you can help it eh."

"Yes sir," Alex responded with a bow, "And thank you again."

"Ay, don't mention it, anything else I can help you boys with?"

"Do you have any swords?" Dante asked.

Gormith did have swords. A large number of swords, but unfortunately none of them were exactly to Dante's liking. They were either, too big, too small, too long or too short. Either the grip didn't feel just right, or the balance felt off. At minimum, he wanted to upgrade from his basic iron blade to a steel one, but even the standard steel swords Gormith had on hand felt uncomfortable and unnatural when he wielded them. The dwarven steel, it turned out, was even less fitting. It was denser and heavier than standard steel and much heavier than iron, which made it burdensome to carry and made swinging it cumbersome, clumsy and slow. The dwarven steel swords looked nearly identical to the iron and steel ones with the exception of perhaps a slight variation of color, but the weight and feel was like night and day. . It had something to do with how Dwarves combined their ores in the smelting process. The formula they used to combine iron and carbon into steel was a secret known only to dwarven blacksmiths and as a result dwarven metal came out harder and heavier because of it.

"Perhaps you'll have more luck with elven steel, or maybe even mythril." Gormith had suggested. Elven steel the blacksmith had explained was in effect the exact opposite of dwarven steel, it was lighter and more flexible than standard metals and was often coveted for its beauty and dexterity when it came to sword making. The only drawback, Gormith had added was it was not nearly as strong as dwarven steel. Yes, it was stronger than iron and he could objectively say it was far superior to human made steel, but blow for blow, over the long term, elven steel could not stand up to the punishment inflicted by dwarven metal and some would even say the orcish made weapons were better if ever it came down to a test of simple brute strength.

"And then there's always mythril," Gormith had told them.

"Shines like sliver, stronger than most steels and is more rare than gold. It's the type of metal blacksmiths dream about. The ore itself is infused with magic they say. A mythril sword will cost you a thousand gold as sure as the day you were born, if you can find one. But even if you could and even if it did, you'd better buy it. You can't hope for better than a weapon than one made of mythril, exceptin' for maybe a saintly blade." Gormith chuckled as he mumbled out his last few words.

"A saintly blade? What's that?" Dante already felt a need to own one, whatever it was.

"A weapon belonging to a sword saint. Devil Fang Daggers, the Destiny Spear and all that. I mean they're not real of course, just legends, but then you lads aren't from Deos so you may not know the stories. The best you can hope for is a mythril sword, and until you can find one, I think maybe elven steel will be a good fit for you, but in the meantime, I suspect you'll just have to make do with that iron sword like you have been."

Dante wasn't exactly disappointed at not getting a new sword right away, but he felt excitement at the possibilities. In past Dragon Dale games upgrading to stronger and better weapons was an integral part of the game, but in the 'real world' of Deos, maybe upgrading every few levels didn't' make sense if your experience didn't match.

"Gormith, I need some new armor as well, but am partial to leather, do you have anything for me?" Dante asked.

"Leather eh? Yes, you young swordsmen usually do like that sort of thing. Well, I deal mostly in metal, but I do often trade with this half-orc chap who is a very good leather worker. He sells a lot of his items through me because, well... most people don't trust half-orcs, but believe me when I say I can vouch for his work, its second to none." Gormith disappeared into the back of his shop and came back out with multiple pieces of stiff black armor. "He called it Night Raider Armor. I can't give you too many details about it other than its black and it's made of leather. Everything else only Maar would be able to tell you."

"Maar?" Dante repeated looking over the armor set.

"Yes," replied Gormith, "that's the name of the half-orc bloke that made it."

There was a dark black leather chest piece accompanied with greaves, and matching boots. Each piece was fastened snugly with black rivets, giving the armor one flush and fluid dark color throughout. The inside of each piece was lined with soft black fur meant to serve as a cushion between the hardened leather and the wearers body. It looked, from Dante perspective, no less than amazing, and at the very least was an upgrade from the armor that he currently wore, at least that was his assumption. Then in an effort to be sure, he scanned it.

Night Raider Leather Armor SetQuality: Outstanding

Condition: Remarkable

A set of leather armor crafted with special care and strict attention to detail. Its dark black color does well to conceal the wearer at night. The material is made from the hides of the black wolves of the Illdershire plains, hence its dark appearance and the swift and deadly movements its wearers seem to possess.

"How much?" Dante asked running his finger across the fur lining of the armor's interior.

"I'd say fifty gold is fair price for something like that."

"I can do fifty gold. I'll take it."

"Good, you just got yourself some new armor then." Gormith said in response. "Now lads, I don't want either of you to take this the wrong way, but I do have to point out that the two of you are running up quite the tab. How exactly do ye plan on paying for all of this? I hate to be a stickler but of course you know I can't exactly be giving you any of these goods until the golds is in me hands. The last time I had to wait for a noble family to make good on a deed of sale it took a whole bloody moon before I saw single coin."

"I'm sorry," said Alex looking a little confused. "I don't know what you mean exactly."

"I mean," started Gormith, "That if you need to contact House Oreheart for them to send you the coin for this purchase or if you want me to send a deed of sale to your kin in Oningrad or back to Urthland or what have ye, I'll gladly hold these items for you both, but I can't let you go out adventuring with them until the deed of sale is fulfilled and I'm paid in gold. I'm sorry lad, I like ye and all, but business is business."

"Oh that?" said Alex looking relived, "Well, we'll pay you in gold right now." Alex reached inti his pack and removed a bulging coin pouch. "This is one hundred gold. It should cover the chainmail armor and the axe which came up to ninety gold, please consider the remaining ten coins to be a deposit on the shield while I go back to the inn and get the rest."

Gormith looked dumbfounded, "Boy-o, you're telling me you're just walking around with a small fortune in your pack?"

"Here is my fifty for the night raider armor," said Dante, placing his gold in five neatly placed stacks of ten. "And also, there's this." Dante pulled from his pack the black wolf pelt that Hernandez had skinned for him from their first fight and his first kill after arriving in Deos. He lay the wolf skin atop the counter near the coins. "Can you see if Maar can make a cloak or a mantle from this? I'll leave another five gold to cover cost or fees. We'll be back in Abilene Bay after we're done in the swamp, I can come by and pick it up then if he's done." Dante added another small stack of coins to the counter to join the others.

"Bloody hell, who walks around with this type of gold on their person?" Gormith asked.

"I assumed everyone did." Alex replied.

"No, everyone doesn't. I'll see what Maar can do about the pelt but I can't make any promises." Gormith grabbed a nearby bin and began sweeping the coins off the counter and into the bucket. He seemed eager to get them out of sight, as after he cleared the counter, he quickly grabbed the large coin bag placed it into the bin atop the other coins and recklessly heaved both items into the back of his shop. The dwarf then hobbled back towards the counter with a bewildered look in his eye and a bit of sweat on his brow.

"Everything ok?" Dante asked.

"Yes, yes everything is fine, I just wasn't expecting you to spill out one hundred and fifty-five gold coins like that. I haven't seen that much gold in a long time, didn't want nobody else seeing it either. Abilene Bay is a safe place, but gold can make men do strange things, you boys would do well to remember that too. Be careful with that coin."

"We will," said Alex, "thanks for the advice."

"Gormith one last thing," Dante added, "you mentioned horses earlier. Where could we go to maybe rent or buy a few horses to help speed us along our way."

"You can't," Gormith replied "No stable master with a horse worth riding is going to rent one out to you for just for you to take it down to Hell Hearth Swamp, it's too risky. And you shouldn't go and try and buy a horse to take to the swamp for the same reason. Horses are built for speed, that's how they survive in Deos, they outrun most other things that might want to eat them. Hell Hearth Swamp is a slow miserable grind, with all the mud and the muck about the place there ain't much running that can be done, which defeats the entire point of having a horse. It'd be the equivalent of throwing money down a well. You'd spend half of every waking moment trying to either pull the horses out of mud pits or help them to avoid them altogether. No, you'd be much better off getting a Juxia instead."

"A what?"

"A Juxia, not nearly as fast as a horse, but it has a three toed hoof, makes it easier for it to navigate difficult terrain. Plus, juxia aren't nearly as excitable as horses, they don't spook, so even if one does get stuck in mud they are a lot easier to guide out than a horse. Aside from that a juxia always knows how to find its way back home, they are resilient little buggers, so if ever you are in dire straits, you could always give it a slap on the backside and tell it to return. Might could carry you back to safety or at least carry a message, so your kin knows what happen to ye. You'd be surprised at how many people just disappear out there without a trace."

"I could imagine," said Dante solemnly.

"Yeah well you can get a juxia or a horse at the stables on Aldawan Way, that's east of here. Tell them I sent you."

"Ok, we will. Thank you Gormith."

"Ay, no thanks necessary, you boys have made it an eventful morning to say the least."

"I'm going to go get the rest of that gold now, I just have to run over to the Grand Opal, please hold that shield for me until I get back."

"The Grand Opal, blimey, that place has to cost nearly three gold per night."

"Five," Alex yelled over his shoulder as he and Dante exited the shop, "But it's worth it."

"Five gold per night, just to lay yer bloody head on a pillow. Guess it's true what they say about the Orehearts after all. Richest bleeding dwarves in Oningrad." Gormith was still muttering as he turned back to the forge to work the bellows, and breathe life back into the flames.

***

"Do you know what's funny?" Robyn asked Morrigan as they walked casually down the streets of Abilene Bay, "I don't think I've ever had access to this much money back at home."

"Not even close, for me. I don't even know what it feels like to be this rich," Morrigan replied.

It was early in the afternoon, and Morrigan and Robyn were headed back to the inn after having spent most of the day shopping for supplies.

"I kind of feel like Julia Roberts in ⊠*Pretty Woman*'." Robyn said with a smile.

"You know? I've never actually seen ⊠*Pretty Woman*'." admitted Morrigan.

"You've never seen ⊠*Pretty Woman*'!?" responded Robyn with unparalleled surprise. "Oh my God Morrie, one of the first things we have to do once we get back home is have a movie night. You have to see 'Pretty Woman' it's so good."

"Yeah," Morrigan replied with a humoring chuckle and downcast eyes. "We should do that, that would be fun."

A silence passed between them. Robyn noticed that lately Morrigan become quiet every time someone mentioned going back home. She was about to bring it up it when they were interrupted.

"Ahem." An Elven man, tall and lean, walked behind them with a large number of boxes and packages in his arms and nearly just as many more bags hanging from his already full hands. He made a noise, clearing his throat in an obvious attempt to get the attention of the women walking in front of him.

"Oh,"said Robyn looking back at him, "Don't worry it's not much further, just right up ahead here."

The elven gentleman, as it turned out was the assistant clerk to one of the shops, they had visited on Market Street. The shop owner, so impressed with the amount of gold they had spent in his shop on that morning, insisted that his clerk assist them in carrying all of their purchases back to the Inn, which was good because they had made a large number of purchases.

"I still can't believe we bought so much this morning, and I can't believe all you bought was books." Said Robyn speaking back to Morrigan once again.

"Well, I am a mage, and mages expand their knowledge base by studying and understanding magic, so I figured books were an ideal investment for me. Besides, that's not the only thing I bought." Which was true. Morrigan was wearing a pair of large golden hoop earrings, which were designed, according to the shop she bought them from, to allow her mana pool to regenerate faster. She also had a new nose ring. A small, subtle diamond glistened where there had previously been a silver stud. This too was meant to help harness her magical power more efficiently, to help her focus her spells with more clarity and purpose. The hoop earrings had cost ten gold, and the nose ring another seven.

She had also purchased new robes, a cloak, new boots, potions, ethers, a component pouch for spells that needed components, a list of common components used in most spells and a mortar and pestle for any ingredients she found along the road that needed to be ground up and made into components for said spells. She also purchased a silvered dagger to replace the simple dagger she currently owned but rarely every used, mostly because she felt it was better to have a dagger and not need it then to need a dagger and not have it, and she upgraded to a slivered dagger because she knew some monsters, particularly undead ones were weak to weapons coated in silver. She didn't know what they would be facing in Hell Hearth Swamp and she desperately hoped whatever it was it was at least alive when it came after them, but if the entire idea of their preparation plan was that it was better to be safe than sorry, she definitely wanted to air on the safest side possible.

The books that prompted Robyn's comment were a set of five that she purchased from a bookstore that they happened across in a far-off corner of Market Street. They had cost Morrigan fifteen gold and ranged from a variety of topics ranging from the basics of elemental magic conjuration to the advanced theory surrounding the summoning of extra planar spirits. The books themselves did not contain spells as the bookshop clerk had explained, but rather it explained the concepts and underlying ideologies behind the different schools of magic, allowing someone with a working understanding of mana to then create their own spells. In addition to the books on magic, Morrigan had also purchased one other book, a book encompassing the history of the Land of Deos apparently written by a scholar named Alder Mere Frane. The history book, however, was not for Morrigan, that she had purchased for someone else in their group.

"Yeah, I guess you did. So..." said Robyn mischievously, "are you going to take Dante back to that bookstore we found?"

"What? Why would I do that?" Morrigan asked.

"Well, when we were in there you kept saying how much you thought he's like the place, and you were asking me what types of books I'd think he'd like and just all types of really surprising questions that I really hadn't expected from you." Robyn face was contorted in a glee-filled devilish grin.

"I did not." Morrigan protested, "I mentioned that he would probably like the shop *one time*, based off the fact that he a know-it-all who is always obsessing over any and everything Deos or Dragon Dale related. *And* I tried to find books for both you and Alex as well remember, but you told me you only listen to audiobooks and that you didn't take Alex for much of a reader."

"Ah the lady doth protest too much methinks."

"I thought you didn't read." Replied Morrigan, rolling her eyes.

"What do you mean?"

"That's a quote from Hamlet... by Shakespeare." Said Morrigan exasperated.

"Oh, is it? I heard it on an episode of ⊠*Golden Girls*⊠ and I've been saying it ever since."

"Oh my God, you are impossible."

"Impossible not to love." Robyn countered.

"Well, the jury is still out on that one." Morrigan replied with a smile.

"Ah yes, Jacobs my good man, it looks like we are here, the Grand Opal!" Robyn said in a loud and proper voice, or at least the best impersonation she could do of proper.

"That is actually Jacoby madame." Responded the Elven shop clerk.

"Yes, that's what I meant of course. Please feel free to drop those packages at the front counter and I'll have them taken up to our room by the inn staff."

"Yes, right away madame." Jacoby responded, hurriedly making his way inside the Grand Opal ahead of Morrigan and Robyn in an effort to relive himself of the heavy boxes and bags as quickly as possible.

"What now?" asked Morrigan.

"Well, I got nearly everything I was looking for with the exception of a plunder's pouch or some other type of magical bag that can hold a lot of items without taking up a lot of space. I'm going to go grab some more gold out of my room and see if I can find that shop that Shinto bought the seashells from, something tells me they would have something like that." Said Robyn as the two of them walked in through the doorway of the Grand Opal. As they did Jacoby came bounding out, so fast that he actual almost came crashing into them.

"Apologies madame, if there is nothing else, I'll make my way back to the shop."

"I think that just about covers it." Said Robyn flicking a gold coin into the air into Jacoby's direction, the elf snatched it out of the air, mostly out of reaction and the looked into his hands with wide eyes.

"Thank you, Madame. You are indeed too kind."

"Stay Cool Jacoby." Robyn replied with a wink.

"Of course, milady." Jacoby responded looking a bit confused before scurrying away as fast as he could as he was afraid, he would be asked to do something else.

"What is wrong with you?" asked Morrigan.

"Just keeping up appearances." Answered Robyn giving her hair a dramatic swish and twirl as she spoke. A gesture that made Morrigan laugh out loud. "Oh look, there's Dante now," said Robyn, spotting him sitting alone in a corner of the inn's large and opulent entry longue. He sat near a window, looking completely lost in thought. "I wonder what he's thinking about?" Robyn asked in a low voice. "Go check on him, it's you job as Vice-President of the Adventuring Company."

"That's not a real position."

"Of course it is. As Treasurer, my job is money, now excuse me while I tend to my job while you tend to yours." And without another word, Robyn turned and hurried off towards the stairwell that lead up to the private rooms each of them had rented to themselves.

Morrigan moved over towards the front desk, grabbed one the books she had purchased from the bookstore and begin making her way towards Dante in the corner.

Dante was indeed lost in thought. His mind shuffled endlessly over the ideas of spirit tomes, tarot cards, spirit crystals and the constant threat of Pope. Surviving their expedition into the swamp was his most pressing and urgent priority but now mythril swords and saintly blades and become another thing to consider. He needed answers but all he had was questions.

"Hey stranger." Said a sweet and melodic voice from beside him, cutting in on his thoughts and bringing him back into the lounge of the Grand Opal Inn. Before he even turned his head, he smelled the scent of white nectarines and peach blossoms and knew that it was Morrigan that had called out to him. He turned and looked and found that he was right.

"What are you doing over here by yourself? Daydreaming again?" she asked with a smile.

"No," responded Dante with a smile of his own, "Waiting on Alex to come down. Just sitting here thinking about everything that we need to do."

"Thinking about all the ways things can go wrong?" Morrigan asked sitting down in an empty chair beside his.

"Nah, not that at all, Dante answered with a nod of his head. "Trying to figure out what I need to do to make things go right. I can't... we can't afford to lose anybody on this little expedition."

"Well, we can afford to lose Pope I think."

Dante laughed, "Yeah maybe Pope, but definitely not anybody else and if we can get Stephen back, we just may be able to get some questions answered."

"I guess that's true, just seems like such a big risk though, aren't you a little worried."

"I am. I mean to be traveling deep into Deos with Pope who we know can't be trusted, based off a lead he gave us, its crossed my mind a million times that this could all be an elaborate trap and I'm walking us right into it."

"I understand how that can be concerning."

"And then of course taking into consideration your point and I'm asking myself, why am I risking our lives to save someone that we barely know? Especially when I actually had the opportunity to trade this whole problem away in return for exactly what we have been looking for, a way home."

Dante was quiet for a moment, and Morrigan not sure how to respond was quiet as well.

"But you know? As risky as it is, as many doubts exist, I simply wouldn't be able to live with myself if I didn't go through with it. I- I can't really explain it, but I have to complete this quest, not only for Stephen, but also for myself. And because of that, I don't really feel like it's fair how I've drug you guys along with me on this. I think it may be best if I just went to Hell Hearth Swamp alone, just me and Pope and his men and then you guys can go ahead and start the search for Floggins."

"No," said Morrigan almost immediately, "no we're not doing that. We are all going to get Stephen back and we are going to find Floggins and then we are all going to find our way back home. Together."

She reached out her hands and grabbed his and as she did, she flashed Dante a weak smile. He could see both fear and doubt in her eyes but he could tell that she was attempting to be strong for the both of them and that, that bravery in the face of fear, he appreciated.

"The fortune teller," Dante began, still staring into her eyes, "When she told me my fortune, she whispered in my ear about how back on Earth my mother had just died, and my two older brothers who I have always looked up to, currently hate each other all of which left me feeling alone and isolated. I dropped out of college and secluded myself to my mom's house playing old Dragon Dale games trying to escape my problems and now that I've been pulled into the same world that I was trying to retreat to, all I want to do again is escape. All I do she said, is run away, and the scariest part is, everything she said was so right, that I couldn't deny a single word of it, even if I wanted to." Dante let out a deep breath. He wasn't sure why he had just told Morrigan that, he wasn't sure why he would have told anyone that, but there was something in the way she had looked at him, something about the way she had tried to console him. It had felt caring, understanding, selfless. That, he felt, at the very least demanded his honesty in return.

"My real name is Makeda Morrison," said Morrigan quietly, "Oddly enough, I know what it's like to feel alone in the real world." She smiled and sort of shrugged, she broke eye contact with Dante and instead focused on the empty space in front of her as she spoke. "I'm a gamer and I have a streaming channel with a small following, but when I log off, I feel empty and hollow.

"I had a brother, an older brother, and like you I idolized him. He was the one that got me into video games to begin with. My parents... they spilt up when I was young. My dad moved off to a whole other state and started a new family and left me and my brother and my mom to fend for ourselves. My mother didn't handle that too well. She developed a drug habit that spiraled out of control, and it was left to my brother to take care of the two of us even though he was just a kid. He did a good job though. He was pretty much the closest thing I had to a parent from the age of eight to sixteen."

Dante stared at Morrigan as she spoke, sunlight cascaded in through the nearby window and bounced off of her dark brown skin in reflections of gold.

"We lived with my grandmother," she continued, "but he took care of me. Everything I needed he went out and got it. Bought me my first console, and without me even asking he would bring home all of these cool games and we would stay up all night and play them together." Tears begin to roll down the sides of Morrigan's face. "By the time I got halfway through high school though he had started running with this really bad crowd. I um.. I talked to him about it... a few times actually. But he told me he had it all under control and that he was just setting things up so I didn't have any worries when it was time for me to go to college." She sniffled hard. "He was um, killed. He was murdered in my junior year of high school. He didn't even get to see me graduate. Both of my parents came to the funeral, and they tried to make nice with me. My dad, who I hadn't seen in eight years told me I could come live with him and his new family, and my mom told me she had been clean for a year and wanted a chance to start over." Morrigan, looked directly at Dante.

"I told both my parents if given the chance I'd gladly trade both of their lives to have my brother back." She said before slowly looking away again. "Needless to say, there was no reconciliation. I went back to living with my grandmother and the next year graduated from high school and then after that left for college. It was in my freshmen year that I started the gaming and streaming channel, the whole Morrigan Le Bey thing, and for the most part it went really well. Gaming just always made me feel close to my brother again, you know?"

Dante nodded in agreement; he did know.

"Then, I don't know after about a year, year and a half, I got a call from my grandmother. She told me my mother had relapsed and died of a drug overdose. My mother who I hadn't talked to since my brother's funeral, who my last words to were 'I'd gladly trade your life for his' had died. I was distraught. Then add to that there was this stupid scandal with my streaming channel where people were saying it wasn't me playing but it was actually my brother. Normally I could care less what people think, but I mean my brother was gone. And now my mother was gone too, and it just all felt like so much." And then Morrigan, or rather Dante was sure that this was Makeda that looked at him, in much the same way that he had moments ago looked at her, only her eyes were full of tears that she was no longer fighting back.

"Then the fortune teller, whispered in my ear that after losing my brother and then my mother, I tried to kill myself. I tried to commit suicide but failed. Then she told me that I pretend to be strong because in reality my greatest fear is that I am weak. Too weak to save my brother, too weak to save my mother and now too weak to save myself."

Dante felt his own eyes watering as he struggled to keep his composure.

"And the worst part," Morrigan continued, "Is that like you, I knew it was all true the moment I heard her say it." She looked down into her lap, and the used her hands to wipe her face. Dante used the moment to quickly do the same. "Sometimes I think that maybe I was successful after all, maybe I'm dead and all of this, all of Deos is my afterlife. Maybe this is my punishment."

"Makeda Morrison." Dante reached out and squeezed her hand and said her name aloud almost as if to signify she was solid and present before him. "This is not the afterlife I promise you, it's not, and to prove it, we'll get out of here and get back home, together. How does that sound."

"That..." Morrigan looked up at Dante. "That sounds good." She replied not a hint of doubt in her eyes.

***

"Oh yeah, I almost forgot. I got you something."

"You got *me* something?" Dante asked in disbelief.

"Yeah, when we were out shopping, we found a bookstore and I figured you liked books so... I grabbed this for you." Morrigan reached out with both hands and passed Dante the book on Deosian history.

"How-how did you know I liked books?" asked Dante looking dumbfounded.

"It wasn't much of a stretch. After you told us that you changed sports in high school so you could go to some haughty private college it was pretty obvious that you were a giant nerd." She laughed and Dante laughed as well.

"I guess my secret's out."

Dante opened the book to its title page.

A Comprehensive History of the Land of Deos as Collected and Retold by Alder Mere Frane Volume I

Dante rubbed his fingers across the hand inked letters. "This is an amazing gift, Morrigan. Thank you."

Morrigan didn't answer, but she couldn't hide the blush creeping up her face.

Chapter 39: The Brothers Battle

Malcolm sat alone at an empty table in the visitation area of San Marcos State Correctional Facility. Why, was a bit unclear to him, he wasn't expecting a visit that day, or anytime soon actually. Kiesha, his girlfriend, was the only person that came to visit him, and she wasn't set to come back for a couple of weeks. He had been forcing her to space out her visits more and more. He told her it was because he needed her to focus more on running the bookstore and the antique shop, and to help look for his missing brother, which were all true, but it was all so because she was becoming very distracting. Her constant visits were beginning to serve as a reminder to the amount of time he had been sentenced to, a reminder of what and who he was missing while trapped inside that prison. If he was going to get through multiple years in San Marcos, he was going to need to focus on doing the time, and weekly visits for a beautiful woman actually made that more difficult, not less. And for that exact reason he hoped that this wasn't some surprise visit she had planned despite his request to do otherwise. He hoped that it wasn't her, while at the same time a small part of him hoped that it was. Besides, if it wasn't Kiesha, who else could it be.

After only a couple of minutes of waiting, his question was answered. Through the large remotely operated doors walked Bryan Battle, Malcolm's older brother. He wore a dark gray suit, black leather shoes and moved with a kind of arrogant authority of someone employed by the government. It was funny from Malcolm's perspective, Bryan had always carried himself like a cop, even when they were kids, now he carried himself like a fed, for all intents and purposes, a super cop. Always the over achiever.

Without so much as cracking a smile Bryan marched up to the table and sat down across from Malcom and stared at him, glaring the entire time.

Malcolm, looked from side to side, then at his brother.

"Bryan, what the hell are you doing here?" Malcolm asked in a whisper, "And why are you staring at me like that?"

"Why do you think I'm here?" Bryan replied and in one fluid motion he removed a folded sheet of paper from his suit jacket pocket and slammed it on the table.

Malcolm winced from the loud noise and looked around to see if they had perhaps caught the attention of a guard. They had. "Hey man, can you bring it down a notch. What is this anyway?"

"Look at it."

Malcom unfolded the sheet of paper and read it, "It's the letter I sent you. So, you got it?"

"Yeah, I got it, the question is why are you sending me letters Malcolm?"

"Did you not read the letter? Dante's missing."

"No, you *think* Dante's missing, based on the fact that he won't talk to you. And what else? A bunch of conjecture and conspiracy theories and for that you send letters from a prison to *my job*. Are you insane, or are you really just that selfish?"

"Am I really that selfish?" Malcolm repeated in disbelief, "No, the question is, are you really this stupid? I sent the letter to your job because I don't have a phone number or home address for my own brother! Hell, even that letter was sent to your old office with the army. I had to hope it would get forwarded to whatever rock you're hiding under these days."

"Did it ever cross your mind that maybe I don't want to have anything to do with my lying, thieving no good criminal brother and that's why he doesn't know how to get in contact with me."

"Hey, this no-good criminal brother of yours was the one helping Ma pay the mortgage when you were off playing soldier trying to be like Pop remember? Man, you know what, I don't have to explain myself to you. If you're so ashamed of me then why exactly in the hell are you here Bryan?"

"I'm here *Malcolm*, to tell you very clearly and very plainly that whatever con you're planning, whatever scheme you're coming up with I'm not buying it and I don't want any part of it. I don't know if you need money or if you think I can pull some strings to get you a lighter sentence but its-"

"I don't need any money from you." interrupted Malcolm looking offended "And believe me when I say that I would serve a hundred years in prison before I asked you to come down off of your high horse and help shave one day off of my sentence, you self-righteous-"

"Then *why* are you bothering me?"

"Are you really as dumb as that suit makes you look? Because Dante is missing!"

"Dante is not missing." Said Bryan pulling something else from his suit pocket. It was a cellphone. He tapped the screen, input a code to unlock the device and then opened up a program that loaded itself to reveal a picture of Dante wearing jeans and Milgrad sweatshirt. He was holding a lacrosse stick and standing on what looked to be a sunny and bright university campus. Below the picture was a caption that read: *It's good to be back, can't wait to start the new season.*

"He posted it two days ago to his Foto Flixir account. You know what that means? That means he's not missing. It means he's fine. It means like me that he just doesn't want to talk to you."

Malcolm leaned in close to the phone and stared hard at the image on the screen then grimaced.

"You have to be the world's dumbest super cop and the worst big brother to ever exist." Said Malcolm boldly. "That's a doctored photo."

"What?" Bryan pulled phone closer and studied it.

"Dante posted another photo nearly identical to that one months ago, the only difference being the campus in the background didn't look nearly as sunny and warm as it does in that picture, it looked cold and windy, probably because he posted the original picture back in February, right before the season started. Whoever posted that just took his old photo and tampered with it to make it look more recent. That caption doesn't even sound like something Dante would say."

Bryan stared at the image. Now that he looked at it more closely, the coloring did seem a little off, not to mention that he had also thought it a little odd that Dante had been wearing a sweatshirt in July, but this didn't mean the photo was doctored. This is what college kids did, they put filters and color grading on their images to make them look older or cooler or... something, and he was he to judge the fashion choices of a twenty-year-old, the wore shorts in the winter, sweaters in the summer and did a bunch of other things that didn't make sense. No, this was Malcolm's con at work, it was making him second guess everything, even his own eyes. That's how manipulative his younger brother was.

"Scroll down." Said Malcolm as if sensing his hesitancy. "Scroll down and you'll see he has another picture just like that one."

Bryan tapped on Dante's individual profile and begin scrolling through his pictures. There wasn't a lot but there was enough to make him feel like searching through them all was a pointless endeavor, until... Bryan froze. There it was. Halfway down Dante's profile, a picture, nearly identical to his most recent post. Nearly. Same, pose, same clothing, same campus, the only difference was one looked like it was taken in winter and the other looked to be taken in the summer. And then there was one other key difference that made Bryan's mind nearly do a cartwheel inside of his skull.

"You know how I know that was a doctored picture?" asked Malcolm, "Because I was in it. I went up to the school to visit right before the season started and he and I took that picture together. And now, someone's cut me out of the photo and reposted the picture claiming to be Dante."

"We don't- we don't know that yet for sure." Said Bryan hesitantly he was still staring at his phone, still swapping views between the two photos. It was true. In one photo, Dante was standing alone on his college campus, and then in the exact same picture, posted months before, Dante was standing next to Malcolm. Smiling a confident and happy smile, lacrosse stick in hand, same jeans same Milgard sweatshirt. In the latter post Malcom had not been simply cropped out of the picture, he had been removed, perfectly and precisely edited out. It was as if he was never even there. Whoever had doctored the photograph had done a really really good job.

"What do you mean, 'we don't know'? We do know! I just told you! You just saw! For god's sake have you even tried to call him?"

"Yes, of course I have." Said Bryan sounding a little taken off balance.

"And... what happened?" asked Malcolm becoming more and more impatient.

"His phone kept going straight to voicemail." Bryan replied in a low voice.

"Voicemail." Malcolm laughed. "No one's heard Dante's actual voice in nearly two weeks and now someone is posting doctored photos to his social media accounts, but you, you still think we can't know for sure. Right, of course. Bryan Battle, the resident family hero, shows up right at the nick of time and does absolutely nothing to make the situation better. You know what? You-you were right from the start. I was wrong to send you that letter. I was wrong to ever assume that you could be of help to anyone aside from yourself. Just, man just leave get out of here. I'll find Dante on my own."

Malcolm went to stand when his brother's voice cut into him low and harsh.

"Shut up and sit down." Bryan said in a tone that usually proceeded fist fights in their childhood. They were both adults now, not to mention sitting in a prison visitation room, but knowing both himself and his brother, Malcolm still didn't think that was enough to deter them from wanting to punch each other, let alone acting on it. "In case you've forgotten you're in prison, idiot, you're not going to be finding anything except the inside of a cell. Now I'll admit that doctored photo is a bit odd."

"Odd?" said Malcolm loudly.

"Will you let me finish!" Bryan snapped. "Like I said. The photo is odd, I'll give you that. Add that to the lack of communication and that is some cause for concern, *but,* that doesn't mean he's missing. For all we know *he* could have cut you out of that photo. *Now...*" Bryan spoke up before Malcolm could interrupt. "In order to put this whole thing to bed I will personally go and check on Dante myself, see what's going on, make sure he's alright, prove that he's not missing, and then once I do, Malcom, I don't want you to ever contact me again. Am I clear?"

"Brother," said Malcolm, "you've never been more clear about anything in your entire life."

Chapter 40: Fang and the Gang

"What, exactly, is that?" Morrigan looked equal parts awed and disgusted as Alex gently stroked the neck of a large four-legged animal that stood nearly half a foot taller than the dwarf. The creature looked like a primitive horse, panting through its half-open mouth while observing the world through dim, lidded eyes.

"This is Dapple," said Alex casually. "He's a juxia."

Dapple the juxia, looked like a horse, crossed with a tapir. It's a bulky body had long lean legs with a different number of hooved toes on nearly every foot. Four toes on each of its back feet and three toes on each of its front. I had small pointed ears, large dark eyes and a short flexible snout of a nose, that was almost, but not quite elephant like, mostly due to its lack of size.

"We bought him from one of the stable houses yesterday." Said Dante.

"He is sooo cute!" said Robyn excitedly, running up next to Alex and petting the juxia, who gave out a satisfied snort.

"Not the words I would have used." Mumbled Morrigan.

"He's supposed to make it easier for us to get through the swamp." Dante added.

"Why not just buy horses?" Morrigan asked.

"Apparently most horses don't travel through mud and water as well as old Dapple here, and those that do, were very very expensive." Said Alex, handing Robyn an apple which she could use to feed the animal.

"Well, that makes sense, but why do we only have one Dapple? Where are the other Dapples?"

"Yeah, about that." Began Dante. "When we talked to the stable master, he told us that Juxia aren't really the best mounts. They're not very fast. Over the course of a day, they move about as far as we do, plus, he also explained that if you don't have a lot of experience with animals, riding a mount all day is just as nearly as taxing as walking."

"Apparently 'animal handling' is a category of skill that you have to develop like swordsmanship or blacksmithing." Added Alex. "He suggested we get one juxia to use as a pack animal to carry our gear, but then he also recommended that we take turns riding it so we could begin to develop our 'mount riding' skill as we travel to the swamp and back."

"Ooh, I want go first!" said Robyn enthusiastically.

"Nothing in this place is ever simple, is it?" asked Morrigan dismissively.

No," said Dante smiling, "I don't think it is."

The party was standing just outside the southernmost city gate of the Abilene Bay's outerwall. The sun had risen not but a few moments before and the air was still moist with early morning dew. Alex was dressed in his new chainmail armor set. On his back hung the perfectly crafted shield, the image of Onin Mountain painted on its face. The shield looked just as impressive outside the shop as it did inside. Dante couldn't help but think how the large metal disc made Alex's old shield seem like a toy by comparison.

As for Dante himself, he too was sporting his upgraded armor. The night raider leather fit his body like a glove, the fur lined interior made it not only soft and comfortable, but easy to move in as well. He felt lighter, leaner and at the same time not the least bit exposed. He had made it up in his mind that once they returned from the swamp, if his wolf pelt had been fashioned into something useful, he would have to meet this Maar, the half-orc leather worker that did such amazing work.

Morrigan's original robe and pelerine cloak had been replaced with a sort of custom-made tunic, form fitting and so long that initially Dante mistook it for another dress, that is, until he noticed the pants and knee-high leather boots that she wore underneath. Over her shoulders she wore a hooded cloak the color of deep dark purple and around her waist she, like Shinto, wore her spell book attached by straps and buckles.

Robyn had moved away from the hardened and stiff leathers that she wore previously and had exchanged them for soft and supple leathers that looked more like cloth. Strapped to her waist were new twin daggers made from elven steel, half a dozen throwing knives, a new, smaller single-handed crossbow all of which she concealed discreetly under a forest green wanderer's cape draped like a poncho.

The remainder of their equipment, the items that had previously been carried in the furca, the pots, the tools, the one tent which they had upgraded to two tents, was saddled onto Dapple. In addition to that the juxia held stores of food, a change of clothes and a stockpile of health potions, antidotes and ethers. They had spent five hundred and fifty gold on the potions alone adding to the cache they already carried, a justified expense considering their party lacked a healer. The health potions and antidotes would be the only thing standing between them and certain death should anyone's HP drop too low.

"Where is Pope?" Robyn asked as she continued to pet Dapple gently on the neck. "He's late."

"Maybe he's not coming," suggested Alex as he finished tying down the juxia's saddle bags. "Maybe it'll just be us."

"I wouldn't count on it," said Dante.

"And you'd be smart... homeboy." Said a somewhat unfamiliar voice from behind them.

Dante and the others turned and found Pope standing alongside someone they had not seen before, at least not since arriving in Deos.

"Fangloski?" said Alex in disbelief.

"In the flesh, but please, the name is Fang, just Fang. I don't walk around here calling you Rumpelstiltskin, so I'd appreciate it if you would refrain from using my real name as well okay short stack?"

He was taller than he had been on Earth. Bulkier too. He was still human, but only barely by Dante's estimate. He had, at least in his own mind, perfected himself and apparently for Arnold Fangloski that meant becoming bigger and stronger. He wore boots and pants made of animal hide and over his torso, a thin sleeveless shirt that also looked to have been made from the skin of some once living thing. His only armor was a large metal pauldron on his left shoulder, fitted with a leather strap and an assortment of heavy metal studs. On his back hung a double-bladed axe large enough to cleave a full-grown tree in half. He was without a doubt a barbarian, and made Danger Duke, the only other barbarian they had encountered up to that point, look like the joke he was intended to be.

"What are you doing here?" asked Dante, his hackles already up by Fang's presence.

"Well, my mother has a birthday coming up and I was hoping to find her something nice... What do you think I'm doing here?"

"Fang is the defacto leader of team 10 and as such has become one of my most trusted lieutenants," Pope said, in a tone intent on making Dante jealous. It didn't work. "He will be accompanying us to Hell Hearth Swamp to complete the quest."

"We're not going into Hell Hearth Swamp with him," said Dante forcefully.

"You don't have a choice," Fang replied, crossing his arms in front of him. The changes to his body had made his voice deeper, slightly raspier, but it still dripped with sarcasm and condescension. "But to satisfy my curiosity... tell me why not?"

"Well for one, you're an idiot who's pretty much guaranteed to get us killed, and two, I don't like you." Dante responded aggressively stepping towards Fang as he spoke.

"You sure got a big mouth for someone who let their game guide die. If you're so scared, why don't you run back into the city and let me, and *my* team handle this one home boy? Maybe you and your three girlfriends would be better off forming a cheerleading squad." Fang replied, unfolding his arms, and stepping towards Dante as well.

"Call me 'home boy' one more time and we're going to need to collect two sets of flowers from that swamp." Dante said through gritted teeth.

"Fangloski is an able-bodied combatant who successfully led his group to the safety of Abilene Bay, just like you Dante. He's also a gamer, just like the rest of you. I trust him and believe he can help us get the job done. That's why he was my personal choice for this mission. Me and one of my men, along with the four of you. That was our agreement. I have chosen Fang. You all still have us outnumbered two to one, and all of you are gamers. If that doesn't inspire confidence, I don't know what will."

Dante and Fang stood face to face, staring at one another, each refusing to blink. Dante had to look up slightly due to their height difference. He assumed that Fang's bad knee was no longer a factor, not that it mattered. The moment the barbarian blinked he would punch him in the throat, or the nose or the chin, a soft target was a soft target, it didn't matter how many muscles you had.

"Fang," said Pope from behind the barbarian. "Stand down, I'd like to get this quest started sometime this morning."

Fang cut his eyes at Dante and then slowly took a step backwards.

"Maybe later then there quarterback. Now grab that butt ugly horse of yours and let's move out. The captain's waiting."

"Run along like a good dog." Dante replied in a low whisper. "Your master is calling you."

With tensions already near breaking point, the group of six headed south. The early morning air was cool, and far off to the east Dante could see the sparkling waters of the Tethys Sea and the sandy beaches of the Sunblind Coast. The plan was to march south for about six miles and then west for the rest of the day, in the process they would cross over two bridges, one carrying them over the Triton River and the other taking them over the Phobos. Afterwards they would run into the eastern outer wall of the Black Wood, which they could then follow, at a safe distance, south to the Erebus River. After crossing the Erebus, they would be directly in front of Hell Hearth Swamp. Easy enough.

After a couple of hours, Robyn decided to mount Dapple and take the first shift at attempting to unlock the mount riding skill.

"Hey! Do you guys know where we are?" Robyn asked once she'd settled onto Dapple's back.

"We're just a ways out from the first bridge." Dante answered. "The Triton River is just up ahead."

"No, not that." said Robyn dismissively. "We're in the Wizard of Oz."

"What?" Dante was confused.

"The Wizard of Oz, we are in the Wizard of Oz."

"Um no, we're in the Land of Deos," said Alex. He held a rope and guided Dapple forwarded as they walked. The path was clear and well-traveled, but it was not an openly paved road like the Merchant Road had been.

"No, I know we're in Deos, but I'm saying, it's like we're basically in the Wizard of Oz. Think about it, Deos is like the Land of Oz and our group is like Dorothy and her friends."

"Mmmm, I don't know Robyn, that's a stretch." Said Morrigan reluctantly.

"No, no look. Dante is the Scarecrow, right? Because he's the brains of the operation. He's the smart one."

"Wait," said Alex, "I thought the Scarecrow was out looking for a brain because he wasn't smart."

"Dear God Alex, no wonder you don't get it. Everything they were looking for they already had. It took the journey for them to realize that. Have you ever even seen the Wizard of Oz?"

"Of course I've seen it."

"Well then like I said. Dante is the scarecrow because he's smart. Alex you are the tin man, one because you are sensitive, and two because you carry an axe."

"Sensitive?" said Alex.

"And I guess you're Dorothy?" asked Dante.

"No, or course not. Morrigan is Dorothy."

"Me?" said Morrigan surprised.

"Yes, technically Dorothy is a witch. After her house falls on the Wicked Witch of the East Glinda ask her if she's a good witch or a bad witch, then she gets the Ruby Slippers, a magic item, worn previously by a powerful magic user."

"I'm sorry, I don't follow." Said Morrigan.

"Dorothy kills a witch, is recognized by another witch as a witch and then inherits an item that traditionally only belonged to witches. That qualifies Dorothy as a witch, and another term for witch is..."

"A mage," said Dante

"The Scarecrow strikes again. Dorothy is a mage, Morrigan is a mage. Therefore, Morrigan is Dorothy."

"So that makes you the cowardly lion? You're okay with that?" asked Dante.

"Well, considering I strike from the shadows, don't intend on fighting anyone mano y mano and add in the fact that I'm agile like a lioness. Yes, I'm okay with that. So, you see the Tin Man is a tank, the Scarecrow and Lion are Melee Damage Dealers and Dorothy is a magic user. It's us! We are in the Wizard of Oz."

"You've really managed to turn the Wizard of Oz into an RPG? How long have you been thinking about this?" Dante asked.

"My entire life." Robyn replied with a sigh of relief. "My entire life."

Dapple let out an argumentative huff.

"Oh, don't worry boy, I didn't forget about you. You're Toto."

Dapple released a gleeful snort. He didn't know what a Toto was, but he enjoyed the idea of being included.

"How are any of you even still alive?" asked Fang.

"Don't worry Fang, I didn't forget about you either, you can be the flying monkey," said Robyn snidely.

The group crossed a rope bridge over the Triton River and came into a large open savannah. Tall thin grasses and a sparse population of trees brought to mind images of sub-Saharan grasslands that Dante had previously only seen in books. The space between the Triton and the Phobos seemed serene and reminded Dante of the Jua Valley and he wondered why no one had settled these areas before now. They kept walking, moving forward peacefully with resistance from nothing except the occasional breeze. After a couple of hours, Morrigan and Robyn changed places and Morrigan rode Dapple for a way but after only an hour decided she liked walking better and Robyn climbed back into the saddle.

Before long they found themselves crossing the Phobos River via an old rickety rope bridge that was in slightly worse condition than the previous one, but still allowed them to cross with little trouble.

Then after crossing the second river and perhaps another hour of walking, after feeling quite productive and considering breaking for a long lunch, that's when they heard it. It sounded like giggling. High-pitched whiny giggling. Dante heard it first and didn't immediately know what it was, but the brown fur covered figures moving low in the high grass nearly a hundred yards out soon gave it away.

A pack of hyenas came bounding towards them. They did not move as nearly as quiet or as graceful as the wolves of Illdershire. Instead, they sped forward with reckless abandon, foaming at the mouth, yipping, snarling, and growling as they ran, rushing forward like excited dogs at mealtime.

We've got company!" Dante shouted, unsheathing his sword.

"What part of The Wizard of Oz is this?" asked Alex readying his shield in front of him and pulling his axe from his belt.

Robyn swung her legs around to one side of the juxia's saddle and jumped down from Dapple's back. "The part where I say, I don't think we're in Kansas anymore."

Fang pulled his axe from his sling on his back and then looked at Dante. "What do you say quarterback, how about a little competition? Whoever kills the most hyenas wins."

"Just try not to get eaten alright?" Dante responded.

"Cut the chatter." Said Pope. "We have thirteen hostiles incoming. Keep an eye out make sure we don't get surrounded."

The hyenas closed in fast. Pope lifted his crossbow and without hesitation began firing. His first bolt hit one hyena in the shoulder, it flinched but otherwise kept charging forward, the second bolt hit the same hyena dead center between the eyes, dropping it where it stood. Pope fired again, aiming for another hyena's head but only slightly missing hitting it instead in the chest. The animal's, health bar dropped by only half and yet it kept charging. Another cross-bow bolt flew across the field, hitting the same wounded hyena and downing it. Dante looked back to see Robyn holding her compact crossbow in hand, its single shot fired, and its target hit for a clean kill.

"Does that one count for you or me?" she asked Pope who was pulling the levers back on his large multi-shot crossbow in preparation to shoot again.

Dante looked back to the hyenas, they were nearly half a football field's distance out and closing fast. They had killed two and had roughly eleven more to contend with. He took a moment to scan one.

Spotted HyenaLevel 5

Often identified by their loud and disconcerting bouts of what sounds like maniacal laughter, the spotted hyena, roams the vast grasslands found south of Abilene Bay constantly in search of prey. These vicious pack hunters and scavengers attack there targets relentlessly oftentimes overwhelming larger foes with superior numbers in combination with their powerful bites. While the spotted hyena is a formidable predator not to be taken lightly, the experienced adventurer knows that the real threat that these creatures pose is the company they keep. As the old saying goes. Where there are hyenas, there are hyenadons and where there are hyenadons, there are Gnolls.

Dante's mind was flooded with information and simultaneously the HP bar of each hyena popped alive with color.

"We need to get rid of these things quick!" Dante yelled.

"No really? I was thinking we stretch out a blanket, have a picnic, make a day of it!" Fang shouted over his shoulder.

"No you don't understand, they're going to lead more dangerous enemies to our location." Dante was shouting and suddenly he realized why. There was a loud roar increasing in volume behind them, like they were standing next to a furnace about to explode. Dante looked back at Morrigan to find her not only muttering, but also conjuring an orb of twisting churning fire between her two open hands.

"Agni, ignis, incendium." She muttered, rolling her hands around the proximity of the fiery orb. "Agni, ignis, incendium." She repeated this time louder than she had before. "Agni! Ignis! Incendium! Flame Sparrow!" she shouted thrusting her hands forward in one powerful push. The flaming orb broke itself into four smaller motes of fire that formed into the shape of small birds and soared through the air with a whistling screech. The fire sparrows flew in pairs, and moving as if they were real birds, they slammed into two of the charging hyenas. Upon contact the sparrows exploded in a burst of flames, engulfing the targeted hyenas in bright orange fire, the dog like creatures panicked under the stress of the flames and begin to run in circles seeking relief, bumping into and burning some of the other nearby hyenas in the process.

Two more down, nine left and now they were on top of them.

"For Oningrad!" Alex screamed. A number of hyenas, who seemed to have alternate destinations in mind immediately changed their trajectory and flung themselves at the dwarf. Alex's war cry ability was like a net, but Dante knew that it wasn't all encompassing and as a result he captured the attention of only about four of the charging hyenas. The rest were heading to Robyn and Morrigan, who weren't equipped to take heavy damage from multiple enemies. Whatever happened, he couldn't allow a hyena to get past him.

The first one in the charge order slammed into Alex's shield with a loud audible crunch as the animal's skull collided with the metal shield. It hit the ground in a slump and then directly behind it three more hyenas came running all eager to take their turn at the dwarf. They were forced to jump over or dash around the overeager hyena in the front, slowing them down just enough that they were able to survive their head-on collision with the shield. Alex stepped backward one step at a time, fending off the hyena's with his shield and axe in concert, not necessarily doling out damage, but more so keeping the animals focused on him and their attention off everyone else.

While Alex did that, five more hyenas not captured by his war cry, dashed pass. With speed, Fang dashed into the open space that the hyenas had begun to flood through and with a monstrous roar he lifted his axe high above his head.

"Executioner's Swing!" he bellowed in a voice that echoed across the grassland, and then with near perfect timing and powerful force he brought his axe down on to one of the hyenas, cleaving it in half.

Of the four remaining, two of them froze in the wake of his attack. Their mindless charging apparently stunted by the encounter with something far more savage and vicious then themselves. In that instant, they cowered in the wake of the barbarian, not sure if they should attack or retreat.

That left two hyenas free, both of which seemed determined to sink their teeth into Dante. Perfect, he thought. It made what he was planning to do much easier.

Dante rushed toward the charging hyenas and then, at the exact moment the two beast lunged themselves at him, he raised his sword.

"Lightspeed Slash." Dante called out forcing his will into his sword, as he did, the pouncing hyenas seemed to freeze in the air. They moved slowly through space, trapped in an attempt to lunge out and bite at Dante. It was better than anything he could have hoped for. It seemed as if he had slowed time, but in reality, he knew that he was, in that moment, simply moving extraordinarily fast. Knowing the effects of his ability only lasted briefly, Dante dragged the now semi-solid blade of his sword across the body of one hyena, then the other, and then at the risk of being greedy he dove forward, hit the ground in a roll between the two of them and came up just within arm's reach of a third hyena that was frozen in place not only by Dante's speed, but also by Fang's intimidating presence. He could feel time speeding up around him, or rather himself slowing down, but right before things evened out, he thrust his blade forward piercing it through the body of the animal he had just moved toward.

Time snapped back to attention and all at once three hyenas yelped out barks of agony as Dante seemed to move like a blur of man and metal, his sword severing clean through two hyenas and piercing a third before the beasts themselves could register what was happening. Every hyena Dante's sword had touched fell to the ground in a heap while Fang looked on, dumbfounded.

"Did you just kill my target?" asked Fang, momentarily taking his eyes off of the remaining hyena that cowered in front of him.

"One for you, three for me," Dante replied.

But before Fang could respond multiple shards of ice came flying across his field of vision each one slamming themselves into the still frightened hyena that he had momentarily looked away from. There had to be at least five large shards of solid ice each one as sharp as a dagger, and all of them had plunged into the hyena, dropping its HP to zero in an instant. Both Dante and Fang looked back at Morrigan who still had the remnants of frost emanating from her hands.

"Three for me," She said with a single raised eyebrow and a smirk.

"Damn it" muttered Fang under his breath. He looked over to the dwarf.

Pope's reloaded crossbow had claimed another one, though the captain made no comment about it.

And now that Alex was left with just one enemy to contend with, his one-handed axe made quick work of the last remaining hyena.

"That's two for me as well." He said, placing his shield onto his back once again.

"Wait a minute. Did I only get one kill?" asked Fang to no one in particular.

"Guess you lose," said Dante wiping his sword clean of blood and then placing it back into its sheath. "And now we need to move."

"No, no hold on a second," Fang said pointing at Dante accusingly, "You, you and her. I had two hyenas intimidated and you kill thieves stole them from me. I should have three."

"We're all in the same party," said Morrigan, "It doesn't matter who makes the kill we all get the experience points."

"Then why were you keeping count?" Fang said angrily.

"Well, I didn't want anyone to think I was incompetent and only killed one hyena," said Morrigan.

"See, I knew it!"

"We don't have time for this. We need to get out of here," snapped Dante.

"No way, don't try and change the subject. I demand we count those two stolen kills for me. That means I had three and I win."

"Fang no one cares how many kills you had, the battle is over, the hyenas are dead and now we need to leave. Now!"

"What's the rush?" Pope asked inquisitively.

"The hyenas," Dante explained, "they're scouts for larger more dangerous monsters, namely hyendons and gnolls."

Hyenadons? Gnolls? What are these exactly?" Pope asked.

"A hyenadon would be a lot like the things we just fought, only bigger," said Fang, insinuating he didn't see the point in all the fuss Dante was making.

"Yeah, and I'd imagine it would take a lot more than two cross bow bolts to take it down." Dante interrupted. "A hyenadon is basically a hyena crossed with a grizzly bear, its monstrous."

"And Gnolls?" asked Pope.

"Gnolls are beast men... they're a monster race. They're humanoid like hyenas. They walk on two legs, they fight with weapons, and they think. They aren't just animals acting on instincts and that makes them the most dangerous one of the three. Now if hyenas are present in the area, then the other two can't be far behind. So, we need to move and move now."

"Agreed," said Pope, "Let's head out immediately. We have six hours of daylight left let's get as close as we can to that Erebus River crossing."

"Captain, what about our loot, we need to skin these things, at least get the mana crystals."

"Leave them," said Pope. "There will be plenty of time for that later. For now, we march."

Fang complied though he didn't look happy about it, and together the group began to move west. No one bothered attempting to ride on the back of Dapple and instead Alex gently led him at a speed that was consistent with the rest of the group. The juxia was the only one who seemed to move across the savannah with no great concern, the juxia and Fang. Everyone else was continuously checking their surroundings, looking deep into the distance for the slightest hint of movement, listening intently for the sound of canine-accented laughter and scanning their every direction for any possible or oncoming threat. Large birds circled high above the remnants of their earlier battle. A few times Dante looked up into the bright afternoon sky and to the east back toward the Triton River and the city of Abilene Bay, he could see large birds circling high up above and he knew that vultures or some other type of flying scavengers had found the remnants of their earlier battle.

"You know," said Fang after they walked for nearly an hour and a half in a paranoid silence, putting nearly five miles between themselves and the downed hyenas. "You guys fight pretty well for a group of losers; I was actually surprised. I mean, never expected you to be a kill thief quarterback, but I have to admit, there is something about a cheater that I inherently respect. The desperation to win, the competitive spirit. It's admirable."

"Now I'm surprised," said Morrigan.

"Why's that?" asked Robyn.

"I never expected Fang would know how to use a word like 'inherently'," she said dryly.

Robyn and Alex laughed. Fang fumed. Pope continued walking. Dante couldn't help but smile to himself, but as he did, he thought about what the barbarian had said. They had fought well, something he would have had to attribute to the tutelage of Shinto. Though short, their time together had proved invaluable in more ways than one. The half-orc cleric had helped them refine and clearly define their party roles when engaged in combat. As the tank, it was Alex's job to hold enemy attention, and in a sense to block for the rest of the team almost like an offensive lineman would. In essence he would take a beating and the more heat or hate he could take the better off they would be, and as dangerous as this was, his sturdy build and ability to use his shield to stave off attacks made him ideal for the job. Morrigan's role was to stay at range and fire off spells damaging enemies from a distance. As a mage Shinto explained that she wasn't made to take hard hits, in order not to hinder her spell casting, her armor was light and didn't offer much protection, that meant she had to avoid physical combat as much as possible and keep the battle on her terms whenever at all possible. Robyn's role was similar with some key differences. Her job was also to inflict damage, but not only damage, chaos as well. Like Morrigan Robyn was not equipped to take on a large number of attacks, but unlike Morrigan she did her best work at close range, as a result Robyn's job was to sneak around the battlefield attacking enemies from behind and while they were unaware, perhaps busy with someone else they deemed more of a threat, then afterward she was meant to slink back into hiding and find a new target whittling away at the enemies while doing her best to remain unnoticed. Dante's role, coincidentally was a lot like that of a quarterback. Shinto had explained as a swordsman, he was well equipped enough that he could take a hit, even if he could not take as much abuse as Alex could, and with a weapon like a long sword he could deal large amounts of damage quickly and efficiently with well placed attacks as long as he was fast and smart about how he moved. As a result, it was his job to know the position of everyone on the battlefield and offer his support where it was needed. If Alex was taking too much hate, it was Dante's role to pull it off of him. If an enemy broke through the line and was closing distance on Morrigan he had to be the one to jump in front of her. If someone spotted Robyn and she couldn't get out of sight, he had to go and distract them so she could get away again. And whenever everything was going smoothly, or if absolutely everything was going wrong, he was to find the strongest thing on the battlefield and hack away at it until it died. Either that or determine that it was time to retreat. That was his role, at least according to Shinto.

It was funny, the role of tanks, damage dealers, healers and even party leaders Dante had already been familiar with, but it wasn't until Shinto had put things in perspective that in Deos, when a member of the party fails to fulfil their role someone might die, did things seem to take on new meaning.

"We can make camp here for the night," said Pope.

"Here? Isn't this kind of... out in the open?" Alex asked looking around as if hoping to find a better place pitch a tent.

"Do you have a better suggestion?" Pope asked in a tone that suggested that he wasn't really expecting an answer.

"Dante what do you think?" Alex asked aloud, prompting Robyn and Morrigan, to turn and look at Dante.

The unexpected influx of attention caught Dante by surprise and for a brief moment he froze. What did he think? Well, to the west only a few hundred yards away was the Black Wood. Back east too far to see with the naked eye was the Phobos River. And then to their immediate south, based off what Dante was reading on the map, was an area called The Hard World. From what he knew it was a rocky canyon that at their current levels, was best to be avoided at all cost.

"Well, it's better to hug the tree line and stay as far from it as possible then to wander to far south too soon and end up in an area worse than Hell Hearth Swamp. It'll be night soon and as best we know nothing has followed us so, yeah. I think we're good here."

They quickly constructed their tents and built a fire. "Some of that hyena meat would have been good right about now." Fang said, sitting down a few yards in front of his own crudely constructed tent.

"Yuck," said Robyn, "that sounds gross."

"We can't afford to cook anything anyway." Dante commented. "The fire is risky as is, but the smell that cooked meat gives off is guaranteed to attract predators."

"You worry too much, quarterback," said Fang, leaning back on his elbows in the grass.

"Worrying has kept us alive," said Alex, opening another bag apparently stored with food, which he reached into and begin removing bread, cheese and randomly assorted fruits and vegetables and passing out rations.

"We need to discuss watch for the night," said Pope as he was handed a chunk of hard bread. "I'll take first shift. Someone can relieve me in a few hours."

"There's no way I'm falling asleep with you on watch alone." Dante replied, almost before Pope had even finished his statement.

A silent tension filled the camp.

"Dante," said Pope is a calm and steady voice, "I would have thought we would have built some trust by now."

"We'll do first watch together." Dante said ignoring Pope's comment.

"Robyn and I will take second watch then," said Morrigan.

"We will?" asked Robyn.

Fang went to his tent almost immediately once it was established, he did not have watch duty, but the others lingered around the fire a bit longer.

There arose an awkward silence as Dante, Morrigan Alex and Robyn sat quietly and continued to watch the flickering flames of the campfire, each member of the party seemingly refusing to retire for the night, even after their shift had been set.

"You all know the point of setting night watch in shifts is so that all of us get at least some sleep over the course of the night." Pope remarked.

"Well, since we're all sitting here, I have to say, I haven't been able to figure out for the life of me how you all have survived in the wilderness, with just the four of you." When Pope spoke, Dante thought, he almost sounded like a normal person. "It was difficult for me and my men, and it was nearly twenty of us. But after today, after seeing you all in action. It makes sense. The four of you have grown a lot since we were last together."

"Why are you talking like that?" Dante asked, "Like we're old friends? The last time we were together we pounded my face into the dirt and threated to kill us if we didn't do as we were told. You compared me to a dog for god's sake."

"Dante," said Pope smirking from across the orange flames of the fire, "I thought I explained that it was nothing personal. The things that I've done, they were nothing against you, the truth of the matter is, I like you, you remind me a lot of myself actually."

"I'm nothing like you!" Dante said angrily.

"You see, that's what I mean." Pope said with a chuckle, "You take it all so personally, but that's what makes you a good leader. You're passionate," Pope emphasized the last word with a clenched fist, an uncharacteristic show of emotion was beginning to leak out from the captain as he spoke, as if the flames from the fire was drawing out something buried deep within him. "And your friends can see that, that's why they follow you like they do. That's why they have become so loyal. However, emotion can also be a liability, it clouds the mind, distracts the judgment. That's where you and I differ."

Now it was Dante's turn to chuckle, "You think that's where you and I differ. Pope I don't even think you're human anymore. I don't think you've ever been."

Pope smiled a large grin that could be seen beyond the flames and the sight of it made Dante want to reel back in horror.

"Oh, I was human once, a long time ago. I was a husband... a father."

Pope reached into his collar and pulled the small golden locket from underneath his armor. He stared it for a moment.

"I've been a soldier most of my life." Pope said, almost reluctantly. He continued looking at the locket as he spoke, it was as if his eyes were glued to it. "It's the only thing I've ever been good at, at least until I became a father. I used to be in a Special Ops unit, one that got sent on a lot missions that most of us weren't expected to come back from. After a while you get used the idea of dying and when you get to that point the fear fades and a suicide mission is just another job, just another day at the office. After I got married and had my daughter I was still being deployed on the dangerous missions, but in between deployments, I had this precious, innocent, sweet little girl that made life worth living." Pope smiled down at the piece of children's jewelry as if it could smile back, but this time, it wasn't one of his smug arrogant smirks, instead, it was a kind of sad, melancholy smile and it was hard to tell through the dark and the orange of the flames, but it looked as if his eyes were glistening.

"Then, from out of nowhere she got sick. She went from playing with stuffed animals, hosting tea parties and asking me to read her bedtime stories, to spending her days and nights in a hospital. She was six years old when she was diagnosed. A rare form of brain cancer. We never even got to celebrate her seventh birthday.

"Up to that point in my career, I had run over fifty-five highly classified missions, all of them successful." Pope looked up from the golden locket, the shimmer and glint in his eyes gone, replaced only with a grim and hollow expression that could be seen clearly even in the low light. "Now imagine being a soldier, trained to survive any and every scenario imaginable, trained to kill, protect, defend and then suddenly, the only thing truly worth defending, the only thing truly worth protecting, the only thing that you would have gladly traded your life for, you had to sit by and watch slowly wither away right in front of you. That's enough to kill any man's humanity I think."

"Oh my God," said Robyn, "that's terrible, I- I'm sorry."

"It's funny that you mention God," said Pope, "I spent a lot of time angry at God, blaming God, asking God why me, why my little girl. But then after going so long and hearing nothing back but absolute silence, I made a realization. There was no God, and I was simply taking things too personally."

The night passed into morning without incident and upon sunrise the party broke camp and immediately resumed their trek south following the tree line of the Black Wood. Dante recounted the story that Pope had told them the night before, about the daughter he had lost and how it had turned him into the man that he was today. Honestly Dante couldn't say how much of it he believed versus how much of it he had to assume Pope had made up. He supposed the captain could have been telling the truth about his painful past. But to what end? Why would *he* share such a thing with *them*? Was it to prove that he too was a human being who felt the pain of grief and the hurt of loss, or was it to lull them all into some false sense of security?

They moved through the next day with uncomfortable ease. The savannah was empty with the exception of large black horned rhino that always seemed to be far off in the distance, grazing on the high grass. There was no sign of hyenas, hyenadon or gnolls. After some time, Dante had a go at riding Dapple, sliding himself into the saddle. He immediately saw why Morrigan had preferred walking as in order to stay upright and not feel like he was about to fall over one way or the other, Dante was forced to squeeze with his buttocks and hold on with his thighs, an effort that after a while left him sore. An hour later, he dismounted and decided to walk again.

"I say we get a bit closer and call it a day," said Pope when they came in sight of the Erebus river in the distance.

"We're so close, shouldn't we cross over?" asked Fang.

"It'll be dark soon and we don't know what's waiting on the other side." Added Dante. "And we want to avoid camping next to the swamp if possible. If we camp for the night now, then wake up and get an early start tomorrow, we'll give ourselves the most amount of time to get in and out of the swamp."

"Agreed," said Pope, nodding along with Dante's comment. "Glad we're all on the same page."

They set up the tents and a campfire and quickly resolved that Fang and Alex would take the first watch since neither of them had a watch shift the previous night, Dante and Pope would take second watch, relieving them after a few hours. Satisfied that he and Pope were on the same schedule allowing him to keep an eye on the captain, Dante retired to the tent that he and Alex shared, laid down on his bed roll and closed his eyes to get some rest. The night before Dante had reviewed his spirit tome and found that the thirteen hyenas that they had slain had yielded a total of 1,625 experience points and he now had a total of 21,425 experience points but had yet to reach level seven. That meant that the hyenas were worth 125 points each, technically making them some of the weakest monsters that they had encountered since coming to Deos. That night as he fell asleep, he dreamed about talking hyenas asking him to take a quest deep into the swamp and in exchange they would make him a gnoll and allow him to eat first whenever they captured prey, in the same dream he began losing experiencing and dropping down in levels, unlocking new skills in a category called Grief and Misery and mastering an ability called Paranoia. During the most intense moment of the dream, he could smell something burning and her his brother Malcolm calling his name or was it his brother Bryan. It was hard to tell which because he could only really hear them and not see them. He listened intently trying hard to make out what it was that they were saying. Was that... shake up? No, maybe they were saying... Dante, make up?

"Dante! Wake Up!"

Dante's eyes sprung open to find Alex standing over him drenched in sweat and dripping blood from a small cut on his forehead. He was filthy, covered in dirt and ash and he had a wild look of panic in his eyes.

"We're under attack! It's the Gnolls, they found us!" he screamed.

How? When? Dante was confused, disoriented. What was going on? Was Pope behind this, had this been his plan all along?

"Dante we have to go! Come on, we have to go now!" Alex screamed. The dwarf pulled Dante to his feet and led him out of the tent. Outside the campsite had been turned to a warzone. Both Pope's tent and Fang's tents were on fire and as a result a thick black smoke filled the air around them. Morrigan helped pull Robyn from inside the tent they shared and as she did a large creature covered in fur but shrouded by the smoke approached. Morrigan summoned a powerful wind that sent the creature flying, then she pulled Robyn free from the tent and the two of them came running. Dante saw something large and metal move in his peripheral vision and without thinking he summoned his sword into his hand and lifted it in a defensive position protecting his head and neck. Near moments after raising his sword it was met with tremendous force bearing down upon it and Dante turned to find himself staring at a monster the likes of which he could have never truly imagined.

It was at least six and a half feet tall, but its hunched and crooked back robbed it of at least three inches. It had the undeniable face of a hyena and it pressed its snarling snout in close to Dante's face. The rusted, and battered axe it wielded shot sparks as it pressed hard on Dante's long sword. Foam and drool dripped from the thing's exposed teeth. It was covered in fur and dressed in tattered pieces of old armor. It was a demon from a nightmare, hungry for flesh. The beast man freed his axe from the stalemate with Dante's sword and raised both arms for another attack when two large crossbow bolts came thudded into its chest, a third into its eye. It drew back, reeling.

Pope aimed down the sight of his crossbow while behind him a battle crazed Fang swung his axe wildly at anything that moved. The sight of the captain jump-started Dante's brain back into action.

"I only slowed it down. I didn't kill it," Pope called out.

The wounded Gnoll was still standing. With one fluid movement it pulled the bolt from its eye, letting out a pain filled roar. Dante lifted his sword pointed it toward the advancing Gnoll and activated his ability.

"LightSpeed Slash" he called out, dashing toward the creature. He lifted his semi-solid blade for an attack and set a course for collision. But the gnoll didn't slow as he should have. His axe still moved with speed to a position directly before Dante's neck. Dante tacked left, batted the axe with his own sword. The effects were immediate. The Gnoll's weapon was violently deflected leaving the beast man's chest and face unguarded. As quickly as he could Dante pulled his whip like sword across the gnolls body two times before the effects of his ability wore off. The two well placed slashes dropped the Gnoll down to zero HP and it fell to the ground, lifeless. But just as quickly as one hit the ground, more gnolls appeared, each brandishing a weapon and bared teeth. Morrigan fired her ice shards into a crowd of them, hitting two, one in the leg, another in arm, but three others lifted shields and blocked the magical attack, protecting themselves from taking any damage at all.

Fang swung his axe and caught one by the leg but in the process was struck in the back with a spear. Alex blindsided the gnoll with his shield before he could do any more damage to the barbarian, but the pain sent Fang into even more of a frenzy, he attacked ever more feverishly, catching gnoll after gnoll with his axe. Yet the monsters advanced. For every gnoll killed, there seemed to be two more to take its place. Pope fired his cross bow again, unloading into a nearby gnolls chest and then using a dagger to finish him off only to have the use the cross bow again, this time as a shield to stop another gnoll from decapitating him.

"This is no good!" Dante called out, "We have to retreat, we have to run."

"Make for the bridge!" Pope yelled.

"Everyone, run for the bridge!" Dante screamed swing his sword wildly in an attempt to keep the gnolls at bay.

Robyn took off first, she bolted toward the river and with inhuman agility launched herself on Dapple. The juxia had trotted out a safe distance when the attack began, and then stubbornly stopped cold in its tracks despite the chaos, watching the battle unfold at the campsite.

"Hyah!" Robyn yelled and immediately Dapple lurched forward with speed that he had never used since they had left Abilene Bay. She pulled hard on his reins and he turned and together they charged head first back toward the fighting.

Dante deflected two more random sword strikes, stumbled backwards and then twisted his torso and began running in the same direction. As he turned, two birds made out of flames can screeching past his head and slammed into a gnoll behind him exploding on contact. Dante didn't look back to see how much damage the spell had done. He barreled forward in an all-out sprint grabbing Morrigan by the arm and pulling her along with him as he passed her. She was still trying to form spells, but Dante could see her status box and knew that her MP was already down to half.

"We have to get to the bridge! Go, I'll cover you."

"I'm not going to leave you guys here!"

"I'll cover you now and you cover us once you've crossed the bridge." Dante yelled.

She turned and broke into a run toward the river. Dante turned and saw Alex fending three gnolls from behind his shield, he dashed to his side and impaled one with his sword, and then tried to slash another but the second gnoll blocked the attack with its own weapon and then punched Dante in the jaw with a fur covered fist. The attack caught Dante by surprise, knocking him off of his feet and onto his back. He rolled hard to his right to avoided being cleaved in two by a falling sword and the scrambled back up to his feet and performed a light speed slash that allowed him two open attacks across the gnolls chest and a piercing thrust that not only sunk his sword deep into the stomach of the gnoll that had punched him, but it also pierced the back of the one still engaged with Alex. Dante stumbled backwards as he pulled his sword free and both gnolls fell to the ground from their wounds.

"Pope, Fang, we're leaving!" Dante shouted with all the air left in his lungs and with what little opening he and Alex had, they bolted.

They sprinted away from the campsite and toward the river with all the strength they could muster. Originally when they had set up their camp the river hadn't seemed that far, but now, it seemed like miles away. Dante pushed his body to run as hard as he had ever run before. His muscles burned and his chest ached as he reached and stretched. He couldn't hear anything anymore, only the sound of his own labored breathing and the rhythmic footfalls of his feet as they pounded into the dirt. Pain shot through his body with every step, a grim reminder that he couldn't stop, regardless of the pain, no matter how much it hurt, he couldn't stop until he crossed that bridge, because tonight, he was running for his life.

Robyn and Morrigan crossed the bridge first on the back of Dapple. Robyn turned, saw Morrigan running and pulled her up on to the juxia's back. Dapple sped across the rope bridge without the slightest bit of hesitation. The bridge rattled and shook under the juxia's weight, but with the animal's speed and balance, Robyn and Morrigan found themselves across the bridge before they could register an emotion of fear or uncertainty. The rope bridge was suspended roughly forty feet above the river's surface and was supported by high cliffs on each side of the water. The bridge itself was narrow, no more than four feet in width, forcing anyone crossing the river to so in a single file line. Dante reached the bridge next, followed by Alex, then Pope and lastly Fang. Behind them were nearly a dozen more gnolls, and they had someone new with them.

In a burst of cold and blue magic energy, Morrigan flung large shards of ice the length of the bridge to the other side of the river in an attempt to hit any gnoll who gave chase to the rest of the party. However, now there was something else on the other side of the river, and when the ice shards hit it, they seemed to bounce off of its large muscular body with seemingly no effect. Tethered to a rope being held by two gnolls both of which held short leather whips, was an animal reminiscence of some twisted four-legged creature from some forgotten part of hell. It looked similar to the hyenas from the day before only it was the size of small car, and its every predatory feature was accentuated to a nightmarish degree. The gnolls holding the rope cracked their whips across the creature's back and the beast snarled and roared in anger. Then, for the first time since the attack began, one of the gnolls spoke.

"They flee to the river! They are trying to escape! Release the hyenadon!"

"But she leaves nothing but scraps and bones." Said another gnoll.

"Better scraps and bones then nothing at all! Release her!"

And then without another word, they released the ropes. The hyenadon launched itself forward hurtling toward the rope bridge, trampling and bulldozing other gnolls in its wake. Speeding with unhampered fervor towards the fleeing adventurers.

"Guys, hurry it up!" Morrigan screamed.

Dante looked back, saw what was coming, and unlocked a reserve of energy that he didn't know he had, carrying him the remaining distance across the bridge where he fell to his hands and knees in an effort to try and catch his breath. Alex followed suit, then Pope, but before Fang could exit the bridge the hyenadon had reached the edge of the river on the eastern side. When the monster stepped on the bridge, the entire structure shook and buckled, so much so that Fang had to grab hold to the rope railing to keep from flying off and plunging down into the cold river below.

"Fang, move it!" Dante yelled as the hyendon began making its way across the bridge as well, the gnolls with whips behind it urging it along.

The barbarian looked back, saw the large beast moving cautiously across the flimsily bridge and turned back toward the western edge where the rest of the party stood waiting for him. He moved slowly and deliberately forward still holding on to the sides of the bridge in an effort to keep his balance as the hyenadon's movements shook the now somewhat questionable structure. After only a few more steps Fang made it to the other side of the bridge and then before anyone could say a word, he lifted his axe and severed the rope holding the bridge to the western bank. Instantly the bridge fell from under the hyenadon dropping it forty feet into the rushing black river below and trapping a large group of angry gnolls on the other side of the water.

There was a momentary silence on the western bank.

"What in the hell just happened?" Asked Dante, hands on his knees, still struggling to catch his breath.

"Well..." answered Fang, "I can't say for sure, but I think we crossed the river and made it to Hell Hearth Swamp."

Chapter 41: Hell Hearth Swamp

The group sat in the pre-dawn darkness, under a moonless sky, awaiting the sunrise. They didn't bother lighting another fire, and even in the dead of night none of them had trouble staying awake. The aftereffect of having your camp raided by blood thirsty gnolls and their pet hyenadon was like ingesting large doses of caffeine. They were all wired.

"And to top it off the bridge is gone, so on top of everything else we're going to have to find a way back across the river once we've made it out of the swamp," said Alex in a hushed whisper.

"Let's not get distracted by future circumstances beyond our control," said Pope in a low voice. "We can worry about that part of the mission once we get to it, for now we have to stay focused on the task at hand. Get to the swamp, find the flower, get out of the swamp."

As soon as the party found that they had enough sunlight to see, they continued their walk west and within a couple of hours of dawn found themselves standing on wet soggy ground. The large dark colored trees of the black wood now stood tall and erect to the north, while a smaller number of desolate and withered trees, twisted and gnarled by time and the dark brackish water, lay spread out before them. The further they walked the wetter and muddier the ground became as the grass of the savannah gave way to stiff stalks with blades edged with saw-like teeth.

"I think its safe to say we are officially in the swamp now," Robyn commented, attempting to swat away another insect.

"At least the outer edge." Dante looked up at the sky. "Its still pretty early and we've got plenty of daylight, but what we need is supposed to be deep in the heart of the swamp. I figure we got about eight hours to get in there find it and get out." Dante dropped down to one knee and began rifling through his pack.

"What are you doing Quarterback? If you're in a hurry, we need to get moving."

Without saying a word, Dante came back up with a vial filled with bright red liquid which he then tossed to the barbarian.

"Health Potion. Drink up. You took a lot of damage from that fight last night and you haven't gotten any real rest since, so your HP still hasn't recovered. Everyone, take a health potion or an ether now. We don't know what we're going to run into in the swamp."

"Good thinking," Said Pope. "Let's take five for first aid. Move out immediately after."

Both Alex and Pope consumed a health potion for the sake of their HP and Morrigan drank a vial of ether in order to retore her depleted mana pool. Dante also drank a health potion; it was viscous and thick, the consistency of cough syrup and the flavor of a sugary sweet fruit juice with a chalky aftertaste that left him smacking his tongue against the roof of his mouth. The liquid burned in his chest like a strong drink and at the same time he could feel the random cuts and bruises of the last few hours recede. Dante could see and feel his HP bar refill from two-thirds back up to full health in a matter of seconds.

A familiar ringing in the ears reminded Dante of other possible advantages and he took an additional moment to summon his spirit tome.

-Five Bloodpack Gnolls have been defeated.

-You have gained 4,000 Experience points!

-A Grassland Hyenadon has been defeated.

-You have gained 1,000 Experience points!

-You have obtained Level 7, Congratulations!

- You have a total of 26,425 Experience Points

He had reached level seven. That was good, that was very good. He hadn't unlocked any new skills or abilities, but every level increase came with a bump in stats, and any increase to attack, defense, or any expansion of the health pool, especially at this juncture, was critical to their survival.

"We've leveled up again." Dante announced.

"Sweet," said Fang finishing off a health potion of his own. "Let's go do this."

The ground went from soggy and saturated to flooded. Large pools of gathered water that looked like a collection of small ponds in an open field while between them, a barely visible mud path tracked a walkway within the marsh. The ankle deep water, which sat on a bed of thick black mud, pulled at their every step. Small fish skittered underneath the surface of the water fleeing in the adventurer's wake while long legged cranes took flight at the sound of their approaching splashes. The swamp was a labyrinth of mud, water and sawgrass that seemed to force the adventurers to move in a series of random directions based off of *its* whims, as opposed to their own decisions. Dante began to worry a day wasn't near enough time to make it in and back out again.

Before long they found themselves near the distant trees. Dante felt a growing heat against his chest, reached inside his armor and removed the spirit crystal from underneath his chest plate. The gem was glowing.

"Well, that's new," Dante said.

"The fortune teller," said Pope. "She said that the crystal was key to finding the flowers, perhaps this means we're close?"

Dante was pointed deeper into the swamp, he turned and faced the direction from which they had just come and the light of the spirit crystal faded and the warmth dissipated. He turned back toward the direction that they were walking, and the light and the warmth returned, this time brighter than it had before.

"It must be pointing us in the right direction." Said Robyn, "We just have to follow it to the flowers."

The party continued, following the light of the crystal through a maze of mud and saw grass. Twice they came upon large alligator creatures partially submerged in the dirty water. Cautiously the adventurers crept passed the prehistoric reptiles, avoiding a fight and the potential danger that came along with one. However, by the time they encountered a third alligator they had no choice. It lay directly across their path.

Dante scanned it and found that it was called a Bull Gator, a level ten creature adept at fighting both on land and in the water. He knew it had a basic yet effective tactic of grabbing its prey in its powerful jaws and then dragging them down into the deeper depths of the swamps many wading ponds, drowning and then eating its victims. Quickly they formed a simple strategy of their own to lure the gator off the land trail that it rested upon and bring it to a small clearing, one still covered in muddy water and saw grass but at least large enough to allow them to surround the creature and use their superior numbers to their advantage.

Their plan was based on a classic MMO fighting style. Robyn would pull the gator. Using her hand crossbow and relative speed, she positioned herself at a safe distance from the sun basking reptile, and then fired at it with her single shot ranged weapon. Her crossbow bolt hit the gator but then bounced off of its hard skin doing only minimal damage but still managing to get the creature's attention.

Angrily, and as expected, the bull gator aggressively sped forward giving chase to its attacker. With a considerable head start Robyn scrambled through the mud and back to the clearing only a few yards away where the rest of the party stood waiting for the gator to get within striking distance. Robyn made it to the clearing first, sprinting past Alex who stood waiting for her with his shield in hand. As Robyn made it to the safety of her friends the bull gator continued to barrel forward, determined to capture kill and devour the rogue along with anything else that got in its path.

As it charged forward Pope begin to fire bolts from his own crossbow. Larger and more powerful than the single-handed crossbow Robyn had wielded, Pope shots did more damage to the creature's considerable HP bar, but not nearly enough to slow its charge. In fact the gator seemed to now move even faster, its attention now changed from Robyn to Pope. However, before it could move much further, Morrigan sent shards of ice flying in the creature's direction, they hit the large reptile with impact, although this time the ice shards didn't cover everything they touched in a thin layer of frost, but instead any water that came into contact with the spell was flash frozen into solid ice. Dante watched as a large chunk of the gator's health bar vanished as a result of the spell and its movement speed, hindered by ice covered limbs and ground, was greatly slowed.

The gator finally reached the clearing, its attention now clearly focused on Morrigan, but before it could attack Alex activated his War Cry ability, forcefully grabbing the creature's attention then raising his shield in preparation for the monster's attack. Dante and Fang ran up on both sides of the monster to surround it and position themselves to attack. The gator opened a large mouth filled with long pointed teeth and jaws that looked as if they could snap a man in half. It swung its large head from side to side warding off its many attackers and attempting the to dislodge the hard metal casing from around the turtle like dwarf so that it could crush his skull between its teeth. Pope fired additional shot from his crossbow which found itself to be more effective at close range. Dante and Fang took turns hacking away at the creature whenever it turned away from one of them in an effort to either protect itself or snap at Alex. The Bull Gator's health bar slowly dropped under the onslaught of the parties repeated attack but right when it looked as if they had the monster cornered, it rolled.

It was a violent flailing and desperate roll, like something Dante had seen alligators and crocodiles do on nature documentaries. It was, he realized a special attack, one with a ranged area of effect designed to hit multiple targets. Sadly, Dante realized all of this too late, since once the gator initiated his death roll, the force generated by the creature in addition to its flailing limbs caught everyone by surprise. The bull gator's tail caught Fang in the chest, knocking him into the nearby pond behind them, the sheer force of the spin knocked Dante off of his feet and the equivalent of a spinning headbutt knocked Alex off of his feet and on to his back. When the spin stopped, the tables had been turned and the gator that had been surrounded and well on its way to being defeated was not standing over two prone combatants and a third that was pulling himself out of the water.

The gator, seeing that it now had the advantage, charged toward the downed dwarf, mouth open, hissing and growling as it rushed forward. Shards of ice rained down on the gator and its open mouth, just like it had previously the magic spell flash froze all the water it touched momentarily stopping the bull gator in its tracks. The pause caused by the spell gave just enough time from Alex to get to his feet and then swing around a full 360 degrees slamming forcefully into the monster shield first a newly unlocked ability referred to by the Dwarf as Shield Bash. The resulting collision shattered the ice that had covered the gator's body as well as dropped its HP bar well passed zero ending their battle.

They were awarded 1,000 experience points each for defeating the bull gator. Dante touched the dead creature, pulled from it a decent sized mana crystal and gave it to Robyn who placed the item into one of Dapple's saddlebags. Fang took a number of the gator's teeth and then used his axe to chop off the creature's muscular tail.

If this were the game version of Dragon Dale, they would set up camp and pull in bull gators one by one, killing them to farm crystals and gator tails. But without a healer in the group and the constant threat of death lingering in the air things like experience parties were simply too great a risk for the adventurers of Deos at least in some areas.

The party moved, still following the glow and warmth of the spirit crystal. Before long they noticed that the plant life had begun to change. The sawgrass remained, but now along with it they also began to see fat white pod like plants, that sat atop broad green leaves. At the top of the pod like body of the plant was an opening and curiously upon discovering the new specimen of flora, Fang approached it and pushed his face in close to the plump white pod and its opening.

"You guys see this, kind of looks like a cabbage. You think its edible?" Fang asked, moving in for a closer look.

"No, don't!" Dante called out attempting to stop the barbarian. But it was too late. Once Fang approached the pod and leaned in close, without even touching it, the bulbous white body of the plant heaved and spewed from its top a spray like mist, that hit Fang directly in the face. He reeled backwards swatting and batting at the air. The contents of the pod emptied out into the air above it, but only after Fang inhaled a lungful of the mysterious gas.

The barbarian choked and gagged at first in surprise and embarrassment, but then Dante noticed a slight change in his breathing as he started to wheeze.

"What the heck was that?" Fang rubbed his face and spit to get expel whatever it was he had breathed in. He looked around at the others embarrassed, expecting them to burst out into of wild fits of laughter, but was met only with looks of grave concern.

"That was a Gas Pod," said Dante. "I recognize them from past games. If you get too close, they react by releasing tiny spores into the air. The spores are toxic and even breathing them in is poisonous."

"Poisonous?" Fang wheezed, "I don't feel poisoned. I feel fine actually. I must be..." He struggled to take another breath, "Immune."

"Well, that's odd because you look really, really bad," said Robyn. In a short time Fang's peach-colored skin had become tinted with a sickly shade of green and large beads of sweat had to gathered on his forehead.

"No, I'm fine, let's keep going," Fang wheezed before his words became a garbled mumbling. He attempted to take a step forward before dropping to one knee, then grabbing hold to his torso in pain.

Dante looked to his status box and saw his HP bar slowly depleting.

"He's poisoned," Dante called out. "We need to give him an antidote."

"Nah, I'm fline" Fang muttered around a fast-swelling tongue.

Alex grabbed one of the vials filled with green liquid from Dapple's saddle bag and rushed over to the barbarian, who was still down on one knee. Alex first tried handing the vial to Fang, only to have it waved away, and when the dwarf tried pouring the potion into Fang's mouth for him, he was met with a struggle surprisingly well-coordinated for a man positioned on one knee and only using one arm.

"He inhaled a lot of that gas. He needs to take that antidote now," Morrigan said.

"I didn't think poison made you confused and combative," said Robyn.

"It doesn't," said Dante, "Or at least it didn't in the games."

"We don't have time for this." Pope walked over to Fang, stood behind him and grabbed him by the chin and back of the head as though he were preparing to break Fang's neck with the intention of leaving him there in the swamp, but instead he pulled and held his face up toward the sky. "Pour!" Pope shouted to Alex. "Now!"

Alex obliged, pouring the green liquid down Fang's throat as Pope held him, forcing his mouth open and refusing to let him so much as turn his head. Once the vial was empty, Pope forced the barbarian's mouth closed, pinched his nose closed and held him still until he swallowed. After the captain was satisfied that the antidote had been ingested, he released Fang, who dropped to the ground in a pile.

"Put him on the back of the animal, let's keep moving."

It did not take long for Fang to come back to his senses and resume walking after taking the antidote, which was good, at least in Dapple's opinion. For the juxia it wasn't an issue of the barbarian being too heavy a load to carry, it was more that he'd never received a formal apology for being called an ugly horse a few days' prior, an insult that the juxia felt was unnecessary and quite frankly out of line.

Soon the party found themselves in a section of the swamp inundated with gas pods. The bulbous white flowers grew scattered throughout the marshland, both on and off the mud trail that the party needed to use to navigate. In the distance, one of the spore filled plants hiccupped, spewing poison. In the water near the pod the top of a bull gator's head quickly dropped beneath the water, the apparent culprit for setting the pod off in the first place.

"Ah crap..." mumbled Fang, "How many more of those antidotes did you bring, quarterback?"

"We've got five left." Dante answered looking out at the field of toxic landmines that they now had to navigate their way through. The crystal around his neck was telling his which way to go, now the difficult part was going to be doing it. They moved forward stepping carefully as they went cautions to stay a safe distance away from any of the highly reactionary plants. Dante noticed now that a lot of the animals that had occupied the outer regions of the swamp were now absent, the small minnow-like fish that skittered around the shallows, the fat toads that sat along the edges of the ponds and even the pesky insects were now all missing. The only movement Dante saw now was either that of Hell Hearth bull gators or that of a slithering kind from some unknown mostly unseen serpent, that did an alarmingly good job of keeping itself hidden.

Yet no matter how worrisome the patrolling dinosaur-like alligators and nearly undetectable and highly venomous snake seemed to be, the most pressing concern was that every time one of these creatures moved they unintentionally set off another gas pod, filling the air with poison and forcing the party to either stop where they were or move more quickly in order to avoid inhaling a lung full of toxic spores and end up in the same state as Fang had been.

They moved forward slowly, fighting through the water, mud, heat and poison spraying plants, advancing by what felt like an inch a minute. Then right when it felt like they were finally starting to build up some sort of rhythm and momentum in their march, a sudden and loud chorus of high-pitched squawking startled them all. They looked up to see a large flock of small black birds take flight. They scattered into the sky, fluttered left, then right, and then in mid-air shifted their direction and began flying aggressively in the group's direction.

"Guys, these birds are acting kind of strange!" Dante called out pulling his sword from its sheath.

"It's just a murmuration," said Morrigan looking up in the sky at the flock's curious movement.

Then one of the birds, one much further ahead of the larger flock shot past the members of the group at about head height. It sped passed the adventurers like a bullet and when it was gone Dante noticed that he had been left with a small cut underneath his left eye. Blood pooled and then dropped down his cheek from the small red scratch. Two more birds shot past, leaving Dante with yet another scratch, and then another. Then Fang, Robyn and Alex each all found themselves with small scratches and cuts as a series of the birds zipped through their ranks.

"No," said Pope as one of the birds bounced off of Alex's shield and fell to the ground in a broken heap. "They are moving in an attack formation!" the captain lifted his crossbow and fired into the mass of the flock that had yet to reach them, hitting one of the birds near the front of the charge. The bolt hit the bird through the chest killing it instantly and sending it careening to the ground in like a tiny meteor of black feathers. Upon impact the large flock immediately changed direction moving as if they were all one large organism as opposed to nearly a hundred or so of individual birds. They pulled up, banked hard to the right and then turned around positioning themselves for another pass. They moved like a small living mist or black sentient cloud shaping and remolding itself in the air like a large free form undulating wave. If Dante hadn't known that what he was seeing was made up of a group of angry birds he would have been horrified by their otherworldly and alien like movement. In reality even knowing that they were birds didn't exactly stop him from being horrified by what he was seeing. He looked around himself and wondered how they would possibly shield themselves from incoming barrage especially when one wrong move might end up leaving them with a face full of poison gas.

"Flame Sparrow!" Morrigan screamed. The flock of flames flew forward and collided with the living swarm of black birds, exploding in a series of mid-air fireballs that engulfed bird after bird. The black birds slammed into the fireballs as if it were a red wall. Once nearly half of the birds had perished in the flames the other half abandoned the attack flying off squawking in the opposite direction, while the birds that had failed to escape fell from the sky as small flaming motes of fire and feathers, most of them landing in the swamp water, extinguishing themselves in a plume of black smoke. A smoldering bird fell near a bulbous white plant, which spewed forth its poisonous mist. What happened next surprised everyone. The poisonous mist burst into flames when the bodies of the flaming birds came into contact, causing columns of fire to shoot into the air. This set off a chain reaction, with burning birds setting off pod after pod of brightly burning pillars of fire all over the marsh and suddenly Dante realized that the designation of Hell Hearth seemed like more than a fitting name for swamp, in fact, he was convinced no other name would do.

Dante and the others stood stock still, holding their position until the swamp's erupting fires died down and the burning world around them receded to nothing more than the smell of scorched ozone. The swamp itself was still fully intact and had they not been there a moment before, no one in the party would have believed that the sky itself had just been on fire.

Now that most of the gas pods in the immediate area had expelled all of their contents and the aftereffects of Morrigan's spell had set that highly flammable content ablaze, the party moved through the swamp more steadily and expediently then they had before. Dante knew that the gas pod plants took days to rebuild enough toxic spores to be dangerous again after spewing its mist into the air, allowing them to move with at least one less concern for the general time being. The walked on, following the crystal through turn after turn, all the while glowing brighter and warmer on Dante's chest. They trudged through deep water and mud, constantly checking the sky for the sentient swarm of black birds, the ponds for the patrolling bull gators and the trail for any new and as of yet to be disturbed gas pods. Deep down a part of Dante felt relieved that the swamp held up to its reputation of being difficult and deadly, as he reasoned that they were indeed in over their heads, and that if had they been a few levels higher, while they still might have been having a difficult go of things they would have had an easier time then they were having now, but however, if they had made it as far as they had thus already and faced little to no resistance then Dante would have been worried that something far more sinister than gas pods and bull gators was lurking underneath the surface of the swamp, but now he was convinced that this was a sufficient enough hell.

About three and a half hours from the start of their expedition into the swamp, after taking innumerable twist and turns that left Dante incapable of calculating with even the slightest degree of accuracy how far they had traveled throughout the day, the party found themselves stepping into a large clearing. An open space in the swamp that left the ponds behind and held instead a large muddy field, filled with saw grass, gas pods and the occasional mangrove tree. Upon reaching the clearing, Dante, after considering how much time they had already spent venturing into the swamp, begin to deliberate on if now was the right time to turn around and begin trying to make their way out of the swamp. After all, they probably only had about four hours of daylight left and it would take them at least that amount of time to make their way back out, going the way they came, if they could even remember it. But then, before he could suggest turning back, the spirit crystal begin to glow much brighter and hotter than it had before, so much so that everyone in the party turned to look at the jewel around Dante's neck as it began to lift up of its own accord and pulled Dante forward a few steps, as if to point in a distinct direction clear across the marsh. Then without warning, the crystal stopped glowing, stopped radiating heat and dropped softly back down to his chest. Dante's eyes followed the line of sight created by the crystal and realized that across the field, there in what had to be the middle of the swamp, some fifty yards away from where they currently stood, was a small dilapidated little wooden shack.

It sat near the far edge of the clearing under the shadow of a group of mangrove trees that undoubtedly marked the entrance into the labyrinth like corridors that lead back into the swamps mud trails and gator ponds. The shack was built up on a small wooden frame that elevated it slightly out of the mud and water, while beneath it where Dante expected to see maybe sawgrass or gas pods, he saw instead bright white flowers that grew in great big bushels. Beautiful, pristine flowers, that even from a distance looked out of place surrounded by the mud and muck of the swamp.

"It's them!" Shouted Dante. "The flowers we're looking for. They're right there!" He yelled and began to move quickly toward them, not quite willing to go into a sprint, but far too excited to simply walk, he split the difference and broke out in a slight jog as he made his way to the hut, he could feel the others keeping pacing with him, a clear amount of enthusiasm in the air as they had finally made it. They had found the Death's Head Rose. Now all they had to do was grab a couple and then make their way out of this gods forsaken swamp, and everything would be okay.

It was about then, directly in the midst of that thought and about halfway to the distance of the hut and the flowers that sat beneath it when Dante noticed that to his left was a log. A large, half-rotted and incredibly heavy looking log, that just so happened to be oddly hurtling through the air and towards his head with incredible speed. A lifetime of athletic training in combination with basic human survival instinct took control of Dante's body moving it before he even had time to process what was happening.

"Duck!" he yelled out almost as an afterthought as his body semi-autonomously went through the motions of planting his chest in the mud, narrowly avoiding the flying wooden projectile, clearly aimed at his head. From the position of the cold wet ground, he looked over to his right and saw the log fly over him and his friends then tumble across the field end over end landing some ten yards away, leaving large deep gashes in the mud marking each of the places it had made impact. He was relieved to see that no one in the party had been hit by this chunk of rogue timber, that they had either spotted it same as he had, or that his warning had prompted them to take cover. But then, when he looked back to his left, trying to find out why the better portion of a tree would suddenly come flying out of nowhere in an attempt to blindside them, all relief, color and hope for the future quickly drained from his face.

It came from the edge of the clearing, bounding out from shadow of the sprawling and twisted mangrove trees. There was a chance that it had been there all along, that it had watched them come into the clearing and lurked there between the trees until they got close enough for it to launch its attack. If it had, it would have been nearly impossible to spot until it started moving, but not because it was hiding, only because its skin was the same brackish green color as nearly everything else in the swamp. It was easily nine feet tall and came pounding forward like a gorilla on the charge. It moved with a kind of straddle and a hop as its long gangly arms planted meaty green fist into the mud helping to propel it forward in concert with its large, clawed feet. It had small yellow eyes that sat beneath a protruding brow and above a large bulbous nose all of which were positioned atop a wide snarl full of long, sharp teeth, each of them crooked, jagged, and stained. It wore nothing but a loin cloth, a dirty brown rag that covered only the minimal portion of a tall, lanky and what looked to be, emaciated body. It looked hungry. It looked wild and feral and enraged and despite all that it looked like it still had sense enough to hate.

It was strong, as was evident from its heaving of the log across the clearing, but now Dante was also realizing that it was fast as well. It moved with a rudimentary and primitive gait, lacking both form and grace, yet and still it moved with the speed and power of a natural disaster and Dante knew that in a mere matter of moments it would be upon him. He scanned it, though, in truth he already knew what it was, of that, there was no doubt. It was a swamp troll, a deadly a dangerous monster by every stretch of the imagination and in every incarnation of past Dragon Dale games. The only question now was how dangerous was this one specifically.

Swamp TrollLevel 12

Monstrous beastmen known for their ferocity and insatiable appetites, trolls hail from a variety of regions throughout Deos, each variation having its own separate and unique traits. A few things all trolls have in common however are their overwhelming strength, exceptional speed and their incredibly fast regenerative abilities. A troll's wounds heal quickly, so fast in fact that most attacks made against them seem to only anger the already ill-tempered beastmen more than anything else. The only way to slow a troll's ability to regenerate is with fire or acid, but beware, being threatened with such actions sends a troll into a frenzy, focusing all of their hate and rage at the attacker. Swamp Trolls in particular are also known to...

"Dante move!" yelled Alex from behind him cutting in on the information flooding his thoughts.

He looked up to see that the troll had covered much more ground much faster than even he had anticipated and was now positioned only a few feet from him with a single fist held high above its head. With wide fearful eyes Dante forced himself to roll away from the direction of the monster, moving at what appeared to be the last possible moment, as in nearly the same instant the troll brought its raised fist down with all the speed and force of a runaway train, slamming it into the mud so hard that it left a small crater in the spot that Dante had been less than a second prior. A slight aftershock of force from the blow's impact with the ground washed over him as water and mud splashed in every direction.

The troll let out an intimidating ear-splitting sound that was part guttural grunting and part bestial roar, a sign of frustration, Dante assumed, at the fact that it had narrowly missed both of its initial attempts to squash him like a bug. It appeared to be preparing for a third when a series of ice shards slammed forcefully into its torso causing ice and frost to spread across its body as if it were trying to engulf it in some type of crystalline cocoon. Dante took this as an opportunity to scrambled up this his feet as the troll looked down at itself and saw the large javelin like shards of ice protruding from its body and with one powerful sweep of its arm knocked them all away as if they were nothing more than icicles. The ice and frost fell away with the discarded shards and the holes they left in the creature's body sealed themselves up almost immediately upon their removal.

Dante cursed under his breath, but before he could say anything aloud crossbow bolts came flying from behind him, each one smacking the troll center mass, square in the chest. Well three in the chest and then one additional bolt in the stomach. That had to be three from Pope and then one from Robyn, Dante knew without looking the troll however didn't bother pulling these out. It let out another guttural roar and looked from adventurer to adventurer deciding who would be its next target. Alex dashed forward with his axe and shield in hand and without hesitation activated his war cry ability.

"Come to me you ugly..."

"Alex no," Dante shouted, "This thing is level 12, we need to pull back."

"Executioner Swing!" yelled Fang charging the troll with his own axe raised. Completely focused on Alex the monster hadn't noticed the barbarian allowing Fang a clean hit to the creature's blind side. He buried the axe deep into the troll's left shoulder blade, to which the troll merely paused for a moment, looked back at the large two-handed axe lodged in its back, and then reached around with its right arm removed the blade and flung it carelessly into the mud. The axe came out covered in troll blood and then flew some twenty yards in an odd direction away from the fight as the monster focused its attention back on to Alex, ignoring Fang completely.

Dante observed the troll's status box, its HP had dropped by maybe a little less than ten percent, but even as he stood there, the monster's health pool was refilling of its own accord, its regenerative powers fast at work. The wounds on its chest had stopped bleeding and sealed themselves around the protruding crossbow bolts while the HP bar returned to full capacity.

The monster wielded a heavy hand armed with long sharp claws aimed straight at Alex's head. It swung with a powerful back hand first, a blow that Alex met with his shield. There was a resounding boom as troll met metal, and while the monster didn't flinch in the slightest, Dante noticed Alex slid backwards several feet from the sheer force of the blow alone. The troll followed up immediately with a straightforward punch into the shield. Alex stumbled. The troll brought both fists together and raised them high over its head, preparing to bring them down like an axe onto the skull of the dwarf. It was then that Dante dashed forward, and with sword in hand activated lightspeed slash.

In the time dilatated version of reality that Dante now occupied the troll had left itself over exposed, an opportunity of which the swordsman intended to take full advantage. Dante thrust his semi-solid blade directly into the armpit of the troll, and then with all the strength he could muster dragged the weapon to the right, ripping it out of the monster's chest and then forcefully across the creature's rib cage. When time snapped back into focus the ramification of Dante's attack hit the troll all at once, slightly knocking it off balance and temporarily disabling the shoulder that Dante had attacked. It abandoned the double fisted axe punch and clenched at its wounded right side instead, looking over at Dante with a hate filled snarl. As the wounds started to heal themselves almost immediately, the troll set out to return the favor.

It swung. Dante ducked, the troll reached out with its large clawed left hand to grab the adventurer, Dante dove into the mud and rolled out of reach. Alex activated war cry once again, forcefully pulling the monster's attention to himself. The interruption was well timed for the beastman. In one fluid movement, the monster pivoted to its left and chamber punched Alex with the force of a howitzer cannon. The attack hit the dwarf's shield, but the impact and power of the comparatively high-level monster knocked Alex off of his feet and sent him flying like a dwarven missile. He hit the mud with a thud and continued tumbling in the same direction until he crashed violently into the same tree log that the troll had thrown into the clearing earlier.

Robyn screamed Alex's name and then ran to his aid. The dwarf's HP bar had dropped to less than thirty percent. Meanwhile the troll's health had fully restored. Then almost as if basking in its superior might the troll stood to its full height and began slowly walking toward the downed dwarf, apparently with the intentions of finishing off its first victim, but he was stopped by a resounding explosion. Bewildered, the creature looked down to find a large gaping hole in its torso. Troll blood, nearly black in color gushed from the wound. The troll, in disbelief, held a hand up to the wound and then examined the blood covered claws. The creature along with Dante, Morrigan, Fang and Robyn all followed the troll's line of sight from the wound itself back to its source where each of the was surprised to see Pope standing with an outstretched arm and gripped in his hand was a gun, the tip of its barrel still smoking.

The gun had a long metal barrel, supported and framed by an intricately carved wooden stock that curved gently gracefully at the back end to form the handle grip and butt. If Dante hadn't known any better, he would have assumed that the captain was holding some type of single barrel sawed-off shotgun, but from what little he knew about firearms in combination with the massive amount he knew about Dragon Dale, he reasoned that this had to be a flintlock pistol. Powerful weapons in the Dragon Dale games, but often considered unpredictable in the wrong hands, not to mention slow and cumbersome due to the complicated reloading process. It was a specialized weapon used by only the most adept marksman. Dante should have known that Pope would end up getting his hands on one at some point.

Everyone seemed stunned at the appearance of the flintlock pistol, from the adventurers to the troll. Dante noticed that the wound inflicted by the burning metal bullet was taking much longer to heal than the other injuries that the troll had suffered up to that point. The gaping hole in its abdomen lingered and the blood pouring from it only slowed after a few seconds, and even then, the wound didn't close as the other had did, it kept pulsing blood.

Being shot had upset the creature. After examining its abdomen, the troll launched itself at Pope with a new level of disdain. It swiped at him relentlessly with its massive claw covered hands. The captain seemed not the least bit deterred at engaging the monster in close quarters combat. He dodged the first attack by leaning out of range, moving like a seasoned boxer avoiding a punch. The second swipe he ducked beneath, anticipating the trolls attack ahead of time. The third, an overhead swipe meant to nail him into the mud, he side-stepped and then countered by rising hard and fast and bringing with him the knife in the reverse grip, slashing it across the trolls exposed face. Pope bounced back out of the immediate range of the monster's next attack, and it stared at him with newfound hate as the bleeding cut across its face sealed itself shut, then vanishing as if it never existed to begin with.

Alex was disoriented and in pain, but Robyn helped him to a sitting position and handed him an open vial of red liquid. Just then Fang reappeared, axe in hand, swinging ferociously at the troll, striking it in the back. It turned and took a wild swing in his direction, but he had already moved out of range. The moment the troll turned its back Pope stepped forward and hit the Troll three times in quick succession with his knife.

"Morrigan!" Date called, grabbing the mage's attention. "Fire stops it from regenerating, but we have to time it just right! If you burn it, it's going to come after you."

"Got it!" Morrigan called out in response and immediately she began her ritual chant.

Dante jumped into the air and brought his sword down hard across the trolls back, hit the mud on both feet and then launched himself as far away from the monster as he could. The troll turned towards the direction of the attack only to find Dante already gone and then received another axe blow to its left side. It roared in frustration and swung wildly for the barbarian's head. Another mistake, it left itself open for Pope to stab it multiple times in the ribcage. It tried to take the captain out with an elbow, only to find Dante had thrust his sword into the creature's neck. The troll roared in anger. Each time it turned it was attacked from another direction by another adventurer who then quickly scrambled out of the way of the troll's next attack. They slashed poked and skewered the troll from every angle imaginable, but yet and still, Dante could tell that they were not making much progress toward bringing the thing down. Every wound they inflicted the troll simply healed. Even the gunshot wound was nearly gone.

In the corner of his vision, in between dodging swiping claws, Dante saw Alex rise to his feet, a sign that Morrigan must have taken as her cue because in almost the same instance he heard her shout.

"Flame Sparrow!"

And then he heard the familiar screech and whistle of her conjured birds as they soared towards the furiously swiping troll. The magical spell flew out in the form of three separate birds each of them slamming into the troll in an explosion of fire. The chest head and stomach of the monster were bombarded with flames, it reeled backwards in pain roaring out in agony. The troll didn't burst into flames, but when the fire and smoke subsided, he could see the places where the spell had made contact were covered in large blistering burns, wounds that didn't seem to be healing. He looked at the Troll's status box and saw the letters BRN next to its name. It now had the 'Burned' effect, a debilitating status similar to poison in that it sapped a victim's hp slowly over time and in the case of trolls, stopped them from automatically healing themselves.

The troll gave a blood curdling scream and charged, launching itself directly at Morrigan. Alex dashed forward and threw himself between the monster and the black mage. The dwarf activated war cry, but to everyone's surprise the troll batted at the shield and kept charging toward Morrigan. Alex tried activating war cry again, but the troll simply ignored it and within a matter of seconds he was on top of Morrigan.

Dante panicked. Mages were what were commonly referred to as glass cannons, they were meant to dish out large amounts of damage, not take it. He knew for a fact that if the troll made one well-placed attack against Morrigan, there would be no surviving.

Morrigan took a step back and pushed her hands forward forcefully perhaps in an attempt to cast a spell similar to the one she had cast on the gnoll that had gotten to close to her and Robyn during the raid on the camp, however this time it appeared to be ineffective against the troll. Dante's speed had carried him past Alex and placed him a few feet behind the troll as it was raising a fist to attack. He was close, close enough to maybe stick his sword into the trolls back, but if Alex's war cry hadn't been strong enough to take the monster's attention, he couldn't imagine any of his attacks could. He could use lightspeed blade but, in the trolls frenzied state, not even that would be enough to pull the hate away from Morrigan now. He needed something stronger. Something stronger than three attacks compressed into one. But what? Six? Was that possible? Could he stack lightspeed blade and into two, double it, do twice as much damage twice as fast. He had enough MP to do the attack two more times. Maybe that would generate enough hate to steal the monster's attention.

Dante poured his will and mana into his sword and right when he felt he had enough to activate his lightspeed blade ability, he forced even more mana into the blade. He felt his arm begin to shake and vibrate with energy, as if the weapon he was holding was about to explode, and still he didn't stop, he kept pouring more and more mana into the blade, he would use everything he had, freeze time if he had to and perform a hundred attack if he could, even if it killed him in the process. His mind was already made up. He grabbed the sword with both hands and the whole world began to shake violently as if he was holding a jackhammer as opposed to a long sword. He felt his MP empty out into the metal and he squeezed his every muscle to hold the sword steady. He felt himself screaming. It seemed like the sword was trying to tear him a part and now holding on to it was like holding on to dear life. His muscles ached, strained and then burned. His entire body burned as fought to hold himself to the sword.

Dante stared down at the blade and watched, felt and heard as the vibration in the sword fell into perfect harmony with the vibrations of his own body and when they did, the heat and pain in his arms and chest flowed freely into the blade and all at once and without warning, his sword burst into flames as his mind finally registered the words that he had been screaming all along.

"Burning Blade!"

The world around him came back into view and with no time to think or even marvel at the newly unlocked ability, Dante took the flame drenched sword and buried it into the back of the swap troll. The monster writhed in agony as the sword impaled it, bursting forth from its stomach, its metal blade still on fire. The troll ripped the sword from Dante's hand, but left it planted in its back in the process.

The creature reached around and ripped the sword from its flesh and upon doing so the flames extinguished. With a mental command Dante summoned the sword back to his own hand and in an instant, it vanished from the troll's grip and reappeared in Dante's grasp. The swamp troll bellowed an infuriated roar in Dante's direction and right as it was about to attack a gunshot rung out and the troll was hit in the shoulder. The monster's health dropped to fifty percent and now it looked back and forth from Dante to Pope trying to decide which of them it hated more. The one who had impaled it with fire, or the one who had placed another burning metal ball into its arm.

As it turned out there was no need for it to decide, before it could move on either of them, it took another axe blade into the back. Fang laughed with manical glee as he struck the troll and then retreated. Robyn struck it in the left leg with her daggers, Alex used his axe and shield to cover her retreat, and Dante followed up with another sword strike to the abdomen. The adventurers attacked in rhythm, whittling down the trolls HP from fifty percent to thirty percent, but their rotation of attacking and dodging only lasted for so long before the troll finally caught on and punted the dwarf with a strong kick that sent Alex flying back into the mud once again. The kick was not nearly as powerful as the punch that Alex had suffered earlier, and as a result the dwarf climbed quickly back up to his feet.

The troll was beginning to break down, but so were the adventurers. The march through the swamp in addition to the prolonged fight was beginning to take its toll. The troll swung at Dante with its right arm, missed, and then caught the swordsman with its injured left arm which it swung around, lamely hitting Dante in the stomach and sending him colliding into Fang. The two of them tumbled backwards, crashing into the mud.

Pope grabbed a hold of Fang by the arm and spoke. "Fang, I need a clear shot to finish this thing, but it's moving too much. I need you to get in there and grab it, hold it still so I can finish reloading and take the shot."

"You want me to grapple it while you shoot it?"

Pope grabbed Fang angrily by the leather strap that crossed his chest and pulled his face close to his own. "Now you listen to me, we can't afford to fight this thing forever and at this rate it's going to wear us down before we wear it down and if it starts healing itself again before we finish it off we're all going to die in this swamp, now get in there and grab hold to that thing and I'll signal you to get out of the way once I've lined up a kill shot. That's an order." Pope said forcefully.

Fang took a deep breath, dropped his axe in the mud and turned back towards the others and the rampaging troll. They were indeed struggling. With one arm the troll was repeatedly pounding the dwarf into the mud, his only saving grace was the large metal shield that he hid behind. Dante, Robyn and even Morrigan with her ice shards were attempting to peel the monster free of the dwarf, to no avail. The monster was down to roughly twenty percent of its total health, but it seemed unlikely they could burn through the remainder of the monster's HP before it killed the dwarf and possibly everyone else. They needed to end the battle now. Fang was their last chance.

Fang rushed forward screaming. The troll's head turned to see what the fuss was about and was met with a body-on-body collision. Fang latched on to the much stronger creature, but a disabled arm and deeply wounded body gave him the leverage needed. With his own chest pressed against the troll's chest Fang trapped both of the troll's arms underneath his own and clasped his hands together around the monsters back.

"Fang, what the hell are you doing?" Dante yelled.

"We're going to finish this."

"We?" muttered Dante.

Pope was packing gun powder down the barrel of his gun. The troll struggled to release itself from the barbarian's grip, but once it found that it couldn't, it reared its head, opened its wide gaping mouth and using its long sharp teeth bit down hard into Fang's shoulder. The barbarian let out a loud pain filled yell but held on tightly to the troll.

There was another bang, just as loud and as startling as the previous ones had been. As the echoes of the shot died out Dante noticed the troll's large heavy body had gone limp, and its health bar had emptied out to zero, and Dante knew at once that it had finally been successfully slain. Fang, whose arms were still wrapped tightly around the body of the troll collapsed to the ground as the dead weight of the large unresponsive creature fell on top of him. Dante and the others rushed to his side, grabbed hold to the troll's motionless body and struggled to lift its heavy mass from on top of the fallen barbarian. Fang was nearly catatonic, his eyes rolled into the back of his head and he shook with convulsions.

"What's wrong? Did it crush him? Is he suffocating?" Robyn asked with panic in her voice.

"He's poisoned." Dante said aloud.

"Poisoned how? By what?" Alex asked.

"Troll venom," answered Dante. "A swamp troll's salvia is highly toxic. When he grabbed it and it bit him, he was infected. This looks bad. Its draining his HP a lot faster then the poison from the gas pod did. He's going to need a health potion soon but we'll need to give him an antidote first."

"They're all in Dapple's saddle bags," said Morrigan.

"I'll go and get them!" volunteered Robyn, running off toward the Juxia who stood near the edge of the clearing.

"Why would he grab hold to the troll in the first place?" asked Alex.

"Because I told him to," said Pope coldly.

"And why would you do that?" asked Dante anger rising in his voice.

"There was no clear shot with all of you diving in and out of my line of fire, so I ordered Fang to grab hold of the troll so I could take the kill shot."

"You ordered him?" said Dante appalled. "Your order might have got him killed."

"It was a calculated risk," said Pope placing his flintlock gun back into the band of his waist at the small of his back. "and in the end, the troll is dead and Fang is alive, so mission accomplished."

"Mission accomplished? Are you serious?"

"Here's an antidote and a health potion too!" said Robyn with two small glass vials in her hands. She passed them to Dante who took them both and began administering them to the Fang. He started with the antidote, which they poured down the barbarian's throat in much the same manner that they had done earlier that day. Upon doing so the convulsions, eye rolling, and the steadily declining HP immediately stopped but Fang remained unresponsive. The wound on his shoulder was still bleeding as well as a number of other cuts and scrapes that he had accumulated during the fight. In addition to that Dante noticed his overall health bar was down to only one third of its total size, meaning that the troll venom had eaten thorough about twenty percent of his HP bar in minutes. Next, they gave him the health potion and upon swallowing it the wounds on his body began to heal themselves in much the same way the troll had been healing itself, only Fangs wounds were healing much slower. Then Dante noticed that Fang's health only refilled up to about the forty percent mark and then stopped.

"It's the troll venom," said Dante. "It's limiting the effects of the healing potion. We're going to have to wait for the aftereffects of the poison to fade over time. Until then each health potion is only going to heal a small amount of health."

"Well, we've found the flowers and we know the way back out is manageable, pick him up, place him on to the back of that animal and let's get out of here," said Pope.

"You're sick do you know that?" said Robyn.

"Yes," said Pope, "sick, but efficient and effective. Now let's move. We don't have much daylight left."

Dante and Alex pulled Fang up to his feet. The barbarian had begun to stir after the health potion but still seemed fatigued and disoriented. His head lolled and rolled between his shoulder as his feet fumbled clumsily across the water saturated swamp ground. Together they all approached the small, dilapidated shack in the center of the clearing when Dante noticed for the first time, smoke coming from the chimney of the small house. Then, before they could get close enough to pick a single flower, the front door of the tiny wooden hut creaked open, and a small, wrinkled, pale skinned woman peered out from the dimly lit room inside. At first, she merely poked her nose through the crack of the door as if answering a knock that no one had made, but then, when she saw that no one was close to the hut as of yet, she opened the door fully and with slow and deliberate steps walked out of the door, down the stairs and out into the open and muddy field to meet the adventurers who themselves had stopped and were now all staring up at the sight of her, stunned by her sudden appearance.

"Is that the fortune teller?" asked Morrigan.

"What's she doing here?" said Dante. He looked at Pope for answers expecting to see some type of smug grin, but instead found the captain to be wearing an unfamiliar expression of angry confusion.

"What's the meaning of this?" asked Pope, pulling his crossbow from his back at the same time.

"How did you get here before us?" asked Robyn.

"An old woman has her ways my dear," said the fortune teller as she moved slowly across the muddy field.

"Why would you have us travel all the way out here if you knew a faster and safer way to gain access to these flowers? Explain yourself!" Pope drew his crossbow.

"Captain Pope, calm down you can't shoot a defenseless old woman," exclaimed Robyn.

Pope pulled a lever on his cross bow and a large bolt loudly moved into place. "I can and I will unless I get the answers, I'm looking for right this instant."

The fortune teller smiled. "Such a tenacious young man. You remind me of my son," she said in her wispy and metallic voice. "Resolute and at the same time cautious, these are good qualities in a leader yes, these are also good qualities in an old mother. Old mother must be sure we are away from prying eyes and an old mother must also be sure that the children who made such a request are worthy of a blessing such as this."

"So, you're saying this was all a test?" Dante commented. "You didn't really need the flowers at all, you were just testing us?"

"Do not be angry with an old mother," said the fortune teller dropping her head bashfully, "I am merely an elderly elven woman who follows the old ways, and it is the sacred traditions of Deos that tell us a reward is given for a task well done. In order for an old mother to reward you she had to first give you a task. For we have a saying, 'No good deed must go unrewarded, and no reward should go undeserved.' And now that your task is complete young one, your reward can be bestowed." The fortune teller reached out a long thin arm with her spider like hand splayed open with her palm pointed up and out toward Dante. "Now give me the crystal my child and I shall give you your reward."

The spirit crystal hung from Dante's neck, it dangled freely on the black cord necklace dislodged from under his armor during the course of his battle with the troll. The fortune teller was still some fifteen feet away from him, a distinguishable distance considering how slow she moved in the thick mud of the swamp, but not distinguishable enough when Dante reflected on his conversation with her in the marketplace her and tendency for spontaneous burst of speed that mysteriously put her in places, she ought not be much quicker than she ought to be there. A pattern of behavior Dante noticed based on her current appearance in the swamp, that seemed to be becoming a sort of odd trend for the mysterious old woman. In fact, if Dante had to describe the fortune teller, odd and mysterious were truly the only words that came to mind at the moment. She had sent them on a wild goose chase into the middle of a dangerous swamp, just to test them, only to show up there herself not only alone, but with the appearance of not having had even the slightest problem getting there. And now once there, she was in the swamp, much like she was in the city uncomfortably eager to get her hands on to Stephen's spirit crystal. Dante had not forgot the offer she had made him to exchange the crystal for information on Sandberg and now here she was again, in the middle of Hell Hearth Swamp, telling them the ingredients that she sent them there for were actually not needed in the slightest and all she needed now, once again, was the crystal. Dante felt something lurch in the pit of his stomach.

"No," Dante said shaking his head. "This doesn't feel right. I don't know who you are or what you're up to, but I don't trust you and I can't give you this crystal."

"I happen to agree," said Pope. "Enough of your games old woman, show us how you got here so quickly, did you travel by boat, or perhaps there are a series of tunnels underneath that hut of yours."

"Who I am, how I got here are all unimportant. The only thing that matters is that now I am here and that which you all seek is here at hand. Now boy give me the crystal and receive what you have earned."

"I told you," said Dante. "I'm not giving you this crystal under any circumstance." He braced and reached for his sword. A part of him felt guilty, pulling his weapon on an old woman, but he was well aware in Deos, nothing was as it seemed, and it was obvious that this old woman was much more than met the eye.

"Ah yes, children at times can be quite foolish, but it is up to an old mother to make the proper decision for them when they cannot make it for themselves. Come now, since you seem reluctant to receive your reward, mother will help make it easier for you to accept it by simply not giving you a choice."

It took a moment for Dante to process exactly what the old woman was saying, and by the time he did she had turned her hand from palm-up to palm out, and then with a hard and sudden jerk she clenched her hand into a fist and yanked inward as if she was snatching something out of the air. As she did, the crystal around Dante's neck lifted, heaved forward, and then ripped itself from the coto-coto silk cord necklace and went flying into the open and waiting hand of the fortune telling woman.

Dante unsheathed his sword, shrugged Fang from his shoulder and dashed forward in chase of the crystal. Simultaneously Robyn leapt towards the old lady as Pope pulled the trigger of his crossbow aimed directly at the head of the old woman. Before anything made impact with the old woman, the fortune teller gave a swish of her wrist, dragged two fingers upward and Dante, Robyn, Morrigan, Alex, Fang, Pope and even Pope's crossbow bolt all froze before levitating into the air. Dante felt his body stiffen as his feet left the ground and began to float upward completely out of his control. He struggled to force himself back down, waving his arms as though trying to swim through the air only to find all of his movements had been dramatically slowed. It was like being encased in a bubble of thick viscous liquid, only there was no visible bubble to see and no liquid to feel. He and the others were merely floating there in midair some six feet off the ground with all of their motor functions greatly reduced.

Below them the fortune teller stood there looking up at them, nodding and smiling the crystal still in her hand, and just when Dante thought she might scurry back to the hut in an effort to make her escape, or perhaps strike them with another spell to finish them off, she instead looked down at the glimmering jewel gripped loosely in one hand and pointed at it with the outstretched fingers of the other. In a low mumbling voice, she began chanting words in a foreign and ancient language Dante could not even hope to understand. As her chant continued the crystal begin to glow, it went from a dull luster to a bright hot burn in a matter of seconds. It lifted up from her hand and floated freely in front of her. She dipped down deep and dragged both hands up towards the crystal like a composer bringing a symphony to a crescendo. As her arms went up the crystal grew even brighter, the jewel itself no longer visible only swirling patterns of light and energy like a small pink star. As the crescendo reached its peak the old woman twisted her arms and pushed outward toward the bubbling star and then brought her two hands together in a decisive clap. The crystal and all of the energy and light surrounding it collapsed in upon itself and then burst open with a wave of force and a flash of light and suddenly, where the star had been a fully formed Stephen appeared.

Stephen's unconscious body floated softly downward and then the moment it made contact with the muddy swamp ground the spell holding Dante and the others broke, and each dropped from the sky, slamming into the mud with a thud. Dante scrambled to his feet and he and Robyn hurried over to the outstretched body of the game guide while Alex and Morrigan helped a still semi-conscious Fang to an upright position in order to avoid suffocating face down in the mud. Pope simply stood and stared from Stephen to the old woman and then back to Stephen again, stunned.

"You-you brought him back," said Dante, feeling Stephen's neck for a pulse and finding a small rhythmic thump underneath the warm skin.

"As promised," said the fortune teller looking at Dante, but after a brief pause, she turned her head towards Pope. "Your proof, my lord."

"Proof?" repeated Dante. "What is she talking about."

"How does it work?" Pope stammered. "Does it only work on those who have been formed into crystals? Does it only work on those who have died in Deos?"

"There are no such limits my lord, not for those with the knowledge and the training. In fact, if one had the knowledge, one could even accomplish that which ye truly desire, but I must forewarn you, these things, they have a cost."

"Pope, what is she talking about? What's going on?"

"And you have this knowledge?" Pope asked the fortune teller, ignoring Dante completely.

"Mother knows many things."

"And the cost then? What fee do you demand?"

"What you seek my lord is personal and must be done by your own hand. I cannot do it for you, but if you so desire, I can guide thee down the path."

"What's in it for you?"

"I ask only that my lord allow a poor old woman to travel with him as a teacher and mentor, and in that way thy company and companionship shall be my reward. For you see I am old and lonely, and my lord desperately reminds me of my own son, and that feeling alone warms my heart and is more than payment enough." The fortune teller extended her spider like hand towards Captain Pope as if offering it to him to shake.

Pope looked at it and then took the woman's hand into his own. In the distant sky there was a clap of thunder, and light drizzling rain began to fall down upon the swamp.

"By the ways of old, in the sacred traditions of Deos, it is customary for a pupil who has been accepted by a teacher as her student, to kneel and seal the agreement made between the two of them with a kiss to the back of her hand. This is done to acknowledge her as the master and mentor and him the student and apprentice."

Pope cut his eyes at the woman.

"Pope, we need to get both Fang and Stephen out of here. They need help," said Dante, still crouching by the side of the unconscious cleric.

"It is only a formality," said the fortune teller as if Dante was not even there. "You will undoubtedly be the master, and I merely the instructor."

Pope looked over to Stephen whose chest moved up and down gently with each unconscious breath. The same Stephen that had been crushed and lifeless the last time Pope had lays eyes on him but was now living and breathing once again. The impossible made possible.

"Pope." Dante called out. He was crouched over Stephen, his eyes confused and pleading, he really did, Pope thought, remind him of himself, or perhaps he simply reminded him of someone he used to be. Pope turned back to the fortune teller, and with her hand in his he slowly dropped down to one knee and pressed his lips to the back of her cold pale hand.

The old woman blushed and then let out a muffled laugh that was more reminiscent of a cackle than the girlish giggle she had intended it to be. As Pope rose from his kneeling position, the old woman bowed to him in a shallow curtsy.

"It is done," she said in her bloody, piano string voice.

"Good, but now I need to return to Abilene Bay. I need to report to my superiors, and I need to have something sent over immediately."

"And what of them?" asked the fortune teller motioning towards Dante and the others.

"What of them," Pope responded dismissively. "Once we return to the city, we will go our separate ways."

"I see, so they are... nonessential?"

"Yes," replied Pope now staring Dante in the eyes as he spoke. "Nonessential would be a good way to explain it."

"Pope!" yelled Dante with clenched fist, a visible rage bubbling up within him. "What are you doing? You promised..."

"Good," said the fortune teller, "then we shall be off." With a flash of purple crackling energy the old woman and Pope vanished, leaving Dante and the others sitting alone in the pouring rain, in front a dilapidated shack in the center of mud-covered Hell Hearth Swamp.

Chapter 42: The Captain's Request

"Mr. Chairman." Said Johnson excitedly. "We've received a new communication from Captain Pope. It contains some... promising and yet alarming news. Apparently, he has confirmed the ability to fully restore the injured from a near death state. Now he is preparing to determine if he can use the same method to restore living tissue from dead tissue. But um, he has also requested that the company exhume and send over to Deos the remains of Tabitha Pope."

At this Johnson looked around the boardroom nervously before continuing with his report. "He has stated that since he is the father of the deceased, he feels this would be the least complicated, from an ethical standpoint, as he states, and I quote 'I am formally authorizing the transfer of the body and fully absolving Dytorus Corp of any wrongdoing in the process making this request.'"

There was silence in the room as the chairman simply stared at Johnson for a long moment.

"Fascinating, just absolutely fascinating," said the VP of Tactical Operations, an overweight and balding executive that in the previous board meeting had been wearing a black suit and who just so happened to also be wearing a black suit in the current meeting. "The idea of restoring living tissue from dead. If successful just think of the profit margins!"

The boardroom erupted in chatter.

"Think of the medical applications," said one of the executives.

"People will pay a fortune in the resurrection of dead pets alone."

"All we need is confirmation and verifiable data that it can be done, and we can begin drawing up projections for announcement, release and distribution no later than the next fiscal year."

Murmurs of agreement and excitement filled all corners of the room, until a manicured yet masculine fist slammed down hard on the expensive mahogany table.

"Let's all get one thing straight right here and right now," said the Chairman, a distinct look of anger on his face. "There is no way in hell that I am digging up the grave of a child and sending her body to another dimension to be experimented on. Sweet Mother Mary, even I have my limits for God's sake."

"Completely out of line sir," agreed the executive directly on his right.

"A bridge to far!" cried another.

"Studies show grave robbing is still highly frowned upon by sixty-five percent of the general population, a move like this could spell disaster for our stock prices."

"Everyone quiet," commanded the Chairman. "Johnson, prepare a statement. I want a response communicated back to the Captain Pope right away."

"Of course, sir. We'll take care of it right away sir." Johnson scribbled something onto a piece of paper and then hurriedly passed it to an executive in a dull grey suit, who then leaned back and slyly passed the note to Frank and Sara who were once again sitting in an isolated corner of the boardroom, and who were, up to that point, being thoroughly ignored.

"Send this message back to Pope right away, confirm once it's been sent and let me know the moment anything else comes through," said the grey suited VP of Player Correspondence in a low whisper to Frank. Frank took the paper from the executive and then handed it to Sara, at which point both of them stood and slowly exited the boardroom while everyone else present pretended they were never there in the first place.

In Deos, in a quiet corner of Abilene Bay, the black fire brazier roared back to life and much to his surprise Captain Pope received a response. Unfortunately, however, the response was not at all what the captain had hoped for. He gripped tightly to a singular piece of parchment that read simply,

"Request denied."

Pope read the response multiple times. Just two words. No explanation, no follow-up, just a flat-out 'No'.

"Bureaucrats," mumbled Pope to himself. He crumpled the reply in his hand. He was close now, on the brink of the unimaginable and he wasn't about to let anyone get in his way, including Dytorus Corporation.

"Not the news you were hoping for. Not to worry, there is much to learn before you are ready for that step, but in the end, the remains of the deceased will be needed in order to restore them," said the old woman from behind Pope. She seemed a short distance away from him, but he got the feeling that she was reading over his shoulder.

"That won't be a problem," Pope responded coldly. "If they won't send me what I need, then I'll just have to go and retrieve it myself.

Chapter 43: A Death Deferred

Over the course of a day, the swamp's drizzling rain had turned to an unrelenting downpour that persisted without interruption. Dante, Alex, Robyn and Morrigan along with a still partially incoherent Fang and a fully unconscious Stephen, had managed to navigate their way out of the swamp with minimal conflict, by using an extreme amount of caution and nerve-wrecking amounts of patience.

After Pope and the fortune teller teleported into oblivion, Dante and the others took cover inside the crumbling shack in the center of the clearing. Looking at the map and taking cover from the rain, they reasoned that Hell Hearth Swamp was not as wide as it was long, and for all intents and purposes, they were just as close to the western edge of the swamp as they were to the eastern edge through which they had entered. In addition, they also noted that there was nothing waiting for them back in the easterly direction other than angry gnolls and a destroyed bridge which they had no way of crossing, and as a result, they begin their trek west, following the mud-covered trails through the swamp in search of a new exit from Hell Hearth.

They placed a still weakened Fang on the back of Dapple and then used the frame of an old wooden bed from the hut to build a stretcher upon which they laid Stephen, allowing Dapple to pull it behind him like a makeshift sled. They moved through the swamp at a snail's pace, constantly on the lookout for bull gators, swamp trolls and roving swarms of flitty black birds. The constant pitter of rain, which at first seemed like hindrance turned out to be a blessing in disguise. The rain apparently had an odd effect on the swamp. Something about the falling water effected the sensory perception of the gas pod plants, prompting them to stop spraying their poison mist and instead fully open their pods to soak up the fresh rainwater. The falling rain also brought the bull gators to the surface of the ponds in which they waded, making them easier to spot and avoid. The black birds were conveniently absent, perhaps somewhere taking cover from the rain, perhaps purposely avoiding the adventurers, or more accurately avoiding Morrigan and her sparrows of fire. After about four hours of trudging through the rain and mud the party found themselves at the western most edge of the swamp.

Now the waterlogged terrain and the poison filled gas pods lay behind them, and an open field of green windswept grass stretched out before them. They were covered up to their knees in mud while their clothing and armor was soaked and heavy with rain. The sun retired behind the western horizon, signaling the day's end and the coming of another Deosian night.

It was around then, at the onset of dusk and about a mile outside of the swamp that Dante and the others decided to stop their march. They positioned themselves under a large, isolated tree where they created a makeshift lean to, in order to protect them from the rain and then used what little dry wood they could find to build a fire before finally sitting down to rest.

"I never thought I'd say this, but man I really miss the Merchant Road," said Alex. "When we first got here, I took for granted how civilized it made this place feel, without it leading us to our next destination it just feels like we're hopelessly lost out here in the middle of nowhere."

"That's because we are hopelessly lost, you idiot," said Fang. He held one hand over a bloody bandage across his chest and another clenching his head. Apparently since emerging from his poison induced stupor, he had been suffering from a terrible headache not to mention the wounds incurred in their last fight had continued to throb with pain. The combination of these two ailments had seemed to put the barbarian in a particularly foul mood. At least that's what the other adventurers told themselves.

"I understand you're upset, we all are, but that's no excuse to be rude," said Robyn in response to Fang's comment.

"Rude?" Said Fang looking up from the hand that held his aching head. "We're about to die out here in the dark and the rain and you're worried about me being rude?"

"No one is dying," said Dante.

"Says you," replied Fang, "but my bloody chest and aching head say otherwise. Besides we don't know where we are or where we're going. You all drank all the health potions in the swamp, I'm bleeding like a stuck pig, and the whole reason we're out here is nothing but dead weight. I'm sure you all love believing in the power of positivity but I'm positive we'll all be dead by morning."

"Has it occurred to you that the only reason that we're even in this predicament is because your boss abandoned us and disappeared with that fortune teller lady, *after* he got you mauled by a troll just so he could get a clear shot at it?" asked Morrigan.

"Yeah, well... what we did worked, we actually killed it thought didn't we? Besides we wouldn't have had to take such drastic measures if the rest of you were pulling your own weight."

"Bro, we just literally *pulled* you out of the swamp, after you went and got yourself badly poisoned for a *second* time." Alex snapped.

"I wouldn't have needed you to pull me anywhere if you would have been able to take a punch and if the rest of you had been able to actually deal some damage."

"Are you really saying this is our fault?" asked Robyn.

"Well, it ain't my fault." Fang replied.

"We never said it was, we all know whose fault it is."

"It's my fault." Dante interjected. He looked up at the other members of the party as he spoke, a momentary reprieve from angrily stabbing at the campfire with a stick.

"Bro?"

"It's my fault for ever having thought for a moment that Pope could be trusted."

"Dante," said Morrigan, "you couldn't have known what Pope was planning. Honestly, I don't even think he planned it; things just seemed to happen one after another."

Dante stood, stick still in hand. "Couldn't I though? Shouldn't I have known he was up to something? Pope showed us that he was a lying, self-serving manipulator that would use anyone at his disposal to get what he wanted. I knew that. And the moment we left Abilene Bay I knew in my gut that he was up to no good. I knew he was going to turn on us and still I couldn't stop him." Dante was shaking with anger as he spoke. "Since we've gotten to Deos, he's always been two steps ahead of me. First, he pounds my face into the dirt and then he's working with magic users that can resurrect people and teleport. I'm supposed to know how Deos works. The world, the rules, Dragon Dale is supposed to be my strong suit, and now Pope has even beat me at that." Dante snapped the stick in half and threw both ends into the fire. The flames roared up angrily as if in synch with his mood. "I suggested we come here to help Stephen, I let Pope get the jump on us again. If anyone is to blame, it's me."

"Finally. At least one of you is taking accountability," said Fang.

"Do you ever shut up?" Robyn asked.

"Don't you tell me to shut up."

"How about you grow up then."

"You grow up!"

"Wh-Where am I?" a voice called out weakly, "Wh-whats going on?"

"Stephen?" said Alex, "You're awake. Hey guys, Stephen's awake."

"W-water."

"Yeah of course, I'll get you some water," said Alex grabbing a waterskin and gently placing it up to the resurrected cleric's lips.

"Stephen, how are you feeling?" asked Dante.

"What do you remember?" asked Morrigan.

"Do you know how to get us home," asked Robyn.

"I-I... what happened? Stephen said.

"Well, I think that answers all three of those questions," said Fang.

"I remember leaving Illdershire to go and do a quest to kill raptors, I think. We fought a big one, if I'm not mistaken and we won. Then on the way back, I was..."

Stephen looked up at Dante, his dark eyes intense. "I was about to tell you the truth. I was about to tell all of you the truth about Deos, but then... that's all that I can recall, from then on its nothing but darkness and distant voices, all like some type of weird dream and then I wake up here."

"You did tell me the truth," Dante replied. "Right before you died. That was nearly two weeks ago."

"Died?"

"After we killed the Alpha Raptor, we were attacked by another monster. It um, grabbed hold to you before anyone knew what was going on. You didn't make it, but before you died you told me the truth, you told me that we are not in a video game."

"What do you mean I died? I couldn't have died if I'm here talking to you now. That's what I was trying to tell you all, this place only seems like a video game but, but here just like back home, once you die, you're dead."

"Normally yes," said Morrigan, "but that day we just so happened to be traveling with another cleric as well, a half-orc, remember?"

"Vaguely," said Stephen.

"He cast a spell that preserved your consciousness into something they call a spirit crystal and we used that to bring you back to life. A bunch of stuff happened in between but we can tell you about that later."

Stephen was silent. Dante noticed that his mouth was tightly closed but that his rate of breathing in and out of his nose was steadily increasing. Dante wondered if he was hyperventilating or perhaps having some sort of panic attack based off of the information, they had just given him.

"Are you okay? Dante asked.

Stephen didn't say anything, he simply shook his head 'no', closed his eyes, titled his head back and swallowed hard. He rubbed his hands across his face, as if he was trying to wipe away the signs of an imminent mental break.

"How," Stephen said finally, "How did you all bring me back? The other cleric?"

"No," answered Dante, "Actually Pope found some woman capable of performing resurrection magic. She lured us out into the middle of the swamp with the promise of helping to restore you and when we got there, she brought you back, and then her and Pope disappeared leaving us there with your unconscious body. I was surprised that she helped us at all. Ever since I met her, she had been trying to get your spirit crystal for herself."

"My what?" asked Stephen.

"Your spirit crystal," answered Robyn, "It was like the physical representation of your soul in the form of a jewel. Dante's been carrying it around Deos since... well you know." She said beginning to get the impression that repeating that he died was somewhat upsetting. "Apparently spirit crystals are very valuable items."

"Especially to necromancers." Said Morrigan, "Which I'm pretty sure that the fortune teller is, that's how she was able to bring you back."

"And now she and Pope are working together, which means we have to assume, he is attempting to become a necromancer too." Said Dante.

"Is that even possible?" asked Alex, "He's not a magic class to start with, can he really change classes like that."

"I think a large part of her bringing Stephen back was proving to Pope that she had the power to do so. That why he was so adamant on restoring you," Dante said to Stephen. "For someone like him the idea of controlling life and death probably seems like an opportunity too good to pass up."

"As a necromancer he could raise an entire army of undead," said Alex. "Pope is scary enough as is, I can't imagine him with a horde of zombies at his command."

Stephen groaned and rubbed his face with his hands again. "Dytorus Corps' entire reason for coming to Deos was to plunder its magical resources. To harness the power that resides here and turn it into a viable commercial product back on Earth. Consumer goods made of magic but disguised as advanced technology is one thing, but what they really want is high level magic powerful enough to be weaponized and sold to governments or militaries. The capability to bring a loved one back to life sounds like the type of business opportunity that Dytorus Corp would be foaming at the mouth over."

"Be that as it may, I don't think either Pope or the Dytorus Corp know what they are getting into by delving into necromancy." Said Dante, "In the video games, necromancy is a very dark, very powerful school of magic where the spells can just as easily destroy the caster as the target. There's no reason to believe things will be any different here. I'm not sure what Pope is planning but I'm starting to think he may be in over his head."

"Wait a second guys, this could be good for us," said Alex, "This may be the break we need. While Pope is distracted with his necromancy lessons, we can take this time to find Sandberg and get home."

"You all know about Sandberg?" Stephen asked.

"We know he's here on Deos and that he may have a way of traveling back to Earth," said Robyn proudly.

"Only problem with that idea is the fortune teller," said Dante. "She's clairvoyant, so I'm pretty sure she already knows where Sandberg is to begin with, she was the one that gave us his Deosian name after all. Besides the first thing we have to do is figure out where we are and then figure out where we're going."

"Well, that puts us in a bind."

"Just like I said," Fang added abruptly. "We'll be dead by dawn."

Dante stared down at the high growing grass that surrounded their makeshift camp and realized that he recognized some of the plants nearby. He pulled up a handful of bright green plants with small white and yellow flowers crowned at the top of them. Yarrow as he recalled. He tossed the plants over to Fang.

"Chew that up and place it on to your wound. It'll help heal it."

"Do what?" Fang replied, appalled.

Dante ignored his response and began shuffling through his own pack removing from it a large seashell carefully wrapped in cloth.

"And what are you going to do with that? Listen to the ocean?"

"No," said Dante calmly. "I'm going to use it to call a friend for help."

Chapter 44: One Night in Langune...

"Friend?" said Fang with a chuckle. "In case you forgot everyone else you know *in this world* is back in Abilene Bay. Which is where I should be, not stuck here with the rejects," Fang muttered.

"You're stuck with the rejects because Captain Pope left you behind, remember?" said Robyn.

"Probably that senile old lady's doing. Not that it's any of your business. You'd be much better off asking yourself if anyone will hear that stupid conch shell horn out here in the middle of nowhere?" Fang spoke snidely.

"It's not a horn," said Alex. "It's a magic sending shell."

"Well unless it's going to 'send' us to the nearest town, then you might as well throw it in the fire because it's useless," Fang replied.

"Will everyone be quiet so he can actually use it please," said Morrigan

When Dante first spoke into the seashell it responded only with an awkward and prolonged silence. But then, after another moment, he heard the faint sound of a voice radiating from the opening of the shell. It started off weak and low, but after only a couple of seconds the familiar deep voice of the half-orc cleric reverberated clearly from the large seashell as if he was somehow trapped inside.

"Dante? Can you hear me?"

"Shinto, yes we can hear you."

"Ah good, I didn't expect to hear from you so soon. Have you found your Urthlander friend already? Is this a call to say goodbye?" asked Shinto.

"No, no I'm afraid not," said Dante painfully. Now that he'd pulled out the shell and heard the half-orc's voice, he felt ashamed at having to reach out and ask him for help so soon. It hadn't even been a week. "Shinto, we're actually in a bit of trouble. We need your advice."

"Trouble?" said Shinto with an edge of concern in his voice.

"Yes, we're all okay, but we're stranded and for all intents and purposes, lost, outside of Hell Hearth Swamp."

"Hell Hearth Swamp? What brought you there?"

"We found someone to restore our friend from the spirit crystal, which we were able to do, but now we're stuck and lost. We're on the western edge of the swamp. Stephen is disoriented and we have someone else with us who is injured as well. We really didn't know what else to do, so we... we called you."

The shell was quiet.

"Shinto? Are you still there?"

"Yes," said the Half-orc solemnly. "I'm still here. You say you found someone to resurrect your friend from a spirit crystal?"

"Yes," said Dante. "Stephen. He's right here with the rest of us. He seems exhausted, and his memory is fuzzy, but other than that he appears to be okay."

"Tell me, if you look to the north can you see the Black Wood in the distance?"

Dante looked up from the sending shell, and in the waning light of dusk, off in the far distance, directly to the right of the setting sun, he could see the shadowy silhouette of an ocean of black trees.

"It looks pretty far away but I'm sure that's the Black Wood. If I had to guess, I'd say it's at least half a day's walk from where we are now."

"Good, that means you came out of the swamp closer to the northern end than the southern end, that also means we aren't that far from one another."

"Wait?" said Robyn. "You're close by?"

"Relatively," replied Shinto. "If you march west for a full day, you'll run into the town of Langune. You can't miss it; it sits just above the Merchant Road. I will meet you in Langune by

sunset tomorrow."

"Thank the gods, the Merchant's Road," said Alex.

"Be careful," replied Shinto. "You all are starting to sound like real Deosians." Even through the shell Dante and the others could hear that Shinto spoke with a smile as he made that last comment, and the half-orc's playfulness brought a smile to each of their faces.

The group said their goodbyes and once the shell went silent, Dante re-wrapped the magic item in cloth and placed it carefully back into his pack.

"Did you just have a full-blown conversation with a seashell?" asked Stephen

The night passed without incident. Dante and Morrigan sat in front of the campfire, discussing their Deosian reading habits. Dante told her about the interesting and odd bits of information that he had stumbled across while reading the book she had found for him in Abilene Bay, and Morrigan described the intricate and complicated spell instructions she had been studying in the book from Shinto.. Their conversation, Dante noticed involved a lot more smiles and laughter than any of their past conversations had and he also found himself being far more charming and funny then he had been in quite a long time. Before either of them knew it, hours had passed and they soon found their conversation being interrupted by Robyn and Alex, who had awakened to relieve them of their night watch duties.

The morning came and immediately upon first light the party rose and began their march west per Shinto's directions. They were careful to keep the Black Wood to their north as they moved cautiously but quickly through the open green fields. Dante, Morrigan, Robyn and Alex had in their short time in Deos learned to travel over large distances with a certain amount of efficiency and speed but seeing as to how the two additional members of their party were not at peak health, they found themselves slowing down so that Fang and Stephen could keep pace. The bright green grasslands reminded Dante of the Illdershire Plains only it was conveniently absent of cockatrice raptors and large black wolves. The sun rose, hung languidly overhead and then began to dawdle and slope toward the horizon once again. Dante took a moment while they were walking to check his spirit tome.

-A Bull Gator has been defeated.

-You have gained 1,000 Experience points!

-Forty-Five Hell Hearth Starlings have been defeated.

-You have gained 1,125 Experience points!

-A Swamp Troll has been defeated.

-You have gained 2,000 Experience points!

-You have unlocked a new ability "Burning Blade"

-"Burning Blade" has been added to the skills and abilities list.

-You have fulfilled the primary objective for the quest, "A Fool's Errand in Hell Hearth Swamp"

-You have gained 2,500 Experience points!

-You have fulfilled the primary objective for the quest, "How to Resurrect Friends and Influence People"

-You have gained 5,500 Experience points!

-You have obtained Level 8, Congratulations!

- You have a total of 38,550 Experience Points

Level 8. They had entered the swamp at a freshly attained level 7 and exited a day later a full level higher. High risk, high reward. At least they had survived the swamp and lived to tell the story. Dante closed his spirit tome and looked up to find that he could see a town in the far distance. It had to be Langune. He held his hand up horizontally, placing his index finger just beneath the sinking sun and then counted how many fingers between it and the far-off horizon. It was a trick that Shinto had taught them in the Jua Valley for calculating how much time was left before nightfall. He counted three finger lengths between the sun and ground. That gave them roughly three more hours of daylight before sunset, and with that much time he reasoned they would make it to Langune an hour before sundown.

Langune was a farming town. Small homes and vast tracts of plowed fields stretched to the horizon as they entered the town at dusk. The few people on the streets paid little attention to Dante and his friends as they made their way to a tavern and inn called the Six-Fingered Bowman.

An attendant took Dapple to the stables while Dante and the others made their way up to their pre-appointed room. The plan was to drop off their belongings and then find themselves a hot meal while they waited for Shinto to return from whatever errand he was on as they had expected him to meet them in front of the inn, or at least in the lobby of it. The fact that he had arrived in the city before them was evident considering he had already reserved a room and forewarned the inn staff, an older halfling woman, of their arrival, however, the fact that he had yet to make an appearance seemed a bit odd. At least to Stephen and Fang, to Dante, Morrigan, Robyn and Alex, it seemed like a matter that was less then trivial. If Shinto said he would meet them there, then he would meet them there, for them there was no question. Which is why when they turned the key to open the door for their assigned room, and found a quiet and contemplative waiting and side, they were only partially surprised.

"Shinto!" Shouted Robyn at the sight of the half-orc who was standing with his back to the door, staring out of the small window of the second-floor room. At the sound of his name, he turned to reveal a warm and kindly smile, that despite the oversized tusk that protruded from his bottom jaw, still somehow seemed welcoming and sincere.

"Greetings." Said the cleric, who had to brace himself as Robyn threw herself into him and hugging him as if they had not seen one another in years. Shinto patted her softly on the back and chuckled as she released him. "I see you all have made it. I take it you had no trouble finding the town or the inn?"

"No," replied Dante, "It was just where you said it would be."

"Good, good, that's very good indeed, now tell me, why were you all in Hell Hearth Swamp?"

As the group recounted their adventures since they'd parted ways, Shinto listened intently, never interrupting or stopping them for clarification, even when they spoke over one another or argued the details of a particular part of the story. His green eyes simply shifted from person to person until they worked out the specifics and relayed to him the details of the event to the best of their collective memories.

"And that's when we used the sending shell to reach out to you," said Dante.

At the obvious conclusion of their story the half-orc leaned back, deep in thought. "Normally," he began, "a mage of such skill and power is rare. Particularly of the skill and power you all have described, and normally amongst mages, that makes them very well known, but I must confess I have no such knowledge of an elderly elven woman who from what you all have said appears to have a mastery of divination, transmutation, chronomancy and necromancy. There are mages who practice their arts in secret but for someone to seemingly display such a broad level of knowledge and skill, it seems nigh impossible for them to have gone unnoticed for so long." Shinto looked up from his thoughts and with a look of concentration his eyes fell upon Stephen. "Master Stephen, would you be opposed to an examination? I would like to check something."

"Um, yeah I guess that would be okay," Stephen replied.

"Do we need to leave the room?" asked Robyn, standing as if she expected Stephen to begin undressing as if in a doctor's office.

"No, that won't be necessary," replied Shinto with a smile. With a sudden surge of power, Shinto's right hand begin to glow with shimmering green light, and around it the same circular dials that had appeared aboard the ferry encapsulated his hand and rotated in a series of alternating directions as if they were attuning themselves to some to some unseen cosmic clock. A ray of green light cast from Shinto's brightly glowing hand began to move up the body of the game guide, starting at his feet and moving the length of his body.

"The reformation of a physical body from a spirit crystal is a fragile and difficult process," said Shinto as his light moved up Stephen's body. "It is difficult to do without error, as one is basically reconstructing the body with the power of will. Small mistakes made during this process usually imperceivable at first glance, over time may manifest as different forms of illness, physical deformities and eventually madness."

Stephen looked decidedly unhappy at this news.

The party members exchanged curious glances, each of them a bit worried at the thought of what Shinto might find. Dante looked over at the cleric as he continued his examination, the light moving up Stephen's body as if he were doing some type of magical x-ray. Dante noticed that even Shinto's eyes were a glow with the same green light as his hands.

"In addition," the half-orc continued. "The reconstruction of a body from nothing also affords the caster the opportunity to input their own influences into the reconstruction, leaving the resurrected individual bound to the caster's will, and in effect, under their control, even if they are not aware of it." The light moved over the top of Stephen's head and then as if Shinto had flipped a switch, the light went out. The rotating dials moving around his glowing hand vanished and Shinto blinked away the glow from his eyes. "That is interesting," Shinto remarked.

"What is it?" asked Stephen, "What's wrong? What did she do to me?"

"Your physical body has been reconstituted from the Deosian atmosphere and reconstructed into flesh. It has been restored perfectly and there are no traces of lingering necromancy magic in your system." Shinto paused for a moment. "What was the name of the fortune teller that sent you all to the swamp?" he asked looking up at Dante with a hint of concern in both his eyes and his voice.

"Um," Dante thought for a moment. "What was her name?" He racked his brain trying to remember.

"She never gave us a name," said Morrigan, "She just kept referring to herself as Old Mother."

"That's right," Dante said, realization dawning. "Mother is the only thing she ever called herself."

Shinto looked back to Stephen. "As perfect as the resurrection may have been, being remade takes a toll on the mind and the spirit, I'm going to cast a healing spell that puts you into a deep sleep, but once you awake, you will feel much better. Do you understand?"

"Um yes," Stephen said shaking his head, clearly overwhelmed by both the information he was receiving as well as his up-close interaction with Shinto. "Thank you, you know, for your help."

"It is my pleasure," said the half-orc, and released a golden wave of light that washed over Stephen who almost immediately closed his eyes and slumped over into a deep sleep. Shinto caught the game guide before he fell forward and laid him down across the small hay-stuffed mattress and wooden bed frame.

"Now for you," said Shinto, looking at Fang.

"Me, what about me?" replied Fang, standing on the other side of the room. Shinto stood and began to move toward the barbarian who stiffened as if ready for a fight.

"You were bit by a swamp troll, correct? Poisoned by troll venom? Health potions have been rendered ineffective, you're having trouble sleeping, resting, and recovering hit points, even after taking an antidote?"

"Well, yes, but that was a day and a half ago, I'm fine now," Fang lied, the bloody bandages still wrapped around his collarbone told a different story, and a health bar stuck at the seventy-five percent mark reinforced it. Fang braced himself as Shinto closed in on him, and then defiantly stuck out his chest as the half-orc got within striking distance.

Shinto lifted a hand toward the barbarian and instinctively Fang rose a forearm to block it, but only in futility as Shinto was both too fast and too strong to resist. Before Fang could offer any real protest, Shinto had a firm grip on the barbarian's wounded trapezius muscle and right as Fang was about to call out in pain, a warm golden glow radiated from Shinto's hand. Dante watched as Fang's face went from a painful wince to a confused and bewildered stare as his health bar slowly increased from the seventy-five percent that it had been stuck on since they left the swamp to completely full in a matter of minutes.

"Swamp Troll venom is a particularly potent poison that not only leaches one's health, but thins the blood, making any attempts at recovery much more difficult, if not impossible. Antidote only treats part of the issue. What you needed was an anti-venom, a potion used for stronger more lethal poison that have more than one effect."

Fang rolled his shoulder, amazed to apparently have the full range of motion once again.

"I've neutralized all remaining traces of the venom and restored your hit points; you should be as good as new," said Shinto.

"Th-thanks," said Fang, clearly unsure of what had just happened.

"Shinto," said Dante. "We did get one other thing from the fortune teller, the man that we're looking for, Sandberg, she gave us another name. She said here in Deos he goes by-"

"I think," said Shinto abruptly, before Dante could finish his sentence, "that we've actually had enough excitement and mystery for one night. For now, I recommend that we all get some rest. We have a lot of traveling to do tomorrow and we can discuss any additional concerns in the morning as we prepare to head out."

"Oh, okay," said Dante.

"I've reserved a second room for Morrigan and Robyn, but I imagine the rest of us are fine staying here. I assume it is better than where you all have spent the last couple of nights at least."

"That works or me," said Alex.

"What other choice do I have," muttered Fang.

"Then it's settled," said Shinto. "Gentlemen, if it's all the same to you, I tend to get very hot at night so I will take a spot by the window if you all don't mind."

Chapter 45: A Bad Dream

Ever since arriving in Deos and becoming aware that they were in fact not inside a videogame Arnold Fangloski had been having very odd and off-putting dreams to say the least. So, when he found himself standing in the completely deserted streets of Langune under the light of twin moons too large to be real, even for Deos, he assumed that he was dreaming, but when the lone figure of a hunched over old woman appeared some thirty feet in front of him, he admittedly became nervous. He attempted to turn away from the old woman, to move through the empty streets of Langune and find his way back to the inn, back to the others, or at least back to something familiar. But every time he moved away; the figure of the old woman somehow came to be closer to where he stood. He cursed under his breath, this dream had nightmare written all over it, and he knew from experience that all you could do in a nightmare was let the terror play out until you mind was done torturing you and you woke up screaming and covered in a cold sweat.

Multiple attempts to escape had brought the old woman merely a few feet from him. Her back was turned, leaving him unable to see her face, but even then, something about her seemed familiar. He imagined that any moment she would turn around with the face of a gnoll, or perhaps a troll, scare the life out of him in some unbearable and traumatizing way. It was funny, his knowledge that he was in a dream, his assumption of what was to come and the full realization that none of it was real and therefore could not hurt him, did absolutely nothing to make the situation any less terrifying.

Now the woman stood close enough to touch. He could hear her on the other side of her dirty dark brown robes, singing to herself in a low gravelly voice some type of strange and peculiar song, one that Fang was sure he had never heard before. As she continued, seemingly oblivious to his presence Fang realized, that the woman was singing in a language that he did not understand. She rocked back and forth, mumbling a garbled mess of words in a simple rhythmic cadence that indicated it had to be a song, or perhaps even a lullaby designed for children. And then purely out of curiosity Fang stepped towards the woman and reached out to touch her shoulder.

She moved faster than he thought possible and before his hand could graze the hem of her robe, she turned to face him. He was surprised to see the face of an elderly wrinkled woman looking up at him as opposed to some eldritch horror, but he then found himself even more surprised by what the old woman then said.

"Hello, young one. An old mother is glad to see you in better health. You did not look well upon our last meeting."

"What are you talking about? Who are you?" Suddenly Fang wasn't sure he was dreaming.

"Oh me, well, who I am is not important. What is important is who I bring thee." The old woman smiled a hideously wrinkled and ugly smile. "My child, you and I serve the same master, and as a result old mother has brought him to you via the dream talk." The old woman moved aside, seemingly stepping out of existence, only to be replaced by Captain Pope.

"Fang, I'm glad to see you are well. What is your location?" Pope spoke as if this was all normal. As if he had not just stepped into being just moments before and as if they were not in actuality talking inside the confines of Fang's own mind inside a dream.

"What's my location? I'm sitting outside the swamp you left me in." Fang said hotly. "Now what's going on here, what type of dream is this? Is-is this because of that troll venom, am I hallucinating."

"Listen here, I don't have the time or the patience for your whining. Now where are you?"

"I'm-I'm in a town called Langune." Fang replied. "With Dante and the others. We're staying at an inn called the Six-Fingered Bowman."

"Good." Said Pope satisfied. "Meet me on the street, out in front of the inn. I'm going to come and get you. You're needed back here."

"Wait, what? What do you mean you need me? You-you just left me for dead. Captain what's going on?"

"Look son, you need to understand I'm never going to put you in any type of situation that I think you can't handle. Now I left you behind in the swamp because I needed to attend to business elsewhere, but I needed you to keep an eye on Dante's group, and that is exactly what you've done. Now I'm planning something big, and you are one of my most trusted lieutenants, which is why you are now needed back in Abilene Bay, but if you are going to question my every order and second guess my every command anytime I just so happen to hurt your feelings, then maybe I've made some type of mistake. Maybe I need to find someone us to help lead my men through this next mission. A mission I might add that is going to be vital to our success and longevity here in Deos. So, you tell me soldier. Did I make a mistake? Are you staying there with Dante and his rag tag group of renegade gamers, or are you with us? Do I need to find someone else to lead my men or are you the man for the job?"

Fang stared at Pope for a moment. His hard and stern face was unwavering. He was truly a man without fear, without weakness and now he was telling Fang that he needed him, that he trusted him. Maybe he was right. Maybe he was being to overly emotional about what happened in the swamp. There was no point in getting hung up on that, they did what needed to be done and it had worked. Case closed. And now was his chance to be a part of something, to be a part of something great, he couldn't let fear or emotions get in the way of that.

"No sir, you didn't make a mistake. I am the right man for the job," Fang replied.

"Good soldier, that's what I like to hear. Now meet me outside in front of the inn. I 'll be there for you in a few minutes."

"Yes sir, I'll head out right away."

Fang awoke immediately. He opened his eyes to the darkened inn room that he was currently sharing with Dante, Alex, Stephen and Shinto. Moonlight poured in from a nearby window casting just enough light for Fang to see that everyone appeared to be in a deep and restful sleep. Shinto the half-orc cleric, the one that had healed his shoulder was stretched out on the floor by the window with his mouth open loudly snoring, While Alex and Stephen occupied one of each of the beds and Dante was face down on a stack of bedrolls that he had formed into a makeshift bed of his own. Quietly Fang rose from his own bedroll and moved stealthily across the room. As delicately and as silently as he could he poked and prodded his way through a number of open packs that lay on the floor, rummaging through the items that lay inside. Multiple times he looked over his shoulder, checking the others for movement or sound, but they slept like the dead and the only sound that radiated from the room was the loud snoring of the half-orc cleric. Fang checked the packs again, securing each of the items he felt were necessary for the next part of his own journey and then with one final look back at the others, he crept out of the room, silently closing the door behind him. Shinto's loud snoring continued as Fang crept out of the door, down the hall and down the stairs to the first floor of the Six-Fingered Bowman. It was at that point that the half-orc stopped snoring. Once he was convinced that Fang had gone, Shinto opened one eye to ensure that he had indeed left the room.

In front of the inn, Fang stepped out onto the Merchant's Road and into the night air. It was cool and quiet, the streets on Langune were deserted. For a moment he wondered if the whole thing had really been a dream, if he had jumped up and ran outside in the dead of night because a dream had told him to, and then right when he considered turning around and going back inside, a crackle of energy and a purple flash of light changed his mind. Out of the night, both Captain Pope and the old woman appeared on the streets of Langune.

"Let's go," Pope said by way of greeting. With another crackle and flash of purple the three of them disappeared.

Up on the second floor of the Six-Fingered Bowman, Shinto watched everything unfold under the attentive gaze of his bright green eyes. Then once the streets of Langune were empty once again, he rolled over and went to sleep for real this time.

Chapter 46: The House of Battle

Bryan Battle, eldest of the three Battle brothers, stood in front of his childhood home reluctant to enter. It was a difficult thing to acknowledge that he was afraid to return home. The most annoying part of making such a self-realization was admitting that his brother Malcolm had been right . He had been selfish. He had spent more than half of his life avoiding confronting the past, because his old home, the house that stood before him, represented a part of his life that he had always been anxious to leave behind. But after having exhausted all other avenues in the search for his mysteriously absent baby brother, he had no choice. All roads lead to home.

His hope was that Dante was holed up inside, watching movies, playing video games and refusing to answer the phone. He had looked for him absolutely everywhere else that there was to look. He had called him multiple times only to receive no answer. Texted him more than he felt comfortable saying aloud and never received a single response. He even reached out to him via social media. He sent multiple messages to his Foto Flixer account only to be met in return with dead silence. He used his government connections within The Agency to check flight records, hotel receipts and even Dante's bank card transaction and it all checked out. Dante had boarded a flight from California and returned home. The only issue being, no one had actually confirmed seeing him do it. Aside from checking the paperwork, Bryan had retraced Dante's steps from the hotel to the airport questioning anyone who may have come in contact with him. Everyone to whom Bryan had shown a picture, remembered seeing Dante, but they couldn't recall if they had last seen him coming or going. In fact, Bryan couldn't really find anyone who could recall physically laying eyes upon Dante since his return from California. What was even more unusual was when he prodded further, he was somewhat surprised to find that even before his trip to California, Dante had not been seen in months.

At Milgard University, Bryan discovered that his brother left campus shortly before their mother's funeral and had not returned since. His coaches, teammates and friends all told Bryan the same thing, after the funeral, Dante stopped taking calls, returning messages or corresponding in any way. He had disappeared, a symptom, they had all assumed, of his grief, and would, if left alone, return when he was ready.

Bryan had spent days following leads and chasing down information all of which led to where he currently stood. Outside his childhood home, the last possible place his brother was known to be. He used his key to let himself in and saw, before anything else, a large mound of mail on the floor. The mail slot, which normally deposited letters neatly into a small basket to the right of the door had filled to capacity and as a result the additional mail continuing to be received went careening off the top of the already full basket and began to stack up in a messy pile in front of the door. Bryan picked up the mail from the floor and then removed the letters filling the overstuffed basket as well.

"Dante! You home?" Bryan called out, setting the armful of mail on a small table near the door.

He stepped further inside the modest three-bedroom house to find it nearly exactly as he remembered, if not only smaller. The living room was just as his mother had always kept it. The furniture was old but well-kept, as was *almost* everything else in the house. Certain things had been redone, updated, but not in an attempt to make the house look more modern, but more so in an attempt to refresh and renew the same look that it already had. The stained carpet in the living room, where once a stain created by a cup of spilled Kool-Aid, knocked over in the midst of a fight between Malcolm and himself over who's turn it was to play 'Hero-Man 3,' was now gone. In fact, the carpet had been replaced altogether, and not only that but so had the tile floors in the kitchen as well. The wall in the hallway near the bathroom, which used to be graced by a self-portrait of Dante drawn in magic marker, had been painted over with a new coat of paint. The bathroom had been updated, as had the appliances in the kitchen.

Bryan frowned. Had Malcolm been funneling his dirty money into their mother's house under the guise of home improvements only to sell it out from under her? No, not even Malcolm was that stupid, he knew that if he did that then Bryan would kill him himself, and with his current job and skill set, he'd get away with it too. No, he must have been waiting for her to pass and then he must have been planning to sell it then. That sounded more like his style, the long con.

A walk through the kitchen revealed a refrigerator full of soda and energy drinks, one open and only half full. In the corner by the trash can were a number of empty pizza boxes stacked neatly atop one another. Bryan looked at the box on the top and saw that it had a receipt taped to the box. The pizza was delivered three weeks prior, placing it roughly at the time right before Dante's trip.

Bryan walked deeper into the house, passing the first two bedrooms that used to belong to him and his brothers and walked into his mother's room. It, like the rest of the house had changed in only the smallest ways. The bed was new, smaller than what he remembered growing up, but not because his angle of perspective had changed, but because it was actually a different bed. The bed that had occupied the room during his childhood was gone. The king-sized bed that his mother had once shared with his father, the one that he remembered bouncing on while his father encouraged him to see how high he could go, the one that he remembered piling into with both his parents and a little Malcom and with an as of yet unborn Dante still in his mother's stomach. The bed that his mother slept in alone after his father died, the one that she would lay in crying, right up until he knocked on the door and then she would wipe her eyes and straighten her face and pretend that she was not in unspeakable pain after losing her husband. That bed had been replaced with a sleek, auto cooling, auto heating, massage you in your sleep type of bed, that once again Bryan assumed Malcom purchased, even though he was sure his mother could not have wanted it.

Bryan left his mother's room and went into the bedroom that he assumed now belonged to Dante. It was the one room that had changed the most in the entire house. There was a large flatscreen television set squeezed into the corner of the room, with a new high-tech video game console beneath. Football trophies took up nearly every available shelf space and the walls were covered in posters and framed certificates of completion for nearly every game in the Dragon Dale series.

Ha, Dragon Dale, Bryan used to love that game. He would stay up playing it all night. Malcolm and Dante would even sit there watching him play and as he progressed and had new characters join his party, he'd name them after his brothers so that they could feel like they were part of the game as well. Sometimes he'd even let them do the fighting, and he'd just handle the exploring and talking and discovering, all the boring parts. Eventually they started playing themselves, and he would show them the ins and outs of the game, where to find the best weapons, how to beat the toughest bosses and the best places to go to collect gold. At one point, everyone in the house was a Dragon Dale fanatic, each one of them with their own theories on how to do which part of the game the best. Eventually Bryan outgrew video games, but he never did enjoy playing anything as much as he enjoyed playing Dragon Dale with his little brothers watching and playing with him.

The rest of the room was pretty much as Bryan would have expected. Empty soda cans set near a bean bag chair close to the oversized television and a random assortment of clothes lay strewn across an unmade bed. Bryan took another look at the clothes on the bed. There were shorts, t-shirts, and a couple of pairs of jeans, three pairs of shoes on the floor nearby. He looked inside the closet for some type of empty luggage but couldn't find a suitcase, duffle bag or even a backpack for all of his efforts. He marched out of Dante's room and into the bathroom and found that his brother's toothbrush was missing as well. He went back into Dante's room and looked around before allowing his eyes to settle on the large flat screen television. He reached down and powered it own and then grabbed one of the controllers to the video game console. The screen flashed with a series of logos before settling on the home screen. It had been years since Bryan had played a video game, but he knew enough to know that consoles today were nothing more than dedicated computers systems, and all computer systems logged info. He cycled through a number of screens until he finally made his way to his brother's profile details. Overview, Friends, Games. Bryan scrolled over to games and a list of what looked like over forty games, each with a small image of the games cover next to its title. They were automatically sorted by a filter at the top of the screen labeled "most recently played" and there sitting at the top of the list was Dragon Dale 7 Online, last played: three weeks ago.

Bryan, a career military man who considered himself logical and pragmatic in most situations, even when people were shooting at him, suddenly found himself beginning to worry. Malcolm, it appeared was right once again, their little brother was missing.

Part IV

Chapter 47: The Mythril Caravan

"What do you mean Fang's gone?" Dante stood in the middle of the room, looking around as though expecting to discover Fang still hiding in a corner. "Why? Where would he have gone?"

"Looks like he rummaged through some of our stuff before he left, too. I'm missing some of my gold not to mention my last jar of pickled peregrine fruit," Alex huffed with indignation. "I love pickled peregrine fruit."

"But I don't understand, why would he leave?" asked Robyn.

"He wasn't alone," said Shinto calmly. It was only just after dawn, the primary light in the room was from a candle beside Shinto, who thumbed leisurely through the book he usually kept buckled to his waist. He didn't to look up as he spoke.

"Wait, what?" said Dante. "You saw him leave?"

"I did," said Shinto unenthusiastically.

"Why didn't you stop him?"

"I was unaware that restrictions had been placed upon his autonomy," Shinto said, looking up from his book. "Was it your intention that I keep him here, against his will?"

"Well, no I didn't mean it like that."

"Is it not true that you all removed yourselves from a group forcefully holding you against your will?"

"Yes, fine, but we aren't like them," said Dante, in an attempt to regain some type of foothold in the conversation.

"No, I didn't think you were," said Shinto, his point made for him.

"Did you at least see who he left with?" asked Dante.

"Of course," Shinto replied, turning back to his book. "He was with the man you call Pope, and the woman who I assume was the fortune teller."

"What!?" said Dante, Alex, Robyn and Morrigan in unison.

"Shinto why didn't you think it was important to tell us this. Pope has been terrorizing us since we arrived in Deos, and now that he has that fortune teller on his side there's no telling what he's up to!"

"Last night their only goal seemed to be to get your friend and get out of town as soon as possible."

"Fang's not our friend. He works for Pope and Pope can't be trusted. Even after he almost got Fang killed in Hell Hearth Swamp, the first thing the big oaf does is go running back to his side like a lost puppy. He even ransacked our stuff on his way out."

"One thing I've learned in all my years is that you have to allow people to be people if they are ever expected to change for the better."

"Even when they're untrustworthy thieves to begin with?"

"Dante, I assure you, the most important thing is those that remain here, remain by choice, and those that leave, do so for their own reasons." Stephen, who sat quietly in the corner, nodded his agreement. "What is far more important is discussing what comes next for you and your group. Last night didn't you say there was something else you wanted to talk to me about?"

Dante let out a sigh of resignation. "Well yeah. Sandberg. I found out in Deos he goes by the name Floggins, Alabaster Floggins. Do you know how to find someone by their Deosian name?"

"Alabaster Floggins?" said Shinto curiously. "That's who you all have been searching for?"

"Why," answered Robyn. "Have you heard of him?"

"But of course," answered Shinto. "I know him. Professor Floggins is well known in Deos. He is a famous inventor who resides in Hemara-Balgrad. A city that sits in the Hathorian Mountains to the north just beyond Illdershire and Bleeksborough."

"Finally, some good news," said Morrigan. "I say we don't wait around for our luck to change, let's leave right now. Shinto will you come with us? At least as far as to Bleeksborough? Illdershire?"

"I can do you one better," said the half-orc "I'll accompany you all the way to the city of Hemera-Balgrad and introduce you to Professor Floggins myself and what's more, we don't even have to walk."

"What?" said Morrigan partly laughing, confused by the clerics offer.

"The Mythril Caravan will be passing through Langune today. The six of us can hitch a ride. We'll make it to Hemera-Balgrad in a quarter of the time it would take us to get there traveling on foot."

"The mythril what?" asked Stephen from his position in the corner.

"The Mythril Caravan is a convoy that travels along the Merchant's Road constantly moving from town to town. It journeys unceasingly and stops to rest only inside of cities. There it lets off and picks up new passengers. As you all know, it can be difficult and dangerous to traverse the unforgiving wilderness of Deos, especially alone, the Mythril Caravan offers a solution for merchants and Deosians residents to move from city to city in relative safety and ease as long as they catch the caravan as it passes through their town. It runs throughout Deos, albeit on a very tight schedule."

"Well, how about that," Robyn smiled widely. "Things are starting to go our way."

"Please," responded Dante in a low solemn tone, "don't jinx it."

At high noon under a bright sky, the caravan appeared. It wasn't even close to what the adventurers expected. No wagons, horses, or long and ricket line of independently drawn carts.

At the head of the caravan was a monstrous machine of iron and wood. A mana engine. It was as if a large metal furnace had been turned over on its side and put on wheels. The front end of the engine had a scoop like brush guard strong enough to plow through a building. The engine itself mounted a wide funnel-like smokestack which spewed the iridescent blue smoke of burning mana crystals. As the beast pulled into Langune, a bell and a steam-powered whistle tolled and screamed.

"It's a train!" said Robyn with joy.

"Well, it can't be a train," said Alex. "There are no tracks. What does it run on if there are no tracks?"

"The Mythril Caravan can only operate on the Merchant's Road," answered Shinto. "It's an airship engine that has been magically modified to operate on land. It is the work of Professor Floggings, actually."

"Floggins made this?" asked Dante, more to himself than anyone else.

Behind the engine was a series of eight or nine long wooden carriages big enough to easily carry over a dozen people. Each was latched to the next and each bustled with activity. The last carriage in line held a stable of horses and other animals, men dressed as guards lead a couple horses out of the car, mounted them and then rode on ahead towards the direction of Illdershire without so much as looking back. The next to last carriage was being loaded and unloaded with containers. With the appearance of the Mythril Caravan, Langune had burst into life. Townsfolk spilled out to the street in droves, everyone buying or selling food, goods, wares or souvenirs to or from the people in the carriages. All transactions were conducted through the small carriage windows as guards armed with swords and stern faces determined not to let anyone onboard without a ticket. Tickets which could appernatly only be purchased from a Dwarven man who had stepped off one of the carriages barking the going rate as well as availability of open seats aboard the Mythril Caravan.

"Tickets! Caravan tickets here! Common car, five silver! First car, three gold! Fifteen tickets left! Get your caravan ticket here! Next stop Illdershire, Bleeksborough, Hemera-Balgrad and Oningrad!"

"Six tickets for a common car?" asked Dante.

"Of course not!" Robyn answered gleefully. "We're springing for first class!"

The interior of the first-class passenger carriage was larger than what seemed possible on the outside, and what should have been able to hold a dozen comfortably, easily took two. Seating was in leather-like banquet booths with small tables between them while an intricately woven carpet ran up the center aisle. The group found two empty booths across the aisle from one another and sat in elegant comfort.

"It's like the Grand Opal all over again!" said Robyn, as she took a seat next to Morrigan in one of the empty booths.

"It is, isn't it," said Alex with a smile, as he and Dante sat opposite.

"What is the Grand Opal?" asked Stephen sitting beside Shinto across the aisle.

"The Grand Opal was this fancy hotel we stayed in while in Abilene Bay. It was like we were celebrities or something. You would have loved it," answered Robyn enthusiastically.

"Yes," said Stephen smiling weakly. "I'm sure I would have." There was an elephant in the room and had been ever since the moment of Stephen's restoration, they had simply been so busy scrambling from one moment to the next none of them had found the time to address it.

"I've not thanked you all for what you've done for me," Stephen said, swallowing hard. Dante couldn't help but notice the difference in boldness and body language compared to the person he first encountered in the Last Legend Headquarters. His voice was low and monotone, his eyes dull and empty. "I know it couldn't have been an easy decision to make... to um... risk your own lives to save mine, someone you barely know. Someone who was not completely honest with you about what you all were being pulled into here in Deos. If it's any consolation, it was always my intention to tell you all the truth." He lifted his head and a strength seemed to return to his eyes. "My mission was to keep you all safe then blow the whistle, bring Dytorus Corp down. All of us together. As it turns out, I couldn't even keep myself alive."

"It's not," said Morrigan quietly.

"What's not?" asked Stephen.

"Any consolation."

"Morrigan, cut him some slack," said Alex ruefully.

"Why?" Morrigan replied. "Dytorus Corp may be the reason we're here but his 'good intentions' didn't do anything to stop it. As pure as his "intentions" may have been, he deceived us, and as a result we're all stuck here and still in real danger. Worst of all, he still hasn't even apologized."

"Yea," replied Alex. "You're not wrong, but he literally died. I think we can give him a bit of a break."

"No," interrupted Stephen. "She is right. I could have gone public with what I knew about what Dytrous Corp was planning long before any of you were involved, but the truth is, I was afraid. First, I was afraid no one would believe me, and then I was afraid of what the company would do to me and the people I cared about once they found out I had tried to expose them. I figured if I had two hundred witnesses to support my claims, then the world would have to believe me and that with so many voices, I would be protected. So, I volunteered to participate as a game guide. I lied to you all and though I like to think I was working toward some greater good, I see now how delusional I really was. I helped bring you all here, you didn't volunteer for this. I did. All because I was a coward and for that I am truly sorry."

"For the record, Dante was the one that was adamant about us doing whatever it took to save your life. Alex and Robyn were more apt to agree with him then I was. I was openly against it."

"Morrigan don't," said Robyn, but Morrigan lifted a hand cutting her off.

"He's the reason that we were able to restore you, and like I said, at first I didn't agree. But now, in retrospect, I see that Dante was always right. We are trapped in this world, somewhere between a video game and hell and all we really have while we are here is each other. The smartest thing we can do now, regardless of how we got here, is to hold on to one another with everything we have because that is our best chance of getting back home." Morrigan leaned across the aisle and placed her hand on Stephen's hand. "I'm not happy you lied, regardless of your intentions, but I am glad that you're alive and that you're with us. Now that we've addressed this whole awkward thing, please stop looking guilty and depressed and get back to your old corny self-okay?"

Stephen blinked tears through his choked laugh. "Thank you Morrigan," he said. "Thank you all."

There was a loud shrill whistle, a distant clang of a bell and the carriage jerked, beginning its journey towards the next destination.

"And we're off," said Shinto quietly.

Chapter 48: Hemera-Balgrad and the Amazing Professor Floggins

The powerful mana engine of the Mythril Caravan rumbled to life, the carriage shuddered as it pulled the attached carriages north along the Merchant's Road. The Deosian landscape passed by the carriage windows slowly and then, in a blur, as the train caught speed. Robyn leaned against the carriage window looking out, a look of contentment on her face. The quiet rumblings of the passengers and the gentle vibration of the carriage gave her a feeling of nostalgic bliss, reminding her of one of the few good memories she had from her childhood.

Her eyes drifted to land on Dante, who looked, she noticed, how he nearly always looked, deep in thought. Dante was handsome in a traditional way. The All-American homecoming king, Mr. Popular, leader of the cool kids, one of the types that Robyn didn't normally get along with, but Dante was different. He wasn't the arrogant, self-centered jerk she had expected upon first meeting. In fact he was a humble and insightful gentleman, a prince out of a storybook. She could see why Morrigan liked him the way she did, even if she did try to deny it.

"Hey there fearless leader, you've been pretty quiet since we boarded the caravan, what's on your mind now?" Robyn asked.

Dante snapped from his reverie, answering immediately. "I'm trying to figure out exactly how this caravan ride is going to go wrong."

"Why does it have to go wrong?" asked Robyn.

"It's a classic RPG trope. The heroes finally catch a break, seems like its smooth sailing to the finish line and then boom, something falls out of the sky and completely derails an otherwise full proof plan. Originally, I suspected the caravan would be hijacked by bandits, but that almost sounds too obvious."

"Kobolds," said Alex. "We'll be attacked by kobolds, I bet."

"My gold is on goblins," said Robyn. "A horde of angry little goblins coming from every angle."

"I'm calling it now," said Morrigan. "Halfway there a gargantuan red dragon swoops down out of the sky and carries more than half of the caravan away."

"Interesting, are we in the half that gets left behind or the half that gets carried away?"

"With our luck, both," said Morrigan. The entire party burst into raucous laughter.

The caravan moved on un-harassed by bandits, kobolds, goblins, or dragons. They traveled north, reaching Illdershire in three hours, and Bleeksborough in a total of six. Most everyone who passed through the first car were merchants. The Mythril Caravan was as much a mode of transportation as it was a center of commerce and trade. Merchants who were not even passengers in the first car were allowed into the carriage to peddle their wares, and Robyn had soon purchased for the price of a few gold pieces, resin from both the Boswellia tree and the Commiphora bush, dried waxy sap of an exceedingly strong smell normally used to make perfumes. Robyn had no intention of making her own fragrance, but couldn't pass up the opportunity to buy something from the roving market on wheels.

Twelve hours had passed by the time they approached the city of Hemera-Balgrad. Dante had spent most of the ride, when not sleeping or staring out of the window, deeply engaged in the *Comprehensive History of the Land of Deos Volume One*. It held a wealth of information about Deos, some of which mirrored Dante's in-depth knowledge already learned from the Dragon Dale video games, and some additional information.

Hemera-Balgrad, Dante knew from his experience as a gamer, was a medium sized city, known mostly for its technological advancements and its exceedingly high population of gnomes. It was never central to any of the game's major plot lines, but served as an innovative mountain town and last major stopping point before the Dwarven city-state of Oningrad, which was comparable in size and importance to Abilene Bay. Due to its proximity to the Dwarven capital, Hemera-Balgrad was often referred to as the gateway to the north. What past Dragon Dale games had not communicated that the writings of Alder Mere Frane did, was that Hemera-Balgrad had begun as a hybrid settlement among both dwarves and humans, however after about two hundred years, gnomes migrated to the city. Gnomes, who are small in stature and lacking in physical prowess, make up for their deficiencies with a natural affinity toward cleverness, innovation and invention. Their resettlement in Hemera-Balgrad brought with it an unprecedented boom in mechanical and alchemical advancements, pushing the city forward as a hub for clockwork technology and mana crystal infused machinery. It was not too much of a surprise then, at least to Dante, that once the Mythril Caravan had made the arduous climb up the Hathorian Mountains via the ever-persistent Merchant's Road, they saw unfold before them, carved directly out of the side of one the mountains, a multi-leveled city built out of wood, metal and stone.

The Merchant's Road cut a swath through the heart of Hemera-Balgrad like a river running through a canyon. The city grew upward on either side of the road along the canyon walls. The walls of the artificially dug canyon, hacked into the mountain as if some colossal titan has tried to split the mountain open with an axe, formed a multi-tiered city directly in the face of the exposed rock. There were four tiers total, one stacked directly atop the other and each one roughly two to three stories in height. Mid-air bridges connected one side of the canyon to the other at every level, so the effect upon entering the town at the lowest tier was that of endless stone bracers attempt to pull the two sides of the cleaved mountain back together again.

The Mythril Caravan let Dante and the others out on the first level of Hemera-Balgrad. The walls of the city extended upwards for another one hundred feet, at the end of which was the mountain's split peak and the now velvety dark evening sky. Dapple had disembarked from the caravan along with the rest of the party and placed in an animal stable on the first level. However, while the Juxia situated himself to the mountain elevation, Shinto took Dante and the others to a mechanically operated lift that would take them all up to the third tier of the city. As Shinto guided them through the streets or more aptly named rows of the first tier, they noticed that the residential apartments, shops even taverns were all built directly out of the face of the rock. The buildings, or structures that resembled buildings were fashioned with wooden doors and shingled roofs, wooden support beams held up second floor balconies and windows with thick layers of glass allowed occupants to peek out of third floor rooms. Lanterns jutted out from the canyon walls, and with bright golden flames illuminated the city with a soft and subtle glow that reminded Dante of electric powered streetlights.

They entered the lift to find it operated by a small man no taller than four feet in height. He was shorter than even Danger Duke had been with a face distinguishably more round and a small button nose as compared to the barbarian halfling. He pulled on a series of complicated levers and at his command the large metal box shifted upward along a hollowed-out track cut into the canyon wall. Dante looked around curiously as a cascading number of clicks and hisses began to escape from nearly all directions surrounding the large metal box.

The gnome smiled. "First time in a verti-mover, I suppose?"

Dante looked around the large metal lift, it looked like a homemade service elevator and felt about half as sturdy. "You could say that."

"You can always tell a first timer," said the lift operator. "They're always looking around trying to figure out how the thing works."

There was a distinct clicking of metal gears and the almost snake like hiss of unseen valves releasing enormous amounts of pressure. "Is it mana-engine that powers this whole thing?" Dante asked.

"A very good guess, but it's steam powered, mana-engines are much too costly and powerful to use for anything aside from airships. But steam power however, it's used to operate a lot of the mechanicals here in the city."

"Steam powered mechanicals," repeated Robyn.

"Oh yes," said the lift operator. "The Hemera-Balgrad claim to fame."

The lift stopped with a jerk and the operator wound a crank that prompted two adjoined doors to open, revealing a stone walkway. Alex stepped a foot from the lift when Shinto stopped him.

"This is only tier two; we are going up to tier three," said Shinto motioning his head to a row of buildings thirty to forty feet higher. A human woman and two dwarven woman entered the lift, followed by two human men, two dwarven men and a group of four gnomish men. Each corresponding group spoke quietly among themselves.

Moments later the lift stopped on Hemera-Balgrad's third tier where Dante and the others disembarked. It was not until Hemera-Balgrad was seen from the upper tiers that the grand scale of the mountain town could be fully appreciated. They crossed a bridge that took them from one side of the canyon to the other stopping once to marvel at the view before stopping before an enormous building.

"This is it," said Shinto. "The workshop of Alabaster Floggins, the most famous inventor in all of Hemera-Balgrad."

Just then from inside the building there was a loud bang, a flash of blue light and slowly a deep dark purple smoke begin seeping from the uppermost windows of the building.

Dante, Shinto and the others entered the building to find a trio of humans in what looked like white lab coats, coughing profusely as they exited the building. Their faces were stained with blue and purple soot and each of them seemed desperate for fresh air.

"Do you need assistance?" asked Shinto.

"We are fine," replied one of the men between coughs. "An experiment gone wrong." He pushed his way past the group hacking and coughing with every step.

"Is that not Floggins?" asked Dante excitedly.

"No, of course not." Shinto replied without even bothering to look back.

After each of the humans had pushed their way through, a dwarf stumbled down from the staircase that led up the workshop's loft style second level, the apparent source of the experiment gone wrong. The dwarf like the humans who had come out before him, also wore a white lab coat and had a face covered in blue and purple soot.

"Professor Floggins," Shinto called out. "Where is he?"

The dwarf looked up at Shinto through a haze of purple smoke and a look of recognition dawned on his face. "He's at the alchemical station."." Said the dwarf as he came down the steps. He stopped for a moment and choked out four to five consecutive coughs spewing out a cloud of purple mist from his lungs in the process.

"Are you sure you all are, okay?" asked Stephen.

"Yeah laddie, we'll be fine. It's just a little alchemical misfire, happens all the time."

The second story of the warehouse was covered in thick purple smoke. It was hard to breathe and impossible to see. Dante squinted his eyes to see a small figure moving within the confines of the smoke. Clicking and hissing of gears and valves graduated to humming and droning and then suddenly, the thick purple smoke filtered from the room, revealing a single solitary gnome.

Like everyone else that had stumbled from the workshop, the gnome wore a white coat. He stood in the center of what Dante could only describe as an old-world laboratory filled with hastily stacked papers, empty and half full glass containers, random coppers wires, copper gears and copper tubing, along with an assortment of clockwork mechanisms in various states of disrepair all strewn about the place in such a chaotic fashion, that at first thought, Dante had assumed that the explosion had left the lab in disarray. But upon closer inspection he resolved that what he was seeing was in fact the labs natural state of being. The gnome himself wore a pair of thick leather and copper rimmed goggles, positioned off of his eyes and on the top of a balding head. The lenses were covered in thick purple soot, much like the outer edge of the gnome's round face.

"Well, what is this? Did the council send you that quickly after one little explosion? I assure you all of my paperwork and permits are in order for any and all alchemical experiments run out of this lab. It's all been approved and is quite on the up and up, there is no need for the Philosophers' Council to watch over me like a hawk."

"Professor, we're not from the council. It's me Shinto."

"Ah, Shinto so it is you! Sorry about that, thought you were one of those government dogs here trying to shut down my lab again. How are you doing my boy? To what do I owe the pleasure?"

"It's good to see you to Professor, I've come to introduce you to some friends of mine."

"Oh yes, yes of course, a friend of Shinto is a friend of mine."

"Well in that case Professor Floggins," Shinto said with a slight bow, "Dante, Morrigan, Robyn, Alex and Stephen."

"Ah yes, pleased to meet you, pleased to meet you all. I think it's safe to say you're all adventurers from the look of you. Come to Hemera-Balgrad for top quality gadgetry and alchemical contraptions, I suppose? Shinto said he'd come introduce you to old Professor Floggins eh?"

"Well, not precisely," said Dante stepping forward. "We are adventurers, and Shinto did bring us here to meet you, but we're not looking for Professor Floggins exactly, we've come in search of Benjamin Sandberg."

"What's that?" Floggins looked taken aback.

"You see Professor, these adventurers are not from Deos, they are from Urthland," said Shinto.

"Earth... land." Floggins had turned as white as a sheet. "Well knock me over with a feather," said the gnome, falling back into a miniaturized armchair. "I guess you finally found me."

"You're referring to Dytorus Corp, I assume but we're not with them. That's actually why we're here. Dytorus Corp lied to us and sent nearly two hundred people here to Deos under the guise of a video game beta test. We found out that you might be hiding here in Deos and came looking for you. We need you to help us get back home. You're our only hope. We have to go back and get help so we can come back for all of the other gamers that are trapped here."

"Wait, wait, wait. Wait just a second young man. Please this is a lot of information. I need you, if you can, to simply start from the beginning."

On the second floor of the workshop, as the evening crept late into night, Dante told Benjamin Sandberg, currently known as Alabaster Floggins, the entire story of how he and his friends had come to be in Deos. From the character creation process all the way to their Mythril Caravan ride to Helmera-Balgrad to meet him, the man, or rather gnome capable of solving all of their problems. Sandberg listened to their story intently and with great interest. His head darted from adventurer to adventurer every time a new party member stepped forward to tell a different part of the story. He stroked his grey colored beard with grave concern when they told him the details of Stephen's death and then clenched it in shock when they walked him through his restoration. He sneered at every mention of Dytorus Corp and by association any mention of Pope and whenever they talked about their encounters with gnolls, or trolls, or ogres or shaugin or raptors, he seemed to slide up to the edge of his seat. By the time they had finished bringing him up to speed, Floggins lay back in his chair as if he had just been on an emotional rollercoaster.

"So, you see sir," said Dante, "Dytrous Corp does know that you're here and they are looking for you, but we wanted to make sure that we found you first. You are our last hope for returning home, now I know it's a lot to ask but if you would be willing to send us back to Earth, we can get help for the other gamers that are trapped here as well."

Floggins frowned. "I'm sorry kiddo, I wish I could help you; I really do. But I don't have means to send you or anyone for that matter back to Earth."

"I don't understand. You, along with Arthur Hirsch and Michael Edwards had to discover the original portal to Deos over forty years ago. Your presence here proves that. You all had to have the ability to travel back and forth between Deos and Earth, how else could you have made the video games in such detail?"

"At one point, yes. We were able to jump back and forth between worlds, but really wasn't because of anything we did. You see, us even coming to Deos for the first time was an accident. Arthur, Michael and I were all professors at Central State University of Mathematics and Technology. For fun we had started a weekend project of trying to build a teleporter in my garage. It was a completely theoretical experiment, nothing we ever expected to work, but then one day it just turns on and starts beeping and next thing I know, the three of us wake up inside a temple here in Deos. Turns out an evil cult over here tried to summon their dark primordial god of death and destruction to wreak havoc on their enemies, and the machine we were building picked up the signal being sent out from the device they were using to summon their dark lord." Floggins paused for a moment, lost in the thoughts of his past.

"Well then what happened?" Alex asked.

"Well, we stole their device of course." Floggins replied, getting back on track. "It was the key to everything. It was that device, which had now somehow been calibrated as a kind a bridge between our two worlds that allowed us to jump back and forth at will."

"So..." Robyn said impatiently, "Where is it now?"

"Oh, I destroyed it."

"Destroyed it" Dante shouted in surprise. "Why would you do that?"

"Because my partners sold out to a soulless corporate entity. We created the Dragon Dale video games as a way to share Deos with the rest of the world without putting it in danger. Then they go and turn over our company, our home and everything we built for a few measly dollars. So, I did what I had to do. I fled to Deos and destroyed the device."

"But... but they already discovered a portal of their own, why destroy the device?" Dante asked.

"Portals have limitations. They can only be opened and closed from Earth. The device could be activated from either side, at will. As I said, it was the key to everything, which is why I could not allow it to fall into the wrong hands."

Floggins lifted his arms and let out a sad chuckle, "This was to be my retirement plan. I never imagined that they would send children here. I never imagined I would ever need to use the device again."

"So that's it," Morrigan whispered. "We really are trapped here."

Chapter 49: Penumbra Nights

If Fang was being honest, everything seemed a bit weird. He and Pope had left the convenience and comfort of Abilene Bay for some small, backwater, one horse town on the edge of a valley that rarely ever saw the light of day. Penumbra was a day's journey south of a placed called Caligo Nyx.

Penumbra received about six hours of daylight between sunrise and sunset. Twice as much as some of the locations deeper into the Nightlands, namely Caligo Nyx, which some of the game guides described as a type of Deosian Las Vegas, a city where the nights were long, and the party never ended. But Penumbra was no Vegas, it wasn't even Reno. It was, if anything, more like a Sleepy Hollow, emphasis on the sleepy.

There was only one tavern and one inn in Penumbra, the Misty Shadow, and it was currently being occupied by Fang, Pope and 45 gamers, games guides and combat consultants. Pope's command had grown. Their presence, without the slightest hint of violence, had, just by sheer numbers alone, forced the locals out of the tavern.

Fang sat in the back of the tavern, watching in contemplative silence as Pope gave what appeared to be the makings of a rousing speech to his engaged but captive audience.

"Warriors," Pope called out, both his voice and arms raised in order to gain the attention of everyone in the room. It did not take long before all eyes were on him. "Now when I address you as warriors, I want you to know that I do so with intention. I call you warrior because that's what each of you are." He paused and stared into the room with bright blue penetrating eyes. "All of us did not come to this place with the same goals in mind. Some of us did not even come here of our own volition. Yet everyone here in this room, at this moment, has proven that even in an openly hostile world, under the most harsh and unforgiving conditions, that if you are given just the slightest fighting chance, you'll not only survive... you'll thrive." Pope's eyes lit up as he spoke, and an uncharacteristic show of emotion flashed across his face. "I don't know how many of you know this, but we're special here, and not because we are from Earth, but in spite of it. Did you all know that they've run 18 missions into Deos and every last one of them has ended in dismal failure. None of them, not one has accomplished what we have accomplished up to this point."

"They all died!" he continued with a shout. "I'm talking about the scientists, the soldiers, the top minds of the age. They couldn't hack it. So, they called me, they tricked you and they sent us here as a last resort, and we lived. I want you all to take a moment and think about that." Pope leaned forward as he spoke and his outstretched arms swept over the tavern emphasizing the all-encompassing nature of his message. "Earth sent their best and their brightest and they could not cut it and then when they had no other option, they went and got us." Pope paused again.

"On Earth," he began again. "A lot of you had nothing, were nothing. Now, I don't say that to pass judgement I only say it as a statement of fact. The truth of the matter is, I handpicked most of you. And I know you were nothing because, I too was nothing. I was forced out of the military, had my family taken away from me, lost my career, lost my livelihood. I had nothing. I *was* nothing! The world had broken me."

Pope's eyes were closed, his clenched fist bobbed back in forth before him as he ruminated on all he had lost. The room was silent, every person hanging on to his every word.

"A lot of you know what that feels like, to be broken by the world. But tell me this, how is it that on Earth we can be broken down, destroyed and crushed into dust, but here in the unforgiving world of Deos, where the best and brightest of Earth couldn't last a week, we thrive... I'll tell you why, because this world, as harsh and as visceral as it may seem, has given us all something that Earth never did... a fighting chance." Murmurs of acknowledgement rippled through the room. Pope paused before continuing, "Deos is honest, straightforward, transparent. If something wants to kill you, it tries to kill you, it doesn't smile in your face then stab you in the back. It doesn't pretend it's trying to help you, all the while hurting you at every opportunity. In Deos you get a fighting chance, and we in this room have proven that was all we ever needed."

"Now, the way I see it, we've got two options. We can stay on mission and keep working for our overlords at the Dytrous Corporation. We can continue being cogs in the machine, pawns for some faceless corporate executives who don't care if we live or die so long as the reap the benefits of our blood, sweat and tears. Or we can, for the first time in our pathetic and miserable lives make a decision that makes sense for us and take our rightful place as rulers here in a world where we've already proven we can succeed."

The murmurs in the crowd grew louder.

"Destiny has chosen the men and women in this room to do what no others before them could. Back 'home' you were outcasts wasting you lives playing video games; here you're warriors. Real, genuine warriors. Are any of you prepared to give that up? Do you really want to go back to being mindless, soulless robots waiting on your turn to die? Or would you rather take the fighting chance you never had on Earth and use it to forge a new Deosian Empire!"

Someone let out a resounding *whoop* that spread across the room like wildfire and the next thing Fang knew, the entire tavern was on its feet, yelling, stomping hooting for the start of a new Deosian Empire led by none other than Captain Marcus Pope himself. Fang did not yell, hoot, or stomp. Instead, he rubbed his once wounded shoulder tracing his fingers across the scars from the healed over troll bite.

Pope raised a hand and the room fell once again to silence.

"In order for us to embrace our destiny here, we must first separate ourselves from the people who seek to manipulate us from a world away. In order for us to be free, we must declare our independence and we must prepare for nothing less than revolution. Who's with me?"

Again, loud shouting thundered through the room. Pope raised a hand for silence.

"We will go back to Earth one last time, back into the heart of the Dyrtous Corporation, take the magic items they have plundered from this land and use those items to help build a new home here for ourselves, a home where a warrior lives by his or her own merit and not by how well they can siphon off the hard work of others."

Next to Fang, an enthusiastic cat man with an eye patch shouted approval while the halfling next to him looked on with a worried frown. A few more of the gamers didn't seem particularly moved by Pope's rousing speech, but they were in the minority, on the whole, the group had been stirred into a frenzy and seemed prepared to follow Pope wherever he led.

Fang made his way through the crowd toward Pope.

"Ah, Fang. Just the man I was waiting for," Pope said, extending his hand in Fang's direction.

"Can I talk to you for a second?"

"Of course, but now is not the time. We need to prepare for the mission, and we have a lot to discuss. Come with me."

Fang followed Pope behind the bar and through a door that led to a dimly lit back room. The room was occupied with several other adventurers from the group, most of whom Fang recognized. Lansing, the elven archer and combat consultant that could normally be found at Pope's side; Corrine, the half-elf mage and game guide from team seventeen; Roberts, a half-orc battle guard and combat consultant also from team seventeen; Eliot a dwarven battle guard from team twelve; the Kalgari with the eye patch and the split ear and two adventurers that Fang did not know by name but was sure were gamers and not consultants or guides. And then there was also the old woman. The fortune teller they had met in the swamp and had teleported them from Langune to Abilene Bay in the blink of an eye. The old witch sat quietly in a dark corner of the room, smiling to herself. The rest stood around a circular table and when Pope and Fang walked in, they looked up in anticipation. A small fire burned within the confines of a metal brazier.

"Is everything ready?" Pope asked, his voice returned to its steely tone.

"Yes sir," responded Lansing. "We need only to send the message to HQ."

"Good," Pope said. "Take this down." On command Lansing pulled out a quill dipped it in ink.

"Captain Marcus Pope reporting. I have made extensive progress towards stated objective number one. We have at this time secured live samples of local flora and fauna. We have secured medicinal plants with miraculous healing properties as well as potions and elixirs what have been proven to mend broken bones and cure potent poison in a matter of minutes. We have captured local wildlife with innate magical ability, in pairs ideal for breeding, study, or dissection. Lastly, we have also secured a large and fully intact spell book, a very rare and high-quality item even by Deosian standards. It is in good condition, ideal for study and research. With these items secured and prepped for delivery I am requesting immediate extraction. Please activate a return portal at the coordinates specified below in forty-eight hours from receipt of this message. I will be returning to Earth temporarily to deliver the secured samples before returning to Deos to continue the mission.

End message.

"Did you get all of that?" Pope asked.

"I did." said Lansing finishing writing as he answered. "And the coordinates?" he asked.

"Fifteen miles west of our current location on the eastern edge of the Hathortian Hills." Pope said pointing at a map that lay spread out on the round table that they all surrounded.

Lansing transcribed the longitudinal and latitudinal coordinates to the bottom of the parchment.

"Good," said Pope. "Send it."

The elven archer dropped the letter in the small fire and everyone in the room watched as it burned to ash. Once the piece of parchment had completely disappeared, the old woman stood from her seat in the corner of the room.

"Who is your best mage?" she asked in her withered voice like nails on a chalk board.

"Corrine," said Pope, to which the half-elf woman stepped forward.

The old woman extended a pale and wrinkled hand prompting the game guide to hold out her own.

"This is a teleportation ring," said the fortune teller. "It holds two charges and requires an incantation, which must be spoken in elven to activate it, but do not worry my child, Old mother will teach you the words."

"Hernandez's bag," Pope demanded, reaching out an open hand. Roberts reached down under the table and handed Pope a large brown burlap sack, which Pope took before turning his attention back to the fortune teller. "Are you sure two days in enough time for your spell to take effect?"

"Yes, my lord, two days will be plenty," the old woman responded with a bow.

Pope pulled from the bag three smooth white eggs the size of a human head.

"I will prepare them for you at once," the old woman said with a smile.

"Good, the rest of you know your roles, let's get to work."

At Pope's command everyone in the room scattered. Fang wondered if Pope's inner command center had always been run this way, or if he was only just being allowed inside. Before he could ponder further, Pope turned to him and said, "You had something you wanted to talk about?"

Fang froze. He had asked to talk to the captain not five minutes ago, but now, in that present moment, after hearing his speech and witnessing what he had just seen in that room, he couldn't fathom in the slightest sense what he could of possibly have to ask this man. He was in over his head. Captain Pope was a powerful man and a cold hearted and calculated tactician who commanded people like they were pieces on a chess board. Even being in the same room with him was dangerous, and suddenly Fang realized that he felt very uncomfortable.

"Oh yes, I just wanted to ask, what is my role in the plan... sir."

"I'm going to take a small tactical team into Dytorus Headquarters. Don't worry, you've already proven yourself in the field," said Pope, slapping Fang on the shoulder with a heavy hand. "I need you to hold down the fort here and keep an eye on the gamers that stay behind. Make sure no one does anything stupid while I'm gone." Pope leaned in close to Fang and for a moment the barbarian held his breath, afraid that the captain had found a way to read his mind, sense his uncertainty. "Take note of who you work well with. Once I return, I want you and your handpicked team to start taking missions of *your* choosing. We're building an army, and I'm going to make you one of my top lieutenants. Welcome to the newly formed Knights of Penumbra." Pope leaned back and extended a hand to Fang to shake.

"Thank you, sir." said Fang, returning the handshake with a tight-lipped smile.

Arnold Fangloski exited the back room and made his way out of the Misty Shadow Tavern and Inn. Fang had taken up residence in what had previously been the blacksmith's shop. The barbarian made his way past the long dead forge and the old and rusted armor to the back room that he now used as living quarters. He pulled his personal belongings from under a wood framed straw bed, opened his pack and removed a large seashell gently wrapped in cloth.

Chapter 50: A Fighting Chance...

"We're never going home. That's it, we're going to die here," said Alex, throwing his hands in the air.

"We may as well start shopping around for apartments and looking for day jobs. I mean unless you guys want to keep being adventurers in which case, we'll probably all be dead by next month so no need to sign a lease," said Robyn.

Dante walked backward blindly until he just so happened to find an armchair in which he plopped down, dropping his head into his hands, and rubbing them slowly over his face as if he was trying to wipe away the feeling of disbelief which had set itself into his facial expression.

"Guys, come on. It's not over yet. There has to be something we can do, some other options we can pursue," said Stephen.

"It's useless," said Morrigan. "Aside from Sandberg the only people that could get us back to Earth is Dytorus Corp, and the only way through them is through Pope, and for us, that's not an option."

"Well now, don't look so glum," said Floggins. "I'm sure there is something I can do to help, just give me a moment." The old gnome unraveled scroll after scroll, throwing each one over his shoulder upon realizing it was not the one he was looking for.

"Do you guys hear something?" said Dante. He looked around the room for the source of the noise. The voice grew stronger and more distinct with each passing moment. He looked over at Shinto, the half-orc sat quietly in a corner, a bewildered look of recognition on his face.

"Do you hear that?" Dante asked aloud.

"I hear you talking," said Alex.

"No, not me, a voice that sounds far-off, but still... in the room."

"Oh God, it's finally happened. He's losing it, he's cracked up," said Robyn.

"Everyone be quiet!" said Dante, struggling to hear the voice once again. "Shinto do you hear that?"

Shinto stood. "Yes... I do. It almost sounds like..." The half-orc opened his pack and pulled from it the sending shell, which bellowed with the clear and distinct voice of Fang from the other end.

"Hello! Hello! Is this thing working. Can anybody hear me? Pick up! How do I know if this piece of crap is on or not? Hello? Shinbo? Dante? You there?"

"Hello?" said Shinto into the shell. "We can hear you."

"Thank god, finally. Shinbo? Is that you? Are Dante and the others still with you? Are you all still in Langune?"

"It's Shinto!" Dante took the shell. "Why does it matter to you where we are. You left us remember? And you stole our sending shell."

"Quarterback! Thank god you're there I was hoping you were still with your orc friend. Listen we have a problem."

"Fangloski, you know what, you really got a lot of balls using this shell to call us after stealing it. What is this some type of weird flex?"

"Damnit quarterback, will you shut up for a second and listen!" Fang's voice trembled with tension. "There isn't much time. It's Pope. He's planning to go back to Earth."

"What!?" said Dante, Alex, Morrigan, Robyn and Stephen all in unison.

"He's lost it! Dytorus Corp is going to open a portal for him in two days. He's planning to go back there and take something from the headquarters building and bring it back here to Deos. He says they have magic items hidden there."

"That's true," said Stephen. "Dytorus has a number of magic items from past expeditions into Deos."

"Pope wants them, and he intends to take them by force. He's decided to sever ties with Dytorus Corp. Aside from this shopping trip, he has no intentions on going back... *ever.* He is going to maroon all of us here, then he plans to form an army and take over Deos."

"What? He's planning to what?" Dante's mouth hung open in disbelief.

"Dante. You have to get here, and you have to stop him."

"Wh-where is... where is here?" asked Dante, still dumbfounded by turn of events.

"A small town called Penumbra, about a day's travel from Abilene Bay. Pope sent a message to Dytorus asking them to open a portal in a valley at the edge of the Hathorian Hills. The portal is set to open at dusk two days from now. I will gather any gamers willing to stand up to Pope and meet you there.

"Quarterback, I didn't see it before, but I see it now. Pope is not like you or me. He's going to get us all killed if we don't do something about it right now."

"Yeah," said Dante into the shell. "I know.... Look, Fang I believe you. We'll be there."

"Good, good glad to hear it. Remember, two days from now at the western edge of the Hathorian Hills just east of Penumbra. The portal opens at dusk."

Dante wrote down the coordinates on a piece of lab paper and then he and Fang signed off. A stony silence filled the workshop.

"So, I thought Dante was cracking up, turns out it was Pope," said Robyn.

"If he carries out these plans, if he attacks Dytorus he cuts off any escape to Earth for good," said Morrigan.

"While sudden and not ideal, this does pose an interesting opportunity for your party," suggested Shinto. "If you all can stop Pope, the portal back to your world will be wide open and you all can walk right through returning home, in addition to that, it would appear you don't even have to fight this battle alone, you have backup."

"Good points," said Alex. "But how do we get to the Hathorian Hills in two days? It's well out of walking distance."

Floggins who had stopped his frantic search through his papers and books to listen to the conversation with Fang, moved quickly to a scroll that now sat discarded on the floor. "I may be able to help," he said. He unfurled the scroll and nodded approvingly. "Yes, yes this just might work after all. I've been working on this prototype airship. It's an advanced glider that's lifted high into the air by a hot air balloon. Once it gets high enough, the glider is released, and you ride the air currents to your destination. It's designed to carry its occupants over very long distances within a very short time. The only issue has been making it light enough to ride the wind yet strong enough to survive multiple flights. That particular design point has been difficult to nail down, so in truth its only really good for one use." Floggins cleared his throat. "The landing can be a bit rough, if you know what I mean, but at the moment this is all I have."

"Then I think this will just have to do," said Dante.

"I agree," said Morrigan. "At this point it's all or nothing. We have to get to that portal before it closes. Book us five seats in the glider."

"Six seats," said Shinto. "I dare not bow out now."

"Very well then. The trip will take about eight hours by air, giving you all a day and a half to prepare and giving me the same amount of time to make final adjustments to the ship. So get some rest, explore the city and in 36 hours you'll set sail for a final confrontation with your arch nemesis. Now, I have work to do, goodbye!"

And with that, the adventurers were dismissed.

Chapter 51: Executive Approval

"Sir we've received communication from Captain Pope. He's requesting we open the door for a return trip."

"What's happened? Has he abandoned his mission?" asked the chairman.

"No sir, quite the contrary, says he's made major progress. He claims to have a number of medicinal plants, potions and elixirs that can cure disease and instantly heal wounds. Um a few live samples of the local wildlife, and also sir he says he has a spell book."

"A spell book?" Said the chairman his eyes growing wide and dewy.

"Yes sir, an actual book of spells, fully intact, quite large and quite well used from his description, an ideal situation for our research needs."

Well, this Pope is proving to be somewhat useful after all, glad to see this latest expedition hasn't been a complete and total waste of time."

"Yes sir, we lost a number of good men on those previous attempts in before now sir."

"Ah yes, of course... that's what I meant...the men... we lost a lot of good men."

"Is it safe to assume that you approve of the portal activation for Pope's return trip then sir?"

"Oh yes, bring him through, have him bring forth that beautiful bounty of health wealth and progress for all of human civilization!"

"Consider it done sir. We will be set to open the portal in 24 hours."

"Aha perfect! I'll be there."

"I'm sorry sir, you want to be present at the lab when he returns?"

"I'll be winning the Nobel Prize someday for the work I'm doing here, I'm not going to miss the moment my soldiers march in with the first spoils of war."

"Good point sir, I'll let the other executives know, perhaps its best that we are all present."

"Yes, yes of course. Oh, and Johnson, has Pope mentioned anything else about... dead kids and digging up graves and anymore nonsense like that?"

"No sir, not a word."

"Good, good. Thought we were losing the old boy for a minute there. Probably just the pressures of the place momentarily getting to him, I guess. Glad he came back to his senses."

"Yes sir, so am I."

Chapter 52: The Maiden Flight of the Swan Song...

Dante had butterflies in his stomach. The feeling had normally been reserved for big football games or important lacrosse matches. Now, he wasn't sure if the pre-game jitters were due to the impending final confrontation with the psychotic yet capable Captain Marcus Pope, or, if it had anything to do with him being a passenger on the maiden flight of a prototype airship in a faraway land.

"Dante, you ready?" asked Alex. "They're expecting us up on the Aeropad."

In the bright light of day, Hemera-Balgrad was a beehive of commotion, steam engines hissed, venting hot air through shrill high-pitched whistles, while large mechanical clockwork gears shifted through interlocking teeth in order to operate cranes and lifts, construction equipment that carried lumber, stone and other goods from one tier to another. Dante, Alex and Stephen crossed a bridgeway taking them over the expansive mountain crevice that split the city in half and the nearly ninety-foot drop to the open courtyard below. They reached the western side of the third tier where they found and entered Floggin's workshop.

"Question," said Alex. "What do we call the professor. Sandberg or Floggins? I keep getting it confused."

"I'm guessing," said Dante as they entered the front door of the workshop, "Since he came here to live out the rest of his life under the assumed name Floggins, we should call him Floggins. If we make it back to Earth and he decides to one day return, then we can call him Sandberg."

"Yeah, that makes sense. Well, Professor Floggins says he has a lift in the back of his workshop that will take us all the way up to the summit level, that's where we'll find the aeropad."

"Hey look." Said Stephen, pointing ahead of them. "There's Robyn. She must be headed up as well."

Robyn was in the workshop, only she wasn't making her way to any backroom lift, she was instead involved in an in-depth conversation with one of Professor Floggings' assistants.

"So, were you able to do all of the things we discussed?" she asked the same male human assistant that a day and a half prior they had all seen stumbling out of the workshop in a white lab coat and shrouded in a cloud of dark purple smoke.

"For the most part, yes," said the assistant. "But none of these items have been thoroughly tested. At this point they are all merely theoretical prototypes. I don't know if they are safe."

"We're about to fly in a theoretical airship. What's the point in worrying about a few smoke bombs and a modified crossbow?" Robyn's words had an odd way of cutting past one's psychological defenses, yet still somehow coming across as persuasive. It was as if her every proposal was a 'triple dog dare' that even the most mature individual had a hard time resisting. Her approval, it appeared, was a highly sought-after commodity, even if it was done so begrudgingly.

"Yes, well in that case, if the professor has approved it. Here are the fog capsules. I used the resin you gave me, distilled it into a liquid and then infused that with a special mana treated water. I then took that mixture and ran it through an alchemical process turning it into a fog which I then condensed into these thin glass orbs." The assistant handed her a small pouch from which Robyn removed a small cloudy glass sphere the size of a marble.

"Be careful," warned the assistant. "If the glass breaks the condensed fog inside will escape. Both breathing and seeing within the confines of the fog will be impossible. The amount of resin you gave me was enough to make nearly a gallon of perfume. I've used it all to make a total of six of these capsules."

"Excellent. You've out done yourself." Robyn said, flicking the cloudy marble into the air and catching it before the assistant's panicked eyes. "And my second request?"

The assistant let out an exhausted sigh, then before saying another word turned around and hefted a crossbow out from beneath a nearby workstations. The crossbow, Dante noticed looked similar to what Robyn already owned, however this one, as opposed to being loaded with a crossbow bolt was instead loaded with a heavy metal grappling hook.

"Luckily Professor Floggins already had schematics for an item such as this, only he calls his a Grappling Shot."

"Milo my man you are a certified genius," said Robyn as she took the modified crossbow and attached it to her belt.

"Actually, it is Professor Floggins who is the genius, everything you have requested I have created based off of his original processes and or designs."

"Yes, well I am sure the Professor will be proud of the work you've done here and if my friends and I somehow manage to survive this test flight and aren't in another world by this time tomorrow, I'll owe you a favor," Robyn said with a wink.

"Oh yes," said Milo. "The uncivilized lands beyond the Tethys Sea. Quite a dreadful place I've heard. I must say, I don't envy you lot at all."

"Hello boys," said Robyn cheerily at the site of her friends. "When did you walk up."

"Right when you started receiving special request items from the lab assistants," said Dante.

"Well, we are heading off to a final confrontation with Pope, never know what might come in handy. You guys heading up to the air pad thingie?"

"The Aeropad," corrected Alex.

"That's what I said," responded Robyn. "Are you guys ready to head up or not?"

The summit was the peak of Mount Hemera, one of the tallest mountains in the Hathorian mountain range and the one the city of Hemera-Balgrad had been carved into. The platform was made of iron, upon which waited a wooden bird-like wedge with heavy outstretched canvas wings . Dante imagined Leonardo Da Vinci would have designed something similar had he built an airship in Deos. Above the wooden craft was an oversized oblong balloon, attached by a series of nets and ropes and now filling with heated air, dispensed from bellows that spouted bright orange flames like the burners of a hot air balloon.

"Ay yes, you all are here. Welcome," said Professor Floggins enthusiastically, the wind blowing off the mountain peak nearly drowning out his voice. "This is the ship. I call it the A.G. Swan Song."

"A.G.?" repeated Stephen.

"A.G. for Aerial-Glider."

"You named the airship the 'Swan Song'?" asked Dante.

"Seemed fitting."

Dante shrugged, he didn't have the wherewithal to explain irony.

"The ship's operation is simple really. Pull lever one to release the ship from the dirigible. Operate lever two to control the pitch, lever three to control the yaw and lever four to control the roll. Pull lever five to deploy the backup balloon if you need to regain altitude, its filled with an alchemical gas that expands quickly. In a jam its worth a try. Lever six and seven each will deploy parachutes meant to slow the decent of the aircraft and lever eight will deploy landing gear. Now that I think about it, try not to use lever five during flight. I designed it for after landing so that the ship can actually make it back. That is, if it lands in one piece. I'm not sure how well the parachutes will slow the craft. As you know, it's not been tested."

"Wait, what does lever five do again?" asked Robyn.

"That may as well have been in Greek, there is no way any of us are qualified to fly this thing," said Morrigan.

"Please tell me you got some of that," Alex whispered to Dante.

"I got the first half in case anybody else got the second half," said Stephen.

"I remember it all. We'll be fine," said Shinto reassuringly.

Floggins' dwarven assistant wound a large crank which pulled the ship's canvas wings in to lay flat against the side of the hull, before disconnecting the bellows and pulling them away from the now completely filled hot air balloon that floated above the tied down ship. With the wings reeled inward, the ship looked less like a large bird and more like a wooden space capsule. Dante, Alex, Morrigan, Robyn, Stephen and Shinto clambered on board the A.G. Swan Song via a dwarf sized hatch panel in the back of the enclosed ship. The interior of the glider looked like a small one room cabin. There were seven seats, one more than what they needed, but barely enough head room to stand.

One seat sat in the pilot's positions, in arm's reach of all eight of the ship's control levers with a set of three chairs positioned to both the left and right side of the captain's chair, each set facing the other.

"Alright, go ahead and grab a seat," said Floggins, standing in the hatchway of the ship's back entrance. "I will release the ropes and launch the ship in five minutes. Most important, you must remember to keep the Hathorian mountains in your view and you can follow them west all the way to the hills." The gnome stepped out of the doorway and the hatched closed with a decisive bang. A circular glass viewport in the entry door and a large rectangular one on the ship's front end allowed the adventurers to see Floggins' assistants from inside the Swan Song; either an enchantment or really good soundproofing left them unable to hear anything beyond the confines of the ship.

"Okay, so who's gonna fly her?" asked Alex.

There was an awkward silence.

"Shinto is the only one who remembers all of the instructions," said Robyn.

"He can tell us the instructions, that doesn't mean he has to fly it," said Morrigan.

"Did anyone on Earth have any experience flying planes before?" asked Stephen. "During character creation, some real-world experiences translate into Deosian abilities."

Another awkward silence.

"The trip is long; we will need multiple pilots," said Shinto.

"Stephen, you said you remember the first half of the instructions, you take the first leg." Dante said "Shinto can support. Once we get airborne, we'll figure the rest out from there."

Stephen strapped himself into the captain's chair while everyone else took a seat behind him. Leather straps crossed the chest of each occupant and a hook connected to the end of the strap latched on to an anchor point at the base of each seat. There were three decisive bangs at the back hatch, and from his seat Dante could see Milo retreating from the Aeropad platform. The ship shifted, and then lifted. They had been untethered. They were off.

The Swan Song floated upward higher and higher above the mountain peak. An additional circular viewport at the bottom of the ship allowed the adventurers to look below them and watch as the city of Hemera-Balgrad went from a sprawling metropolis beneath their feet to a hardly recognizable anthill that they had to struggle to see there the ever-increasing cloud cover that had begun to gather around the ship.

"How high are we?" asked Alex.

"There is an altimeter up here," said Stephen, "It says we're nine thousand... paces up."

"Paces are like feet," said Dante, answering the questing before anyone asked.

"We pull the first lever at ten thousand paces," said Shinto. "Mount Hemera's peak is six thousand five hundred paces high."

"We're rising fast," said Stephen "nine thousand two hundred... nine thousand three... four... five..." Stephen placed his hand on the first lever.

"I really hope this ship doesn't fall apart in mid-air," said Alex, "or crash into a mountain, or get attacked by some giant flying bird."

"Nine thousand six."

"Alex!" yelled Dante. "That's not helping."

"Nine thousand seven."

"What?" said the dwarf confused, "I thought naming worst case scenarios relieved tension, like on the Mythril Caravan."

"Nine thousand eight."

"Not the same. It's just not the same at all."

"Nine thousand nine."

"Dear God, why do I have to die like this? Penniless and listening to these two argue about nothing!"

"Ten thousand feet!" called out Stephen.

"Hold on everyone!" yelled Shinto.

Stephen yanked the first lever downward and the ship responded with a violent jerk as the it detached from the balloon and the compactly folded wings unfurled themselves to their full length. The Swan Song bobbed as if it were about to do a nosedive directly back toward the Deosian continent and then just as suddenly the ship seemed to catch the wind and begin to glide through the air like a gigantic kite.

"It worked," said Stephen, "it's working." He touched the second, third and fourth lever only slightly and the ship responded in turn to each, swaying and shifting with the manipulation of each lever. No one noticed Stephen's deftness with the levers though, they all had their eyes shut tight.

"We're not dead?" asked Robyn.

"Not yet," said Morrigan.

The Swan Song drifted across the sky with relative ease and soon the passengers unclipped themselves to get a better look at the dazzling cloudscape. Out of the front view window the adventurers could see the vast, cloud-filled blue sky laid out before them while through the bottom view window they could see the distant tops of the Hathorian mountains passing beneath.

"It's amazing to think that we're flying with no engine," said Robyn.

"You say amazing, I say terrifying," said Dante.

"How long will it take us to get to the hills?" asked Alex.

"Around eight hours. Everyone should make themselves comfortable," said Shinto.

"How are we going to stay airborne for eight hours?" asked Robyn.

"Before you all arrived at the aero pad, Dr. Floggins was explaining Flyways. He described them as extremely powerful air currents that travel clear across Deos. Apparently, birds use them to migrate from one part of the continent to another. The Professor calibrated the glider to place us directly in the path of a flyway headed toward the Hathoriarn Hills," Morrigan explained.

Just then a jolt vibrated through the ship, shaking the entire wooden frame of the glider. Each plank rattled in its housing and the passengers all sat bolt upright before Shinto assured them it was just wind turbulence. They had a full day of flying ahead of them in an airship with no engine. Dante thought about some of the RPG video games he used to play, not just Dragon Dale but all of his favorite franchises. There always seemed to be an airship ride to the final battle, and now here they were, in Dante's game. Flying off to the final confrontation.

Dante opened up his Spirit Tome.

-You have fulfilled 4 of 4 primary objectives for the quest "Searching for a Stranger in a Strange Land"

-You have gained 8,500 Experience points!

-You have been issued a new quest, "A Portal Home"

-You have been issued a new quest, "The Maiden Flight of the Swan Song"

-You have a total of 47,050 Experience Points

As ever, the journal had taken the liberty of recording the adventurer's highlights, although this time there were not nearly as many as there had been previously. Dante flipped over to his character sheet, the one section he hadn't checked in some time.

- Strength – 26
- Agility – 26
- Constitution – 17
- Intelligence – 22
- Wisdom – 17
- Mind – 17
- Charisma – 17

Dante's stats had grown considerably since first entering Deos almost four weeks ago. Now he was level eight, and his two highest stats, strength and agility, were double what they had been when he started, making him twice as strong and as fast as when they had first arrived. At first he'd felt his body tearing apart from all the marching and fighting, but over time, and after a hot meal and a full night of sleep, he was waking up in the best condition of his life. The only question that remained was had he grown strong enough to get them back home.

After a couple of hours in the pilot's chair, Stephen stood to let Shinto guide the Swan Song, and then after Shinto, Robyn. Alex, Morrigan and even Dante flew the ship for brief intervals of time, but after everyone had operated the controls for what they considered a minimal stretch, Robyn came out as the most comfortable and gifted pilot of the group. As a result, once the adventurers had worked themselves down to less than an hour of flight time left, the rogue became the only reasonable choice as the one to attempt the landing.

"Drop in altitude coming up," said Robyn her eyes glued to the large window where before the the mountain range was beginning to level out and soften into green hills. Stephen stood braced over her shoulder as Robyn pushed the second lever, in direct correlation to her movement the nose of the ship pitched gently forward sending the Swan Song into a downward tilt as opposed to the carefully balanced even keel they had maintained the entire flight.

"We're losing altitude, we're down to nine thousand eight hundred feet," Stephen said, reading off the altimeter.

Below them through the viewport the mountains had all but disappeared.

"We need to drop faster," said Morrigan. "We can't see the mountains anymore, we might already be over the hills."

Robyn pushed the second lever and the Swan Song pitched forward into an aggressive dive toward the ground.

"We're dropping fast now," said Stephen. "Nine thousand three hundred feet. Nine thousand feet. Eight thousand five hundred feet. Eight thousand feet."

"Ummm... that seems a bit too fast," Alex said.

Dante looked back to the lower view port window to see that they had broken from their blanket of clouds and were approaching the ground.

"Seven thousand feet."

The bottom viewport window was now skewed due to the ships downward tilt, but Dante could still see rocky green mountains had long given way to large rolling hills.

"Six thousand feet."

"Even the ship out at five thousand feet" Shinto shouted over the roar of rushing wind. "We're gonna hit the ground too early."

"Crash," shouted Alex. "You mean we'll crash!"

They were still high, but not nearly as high as they had been and if they kept going at this pace, they'd be a smoldering stain on the side of one of those Hathorian Hills before too long.

"Five thousand feet," Stephen yelled out.

"Even her out!" Shinto yelled.

Everyone hold on!" Robyn pulled back hard on the second lever forcing the nose of the Swan Song to come up out of its dive and align with the horizon once again, this maneuver seemed to sling shot the ship even faster through the sky over the Hathorian Hills. Everyone was pulled from their seats from the force of the direction change and Stephen, the only one not sitting, slammed hard into the wall. The ship rumbled and shook. Stephen struggled back to his position behind the pilot.

"We're at four thousand five hundred feet. Still dropping," shouted Stephen.

Dante looked down through the lower viewport window to see the hills below passing by in a blur.

"Four thousand feet."

"We're no longer riding the air current. We're maintaining speed but losing attitude," said Shinto.

The wind turbulence that they had experienced at ten thousand feet had been multiplied dramatically now that they were closer to the ground. Robyn struggled to keep the ship steady as it rolled and twisted.

"Three thousand feet. Two thousand feet."

Robyn pulled the sixth and seventh levers to deploy the ship's parachutes. There was a loud bang as the chutes deployed from the back of the Swan Song. The ship snapped hard as the chutes filled, there was a sound like an explosion before the overpowering tailwinds ripped both parachutes from the frame of the ship.

"We lost both chutes!" said Alex watching out the back window as they flapped into the distance.

"One thousand feet," said Stephen sitting down and strapping himself in.

"Deploying the landing gear," Robyn called out, pulling the eighth lever.

"We can't land at this speed," Morrigan yelled.

"We have no choice we're at five hundred feet. Brace for impact!"

As the ground flashed past through the lower viewport window Dante saw them, a group of at least two dozen people marching across an open green field. Pope and his men moving toward the portal jump point. They were so close. Yet so much stood in the way of achieving their mission.

"There they are." yelled Dante. They're right below us! We have to land now. This is our chance to go home."

For the first time since they had started to descend Robyn turned and looked at Dante. She gave him a slight nod and then turned back to her controls.

"Everyone hold on! I'm going to try something."

Robyn pulled the fifth lever and with another loud bang a large balloon released from the top of the ship, filling itself with alchemical gas lighter than the air around it. The balloon couldn't fight the velocity and ended up being dragged in the ship's wake before snapping free, but not before slowing the Swang Song and disrupting its trajectory. The ship continued to hurtle forward while violently swinging from side to side. Everyone braced for impact.

Just before landing Robyn pulled back as hard as she could on the second lever and the nose of the ship jerked upward so the belly hit the ground first. The impact was a tooth crunching bounce. The second bounce broke the right wing clean off the ship and the third sent the nose into the dirt, the ship sliding twenty feet plowing through everything in its path before stopping at the base of a hill.

Chapter 53: Portal Crashers

Pope and his platoon marched on towards the Hathorian Hills. There were thirty in total, mostly combat consultants and game guides as well as a few of the more enthusiastic gamers. They moved across the large green plain in mass, like army ants on a warpath. Between them, on the shoulders of four combat consultants, they carried a large wooden box.

Pope walked in front with Lansing, Corrine and Roberts close behind. Their destination lay only a hundred feet ahead, a set of stone ruins set right at the edge of the Hathorian Hills, the designated extraction point where in a few moments a portal would take them out of Deos and back to Earth.

Captain Marcus Pope was ruminating on his coming victory when a large wooden bird streaked across the sky. It burst from the clouds like an unsteady rocket, wobbling and juddering before crashing violently into the base of a hill a few hundred yards away. There was stunned silence. Plumes of dust and debris swirled around the wreckage before dissipating in a smoke-like haze to reveal the broken airship.

"Is that the portal?" asked one of the gamers, breaking the awkward silence that possessed the group. "Is that how we get back to Earth?"

"No." replied Pope, already certain who was inside the ship. "That's simply a stray dog trying to follow us home."

The rear hatch of the Swan Song burst open and Dante, battered, bruised and with a small bloody cut over his eye, clambered from the ship, followed by Alex and then Shinto. He reached a hand back inside and helped Morrigan climb out, then Stephen and finally Robyn. The group of adventurers stumbled out of the wrecked airship clapping one another on the backs and laughing in hysterics at their near miss. Shinto brought his hands together, interlocking his fingers and bowing his head as a golden shimmering energy engulfed the huddled group, reversing the effects of the minor scrapes and bruises sustained during their crash. Dante felt his HP bar refill. This was it. The best chance they would get.

"DANTE!" Pope screamed from across the open field. "Way to make a dramatic entrance."

Dante turned to face his nemesis. "The game's over, Pope. We're going home, now!"

"That's the problem Dante, you still think it's a game, and that's why you'll never win!" Pope gave a sweep of his hand and at his command, his soldiers charged.

Dante pulled his sword from his sheath and set his feet, readying himself for the attack. Alex, Morrigan Robyn Stephen, and Shinto were following suit when a voice from their rear called out to them.

"Don't start without us."

"Fang!" shouted Dante in surprise.

Fang stood atop the small hill where the Swan Song had crashed, flanked by four more gamers. They descended and joined Dante and the others at the base of the hill. There was a brief exchange of nods as one group of adventurers joined the other and without another word, they all turned back to Pope's Knights of Penumbra, who had stopped their advance only to launch a flurry of projectiles upon Dante and his friends. Momentarily the sky filled with arrows and crossbow bolts which arced high and to the air and then fell towards Dante and the others like deadly rain.

"Greater Shield," said Shinto, extending his hand out before him. The air around them shimmered and the arrows and crossbow bolts that should have impaled the eleven of them instead bounced off the invisible barrier and fell to the ground.

"Everyone," Dante called out with his sword pointed toward the charging soldiers. "Attack!"

Primal roars erupted from each group as they charged towards one another with weapons drawn. Magic spells launched from the back lines filled the air with burning ozone. Motes of fire and shards of ice flew from both directions, forcing Dante to duck and evade random spell fire as he rushed forward. His heart pounded in his chest, and he could hear his own labored breathing through his ears. His mind had gone blank of rational thought, there only existed the instinctual and singular focus of completing the task at hand.

He felt almost bestial, like the black wolves that sprinted across the Illdershire Plains in pursuit of prey. In pursuit of a goal that ultimately meant the success or failure of the entire pack. He could feel Alex, Morrigan, Robyn, Stephen and Shinto close behind him, and that feeling alone encouraged him to push faster and harder, straight into his enemies. Dante dropped his left shoulder, raised his sword high in his right hand and screamed, the blood burning in his veins.

Dante slammed into a human battle guard, his shoulder landing directly into the man's chest knocking him off of his feet. He felt a small chunk of his HP drop from the impact of the collision but saw that the man he had trampled lost considerably more. Dante ducked, dodging a free flying arrow only to stare down the offending bowman standing some ten yards out from him, his bow already aimed directly at Dante's head.

Before the archer could release his next shot, an axe tumbled over Dante's shoulder, crashing through the archer's bow and burying itself into his collarbone, taking half of his HP bar along with it. Dante looked back to see Alex, shield in one hand and the other still extended from a perfectly thrown axe. Dante nodded to his friend, who nodded back before lifting his shield to block an incoming swing from a short sword and then returning the favor by punching the attacker in the face with a large meaty fist.

The rest of the party spread out, engaging one Penumbra Knight after another, even though their inferior numbers left them at a stark disadvantage. And still they fought. Fang bulldozed his way through the enemy lines, his every step brought with it a deadly swing of his heavy double-bladed axe, each stroke an attempt to cleave someone in two. Robyn concealed herself in the wake of his rampage, sneak attacking the distracted enemies who were too busy attempting to avoid the barbarian to notice the rogue. She plunged her daggers into the back of a half-orc battle guard before disappearing once again into the crowd to fire her crossbow at an unsuspecting mage.

Morrigan stood in the middle of the battlefield, alternating between her flame sparrow spell, the fire birds screeching through the air before exploding on impact, and her ice javelin spell, which covered anything it touched in shards of ice and frost. Shinto fought off multiple attackers, expertly wielding his mace in one hand, while casting healing and protective spells with the other.

Dante crossed swords with a combat consultant, a half-elf male with a steel blade. The two swordsmen pressed into each other with all of their strength. Dante could feel his muscles straining under the stress of the combat consultant's weight against his blade and then without warning Dante stopped resisting and allowed the tip of his swords to drop to the ground, the half-elf found himself caught off guard by Dante's change in strategy and lost his balance. With speed and precision Dante rolled his wrist clockwise and pulled his sword up behind his stumbling opponent and then brought it down hard, slashing the combat consultant across the neck and chest. An act which sent his HP bar plummeting down by half and sent the swordsman falling to the ground writhing in agony.

Pope stood watching, on the raised stone floor of some crumbling and weathered ruin. Lansing stood to one side of him and Corrine to the other. Behind him four more guards were stationed at the corner of a large wooden crate. Dante regripped his sword. This was it. He had fought his way through a veritable army for this precise moment and he had done so without using any of his abilities, without expending any of his MP. He began to channel his mana, the magical energy that burned in his blood. He was ready.

Pope pulled his crossbow from his back and leveled it at Dante who had already anticppated this cource of action. With a lightspeed slash Dante was confident he could dodge a speeding crossbow bolt and close the distance between himself and the captain in an instant. But then, Pope shifted. He took his aim off Dante and placed it onto something in the distance. His face twisted in a vile smirk. Dante followed his line of sight to find that his crossbow was aimed directly at Morrigan.

Pope pulled the trigger. Three bolts flew. Dante activated lightspeed slash but before time could slow the bolts were past him and out of reach. His legs were heavy and unresponsive as if he moved through sludge. The ability wasn't meant for chasing bullets. Lightspeed Slash, Sword Summon, Burning Blade, none of it could help him now when he needed it most.

Morrigan was frozen in a moment, fire leaping from her hands, she had no idea what was coming. In seconds, time would restart and those bolts would slam into her ending her life. In nightmare-like agony Dante could only watch it happen. In that instant he thought back to the moment they had shared in Abilene Bay. How he had promised Morrigan they would make it home together and with every fiber of his being he knew he had to keep that promise, even if it killed him.

Dante's body stretched, his blood burned, his vision blurred as all his intent went into saving Morrigan's life. An intense tingling sensation like that of electricity moved throughout his being as the world around him became a fuzzy blue haze and his surroundings shifted themselves, as if the world was moving of its own accord beneath his feet. His sword vanished, replaced by a bright blue crackling bolt of raw energy. Suddenly, Morrigan was no longer across the battlefield but right beside him, the crossbow bolts were still airborne and still slowed by the effects of his original ability. Without thinking Dante threw himself on the mage as time coalesced. Morrigan and Dante fell in a heap while the crossbow bolts whizzed by overhead, missing them both.

Morrigan hit the ground with a grimace, saw that it was Dante on top of her and stared up at him with shock.

"What just- did you turn into lightning and teleport?" she asked.

Dante looked at his own MP bar at the edge of his sight. It was empty. "I think so." He smiled. "Are you... okay?"

"Oh no..." Morrigan's smiled turned to a frown.

"What? Are you hurt?" Dante asked, panic in his voice.

"No... not me." Morrigan looking passed Dante toward the direction where the crossbow bolts had continued to travel.

Dante scrambled to his feet and rushed across the field. Fang had three crossbow bolts protruding from his chest, each one gushing blood. His HP bar had fallen to nothing but a sliver of red. He dropped down to his knees and was about to fall face first into the grass when Dante caught hold of his limp body.

"Fang! Fang can you hear me?"

"Quarterback." Fang took desperate gasps for breath. "You were right about Pope. He's a real... asshole."

"Don't talk. Just don't talk, I'm going to get you some help." Dante looked around frantically. "Shinto we need help!" he screamed.

Shinto swung his mace with ferocity, sending two enemy combatants airborne, their bodies limp ragdolls under the weight and force of the half-orc's heavy club.

Pope watched with his smug and malicious grin unwavering. Behind him, the air crackled. The fabric of reality itself seemed to rip open as a near ten-foot wall of liquid light materialized out of thin air. It hummed with the resonance of a living thing before Pope and those standing nearby turned and walked through the portal.

"No!" Dante screamed out as they disappeared into the light.

"You go." Said Shinto, taking hold of Fang. "I'll take care of him. Get through the portal and keep it open so the others can come through."

Dante charged the still thrumming portal. He deflected a sword strike, parried another, ducked past an axe swing and knocked two arrows out of the air. Within sight of the portal he found himself on a collision course with a mote of fire streaming through the air. He swung his sword defiantly, metal meeting magic in much the same way a bat connects with a baseball, and with a forceful push, he sent the small ball of fire flying off into the distance. His path now clear, Dante dropped his shoulder and forced his body to move faster. He would barrel through the portal and disrupt whatever plan Pope had in play, he'd stall, keep the portal open long enough for everyone else to come through and together they'd win. And then, right when he was ten feet from the glowing shimmering portal surface, he slammed into what felt like a brick wall.

The force knocked Dante off his feet. He hit the ground disoriented and confused, before climbing to his feet and approaching the portal once again, only to find a solid wall of invisible force blocking his path.

"A barrier spell? Someone cast a barrier spell?"

A familiar cackle filled the air and Dante's heart sank. Thick purple smoke swirled up from the ground before dissipating, to reveal the old fortune teller.

"You did this?" Dante growled. "Don't you understand what's at stake? Drop this spell and get out of here!" Dante screamed and in a fit of rage raised his sword and struck the invisible barrier only to have his blade spring backward like a wooden stick off a rubber tire.

"Such a vicious and ferocious young wolf," sneered the woman. Lifting her hand she pressed it to the barrier as if observing an animal in a glass cage. "Your hunger is great indeed, but unfortunately for you, your fangs are not sharp enough to pierce the heavens."

"I won't let you stand in my way!" Dante screamed, repeatedly striking the barrier with his sword only to have it recoil violently upon impact each time. He gripped the sword in both hands, lifted it high over his head and with all his strength, brought it down on the barrier. Magic and metal collided, but unlike when he had deflected the fire spell, this time there was a distinctive cracking sound and all at once his sword shattered as if it were made of glass, leaving him holding in his hands nothing more than a hilt and the shard of a jagged blade.

"The ferocity, the determination, even the look of desperation and loneliness that you carry in your eyes, it so greatly reminds me of my own son," cackled the fortune teller. She smiled as if his anguish caused her a joy she could not hide. But then she gasped, as if suddenly all of the air had been sucked from her lungs she started out at Dante with an expression of wide-eyed shock. Slowly and almost carefully the fortune teller looked down.

Dante's broken blade had pierced the barrier, the shattered sword now buried into the magic force field up to the hilt, its jagged tip inches from piercing the fortune teller's belly. The old woman let out a breath, and unmistakable sigh of relief, followed by a somewhat muffled and amused laugh. "You pierced my barrier spell," she cackled. "Why, you are full of surprises."

Dante took hold of the hilt with both hands and with bared teeth dragged the broken blade upward ripping a hole in the magic barrier. The fortune teller stepped backward in awe, a smile wide and mischievous spread across her pale and wrinkled face. As Dante struggled to bring the blade up to shoulder height, she placed a hand on its exposed and jagged edge.

"Your journey shall be an interesting one to witness," she whispered, her spider-like fingers balanced delicately on the crooked and wriggling blade. Then, with a flash of purple crackling energy, she vanished, just as Dante ripped a jagged hole large enough for a man to squeeze through.

Chapter 54: Return to Earth

Normally Sara was relegated to the observation room, along with her supervisor Frank, but today she sat in Dytorus Corp's Amphitheater, on subfloor one of the Last Legend Games HQ. Today was not a normal day. Sara, Frank and everyone else that worked on the Deosian Expedition Project, including the Chairman, vice-president Johnson and each of the executives that were invested in the success of the project, were currently seated in the amphitheater. Everyone in attendance from the balcony level to the working stiffs on the middle level were all focused on the lowest tier of the amphitheater, the stage.

Armed guards stood just outside the bullet-proof glass of the stage. A group of technicians stood behind a large metallic console checked readouts and making last minute adjustments in preparation for the main event.

"Mr. Chairman, everything is a go for the portal launch. They are about to start the countdown."

"Very good Johnson, very good. I suppose I should have my writer start preparing my Nobel Prize acceptance speech," said the Chairman with a laugh.

"Portal activation in three... two... one..." One of the scientists at the console hit a large red button.

At first, there was silence. Just before the air on the stage came alive, crackling with electricity, there was the smell of burning ozone. A plasma ball took shape in the center of the stage, rotating like a small sun before flattening and forming a large wall of shimmering liquid light. The portal thrummed loudly, vibrating the glass that surrounded the stage.

"The portal is active, structural integrity one hundred percent," said the engineer who had pushed the red button.

"Doorway is open sir, all that is left is for Captain Pope to step through,' said Johnson.

A second later the portal flashed brilliant bright white light, forcing everyone in the room to cover their eyes. A wave of energy surged through every electrical system and outlet in the room. Lightbulbs exploded and sparks rained down from the ceiling. The amphitheater erupted in chaos as everyone ducked for cover, Sara included. She and Frank retreated to the observation room, in an attempt to avoid the glass and sparks that dropped down on them from above. As a precautionary measure, the amphitheater's automated fire control system activated of its own accord, releasing fire extinguishing mist that filled the room with a light and hazy fog. Upon realizing that nothing was actually on fire, one of the technicians on the midlevel hit a button and loud fans could be heard, whirring to life as the ventilation system activated to clear out the extinguishing spray, revealing a man crouching inside the stage a few yards from the mouth of the portal. Seconds later the stage was cleared and the full tableau of who had traveled through the portal was clear.

The entire room froze as the large figure in the center of the stage stood, unfolding itself to its full height. The guards standing outside the stage raised their guns while everyone else in the room seemed to hold their breath in anticipation. Sara watched silently through the cracked door of the observation room.

"Captain Marcus Pope reporting: Dytorus Employee Number zero-five-niner-six-five-niner-three. Earth reentry confirmed."

"It's him!" said one of the scientists. "It's Captain Pope!"

A cheer erupted. The guards lowered their weapons and one of the scientists behind the console flipped a switch that unlocked and then opened the large glass door leading into the stage.

"Captain Pope!" said the Chairman from his position on the balcony level gesturing like a modern-day Julius Caesar. "Welcome home. What have you brought us back from your expedition?"

Pope's face twisted into its signature smirk.

"I have brought you everything you have requested." Pope raised his arms dramatically, "Judgement, reckoning and doom."

In that moment, one of the figures that had come through the portal with Pope unlatched the door on the wooden crate and three monstrous lizards, covered in feathers and walking on two legs, burst from the box. Their high-pitched screeches pierced the room like bullets while large, snout-like mouths opened wide to reveal needle teeth. Screams of terror came from the occupants of the amphitheater as employees scrambled for the balcony level. One of the guards nearest the stage raised his gun, only to be struck in the chest with an arrow that killed him instantly. Lansing, still in the form of the Deosian elf Sara had helped him create, held upright in his hand a longbow, which he shot through with an arrow from the quiver on his back.

Horrified, Sara and Frank watched as the men and creatures that had come through the portal with Captain Pope opened fire on everyone in the room, killing the armed guards in seconds with nothing more than crossbows and longbows. The monsters they had released ran through the open door of the stage to attack the fleeing people in lab coats on the mid-level. One of the monsters jumped, and in two bountiful leaps had made its way to the balcony level, blocking the only exit out of the room and attacking stunned and dumbfounded executives. Sara watched the Dytrous Corp. President grab the

VP of Tactical Operations by the suit jacket and throw him to the ground before barricading himself in the boardroom, leaving the remaining members of his executive team, including Johnson, banging on the boardroom door begging to be let in.

Back on the stage Pope surveyed the bloodshed and chaos with a look of pride. Sara watched as Corrine, one of the game guides that had entered Deos with Stephen, walk up alongside the captain, place a hand on his shoulder, raise her other hand high in the air and speak. When she finished, both Corrine and Pope vanished in a flash of purple crackling energy. Just then, Frank grabbed Sara by the shoulder and pulled her deeper into the observation room. "Get away from that door," he said. "We need to hide."

"What's going on, why is Captain Pope doing this?" Sara was frantic, unable to believe what she was seeing. Her voice shook with panic.

"This is the same guy that asked them to dig up his dead daughter and send her body over to another world only days ago. I imagine him bringing dinosaurs back here to kill everyone is not really that much of a stretch. Look just get under the desk and stay quiet. I'm going to find something to barricade the door."

"I can help you."

"No!" said Frank forcefully. "Just hide."

Sara did as she was told and wedged herself under the desk that sat facing the black fire brazier and then with a forceful push and a loud bang, one of the filing cabinets where she and Frank kept the physical copies of the player correspondence messages came crashing down in front of the desk. Sara was fully hidden. Through a small crevice between the overturned cabinet and the desk she could see the door to the amphitheater, and Frank struggling to flip the second file cabinet. He grunted with effort as he rocked it back and forth, but before he could get the cabinet to fall the observation room door, flew open, kicked in by Lansing.

The elf walked into the room with his bow strung across his back followed by the screaming from the amphitheater.

"What do you want?" Frank asked with a shaky voice.

"The magic item, the black fire brazier, where is it?" asked Lansing.

Frank stole a quick glance at the overturned cabinet in front of the desk and then turned his attention back to Lansing.

"I don't know what you're talking about."

Lansing moved slowly toward Frank who stood defiant, even though Sara could see from her hiding position that his knees were shaking.

"That's an odd hill to die on," said Lansing coldly, "but to each his own." And with a quick and fluid movement Lansing's arm slashed outwards at Frank. A muffled gurgling sound burbled from Frank before he fell to his knees, gripping his throat as it poured blood.

Sara covered her mouth to keep from screaming. Lansing kicked in the door to the adjoining room which held the black fire brazier, a fire still burning within its metal ring. Lansing kicked over the brass pot that held the flames grabbed the magic fire ring and stormed out of the observation room and back into the amphitheater without so much as a look over his shoulder.

Once she was sure he had left Sara crawled out from under the desk and over to Frank who lay bleeding out on the floor. He was pale and his skin already cold to the touch. He wasn't dead yet. His eyes moved to hers and he opened his mouth to speak. He had a terrified look on his face, before... nothing at all. His face froze, his eyes went blank. It took Sara a moment to realize she was crying. She lost time as she sat weeping over Frank's body, only pulling out of it when she heard a familiar sound from the amphitheater.

The sound of crackling energy sent Sara back to the broken frame of the amphitheater door. She peeked out to see Pope had returned with Corrine and a large burlap sack over his shoulder. With a single shrill whistle, the captain turned and walked back through the portal followed by his men and the monstrous lizards, who heeded his command like trained dogs.

Lansing was the last to step through the portal, only before he did, he fired one last arrow directly into the console. The elf disappeared into the into the wall of liquid light and shortly after the portal vanished, collapsing in on itself like an imploding star. It let off another surge of power, flickering the lights before a loud pop that made the survivors in the room jump in fear.

There were numerous people dead, countless others injured, and all for a reason Sara couldn't fathom. She looked at the stage in a kind of daze, before slowly making her way closer to the spot where Pope had stood during the brief time that he had actually been in the room. She wondered where he and Corrine had disappeared too when they had vanished the way they did and was curious as to why they left so quickly upon their return. She looked down at the stage a bit more closely, and she couldn't help but notice that among the glass and the debris there was something else. Where Pope had returned and walked back into the portal, a trail of clear footprints were left behind, the imprint of Pope's boots in freshly turned over earth.

Chapter 55: The Urthlander Adventuring Company

The gash in the old woman's invisible force field was now nearly as tall as Dante. He turned his body sideways and tried to force himself through the barrier, wriggling between the slit he created as if he were trying to squeeze his body through a partially open door.

He squeezed his head through, a shoulder, his entire right arm, part of his right leg, and then he hit a roadblock. His chest and hips were stuck fast between the barrier opening which from Dante's current position looked like thin and shimmering glass that refused to move or budge no matter how hard he pushed against it. And then his untenable position got worse. Pope and his men were returning, along with their team of hungry cockatrice raptors.

Once they had all exited the portal there was a distinctive and ear-splitting pop before the portal leading from Deos back to Earth simply blinked out of existence.

At the exact same time the barrier spell dissolved. Its sudden and abrupt disappearance threw Dante off balance, and almost as if a rug had been snatched out from under him, he went tumbling to the ground, landing on his hands and knees.

"What have you done?" Dante muttered through tear filled eyes and clenched teeth. His left hand clenched at the ground underneath his palm, his fingers digging themselves into the into the dirt, while his right hands gripped tightly to the hilt of his broken sword.

"I've freed you." Pope responded with a smile.

"How?" said Dante, his voice and body trembling as he looked down at the clump of dirt that he had gathered in his hand.

"Why?" he said in a slightly different tone, a deeper, hollow, desperate voice.

"You!" he looked up toward the captain and his voice changed again, sounding more like a raspy throaty growl than a spoken word. "You did this!"

Dante launched himself at Pope, brandishing his shattered sword as if it were still a whole weapon. With uncanny reflexive speed, Captain Pope lifted his large crossbow in front of his body, blocking the wild and unwieldy sword swing. Dante leaned into the captain with all of his weight and the two of them stared each other down from across their respective weapons.

"I've always liked you Dante, you're smart and strong. Join me! Here you and I can be kings. No, we can be Gods!" Unlike Pope's followers in Penumbra, Dante was not nearly as responsive.

"You've trapped us here. You're insane. I'LL KILL YOU!" Dante screamed inches from Pope's face. His eyes were wild almost feral, and his mouth dripped with a curious combination of drool and foam. Dante felt as if he was losing his mind and every word the captain spoke drove him deeper and deeper into a frenzy. Anger overtook him, the only thing that would slake his rage would be to drive his broken blade into Pope's neck.

Pope twisted his hip throwing Dante off balance for half a second before side kicking him so hard he sent Dante flying, his body was limp as he rag-dolled through the air, tumbling across the grass end over end until he stopped with a jolt. Disoriented, Dante looked up into the serene green face of Shinto. Behind the cleric, Morrigan, Alex, Robyn, Stephen and even Fang all stood at the ready. Their weapons drawn and their expressions steadfast. Like a soothing balm to the soul, immediately, Dante was calmed. The seething hate within him that had moments before overflowed into the form of an uncontrollable rage, had now coalesced into a burning passionate determination. The half-orc helped him to his feet.

Dante realized he had tried to beat Pope at every turn through strength, by overpowering, out maneuvering and even out thinking the captain. Each time, he had engaged Captain Pope alone. As he looked into the eyes of those that had been with him almost every step of the way through the Land of Deos, it hit him. He was not alone.

Together they had overcome petrifying lizard-birds, man-eating plants, rioting townsfolk, tree hugging cats, ogres, gnolls, trolls, a deadly swamp and even death itself. Together they could overcome anything, even Marcus Pope.

Dante turned back to Pope and leveled his broken sword in the snickering captain's direction.

"Black Wolves of the Urthlander Adventuring Company attack!"

Dante charged Pope once again, this time with the full force of his friends behind him. He took three to four steps before a familiar lethargy took possession of his limbs while at the same time his entire body, along with everyone else's, lifted from the ground, softly floating ten feet in the air. There was a muffled cackling and in a swirl of purple smoke, the fortune teller appeared standing next to Pope.

"Why are you helping him?" Dante shouted in frustration.

"I am an old woman and he is my student." The fortune teller responded.

"Such a waste of good soldiers," Pope said. "Kill these 'black wolves' and let's be on our way."

However, before anyone could act on Pope's command, Shinto, who had been focusing all of his energy on completing one movement brought his hands together as if in prayer. "Dispel!" yelled the half-orc and immediately he dropped out of the sky like a stone.

He hit the ground feet first, sticking the landing with the agility of a professional gymnast, even though he was the size of a professional football player. The moment his feet planted themselves in the soil, Shinto bent at the knees and then bolted forward with speed toward Pope and the old woman. Dante watched as he used his left hand to perform a waving motion, covering his right in the glowing purple flaming blade that Dante had grown accustomed to seeing the cleric wielding when he knw he meant business and for a moment he felt sorry for whoever ended up on the receiving end of Shinto's wrath.

The half-orc went straight for the fortune teller, leaping into the air, his purple bladed hand blazing with destructive magical energy. Smiling the old woman raised her arm and with a bright flash, she, Pope and all of his men vanished from the battlefield in an instant. Shinto's spell blade hit nothing but open air before burying itself deep into the ground. Dirt and debris flew in every direction as the impact of his blow left a small crater in its wake. The cleric stood to his feet and as he did the hardened purple flames blinked out of existence.

Dante and his team fell out of the sky. When he'd stood and regained his breath he found it was only his friends and Fang's remaining, though something else still lingered in the air.

"I see the 'Black Wolves' have a trick or two of their own up their sleeve as well." Pope's disembodied voice spoke from somewhere in the air. He let out a laugh that echoed through the small valley. Dante looked in every direction but knew he wouldn't find anything. Pope's voice seemed to emanate from both the inside and outside of his skull.

"Now I would be lying if I said I did not enjoy a good rivalry but make no mistake, Dante, I won't be letting anything interfere with my goals here in Deos. If you get in my way again, I will kill you."

Pope's voice faded away into a distant echo, and Dante and the others found themselves alone in the valley on the edge of the Hathorian Hills.

Chapter 56: Aftermath

Over the course of a day and a half, Dante, Fang and the rest of their adventurers departed from the shadow of Hathorain Hills and made their way back to the Northern Gates of Abilene Bay. Among Fang's team was Orion and Mandrake. The cleric and bard, who had witnessed Dante's outburst in the Sipper and the Sapling so many days earlier. Turns out it had only served to confirm the suspicions they had already been forming about the world of Deos and reinforced that Pope was not to be trusted. The remaining two gamers had also wrestled with unease. They had never met Dante but had heard whispers of the renegade team, so when Fang explained who he was going to help, Maxor, a lavender skinned dark-elf monk, and Aoleon, a panther like female Kalgari ranger, both felt it was imperative they join in.

The newly formed, larger group had spent time discussing what to do next, but all conversations ended at the same reality: They were trapped.

As they approached the towering limestone walls of Abilene Bay, Dante pointed out a muffled and distant, yet familiar voice attempting to penetrate the noise all around them. An observation which prompted Fang to reach into his pack and pull out the sending shell.

"Hello? Hello? Is anyone there? I'm trying to see how everything went. Shinto can you hear me? Did the ship crash? Did the kids make it back home? Hello? Is anyone there?"

Shinto grabbed the shell from Fang's hand.

"Professor Floggins, it's Shinto. I'm here."

"Oh, very good, very good. Am I correct in assuming the mission was a success then?" asked the professor.

"No sir," answered Shinto solemnly, "Unfortunately not. The portal collapsed before they could get through."

"Ah, I am sorry to hear that. Is everyone okay?"

"Yes, we are all intact. We have just arrived at Abilene Bay."

"Excellent. In that case I need you all to return to Hemera-Balgrad at once. I found something that may be of help. Believe me, you will want to hear about it as soon as possible."

"We'll travel back by airship. We'll be there soon."

"I wonder what that could be about?" said Alex.

"Maybe he's found a way for us to get back home," said Robyn hopefully.

"Whatever it is, I'm going to let you all go and check it out," said Fang. "There were a few other gamers in Penumbra who wanted to break away from Pope but weren't willing to face him head on. Before the five of us left to meet you, I told them to come back here to Abilene Bay. Now I need to go find them. Once we've gathered, I'll come find you in Hemera-Balgrad."

"That sounds like a plan," said Dante, relieved that they had even the beginnings of a plan. "Until then, you guys be safe." Fang reached out his hand and he and Dante clamped down on each other's wrist.

Professor Floggins was hopping with excitement to see the adventurers by the time they got back to his lab. His workshop was in an unusually higher state of disarray than it was before they left it, and his assistants were nowhere to be found.

"While you all were out," began the professor, "I continued looking around the workshop for anything that might be of help and I found this." Professor Floggins dropped a large leather-bound book nearly as big as himself on the table.

"And what is this?" asked Morrigan.

"These are my notes on the Antikythera Device."

The group waited patiently for an explanation.

"The Antikythera Device allowed us to travel between worlds, and is the device that will allow you all to return to Earth. These are my notes on how it works, notes on how to rebuild it."

"That's great! That means you can get us home!"

The entire group let out a cheer, but before they got too carried away Floggins interrupted.

"Building the device is complex, its inner working complicated. Honestly it will take quite some time and will require quite a bit of work, not to mention some very rare components that I will need you all to retrieve for me."

"Well, that's not a problem. Just give us a grocery list and we'll get started right away. Right Dante?" said Robyn.

"If I could for a moment," interrupted Shinto before Dante could respond. "I'm afraid you all may be getting a bit ahead of yourselves. Professor Floggins, how long before you are actually ready to get started rebuilding the device?"

"Well, I need to do a more in-depth review of my notes, run some tests, draw up blueprints and that all in addition to my standard work here at the workshop. I'd say it would be at least three months before I could start building the first prototype. I wouldn't be sure of absolutely all of the materials I needed until then."

"Three months?" repeated Alex. "That's a long time."

"Yeah, I was hoping to start treasure hunting as soon as possible." Said Robyn.

"I know you all are anxious to find a way home, but I must remind you that the land of Deos is both dangerous and unforgiving and while you all have experienced a lot in you short time here, I hate to say you have only scratched the surface in regards to all of the possible perils you can encounter once you leave the confines and safety of the cities. Not to mention Captain Pope came to Deos with you all, and now with this advanced and powerful mage by his side, guiding and instructing him, there is no guessing what they are planning to do. Who will take responsibility for Pope and the havoc he has planned?" Shinto looked directly at Dante to answer his question.

"Are you saying that whatever Pope is planning to do is *our* fault? He tricked us!" Alex exclaimed.

"No," said Shinto, "I do not seek to place blame, I merely offer up a question which appears to have only two possible answers. When you *know* there is a madman that poses a threat to the world, what do you do? Make it your mission to stop him, or turn a blind eye and allow it to become someone else's problem?"

"He's right," Dante replied. "Getting home is important, but the truth is, we have every reason to suspect the fortune teller is a powerful necromancer, and now Pope is her student. Knowing that, it would be irresponsible for us to abandon this world and leave Pope unchecked."

"Before we start chasing Pope, we should at least ensure Floggins has everything he needs to start building the device, even if we have to wait three months to get the list of components," said Morrigan. "I think it's better to be safe than sorry."

"I agree," said Shinto, "In the meantime, you all have some considerable growing and learning of your own to do, so I suggest you all come with me, and I will ensure you receive the training that you need. Morrigan, at one time you asked me to mentor you in the study of magic, allow me to take you up on that request once more, only this time much more in-depth. Alex if you are open to the idea, I can teach you what I know of shield craft and melee weapon combat and perhaps some restoration magic. Stephen, if you are willing, I would be honored to tutor you in the ways of the cleric. And Robyn, I can bring you to someone who can teach you in the advanced techniques of stealth and misdirection."

Plans were laid and within days the party left Hemera-Balgrad to travel with Shinto to his home on the other side of the Hathorian Mountains, where they intended to spend the next three months. As they traveled, Dante approached Shinto.

"Shinto, you didn't mention it earlier, but I assume you plan was to train me as well, right?"

"No," replied Shinto calmly. "I do not have the knowledge or ability to train you in the advanced ways of the sword. Besides, if your rival has a teacher who is strong, then you too will need a teacher of incredible strength. I'm taking you to such a teacher."

"I'm confused," Dante said with a nervous laugh, looking up at the half-orc, "Who could possibly be stronger than you?"

Shinto looked at Dante his green eyes sparkling in the Deosian sun.

"I'm taking you to my childhood home to be trained by my master and father, Hassan the Merciful."

***

Marcus Pope sat alone in a cold dark room, the plunder's pouch before him. He reached inside, focused on the item he wished to retrieve and grabbed hold to something solid. Then, through whatever magic that controlled the bag's extradimensional space, a large object inside the plunder's pouch became evident and he pulled out a child-sized coffin still caked with dirt. He laid a gentle hand on the wood and leaned his face in close to its polished surface.

"Soon, very soon," he whispered in a low and fatherly voice, "you'll see. Soon everything will be as it should be. As it should have been all along. Soon, daddy will fix everything."

Pope climbed the flight of stairs out of the dark, cold crypt where his daughter would remain until he was ready for the next phase of his plan. In the kitchen pantry he gently closed and locked the cellar doors behind him. He walked through the kitchen, past the bar and into the open and abandoned tavern of the Misty Shadow. The room, which normally held a number of his men drinking at nearly all hours of the day and night, was empty, with the exception of the old woman who sat quietly at a small table in a dimly lit corner, her attention glued to something in front of her.

Pope saw that the old woman was once again blindly shuffling her deck of tarot cards. Once she was done, she pulled three cards from the top of the deck and lay each of them face down on the small table in front of her before flipping them over in order of left to right. The Fool. The Hermit. The Ace of Swords. The fortune teller shook her head.

"Old woman, you know the boy had a point. I really don't know who you are, or why you're helping me."

"That day on the roads, outside of Abilene Bay, you saved my life. I am merely repaying a debt." She spoke without looking up from her cards.

"You and I both know that's a lie. You could have easily handled those bandits yourself. What is your true motive?"

The old woman looked up from her cards, and without saying a word she pulled three more cards from the deck, this time positioning them beneath the cards already on the table. She placed the first card opposite the fool card and then went from right to left as she laid out the other two cards.

"You are a smart boy." She said, looking down at the cards. There were six of them on the table now, only The Fool, The Hermit and The Ace of Swords, lay face up.

"No, I never imagined you would part with your secrets so easily anyway, otherwise you wouldn't go through such lengths to conceal them to begin with now, would you? Yes, well keep your secrets, so long as our goals align your intentions don't matter to me. But perhaps you can at least tell me your name. I'm tired of calling you 'old woman'."

"Well, your men simply call me Mother," she said.

Pope said nothing until she spoke again with her cackle. "My name is Xinterra," and she flipped over the face down card on the far left of the table. The High Priestess.

"Well Mistress Xinterra, I have retrieved all it is that I need from Earth, so if it pleases you, I will begin my lessons tomorrow."

"Yes, the lessons," she hissed flipping over the middle card to reveal Death.

"Xinterra!" Pope said, attempting to snap her out of her distracted state.

"Do not worry my son, tomorrow we will begin your training and I will guide you down the path to true power and by the time we are done, nothing in Deos will stop you from obtaining what it is you seek."

"Very good then." Pope smiled. "Very, very good." And without another word he walked away.

"Such an ambitious boy," Xinterra mumbled to herself. "Such a cold, ruthless and dangerously ambitious boy." She rubbed her pale, spider fingers over the last face down card then flipped it, revealing The Devil. "Reminds me so much of my own dear son."

***

Malcom Battle was lying across the bed in his cell eating an apple and re-reading the Autobiography of Malcolm X when a guard came to the door.

"Let's go, Battle."

"Huh? Where we going?"

"Battle, I don't have time for this today. I said let's go. Now move it."

Malcom stood up from his bed, threw the apple aside and approached the cell door sticking his arms out of an opening at waist height. The guard, with little concern for the effects of hard metal on flesh, cuffed his hands at the wrist and then dropped and shackled his legs at the ankles. Afterwards he opened the cell and ordered Malcolm to follow him out of the cell block past a number of other cells, where inmates hooped and hollered.

"Battle! Don't let 'em wear you down!"

"X! X! Hold ya head!"

"I see ya Little! They got nothing on you. Never have, never will!"

Malcolm followed the guard to a small room that held one table and two chairs. There he was told to sit and wait. It was in rooms like these that inmates usually came to speak privately with their lawyers. The only thing was, Malcolm wasn't expecting a visit from his lawyer anytime soon, and when lawyers started making unexpected visits that was not a good sign. Malcolm sat alone and in silence in the small room for ten minutes before the door swung open and a guard walked in followed by his older brother, Bryan Battle.

Bryan looked at Malcolm, then at the guard.

"Uncuff him." Bryan spoke with the demand that always used to drive Malcolm up a wall, although it didn't bother him at all this time.

The guard removed the chains, gathered them up and left the room, closing the door behind him.

"Bryan, what the hell is going on? What are you doing here?"

Bryan responded by throwing a backpack into his brother's lap. Malcolm unzipped it. It was full of clothing. In front of him a large stack of papers slammed down on to the small table with a heavy bang.

"What's that?" Malcolm asked.

"That," Bryan replied, "Is a very complex set of paperwork invoking my authority as an agent of the federal government to take whatever precautions I deem necessary to procure and secure the safety of this nation, enforce its laws, safeguard its democracy and protects its citizens."

"What?"

"In short, it means for as long as I deem necessary, I am now solely and personally responsible for you, your whereabouts and your actions for as long as and up until you have been safely returned to this prison."

"WHAT?"

"Put the clothes on," Bryan said. "Our little brother has gone missing, and you and I are going to go find him."

***

Epilogue

Notifications

-You have fulfilled the primary objective for the quest, "Maiden Flight of the Swan Song"

-You have gained 3,000 Experience points!

-You have obtained Level 9, Congratulations!

-You have been issued a new quest, "Survive the Battle of Hathorian Hills"

-You have defeated Lvl 9 Adventurer Davidson in battle. (Non-lethal)

-You have gained 1,000 Experience points!

-You have defeated Lvl 10 Adventurer Silvers in battle. (Non-lethal)

-You have gained 1,100 Experience points!

-You have unlocked a new ability "Lightning Dash"

-"Lightning Dash" has been added to the skills and abilities list.

-Sword Technique Rank Up!

-Your Sword Technique has risen to a rank of 'C'

-You have shattered your sword!

-You have failed the primary objective for the quest, "A Portal Home"

-You have survived The Battle of Hathorian Hills

-You have gained 6,500 Experience points!

-Congratulations, your heroic deeds have earned you the recognition of your peers.

-Your Reputation Rank is currently listed as 'Little-Known Adventurer'

-You have been issued a new quest, "Disciple of the Shattered Blade"

-You have been issued a new quest, "The Antikythera Device"

-You have been issued a new quest, "In Pursuit of a Powerful Rival"

-You have been issued a new quest, "Hassan the Merciful"

- You have a total of 58,650 Experience Points

Afterword

The End

of

Dragon Dale Beta Book 1

“Thanks for reading. If you enjoyed this book, please consider leaving an honest review on your favorite store.”